HOWE'S TRANSCENDENTAL TOYBOX

SECOND EDITION

HOWE'S TRANSCENDENTAL TOYBOX

SECOND EDITION

BY DAVID J HOWE
& ARNOLD T BLUMBERG

First published in England in 2003 by

Telos Publishing Ltd
61 Elgar Avenue, Tolworth, Surrey, KT5 9JP, England
www.telos.co.uk

in cooperation with

ATB Publishing Inc.
33 Silverton Ct, Cockeysville, MD, 21030
www.atbpublishing.com

ISBN: 1-903889-56-1

Cover design by Nathan Skreslet and Dariusz Jasiczak. Logo by Arnold T. Blumberg.
Internal design, typesetting and layout by Arnold T Blumberg. Page top border collages by Nathan Skreslet.

This book was assembled primarily on the same 500mhz Apple G3 Powerbook used to create the first edition, with files stored on a very cool USB Lexar Media JumpDrive. Macs still rule! The book was designed in Quark XPress, with photos and text prepared in Adobe Photoshop, Microsoft Word, and Microsoft Excel. The body text is set in Garamond 3, headers in Comicraft's Exterminate (www.comicbookfonts.com), and the item listings in Gill Sans. This paragraph may seem a bit excessive, but the tech-heads and design devotees out there will want to know, trust me.

Printed in England by Antony Rowe Ltd, Bumper's Farm Industrial Estate, Chippenham, Wiltshire, SN14 6LH

1 2 3 4 5 6 7 8 9 10 11 12 13 14 15

British Library Cataloguing in Publication Data.
A catalogue record for this book is available from the British Library.

THIS book has once again been a labour of love, but it couldn't be done without the help of many individuals and organisations that gave their time and knowledge to the project. Here are some of them, listed in alphabetical order:

Roger Anderson (of the *Doctor Who* Cuttings Archive), Mark Ayres (audio information), David Brunt (final checking and assistance), Brenda Busick (design suggestions), Bruce Campbell (TV and Film Memorabilia), Aran Challinger (Australian Royal Melbourne Show *Doctor Who* Showbag information), Daniel Cohen (Gudi information), Peter Darvill-Evans (W H Allen/Virgin Publishing information), Matthew Fitch (USA Video release dates), Robert Franks (moral support), George at Dapol (general information and confirmations), Gary Gillatt and Alan Barnes at *Doctor Who Magazine,* Laura Gillespie (additional proofreading), Paul Griggs/The Who Cooperative (Audio Adventures information), Mick Hall (collector *extraordinaire*), Paul Harman (website guide), Steve Hill (for his extensive on-line picture archives and information on USA merchandise), Steve Manfred (CBS/FOX video information), Jeremy Rayner and Allen Robinson (WhoLINK; website guide), Kim Holcomb, Linda Taggart and Debbie Thomas of MPT (Maryland Public Television; US pledge drive merchandise), Richard Hollis and Chris Crouch for contacts and information, Shaun Lyon (assistance and general niceness), Steve Manfred (USA Video information), Andrew Pixley (final checking and assistance), Gary Russell (gentleman), Bob Schaefer, Jr. (Japanese *Revenge of the Cybermen*), Steven Scott (The Stamp Centre, The Strand), Nick Seidler (role-playing game information), Stephen James Walker (final checking and assistance), Robin Welch at CMA (trading card assistance), Jeffrey Zyra (Cushing video information).

For help with the Target Books section: David Darlington, Ian Edmond, Arfie Mansfield, Tim Neal, Daniel O'Mahoney, Chris Rednour, Jon Rowe, Gary Russell, Jason Shron.

For help with the comics listing: Finn Clark, Andrew Pixley, David Brunt.

Illustrations have come from the authors' collections as well as from *The Sixties*, *The Seventies* and *The Eighties* books and from the collections of many gracious fans around the world. Thanks also to Marvin Blumberg for searching through old magazines for pictures, and Rosemary Howe, James Howe, and Rochelle Blumberg for scanning many of the pictures included here.

Other thanks to: Chris Avis, Paul Bensilum, Jeremy Bentham, Richard Bignell, Steve Black, Nathaniel Blake, Keith Bradbury, David Brawn, Nick Briggs, Richard Briggs, Rick Brindell, Dave J. Brook, Michael Brooks, Chris Burnside, Immanuel Burton (www.policeboxes.com), Alistair Carnell, John & Carol Chamley, Roger Clark, Tom Coffey, Hugh J. Cregan, Mark Crowder, John Curtis, Richard Davies, Steve Day, Jonathan Dennis, Mike Dennis, Chris Dickinson, Niall Doran, Chris L. Doyle, Brian Edwards, Benjamin F. Elliott, Clive Evans, Tim Everson, Johnny Ffinch, Anthony Forth, Colin John Francis, Galaxy 4, Dave Gaskell, Eric Gjovaag, Scott Goodman, David Greenham, Sarah Hadley, Neil Hagan, Richard Holden, Steve Holland, Peter Ibrahim, Paul James, Steve Johnson, Dallas Jones, Eric Katz, Iain Key, Anthony Keetch, Matthew Kilburn, Ian Knight, Michael Livsey, Allen Machielson, Jenny Martin, Brian Mattocks, Herb McCaulla, Susan Moore, Paul Nagle, Richard Nolan, Lance Parkin, Samuel Payne, Marc Platt, Keith Plummer, Jon Preddle, Ian A. Pritchard, Andrew Raymond, Jac Rayner, Paul Rhodes, Justin Richards, Tim Roll-Pickering, Andrew Rowe, Gordon Roxburgh, S. Rudyk, Paul Scoones, J. Scott, Kieran Seymour, Andrew Shenton, Simon Simmons, Stewart Skardon, Terry Skirko, Gene Smith & Alien Entertainment, Steven Smith, Mark Stammers, Alex Storer, Shannon Sullivan, Liam Teer, 10th Planet, Iain Truskett, Julian Vince, Jan Vincent-Rudzki, Anthony Warwood, Kev West, Ian Wheeler, Martin Wiggins, Tom Winpenny, Colin Young.

Thanks also to everyone who helped with the listings in *The Sixties*, *The Seventies* and *The Eighties* books, especially to Chris daLuca who supplied details of most of the American merchandise from the eighties, and which we were ultimately unable to include in *Doctor Who: The Eighties*.

For pricing, we are grateful to the following shops and individuals for supplying the base information on which the pricing ranges have been developed: Andy Swinden and Ben Keywood (Galaxy 4), Mike Kott (Intergalactic Trading), Andrew (Kulture Shock), Bruce Campbell (TV and Film Memorabilia), Alex Loosley-Saul (The Who Shop)

Personal thanks from David: Given that they have to put up with it all, this is for my wife, Rosemary, and for James and Andrew, sons who know more about *Doctor Who* than perhaps is normal for kids their age!

Personal thanks from Arnold: This one's for Bubben and Papa: Bubben–Here's that book I told you about on December 23, 2001. Don't worry about me, I'll be OK; Papa–It was fun being your companion in all those adventures.

Lastly, if we forgot any of you, we apologize profusely and offer one last round of thanks to everyone who in some way, however large or small, contributed to the book you now hold in your hands.

WE said it last time, and we'll say it again: Don't let the word 'unauthorised' fool you. If you're perusing this book in your favourite book store, and you're wondering whether or not it's worth it, we know how you feel. As collectors and science fiction fans, we've been burned too many times by 'unauthorised' guides and reference books purporting to cover our favourite shows and films, only to discover what a truly lacklustre job the 'authors' really did. The word 'unauthorised' has become, for some, synonymous with 'unprofessional,' and we want to assure you that this is not the case with this book.

Despite the lack of official sanctioning, we have taken great care to ensure that this is the most authoritative and exhaustively researched reference guide to the vast world of *Doctor Who* collectibles. In fact, it's still the only one to date, and as fans and collectors ourselves who value the many wonderful hours of entertainment *Doctor Who* has given us, we would be remiss if we didn't make this book as professional as we could.

The 'unauthorised' trap also brings with it a certain implication of questionable credibility, and that too is unfortunate. Many so-called 'definitive' price guides are nothing more than a poorly assembled catalog of one over-enthusiastic fan's personal collection, with obvious substantial gaps in information and highly unethical pricing information.

We want to assure you here too that our motivation in making this book is a far cry from mere self-aggrandisement. We are first and foremost devoted fans of *Doctor Who*, and we wanted to make a book we would want to own and read ourselves. As a result, our information and pricing data is as accurate as we could possibly make it, and has been compiled and verified by many other dealers, collectors, and experts besides ourselves (a list of our advisors and contributors appears on the acknowledgments page). If we couldn't verify it, we didn't use it; it's as simple as that.

This has been a labour of love for us, and we hope you enjoy it half as much as we enjoyed making it. 'Unauthorised' or not, this is the only guide to *Doctor Who* merchandise around, and we hope you feel it's worth supporting.

One last note: in a project of this size and scope, errors are bound to creep in despite our best efforts. We received many letters and e-mails over the last few years pointing out such errors from the first edition, and we've tried to incorporate all of your corrections, suggestions and additions in this second volume. We are hopeful that this book will continue to grow into the single most exhaustive guide to *Doctor Who* memorabilia in the world, and as such, we ask again for your help in assuring its accuracy and completeness.

If you discover any inaccuracies, or have photos or information that should be included in a future edition, please feel free to contact us directly (our e-mail addresses are listed below). Although we welcome the feedback, please note that we cannot enter into any private communications regarding any aspects of pricing or related collectible topics. While we're interested to know what's out there, we simply can't always respond personally to queries. We hope you'll still feel motivated to write and let us know what you think of our efforts.

In the end, this isn't just our guide to the world of *Doctor Who* merchandise...it's yours too. And now that the series is scheduled for a long-awaited return to UK TV in 2005, this is the perfect time to explore the fun and fascinating universe of *Who* collectibles. Off you go then!

Cheers,
David J Howe (david@telos.co.uk)

Arnold T Blumberg
(the14thdoctor@yahoo.com)

WELCOME to the wonderful world of *Doctor Who* collectibles! If you grew up with the Doctor, joined his adventures later in television repeats or on video and other media, or if you're an SF-TV enthusiast who likes to learn more about the history of science fiction fandom and collectibles, then you've come to the right place.

This book has been a long time in development. Around 1980, when David J Howe had just taken over the running of the *Doctor Who* Appreciation Society's Reference Department, he put together a proposal for a *Doctor Who* merchandise book, together with a draft copy of the same, complete with photographs. The idea for a merchandise guide was discussed with Chris Crouch, then in charge of licensing *Doctor Who* merchandise at BBC Enterprises, and he was keen to see it published. There then followed twenty years of David failing to interest any publisher in doing such a book. Everyone approached saw such a venture as uncommercial. Even during the mid-eighties when W H Allen seemed willing to publish anything with the *Doctor Who* name on, they didn't want to do a book on the merchandise.

In 1991, when work started on David's co-written book *Doctor Who: The Sixties*, Virgin Publishing were asked about doing a merchandise book and, predictably, they turned it down. Therefore David proposed including lengthy sections in *The Sixties* and subsequent books looking at the merchandise as this was the only way that some of the information was going to get published.

Then, in October 1997, David was contacted by Arnold T Blumberg with an outline proposal for a *Doctor Who* merchandise book. At the time, Arnold was Managing Editor at Gemstone Publishing, an American company which specialised in collectible guides. Over the next year, David and Arnold refined the ideas, and, with Gemstone ultimately declining to publish the book, again tried to interest other companies in the project – to no avail. The BBC, Virgin, Boxtree, Titan Books, Schiffer, Krause ... all turned the project down as having no commercial interest.

However, after all this time, David and Arnold decided that the book just had to be published and so decided to go it alone. In November 2000, the first edition of *Howe's Transcendental Toybox* was released to universal acclaim, going through three printings over the next two years. It was inevitable that there would be a follow-up, if only to include all the new merchandise released since the original volume's cut-off date (1999), and of course to correct and refine the material in the first edition. And so David and Arnold planned for a second edition to be released two years after the original *Toybox* achieved such success. Those plans were delayed for various reasons, but with the 40th anniversary of *Doctor Who* arriving in 2003, it seemed the time was at last right for a second edition of the *Toybox*.

Thus is the history of the book you now hold in your hands. We hope you enjoy it, and we hope you find it useful. It's a heady nostalgia trip, but one which we have enjoyed putting together. So set the TARDIS to hover in the vortex, relax with a good cup of hot tea, and join us as we travel back in time to witness the birth of one of the most exciting phenomena of the 20th century – *Doctor Who*!

ABOUT THE BOOK

THIS book documents the entire range of *Doctor Who* merchandise produced and released since the show started on BBC television on the 23rd November 1963, up to the end of 2002. It covers an amazing array of categories and types of items. Included are toys, books, magazines, comic books, records & CDs, videos, and even clothing and toiletries! We've done our best to ensure that the universe of *Doctor Who* collectibles is encompassed in one organised volume. All of the items are listed by category – action figures, books, clothing, etc. For the most part, all the information in this book has been researched through first-hand viewing of the items concerned, while other information has been gleaned from dealer catalogues, records held by BBC Worldwide (who monitor and issue licences for any official *Doctor Who* products), the extensive collections of many fans all over the world, plus reports and reviews contained within such periodicals as *Doctor Who Magazine* and several fan club magazines including *Celestial Toyroom*, the newsletter of the *Doctor Who* Appreciation Society, and several American newsletters and club reports issued during the eighties.

We've tried to make the listings as easy to follow as possible. Each item is listed by an item code (assigned by us in relation to the category in which the item is listed) and its name. In some cases this is the actual name given by the producers of the items, while in other cases we've named an item with an approximate description that best identifies the collectible in question. Because of the sheer quantity of items included, there will be occasions when readers may find it difficult to locate an item as it may not be listed where perhaps it might be expected. Please try alternative locations in these instances: for example a book you expected to find under 'Books, Factual' might be under the 'Books, General' heading, or an 'Activity Book' might be under 'Books, Gaming'. We have tried to apply common sense to the locating of items, and we hope that this sort of confusion will not often happen.

We also list release dates (as accurate as we have been able to determine; sometimes this is just a year, sometimes a year and month, and occasionally the actual date of release) along with any other pertinent descriptive information (manufacturer, distributor, size, colour etc.). A reference number is sometimes listed (a serial number or ISBN code), as well as the original retail price when known. Finally, a current Near Mint value is listed *when it could be reasonably determined* (see our notes on pricing later in this article). Prices are generally given in UK pounds sterling as the UK is where the majority of items were produced for sale, and where Near Mint pricing tends to be more consistent.

CRITERIA

WHILE we were preparing this edition of the book, drafts were seen and checked by several *Doctor Who* fans and researchers around the world. Since the release of the first edition in 2000, we have received many letters, calls and e-mails offering feedback on the material presented, noting items that we should include, and asking questions about why certain items were not contained in the book. This section attempts to explain the scope of the book, and to help readers understand our criteria for including items.

First of all, we decided that we could not include in the first edition anything and everything which could be classed as a *Doctor Who* collectible; there is far too much. Therefore we developed a basic inclusion criterion: items had to have been available to buy commercially, and also needed to be *Doctor Who* items in their own right. Collectible items like autographs, props, costumes, scripts and other production documentation, photographs (except where commercially available), proof copies and other manufacturing trial items are therefore not included as they do not fall into this definition.

There are, of course, some instances where we broke our own rules. The main exception are the comic strips which appeared in places other than *Doctor Who Magazine* (and its variant titles) and a hopefully useful appendix of these appears at the back of the book. We have not listed magazine articles, newspaper articles or any other *Doctor Who* coverage in the press with the exception of particularly relevant editions of the BBC's listings magazine *Radio Times* (those with *Doctor Who* covers in particular).

We have also generally excluded items produced by fans and fan clubs except where these were commercially available or where the person behind them went on to be involved in more significant things in the *Doctor Who* field. Fanzines and fan magazines have not been included. Occasionally, however, we have allowed some fan-produced items to creep in, particularly where they were of note or of professional quality.

We have not generally included promotional items and point of sale items (like the TARDIS and Dalek dump-bins created by BBC Worldwide for video specials in the nineties, or *Doctor Who* standees and other promotional items used over the years). For items to be included, they must have been generally available to buy.

There are some other basic notes on the inclusion of items, and the content of the text, which are worth mentioning:

The initial basis for the information contained in this book were the merchandise listings contained in the books *Doctor Who: The Sixties*, *Doctor Who: The Seventies* and *Doctor Who: The Eighties*. Some descriptive text has been re-used from those publications where appropriate; however, just about everything has been re-checked and in many cases expanded from those original listings.

To keep the list as concise as possible, we assume that the reader has a basic knowledge of *Doctor Who* and the various people involved in its creation and realisation. Notes have been provided as to the backgrounds of several individuals involved in the creation of the merchandise, but these are not all-inclusive, and the intention is not to provide biographical information on the show or its production. For anyone who wants to know more about *Doctor Who* generally, we'd recommend the Telos revised edition of *The Television Companion* (by David J Howe and Stephen James Walker), available from Telos (www.telos.co.uk) and other retailers, as a good starting point.

We also only list those items which were actually released. There is a listing of some announced but unreleased items – or 'ghost' items as they have been termed – in Appendix B.

Where an item has been identified as remaindered, this notation is backed up by documented evidence from either the BBC's files

or those of the publisher concerned. Just because a book has appeared at a reduced price in a discount shop does not mean that it was remaindered. Publishers often allow shops to buy at large discount, and this is not the same as remaindering the book, which occurs when a publisher knowingly sells off their entire stock at a huge discount to clear the warehouse.

Information has been supplied where known. If a description or information is absent, it means that it is not known. We have tried not to assume things in the listing.

We have tried to keep the information factual, and avoided passing opinion on the items except where this forms a part of the background or is relevant to the collectibility or desirability of an item.

With items produced in America in the early and mid eighties, we have done our best to list these, but there was so much produced in a relatively short space of time, it is almost certain that some have been missed. The line between fan-produced items and commercial items is very blurred in this area as well, particularly in categories like T-shirts and badges.

Where books and videos feature foil printing, the chances of there being mis-prints with the foil either missing or mis-aligned are quite high.

Plastic toys can also be found in variant colours from those they were 'officially' released in. These variants are collectible, but are not necessarily worth a great deal more than their 'standard' counterparts.

television home of the Doctor.
c. – circa. Where actual dates cannot be determined, we've used this to indicate uncertain dating.
CBS/FOX – The United States distributor of *Doctor Who* on video.
Audio
C – Cassette
CD – Compact Disk
DVD – Digital Versatile Disk
LP – Long Playing Record
EP – Extended Playing Record
7" – Seven inch single
12" – Twelve inch single
Books
h/b – Hardback.
p/b – Paperback. Either a standard 'A' format paperback or a slightly larger 'B' format version.
lfp/b – Large Format Paperback. A large softcover edition.
l/b – Leatherbound.
ISBN – International Standard Book Number. All published books should have an ISBN allocated to them.
ISSN – Like the book numbering system, but used for magazines and periodicals.
SBN – Standard Book Number. Sometimes used rather than ISBN.
Clothing
S – small
M – medium
L – large
XL – extra large

ABBREVIATIONS

THROUGHOUT this book we employ a variety of abbreviations and acronyms to refer to common terms, company names, and other information that regularly applies to *Doctor Who* merchandise. Here are some of the most frequently used abbreviations:

TARDIS – The Doctor's time capsule, disguised to look like a British police telephone box. The letters in TARDIS stand for Time And Relative Dimension in Space.
b&w – Black and white
BBC – The British Broadcasting Corporation, the

CONDITION

DETERMINING the condition and relevant grade of an item for purposes of pricing in the collectible market is probably one of the most contentious areas of discussion in collectibles today. Philosophical wars are fought in the unlikeliest situations merely to establish whether a book is considered in Fine condition or Near Mint. We advise all those interested in collecting to base the evaluation of an item's condition on the easily identifiable physical factors listed below. Beyond that, we would suggest that when looking to purchase an item, your own desire to own the collectible and your opinion of its condition is all that matters in the end. The choice to buy or not to buy is always yours, and if you're unhappy with the condition of a collectible, whether it's marked as Good or Mint, the power to walk away is always yours as well.

For the newcomer to collecting and the seasoned convention goer alike, we've assembled here a basic list of grading terms and their definitions. Please remember that these are loosely defined areas for purposes of evaluation, and the grade and condition of an item is ultimately a subjective determination made by the seller and the buyer.

The physical condition of an item is probably the primary means of evaluating its value in the marketplace, if only because it relies purely on visual indicators. Other factors in determining value, like rarity and demand, are more esoteric, and require a bit more research. For the most part, although these grades are subjective, the terms and their application will be familiar to most of the collectible community. At the very least, you will be armed with a common language that will allow you to buy and sell in an informed way.

One last note: Since almost all collectibles have been handled at one time or another, it is almost impossible to find any item that can be considered to be in Mint (i.e. "perfect" or original) condition. Therefore we begin our grading range with the term Near Mint, indicating an item that is nearly new in every way apart from the most minor wear. This is the standard upon which we have chosen to base the pricing for this book. Anything less than this, therefore, should theoretically cost less than the prices herein. Variations on this grading scale are used by collectors worldwide in relation to items like comic books, toys, and other ephemera, and serve as a useful 'universal language' in the collectible community.

In general, most collectors follow a grading system that employs the grades of Mint, Near Mint, Very Fine, Fine, Very Good, Good, Fair and Poor. There are distinct variations in the nomenclature and the ways in which these grades are practically applied to each hobby, but

the basic meanings remain the same. Some specific notes on the application of these grades: **NEAR MINT**–The highest grade that can be expected in most collectible categories. Paper items are still bright with little visible wear, lay flat, and if there are any staples they are rust-free. Metal or metallic items retain their lustre and any applied colouring. There is no corrosion or rust, and any working parts (or pins in the case of badges) must still operate. In the case of celluloid badges (those that have a plastic coating to seal in photographic or graphic material), the items must be free of stain or discoloration. There can be no surface scratches or splits.

FINE–Paper items display moderate wear and ageing, including creases and small tears, worn corners, a small amount of browning or yellowing, light rust around staples, and other assorted minor defects. Metal objects still retain about 50-60% of their original lustre. Corrosion or rust may be evident in small amounts, and moving parts may be slightly bent or damaged. Other materials may show scratches, minor dents, discoloration, chipping, and other stress markings.

GOOD–Paper items must still be intact, with no more than a few small pieces missing. Obvious ageing, creases, tears, browning, and other defects are evident but the item is more or less complete. Metal objects have lost almost all lustre and possible applied colouring, with repaired or lost working parts. Other major defects and surface stress are evident, but again the items must be complete. Other materials can exhibit ageing, discoloration, staining, stress fractures, and other obvious wear. Key to retaining this grade is that items must not display so much wear as to make them totally undesirable for collectors.

Again, keep in mind that these are only meant to be general guidelines, and as such they are subject to interpretation depending on the item in question and the collector's desire to obtain it. We have chosen to reflect values that adhere to the upper end of this scale for brevity and practicality.

DETERMINING VALUE

IF there's anything in the world of collectible price guides more contentious than grading condition, it's the actual pricing of individual items. There's no doubt that once again, this must be based at least in part on subjective evaluation, but the credibility of a guide like this must stand or fall on the accuracy, and more importantly, the honesty, of its pricing data.

As most die-hard collectors will tell you, pricing is a tricky thing, based on factors such as condition, demand for the item in question, and its rarity in the marketplace. Is this a common collectible, produced in the hundreds of thousands or millions for distribution to stores? Was this a limited edition release, difficult to find in good condition today? Was this a promotional item, perhaps only available to those connected to someone in the industry and thus an extremely rare item of considerable value?

For the most part, it can be easily determined how rare an item is by finding out how many were made and how many still exist. If, for example, only three intact copies of a certain comic book exist, then it's naturally quite rare. If it was a 1980s issue printed in the millions, it's pretty common. Either way, the rarity of an item is ultimately quantifiable. This is not, however, always true. For example, print runs are known for the majority of the first edition Target novelisations; however, a handful are considerably harder to find than the majority, despite their print runs being of similar magnitude. Manufacturers tend to guard their sales figures rigorously and it can be hard to find out the information. Where known, we have included print run and unit sale information in the listings.

It's an entirely different matter when dealing with demand and condition. Since we've already discussed grading, we must take a moment to examine the concept of demand in collectibles. A book like this is probably already reaching an audience at least mildly if not wildly interested in the subject matter. Therefore, all of the items listed here are in demand to some extent as *Doctor Who* collectors scour the market for treasured items from the past. Some items, however, may enjoy more appeal and demand due to their subject matter. A Tom Baker toy or magazine is arguably more recognizable and more desirable than say, a Colin Baker or William Hartnell item. On the other hand, collectors devoted to the series who grew up watching different Doctors may focus their

efforts on those eras in the show's merchandise history, and for them, a Hartnell or Troughton item may be the most important find of all.

Ultimately, as noted before in matters of grading, a collectible is worth what you think it's worth. Everyone has their own opinion as to how important a collectible is, what minimum condition it must be in to commit to the sale, and how much they're willing to spend. For collectors, the collectible market is not about pounds and pennies or dollars and cents ... it's about the heart and cherished memories. There's no way to put a value on nostalgia, but if both the buyer and the seller can agree on terms, then everyone can be happy. There are a few other factors important in determining the value of an item. Certainly in the case of *Doctor Who*, there is the potential for cross-over appeal. *Doctor Who* fans will naturally be interested in collectibles related to the show, but so might general SF fans, as well as fans of cult television or British pop culture history, for example. Even collectors of robots will want to have the Dalek toys in their possession, and someone interested in obscure plates could be hunting the 1999 *Day of the Daleks* item. If diverse groups of collectors are interested in an item, the chances are it enjoys a higher profile in the market, and subsequently a higher value.

Another significant factor in play where *Doctor Who* is concerned is geography. For collectors on either side of the Atlantic, finding that sought after item may be difficult if the country of origin and its likeliest resting place is miles away. United States fans eager to own *Doctor Who* collectibles may pay much more for UK items that rarely turn up in the States, while UK fans may be willing to value a US or Australian item a bit higher than one they can easily find at the local comic shop.

All of these elements must come into play when determining the value of an item. But even so, it's far more difficult to consider all of these factors in order to print a definitive value in a guide rather than just come to terms between buyer and seller at a convention or in a store. So how did we establish the prices in this book without weighing one factor too heavily or allowing too much bias to enter into the process?

VALUES LISTED

MOST successful, reliable guides today realise that valuing the items listed in their pages involves traversing the most dangerous territory any guide publisher can hope to navigate. In order to guarantee that the values listed are as accurate and as balanced as possible, these guides employ a number of advisors chosen from the collectible community and recognized as experts in their field. These advisors, typically a cross-section of retailers, dealers, professional collectors, and pop culture historians, provide notes and detailed pricing information based on actual sales tabulated during the course of the last year to establish the values for the market in question.

In the case of this book, we contacted and enlisted the aid of many other experts, dealers and collectors, most of whom are listed in the acknowledgments page at the beginning of this book. Their opinions and documented data were invaluable in setting the prices published here. For this second edition, we reviewed all prices in light of market trends, and amendments have

been made where appropriate.

Other prices have been taken from appropriate pricing guides, and from items currently on sale. All items have been priced as for 'Near Mint'. In other words, these are guide prices for an item which is complete, boxed and totally undamaged and unmarked. Any other condition, and you should expect the prices to be lower. The prices in this book have been arrived at by asking the dealers to advise on the prices of items as currently available from them, and also to give conjectural prices for as many other items of merchandise as they can. These prices have then been compared and either supplied as a range (e.g. £5 – £10) or as an average of the values we received (e.g. an item may have been conjecturally priced at £50, £150 and £180, and so the listed price here is around £130). We feel this is the fairest way to deal with prices which can vary wildly. Pricing is an imprecise art, and the value of any item is really what the buyer is prepared to pay. Therefore please take all valuations in this book as a guide only, and the authors take no responsibility for actual pricings or prices paid by collectors.

We have not included any values taken from auctions as these vary wildly and are not an accurate representation of the true worth of an item. While it is true that in the last few years alone, Internet-based auctions have become an intrinsic part of the experience for many pop culture collectors, it remains a difficult task to ascertain the value of an item based on that kind of sales activity. The major Internet auction site eBay, for example, has played a significant role in setting unheard-of records for high prices paid in the comic book collecting community, but the prices realised in an eBay auction usually diverge drastically from prices realised in a traditional convention or retail environment. Is this the way collectibles pricing will be determined from now on, or is this merely one way of looking at the market? For our purposes, eBay and other Internet auction activity did inform some of our thinking, but did not wholly dictate our final decision on the values contained in this book.

Some of the original prices in this book are from pre-1971, which is when the UK moved over to decimal coinage. Here is a brief overview of how that system of currency operated: Pennies (d), Shillings (12 pennies) (s or /), Pounds (20 shillings) (£). So, six pennies is 6d. Five shillings is 5/-. Five shillings and sixpence is 5/6 or 5s6d. Two pounds nineteen shillings is £2 19/- or £2 19s. One pound, ten shillings and sixpence is £1 10/6 or £1 10s 6d. In today's decimal currency, one shilling equates to 5 new pence.

Another issue is that a reader using something other than UK currency may not know how to interpret the values listed in this book. Since conversion rates fluctuate daily, we have decided not to provide conversion tables or other similar data and instead recommend checking conversion rates with established financial institutions or on the web to get a better idea of how to translate the prices in this book.

We cannot stress enough, however, that these prices are merely guidelines. We are suggesting values, not dictating them. Furthermore prices can rise or fall depending on availability and demand. The decision about whether or not an item is worth a certain amount must be the determination of the individual buyer or seller, and the true value of a collectible is however much you as a collector are willing to pay for it. The most important thing is to have fun and enjoy the thrill of collecting.

COLLECTING WHO

SO after all this, you still want to dive in and become a die-hard *Doctor Who* collector? Well, we certainly understand the desire, but we also want to prepare you for some of the pitfalls awaiting you in the world of collectible shopping.

Collecting is a passion, nothing more or less. It comes from an insatiable desire to recover the past, either your own or one that draws you to it although you never experienced it first-hand. You feel the joy and excitement of hunting for that elusive item, finding it, bringing it home and then going out again to begin the quest anew. It's a never-ending search for satisfaction, and the enjoyment comes as much from the chase as the actual acquiring of the treasured collectibles themselves.

Once you're set on beginning your own adventure into the world of *Doctor Who* collecting, you'll want to arm yourself with the necessary tools to make your trip into the collectible world pay off. With all due humility, we would like to point out that you probably couldn't have picked a better starting point than this book. By providing you with as accurate and exhaustive a collection of information on *Doctor Who* merchandise as possible, we hope this book will serve as your blueprint for the collection of your dreams.

blueprint for the collection of your dreams.

Next up, you'll want to scout out the stores, conventions, and dealers who can help you to find the items you're seeking. Some valuable contact information appears in this book through advertisements. The Internet is also a valuable tool for tracking down the collectibles of your choice. Besides using search engines and commercial sites to locate real-world establishments, you'll want to spend some quality time with eBay or the countless other auction sites now spreading across the web. These sites usually feature dozens if not hundreds of *Who* related collectible auctions every day. There is even now a website specifically devoted to the buying and selling of merchandise related to *Doctor Who* and several other genre shows, Mallarkey (www.mallarkey.com).

Joining clubs and attending conventions will provide you with even more knowledge and first-hand experience with dealers and collectibles. Also, despite the all pervasive nature of the Internet and the many resources at your disposal, never underestimate the potential of those classic low-tech venues – flea markets, jumble sales and second-hand shops. Local events like thrift stores and even boot sales can yield some impressive gains if you pay attention. That treasured wind-up Dalek may mean nothing to the family selling it off with their

eclectic collection of stained glass lamps and wood carvings, but it may be the Holy Grail to you. Keep your eyes open and collecting bliss will be yours.

SELLING WHO

YOUR wife is worried that you spend more time playing your *Doctor Who* pinball machine than you do talking to your kids, and she's also not too thrilled about that life-size TARDIS sitting out on the lawn. Or maybe your husband thinks you've forgotten about him now that you've completed your shrine to Paul McGann and have taken to wearing surgical scrubs around the house.

Every collector faces a point sometime in their life when the necessity of selling some if not all of their collection looms large and ominous. It's not something most of us who are dedicated to collecting are geared for, but it may just be an unavoidable event. There are also those who wish to change interests and find a way to translate that collection into money for other purposes, or maybe you're just tired of all the multiple copies of *Doctor Who Magazine* lying around the house. However large or small the need, there are things every collector needs to know about selling their collection, and here are a few useful tips for just such an occasion.

The prices listed in this book reflect a consensus of opinion concerning the values of the items listed, but don't expect to get that price when selling an item to a dealer at a show or store. Dealers will likely only offer a percentage of the assumed market value, since they too want to make a profit.

Ultimately, you will have to decide whether to sell your collection piecemeal or as a whole unit. Dealers can often make a good deal on an entire collection, but you may lose out if one or two items are of themselves higher in value than the rest. You do however gain the advantage of unloading your collection in one easy step.

Selling piece by piece is a far more laborious process and requires more commitment on your part. Today there are many options that make such a plan more convenient. Besides setting yourself up as a dealer at a flea market or convention, you might consider putting your collection on-line and advertising its availability, whether through a site of your own (if you're so inclined) or through auction sites like eBay, trading sites like Mallarkey, or the *Doctor Who* newsgroups. If you choose to go this route, always be sure to read any and all rules pertaining to running auctions thoroughly to be sure you don't violate any important stipulation on the part of the site hosts. Other options include advertising in club or other trade publications, and offering collectibles via mail order, but in all cases you must weigh the potential profits against the cost of advertising, operation, and other expenses.

REPRO, RESTORED & 'CREATED' ITEMS

BEFORE we finish our brief tour through the world of *Doctor Who* collecting, we should note two important things to watch out for when hunting that elusive piece of merchandise. Often in the collectible market, two kinds of items surface that may or may not hold any value for the collector, but may succeed in confusing or even fooling you into thinking you have a rare item when in fact you've paid far more than you should have for something that's lower in value or even worthless.

Restored items are those collectibles which have been repaired or otherwise altered to restore them to something resembling their original condition. This could involve glueing broken parts, whitening paper (a costly but often effective process), repainting scratched surfaces, or any of a number of other major to minor alterations. For the most part, reputable dealers will be up front when selling a restored item, but there are those unscrupulous types who will attempt to pass off a restored collectible as a Mint condition one. Whether they are the honest sort or not, a restored collectible will never be quite as valuable as an original one in Mint condition. At best, you should consider an expertly restored item to fall around the Fine price for a comparable unrestored item.

Far worse than restored items, at least as far as the novice collector and easy identification are concerned, is the reproduced or fake item. These are, put simply, fabricated items made to look like authentic collectibles. They can be items that were never actually produced, or they can be facsimiles of licensed products that have been painstakingly designed to fool the collector into believing them to be the real thing.

A recent sidestep in the category of the repro or fake item is the 'created' collectible. Fuelled by the accessibility and ease of use of sites like eBay, many less-than-trustworthy types have started simply manufacturing previously non-existent collectibles by buying easy-to-obtain mass-produced items like CDs and clock-making kits, metallic lighters, and badge-making machines, and then applying various celebrity and pop culture images to them to create a collectible for auction on the Internet. The result is a torrent of *Doctor Who* merchandise that was never licensed or produced by any established company.

The best weapon against illicit merchandise and the dealers that sell such items is knowledge. Being well versed in your chosen collectible field will go a long way to prevent you from being swindled in a deal. In some cases, your awareness of the details of your collectible history will enable you to spot fakes and reproductions easily by identifying incorrect copyright dates, inaccurate details, or other telltale signs.

Another defence is an established relationship with a reputable dealer. If you know your dealer well enough, chances are you won't be in danger of buying phoney merchandise. Be aware, however, that even honest dealers sometimes acquire repros or fakes without realizing it themselves. Always remember the tried and true axiom: "Let the buyer beware". But don't let it ruin the fun, either. The more you collect, the more informed you will be. A knowledgeable collector is a safe collector.

ANOTHER PERSPECTIVE

IN the United States, there's always been a certain additional mystique to collecting *Doctor Who* memorabilia. For one thing, until the mid to late eighties, there simply weren't that many places you could go to even find *Who* collectibles. Stores rarely carried them, apart from the SF and specialist comic shops, and when they did, there might be one or two copies of *Doctor Who Magazine*, a few FASA figurines and modules (usually 12 copies of the same one), and that was basically it. Without years of exposure, and with only a small number of PBS stations carrying the show (and regularly berating fans – excuse me, 'Whovians' – during their twice yearly pledge drives for not calling in and bequeathing their annual salaries to the station for the privilege of watching that wacky Time Lord), the American collectible marketplace was slow to recognize the value of *Doctor Who* merchandise. And so US fans dwelled in darkness.

Don't miss the fabulous DALEK BADGE

DALEK 1/3d

MINI DALEK 9d

DALEK

DALEK

At your local Woolworth Store.

This changed during the late eighties, and ironically, as *Doctor Who* ended its long reign on the BBC in the UK, the United States fanbase exploded, resulting in many more and plentiful tie-in items than ever before. Today, *Doctor Who Magazine* is much more reliably distributed through the same comic shops that used to receive a few issues every six months or so. And thanks to the increasing popularity of collectible transactions on the Internet, of course, the availability of *Doctor Who* collectibles no longer depends on where in the world you are. Simply go online, visit eBay or Mallarkey or some other comparable site, and luxuriate in all the wonderful choices: old Target novels, Sevans models, that porcelain TARDIS you always wanted, and much more. Even as the show's exposure has fluctuated on American PBS stations as well as cable and satellite services, the Internet has remained the single best place to collect and connect with *Doctor Who*.

So as we enter a new millennium, the world of *Doctor Who* collecting has truly become a worldwide phenomenon, unchained by any geographic boundaries. Whether you're a British fan who remembers hiding behind that clichéd sofa and cowering from the Daleks or the Cybermen as they stalked towards you in eerie black and white, or you're an American fan who first encountered that scarf-wearing, curly-haired, toothy Bohemian as he battled the Wirrn or the Sontarans and later thrilled to the final showdown between a more dashing, romantic Doctor and his leather-jacketed arch-nemesis, or perhaps even someone who first fell in love with *Doctor Who* via novels or audio dramas and then discovered the television series that spawned them, the universe of *Doctor Who* collecting is yours. British, American, Australian, Canadian, and everyone in between – we're all linked together by our love for a quirky BBC TV series that took us on journeys to distant worlds and times, and we can all share in the fun of collecting *Doctor Who* memorabilia.

A BRIEF HISTORY OF DOCTOR WHO MERCHANDISE

THE history of *Doctor Who* merchandise really begins with the Daleks. Today it is hard to imagine the impact that the Daleks made on the British television-watching population at the very end of 1963. Anyone who grew up at that time will probably recall games of 'Daleks versus Thals' being fought in the school playground, and anyone who missed an episode felt left out all week, unable to join in the speculation as to how the Doctor would win through in his latest adventure.

From the point at which the Daleks first appeared – in the second episode of *Doctor Who*'s second story – the BBC started to receive letters asking about them. Inevitably, people wanted to know where they could get a Dalek of their own from, and this led to questions about the availability of toys and other Dalek-related merchandise. It took some time for the BBC to react to this.

In the nineties, television shows and films with marketable potential are geared towards just that fact, and the issuing of licences to produce tie-in merchandise is all done as part and parcel of the show that is being produced. Film production companies have not been slow to realise that you can make more money from lucrative merchandise deals than you get from the film itself – in the case of *Star Wars: The Phantom Menace*, more was spent on the production of merchandise and promotion than the film cost to make. It can also be argued that the film is a necessary annoyance in order to get as much merchandise out in the shops as possible.

Things were very different in the sixties. For there to be any tie-in merchandise at all, a show had first to find its audience – there had to be a demand, and the idea of creating that demand artificially as happens today had not been thought of. Therefore it took until June 1964 before the first item of *Doctor Who* merchandise was released. This was *The Dalek Book* published by Souvenir Press. After this, and with the promise of a further Dalek adventure before Christmas 1964, the race was on to release the first Dalek model for Christmas.

The BBC had been caught completely off guard by the burgeoning popularity of the Daleks – after all, many people in the Corporation quietly felt that this new programme *Doctor Who*, with its young and inexperienced producer, would and should fail. Clearly they were wrong.

The BBC had a small department for overseeing merchandise tie-ins to their programmes – *Dixon of Dock Green*, *The Flowerpot Men*, *Z-Cars* and *Andy Pandy* had all spawned spin-offs before *Doctor Who* arrived – but the scale of the Dalek boom defeated them. This is not really suprising as the "department" consisted of just one person, Roy Williams. With pressure to sort out the licensing of *Doctor Who* growing, Williams decided to give over the job of dealing with all the interested companies to an Australian entrepreneur, Walter Tuckwell, whose organisation, Walter Tuckwell Associates Ltd, already handled several BBC copyright programmes. Tuckwell took responsibility for liaising with the external companies and issuing them with licenses and the BBC created a new post, that of Exploitation Manager, to deal with the copyright

From an October 1965 'ABC Minors Special' magazine (produced by a UK cinema chain), this picture captures the excitement of Dalekmania at a Woolworths in Romford. Note the Dalek playsuit.

agreement and clearance procedures. This role was taken by Williams and one of his first tasks was to try and sort out the ownership of the Daleks. Eventually, Terry Nation and his agents managed to secure a fifty per cent ownership deal with the BBC, making the Daleks one of the few *Doctor Who* monsters the dramatic rights to which are legally co-owned by both the BBC and by the writer who created them. The dramatic rights in the majority of the monsters is wholly owned by their creators, with the BBC only able to claim ownership of their design, a fact that many companies and individuals in the eighties and nineties exploited with regards to audio and video productions, gaining permission from the owners of the dramatic rights, and altering the design of the various characters and creatures so the BBC's agreement was not required.

In mid-1965, Tuckwell ran an eighteen-page advertisement feature in *Games and Toys* magazine to promote all the companies he had interested in producing Dalek-related merchandise. Tuckwell's success stemmed from the fact that his company would actively approach other companies and suggest that they might be interested in a Dalek or *Doctor Who* variant of something that they already manufactured: like the 'Linda' snowstorms, the various anti-Dalek guns or the jigsaws. This pro-active approach is used today by television and film promoters for new product, but the BBC traditionally tends to license *Doctor Who* items when interested parties come to them, or when an obvious opportunity presents itself.

Tuckwell's aim was to get all the Dalek and *Doctor Who* products he had arranged licences for into the shops for Christmas, and his approach worked admirably. Fliers also listing available toys and games were distributed at all the cinemas showing the new film *Dr. Who and the Daleks*, thus raising public awareness of just what could be bought, and any child who did not receive a Dalek in their stocking for Christmas 1965 would have been sorely disappointed.

Given that television was still a relatively new form of entertainment, and not that many families had it, or even could afford it, it is arguable that it was the combined efforts of Tuckwell, and the two *Doctor Who* cinema films, that brought the adventures of the Doctor to a wider audience, and thus ensured it a place in the hearts and minds of an entire generation of children and adults. It is difficult today to recognise Tuckwell's achievement. We are used to being assailed every Christmas by a different marketing ploy to get us to buy toys: whether they be Buzz Lightyear, Furbys, Thunderbirds, talking Teletubbies or *Star Wars* items. Back in 1965, this did not happen, and the arrival on every toyshop shelf of Daleks in every imaginable form, from badges and transfers to models, jigsaws and slippers via sweet cigarettes, comic strips and cinema films, must have been an amazing thing to experience.

This high level of success continued throughout 1966, but by 1967 the bubble seemed to have

From the same 'ABC Minors Special' magazine, this Woolworths in Hereford has been inundated with Daleks.

burst. The Daleks were slipping in popularity, and the BBC were unable to come up with anything which generated the same degree of interest. No one seemed to want to market the Cybermen (a fact which prompted their co-creator and copyright holder Kit Pedler to write several letters to the BBC querying the lack of promotion); and although there was interest expressed in the Quarks in 1969, contractual problems between the BBC and the robots' creators prevented the licensing of any products.

Up until the end of the sixties, very little merchandise unconnected with the Daleks was released. In many ways, the Daleks made and broke *Doctor Who* merchandising, as manufacturers and publishers seemed reluctant to produce *Doctor Who*-related as opposed to Dalek-related items. In fact, in the late sixties, the combination of post-Dalek apathy and Patrick Troughton's reluctance to publicise the programme resulted in *Doctor Who* tie-in products all but disappearing from shop shelves. In addition, Walter Tuckwell had moved on from looking after the *Doctor Who* properties and their administration had reverted to Roy Williams at the BBC.

In the late sixties BBC Exploitation was merged with BBC Radio Enterprises and renamed BBC Licensing, at the same time taking on responsibility for a series of increasingly popular BBC-orientated public exhibitions. The mandate of the department was, as its original title suggested, to exploit BBC properties through the licensing of merchandise rights. The department would do what they had employed Tuckwell to do: actively go out and suggest products to manufacturers as well as acting as a reference point for anyone who wanted to produce something connected with a BBC programme. In the seventies BBC Licensing became subsumed within BBC Enterprises, a company set up specifically to handle all aspects of the marketing of BBC programmes.

Although there were a large number of *Doctor Who*-related products produced during the seventies, it was rare for any of them to do really well. The days of the mid-sixties Dalek boom were over and most licensees had no more than one royalty payment to make to the BBC. In many cases, only the initial licence fee was paid, the product selling insufficiently well to cover even that advance. The one major exception to this rule was the range of novelisations based on the series, which formed the single most profitable area of *Doctor Who* merchandising in the seventies.

In the late seventies, Roy Williams was joined in running the licensing division of BBC Enterprises by Chris Crouch and between them they looked after this side of the organisation through the eighties. *Doctor Who* formed a large part of their workload as there was ever more interest in the production of spin-off items. By the start of the eighties, the BBC had effectively split into two separate organisations: BBC Television, which made and transmitted programmes; and BBC Enterprises, which exploited the programmes commercially.

Whereas in the sixties and seventies, the interest in *Doctor Who* items had been primarily from established book publishers and toy manufacturers; in the eighties, it was the small fan-led concerns which dominated. Organisations like Whomobilia, BCP Promotions, Sevans Models, Who Dares Publishing, Reeltime Pictures and Mediaband had all come into existence through a fan demand for product, and in many cases were set-up and run by fans. There were numerous demands for licences for small, one-off projects which the BBC were generally reluctant to grant, feeling that the time and effort to issue a licence would not be justified by any financial return.

Along with the swell of demand for *Doctor Who* product came the establishment of a second key line, which, together with the ongoing ranges of novelisations and factual hardback books, would go on to dominate *Doctor Who* merchandise into the nineties. This was BBC Video's catalogue of *Doctor Who* releases. BBC Video was, along with BBC Records, another division of what was to become BBC Worldwide. There were also some casualties with World International Publishing's *Doctor Who* Annual, up to that point the longest running range of *Doctor Who* merchandise, ceasing publication following the 1985 release of an Annual for 1986. Fine Art Castings also underwent a boom and a subsequent decline during the decade, producing an impressive range of metal miniatures.

Another factor in the eighties were the great technological strides that placed the ability to create basic merchandisable items like tee-shirts and badges into the price range of just about anyone. Because of this, it is almost impossible to document accurately all the items issued during the decade in question. A large number of unofficial and unlicensed items appeared, often being produced in small numbers and sold exclusively at *Doctor Who* conventions both in the UK and in America.

The eighties were also when fandom really took off in America, and with it came additional problems for Williams and Crouch. It became increasingly hard to administer what all the fan groups and conventions were doing, and a great number of unlicensed items were released. To try and combat this, two American groups were given licences to produce (or to subcontract to others) *Doctor Who* goods. These were the Spirit of Light organisation who were organising an annual *Doctor Who* convention patronised by producer John Nathan-Turner and the then-current stars of the show, and Barbara Elder, a fan who had become involved in running a North American section of the UK fanclub, the *Doctor Who* Appreciation Society, and who set up both the Barbara Elder Corporation and Nightstar Ltd to facilitate the release of *Doctor Who* goods.

When Williams retired, Crouch continued to run the department until the BBC underwent another reorganisation, and BBC Enterprises became BBC Worldwide. Responsibility for licensing then passed to Richard Hollis within the licensing division of BBC Worldwide, and, at the time of writing, there is a team of people who actually handle the individual properties, as well as other departments which look after America, Europe, Australasia and so on.

The nineties saw the continuation of the successful *Doctor Who* merchandising lines: the videos through BBC Worldwide; Marvel Comics' *Doctor Who Magazine*, which survived changes in corporate direction when the Italian firm Panini was acquired by Marvel in the '90s and given publishing control of the magazine; and Virgin Publishing's ranges of original *Doctor Who* fiction

Has the second Dalek invasion of Earth begun? Compare this classic Marx Dalek toy ad from the 1960s, proclaiming that "Daleks have invaded toyshops!" with this Product Enterprise Ltd ad from 2001, announcing that their new Talking Daleks were "Invading this season!" It seems no matter what the era, the mutants from Skaro will be there to fill collectors' shelves.

and non-fiction books which were taken over by BBC Worldwide themselves in 1996. These ranges were joined by Big Finish's range of original *Doctor Who* audio adventures, as well as Harlequin Miniatures ever-expanding range of metal models, new soundtrack CDs and many other examples of *Doctor Who* merchandise.

As the series approached its 40th anniversary year in 2003, there was an ever-growing torrent of *Who*-related merchandise flooding specialty shops and online retailers. Product Enterprise Ltd was granted the master toy licence by BBC Worldwide after impressing fans worldwide with their line of '60s-like Dalek Rolykins and their larger-scale Talking Daleks. By the end of 2002, Dalek Roll-A-Matics, a foot-tall radio controlled Dalek, and a Talking Cyberman complete with Cybermat had joined the Talking Daleks. Once again the Daleks were leading the charge into shops and collectors' homes.

Meanwhile, Big Finish began an exciting new chapter in the *Doctor Who* saga by producing licensed full-cast audio dramas featuring many of the original actors from the television series. For many fans, it was as close to a revival of the show as they would get for some time, and the BF crew expanded their efforts to include spin-off series based on popular companion Sarah-Jane Smith and, of course, those dependable Daleks.

Telos Publishing also took up the gauntlet by introducing a new range of *Doctor Who* fiction in the form of limited edition hardcover novellas.

At press-time, the series was set to end in 2004, but not before releasing a line of highly collectible books.

From a humble one-man operation in the sixties, the licensing and exploitation of BBC properties has become big business. *Doctor Who* still forms a major part of that operation, and, by the end of the 20th century, was the only BBC property, not currently in production, which enjoyed books, videos and audio releases being produced on an ongoing schedule by BBC Worldwide. The bulk of their other licensing lies with shows like *Teletubbies*, *Postman Pat*, *Fireman Sam*, *Pingu*, *Fimbles* and other children's shows, plus tie-in books and videos for currently airing shows like Delia Smith's popular cookery programmes, numerous gardening and home improvement shows, and tie-ins to one-off productions and ongoing series like *Neverwhere*, *Red Dwarf* and *Walking With Dinosaurs*.

So where will the *Who* merchandising juggernaut go next? As before, the Daleks remain the singlemost exploitable image from the series for any number of product lines; it seems clear that as long as fans are willing to buy the nasty pepperpots, there will be an endless variety of them available. The new frontier of DVD has enabled BBC Worldwide to begin a new cycle of releasing classic stories now that the series has completed its run on VHS video tape, and BBCi, the network's online presence, has even found a way to present all-new *Who* via the embryonic

medium of webcasting. As this book goes to press, we await the debut of Richard E. Grant as the Ninth Doctor in a 40th anniversary animated webcast as well as the return of the live-action series itself in a new production scheduled to air on BBC1 in 2005. Will these new incarnations spark a resurgence in *Who* merchandising? You know what the Doctor says about time telling...

AAP-004 (selected cards and Elizabeth Sladen brochure)

ARTIST PROMOTIONAL ITEMS

THESE are not *Doctor Who* items in the strict sense of the term, but goods which are commissioned by and are associated with the actors and actresses who appeared on *Doctor Who*. They are usually based around current, newly-taken photographs.

AAP-001 Sophie Aldred Photographs
1989, Mediaband, UK
Mediaband arranged two sets of photographs of the stars of *Doctor Who*. These were not images from the program, but new photographs of the actors concerned.
OP: various   NM: £3 each

AAP-002 Sylvester McCoy Photographs
1989, Mediaband, UK
OP: various   NM: £3 each

AAP-003 Photographs
1994- , TTL, UK
Original images by Robin Pritchard, many produced to tie in with Reeltime Pictures' *Myth Makers* video releases. TTL also sold some of designer Raymond P Cusick's stills, plus some from actor Rick Lester taken on location for *Day of Daleks*. See also SPH-012.

AAP-004 Character Photographs, Postcards, Mugs, Brochures
1996- , Cineffigy, UK
Produced by Ian Burgess for *Doctor Who* stars Colin Baker, Nicola Bryant, Elisabeth Sladen, Carole Ann Ford, Sophie Aldred, Sylvester McCoy and others.
OP: various

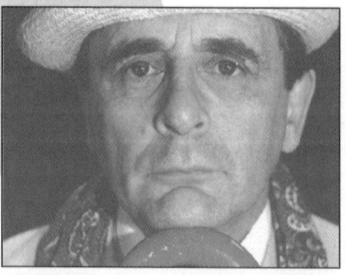

AAP-004 (three more examples)

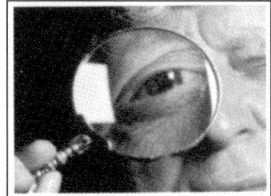

AAP-005
(selected cards)

AAP-005 Tom Baker Postcard Pack
1999/11, Tree Root Productions Ltd, UK
Set of 6 postcards featuring Tom Baker in costume.
Includes a promotional card and a special TARDIS
cover. A set of nine cards was also available for the
same price through several UK retailers.
OP: £4.99

AAP-006 Tom Baker Posters
1999, Tree Root Productions Ltd, UK
Set of five A5 posters. Same images as on the 1999
Tree Root Productions Postcards.
OP: £25.00 set   NM: £22 set

AAP-007 Colin Baker Photographs
2001/08/23, The Stamp Centre, UK
Two 8"x10" photographic images of Colin Baker.
Signed by Baker.
OP: £15 each

AAP-008 2003 Calendar
2002/11, Cineffigy, UK
Black and white photographic calendar featuring pho-
tographs of: Colin Baker; Carole Ann Ford; Nicola
Bryant; Mark Strickson; Sophie Aldred; Louise
Jameson; Nicholas Courtney; Deborah Watling;
Sylvester McCoy; Wendy Padbury.
OP: £17.99

AAP-008

ABF-001

ABF-002

AUDIO, BIG FINISH DRAMAS

IN 1999, Big Finish Productions began releasing a series of full-cast audio dramas reuniting all of the surviving Doctors (bar Tom Baker) with many of their companions (and a few new ones) for all-new *Doctor Who* adventures. The stories were originally released in both CD and cassette versions, but the cassette releases were phased out in 2000. Note: Big Finish do not specify release dates for their products, just the month of release.

ABF-001   *Doctor Who: The Sirens of Time* (Nicholas Briggs)
1999/07/19, Big Finish Productions, UK
Twin CD/Cassette. Cover by James Arnott. The first in a new range of original *Doctor Who* adventures on audio. Starring Peter Davison, Colin Baker and Sylvester McCoy.
REF: BFPDWCD7Z OP: £13.99/£9.99

ABF-002   *Doctor Who: Phantasmagoria* (Mark Gatiss)
1999/09/04, Big Finish Productions, UK
Twin CD/Cassette. Cover by James Arnott. Starring Peter Davison and Mark Strickson.
REF: BFPDWCD6PA OP: £13.99/£9.99

ABF-003

ABF-004

ABF-003   *Doctor Who: Whispers of Terror* (Justin Richards)
1999/11/01, Big Finish Productions, UK
Twin CD/Cassette. Cover by James Arnott. Starring Colin Baker and Nicola Bryant.
REF: BFPDWCD6ZA OP: £13.99/£9.99

ABF-005

ABF-006

ABF-004   *Doctor Who: The Land of the Dead* (Stephen Cole)
2000/01, Big Finish Productions, UK
Twin CD/Cassette. Cover by Peri Godbold. Starring Peter Davison and Sarah Sutton.
REF: BFPDWCD6CA OP: £13.99/£9.99

ABF-007

ABF-008

ABF-009

ABF-010

ABF-011

ABF-012

ABF-013

ABF-014

ABF-015

ABF-016

ABF-005 *Doctor Who: The Fearmonger* **(Jon Blum)**
2000/02, Big Finish Productions, UK
Twin CD/Cassette. Cover by Clayton Hickman. Starring
Sylvester McCoy and Sophie Aldred.
REF: BFPDWCD7R OP: £13.99/£9.99

ABF-006 *Doctor Who: The Marian Conspiracy*
(Jacqueline Rayner)
2000/03, Big Finish Productions, UK
Twin CD/Cassette. Cover by Clayton Hickman. Starring
Colin Baker.
REF: BFPDWCD7CA OP: £13.99/£9.99

ABF-007 *Doctor Who: Red Dawn* **(Justin
Richards)**
2000/04, Big Finish Productions, UK
Twin CD/Cassette. Cover by Clayton Hickman. Starring
Peter Davison and Nicola Bryant.
REF: BFPDWCD6QA OP: £13.99/£9.99

ABF-008 *Doctor Who: The Genocide Machine*
(Mike Tucker)
2000/05, Big Finish Productions, UK
Twin CD/Cassette. Cover by Clayton Hickman. Starring
Sylvester McCoy and Sophie Aldred.
REF: BFPDWCD7S OP: £13.99/£9.99

ABF-009 *Doctor Who: The Spectre of Lanyon
Moor* **(Nicholas Pegg)**
2000/06, Big Finish Productions, UK
Twin CD/Cassette. Cover by Clayton Hickman. Starring
Colin Baker and Nicholas Courtney.
REF: BFPDWCD7CB OP: £13.99/£9.99

ABF-010 *Doctor Who: Winter for the Adept*
(Andrew Cartmel)
2000/07, Big Finish Productions, UK
Twin CD/Cassette. Cover by Clayton Hickman. Starring
Peter Davison and Sarah Sutton.
REF: BFPDWCD6CB OP: £13.99/£9.99

ABF-011 *Doctor Who: The Apocalypse Element*
(Stephen Cole)
2000/08, Big Finish Productions, UK
Twin CD/Cassette. Cover by Clayton Hickman. Starring
Colin Baker and Lalla Ward.
REF: BFPDWCD7CC OP: £13.99/£9.99

ABF-012 *Doctor Who: The Fires of Vulcan* **(Steve
Lyons)**
2000/09, Big Finish Productions, UK
Twin CD/Cassette. Cover by Clayton Hickman. Starring
Sylvester McCoy and Bonnie Langford.
REF: BFPDWCD7FA OP: £13.99/£9.99

ABF-013 *Doctor Who: The Shadow of the
Scourge* **(Paul Cornell)**
2000/10, Big Finish Productions, UK
Twin CD/Cassette. Cover by Clayton Hickman. Starring
Sylvester McCoy and Sophie Aldred.
REF: BFPDWCDSS1 OP: £13.99/£9.99

ABF-014 *Doctor Who: The Holy Terror* **(Rob
Shearman)**
2000/11, Big Finish Productions, UK
Twin CD/Cassette. Cover by Clayton Hickman.
Starring Colin Baker.
REF: BFPDWCDSS2 OP: £13.99/£9.99

ABF-015 *Doctor Who: The Mutant Phase*
(Nicholas Briggs)
2000/12, Big Finish Productions, UK
Twin CD/Cassette. Cover by Clayton Hickman. Starring
Peter Davison and Sarah Sutton.
REF: BFPDWCD6CC OP: £13.99/£9.99

ABF-016 *Doctor Who: Storm Warning* **(Alan
Barnes)**
2001/01, Big Finish Productions, UK
Twin CD. Cover by Clayton Hickman. Starring Paul
McGann. Introduces a new companion for the 8th
Doctor, Charley Pollard, played by India Fisher.
REF: BFPDWCD8B OP: £13.99

ABF-017

ABF-018

ABF-019

ABF-020

ABF-021

ABF-022

ABF-023

ABF-024

ABF-025

ABF-026

ABF-017 *Doctor Who: Sword of Orion* (**Nicholas Briggs**)
2001/02, Big Finish Productions, UK
Twin CD. Cover by Clayton Hickman. Starring Paul McGann. Features the Cybermen.
REF: BFPDWCD8C OP: £13.99

ABF-018 *Doctor Who: The Stones of Venice* (**Paul Magrs**)
2001/03, Big Finish Productions, UK
Twin CD. Cover by Clayton Hickman. Starring Paul McGann.
REF: BFPDWCD8D OP: £13.99

ABF-019 *Doctor Who: Minuet in Hell* (**Alan W Lear and Gary Russell**)
2001/04, Big Finish Productions, UK
Twin CD. Cover by Clayton Hickman. Starring Paul McGann and Nicholas Courtney.
REF: BFPDWCD8E OP: £13.99

ABF-020 *Doctor Who: Loups-Garoux* (**Marc Platt**)
2001/05, Big Finish Productions, UK
Twin CD. Cover by Clayton Hickman. Starring Peter Davison and Mark Strickson.
REF: BFPDWCD6PB OP: £13.99

ABF-021 *Doctor Who: Dust Breeding* (**Mike Tucker**)
2001/06, Big Finish Productions, UK
Twin CD. Cover by Clayton Hickman. Starring Sylvester McCoy and Sophie Aldred. Also features the Krill from the BBC novel *Storm Harvest*.
REF: BFPDWCD7T OP: £13.99

ABF-022 *Doctor Who: Bloodtide* (**Jonathan Morris**)
2001/07, Big Finish Productions, UK
Twin CD. Cover by Clayton Hickman. Starring Colin Baker. Also features the Silurians.
REF: BFPDWCD7CD OP: £13.99

ABF-023 *Doctor Who: Project: Twilight* (**Cavan Scott and Mark Wright**)
2001/08, Big Finish Productions, UK
Twin CD. Cover by Clayton Hickman. Starring Colin Baker.
REF: BFPDWCD7CE OP: £13.99

ABF-024 *Doctor Who: Eye of the Scorpion* (**Iain McLaughlin**)
2001/09, Big Finish Productions, UK
Twin CD. Cover by Clayton Hickman. Starring Peter Davison and Nicola Bryant.
REF: BFPDWCD6QB OP: £13.99

ABF-025 *Doctor Who: Colditz* (**Steve Lyons**)
2001/10, Big Finish Productions, UK
Twin CD. Cover by Clayton Hickman. Starring Sylvester McCoy and Sophie Aldred.
REF: BFPDWCD7U OP: £13.99

ABF-026 *Doctor Who: Primeval* (Lance Parkin)
2001/11, Big Finish Productions, UK
Twin CD. Cover by Clayton Hickman. Starring Peter
Davison and Sarah Sutton.
REF: BFPDWCD6CD OP: £13.99

ABF-027 *Doctor Who: The One Doctor* (Gareth
Roberts and Clayton Hickman)
2001/12, Big Finish Productions, UK
Twin CD. Cover by Clayton Hickman. Starring Colin
Baker and Bonnie Langford.
REF: BFPDWCD7CR OP: £13.99

ABF-028 *Doctor Who: Invaders from Mars*
(**Mark Gatiss**)
2002/01, Big Finish Productions, UK
Twin CD. Cover by Clayton Hickman. With Paul McGann.
REF: BFPDECD8F OP: £13.99

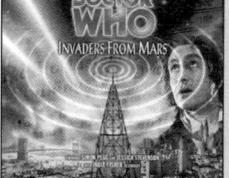

ABF-027

ABF-028

ABF-029 *Doctor Who: The Chimes of Midnight*
(**Robert Shearman**)
2002/02, Big Finish Productions, UK
Twin CD. Cover by Clayton Hickman. With Paul McGann.
REF: BFPDWCD8G OP: £13.99

ABF-030 *Doctor Who: Seasons of Fear* (**Paul
Cornell and Caroline Symcox**)
2002/03, Big Finish Productions, UK
Twin CD. Cover by Clayton Hickman. With Paul McGann.
REF: BFPDWCD8H OP: £13.99

ABF-029

ABF-030

ABF-031 *Doctor Who: Embrace the Darkness*
(**Nicholas Briggs**)
2002/04, Big Finish Productions, UK
Twin CD. Cover by Clayton Hickman. With Paul McGann.
REF: BFPDWCD8J OP: £13.99

ABF-032 *Doctor Who: The Time of the Daleks*
(**Justin Richards**)
2002/05, Big Finish Productions, UK
Twin CD. Cover by Clayton Hickman. With Paul McGann.
REF: BFPDWCD8K OP: £13.99

ABF-031

ABF-032

ABF-033 *Doctor Who: Neverland* (Akan Barnes)
2002/06, Big Finish Productions, UK
Twin CD. Cover by Clayton Hickman. With Paul McGann.
REF: BFPDWCD8L OP: £13.99

ABF-033

ABF-033.5 *Doctor Who: The Maltese Penguin*
(**Robert Shearman**)
2002/08, Big Finish Productions, UK
Special CD initially given free to subscribers to Big
Finish's range. Numbered 33 and a half. Single CD.
Starring Colin Baker. Released for sale at £9.99 in
December 2002. Cover by Lee Binding.
REF: BFPDWCDSS3 OP: free

ABF-033.5

ABF-034

ABF-035

ABF-034 *Doctor Who: Spare Parts* **(Marc Platt)**
2002/07, Big Finish Productions, UK
Twin CD. Cover by Clayton Hickman. Starring Peter
Davison and Sarah Sutton.
REF: BFPDWCD6CE OP: £13.99

ABF-035 *Doctor Who: …ish* **(Phil Pascoe)**
2002/08, Big Finish Productions, UK
Twin CD. Cover by Clayton Hickman. Starring Colin
Baker and Nicola Bryant. Original edition has number
'34' on the spine. The inlay card was re-issued with
the correct number '35'.
REF: BFPDWCD6ZB OP: £13.99

ABF-036 *Doctor Who: The Rapture* **(Joseph Lidster)**
2002/09, Big Finish Productions, UK
Twin CD. Cover by Clayton Hickman. Starring Sylvester
McCoy and Sophie Aldred.
REF: BFPDWCD7V OP: £13.99

ABF-037 *Doctor Who: The Sandman* **(Simon A
Forward)**
2002/10, Big Finish Productions, UK
Twin CD. Cover by Lee Binding. Starring Colin Baker.
REF: BFPDWCD7CF OP: £13.99

ABF-036

ABF-037

ABF-038 *Doctor Who: The Church and the
Crown* **(Cavan Scott and Mark Wright)**
2002/11, Big Finish Productions, UK
Twin CD. Cover by Clayton Hickman. Starring Peter
Davison.
REF: BFPDWCD6QC OP: £13.99

ABF-039 *Doctor Who: Bang-Bang-A-Boom*
(Gareth Roberts & Clayton Hickman)
2002/12, Big Finish Productions, UK
Twin CD. Cover by Clayton Hickman. With Colin Baker.
REF: BFPDWCD7EA OP: £13.99

ABF-038

ABF-039

AUDIO BOOKS

SPOKEN word versions of previously existing books.

ABO-001a *State of Decay* **Talking Book**
1981/06, Pickwick International, UK
Cassette. Abridged version of the novelisation. Read by
Tom Baker. Blister packed on a book-shaped backing card.
REF: PTB 607 OP: £2.25 NM: £11

ABO-001b *State of Decay* **Talking Book**
1985, Ditto, UK
Re-issue on two cassettes. Two variants of packaging:
two cassettes stuck together with sticky tape; single
box containing two cassettes.
REF: DTO 10517 OP: £1.99 NM: £22

ABO-001a

ABO-001b

ABO-002 *Origins of the Cybermen* by David Banks
1989/03, Silver Fist, UK
Cassette adapted and read by David Banks from his book *Cybermen*. See BFA-021.
REF: TC-DB1 OP: £5.99 NM: £6-£9

ABO-003 *The Early Cybermen* by David Banks
1989/10, Silver Fist, UK
Cassette adapted and read by David Banks from his book *Cybermen*. See BFA-021.
REF: SF-AT2 OP: £5.99 NM: £6-£9

ABO-004 *The Cyber Nomads* by David Banks
1990/02, Silver Fist, UK
Cassette adapted and read by David Banks from his book *Cybermen*. See BFA-021.
REF: SF-AT3 OP: £5.99 NM: £6-£9

ABO-005 *The Ultimate Cybermen* by David Banks
1990/02, Silver Fist, UK
Cassette adapted and read by David Banks from his book *Cybermen*. See BFA-021.
REF: SF-AT4 OP: £5.99 NM: £6-£9

ABO-006a *Doctor Who: Attack of the Cybermen*
1995/08/07, BBC Worldwide Ltd, UK
Single cassette. Abridged version of the novelisation read by Colin Baker.
REF: ZBBC 1776 ISBN: 0-563-38866-8 OP: £5.99

ABO-006b *Doctor Who: Attack of the Cybermen*
1995, ABC Enterprises, AUS
Same catalogue number as UK release.

ABO-007a *Doctor Who: Planet of the Daleks*
1995/06/05, BBC Worldwide Ltd, UK
Single cassette. Abridged version of the novelisation read by Jon Pertwee.
REF: ZBBC 1769 ISBN: 0-563-38826-9 OP: £5.99

ABO-007b *Doctor Who: Planet of the Daleks*
1995, ABC Enterprises, AUS
Same catalogue number as UK release.

ABO-008a *Doctor Who: The Curse of Peladon*
1995/07/03, BBC Worldwide Ltd, UK
Single cassette. Abridged version of the novelisation read by Jon Pertwee.
REF: ZBBC 1768 ISBN: 0-563-38821-8 OP: £5.99

ABO-008b *Doctor Who: The Curse of Peladon*
1995, ABC Enterprises, AUS
Same catalogue number as UK release.

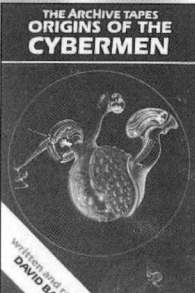

ABO-002

ABO-003

ABO-004

ABO-005

ABO-006a

ABO-007a

ABO-008a

ABO-009a

ABO-010

ABO-011

ABO-012

ABO-013

ABO-014a

ABO-015

ACO-001 (sleeve)

ABO-009a *Doctor Who: Warriors of the Deep*
1995/06/05, BBC Worldwide Ltd, UK
Single cassette. Abridged version of the novelisation
read by Peter Davison.
REF: ZBBC 1771 ISBN: 0-563-38836-6 OP: £5.99

ABO-009b *Doctor Who: Warriors of the Deep*
1995, ABC Enterprises, AUS
Same catalogue number as UK release.

ABO-010 *Doctor Who: Kinda*
1997/08/04, BBC Worldwide Ltd, UK
Single cassette. Abridged version of the novelisation
read by Peter Davison. Also imported for sale in
Australia, no separate ABC Enterprises release.
REF: ZBBC 1770 OP: £7.99

ABO-011 *Doctor Who: The Novel Of The Film*
1997/06/02, BBC Worldwide Ltd, UK
Twin cassette. Abridged version of the novelisation
read by Paul McGann.
REF: ZBBC 1998 ISBN: 0-563-38148-5 OP: £7.99

ABO-012 *Doctor Who: Vengeance on Varos*
1997/11/03, BBC Worldwide Ltd, UK
Single cassette. Abridged version of the novelisation
read by Colin Baker.
REF: ZBBC 1832 OP: £7.99

ABO-013 *Doctor Who: Short Trips*
1998/03/02, BBC Worldwide Ltd, UK
Twin cassette. Read by Nicholas Courtney and Sophie
Aldred. Stories: *Freedom* (Steve Lyons); *Model Train Set*
(Jonathan Blum); *Glass* (Tara Samms); *Degrees of Truth*
(David A McIntee); *Stop the Pigeon* (Robert Perry and
Mike Tucker); *Old Flames* (Paul Magrs); *Degrees of Truth*
(David A McIntee). See also BAT-005.
REF: ZBBC 2147 OP: £8.99

ABO-014a *Doctor Who: Earth and Beyond*
1998/09/07, BBC Worldwide Ltd, UK
Twin cassette. Read by Paul McGann. Stories: *Bounty*
(Peter Anghelides); *Dead Time* (Andrew Miller); *The
People's Temple* (Paul Leonard). See also BAT-005 and
BAT-006.
REF: ZBBC 2223 OP: £9.99

ABO-0014b *Doctor Who: Earth and Beyond*
1998, ABC Enterprises, AUS
Same catalogue number as UK release.

ABO-015 *Doctor Who: Out of the Darkness*
1998/11/02, BBC Worldwide Ltd, UK
Twin CD. Read by Colin Baker and Nicola Bryant.

Stories: *Moon Graffiti* (Dave Stone); *Wish You Were Here* (Guy Clapperton); *Vigil* (Michael Collier).
See also BAT-005 and BAT-006.
REF: ZBBC 2274 CD   OP: £12.99

AUDIO COLLECTIONS

ACO-001 *Doctor Who* **Collectors Edition**
1982, BBC Records and Tapes, USA
Genesis of the Daleks LP, Sound FX LP, Theme Single, poster and 7 photos).
REF: BBC-2LP-22001
OP: $16.98 ($12.95 in a different ad) NM: £35

ACO-001 (contents)

AUDIO DRAMAS

ACTED stories, either originated on LP, cassette or CD, or released commercially following radio transmission, excluding the regular releases of the licenced Big Finish *Doctor Who* series itself, which has its own section.

ADR-001a *Doctor Who and the Pescatons*
(Victor Pemberton)
1976/08, Argo/Decca Record Company, UK
LP/Cassette. An original story written by Victor Pemberton and starring Tom Baker and Elisabeth Sladen. Directed by Don Norman.
REF: LP ZSW 564 / cassette OP: £2.50 NM: £22-£28

ADR-001b *Doctor Who and the Pescatons*
(Victor Pemberton)
1979, World Record Club, AUS
Front cover is a completely different red and blue abstract design, with artwork signed 'Craig Dowsett(?) '79'. The record itself and back cover are otherwise the same as the regular release apart from the copyright and World Record Club information.
REF: WRC R-06037

ADR-001a

ADR-001c *Doctor Who and the Pescatons*
(Victor Pemberton)
1985/04, London Records, UK
LP & Cassette/ Re-issue
REF: 414 4591 LP, 414 4594 cass
OP: £4.50 NM: £16.50-£22

ADR-001d *Doctor Who and the Pescatons*
(Victor Pemberton)
1986, Neuman Communications Corporation, USA
Cassette. Design/Illustration by Laurie Richards, pho-

ADR-001b

ADR-001c

ADR-001d

ADR-001e

ADR-002a

ADR-002b

ADR-002c

ADR-002d

ADR-003a

ADR-003b

tographs by Suzette Gibbs. Inside flap advertises other audio titles featuring Tom Baker: *Journey to the Center of the Earth* and *The Strange Case of Dr. Jekyll and Mr. Hyde*.
REF: Argo 10090 ISBN: 0-88690-249-5

**ADR-001e Doctor Who and the Pescatons
(Victor Pemberton)**
1991/12, Silva Screen, UK
CD/Cassette. Re-issue. Cassette release issued by mistake and quickly withdrawn.
REF: CD FILMCD 707 / cassette FILMC 707
OP: £8.99 NM: £11

**ADR-001f Doctor Who and the Pescatons
(Victor Pemberton)**
1993/10, PolyGram/Speaking Volumes, UK
Cassette. Re-issue.
REF: 844-364-4 OP: £4.99 NM: £9

ADR-002a Slipback/Genesis of the Daleks
1988/11/07, BBC Records and Tapes, UK
Cassette release of the 1985 radio adventure *Slipback* along with a re-issue of the *Genesis of the Daleks* narrated soundtrack. Deleted 01/09/1998. Same as AST-002d.
REF: ZBBC 1020 ISBN: 0563 225572
OP: £5.99 NM: £16.50

ADR-002b Genesis of the Daleks & Slipback
1989, AVC Corporation/The Minds Eye, USA
Twin cassette. Same as AST-002e.
OP: $14.95

ADR-002c Doctor Who: Slipback
2001/01/08, BBC Worldwide Ltd, UK
Re-issue. Single CD. Cover by Max Ellis.
REF: ISBN 0-563-47794-6 OP: £9.99

**ADR-002d Doctor Who: Genesis of the
Daleks/Exploration Earth**
2001/07/02, BBC Worldwide Ltd, UK
Single CD. Re-issue. *Genesis of the Daleks* is presented in a slightly revised and expanded version to the previous LP and cassette releases. This is the first release of *Exploration Earth*, a 1976 radio schools broadcast starring Tom Baker and Elisabeth Sladen. Same as AST-002f.
REF: ISBN 0-563-47857-8 OP: £12.99

**ADR-003a Doctor Who: The Paradise of Death
(Barry Letts)**
1993/11/07, BBC Enterprises Ltd, UK
Twin cassette. Originally transmitted on BBC Radio. This is an extended version.
REF: ZBBC 1494 OP: £7.49 NM: £5.50

ADR-003b *Doctor Who: The Paradise of Death*
(Barry Letts)
2000/03/06, BBC Worldwide Ltd, UK
Twin CD. Re-issue. Cover by Max Ellis.
REF: ISBN 0-563-55323-5 OP: £12.99

ADR-004a *Doctor Who: The Ghosts of N-Space*
(Barry Letts)
1996/02/19, BBC Worldwide Ltd, UK
Twin cassette. Glow in the dark cover. A version with-
out the glow in the dark effect was later released.
Originally transmitted on BBC Radio.
REF: ZBBC 1813 ISBN: 0-563-38883-8
OP: £7.99 NM: £5.50

ADR-004a

ADR-004b *Doctor Who: The Ghosts of N-Space*
(Barry Letts)
2000/06/05, BBC Worldwide Ltd, UK
Triple CD. Reissue.
REF: ISBN 0-563-47701-6 OP: £15.99

ADR-005 *Doctor Who: Excelis Dawns* **(Paul Magrs)**
2002/02, Big Finish Productions, UK
Twin CD Starring Peter Davison and Anthony Stewart
Head with Katy Manning.
REF: BFPDWCDEX1 OP: £9.99

ADR-005

ADR-006

ADR-006 *Doctor Who: Excelis Rising* **(David A
McIntee)**
2002/04, Big Finish Productions, UK
Twin CD Starring Peter Davison and Anthony Stewart
Head.
REF: BFPDWCDEX2 OP: £9.99

ADR-007 *Doctor Who: Excelis Decays* **(Craig
Hinton)**
2002/06, Big Finish Productions, UK
Twin CD Starring Peter Davison and Anthony Stewart
Head.
REF: BFPDWCDEX3 OP: £9.99

ADR-007

ADR-008 *Doctor Who: Death Comes to Time*
(Colin Meek)
2002/10/28, BBC Worldwide Ltd, UK
Triple CD. Issue of a five part *Doctor Who* adventure
originally webcast on BBCi in weekly ten minute
instalments. Cover by Max Ellis.
REF: ISBN 0-563-52823-0 OP: £15.99

ADR-008

ADR-009 *Doctor Who: Real Time* **(Gary Russell)**
2002/12, Big Finish Productions, UK
Twin CD. Cover by Lee Sullivan. Starring Colin Baker.
Release of a story originally presented as a webcast on
the BBCi website.
REF: BFPDWBBCiCD01 OP: £9.99

ADR-009

ADS-001

ADS-002

ADS-003

ADS-004

ADS-005

ADS-006

ADS-007

ADS-008

AUDIO DRAMA SPIN-OFFS

ACTED stories featuring characters and settings from the *Doctor Who* universe but not the Doctor himself.

ADS-001 *Dalek Empire 1: Invasion of the Daleks* **(Nicholas Briggs)**
2001/06, Big Finish Productions, UK
CD. Story features the Daleks.
REF: BFPCDDE01 OP: £9.99

ADS-002 *Dalek Empire 2: The Human Factor* **(Nicholas Briggs)**
2001/08, Big Finish Productions, UK
CD. Story features the Daleks.
REF: BFPCDDE02 OP: £9.99

ADS-003 *Dalek Empire 3: Death to the Daleks* **(Nicholas Briggs)**
2001/10, Big Finish Productions, UK
CD. Story features the Daleks.
REF: BFPCDDE03 OP: £9.99

ADS-004 *Dalek Empire 4: Project Infinity* **(Nicholas Briggs)**
2001/12, Big Finish Productions, UK
CD. Story features the Daleks.
REF: BFPCDDE04 OP: £9.99

ADS-005 *Sarah Jane Smith: Comeback* **(Terrance Dicks)**
2002/07, Big Finish Productions, UK
CD. Story stars Elisabeth Sladen.
REF: BFPSJSCD01 OP: £9.99

ADS-006 *Sarah Jane Smith: The Tao Connection* **(Barry Letts)**
2002/08, Big Finish Productions, UK
CD. Story stars Elisabeth Sladen.
REF: BFPSJSCD02 OP: £9.99

ADS-007 *Sarah Jane Smith: Test of Nerve* **(David Bishop)**
2002/09, Big Finish Productions, UK
CD. Story stars Elisabeth Sladen.
REF: BFPSJSCD03 OP: £9.99

ADS-008 *Sarah Jane Smith: Ghost Town* **(Rupert Laight)**
2002/10, Big Finish Productions, UK
CD. Story stars Elisabeth Sladen.
REF: BFPSJSCD04 OP: £9.99

ADS-009 *Sarah Jane Smith: Mirror, Signal, Manoeuvre* **(Peter Anghelides)**
2002/11, Big Finish Productions, UK
CD. Story stars Elisabeth Sladen.
REF: BFPSJSCD05 OP: £9.99

ADS-010 *Kaldor City: Occam's Razor* **(Alan Stevens & Jim Smith)**
2001/09/01, Magic Bullet, UK
CD. Story features characters and situations from *The Robots of Death*.
REF: KC001 OP: £10.99

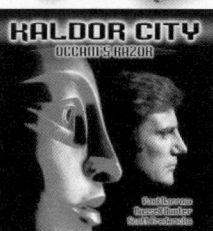

ADS-009   ADS-010

ADS-011 *Kaldor City: Death's Head* **(Chris Boucher)**
2002/04/20, Magic Bullet, UK
CD. Story features characters and situations from *The Robots of Death*.
REF: KC002 OP: £10.99

ADS-012 *Kaldor City: Hidden Persuaders* **(Jim Smith & Fiona Moore)**
2002/11/30, Magic Bullet, UK
CD. Story features characters and situations from *The Robots of Death*.
REF: KC003 OP: £10.99

ADS-011   ADS-012

AUDIO INTERVIEWS

SPOKEN interviews with the subjects concerned.

AIN-001 Tom Baker Audio Tape
1984, Scorpio International, USA
Cassette offered free with any video: 48 min
OP: $15.95

AIN-002 *The Ultimate Interview: Colin Baker talks with David Banks*
1989/10, Silver Fist, UK
Cassette. Audio interview recorded during the tour of the stage play *The Ultimate Adventure*.
REF: SF-UI 1 OP: £5.99 NM: £6-£9

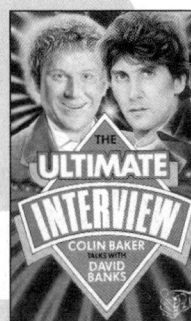

AIN-002

AIN-003 *Pertwee In Person: Jon Pertwee talks with David Banks*
1990/07, Silver Fist, UK
Cassette. Audio interview recorded during the tour of the stage play *The Ultimate Adventure*.
REF: SF UI 3 OP: £5.99 NM: £6-£9

AIN-003

AIN-004

AIN-005

AIN-006

AIN-004 *Who's the Real McCoy: Sylvester McCoy talks with David Banks*
1990/02, Silver Fist, UK
Cassette. Audio interview.
REF: SF UI 2 OP: £5.99 NM: £6-£9

AIN-005 *An Evening With The Doctor: Jon Pertwee*
1996/07, Listen For Pleasure, UK
Twin cassette. Not strictly an interview, but a recording of a performance of Jon Pertwee's one man show made shortly before his death in May 1996.
REF: LFP 7970 ISBN: 1-85848-487-1
OP: £7.99 NM: £9-£13

AIN-006 *The John Nathan-Turner Memoirs*
2000/11, Big Finish Productions, UK
Two double CD sets of Producer John Nathan-Turner narrating his memoirs about working on *Doctor Who*.
REF: BFPJNTCD1/BFPJNTCD2 OP: £13.99 each

AIN-007 *Big Finish Talks Back: The Audio Companions*
2001/06, Big Finish Productions, UK
Single CD. Gary Russell interviews India Fisher (Charley), Maggie Stables (Evelyn) and Lisa Bowerman (Bernice) about playing *Doctor Who* companions in the Big Finish audio dramas.
REF: BFPCDTB01 OP: £6.99

AIN-008 *Big Finish Talks Back: The Writers*
2002/09, Big Finish Productions, UK
Single CD. Gary Russell interviews the writers of the Big Finish eighth Doctor stories.
REF: BFPCDTB02 OP: £6.99

AIN-009 *Big Finish Talks Back: The Nicholas Courtney Memoirs*
2002/11, Big Finish Productions, UK
Triple CD. Nicholas Courtney (the Brigadier) narrating his memoirs.
REF: BFPCDTB04 OP: £12.99

AIN-007

AIN-008

AIN-009

AUDIO, MUSIC

RELEASES of incidental music used in *Doctor Who*.

AMU-001 *BBC Radiophonic Music* by John Baker, David Cain and Delia Derbyshire
1971, BBC Records, UK
LP Contains two stock tracks used in *Inferno*. 'The Delian Mode' and 'Blue Veils and Golden Sands'. This was originally produced as an internal BBC stock disk around 1968, and then commercially released in 1971.
REF: REC25M NM: £11

AMU-001

AMU-002 *Sounds from ... EMS*
1972, Electronic Music Studio, UK
7" flexi and EP versions. A very limited edition 'sampler' disk for electronic music produced using EMS equipment. Both the flexi-disk and the EP contained two *Doctor Who* tracks: 'Axon Attacks' from *The Claws of Axos* and 'Dover Castle' from *The Mind of Evil*. The 7" version contained slightly truncated versions of the music. The disk came in a black card sleeve.
OP: n/a NM: £55

AMU-003 *Moonbase 3/The World of Dr Who* by Dudley Simpson
1973/10, BBC Records, UK
7". Composed by Dudley Simpson, realised by Dick Mills. 'The World of Dr Who' is a suite of music including the Master's theme, the Keller Machine theme and jungle themes from *Planet of the Daleks*.
REF: RESL 13 OP: 48p (?) NM: £11

AMU-004

AMU-004 *BBC Radiophonic Workshop 21*
1979/04, BBC Records, UK
LP/Cassette. Contains the *Doctor Who* theme, the TARDIS take-off effect, and *Minds of Evil*, the Keller Machine theme from *The Mind of Evil*.
REF: REC 354 / ZCM 354
OP: £3.25 (LP) £2.75 (C) NM: £9

AMU-005

AMU-005 *Space Invaded: BBC Space Invaded*
1982, BBC Records, UK
LP/Cassette. This included the 1980 Peter Howell theme, the *K9 & Company* theme and incidental music from *The Leisure Hive*.
REF: REH 442 / ZCR 442
OP: £3.75? (LP) £3.25? (C)

AMU-006 *The Soundhouse: Music from The BBC Radiophonic Workshop*
1983/05, BBC Records, UK
LP/Cassette. Contains a stock track used in

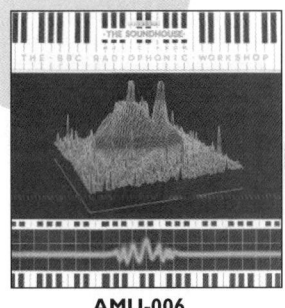

AMU-006

AMU-007a

AMU-007b
(front and back views)

AMU-007b
(misprinted version)

Enlightenment, 'The Milonga'. Another track, 'Macrocosm,' can be heard in the radio play 'Slipback'. It was also once used as the sound effect/music for Longleat's Who Exhibition.
REF: REC 467 / ZCM 467
OP: £3.75 (LP) £3.25 (C) NM: £9

AMU-007a Doctor Who: The Music
1983/02, BBC Records, UK
LP/Cassette. Collection of incidental music and sound effects.
Side One:
TARDIS/Doctor Who (Derbyshire), The Sea Devils, Meglos, Nyssa's Theme (*The Keeper of Traken*), Kassia's Wedding Music (*The Keeper of Traken*), The Threat of Melkur (*The Keeper of Traken*), Exploring the Lab (*Four to Doomsday*), Nyssa is Hypnotised (*Four to Doomsday*), The Leisure Hive
Side Two:
Omega Field Force (*Arc of Infinity*), Ergon Threat (*Arc of Infinity*), Termination of the Doctor (*Arc of Infinity*), Banqueting Music (*Warriors' Gate*), TSS Machine Attacked (*Kinda*), Janssary Band (*Snakedance*), Subterranean Caves (*Earthshock*), Requiem (*Earthshock*), March of the Cybermen (*Earthshock*), Doctor Who theme (Howell)
REF: REH 462 / ZCR 462
OP: £3.75 (LP) £3.25 (C) NM: £16.50

AMU-007b The Five Doctors Picturedisk
1983/11, BBC Records and Tapes, USA
LP. Collection of incidental music and sound effects culled from both *Doctor Who: The Music* and *Doctor Who Sound Effects*. The record features the artwork cover to *Doctor Who: The Music* on side one, and an image of the TARDIS on side Two. A backward mis-printed version and a correctly printed version exist.
Side One:
Requiem (*Earthshock*), March of the Cybermen (*Earthshock*), Termination of the Doctor (*Arc of Infinity*), Banqueting Music (*Warriors' Gate*), Doctor Who Theme, Ergon Threat (*Arc of Infinity*), Exploring the Lab (*Four to Doomsday*), TARDIS take off, The Leisure Hive
Side Two:
Side two of *Doctor Who Sound Effects* (ASO-003a).
REF: BBC 22002 OP: $10.95 NM: £27.50

AMU-007c Doctor Who Picturedisk
1985, BBC Records and Tapes, USA
LP. Collection of incidental music and sound effects culled from both *Doctor Who: The Music* and *Doctor Who Sound Effects*. The record features three photo-graphs against a yellow/green/red partitioned back-

ground on side 1 with three different photographs against the same background on side 2.
Side One:
Side two of *Doctor Who: The Music*.
Side Two:
Side two of *Doctor Who Sound Effects*.
REF: BBC 22004 OP: $12.95 NM: £27.50

AMU-007d *Doctor Who: Earthshock: Classic Music from the BBC Radiophonic Workshop: Volume 1*
1992/11, Silva Screen, UK
CD. Reissue of *Doctor Who The Music* with three additional tracks ('The Worlds of Doctor Who', 'Blue Veils and Golden Sands' and 'The Delian Mode') and missing the Peter Howell version of the theme.
CD/Cassette
REF: FILMCD 709; FILMC 709 OP: £8.99 NM: £11

AMU-008a *Doctor Who – The Music II*
1985/02, BBC Records and Tapes, UK
LP/Cassette. Collection of Incidental Music.
Side One:
The Five Doctors, The King's Demons, Enlightenment
Side Two:
Warriors of the Deep, The Awakening, Resurrection of the Daleks, Planet of Fire, Caves of Androzani
REF: REH 552 / ZCR 552
OP: £4.75 (LP) £4.25 (C) NM: £16.50

AMU-008b *Doctor Who: The Five Doctors: Classic Music from the BBC Radiophonic Workshop: Volume 2*
1992/11, Silva Screen, UK
CD and cassette. Reissue of *Doctor Who The Music II* plus the Peter Howell version of the theme from Volume 1.
REF: FILMCD 710 / FILMC 710
OP: £8.99 NM: £11-£14

**AMU-007c
(front and back views)**

AMU-007d

AMU-008a (LP & cassette)

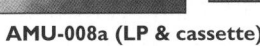

AMU-008b

AMU-009a

AMU-009b

AMU-010

AMU-011

AMU-009a Space Adventures
1987/09, DWAS Reference Department, UK
Cassette. Collection of stock music used on *Doctor Who* during the sixties. Compiled and released by Julian Knott, at the time running the DWAS' Reference Department. Limited edition of 300?
Track List:
'Three Guitars mood 2' (*100,000 BC*), 'Machine Room' (*The Tenth Planet*), 'Little Prelude' (*The Massacre*), 'Asyndeton' (*The Space Museum*), 'Hunted Man' (*The Massacre*), 'Palpitations' (*The Tomb of the Cybermen*), 'Telergic' (*The Tomb of the Cybermen*), 'Andromeda' (*The Web of Fear*), 'Music for Technology: Part One' (*The Tenth Planet*), 'Bathysphere' (*The Space Museum*), 'Spine Chiller' (*The Web of Fear*), 'Space Adventure' (*The Tenth Planet, The Moonbase, The Tomb of the Cybermen*), 'Power Drill' (*The Tenth Planet*), 'Sideral Universe' (*The Tomb of the Cybermen*), 'Frightened Man' (*The Massacre*), 'Meteoroids' (*The Time Meddler*), 'Space Time Music – Part One' (*The Tomb of the Cybermen*), 'Space Time Music – Part Two' (*The Tomb of the Cybermen*), 'Musique Concrete II' (*Inside the Spaceship*), 'Impending Danger' (*The Web of Fear*), 'World of Plants' (*The Space Museum*)
REF: RDMP 1 OP: £3.99 NM: £11

AMU-009b Space Adventures: Music from Doctor Who 1963-1971
1998/10, Julian Knott, UK
CD Re-issue. 28 tracks. Features some additional material. Limited edition of 300.
Additions:
'Desert Storm' (*The Tomb of the Cybermen*), 'Musique Concrete' (*The Space Museum*), 'Blast Off!' (*The Tenth Planet*), 'Astronautics Suite' (*The Space Museum, The Tomb of the Cybermen*), 'Youngbeat' (*The Evil of the Daleks*), 'Spotlight Sequins No 1' (*Terror of the Autons*), 'Mutations' (*Quatermass and the Pit*)
NB: Although 'Youngbeat' appears in the track listing for *The Evil of the Daleks* the music as heard on-screen is not the track included on this CD.
REF: JPD 2CD OP: £19.99 NM: £22-£28

AMU-010 Black Light by Dominic Glynn
1988, Dominitemporal Services Ltd, UK
Cassette. Collection of incidental music from *The Trial of a Time Lord* and *Dragonfire*
REF: RDMP 2 OP: £4.99 NM: £16.50

AMU-011 The Corridor of Eternity by Paddy Kingsland
1990, Julian Knott, UK
Cassette. Collection of incidental music from *Castrovalva* and *Mawdryn Undead*.
REF: JPD1 OP: £6.99 NM: £16.50

AMU-012a *The Doctor Who 25th Anniversary Album* **by Keff McCulloch**
1988/11, BBC Records and Tapes, UK
LP/CD/Cassette. Collection of incidental music. There were four alternate colour schemes for the sleeve.
Track List:
'TARDIS', 'Dr Who' theme, 'Gavrok's Search', 'Burton's Escape', 'The Sting', 'The White Flag', 'Here's to the Future' all from *Delta and the Bannermen*., 'A Child's Return', 'Cemetery Chase' from *Remembrance of the Daleks*, 'Towers el Paradiso', 'Drinksmat Dawning', 'Newsreel Past', 'Guards of Silence', 'The Making of Pex', 'Goodbye Doctor' all from *Paradise Towers*, 'Future Pleasure', 'The Brain' from *Time and the Rani*. 'Dr Who' end title. Also contained '8891 Royale' from a promotional trailer for the 25th season.
REF: REB 707 / ZCF 707 / BBC CD 707
OP: £6.49 (LP) £11.99 (CD) £6.99 (C)
NM: £11-£22

AMU-012a

AMU-012b *Evolution – The Music from Dr Who* **by Keff McCulloch**
1997/05/30, Prestige Records, UK
CD Re-issue of *the Doctor Who 25th Anniversary Album*. Runs at a faster speed to the original release. This CD was repromoted in January 2000.
REF: CDSGP0320   OP: £14.99   NM: £16.50

AMU-012c *Music From Doctor Who: Original Music from the BBC Series*
2002/07, Castle Pulse, UK
CD. Re-issue of the *25th Anniversary Album*.
REF: PLS CD 579   OP: £8.99

AMU-012b

AMU-013 *Doctor Who: The Curse of Fenric* **by Mark Ayres**
1991/07/29, Silva Screen, UK
CD. Incidental music from the story. Cassette version never released.
REF: FILMCD 087   OP: £12.50   NM: £11

AMU-014 *Doctor Who: The Greatest Show in the Galaxy* **by Mark Ayres**
1992/04, Silva Screen, UK
CD. Incidental music from the story. Cassette version never released.
REF: FILMCD 114   OP: £12.50   NM: £11

AMU-012c

AMU-013

AMU-015 *Doctor Who: Ghost Light* **by Mark Ayres**
1993/06, Silva Screen, UK
CD. Incidental music from the story.
REF: FILMCD 133   OP: £12.50   NM: £11

AMU-014

AMU-015

AMU-016

AMU-017

AMU-018

AMU-019

AMU-020

AMU-016 *Pyramids of Mars: Doctor Who Music by Dudley Simpson*
1993/09, Silva Screen, UK
CD. Arranged by Heathcliffe Blair. Selection of musical suites from several *Doctor Who* stories originally composed by Dudley Simpson: *The Ark in Space*, *Genesis of the Daleks*, *Pyramids of Mars*, *Planet of Evil*, *The Brain of Morbius* and 'The Doctor's Theme'.
REF: FILMCD 134 OP: £10.99 NM: £11

AMU-017 *The Best of Doctor Who Volume 1: The Five Doctors*
1993, Silva America, USA
CD. Compilation of excerpts from FILMCD 709 (AMU-007d) & 710 (AMU-008b), plus the 'Terror Version' from FILMCD 706.
REF: SSD 1014 NM: £22

AMU-018 *The Best of Doctor Who Volume 2: The Greatest Show in the Galaxy*
1994, Silva America, USA
CD. Compilation of edited highlights from 'The Greatest Show in the Galaxy' (AMU-014), 'Ghost Light' (AMU-015), and 'The Curse of Fenric' (AMU-013), plus Keff McCulloch's McCoy theme.
REF: SSD 1042 NM: £22

AMU-019 *The Worlds of Doctor Who*
1994/05, Silva Screen, UK
CD. Collection of tracks from previously released CDs.
Track List:
*'Doctor Who' Lambert/Hu, 'TARDIS', 'The World of Doctor Who', 'The Sea Devils', 'The Ark in Space', 'Pyramids of Mars', 'The Brain of Morbius', 'Doctor Who Theme' Howell, 'Meglos', 'The Five Doctors', 'The Caves of Androzani', 'Myth Makers Theme', 'Doctor Who: Terror Version', 'Terror in Totters' Lane', 'The Greatest Show in the Galaxy', 'Ghost Light', 'The Curse of Fenric', *'Return to Devils' End', *'Doctor Who' Hu/Lambert
*Previously unavailable
REF: FILMCD 715 OP: £8.99 NM: £10

AMU-020 *Doctor Who by John Debney, John Sponsler and Louis Febre*
1997/07, Super Tracks Music Group for Debney Production, USA
CD. Paul McGann 1996 TV-Movie soundtrack. Promotional CD only, copies were nevertheless sold through comic stores and distributors.
REF: JDCD 005 OP: $20 NM: £35

AMU-021 Music from *The Tomb of the Cybermen*
1997/05, Via Satellite, UK
CD. Collection of stock music used in *The Tomb of the Cybermen*.
REF: V-Sat ASTRA 3967 OP: £17.99 NM: £45

AMU-022 *Sherlock Holmes meets Dr Who* by Carey Blyton
1999/07, Upbeat Classics, UK
CD. Contains re-scored suites from *Doctor Who and the Silurians*, *Revenge of the Cybermen* and *Death to the Daleks*.
REF: URCD148 OP: £12.99

AMU-023 *Terror of the Zygons* by Geoffrey Burgon
2000/01/24, BBC Music, UK
CD. Includes music from *Terror of the Zygons* and *The Seeds of Doom*. CD Compiled and produced by Mark Ayres.
REF: WMSF 6020-2 OP: £14.99

AMU-024 *Doctor Who at the BBC Radiophonic Workshop – Volume 1: The Early Years 1963–1969*
2000/05/31, BBC Music, UK
CD. Music and sound effects composed by the BBC Radiophonic Workshop and used in *Doctor Who*. CD Compiled and produced by Mark Ayres. Contains material from the following stories: *100,000 BC*, *The Daleks*, *Inside The Spaceship*, *The Keys of Marinus*, *The Sensorites*, *The Chase*, *Galaxy 4*, *The Daleks' Master Plan*, *The Savages*, *The Tenth Planet*, *The Power of the Daleks*, *The Underwater Menace*, *The Macra Terror*, *The Web of Fear*, *Fury from the Deep*, *The Wheel in Space*, *The Dominators*, *The Mind Robber*, *The Invasion*, *The Krotons*, *The Space Pirates*, *The War Games*. Plus versions of the *Doctor Who* theme.
REF: WMSF 6023-2 OP: £14.99

AMU-025 *Doctor Who at the BBC Radiophonic Workshop – Volume 2: New Beginnings 1970–1980*
2000/05/31, BBC Music, UK
CD. Music and sound effects composed by the BBC Radiophonic Workshop and used in *Doctor Who*. CD Compiled and produced by Mark Ayres. Contains material from the following stories: *Inferno*, *The Mind of Evil*, *The Claws of Axos*, *The Sea Devils*, *The Curse of Peladon*, *Planet of the Spiders*, *The Ark in Space*, *The Brain of Morbius*, *The Masque of Mandragora*, *Destiny of the Daleks*. Plus versions of the *Doctor Who* theme. Also contains demo music produced for *The Horns of Nimon*.
REF: WMSF 6024-2 OP: £14.99

AMU-021

AMU-022

AMU-023

AMU-024

AMU-025

AMU-026

AMU-027

AMU-028

AMU-026 *Dr Who – Music From The Tenth Planet*
2000/12/04, Ochre Records, UK
CD. Release of stock music used in the television story *The Tenth Planet*. Released to co-incide with the BBC Video release of the story.
REF: OCH050 OP: £14.99

AMU-027 *Doctor Who at the BBC Radiophonic Workshop – Volume 3: The Leisure Hive*
2002/05, BBC Music, UK
CD. Music and sound effects from the story *The Leisure Hive*.
REF: WMSF 6052-2 OP: £16.99

AMU-028 *Doctor Who at the BBC Radiophonic Workshop – Volume 4: Meglos and Full Circle*
2002/05, BBC Music, UK
CD. Music and sound effects from the stories *Meglos* and *Full Circle*.
REF: WMSF 6053-2 OP: £16.99

AUDIO, OTHER

AUDIO releases which don't easily fit into the other categories.

AOT-001 *The Universe is Big* by **Dr Poo and the Psychic Koalas**
1985, Chase Custom Records, AUS
Mini-album from the cult radio spoof, *Dr Poo*, featuring that show's theme (a vocal performance of the *Doctor Who* music).
REF: CLP7

AOT-002 *Timeflight - The Original Music for the Film* by **Mark Ayres**
1987, Mark Ayres/Reeltime Pictures, UK
Cassette featuring incidental music score from the Reeltime Pictures celebrity parachute jump for charity. DWAS mail-order only.
REF: MAC-01

AOT-003 *Myth Makers The Music* by **Mark Ayres**
1987, Mark Ayres/Reeltime Pictures, UK
A cassette of Mark Ayres' music from the Reeltime Pictures *Myth Makers* series. DWAS mail-order only; limited to about 500 copies.
REF: MART-01 NM: £5.50

AOT-002

AOT-003

AOT-004 *TARDIS* by Jack Mackrel
1988/05, Template, UK
A dance beat EP with added effects intended to suggest the TARDIS on a journey.
REF: TEMPL8.4

AOT-005a *Myths And Other Legends* by Mark Ayres
1990, Metro Music International, UK
12" LP of music by Mark Ayres for the *Myth Makers* video series. Includes demo tracks submitted to the *Doctor Who* office prior to the 25th season and a theme for a proposed Dalek spin-off series. A flexi-disk containing an extract from 'Terror in Totters Lane' was given away free on *Doctor Who Magazine* #167 (1990).
REF: METRO-3 OP: £6.99 NM: £6-£9

AOT-005b

AOT-005b *Myths And Other Legends* by Mark Ayres
1991/08, Silva Screen, UK
CD. Re-issue with some additional material.
REF: FILMCD 088 NM: £8-£11

AOT-006 *Cybertech* by Cybertech
1994/02, Jump Cut Records, UK
Includes two versions of the theme from *Dimensions in Time* as well as a dark version of the *Doctor Who* theme and other music 'inspired' by *Doctor Who*. *Cybertech* is Adrian Pack and Michael Fillis (the latter of whom also appeared in *Dimensions in Time*). CD features a 'secret' track at the end, as the final track continues after a long break.
REF: Cutup CD 005 OP: £12.99 NM: £16.50-£22

AOT-006

AOT-007 *Pharos* by Cybertech
1995/07, Jump Cut Records, UK
More music 'inspired' by *Doctor Who* and Virgin's range of *New Adventures*. CD includes vocal contributions from Jon Pertwee, Sylvester McCoy, Caroline John, Sophie Aldred, and Mark Gatiss.
REF: Cutup CD 010 OP: £14.00 NM: £16.50

AOT-007

AOT-008 *Downtime*: Original Soundtrack Recording by Ian Levine, Nigel Stock and Erwin Keiles
1995/12, Silva Screen, UK
CD. Music from the Reeltime Pictures video drama
REF: FILMCD 717 OP: £8.99

AOT-009 *Shakedown – Return of the Sontarans*: Original Soundtrack Recording by Mark Ayres
1996/01/29, Silva Screen, UK
CD. Music from the Reeltime Pictures video drama.
REF: FILMCD 718 OP: £8.99

AOT-008

AOT-009

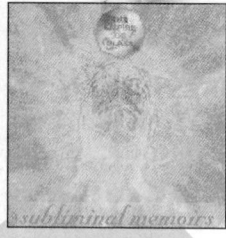

AOT-010

AOT-010 *Subliminal Memoirs* by The Empire of Glass
2000/08, peoplesound.com, UK
CD. Ambient dance music inspired by *Doctor Who* and Virgin's range of *New* and *Missing Adventures*. Available by Internet order only.
REF: ART8087-CD01-00

AOT-011 *Doctor Who: Music from the New Audio Adventures Volume I* (Alistair Lock)
2000/10, Big Finish Productions, UK
Single CD. Music from *Phantasmagoria, The Fearmonger, The Marian Conspiracy, The Spectre of Lanyon Moor.*
REF: BFPCDMUSIC1 OP: £8.99

AOT-012 *Doctor Who: Music from the New Audio Adventures Volume II* (Alistair Lock)
2001/04, Big Finish Productions, UK
Single CD. Music from *Last of the Titans, The Shadow of the Scourge, The Fires of Vulcan.*
REF: BFPCDMUSIC2 OP: £8.99

AOT-011

AOT-012

AOT-013 *Doctor Who: Music from the New Audio Adventures Volume III* (Russell Stone)
2001/07, Big Finish Productions, UK
Single CD. Music from *Red Dawn, Winter for the Adept, The Holy Terror.*
REF: BFPCDMUSIC3 OP: £8.99

AOT-014 *Music from Doctor Who The Eighth Doctor Audio Adventures* (Alistair Lock, Nicholas Briggs, Russell Stone, William Allen)
2001/12, Big Finish Productions, UK
Twin CD. Music from *Storm Warning, Sword of Orion, The Stones of Venice, Minuet in Hell.*
REF: BFPCDMUSIC4 OP: £13.99

AOT-013

AOT-014

AOT-015 *Music from Doctor Who The Fifth Doctor Audio Adventures* (Alistair Lock, David Darlington, Russell Stone)
2002/10, Big Finish Productions, UK
Single CD. Music from *Loups-Garoux, Eye of the Scorpion, Primeval.*
REF: BFPCDMUSIC5 OP: £9.99

AOT-016 *Music from Doctor Who The Sixth Doctor Audio Adventures* (Alistair Lock, Jim Mortimore, Jane Elphinstone)
2002/11, Big Finish Productions, UK
Single CD. Music from *Bloodtide, The One Doctor, Project: Twilight.*
REF: BFPCDMUSIC6 OP: £9.99

AOT-015

AOT-016

AOT-017 *Music from Doctor Who The Excelis Audio Adventures* **(David Darlington)**
2002/12, Big Finish Productions, UK
Single CD.
REF: BFPCDMUSIC7 OP: £9.99

AOT-017

AUDIO, SHEET MUSIC

ASH-001 *Doctor Who* **Theme Sheet Music (Ron Grainer)**
1964, International Music Publications, UK
Music arranged for piano. Purple cover.
REF: Order Ref 4569 NM: £27.50

ASH-002 *Doctor Who* **Theme Sheet Music (Mankind)**
1978, Chappell & Co, UK
Re-issue of the standard 'Ron Grainer' theme for piano. Photo of the group 'Mankind' on the cover.
REF: Order Ref 4569 NM: £5.50

ASH-001

AUDIO, SINGLES

RELEASES which have some connection with *Doctor Who*...some only marginally so.

ASI-001 *I'm Gonna Spend My Christmas With a Dalek* **by the Go-Go's**
1964/12, Oriole, UK
7". The first single from the Go-Go's, a semi-profes-sional Newcastle group comprising Mike Johnson (19), Alan Cairns (20), Abe Harrison (20), Bill Davison (22), Les McLeian (19) and Sue Smith (17). Produced and written by Johnny Worth under his pseudonym Les Van Dyke (spelt Vandyke on the record label). Came with and without picture sleeve. 'B' – *Big Boss Man*.
REF: CB 1982 OP: 5s 11d NM: £83 / £100 with picture sleeve

ASI-002 *Landing of the Daleks* **by The Earthlings**
1965/02, The Parlophone Co. Ltd, UK
7". A Dalley Taylor Production. 'B' – *March of the Robots*. An instrumental, this was initially banned from the airwaves as it contained an SOS Morse message. However it was then reissued without the offending signal.
REF: R 5242 OP: 5s 11d NM: £90

ASH-002

ASI-001

ASI-008b

ASI-008c

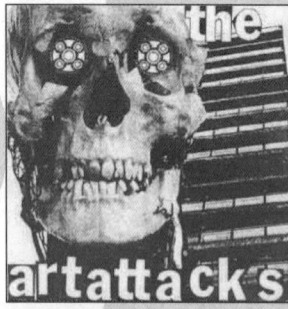

ASI-009
(front and back of picture sleeve)

ASI-003 *Dance of the Daleks* by the Jack
Dorsey Orchestra
1965/07, Polydor, UK
7". A jazzy instrumental inspired by *Doctor Who* and
published by Shadows Music. 'B' – *Likely Lads*.
REF: BM 56090   OP: 5s 11d   NM: £90

ASI-004 *Who's Who* by Roberta Tovey
1965/07, Polydor, UK
7". Written by Lockyer/Bev. Orchestra conducted by
Malcolm Lockyer. 'B' – *Not So Old*. Roberta Tovey
starred in both sixties *Doctor Who* films as the
Doctor's granddaughter Susan. Some in picture sleeve.
REF: BM 56021   OP: 5s 11d   NM: £83

ASI-005 *Eccentric Dr Who, The* by the Malcolm
Lockyer Orchestra
1965/08, Columbia, UK
7". Reworked version of title music from the film
Doctor Who and the Daleks. 'B' – *Daleks and Thals*, a re-
arranged suite from the film's incidental music.
REF: DB 7663   OP: 5s 11d   NM: £90

ASI-006 *Fugue For Thought* by Bill McGuffie
1967/02, Philips, UK
7". Reworked version of incidental music from the
film *Daleks Invasion Earth 2150 AD*. 'B' – *Fair's Fair*.
REF: BF 1550   OP: 5s 11d   NM: £50

ASI-007 *Who's Dr Who?* by Frazer Hines
1968/10, Major Minor, UK
7". Written by L Reed and B Mason. Produced by
Tommy Scott. 'B' – *Punch and Judy Man*.
REF: MM 579   NM: £70

ASI-008a *Who Is The Doctor?* by Jon Pertwee
1972/11/10, Purple Records Ltd, UK
7". Produced and arranged by Rupert Hine. 'B' – *Pure
Mystery*. Upbeat version of the *Doctor Who* theme with
spoken lyrics by Jon Pertwee.
REF: PUR 111   NM: £27.50

ASI-008b *Who Is The Doctor* by Jon Pertwee /
The Sea Devils by the **BBC Radiophonic**
Workshop
1982/83?, BBC Records and Tapes/Gemcon, USA
7". TARDIS image on the sleeve.
REF: BBC-453   OP: $3.50   NM: £22

ASI-008c *Who Is The Doctor* by Jon
Pertwee/*Doctor ...?* by **Blood Donor**
1985/06, Safari Records, UK
7". Re-issue. Picture sleeve.
REF: DOCTOR 1   OP: £2.00   NM: £22

ASI-009 *I Am a Dalek* by The Art Attacks
1978/02, Albatross, UK
7". Picture sleeve. 'B' – *Neutron Bomb*. Punk track with lyrics about becoming a robot.
REF: TIT 1 OP: £2.00 NM: £22

ASI-010a *Dr Who* by Mankind
1978/11, Motor Records/Pinnacle records, UK
7" and 12". Arranged by Mark Stevens and D Gallacher. Produced by Don Gallacher. 'B' – *Time Traveller* (by Mark Stevens). Sleeve of 12" shows an alien head and featured a white slip-band around the sleeve. Reached number 25 in the Radio 1 chart in November 1978. Released in both 12" and 7" formats. Sheet music was available from Chappell & Co. (see ASH-002). The 12" single was first released on the Motor label in blue vinyl, but Pinnacle records then took over Motor and a sticker was placed over the label on some shipments until proper Pinnacle labels could be applied. Shortly after the blue vinyl copies had been released, the record was issued in several other colour vinyls as well (Green, silk grey, yellow, red, a different more translucent blue, and brown - which may have only been for a promo release - are known). The Pinnacle 12" release is known to exist in black, brown, blue, green, grey, white or yellow vinyl with picture sleeve. There are two different Pinnacle labels, both showing four alpine peaks with the sun behind them. The first is printed black-on-silver and the second in full colour.
REF: 7" MTR 001 / 12" MTR 001/12 / 7" PIN 71 / 12" PIN 71-12 NM: £9-£14

ASI-010b *Doctor Who – The Sequel* by Mankind
1984, Motor Records, UK
7" and 12". 'B' – *Dr When*.
REF: MTR001/MTR001T NM: £7-£13

ASI-011 *Dalek I Love You (Destiny)* by Dalek I
1980/04, Back Door, UK
7". 'B' – *Happy/This is My Uniform*. Released with and without picture sleeve.
REF: DOOR 005

ASI-012 *I Wanna Be Doctor Who*
1980, Agro Fish, AUS
Performed by Adelaide group Jackson Zumdish, written by Michael Spargo and Baden Smith, and self-published on the Agro Fish label. 'B' – *Knup In Your Eye* (The Popes featuring Hank Dross/Vatican Records). Limited to 500 copies.
REF: 17171-A OP: $1.99

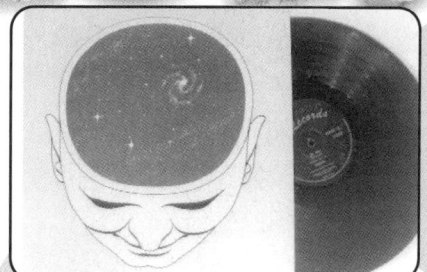

ASI-0010a

ASI-010b
(sleeve and label detail)

ASI-0011

ASI-0012

ASI-013

ASI-014

ASI-015b

ASI-013 *Boys and Girls/Tom Baker* by The Human League
1981/02, Virgin Records, UK
7". The 'B' side of The Human League's 'Boys and Girls' single is a synthesised instrumental tribute to Tom Baker. Vinyl inscribed with 'Thanks Tom'. The picture sleeve features a photograph of Baker. The single was available in gatefold and standard sleeve versions.
REF: VS395   NM: £11

ASI-014 *Doctor ...?* by Blood Donor
1981/05, Safari Records, UK
7". Written by Hale, Coxon. Produced by Steve James and Keith Hale. 'B' – *Soap Box Blues*. Picture sleeve. Environmentally aware track about the Doctor's visit to a future Earth destroyed by pollution.
REF: SAFE 29   NM: £13.20

ASI-015a *K-9 and Co.* Theme by Fiachra Trench and Ian Levine
1982/02, Solid Gold Records Ltd, UK
7". Extended version of spin-off theme. Written by Fiachra Trench and Ian Levine and realised by Peter Howell. 'B' – *Shana the Star Dancer* by Phil Wells. Picture sleeve.
REF: SGR 117   OP: £1.15   NM: £16.50

ASI-015b *K-9 and Co.* Theme / *The Leisure Hive*
1982, BBC Records and Tapes/Gemcon, USA
7". Photo of K9 on sleeve. Realised by Peter Howell.
REF: BBC-456   OP: £3.95 import   NM: £22

ASI-016a *Dr. Who is Gonna Fix It* by Bullamakanka
1982, BBC Records/Gemcon, USA
7". Written by Ovenden, Watson, Young. Produced by Ian Mason. 'B' – *Harlequin*. Bullamakanka were an Australian pop group. Picture sleeve.
REF: BBC 454   OP: $4.00   NM: £16.50

ASI-016b *Dr. Who is Gonna Fix It* by Bullamakanka
1983/11, BBC Records, UK
7". 'B' – *Harlequin*.
REF: RESL 132   NM: £16.50

ASI-016c *Dr. Who is Gonna Fix It* by Bullamakanka
1983, RCL Records, AUS
7". Australian release. 'B' – *Harlequin*. The song also appared on the group's album, *In Search Of*.
REF: 104188A   NM: £16.50

ASI-017 *Doctor In Distress* **by Who Cares**
1985/03/15, Record Shack Records, UK
Written by Ian Levine and Fiachra Trench. 'B' – *Doctor in Distress (instrumental)*. Produced to highlight the hiatus in production of *Doctor Who* in 1985. A video for the song was produced by Reeltime Pictures. Proceedsrom the charity single went to Cancer Relief.
REF: DOC 1 (7") / DOCT 1 (12")
OP: £1.75 (7") £3.50 (12") NM: £13-£22

ASI-018a *Doctorin' The TARDIS* **by The Timelords**
1988/05/23, KLF Communications, UK
7", 12". Written by Chinn, Chapman. 7" Single has 'probably the most nauseating record in the world' written on it. A mixture of Gary Glitter's *Rock and Roll Part II,* The Sweet's *Blockbuster,* the *Doctor Who* theme and samples from *Genesis of the Daleks*. Single got to number 1 in the Radio 1 chart for one week on 12 June 1988. Two versions of the 12" single exist, one with a word balloon around the words at the bottom, and one without the balloon. 'B' – *Minimal,* a slower instrumental version of the *Doctor Who* theme. The 12" also features an extended *Club Mix*.
REF: 7" KLF003 / 12" KLF003T
NM: £9-£22 (for various releases)

ASI-018b *Doctorin' The TARDIS* **by The Timelords**
1988, Possum Records, AUS
7" and 12" with picture sleeve. 'B' – *Minimal*. The 12" also features an extended *Club Mix*.
REF: 7" 104919 / 12" TDS 482

ASI-018c *Doctorin' The TARDIS* **by The Timelords**
1988, DEMIX/Rough Trade, Germany
7" and 12" with picture sleeve. 'B' – *Minimal*. The 12" also features an extended *Club Mix*.
REF: 7" 457004 / 12" 4512004

ASI-018d *Doctorin' The TARDIS* **by The Timelords**
1988, Spitfire/Blanco Y Negro, Spain
7" with picture sleeve. 'B' – *Minimal*.
REF: SP X/S 106

ASI-018e *Doctorin' The TARDIS* **by The Timelords**
1988, Sonet, Sweden
7" with picture sleeve. 'B' – *Minimal*.
REF: T-20109

ASI-018f *Doctorin' The TARDIS* **by The Timelords/The KLF**
1988, TVT Records, USA
7", 12", cassette and CD singles with picture sleeve. Sticker says 'Featuring the "Dr. Who" theme'. The CD single featured false track listings.
REF: 7" 4025 / 12" TVT 4020 / cassette TVT 4023 / CD 4024CD3

ASI-016b

ASI-017

ASI-018g *Gary in the TARDIS* **by The Timelords**
1988/06/13, KLF Communications, UK
12" remix with added vocals from Gary Glitter. *Minimal* is still included, but there is a new third track, *Gary Glitter Joins the J.A.M.S.* 4,000 were released with a picture sleeve. A 10" picture disc cut in the shape of Ford Timelord (the American-style police car on the picture sleeve) was also released without the J.A.M.S. track. Some of these were left uncut and square. In September, a promotional video CD from Phonovision Entertainment was released with a humorous video showing Ford Timelord battling Dalek-like robots constructed from packing crates.
REF: 12" KLF003R / 10" KLF003P / CDV KLFCD003

ASI-018h *Gary in the TARDIS* **by The Timelords/The KLF**
1990s, Possum Records, AUS
12" with picture sleeve.
REF: TDS 491

ASI-018i *Gary in the TARDIS* **by The Timelords/The KLF**
1990s, Somersault, Canada
CD single featuring just about all the tracks previously available on other similar releases.
REF: SOMCD736

ASI-018a

ASI-020

ASI-021

ASI-022

ASI-018j *Doctorin' The TARDIS* **by The Timelords/The KLF**
1991/07, TVT Records, USA
CD single re-issue with some mistitled tracks.
REF: TVT4025-2

ASI-019 The Theme from *Abslom Daak – Dalek Killer* **by The Slaves of Kane**
1990/12, Xenon Records, UK
7" and 12". A flexi-disk containing an extract from this single was given away free on *Doctor Who Magazine* #167 (1990).
REF: XEN-02/12 XEN-2 OP: £3.99 NM: £5.50

ASI-020 *First Class Ticket to Telos* **by Buckfunk 3000**
1998/02, Language Tours, UK
12" LP and CD releases. Credits Kit Pedler, Gerry Davis, and Terrance Dicks for quote from *Revenge of the Cybermen* novelisation. Also credits BBC Stills archive for cover, a squad of Cybermen from *The Five Doctors*.
REF: WORD D7

ASI-021 *Yellow Note Vs. the Daleks* **by Yellow Note**
1999/11, Liquid Sky Music, UK
Double 12" LP and CD releases. Includes samples from the *Doctor Who* theme and Dalek voices from *Genesis of the Daleks*.
REF: JSK 156 / JSK 156 LP

ASI-022 *Who is Dr Who*
2000/10/31, Cherry Red/RPM Records, UK
CD. Compilation of '60s/'70s tribute singles produced by Mark Ayres.
Track List
Doctor Who (original theme) – BBC Radiophonic Workshop
Dr. Who – Eric Winstone and his Orchestra
I'm Gonna Spend My Christmas With A Dalek – The Go Go's
Landing of the Daleks – The Earthlings
March of the Robots – The Earthlings
Dance of the Daleks – Jack Dorsey and his Orchestra
Who's Who – Roberta Tovey with Orchestra
Not So Old – Roberta Tovey with Orchestra
The Eccentric Dr. Who – Malcolm Lockyer Orchestra
Daleks and Thals – Malcolm Lockyer Orchestra
Fugue for Thought – Bill McGuffie
Who's Dr Who? – Frazer Hines
Punch and Judy Man – Frazer Hines
Who is the Doctor – Jon Pertwee
Pure Mystery – Jon Pertwee
Dr. Who – Don Harper's Homo Electronicus
Landing of the Daleks (alt morse vsn) – The Earthlings
Time Traveller (prev. unreleased) – Frazer Hines
REF: RPM 200

AUDIO, SOUND EFFECTS

RELEASES of sound effects used in *Doctor Who*.

ASO-001a

ASO-001a *Out of this World*
1976/10, BBC Records, UK
LP/Cassette. Contains TARDIS take-off and landing effects plus several other tracks which are from *Doctor Who*. These are all uncredited, but include ray gun effects from *The Ark in Space* and jungle effects from *Planet of the Daleks*.
REF: LP REC 225/cassette MRMC 040 NM: £16.50

ASO-001b *Essential Science Fiction Sound Effects Volume 1 (Out of this world sound effects from the BBC Radiophonic Workshop)*
1991/02, BBC Enterprises Ltd, UK
Cassette and CD re-issue.
REF: CD BBC CD 855 OP: £8.99 NM: £16.50

ASO-002 *Disasters - Sound Effects No. 16*
1977, BBC Records, UK
LP/Cassette. The track 'Swarming Insects' is actually Dick Mills' sound effect to the Nucleus's hatching tanks in *The Invisible Enemy*. This is acknowledged in Derek Goom's sleeve notes.
REF: LP REC 295

ASO-001b

ASO-003a *Doctor Who Sound Effects*
1978/05, BBC Records, UK
LP/Cassette. No 19 in the BBC's Sound Effects collection.
REF: LP REC 316/cassette ZCM 316
OP: £2.99 NM: £16.50

ASO-003b *Doctor Who Sound Effects*
1982, BBC Records /Gemcon, USA
LP. Re-issue.
REF: BBC 22316 NM: £16.50

ASO-004a *Sci Fi Sound Effects No 26*
1981, BBC Records, UK
LP. Contains *Doctor Who* sound effects from season eighteen: two from *The Leisure Hive*, two from *Meglos*, one from *Full Circle*, two from *Warriors' Gate*, two from *The Keeper of Traken* and five from *Logopolis*.
REF: REC 420/ZCM 420 OP: £4.99 NM: £13.20

ASO-003a

ASO-004b *Essential Science Fiction Sound Effects Volume 2*
1991, BBC Records, UK
Cassette and CD. Reissue.
REF: CD BBC CD 847 NM: £13.20

ASO-005 30 Years at the Radiophonic Workshop
1993/07/05, BBC Enterprises Ltd, UK
CD. 88 music and sound effects tracks from *Doctor Who*. Stories featured: *The Sensorites, The Dalek Invasion of Earth, The Chase, Galaxy 4, The Underwater Menace, The Macra Terror, The Evil of the Daleks, The Web of Fear, The Wheel in Space, The Dominators, The Krotons, The War Games, Spearhead from Space, The Sontaran Experiment, The Ark in Space, Masque of Mandragora, The Invisible Enemy, Image of the Fendahl, The Invasion of Time, The Ribos Operation, The Stones of Blood, The Armageddon Factor, The Horns of Nimon, The Leisure Hive, Meglos, Full Circle, Warriors' Gate, Castrovalva, Terminus, The Five Doctors, Warriors of the Deep, The Caves of Androzani, Timelash* (music), *The Trial of a Time Lord, Paradise Towers, Delta and the Bannermen, Dragonfire, Remembrance of the Daleks, The Greatest Show in the Galaxy, Silver Nemesis, The Happiness Patrol, The Curse of Fenric, Battlefield, Survival, Ghost Light, Shada, Paradise of Death*. The cover pictured is from a re-issue. The BBC changed it because fans pointed out that the two people pictured on the original cover never worked on *Doctor Who*.
REF: BBCCD 871   OP: £11.99   NM: £16.50

AUDIO, SOUNDTRACKS

RELEASES of *Doctor Who* soundtracks.

AST-001a Daleks, The
1966, Century 21 Records, UK
33rpm 7". 21 minutes long. Adapted from episode 6 of *The Chase* with narration by David Graham. Produced by Des Saunders. Photographic sleeve. Blue C21 label, with the Eric Winstone Orchestra version of the theme and a blue background to the Dalek photograph.
REF: MA106   NM: £45-65

AST-001b Daleks, The
1966, Century 21 Records, UK
Identical to AST-001a except that it features Barry Gray's Supermarionation music (from *Thunderbirds*) instead of the *Doctor Who* theme.

AST-001c Daleks, The
1966, Astor, AUS
This release was on the yellow and black Astor label and featured the original *Doctor Who* theme, had pink lettering on the sleeve and a purple background to the photograph of the Daleks.

AST-002a Doctor Who: Genesis of the Daleks
1979/10, BBC Records, UK
LP/Cassette. An abridged version of the soundtrack to the story, plus narration by Tom Baker written by Derek Goom.
REF: LP REH 364/cassette ZCR 364
OP: £3.75   NM: £22

AST-002b Doctor Who: Genesis of the Daleks
1979, Polygram Records, AUS
REF: 2963 086

AST-002c Doctor Who: Genesis of the Daleks
1982, BBC Records /Gemcon, USA
There is a version with a 1979 date on the package.
LP. REF: BBC 22364

AST-002d Slipback/Genesis of the Daleks
1988/11/07, BBC Records and Tapes, UK
Cassette release of the 1985 radio adventure *Slipback* along with a re-issue of the *Genesis of the Daleks* narrated soundtrack. Deleted 01/09/1998. Same as ADR-002a.
REF: ZBBC 1020 ISBN: 0563 225572
OP: £5.99   NM: £16.50

AST-002e Genesis of the Daleks & Slipback
1989, AVC Corporation/The Minds Eye, USA
Twin cassette. Same as ADR-002b.
OP: $14.95

AST-002f Doctor Who: Genesis of the Daleks/Exploration Earth
2001/07/02, BBC Worldwide Ltd, UK
Single CD. Cover by Max Ellis. The version of *Genesis of the Daleks* is a slightly revised and expanded version of the original release. *Exploration Earth* is a special BBC radio schools broadcast from 1976 featuring Tom Baker and Elisabeth Sladen as the Doctor and Sarah. Same as ADR-002d.
REF: ISBN 0-563-47857-8   OP: £8.99

AST-003a Doctor Who: The Missing Stories: The Evil of the Daleks
1992/07/06, BBC Enterprises Ltd, UK
Twin cassette. Presented by Tom Baker. Release went to no 1 in spoken word chart and was the first spoken word release ever to appear in the Gallup chart (at number 73). Features an edited version of the original soundtrack to the story, plus narration. Deleted 01/09/1998.
REF: ZBBC 1303   OP: £7.49   NM: £15-£20

AST-003b Doctor Who: The Missing Stories:
The Evil of the Daleks
1992, Bantam Doubleday Dell, USA
Twin cassette.
ISBN: 0-553-47164-3 OP: $15.99

AST-004a Doctor Who: The Missing Stories:
The Macra Terror
1992/07/06, BBC Enterprises Ltd, UK
Twin cassette. Presented by Colin Baker. Features the
original soundtrack to the story, plus narration.
Deleted 01/09/1998.
REF: ZBBC 1342 ISBN: 0-563-36682-6
OP: £7.49 NM: £16.50-£22

AST-004b Doctor Who: The Missing Stories:
The Macra Terror
1992, Bantam Doubleday Dell, USA
Twin cassette. Presented by Colin Baker. Features the
original soundtrack to the story, plus narration.
ISBN: 0-553-47214-3 OP: $15.99

AST-005 Doctor Who: *The Tomb of the Cybermen*
1993/06/07, BBC Enterprises Ltd, UK
Twin cassette. Presented by Jon Pertwee. Features the
original soundtrack to the story, plus narration. This was
originally to have been another *Missing Stories* release in
1992 but when video tapes of the story were recov-
ered from Hong Kong and rush-released on video, the
audio release was delayed. Deleted 01/09/1998.
REF: ZBBC 1343 OP: £6.75 NM: £16.50-£22

AST-006 Doctor Who: The Missing Stories: *The
Power of the Daleks*
1993/08/02, BBC Enterprises Ltd, UK
Twin cassette. Presented by Tom Baker. Features the
original soundtrack to the story, plus narration.
Deleted 01/09/1998.
REF: ZBBC 1433 OP: £7.49 NM: £18-£22

ASO-005

AST-001a

AST-001c

AST-002a

AST-003a

AST-003b

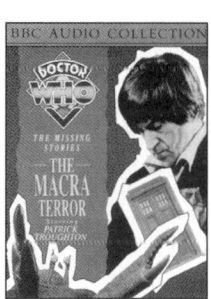

AST-004a

AST-004b

AST-005

AST-006

AST-007

AST-009

AST-008

AST-010

AST-011

AST-012

AST-013

AST-014

AST-015

AST-016

AST-007 Doctor Who: The Missing Stories:
Fury from the Deep
1993/10/04, BBC Enterprises Ltd, UK
Twin cassette. Presented by Tom Baker. Features the
original soundtrack to the story, plus narration.
Deleted 01/09/1998.
REF: ZBBC 1434 OP: £7.49 NM: £22

AST-008 Doctor Who: *The Massacre*
1999/08, BBC Worldwide Ltd, UK
Twin cassette/CD. Features the original soundtrack to
the story, plus linking narration by Peter Purves.
REF: ISBN 0-563-55256-5 (C) ISBN 0-563-55261-1(CD)
OP: £8.99 (C) £11.99 (CD)

AST-009 Doctor Who: *The Web of Fear*
2000/03/06, BBC Worldwide Ltd, UK
Triple CD. Cover by Max Ellis. Narrated by Frazer Hines.
REF: ISBN 0-563-55382-0 OP: £15.99

AST-010 Doctor Who: *Galaxy 4*
2000/06/05, BBC Worldwide Ltd, UK
Double CD. Cover by Max Ellis. Narrated by Peter Purves.
REF: ISBN 0-563-47700-8 OP: £12.99

AST-011 Doctor Who: *The Highlanders*
2000/08, BBC Worldwide Ltd, UK
Double CD. Cover by Max Ellis. Narrated by Frazer Hines.
REF: ISBN 0-563-47755-5 OP: £12.99

AST-012 Doctor Who: *The Macra Terror*
2000/08, BBC Worldwide Ltd, UK
Double CD. Cover by Max Ellis. Narrated by Peter Purves.
REF: ISBN 0-563-47756-3 OP: £12.99

AST-013 Doctor Who: *The Myth Makers*
2001/01/08, BBC Worldwide Ltd, UK
Double CD. Cover by Max Ellis. Narrated by Peter Purves.
REF: ISBN 0-563-47777-6 OP: £12.99

AST-014 Doctor Who: *The Moonbase*
2001/04/02, BBC Worldwide Ltd, UK
Double CD. Cover by Max Ellis. Narrated by Frazer Hines.
REF: ISBN 0-563-47854-3 OP: £12.99

AST-015 Doctor Who: *The Celestial Toymaker*
2001/04/02, BBC Worldwide Ltd, UK
Double CD. Cover by Max Ellis. Narrated by Peter Purves.
REF: ISBN 0-563-47855-1 OP: £12.99

AST-016 Doctor Who: *The Abominable*
Snowmen
2001/07/02, BBC Worldwide Ltd, UK
Double CD. Cover by Max Ellis. Narrated by Frazer Hines.
REF: ISBN 0-563-47856-X OP: £12.99

AST-017 Doctor Who: *The Daleks' Master Plan*
2001/10/01, BBC Worldwide Ltd, UK
Five CD set. Contains *Mission to the Unknown* on disk 1
and then parts 1-12 of *The Daleks' Master Plan* on disks
2-5. Narrated by Peter Purves. Disk 1 additionally contains MP3 files of all episodes minus the narration, PDF
files of the narration scripts, plus PDF and audio file
examples of the quality of the episodes before and after
being cleaned up. Also contains a booklet.
REF: ISBN 0-563-53500-8 OP: £29.99

AST-018 Doctor Who: *The Faceless Ones*
2002/02/04, BBC Worldwide Ltd, UK
Double CD. Cover by Max Ellis. Narrated by Frazer Hines.
REF: ISBN 0-563-53501-6 OP: £12.99

AST-019 Doctor Who: *The Smugglers*
2002/05/06, BBC Worldwide Ltd, UK
Double CD. Cover by Max Ellis. Narrated by Anneke Wills.
REF: ISBN 0-563-53504-0 OP: £12.99

AST-020 Doctor Who: *The Enemy of the World*
2002/08/05, BBC Worldwide Ltd, UK
Double CD. Cover by Max Ellis. Narrated by Frazer Hines.
REF: ISBN 0-563-53503-2 OP: £12.99

AST-021 Doctor Who: *The Savages*
2002/11/04, BBC Worldwide Ltd, UK
Double CD. Cover by Max Ellis. Narrated by Peter Purves.
REF: ISBN 0-563-53502-4 OP: £12.99

AST-017   AST-018

AST-019

AST-020   AST-021

AUDIO, THEMES

RELEASES of all the different versions of the *Doctor Who* theme music.

ATH-001a *Doctor Who* Theme by the BBC Radiophonic Workshop
1964/02, Decca, UK
7". 'B' *This Can't Be Love* (by Brenda and Johnny). The
Doctor Who theme was continuously available until
1988 when it was deleted. Two versions of this single
were available, one with the Decca logo in a rectangle
and the other with the logo in an arch. Re-issued with
the then new Decca logo in February 1972.
REF: F11837 OP: 5s 11d NM: £35

ATH-001b *Doctor Who* Theme by Ron Grainer
1960s?, Decca, AUS
7". 'B'–*This Can't Be Love* (by Brenda and Johnny).
REF: Y7147, 45-XDR32638, 7XDEC563

ATH-001a (both versions)

ATH-001e

ATH-001g

ATH-005a

ATH-005b

ATH-005d

ATH-006b

ATH-007

**ATH-008b
(square CD sleeve)**

ATH-008b (square CD)

ATH-008c

ATH-011

ATH-001c *Doctor Who* **Theme by Ron Grainer**
1973/04, Pye/BBC Records, UK
7". 'B' – *Reg* (by Paddy Kingsland). Plain sleeve.
REF: RESL 11   OP: 48p   NM: £16.50-£22

ATH-001d *Doctor Who* **Theme by Ron Grainer**
1973/05, BBC Records, UK
7". 'B' – *Reg* (by Paddy Kingsland). Silver label.
REF: RESL 11   NM: £16.50-£22

ATH-001e *Doctor Who* **Theme by Ron Grainer**
1973/04, BBC Records, UK
7". 'B' – *Reg* (by Paddy Kingsland). TARDIS sleeve.
REF: RESL 11   NM: £22

ATH-001f *Doctor Who* **Theme by Ron Grainer**
1976, BBC Records, UK
7". 'B' – *Reg* (by Paddy Kingsland). Blue and white
label. Blue & white TARDIS sleeve.
REF: RESL 11   NM: £16.50

ATH-001g *Doctor Who* **Theme by Ron Grainer**
1978, BBC Records, UK
7". 'B' – *Reg* (by Paddy Kingsland). Blue label. TARDIS
in vortex sleeve.
REF: RESL 11   NM: £22

ATH-002 *Doctor Who* **Theme by the Eric
Winstone Orchestra**
1964/02, Pye Records, UK
7". 'B' – *Pony Express*
REF: 7N.15603   OP: 5s 11d   NM: £40

ATH-003 *Dr Who/Dr Who Version* **by I Roy & the
Upsetters**
1973, Panther Records, UK
7". Reggae reinterpretation of the *Doctor Who* theme.
REF: P68

ATH-004a *Doctor Who* **Theme by Don
Harper's Homo Electronicus**
1973/11, Columbia, UK
7". 'B' – World of Sport.
Don Harper composed the incidental music for the
1968 *Doctor Who* story The Invasion.
REF: DB 9023   NM: £55

ATH-004b *Doctor Who* **Theme by Don
Harper's Homo Electronicus**
1973/11, EMI, UK
Appears to have been released on two labels.
REF: EMI 923   NM: £55

ATH-005a *Doctor Who* **Theme by Peter Howell**
1980/10, BBC Records/PRT, UK
7". 'B' – *The Astronauts* (by Peter Howell) T.Baker sleeve.
REF: RESL 80   OP: £1.15   NM: £16.50

ATH-005b *Doctor Who* **Theme by Peter Howell**
1982/02, BBC Records, UK
7".'B' – *The Astronauts* (by Peter Howell) P.Davison sleeve.
REF: RESL 80 OP: £1.30 NM: £13.20

ATH-005c *Doctor Who* **Theme by Peter Howell**
1982, BBC Records /Gemcon, USA
7". REF: BBC 451 OP: $4.00 NM: £16.50

ATH-005d *Doctor Who* **Theme by Peter Howell**
1984/06, BBC Records, UK
7".'B' – *The Astronauts* (by Peter Howell) C.Baker sleeve.
REF: RESL 80 OP: £1.65 NM: £13.20

ATH-006a *Doctor Who* **Theme by Dominic Glynn**
1986/1987, BBC Records and Tapes, UK
7" single.'B' – *Doctor Who (Cosmic Remix)* by Mankind
and Derbyshire theme.
REF: RESL 193 OP: £1.75 NM: £8-£13

ATH-006b *Doctor Who* **Theme by Dominic Glynn**
1986/1987, BBC Records and Tapes, UK
'B' – *Doctor Who (Cosmic Remix)* by Mankind and
Derbyshire theme. 12" single version packaged in a
sleeve with a hologram on the cover and a piece of artwork of the TARDIS console.
REF: ZRSL 193 OP: £3.25 NM: £8-£13

ATH-006c *Doctor Who* **Theme by Dominic Glynn**
1986/1987, BBC Records and Tapes, UK
'B' – *Doctor Who (Cosmic Remix)* by Mankind and
Derbyshire theme. Cassette version packaged in a
sleeve with a hologram on the cover and a piece of
artwork of the TARDIS console.
REF: 12RXL 193 OP: £3.25 NM: £8-£13

ATH-007 *The World of BBC TV Themes*
1989, BBC Records and Tapes, UK
Cassette and CD. Contains full-length McCoy theme.
REF: cassette ZCF705 / CD BBCCD705

ATH-008a *Doctor Who: Variations on a Theme*
1989/11, Metro Music International, UK
12", Four rearrangements of the *Doctor Who* theme by
Mark Ayres (two versions), Keff McCulloch and
Dominic Glynn. Contains; 'Mood Version' (Mark Ayres);
'Terror Version' (Dominic Glynn); 'Latin Version' (Keff
McCulloch); 'Panopticon Eight: Regeneration Mix' (Mark
Ayres). The 'limited' edition had a gold embossed black
sleeve and no track listing on the label, whereas the
'standard' edition had white print on the black sleeve
and a track listing on the label.
REF: 12 MMI-4, 12X MMI-4
OP: £5.50 (12") £6.50 (12" limited edition)
NM: £11-£16.50

ATH-008b *Doctor Who: Variations on a Theme*
1990/02, Metro Music International, UK
Standard CD Re-issue. A picture disk was hinted at for
April 1990 but this was never released.
REF: CD MMI-4 OP: £7.50 NM: £16.50-£22

ATH-008c *Doctor Who: Variations on a Theme*
1990/04, Metro Music International, UK
Limited issue 'square' version of the CD release. This
was actually a square-printed standard CD made square
by cutting off the edges. While it would seem that such
an altered CD would be difficult or impossible to play,
many readers confirm that it can indeed be played.
These square CDs were also individually numbered. A
very limited number of round CDs with square print on
it were later released in a card slip-case.
REF: CDX MMI-4 OP: £11.99 NM: £110

ATH-008d *Doctor Who: Variations on a Theme*
1991/07/29, Silva Screen, UK
CD Re-issue.
REF: FILMCD 706 NM: £11

ATH-009 *Doctor Who On A Mission* by
Cybermen
1996, Academy Street Records, UK
CD and 12". Reworking of the theme. Contains 'Radio
Edit (Vocal)', 'Original', 'K9's Happy Mix' and 'Sonic
Screwdriver Remix'.
REF: D-ACST002 NM: £16.50

ATH-010 *Dr Who* by **Vonal KSZ**
1998/11, Liquid, UK
12" EP recording of four dance mixes of the *Doctor
Who* theme. DJ only promo record, remixed by Vonal
KSZ and Vulture Squadron, in reality Andy Brooks.
Limited edition of 1,000.
REF: LIQ012B OP: £9.99 NM: £11

ATH-011 *Calling Dr Who* by **Raindancer**
1999/05, mp3.com, UK
DAM CD. Title track incorporates the series theme.
Available on the Internet only.
REF: 54317

ATH-012 *Doctor Who* **(The Slaves of Kane)**
2000/12, Xenon Records, UK
CD.
REF: XEN 482

ATH-013 *Traveller* **(ESP)**
2001/07, Neomusica, UK
12 inch single. Contains two versions of the *Doctor
Who* theme (called *Traveller*) and two remixes.
REF: NEO12052

AUDIO, UNLICENSED

DRAMAS which, although not licensed by the BBC, feature characters from the *Doctor Who* series and may be licensed from individual creators.

AUN-001 Audio Adventures in Time & Space
1984-1993, 1998- , Audio Visuals, UK
Cassette only for 1984-1993 series, CD only for 1998- series. This series of unlicensed fan-produced original audio dramas starred Nicholas Briggs as the Doctor and were originally produced by William Baggs, who, after three seasons went on to launch his own BBV series of video and, eventually, audio releases. Season four was produced by Gary Russell. In 1999 Russell became producer of an officially licensed range of *Doctor Who* audio adventures released by Big Finish Productions. Copies of these original tapes are much sought after amongst fans, but are hard to come by. In Canada during the eighties, radio DJ and *Doctor Who* fan Dean Shewring transmitted many of the stories during his daily broadcasts.
Season One – 1984/5:
1. *The Space Wail* by Warren Martyn (aka Gary Russell) (42' 04") featured Michael Wisher as The Judge. The Doctor is played by Stephen Payne for this story only. The title of this release was a play on *Song of the Space Whale*, a story commissioned but ultimately unused for the twenty-second season of *Doctor Who* in 1984.
2. *The Time Ravagers* by Arthur Wallis (aka Nicholas Briggs) (80' 33") featured Michael Wisher as Dalek Voices.
3. *Connnection 13* by Stuart Palmer (38' 21")
4. *Conglomerate* by Arthur Wallis (37' 15"). Was the basis for the BBC Film Club 'Stranger' video *In Memory Alone*.
5. *Cloud of Fear* by Alan W. Lear (60' 44")
6. *Shadow World* by Christopher Rhys and Emma Lindley (aka Richard and Deborah Marson) (50' 00)
Season Two:
7. *Maenad* by Warren Martyn (89' 43")
8. *The Mutant Phase* by Samuel Flint (aka Nicholas Briggs) (99' 27")
9. *The Destructor Contract* by Arthur Wallis (66' 32") plus *Vilgreth* by Arthur Wallis (23' 13")
10. *The Trilexia Threat* by Timothy Holbrooke (aka John Ainsworth) (51' 40")
11. *Minuet in Hell* by Alan W. Lear (62' 57")
12. *Blood Circuit* by Ed Taylor (aka Jim Mortimore) (132' 48")
Season Three:
13. *Second Solution* by Ed Taylor (54' 02") featured Nabil Shaban as Sir Thomas Knevett
14. *The Secret of Nematoda* by Arthur Wallis (71' 13")
15. *Enclave Irrelative* by Alan W. Lear (84' 25") featured Michael Wisher as Maul.

16. *More Than A Messiah* by Nigel Fairs (54' 40"). Adapted by the BBC Film Club for their 'Stranger' video *More Than A Messiah*.
17. *Sword of Orion* by Samuel Flint (89' 13"). Features the Cybermen.
18. *Carny* by Jonathan Boothroyd (aka Jim Mortimore) (66' 21")
19. *Planet of Lies* by Alan W. Lear (135' 52")
Season Four:
20. *Deadfall* by Warren Martyn (87' 51"). Adapted by Gary Russell for Virgin Publishing in 1997 as a non-*Doctor Who* 'New Adventure' novel called *Deadfall*.
21. *Requiem* by Andy Lane (82' 25")
22. *Cuddlesome* by Nigel Fairs (85' 40") featured Michael Wisher as Ronald Turvey
23. *Endurance* by Erica Galloway (aka Nicholas Briggs, Gary Russell and John Ainsworth) (139' 54")
24. *Mythos* by Jonathan Boothroyd (105' 33") plus *Truman's Excellent Adventure* by Warren Martyn (29' 11")
25. *Subterfuge* by Arthur Wallis and Samuel Flint (129' 10")
26. *Geopath* by Stephen Bowkett (91' 09") featured Peter Miles as Sir James Crichton
27. *Justyce* by Erica Galloway (90' 21")
(Details courtesy of the Who Cooperative)

In 1998, Baggs resurrected the 'Audio Adventures in Time and Space' series for a new range of non-*Doctor Who* CD adventures featuring Sylvester McCoy as 'the Professor' and Sophie Aldred as 'Ace'. Following BBC concern over rights, the characters were changed to 'the Dominie' and 'Alice'. BBV also released a range of audio CDs featuring 'Fred', a mysterious traveller in time and space, played by Nicholas Briggs. They have also released two audio ranges with a direct *Doctor Who* connection – rather than just featuring actors who had appeared in *Doctor Who*. The first features K9 (*Adventures in A Pocket Universe*) and the second features monsters from the series (*Familiar Faces – New Adventures*).
OP: £2.00 each (approx) NM: £12

AUN-002 Audio Adventures in Time and Space: Adventures in a Pocket Universe: The Choice (Nigel Fairs)
1999, BBV, UK
CD. Stars John Leeson as the voice of K9 and Lalla Ward as The Mistress.
REF: 13 OP: £8.99

AUN-003 Audio Adventures in Time and Space: Familiar Faces – New Adventures: Zygons: Homeland (Paul Dearing)
1999, BBV, UK
CD. First in a series of CDs featuring the monsters from *Doctor Who*.
REF: 15 OP: £8.99

AUN-004 *Audio Adventures in Time and Space: Adventures in a Pocket Universe: The Search* **(Mark Duncan)**
1999, BBV, UK
CD. Stars John Leeson as the voice of K9 and Lalla Ward as The Mistress.
REF: 16 OP: £8.99

AUN-005 *Audio Adventures in Time and Space: Familiar Faces – New Adventures: Zygons: Absolution* **(Paul Ebbs)** *and Krynoids: The Root of All Evil* **(Lance Parkin)**
1999/10, BBV, UK
Twin CD. Contains two stories. *Zygons: Absolution* features Peter Miles.
REF: 17/18 OP: £13.99

AUN-006 *Audio Adventures in Time and Space: Familiar Faces – New Adventures: Sontarans: Silent Warrior* **(Peter Grehan)**
1999/10, BBV, UK
CD.
REF: 19 OP: £8.99

AUN-007 *Audio Adventures in Time and Space: Familiar Faces – New Adventures: Sontarans: Old Soldiers* **(Simon Gerard and Colin Hill)**
2000/03/01, BBV, UK
CD.
REF: 22 OP: £8.99

AUN-008 *Audio Adventures in Time and Space: Infidel's Comet* **(Colin Hill and Simon Gerard)**
2000, BBV, UK
CD. Story features a Zygon and a Sontaran. This release came with a bonus second disc, numbered Disc 25 in the series, called "On-CD: Music", featuring Mike Nielson's soundtrack music from *Absolution*, *Silent Warrior*, *Cybergeddon* and *Old Soldiers*.
REF: 23 OP: £8.99

AUN-001 Season One: The Space Wail

AUN-001 Season Three: The Secret of Nematoda

AUN-001 Season Three: Sword of Orion

AUN-002

AUN-001 Season Four: Geopath

AUN-003

AUN-004

AUN-005 (cover 1)

AUN-005 (cover 2)

AUN-006

AUN-007

AUN-008

AUN-009

AUN-010
(original cover)

AUN-010
(revised cover)

AUN-011

AUN-012

AUN-013

AUN-014

AUN-015

AUN-009 *Audio Adventures in Time and Space: Familiar Faces – New Adventures: Sontarans: Conduct Unbecoming* (**Gareth Preston**)
2000/10, BBV, UK
CD.
REF: 27 OP: £9.99

AUN-010 *Audio Adventures in Time and Space: The Rani Reaps The Whirlwind* (**Pip and Jane Baker**)
2000/11, BBV, UK
CD. Starring Kate O'Mara as the Rani and Anthony Keetch as Urak. Story continues on from the end of *Time and the Rani*. Initially issued with a sleeve featuring the Rani and a Tetrap, this was withdrawn at the request of O'Mara shortly after release and an alternate sleeve using the same images, but blurred and with a red/blue colour wash , was used instead.
REF: 28 OP: £11.99

AUN-011 *Audio Adventures in Time and Space: Race Memory* (**Paul Ebbs**)
2001/02, BBV, UK
CD. Starring Sarah Sutton as Sarah. Story features the Wirrn.
REF: 29 OP: £11.99

AUN-012 *Audio Adventures in Time and Space: The Barnacled Baby* (**Anthony Keetch**)
2001/07, BBV, UK
CD. Story features a Zygon. Stars Deborah Watling and Clive Merrison.
REF: IV:1 OP: £11.99

AUN-013 *Audio Adventures in Time and Space: The Shadow Play* (**Lawrence Miles**)
2001/12, BBV, UK
CD. Story features the Faction Paradox from Miles' fiction for the BBC Books range of original novels. Also features the Sontarans.
REF: IV:3 OP: £8.99

AUN-014 *Audio Adventures in Time and Space: The Green Man* (**Zoltan Dery**)
2002/02, BBV, UK
CD. Story features the Krynoids.
REF: IV:4 OP: £9.99

AUN-015 *The Killing Stone* (**Richard Franklin**)
2002/07, BBV, UK
Double CD. Non-dramatised reading of a *Doctor Who* story by Richard Franklin on CD1. Interview with Richard Franklin on CD2.
OP: £13.99

BOOKS, ACTIVITY

BAC-001 Dalek Kit, *Daily Express*
1965, Beaverbrook Publishing, UK
A simple paper cut-out kit to construct your very own Dalek. Much sought after today, the kits were sent out free to every entrant of a 'Name a Dalek' competition.
OP: free NM: £33

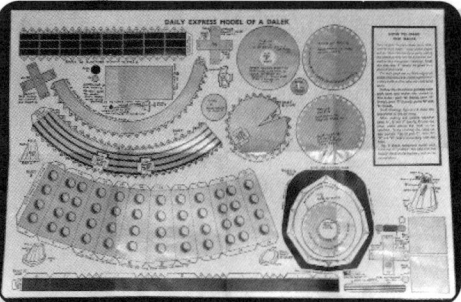
BAC-001

BAC-002 Dalek Painting Book, The
1965/06/17, Souvenir Press/Panther Books Ltd, UK
A book of black and white line drawings to colour in. Cover by Walter Howarth. 350,000 initial print run.
REF: No ISBN OP: 2s 6d lfp/b NM: £44

BAC-003 Paint and draw the film of Dr. Who and the Daleks
1965/08, Souvenir Press & Panther Books, UK
A book of black and white line drawings of scenes from the film to colour in. 350,000 initial print run.
OP: 2s 6d lfp/b NM: £44

BAC-002

BAC-003

BAC-004 Doctor Who on the planet Zactus Painting Book
1966, World Distributors, UK
A single-story painting book. Cover by Walter Howarth.
OP: 1s lfp/b NM: £66

BAC-005 Doctor Who Painting Book No. 1
1966, World Distributors, UK
Line drawings. Cover by Walter Howarth.
OP: 1s lfp/b NM: £82.50

BAC-006 Doctor Who Painting Book No.2
1966, World Distributors, UK
Line drawings. Cover by Walter Howarth.
OP: 1s lfp/b NM: £82.50

BAC-004

BAC-005

BAC-007 Dalek Action Paint 'n Puzzle
1966/03, Souvenir Press, UK
Line drawings, dot-to-dot, complete the picture and other simple puzzles. Cover by Walter Howarth.
OP: 2s 6d lfp/b NM: £44

BAC-008 Dr Who Sticker Fun Book – Travels in Space
1966/03, World Distributors (Netherlands) Ltd, UK
Aside from featuring the image of the Doctor, the insides of these books had little to do with *Doctor Who* as seen on television. Cover by Walter Howarth.
REF: ST 28 OP: 2s 6d lfp/b NM: £110

BAC-007

BAC-008

BAC-009

BAC-010

BAC-011

BAC-012

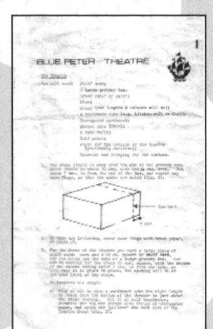

BAC-014 (front)

BAC-014 (back)

BAC-015

BAC-016

BAC-009 Dr Who Sticker Fun Book – Travels in Time
1966/03, World Distributors (Netherlands) Ltd, UK
Cover by Walter Howarth.
REF: ST 29 OP: 2s 6d lfp/b NM: £110

BAC-010 Doctor Who Puzzle Fun No.1
1966/05, World Distributors, UK
Puzzles and line drawings. Cover by Walter Howarth.
OP: 2s 6d lfp/b NM: £110

BAC-011 Doctor Who Puzzle Fun No.2
1966/05, World Distributors, UK
Puzzles and line drawings. Cover by Walter Howarth.
OP: 2s 6d lfp/b NM: £110

BAC-012 Dr Who Colouring Book, The
1973, World Distributors (Manchester) Ltd, UK
The line drawings told a very loose story in which the Third Doctor, his assistant (a sort of cross between Liz Shaw and Jo Grant) and UNIT battled aliens, historical figures, a giant octopus and so on. Several of the drawings were lifted from publicity stills from *Day of the Daleks*, *Terror of the Autons* and *Frontier in Space*, and the cover photograph was from *The Time Monster*.
REF: SBN 7235-3296-6 OP: 10p lfp/b NM: £25-£30

BAC-013 TARDIS Colouring Book
1977, Crosse & Blackwell, UK
Cut-out model of the TARDIS (11.75" x 5 5/8") with 'pop a point' colour pencils. Only available by sending 4 special labels off to the company.
OP: 95p p/b NM: £22

BAC-014 *Blue Peter Doctor Who* Theatre Leaflet
1977/04, BBC, UK
Issued by the popular children's magazine programme to accompany a feature on the show (Mon 25 & Thurs 28 April 1977) when the theatre was constructed.
OP: free NM: £5.50

BAC-015 'How To Build a Dalek' Pamphlet
1978, Time-Life Television/BBC Enterprises, USA/UK
A 6-page US letter-size pamphlet printed on heavy stock. Includes instructions for building a life-size Dalek replica.

BAC-016 Daleks Activity Book, The
1978, Children's Leisure Products Ltd, UK
Contains line drawings, mazes, complete-the-picture, spot-the-difference and other simple puzzles. This and *The Daleks Colouring Book* were rejected by the BBC and the publishers' license terminated. However the books appear to have been published regardless of this. Cover by Tony Gibbons.
REF: ISBN 0-7094-0059-4 OP: 25p lfp/b NM: £22

BAC-017 Daleks Colouring Book, The
1978, Children's Leisure Products Ltd, UK
Contains line drawings (some copied from BBC photographs) to colour in. Features the Fourth Doctor and Davros as well as the Daleks. Cover by Tony Gibbons.
REF: ISBN 0-7094-0058-6 OP: 25p lfp/b NM: £22

BAC-018 Doctor Who Press-Out Book
1978, World Distributors (Manchester) Ltd, UK
The book's publication was delayed after certain pictures of Mary Tamm's Romana were re-drawn at the BBC's request. Although copyright dated 1977, it was not published until late 1978. Print run was 50,000 of which under half sold, the rest being remaindered in 1980. Illustrated by Paul Crompton.
REF: SBN 7235-2454-8 OP: 30p lfp/b NM: £16.50

BAC-017   BAC-018

BAC-019 Doctor Who Colouring Book
1979, World Distributors (Manchester) Ltd, UK
The line drawings told a very loose story featuring the Fourth Doctor and Romana (and one drawing features K9). Some drawings are based on BBC photographs from *Robot*, *The Ribos Operation*, *The Androids of Tara* and *Pyramids of Mars*. Illustrated by Paul Crompton.
REF: SBN 7235-3498-5 OP: 25p lfp/b NM: £11

BAC-020 Adventures Of K9 And Other Mechanical Creatures, The (Terrance Dicks)
1979/09/17, Target/W. H. Allen & Co. Ltd, UK
A selection of simple puzzles. Cover and illustrations by Andrew Skilleter. Puzzles devised by Skilleter's wife. Print run: 60,000 copies.
REF: ISBN 0-426-20067-5 OP: 85p p/b NM: £3-£4

BAC-019   BAC-020

BAC-021 Terry Nation's Dalek Special (compiled and edited by Terrance Dicks)
1979/10/25, Target/W. H. Allen & Co. Ltd, UK
Featured a reprint of a story written by Terry Nation originally for a London newspaper, the *Evening News*, in 1974. Cover and illustrations by Andrew Skilleter. Print run: 60,000 copies.
REF: ISBN 0-426-20095-0 OP: 95p p/b NM: £3-£4

BAC-022 Doctor Who Quiz Book, The (Nigel Robinson)
1981/12, Target/W. H. Allen & Co. Ltd, UK
A book of quiz questions and answers. Nigel Robinson went on to edit the range of Target novelisations in the eighties, and later contributed work to Virgin's 'New Adventures' series of original novels. Print run: 20,000 copies.
REF: ISBN 0-426-20143-4 OP: £1.25 p/b NM: £2-£3

BAC-021   BAC-022

BAC-023

BAC-024

BAC-023 Second Doctor Who Quiz Book, The (Nigel Robinson)
1983/12, Target/W. H. Allen & Co. Ltd, UK
A book of quiz questions and answers. Print run:
20,000 copies.
REF: ISBN 0-426-19406-3 OP: £1.35 p/b NM: £3-£4

BAC-024 Third Doctor Who Quiz Book, The (Nigel Robinson)
1985/10/14, Target/W. H. Allen & Co. PLC, UK
A book of quiz questions and answers. Print run:
35,000 copies.
REF: ISBN 0-426-20212-0 OP: £1.50 p/b NM: £3-£4

BAC-025 Doctor Who Crossword Book (Nigel Robinson)
1982/12, Target/W. H. Allen & Co. Ltd, UK
A book of crosswords. Print run: 30,000 copies.
REF: ISBN 0-426-20138-8 OP: £1.25 p/b NM: £3-£4

BAC-025

BAC-026

BAC-026 Doctor Who Quiz Book of Dinosaurs (Michael Holt)
1982, Magnet/Methuen Children's Books, UK
This series of books was issued to take advantage of
Doctor Who's burgeoning popularity in the early eighties. The content was an uneasy mix of fact and fiction,
using the Doctor and his companions to ask questions about the given subject. Cover illustration by
Geoff Hunt. Illustrated by Rowan Barnes-Murphy.
REF: ISBN 0-416-20430-9 OP: 95p p/b NM: £3-£4

BAC-027a Doctor Who Quiz Book of Science (Michael Holt)
1982, Magnet/Methuen Children's Books, UK
Cover illustration by Geoff Hunt. Illustrated by Rowan
Barnes-Murphy.
REF: ISBN 0-416-20460-0 OP: 95p p/b NM: £2-£3

BAC-027b Doctor Who Book of Science
1985/07, Severn House Publishers Ltd, UK
A hardback library edition.
REF: ISBN 0-7278-1154-1 OP: £5.95 h/b NM: £5.50

BAC-028a Doctor Who Quiz Book of Space (Michael Holt)
1983, Magnet/Methuen Children's Books, UK
Cover illustration by Geoff Hunt. Illustrated by Rowan
Barnes-Murphy.
REF: ISBN 0-416-20450-3 OP: 95p p/b NM: £2-£3

BAC-027a

BAC-028a

BAC-028b Doctor Who Book of Space
1985/04, Severn House Publishers Ltd, UK
A hardback library edition.
REF: ISBN 0-7278-1145-2 OP: £5.95 h/b NM: £2-£3

BAC-029 Doctor Who Quiz Book of Magic (Michael Holt)
1983, Magnet/Methuen Children's Books, UK
Cover illustration by Geoff Hunt. Illustrated by Rowan Barnes-Murphy.
REF: ISBN 0-416-20440-6 OP: 95p p/b NM: £2-£3

BAC-030 Doctor Who – Brain-Teasers and Mind-Benders (Adrian Heath)
1984/11/15, Target/W. H. Allen & Co. Ltd, UK
Adrian Heath was a 16-year old fan of the series at the time he wrote this book. Print run: 50,000 copies.
REF: ISBN 0-426-19860-3 OP: £1.50 p/b NM: £2-£3

BAC-031 Doctor Who Puzzle Book (Michael Holt)
1985, Magnet/Methuen Children's Books, UK
Illustrated by Roger Wade Walker.
REF: ISBN 0-416-26810-2 OP: £1.50 p/b NM: £2-£3

BAC-032a Doctor Who Cookbook, The (Gary Downie)
1985/05/16, W. H. Allen & Co. PLC, UK
A book of recipies donated by various Doctor Who celebrities with suitable Doctor Who titles. Gary Downie contributed to Doctor Who first as an Assistant Floor Manager (AFM), then as a choreographer (on Black Orchid) and finally as a Production Manager on several eighties stories. Cover by Graham Potts. Illustrated by American fan artist Gail Bennett.
REF: ISBN 0-491-03214-5 OP: £6.95 h/b NM: £11

BAC-032b Doctor Who Cookbook, The (Gary Downie)
1986/11/20, W. H. Allen & Co. PLC, UK
Cover by Graham Potts. Illustrated by Gail Bennett. Print run: 10,000 copies.
REF: ISBN 0-426-20276-7 OP: £3.50 lfp/b NM: £6.60

BAC-033 Doctor Who – Build the TARDIS (Mark Harris)
1987/10/19, Target/W. H. Allen & Co. PLC, UK
A large-format cut-out book which could be used to create a cardboard model of the Doctor's timeship.
REF: ISBN 0-426-20323-2 OP: £3.95 lfp/b NM: £11

BAC-034 Doctor Who Quiz Book
1994/01, John Menzies, UK
Small quiz book given away during a 1994 promotion by the newsagent chain. Questions set by John Freeman then editor of Doctor Who Magazine.
OP: free

BAC-029   BAC-030

BAC-031   BAC-032a

BAC-034

BAC-033

BAN-001

BAN-002

BAN-003

BOOKS, ANNUALS

WORLD Distributors (Manchester) Ltd was formed by the Pemberton brothers (Sidney, John and Alfred) just after the Second World War in 1946. The company expanded from humble beginnings selling second-hand books from a cart, and moved into publishing their own books. They first published a *Doctor Who* annual in September 1965 and it contained a mixture of text stories featuring the Doctor and factual articles relating to space travel and science. The second annual included a comic strip and such strips were to remain a staple part of the annuals' contents, which would vary little from year to year. There was, for unknown reasons, no Annual published in 1971 (for 1972).

There are few sales figures available for the *Doctor Who* Annuals, but it is known that the 1981 Annual sold around 61,800 units, the 1982 Annual around 44,500 units and the 1983 Annual around 46,000 units.

Note: (s) indicates a comic strip story.

BAN-001 Dr Who Annual, The
1965/09, World Distributors (Manchester) Ltd, UK
First Doctor. Cover and illustrations by Walter Howarth.
Reputed to have been written by David Whitaker.
Stories: The Lair of the Zarbi Supremo, The Sons of the Crab, The Lost Ones, The Monsters from Earth, Peril in Mechanistra, The Fishmen of Kandalinga
REF: No SBN OP: 9s 6d h/b NM: £35

BAN-002 Dr Who Annual, The
1966/09, World Distributors (Manchester) Ltd, UK
First Doctor. Cover by Walter Howarth.
Stories: The Cloud Exiles, The Sons of Grekk, Terror on Tiro, Mission for Duh (s), The Devil-Birds of Corbo, The Playthings of Fo, Justice for the Glacians, Ten Fathom Pirates.
REF: No SBN OP: 10s 6d h/b NM: £55

BAN-003 Dr Who Annual, The
1967/09, World Distributors (Manchester) Ltd, UK
Second Doctor. Cover by Walter Howarth/Ron Smethurst. Stories and features by Kevin McGarry, J. L. Morrissey, J. H. Pavey, M. Broadley, J. W. Elliott and Colin Newstead, and illustrations by Walter Howarth, David Brian, Susan Aspey and Peter Limbert.
Stories: The Sour Note, The Dream Masters, The Tests of Trefus (s), The World of Asiries, Only a Matter of Time, Planet of Bones, When Starlight Grows Cold,

World Without Night (s), H M S TARDIS, The King of
Golden Death.
REF: No SBN OP: 10s 6d h/b NM: £60

BAN-004 Dr Who Annual, The
1968/09, World Distributors (Manchester) Ltd, UK
Second Doctor. Cover by Walter Howarth.
Stories: Lords of the Galaxy, Follow the Phantoms,
Mastermind of Space, Freedom by Fire (s), The
Celestial Toyshop, Valley of Dragons, Planet from
Nowhere, Happy as Queeg, Atoms Infinite (s), World
of Ice, The Microtron Men, Death to Mufl.
REF: No SBN OP: 12s 6d h/b NM: £65

BAN-004

BAN-005 Dr Who Annual, The
1969/09, World Distributors (Manchester) Ltd, UK
Second Doctor. Photographic cover, showing the
Doctor leaning on the TARDIS console in a publicity
still from *The Power of the Daleks*.
Stories: The Dragons of Kekokro, The Singing Crystals,
The Mystery of the Marie Celeste, The Vampire Plants
(s), Grip of Ice, Man Friday, Robot King (s), Slave of
Shran, Run the Gauntlet, A Thousand and One Doors.
REF: No SBN OP: 12s 6d h/b NM: £60

BAN-005

BAN-006 Dr Who Annual, The
1970/09, World Distributors (Manchester) Ltd, UK
Third Doctor. Cover by World Distributors'
Production Manager Ron Smethurst.
Stories: The Mind Extractors, Soldiers From Zolta, The
Ghouls of Grestonspey, Caught in the Web, Invaders
Invisible, The Dark Planet, Caverns of Horror, A
Universe Called Fred.
REF: SBN 7235-0062-2
OP: 12s 6d (62.5p) h/b NM: £60

BAN-006

BAN-007 Dr Who Annual 1973, The
1972/09, World Distributors (Manchester) Ltd, UK
Third Doctor. Photographic Cover.
Stories: Dark Intruders, War in the Abyss, Hunt to the
Death, Doorway into Nowhere, The Claw, Saucer of
Fate, The Phaser Aliens.
REF: SBN 7235-0179-3 OP: 70p h/b NM: £30

BAN-008 Dr Who Annual 1974, The
1973/09, World Distributors (Manchester) Ltd, UK
Third Doctor. Some illustrations by Edgar Hodges and
Paul Crompton. Comic strips by Steve Livesey.
Stories: Listen – The Stars, Out of the Green Mist, The
Time Thief (s), The Fathom Trap, Menace of the
Molags (s), Talons of Terror, Old Father Saturn,
Galactic Gangster.
REF: SBN 7235-0185-8 OP: 75p h/b NM: £25

BAN-007

BAN-008

BAN-009

BAN-009 Dr Who Annual 1975, The
1974/09, World Distributors (Manchester) Ltd, UK
Third Doctor. Some internal illustrations and comic
strips by Edgar Hodges. *The House that Jack Built* was
written by Keith Miller, the then organiser of the *Doctor
Who* Fan Club. There seem to be two variant editions of
this annual. Some copies transpose the internal colouring: for example pages 18/19 may be printed pink
wheras in another copy they may be purple. This colour
difference occurs throughout the annual.
Stories: The House that Jack Built, Revenge of the
Phantoms, The Time Thief, Dead on arrival (s),
Fugitives from Chance, After the Revolution (s), The
Battle Within, Before the Legend, Scorched Earth.
REF: SBN 7235-0244-7 OP: 90p h/b NM: £20

BAN-010a

BAN-010b

BAN-010a Dr Who Annual 1976, The
1975/09, World Distributors (Manchester) Ltd, UK
Fourth Doctor. Photographic cover. Internal illustra-
tions and comic strips by Paul Crompton.
Stories: A New Life, The Hospitality on Hankus, The
Psychic Jungle (s), The Sinister Sponge, Neuronic
Nightmare (s), Avast There!, The Mission.
REF: SBN 7235-0320-6 OP: £1.00 h/b NM: £11

BAN-010b Dr Who
1975/09, Mulder & Zoon B.V. – Amsterdam, Holland
Dutch edition of the 1976 annual. This edition misses
out the crossword, otherwise the content is the
same...but in the Dutch language.
REF: No. 15.602 OP: h/b NM: £12

BAN-011

BAN-011 Dr Who Annual 1977, The
1976/09, World Distributors (Manchester) Ltd, UK
Fourth Doctor. Cover by Paul Crompton. Internal
illustrations and comic strips by Paul Crompton and
Glenn Rix. This annual, like many of World
Distributors' other 1977 annuals, had a different page
size from all the others (it was 22cm by 29cm as
opposed to 20cm by 27cm).
Stories: War on Aquatica, Cyclone Terror, The Time
Snatch, The Body Snatcher (s), The Eye Spiders of
Pergross, Detour to Disaster, Menace on Metalupiter
(s), Double Trouble!, Secret of the Bald Planet.
REF: SBN 7235-0369-9 OP: £1.25 h/b NM: £9

BAN-012

BAN-012 Dr Who Annual 1978, The
1977/09, World Distributors (Manchester) Ltd, UK
Fourth Doctor. Illustrated by Paul Crompton.
Stories: The Sleeping Beast, The Sands of Tymus, The
Rival Robots (s), A New Life, The Traitor (s), The Sea
of Faces.
REF: SBN 7235-0412-1 OP: £1.35 h/b NM: £8

BAN-013 Dr Who Annual 1979, The
1978/09, World Distributors (Manchester) Ltd, UK
Fourth Doctor. Illustrated by Paul Crompton. Comic
strips by Paul Crompton.
Stories: Famine on Planet X, The Planet of Dust,
Terror on Tantalogus, The Power (s), Flashback,
Emsone's Castle (s), The Crocodiles from the Mist.
REF: SBN 7235-0491-1 OP: £1.50 h/b NM: £7

BAN-014 Doctor Who Annual 1980
1979/09, World Distributors (Manchester) Ltd, UK
Fourth Doctor. Illustrated by Paul Crompton. Comic
strips by Mel Powell and Paul Crompton. Two variants of
this Annual exist: one with the year (1980) on the spine,
front and back cover and title page, and one without.
Stories: X-Rani and the Ugly Mutants, Light Fantastic,
Terror on Xaboi (s), Reluctant Warriors, The Weapon
(s), Return of the Electrids, The Sleeping Guardians.
REF: SBN 7235-6549-X OP: £1.75 h/b NM: £7

BAN-015 Doctor Who Annual 1981
1980/08, World International Publishing Ltd, UK
Fourth Doctor. Illustrated by Glenn Rix. Comic Strips
by Mel Powell. Some copies of this annual were
released with the year '1981' removed from the
cover, spine and page 3.
Stories: Colony of Death, Alien Mind Games, A
Midsummer's Nightmare, Every Dog Has His Day (s),
The Voton Terror, Sweet Flower of Uthe.
REF: SBN 7235-6594-5 OP: £1.95 h/b NM: £7

BAN-016 Doctor Who Annual
1981/08, World International Publishing Ltd, UK
Fourth and Fifth Doctors. Illustrated by Glenn Rix.
Although Peter Davison had been cast as the Doctor,
there were no photographs available of him in costume,
necessitating the use of a photograph of his head only
on the cover. This Annual also saw editor Brenda Apsley
taking an active role in managing the content and a factual piece about the TARDIS appeared along with the
space related features. Some copies of this annual were
released with the word 'Annual' removed from the
cover, spine and inside front cover pages, leaving an odd
yellow space under the logo. As with the previous annual, versions exist with and without the date.
Stories: Inter-Galactic Cat, Conundrum, Planet of
Paradise, Plague World (s), Just a Small Problem …,
The Key of Vaga, Planet of Fear.
REF: SBN 7235-6628-3 OP: £2.25 h/b NM: £8

BAN-017 Doctor Who Annual
1982/08, World International Publishing Ltd, UK
Fifth Doctor. Some illustrations by Glenn Rix.
Contained factual pieces by Brenda Apsley on the

BAN-013

BAN-014

BAN-015

BAN-016

BAN-017

BAN-018

BAN-019

BAN-020

BAN-021

Visual Effects Department, the costume design for the Fifth Doctor, set design and costumes and on Producer John Nathan-Turner.
Stories: Danger Down Below, The God Machine, The Armageddon Chrysalis, On the Planet Isopterus (s), The Haven, The Penalty, Night Flight to Nowhere.
REF: SBN 7235-6653-4 OP: £2.50 h/b NM: £8

BAN-018 Doctor Who Annual
1983/08, World International Publishing Ltd, UK
Fifth Doctor. Factual article on Costume Designers by Brenda Apsley.
Stories: The Oxaqua Incident, Winter on Mesique, The Creation of Camelot, Class 4 Renegade, The Volcanis Deal, The Nemertines, Fungus.
REF: SBN 7235-6685-2 OP: £2.75 h/b NM: £9

BAN-019 Doctor Who Annual 1985
1984/08, World International Publishing Ltd, UK
Sixth Doctor. Illustrations by Mel Powell. Factual articles on Set Design and Special Effects by Brenda Apsley.
Stories: Battle Planet, Day of the Dragon, The Real Hereward, The Deadly Weed, Vorton's Revenge, The Time Savers, The Mystery of the Rings.
REF: SBN 7235-6719-0 OP: £2.99 h/b NM: £10

BAN-020 Doctor Who Annual 1986
1985/08, World International Publishing Ltd, UK
Sixth Doctor. Factual article on Make-Up by Brenda Apsley. The cumulative effect of numerous problems encountered by World in dealing with the BBC and John Nathan-Turner was that the company dropped the *Doctor Who* Annual following the 1986 edition (September 1985). In a letter to the BBC, they explained that the 1985 Annual had not been success-ful for them, and that with the absence of *Doctor Who* from television – this was during the break between seasons twenty-two and twenty-three – they had decided not to proceed with the license.
Stories: The Fellowship of Quan, Time Wake, Interface, Beauty and the Beast, Retribution, Davarrk's Experiment, The Radio Waves.
REF: SBN 7235-6747-6 OP: £3.25 h/b NM: £10

BAN-021 K-9 Annual 1983
1982/08, World International Publishing Ltd, UK
Illustrated by Paul Mark Tams and Glenn Rix. Written by Mike Wilde. Produced to tie in with the *K9 and Company* special, this one-shot annual followed the same format as the standard *Doctor Who* annuals with a mix of text sto-ries and factual pieces unrelated to the subject matter.
Stories: Powerstone, The Shroud of Azaroth, Hound of Hell, The Monster of Loch Crag, Horror Hotel, The Curse of Kanbo-Ala.
REF: SBN 7235-6661-5 OP: £2.50 h/b NM: £15

BAN-022 Terry Nation's Dalek Annual 1976
1975/09, World Distributors (Manchester) Ltd, UK
Illustrated by Edgar Hodges. The Dalek annuals followed the same format as the *Doctor Who* annuals.
Stories: Terror Task Force, Exterminate! Exterminate!
Exterminate!, Planet of Serpents (s), Nightmare,
Flood!!! (s), Timechase.
REF: SBN 7235-0339-7 OP: £1.00 h/b NM: £20-£25

BAN-023 Terry Nation's Dalek Annual 1977
1976/09, World Distributors (Manchester) Ltd, UK
Illustrated by Edgar Hodges. The comic strips were
reprints from *TV Century 21*.
Stories: The Doomsday Machine, Report from an,
Unknown Planet, The Envoys of Evil (s) [The PentaRay
Factor], The Menace of the Monstrons (s), The
Fugitive, The Quest (s) [The Archives of Phryne].
REF: SBN 7235-0384-2 OP: £1.10 h/b NM: £20-£25

BAN-024 Terry Nation's Dalek Annual 1978
1977/09, World Distributors (Manchester) Ltd, UK
Some illustrations by Paul Mark Tams. The comic
strips were reprints from *TV Century 21*.
Stories: The Castaway, The Seeds of Destruction, The
Rogue Planet (s), The Rogue Planet Part 2: Collision
Course! (s), Assassination Squad.
REF: SBN 7235-0421-0 OP: £1.35 h/b NM: £20-£25

BAN-025 Terry Nation's Dalek Annual 1979
1978/09, World Distributors (Manchester) Ltd, UK
Illustrated by Paul Mark Tams. Strips by Walter Howarth.
Tams included a nod to the *Doctor Who* Appreciation
Society – he was a member and edited the society magazine *Tardis* in 1979 – by including their initials 'DWAS' in
a stylised form on an illustration on page 4.
Stories: Blockade, The Solution, The Human Bombs
(s), Island of Horror (s), The Planet that Cried 'Wolf'!
REF: SBN 7235-0490-3 OP: £1.50 h/b NM: £20

BAN-026 Doctor Who Yearbook
1991/07/25, Marvel Comics, UK
In 1991, *Doctor Who* Magazine's editor John Freeman
decided to re-launch the *Doctor Who* annual in a format
similar to those published by World International. The
book also contained factual articles by Stephen James
Walker, Gary Russell, John Nathan-Turner and Sophie
Aldred, and a complete story guide.
Stories: The Meeting (John Lucarotti), Future Imperfect
(Marc Platt), Under Pressure (s) (Dan Abnett), Time on a
Vine (John Lydecker), The Deal (Colin Baker). Illustrated
by Paul Vyse and Alistair Pearson (flyleaf).
REF: ISBN 1-85400-283-X OP: £4.50 h/b NM: £16.50

BAN-022

BAN-023

BAN-024

BAN-025

BAN-026

BAN-027   BAN-028

BAN-029   BAN-030

BAT-001

BAT-002   BAT-003

BAN-027 Doctor Who Yearbook 1993
1992/08/27, Marvel Comics, UK
Stories: Cambridge Revisited (Karen Dunn),
Metamorphosis (s) (Paul Cornell), 'Dream a Little
Dream for Me' (Nigel Robinson), Country of the
Blind (Paul Cornell), Farewells (Terrance Dicks),
Encounter on Burnt Snake Flat (Marc Platt), A Tourist
Invasion (Colin Baker). Illustrated by Paul Vyse. Factual
articles by Justin Richards, David J Howe, John
Nathan-Turner and Andrew Pixley.
REF: ISBN 1-85400-284-8 OP: £4.50 h/b NM: £16.50

BAN-028 Doctor Who Yearbook 1994
1993/09, Marvel Comics, UK
Stories: A Religious Experience (s) (Tim Quinn), Loop
the Loop (Marc Platt), Reconnaissance (Terrance
Dicks), Rest and re-creation (s) (Warwick Gray), The
Changeling Years (Gareth Roberts), Perfect Day (Mark
Gatiss), The More Things Change (Andy Lane), Pulling
Strings (Nigel Robinson). Illustrated by Paul Vyse, Phil
Bevan, Charlie Adlard, David Miller and Brian Hudd.
Factual articles by Marcus Hearn, Andrew Pixley and
Nigel Robinson.
REF: ISBN 1-85400-317-8 OP: £4.50 h/b NM: £16.50

BAN-029 Doctor Who Yearbook 1995
1994/07/28, Marvel Comics, UK
Stories: The Naked Flame (s) (Warwick Gray),
Urrozdinee (Mark Gatiss), Briefly Noted (Justin
Richards), The Hungry Bomb (Gareth Roberts), The
Rescue (David Rodan), The Beast Inside (Daniel
Blythe), One Last Chance (Steve Lyons), Work Is Hell
(Simon Messingham), Blood Invocation (Paul Cornell),
It's Only A Game (Andy Lane). Illustrated by Charlie
Adlard, Alistair Hughes, Brian Hudd, Phil Bevan, Paul
Vyse, Alan Morton, John Ridgeway and Adrian Salmon.
Factual articles by Nigel Robinson, Kevin Davies,
Sophie Aldred and Nicholas Courtney.
REF: ISBN 1-85400-357-7 OP: £4.50 h/b NM: £7

BAN-030 Doctor Who Yearbook
1995/07/27, Marvel Comics, UK
In a departure from the traditional annual format, this
final volume from Marvel was mainly a complete ref-
erence guide to the series written and compiled by
Stephen James Walker and Andrew Pixley. Also con-
tained features and interviews by Austen Atkinson-
Broadbelt, Joe Nazzaro and Sheelagh Wells, Gary
Russell and Gary Gillatt.
Stories: Star Beast II (s), Junkyard Demon II (s)
REF: ISBN 1-85400-377-1 OP: £5.50 h/b NM: £7

BOOKS, ANTHOLOGIES

IT is surprising that there were no collections of *Doctor Who* text fiction by different authors until 1993 when *Drabble Who* was published for the anniversary. With the publication of the first *Decalog* collection the following year, Virgin discovered that the format was immensely popular, and *Decalog* went on to become one of the best-selling *Doctor Who* fiction titles that Virgin ever published. When the BBC took over the fiction license in 1996, they continued publishing an annual anthology, but using *Short Trips* as a generic title.

BAT-001 Drabble Who (ed David J Howe & David B Wake)

1993/09, Beccon, UK
Cover by Paul Vyse. Illustrated by Colin Howard. This thirtieth anniversary collection was published for charity. The book contains 100 pieces of writing, each of which is exactly 100 words long. Contributors include fans of the series, as well as actors, actresses and behind the scenes people who worked on the show. Limited to 1000 numbered copies world wide. Contributions by Dan Abnett, Sophie Aldred, Brian Ameringen, Peter Anghelides, Geoffrey Arthur, Colin Baker, David Banks, Nigel Bannerman, Christopher Barry, Stephen Baxter, Michael Bell, J. Jeremy Bentham, Ness Bishop, Ian Stuart Black, Chris Boucher, Steve Bowkett, Graham S. Brand, Keith Brooke, David Burke, Tim Chapman, Kevin Chitty, Tony Cooke, Nathan Cooke, Paul Cornell, Fiona Cumming, Richard W. Dance, Peter Darvill-Evans, Andrew W. Donkin, Julian Eales, Stan Eling, George Evans, Michael Ferguson, Ian M. Fraser, John Freeman, Stephen Gallagher, Steve Graeme, David Green, Mervyn Haisman, Elizabeth Halliday, Paul Harrington, Alun Harris, Michael Haslett, David J. Howe, Robert Howe, David Inwood, Simon J. Irving, Alison Jacobs, Louise Jameson, Steven Jenkins, Simon Christopher Jones, Andrew Lane, Glenn Langford, Barry Letts, Peter Ling, David Martin, Chaz Mason, Becky Maude, Tim Maude, Graham McKinnon, Adrian Middleton, Brian Milligan, M. R. Morgan, Steve Morgan, Mark Morris, Jim Mortimore, Amanda Murray, John Nathan-Turner, Kate Orman, John Peel, Victor Pemberton, Jon Pertwee, Martin Pollard, Eric Pringle, Justin Richards, John M. Rimmer, Tony Roach, Nigel Robinson, Nicholas Royle, Gary Russell, Robert Sloman, Chris Sparrow, Mark Stammers, Michael E. P. Stevens, Keith Topping, David Tulley, Jan Vincent-Rudzki, David B. Wake, Stephen James Walker, John Wiles and Stephen Wyatt.
REF: ISBN 1-870824-21-0 OP: £8.99 h/b NM: £11

BAT-002 Doctor Who: Decalog (ed Mark Stammers & Stephen James Walker)

1994/03/17, Virgin Publishing Ltd, UK
Cover by Colin Howard. Following pressure from fans to publish fiction about older Doctors, Virgin commissioned an 'experimental' collection of short stories. It was a major success and was reportedly Virgin's top-selling *Doctor Who* fiction title.
Stories: Playback (Stephen James Walker), Fallen Angel (Andy Lane), The Duke of Dominoes (Marc Platt), The Straw that Broke the Camel's Back (Vanessa Bishop), Scarab of Death (Mark Stammers), The Book of Shadows (Jim Mortimore), Fascination (David J Howe), The Golden Door (David Auger), Prisoners of the Sun (Tim Robins), Lackaday Express (Paul Cornell).
REF: ISBN 0-426-20411-5 OP: £4.99 p/b NM: £5.50

BAT-003 Doctor Who: Decalog 2: Lost Property (ed Mark Stammers & Stephen James Walker)

1995/07/20, Virgin Publishing Ltd, UK
Cover by Colin Howard.
Stories: Vortex of Fear (Gareth Roberts), The Crimson Dawn (Tim Robins), Where the Heart is (Andy Lane), The Trials of Tara (Paul Cornell), Housewarming (David A McIntee), The Nine-Day Queen (Matthew Jones), Lonely Days (Daniel Blythe), People of the Trees (Pam Baddeley), Timeshare (Vanessa Bishop), Question Mark Pyjamas (Robert Perry and Mike Tucker).
REF: ISBN 0-426-20448-4 OP: £4.99 p/b NM: £6.60

BAT-004 Doctor Who: Decalog 3: Consequences (ed Andy Lane & Justin Richards)

1996/07/18, Virgin Publishing Ltd, UK
Cover by Colin Howard.
Stories: ...And Eternity in an Hour (Stephen Bowkett), Moving On (Peter Anghelides), Tarnished Image (Guy Clapperton), Past Reckoning (Jackie Marshall), UNITed We Fall (Keith R A DeCandido), Aliens and Predators (Colin Brake), Fegovy (Gareth Roberts), Continuity Errors (Stephen Moffat), Timevault (Ben Jeapes), Zeitgeist (Craig Hinton).
NB: Future *Decalog* books were not *Doctor Who* anthologies. although *Decalog 4* did feature Roz Forrester, a *New Adventures* novel companion.
REF: ISBN 0-426-20478-6 OP: £4.99 p/b NM: £5.50

BAT-005 Doctor Who: Short Trips: A Collection of Short Stories (ed Stephen Cole)

1998/03/02, BBC Worldwide Ltd, UK
Cover by Black Sheep.
Stories: *Model Train Set (Jonathan Blum), *Old Flames (Paul Magrs), War Crimes (Simon Bucher-Jones), The Last Days (Evan Pritchard), *Stop the Pigeon (Robert

BAT-004

BAT-005

BAT-006

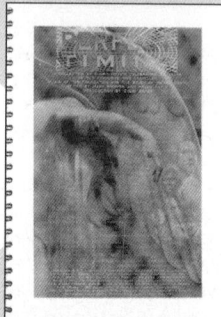

BAT-007a

BAT-007b

BAT-008

BAT-009

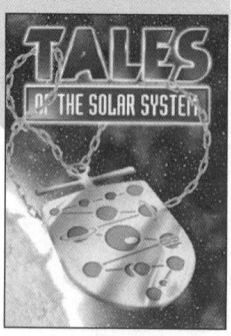

BAT-010

Perry and Mike Tucker), *Freedom (Steve Lyons), *Glass (Tara Samms), Mondas Passing (Paul Grice), There Are Fairies at the Bottom of the Garden (Sam Lester), Mother's Little Helper (Matthew Jones), The Parliament of Rats (Daniel O'Mahony), Rights (Paul Grace), ***Wish You Were Here (Guy Clapperton), Ace of Hearts (Robert Perry and Mike Tucker), **The People's Temple (Paul Leonard).

* Also available on cassette, read by Nicholas Courtney and Sophie Aldred (see ABO-013)
** Also available on cassette, read by Paul McGann (see ABO-014)
*** Also available on CD, read by Colin Baker and Nicola Bryant (see ABO-015)
REF: ISBN 0-563-40560-0 OP: £5.99 p/b

BAT-006 Doctor Who: More Short Trips: A Collection of Short Stories (ed Stephen Cole)
1999, BBC Worldwide Ltd, UK
Cover by Tony Fleetwood.
Stories: Totem (Tara Samms), Scientific Adviser (Ian Atkins), Missing, Part One: Business as Usual (Gary Russell), ***Moon Graffiti (Dave Stone), One Bad Apple (Simon Foreward), 64 Carlysle Street (Gary Russell), The Eternity Contract (Steve Lyons), The Sow in Rut (Robert Perry and Mike Tucker), Special Weapons (Paul Leonard), Honest Living (Jason Loborik), **Dead Time (Andrew Miller), Romans Cutaway (David A McIntee), Return of the Spiders (Gareth Roberts), Hot Ice (Christopher Bulis), UPVC (Paul Farnsworth), Good Companions (Peter Anghelides), Missing, Part Two: Message in a Bottle (Robert Perry and Mike Tucker), Femme Fatale (Paul Magrs).
** Also available on cassette, read by Paul McGann (see ABO-014)
*** Also available on CD, read by Colin Baker and Nicola Bryant (see ABO-015)
REF: ISBN 0-563-55565-3 OP: £5.99 p/b

BAT-007a Perfect Timing (ed Mark Phippen and Helen Fayle)
1998/11, Mark Phippen & Helen Fayle, UK
Collection of Doctor Who related fiction produced to raise money for the Foundation for the Study of Infant Deaths. The book was only available for a donation to the charity. Produced as a spiral bound A5 edition. Cover by Nathan Skreslet. Introduction by Colin Baker.
Stories: The Use Of The Myth (Paul Cornell), Bear Paw Adventure (David J. Howe), Always Let The Conscience Be Your Guide (Mark Clapham & Jim Smith), Birth Pains (Damon Cavalchini), Venusian Sunset (Paul Leonard), From The Cutting Room Floor … (David A. McIntee), Thicket Of Thieves (Kathryn Sullivan), These UNIT Things (Peter Anghelides), Entertaining Mr. O. (Paul Magrs), Masters Of Terror (James Ambuehl & Laurence

J. Cornford), Baron (Count) Dracula And Count (Baron) Frankenstein (Stephen Marley), The Aurelius Gambit (Helen Fayle), Not Necessarily In That Order ... (Paul Ebbs), Child Of Darkness (Daniel Blythe), The Zargathon Menace (Jonathan Morris), One Perfect Twilight (Craig Hinton), Ghost In The Machine (Trina L. Short), The Sixth Doctor Sends A Letter (Charles Daniels), The Great Journey Of Life Ends Here (Gary Russell), Wish Upon A Star Beast (Steve Lyons), Schrödinger's Botanist (Ian McIntire), Second Hand (Rob Stradling), Doing It Right (Alan Taylor), Cheeky Things (Erin Tumilty), Chain Male (Keith Topping), Ascension (Stephen Graves), Caveat Emptor (Susannah Tiller), Doctor-Patient Relationship (Kate Orman & Jon Blum), Worm (Lance Parkin), The Ravages Of Time (Mags L. Halliday), Emerald Green (Mark Phippen), Sad Professor (Nick Walters), Transitions (Daniel Ben-Zvi), Nightmare (Nathan Skreslet), Dark Paragon (Jon Andersen).
OP: £7.99

BAT-007b Perfect Timing (ed Mark Phippen and Helen Fayle)

1999?, Mark Phippen & Helen Fayle, UK
Perfect bound reprint. Additionally features: What if We Went to Italy (Tom Beck).
OP: £15.29 (inc. p&p)

BAT-008 Perfect Timing 2 (ed Helen Fayle and Julian Eales)

1999/12, Time Inc., UK
Collection of Doctor Who related fiction produced to raise money for the Foundation for the Study of Infant Deaths. The book was only available for a donation to the charity. Produced as a perfect bound A5 edition. Cover by Nathan Skreslet. Introduction by Colin Baker.
Stories: A Couple of Drabbles (Peter Anghelides), Darkness Before Me (Jim Campbell), Identity Crisis (Nathan Skreslet), Genesis of the Dustbins (Charles Daniels), A Handful of Silver (Mags L Halliday), Invasion of the Dinosaurs by Sarah Jane Smith (Mike Sivier), Knitworld (Stephen Marley), Goodbye Rembrandt (David J Howe), The Giving Invasion (Paul Leonard), A Cup of Coffee (Daniel Ben-Zvi), Kyreth (Kimberley Yale and John Ostrander), The Effect of Dimensional Transcendendence on Mozzarella Cheese (Diane Duane), Nameless (David Bickley), Painting History (Damon Cavalchini), Black Snow (David Bishop), Safe in the Knowledge (Mark Phippen), Adjudicator's Holiday (Kathryn Sullivan), Part Time, Catching (Dave Stone), Pulp Cutaway (David A McIntee), Isolation (Gareth Humphreys), Quicksilver Bees (Martin Day), First Person (Philip Purser-Hallard), Fishy Business (Lance Parkin), Empty Nest (Jon de Burgh Miller), Cause & Effect (Rebecca Dowgiert), The Hand of the Goddess

(Susannah Tiller), Unseen Rooms (Imran Inyat), This Hollywood Life (Jonathan Dennis), Fangrrl Life (Philip Pascoe), Mysterious Ways (Julian Eales), Memories to Forget (Barry Williams), Touching Indigo (Rebecca J Anderson), Grey (Jon Andersen), Apocalypse Angel (Finn Clark), The Next Universe but One (Dave Owen), A Tapestry of Shadows (Alan Taylor), A Day in the Death of the Land of Fiction (Jim Mortimore and Friends), It's Raining Again (Stewart Sheargold and Paul Magrs), Unlimited (Ian McIntire), Aria for the Broken Hearted (Richard Prekodravac), From the Cutting Room Floor Take 2 – The Crystal Bucephalus (Craig Hinton), Here be Dragons (Helen Fayle), Toy Story (Lawrence Miles).
OP: £15.29 (inc. p&p)

BAT-009 Doctor Who: Short Trips and Side Steps (ed. Stephen Cole and Jacqueline Rayner)

2000/03/06, BBC Worldwide Ltd, UK
Anthology of stories featuring all the Doctors, and including Doctors from other media, like the Peter Cushing version from the films, and the 'Doctor Who' version from the TV Comic strips. Cover by Black Sheep.
Stories: The Longest Story in the World (Paul Magrs), A Town Called Eternity (Part One) (Lance Parkin and Mark Clapham), Special Occasions: 1. The Not-So-Sinister Sponge (Gareth Roberts and Clayton Hickman), Nothing at the End of the Lane (Part One) (Daniel O'Mahony), Countdown to TV Action (Gary Russell), The Queen of Eros (Trevor Baxendale), The Android Maker of Calderon IV (Miche Doherty), Revenants (Peter Anghelides), Please Shut The Gate (Stephen Lock), Turnabout is Fair Play (Graeme Burk), Special Occasions: 2. Do You Love Anyone Enough? (Norman Ashby), Nothing at the End of the Lane (Part Two) (Daniel O'Mahony), The House on Oldark Moor (Justin Richards), Gone Too Soon (Christopher M Wadley), Reunion (Jason Loborik), Planet of the Bunnoids (Harriet Green), Monsters (Tara Samms), Special Occasions: 3. Better Watch Out, Better Take Care (Steve Burford), Storm in A Tikka (Mike Tucker and Robert Perry), Nothing at the End of the Lane (Part Three) (Daniel O'Mahony), A Town Called Eternity (Part Two) (Lance Parkin and Mark Clapham), Special Occasions: 4. Playing with Toys (David Agnew), Vrs (Lawrence Miles).
REF: ISBN 0-563-55599-8 OP: £5.99 p/b

BAT-010 Tales of the Solar System (ed. D Paul Griggs)

2000/06, Bedlam Media and The Unregenerate, UK
An A5-sized spiral bound charity anthology. Cover by Rob White.
Stories: Mercury: The All (Ian J Carter), Lunar: "The Loud Lament of the Disconsolate Chimera" (Gregg Smith), Venus: Blue Venus (Paul Leonard), Mondas:

Research and Development (Richard Jones), Earth: Covert Operations (James Ambuehl), Mars: Wasteland Express (E A Blair), Planet Five: Exodus (John S Drew), Jupiter: Wor Want of a Better Word (Martin Day), Saturn: Saturnalia (Lance Parkin), Uranus: Duty Cools (Jon de Burgh Miller), Neptune: Being an extract from "The Amazing Adventures of Iris Wildthyme on Neptune" (Paul Magrs), Pluto: The Invisible People (Mark Phippen and Leigh Hooper), Charon: Who Pays the Ferryman? (Helen Fayle), Vulcan: Separation Anxiety (Sarah Hadley), Cassius: Watching You, Watching Us, Watching You (James Potter).
REF: No ISBN OP: £4.00

BAT-011 Missing Pieces (ed. Mark Phippen and Shaun Lyon)

2001/02, Napkinhead Publications, USA
A large format perfect bound charity anthology. Cover by Nathan Skreslet.
Stories: Framing Story: Aspects of Evil (Craig Hinton); Tempus Refugit (James Ambuehl and Simon Bucher-Jones); Self Delusion (Jon Andersen); Irresistible Force (R. J. Anderson); The Star Racer (Trevor Baxendale); Where Were You (Tom Beck); A Tale of Monsters (David Bickley); Missing Pieces (Jonathan Blum); The Science of Magic and Vice Versa (aka Attack of the Gluons) (Arnold T. Blumberg); Waste (Daniel Blythe); A Stone of the Heart (James Bow and Erin Noteboom); Going Home (Colin Brake); In the Days of (The Days of (The Days of Our Lives)) (Simon Bucher-Jones); Here Again (Nick Campbell); Letting Go (Jim Catapano); Fiction Paradox (Damon Cavalchini); Fitz Kreiner and the Onion Doom (Stephen Cole); Loose Ends (Sue Cowley); For Queen and Country (Dylan Crawfoot and Peter Petroff); Dinner Conversation (Charles Daniels); Dead Men's Place (Martin Day); Raymond's Room (Keith R.A. DeCandido); The Killing of a Flash Boy (Jonathan Dennis); Time Gained, Time Lost (John S. Drew); Walk a Mile In My Shoes (Julian Eales); Juggling (Zoe Ellis); The Billion Year Heart (Steve Emmerson); The Last Song I'll Ever Sing (Simon Exton); Bedlam (Helen Fayle); Fear and Logarithms in Las Vegas (Matt Fitton); Coda (Joshua Lou Friedman); Revolver (Simon John Gerard); Eurydice's Reprieve (Greg Gick); Oblivion Lurks Near the Coffee Machine (Sietel Singh Gill); The Isidore Corporation (Sarah Hadley); Watch Out! Watch Out! (Mags L. Halliday); Old Scores (Bret Herholz); Mind Over Matter (David J. Howe); A Time To Choose (Olivia James); The Ashes of Eden (Lorelei S. Jordan); Eye of the Beholder (Tom & Alryssa Kelly); The Breach (Daniel Kukwa); How the Mighty... (Shaun Lyon); In the Frame (Steve Lyons); Should Have Been Dancing (Paul Magrs); A Whisper of Light (Matt Marshall); Outside Forces (Greg McElhatton); The Doctor & the Dragon (Bradley McGrath); Time Out (David A. McIntee); Fathers,

Friends, and Other Objects of Hate (Ian McIntire); In vino veritas (Mark Michalowski); The Memory of Stones (James Middleditch); Fate Healer (Jon de Burgh Miller); A Moment to Myself (Mansoor Mir); The Silent City (Jonathan Morris); Shadows Cast (Mike Morris); Iris Explains (Lance Parkin); Tea With Cthulhu (Lars Pearson); On The Town (John Peel); Brought to Book (Mark Phippen and Paul Leonard); While Stocks Last (James Potter); Head in the Sand (Gary Russell); The Arches (Cavan Scott and Mark Wright); A Winter's Tale (Rob Shearman); Tee Time (Trina L. Short); The Dark Domain (Nathan Skreslet); The Puppet King (Dale Smith); Just Love (Gregg Smith); The Painting (Robert Smith?); Casket 44 (Alex Steer); Magnificent Folly (Deborah Stevens); An Inconsequential Death (Dave Stone); Of Chocolates and Queens (Kathryn Sullivan); The Art of Compassion (Alan Taylor); Blind (Witold Tietze); All the Time in the World (Susannah Tiller); Disturbance at the Heron House (Keith Topping); Rock and a Hard Place (Mike Tucker); A Renegade's Manifesto (Angela P. Wade); The Great Eskape (Nick Walters).
REF: No ISBN   OP: $25 lfp/b

BAT-012 The Cat Who Walked Through Time (ed. Tom and Alryssa Kelly)

2001/02, Tom and Alryssa Kelly, USA
A Quarto-sized spiral bound charity anthology. Cover by Carolyn Edwards. 250 copies produced, then a 50 copy reprint.
Stories: The Real Tale of Bast (Kirstin Jones), Food For Thought (Tom Kelly), The Purrfect Companion (poem) (Sandy Adams), The Telling Box (Shaun Lyon), Catspaw (Mark Phippen), Missing Pages (Gordon Dempster), Precious Moments (Greg McElhatton), Pull Over! (Adrean Clark), Gauge (Leigh Hunt), All In A Day's Work (Andrew Lawston), Stories (Stuart Bentley), Unwelcome Guests (Jim Catapano), Time Stalking (Kathryn Sullivan), Badge of Honour (Mark Smith), Eight Cats (Paul Cornell), Stray Mechanism (Stephen Cole), The Cat Who Walked Through Sevilla (Tom Beck), Keeper of the Peace (Sietel Singh Gill), Delayed Reaction (Jennifer G. Tifft), Ripples in the Water (Steve Lake), Putting the Cat Out (Peter Adamson), Cold In The Sun (Nick Campbell), Happy To Be Here! (Annie Marshall), Morphic Resonance (Arnold T. Blumberg), The Big Cat (Simon Bucher-Jones), Siens Fikshen (Stewart Sheargold), Cats and Circuses (Ana Cotton), Done With Mirrors (Jonathan Dennis), Feral Planet (Jay McIntyre), Talking's Good for You (Matt Marshall), Messiah (Lance Parkin), Doctor Who: The Last of Forever (John Clifford), The Cats From Outer Space (Trina L. Short), K9? (Naomi Jacobs), Territorial Markings (Dale Smith), Doctor's Orders (Heidi Linda), The Cat At The End Of The Lane (Jamas Enright), Doctor Who And The Terror Of The Rani (Alden Bates), Whovian Rhapsody: A filk (Erik Pollitt), Dinner In Belgravia (Diane

Duane), GMO (Kate Orman), The Catseye Diamond (Tim Rush), Broken Dreams (Alryssa Kelly), A Beautiful Day (James Ambuehl & Sarah Hadley), Crescendo (Susannah Tiller), Mr Tibbles Saves The World (John H. Toon), Bad Dog (Christopher Taylor).
REF: No ISBN OP: $20

BAT-013 Walking in Eternity (ed. Julian Eales)
2001/05, Factor Fiction, UK
An A5-sized perfect-bound charity anthology. Cover by Nathan Skreslet.
Stories: In the Sixties (Paul Magrs), Pop Culture Reference (Scott Longmuir), Over Your Shoulder (Simon Exton), Wetware (Alex Steer), Changing Rooms (With No Doors) (Mark Michalowski), What Does it Profit a Man? (Arfie Mansfield), Hall of Me (Mike Collins), Satisfaction Guaranteed (Arnold T. Blumberg), Biggles and the Fractured Dimension (Finn Clark), Mercy (Kelly Hale), Dark Time (John Smith), The Wee Man (Iain Hepburn), Cracks in the Pavement (Robert Parker), What a Gun Does (Paul Dale Smith), Dr Who and the Zodiac of Death (David Bishop), The Rainbow Man (Robert Smith), Analysis (Mark Clapham), Pulp of the Black Lotus (Simon Bucher-Jones), Eucatastrophe (Mags L. Halliday), Caught in Margate: The Itching (Matt Marshall), Cabinet of Changes (Phil Purser-Hallard), Feeding Frenzy (Stephen Gallagher), True Colors (Steven Kitson), To Catch a Fox (Philip Parneker), The Courage of My Convictions (James Potter), Doctor Crypptic (Jon DeBurgh Miller), Davros: The Early Years (Rubert Booth & Barry Williams), Constance (Paul Ferry), Timebomb (Kathryn Sullivan & Selina Lock), The Feast of St Crispin Crispianus (Louise Sellers), Man of Smoke and Dust (Sarah Hadley & Nick Campbell), Executive Action (Lance Parkin), Out of the Shadows (Dave Whittam), Bell, Book and Candle (Jay Eales), Foule Deeth (Nick Lancaster), Thorns (Helen Fayle), No Regrets (Phil Hall), Loving in a Box (Rich Johnston), The Resurrection Event (Dave Stone), Dreams Per Chance (Ian McIntire), A Tale of Two Teachers (Paul Castle), Iris Wildthyme & The Spiders From Magrs (Alan Taylor), Don't Mention the War! (Jonn Elledge), Hanging Chads (Jonathan Dennis)
REF: No ISBN

BAT-014 Lifedeath (ed. Kereth Cowe-Spigai and Patrick Neighly)
2001/07, Ambrosia Press, USA
Anthology raising money for Amnesty International. Cover by Anne Marie Horne.
Stories: My Brother and the Doctor (Ben Brown), At the Beach (Simon Bucher-Jones), Something Terribly Important (Evan Waters), An Act of Terrorism (William Billingsley), Hayat (Doris Speed-Keller), Raisin Jack and the Dead Gang (Chris Heffernan), The Unpublished Diaries of Ian Chesterton (Patrick Neighly), Acts of Kindness (Alex Steer), Interlude (Peter Angelides and

BAT-011 **BAT-012**

BAT-013 **BAT-014**

BAT-015

Stephen Cole), Who Tortures the Torturers? (Jamas Enright), A Meeting of Minds (Craig Hinton), Liberation (Kereth Cowe-Spogai), Key to the Future (Mark Phippen), Seasons of Fear (Paul Cornell), Grandmother Clause (Phil Pascoe), Going Nowhere (David Agnew), Skulduggery? (Keith Topping and Suzanne M Campagna).
REF: No ISBN p/b OP: $15

BAT-015 Doctor Who: Short Trips Zodiac (ed. Jacqueline Rayner)
2002/12, Big Finish, UK
Anthology of stories themed around the signs of the zodiac. Cover by Clayton Hickman. Range editors: Gary Russell and Ian Farrington. Managing editor: Jason Haigh-Ellery. Internal illustrations by Jim Sangster.
Stories: Aries: The True and Indisputable Facts in the Matter

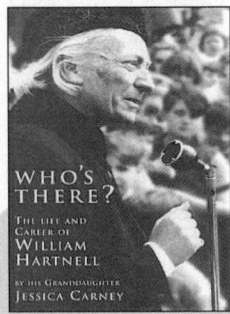

BAU-002

BAU-001

BAU-003

BAU-004

BAU-005

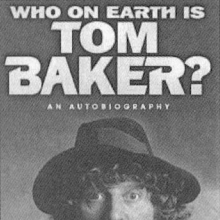

BAU-006a

BAU-006c

of the Ram's Skull (Mark Michalowski), Taurus: Growing Higher (Paul Leonard), Gemini: Twin Piques (Anthony Keetch), Cancer: Still Lives (Ian Potter), Leo: Constant Companion (Simon A Forward), Virgo: Virgin Lands (Sarah Groenewegen), Libra: The Switching (Simon Guerrier), Scorpio: Jealous, Possessive (Paul Magrs), Sagittarius: Five Card Draw (Todd Green), Capricorn: 'I Was A Monster!!!' (Joseph Lidster), Aquarius: The Invertibrates of Doom (Andrew Collins), Pisces: The Stabber (Alison Lawson). Introduction and links by Jim Sangster.
REF: ISBN 1-84435-006-1   OP: £14.99 h/b

BOOKS, BIOGRAPHIES

THIS section is limited to works by and about the actors who played the Doctors and the Companions. We have not included books by others involved in the television industry which mention *Doctor Who* as part of a wider picture.

BAU-001 *Moon Boots and Dinner Suits* (Jon Pertwee)
1984, Elm Tree Books/Hamish Hamilton Ltd, UK
Jon Pertwee's first autobiography covers his life up to the end of the Second World War.
REF: ISBN 0-241-11337-7   OP: £8.95 h/b   NM: £66

BAU-002 *Who's There: The Life and Career of William Hartnell* (Jessica Carney)
1996, Virgin Publishing Ltd, UK
Jessica Carney is the real-life grand-daughter of actor William Hartnell. This book reportedly sold around 2,000 copies.
REF: ISBN 1-85227-514-6   OP: £15.99 h/b

BAU-003 *Doctor Who: I Am The Doctor* (Jon Pertwee & David J Howe)
1996/11/21, Virgin Publishing Ltd, UK
Completed just a week before Pertwee's death. The book covers Pertwee's *Doctor Who* work, as well as featuring sections on *The Navy Lark* and *Worzel Gummidge*. Print run: 6,000 copies which sold out almost immediately.
REF: ISBN 1-85227-621-5   OP: £16.99 h/b

BAU-004 *Films, Farms and Fillies* (Frazer Hines)
1996/10, Boxtree, UK
Although more associated with the ITV soap opera *Emmerdale*, this autobiography by Frazer Hines is of interest to *Doctor Who* fans.
REF: ISBN 0-752-21155-2   OP: £5.99 p/b

BAU-005 *Five Rounds Rapid!* (Nicholas Courtney)
1998/11/19, Virgin Publishing Ltd, UK
Edited by former *Doctor Who* producer John Nathan-Turner. Covers Nicholas Courtney's life and career.

BAU-007

BBE-001

BBE-002

BBE-003

Print run: 6,000 copies.
REF: ISBN 1-85227-782-3 OP: £17.99 h/b

BAU-006a *Who On Earth Is Tom Baker?*
1997/10/06, HarperCollins Publishers, UK
Tom Baker relates his life story in ribald fashion. The
hardback edition reportedly sold around 35,000 copies
thanks in part to heavy promotion by the publishers.
REF: ISBN 0-00-255834-3 OP: £17.99 h/b

BAU-006b *Who On Earth Is Tom Baker?*
1997/10/06, HarperCollins Publishers, UK
Twin cassette. Read by the author. A single tape promotional extract was also available to reviewers and
trade, but not for sale. Abridged from the book.
REF: HCA 492 ISBN 0-00-105365-5
OP: £8.99 cassette

BAU-006c *Who On Earth Is Tom Baker?*
1998/10/06, HarperCollins Publishers, UK
'A' format paperback edition.
REF: ISBN 0-00-638854-X OP: £6.99 p/b

BAU-007 *Jon Pertwee: The Biography* (**Bernard
Bale**)
2000/05/15, Andre Deutsch, UK
Official biography of Pertwee.
REF: ISBN 0-233-99831-4 OP: £17.99 h/b

BOOKS, BBC/8TH DOCTOR

IN 1995, with the production of a new *Doctor Who*
film underway and the possibility of a new series also
in the offing, BBC Worldwide declined to renew
Virgin Publishing's license to publish original *Doctor
Who* novels as they wished to pick them up themselves. Thus in May 1996, the last of Virgin's 'New
Adventures' books was published, and in June 1997,

the BBC started their range with Terrance Dicks' *The
Eight Doctors* and Keith Topping and Martin Day's
The Devil Goblins from Neptune. The initial editor at
the BBC was Nuala Buffini who oversaw the first six
or so releases before leaving to join Hodder Headline,
and Steve Cole took over the reins of the BBC range.
Cole eventually left in 2000, to be replaced by Justin
Richards. The BBC released two novels a month,
except for December. From September 2002, the
schedule changed to one book a month.

BBE-001 *Doctor Who: The Eight Doctors*
(**Terrance Dicks**)
1997/06/02, BBC Worldwide Ltd, UK
Cover by Black Sheep.
REF: ISBN 0-563-40563-5 OP: £4.99 p/b NM: £7

BBE-002 *Doctor Who: Vampire Science*
(**Jonathan Blum and Kate Orman**)
1997/07/07, BBC Worldwide Ltd, UK
Cover by Black Sheep
REF: ISBN 0-563-40566-X OP: £4.99 p/b NM: £7

BBE-003 *Doctor Who: The Bodysnatchers* (**Mark
Morris**)
1997/08/04, BBC Worldwide Ltd, UK
Cover by Black Sheep.
REF: ISBN 0-563-40568-6 OP: £4.99 p/b NM: £7

BBE-004 *Doctor Who: Genocide* (**Paul Leonard**)
1997/09/01, BBC Worldwide Ltd, UK
Cover by Black Sheep.
REF: ISBN 0-563-40572-4 OP: £4.99 p/b NM: £7

BBE-005 *Doctor Who: War of the Daleks* (**John Peel**)
1997/10/06, BBC Worldwide Ltd, UK
Cover by Black Sheep.
REF: ISBN 0-563-40573-2 OP: £4.99 p/b NM: £7

BBE-004 **BBE-005**

BBE-006 **BBE-007**

BBE-006 *Doctor Who: Alien Bodies* **(Lawrence Miles)**
1997/11/24, BBC Worldwide Ltd, UK
Cover by Black Sheep.
REF: ISBN 0-563-40577-5 OP: £4.99 p/b NM: £7

BBE-007 *Doctor Who: Kursaal* **(Peter Anghelides)**
1998/01/05, BBC Worldwide Ltd, UK
Cover by Black Sheep.
REF: ISBN 0-563-40578-3 OP: £4.99 p/b NM: £7

BBE-008 *Doctor Who: Option Lock* **(Justin Richards)**
1998/02/02, BBC Worldwide Ltd, UK
Cover by Black Sheep. Claw by Colin Howard.
REF: ISBN 0-563-40583-X OP: £4.99 p/b NM: £7

BBE-009 *Doctor Who: Longest Day* **(Michael Collier)**
1998/03/02, BBC Worldwide Ltd, UK
Cover by Colin Howard.
REF: ISBN 0-563-40581-3 OP: £4.99 p/b NM: £7

BBE-010 *Doctor Who: Legacy of the Daleks* **(John Peel)**
1998/04/06, BBC Worldwide Ltd, UK
Cover by Black Sheep.
REF: ISBN 0-563-40574-0 OP: £4.99 p/b NM: £7

BBE-011 *Doctor Who: Dreamstone Moon* **(Paul Leonard)**
1998/05/04, BBC Worldwide Ltd, UK
Cover by Black Sheep.
REF: ISBN 0-563-40585-6 OP: £4.99 p/b NM: £7

BBE-012 *Doctor Who: Seeing I* **(Jonathan Blum and Kate Orman)**
1998/06/01, BBC Worldwide Ltd, UK NM: £7

BBE-008 **BBE-009** **BBE-010** **BBE-011**

Cover by Black Sheep.
REF: ISBN 0-563-40586-4 OP: £4.99 p/b NM: £7

BBE-013 *Doctor Who: Placebo Effect* **(Gary Russell)**
1998/07/06, BBC Worldwide Ltd, UK
Cover by Black Sheep.
REF: ISBN 0-563-40587-2 OP: £4.99 p/b NM: £7

BBE-014 *Doctor Who: Vanderdeken's Children* **(Christopher Bulis)**
1998/08/03, BBC Worldwide Ltd, UK
Cover art by Colin Howard, design and composition by Black Sheep.
REF: ISBN 0-563-40590-2 OP: £4.99 p/b NM: £7

BBE-015 *Doctor Who: The Scarlet Empress* **(Paul Magrs)**
1998/09/07, BBC Worldwide Ltd, UK
Cover by Black Sheep.
REF: ISBN 0-563-40595-3 OP: £4.99 p/b NM: £7

BBE-016 *Doctor Who: The Janus Conjunction* **(Trevor Baxendale)**
1998/10/05, BBC Worldwide Ltd, UK
Cover by Black Sheep.
REF: ISBN 0-563-40599-6 OP: £4.99 p/b NM: £7

BBE-017 *Doctor Who: Beltempest* **(Jim Mortimore)**
1998/11/16, BBC Worldwide Ltd, UK
Cover by Black Sheep.
REF: ISBN 0-563-40593-7 OP: £4.99 p/b NM: £7

BBE-018 *Doctor Who: The Face Eater* **(Simon Messingham)**
1999/01/04, BBC Worldwide Ltd, UK
Cover by Black Sheep.
REF: ISBN 0-563-55569-6 OP: £4.99 p/b NM: £7

BBE-012

BBE-013

BBE-014

BBE-015

BBE-016

BBE-017

BBE-018

BBE-019

BBE-020

BBE-021

BBE-022

BBE-023

BBE-024

BBE-025

BBE-026

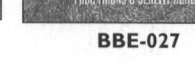

BBE-027

BBE-019 *Doctor Who: The Taint* **(Michael Collier)**
1999/02/01, BBC Worldwide Ltd, UK
Cover by Black Sheep.
REF: ISBN 0-563-55568-8 OP: £4.99 p/b NM: £7

BBE-020 *Doctor Who: Demontage* **(Justin Richards)**
1999/03/01, BBC Worldwide Ltd, UK
Cover by Tony Fleetwood.
REF: ISBN 0-563-55572-8 OP: £4.99 p/b NM: £7

BBE-021 *Doctor Who: Revolution Man* **(Paul Leonard)**
1999/04/05, BBC Worldwide Ltd, UK
Cover by Black Sheep.
REF: ISBN 0-563-55570-4 OP: £4.99 p/b NM: £7

BBE-022 *Doctor Who: Dominion* **(Nick Walters)**
1999/05/10, BBC Worldwide Ltd, UK
Cover by Black Sheep.
REF: ISBN 0-563-55574-2 OP: £4.99 p/b NM: £7

BBE-023 *Doctor Who: Unnatural History* **(Jonathan Blum & Kate Orman)**
1999/06/07, BBC Worldwide Ltd, UK
Cover by Black Sheep.
REF: ISBN 0-563-55576-9 OP: £4.99 p/b NM: £7

BBE-024 *Doctor Who: Autumn Mist* **(David A McIntee)**
1999/07/05, BBC Worldwide Ltd, UK
Cover by Black Sheep.
REF: ISBN 0-563-55583-1 OP: £5.99 p/b

BBE-025 *Doctor Who: Interference Book One* **(Lawrence Miles)**
1999/08/02, BBC Worldwide Ltd, UK

Cover by Black Sheep. Features the Eighth and Third Doctors.
REF: ISBN 0-563-55580-7 OP: £5.99 p/b

BBE-026 *Doctor Who: Interference Book Two* **(Lawrence Miles)**
1999/08/02, BBC Worldwide Ltd, UK
Cover by Black Sheep. Features the Eighth and Third Doctors.
REF: ISBN 0-563-55582-3 OP: £5.99 p/b

BBE-027 *Doctor Who: The Blue Angel* **(Paul Magrs & Jeremy Hoad)**
1999/09/06, BBC Worldwide Ltd, UK
Cover by Black Sheep.
REF: ISBN 0-563-55581-0 OP: £5.99 p/b

BBE-028

BBE-029

BBE-028 *Doctor Who: The Taking of Planet 5* **(Simon Bucher-Jones & Mark Clapham)**
1999/10/04, BBC Worldwide Ltd, UK
Cover by Black Sheep.
REF: ISBN 0-563-55585-8 OP: £5.99 p/b

BBE-029 *Doctor Who: Frontier Worlds* **(Peter Anghelides)**
1999/11/28, BBC Worldwide Ltd, UK
Cover by Black Sheep.
REF: ISBN 0-563-55589-6 OP: £5.99 p/b

BBE-030 *Doctor Who: Parallel 59* **(Natalie Dallaire & Stephen Cole)**
2000/01/03, BBC Worldwide Ltd, UK
Cover by Black Sheep.
REF: ISBN 0-563-55590-4 OP: £5.99 p/b

BBE-030

BBE-031

BBE-031 *Doctor Who: The Shadows of Avalon* **(Paul Cornell)**
2000/02/07, BBC Worldwide Ltd, UK
Cover by Black Sheep.
REF: ISBN 0-563-55588-2 OP: £5.99 p/b

BBE-032 *Doctor Who: The Fall of Yquatine* **(Nick Walters)**
2000/03/06, BBC Worldwide Ltd, UK
Cover by Black Sheep.
REF: ISBN 0-563-55594-7 OP: £5.99 p/b

BBE-033 *Doctor Who: Cold Heart* **(Trevor Baxendale)**
2000/01/03, BBC Worldwide Ltd, UK
Cover by Black Sheep.
REF: ISBN 0-563-55595-5 OP: £5.99 p/b

BBE-032

BBE-033

BBE-034

BBE-035

BBE-036

BBE-037

BBE-038

BBE-039

BBE-034 *Doctor Who: The Space Age* (Steve Lyons)
2000/05/01, BBC Worldwide Ltd, UK
Cover by Black Sheep.
REF: ISBN 0-563-53800-7 OP: £5.99 p/b

BBE-035 *Doctor Who: The Banquo Legacy* (Andy Lane & Justin Richards)
2000/06/05, BBC Worldwide Ltd, UK
Cover by Black Sheep.
REF: ISBN 0-563-53808-2 OP: £5.99 p/b

BBE-036 *Doctor Who: The Ancestor Cell* (Peter Anghelides & Stephen Cole)
2000/07/03, BBC Worldwide Ltd, UK
Cover by Black Sheep.
REF: ISBN 0-563-53809-0 OP: £5.99 p/b

BBE-037 *Doctor Who: The Burning* (Justin Richards)
2000/08/07, BBC Worldwide Ltd, UK
Cover by Black Sheep.
REF: ISBN 0-563-53812-0 OP: £5.99 p/b

BBE-038 *Doctor Who: Casualties of War* (Steve Emmerson)
2000/09/04, BBC Worldwide Ltd, UK
Cover by Black Sheep.
REF: ISBN 0-563-53805-8 OP: £5.99 p/b

BBE-039 *Doctor Who: The Turing Test* (Paul Leonard)
2000/10/02, BBC Worldwide Ltd, UK
Cover by Black Sheep.
REF: ISBN 0-563-53806-6 OP: £5.99 p/b

BBE-040 *Doctor Who: Endgame* (Terrance Dicks)
2000/11/06, BBC Worldwide Ltd, UK
Cover by Black Sheep.
REF: ISBN 0-563-53822-8 OP: £5.99 p/b

BBE-041 *Doctor Who: Father Time* (Lance Parkin)
2001/01/08, BBC Worldwide Ltd, UK
Cover by Black Sheep.
REF: ISBN 0-563-53810-4 OP: £5.99 p/b

BBE-042 *Doctor Who: Escape Velocity* (Colin Brake)
2001/02/05, BBC Worldwide Ltd, UK
Cover by Black Sheep.
REF: ISBN 0-563-53825-2 OP: £5.99 p/b

BBE-043 *Doctor Who: Earthworld* (Jacqueline Rayner)
2001/03/05, BBC Worldwide Ltd, UK
REF: ISBN 0-563-53827-9 OP: £5.99 p/b

BBE-044 *Doctor Who: Vanishing Point* (Stephen Cole)
2001/04/02, BBC Worldwide Ltd, UK
REF: ISBN 0-563-53829-5 OP: £5.99 p/b

BBE-045 *Doctor Who: Eater of Wasps* (Trevor Baxendale)
2001/05/07, BBC Worldwide Ltd, UK
REF: ISBN 0-563-53832-5 OP: £5.99 p/b

BBE-046 *Doctor Who: The Year of Intelligent Tigers* (Kate Orman from a story by Jonathan Blum and Kate Orman)
2001/06/04, BBC Worldwide Ltd, UK
Cover by Black Sheep. Includes a map by Carolyn Edwards.
REF: ISBN 0-563-53831-7 OP: £5.99 p/b

BBE-047 *Doctor Who: The Slow Empire* (Dave Stone)
2001/07/02, BBC Worldwide Ltd, UK
Cover by Black Sheep.
REF: ISBN 0-563-53835-X OP: £5.99 p/b

BBE-048 *Doctor Who: Dark Progeny* (Steve Emmerson)
2001/08/06, BBC Worldwide Ltd, UK
Cover by Black Sheep.
REF: ISBN 0-563-53837-6 OP: £5.99 p/b

BBE-040

BBE-041

BBE-042

BBE-043

BBE-044

BBE-045

BBE-046

BBE-047

BBE-048

BBE-049

BBE-050

BBE-051

BBE-052

BBE-053

BBE-054

BBE-055

BBE-049 *Doctor Who: The City of the Dead* **(Lloyd Rose)**
2001/09/03, BBC Worldwide Ltd, UK
Cover by Black Sheep.
REF: ISBN 0-563-53839-2 OP: £5.99 p/b

BBE-050 *Doctor Who: Grimm Reality* **(Simon Bucher-Jones and Kelly Hale)**
2001/10/01, BBC Worldwide Ltd, UK
Cover by Black Sheep. The original review copies of this title featured a printing fault whereby page 150 replaced page 146. This was quickly corrected and the error only occurred in early review copies.
REF: ISBN 0-563-53841-4 OP: £5.99 p/b

BBE-051 *Doctor Who: The Adventuress of Henrietta Street* **(Lawrence Miles)**
2001/11/05, BBC Worldwide Ltd, UK
Cover by Black Sheep.
REF: ISBN 0-563-53842-2 OP: £5.99 p/b

BBE-052 *Doctor Who: Mad Dogs and Englishmen* **(Paul Magrs)**
2002/01/07, BBC Worldwide Ltd, UK
Cover by Black Sheep. The 100th BBC *Doctor Who* novel.
REF: ISBN 0-563-53845-7 OP: £5.99 p/b

BBE-053 *Doctor Who: Hope* **(Mark Clapham)**
2002/02/04, BBC Worldwide Ltd, UK
Cover by Black Sheep.
REF: ISBN 0-563-53846-5 OP: £5.99 p/b

BBE-054 *Doctor Who: Anachrophobia* **(Jonathan Morris)**
2002/03/04, BBC Worldwide Ltd, UK
Cover by Black Sheep.
REF: ISBN 0-563-53847-3   OP: £5.99 p/b

BBE-055 *Doctor Who: Trading Futures* **(Lance Parkin)**
2002/04/08, BBC Worldwide Ltd, UK
Cover by Black Sheep.
REF: ISBN 0-563-53848-1   OP: £5.99 p/b

BBE-056 *Doctor Who: The Book of the Still* **(Paul Ebbs)**
2002/05/06, BBC Worldwide Ltd, UK
Cover by Black Sheep.
REF: ISBN 0-563-53851-1   OP: £5.99 p/b

BBE-057 *Doctor Who: The Crooked World* **(Steve Lyons)**
2002/06/03, BBC Worldwide Ltd, UK
Cover by Black Sheep.
REF: ISBN 0-563-53856-2   OP: £5.99 p/b

BBE-058 *Doctor Who: History 101* **(Mags L Halliday)**
2002/07/01, BBC Worldwide Ltd, UK
Cover by Black Sheep.
REF: ISBN 0-563-53854-6   OP: £5.99 p/b

BBE-059 *Doctor Who: Camera Obscura* **(Lloyd Rose)**
2002/08/05, BBC Worldwide Ltd, UK
Cover by Black Sheep.
REF: ISBN 0-563-53857-0   OP: £5.99 p/b

BBE-060 *Doctor Who: Time Zero* **(Justin Richards)**
2002/09/02, BBC Worldwide Ltd, UK
Cover by Black Sheep. With this book the BBC novels went to publishing a single title each month.
REF: ISBN 0-563-53866-X   OP: £5.99 p/b

BBE-061 *Doctor Who: The Infinity Race* **(Simon Messingham)**
2002/11/04, BBC Worldwide Ltd, UK
Cover by Black Sheep.
REF: ISBN 0-563-53863-5   OP: £5.99 p/b

BBE-056

BBE-057

BBE-058

BBE-059

BBE-060

BBE-061

BBP-001

BBP-002

BBP-001 *Doctor Who: The Devil Goblins from Neptune* **(Keith Topping & Martin Day)**
1997/06/02, BBC Worldwide Ltd, UK
Dr 3. Cover by Black Sheep.
REF: ISBN 0-563-40564-3 OP: £4.99 p/b NM: £7

BBP-002 *Doctor Who: The Murder Game* **(Steve Lyons)**
1997/07/07, BBC Worldwide Ltd, UK
Dr 2. Cover by Black Sheep.
REF: ISBN 0-563-40565-1 OP: £4.99 p/b NM: £7

BBP-003 *Doctor Who: The Ultimate Treasure* **(Christopher Bulis)**
1997/08/04, BBC Worldwide Ltd, UK
Dr 5. Cover by Black Sheep. Alien by Colin Howard.
REF: ISBN 0-563-40571-6 OP: £4.99 p/b NM: £7

BBP-003

BBP-004

BBP-004 *Doctor Who: Business Unusual* **(Gary Russell)**
1997/09/01, BBC Worldwide Ltd, UK
Dr 6. Cover by Black Sheep.
REF: ISBN 0-563-40575-9 OP: £4.99 p/b NM: £7

BBP-005 *Doctor Who: Illegal Alien* **(Mike Tucker and Robert Perry)**
1997/10/06, BBC Worldwide Ltd, UK
Dr 7. Cover by Black Sheep.
REF: ISBN 0-563-40570-8 OP: £4.99 p/b NM: £7

BBP-006 *Doctor Who: The Roundheads* **(Mark Gatiss)**
1997/11/24, BBC Worldwide Ltd, UK
Dr 2. Cover by Black Sheep.
REF: ISBN 0-563-40576-7 OP: £4.99 p/b NM: £7

BBP-007 *Doctor Who: The Face of the Enemy* **(David A McIntee)**
1998/01/05, BBC Worldwide Ltd, UK
The Master. Cover by Black Sheep.
REF: ISBN 0-563-40580-5 OP: £4.99 p/b NM: £7

BBP-008 *Doctor Who: Eye of Heaven* **(Jim Mortimore)**
1998/02/02, BBC Worldwide Ltd, UK
Dr 4. Cover by Black Sheep.
REF: ISBN 0-563-40567-8 OP: £4.99 p/b NM: £7

BBP-005

BBP-006

BBP-009 *Doctor Who: The Witch Hunters* (**Steve Lyons**)
1998/03/02, BBC Worldwide Ltd, UK
Dr 1. Cover by Black Sheep.
REF: ISBN 0-563-40579-1 OP: £4.99 p/b NM: £7

BBP-010 *Doctor Who: The Hollow Men* (**Keith Topping & Martin Day**)
1998/04/06, BBC Worldwide Ltd, UK
Dr 7. Cover by Black Sheep. Scarecrow by Colin Howard.
REF: ISBN 0-563-40582-1 OP: £4.99 p/b NM: £7

BBP-011 *Doctor Who: Catastrophea* (**Terrance Dicks**)
1998/05/04, BBC Worldwide Ltd, UK
Dr 3. Cover by Black Sheep.
REF: ISBN 0-563-40584-8 OP: £4.99 p/b NM: £7

BBP-012 *Doctor Who: Mission: Impractical* (**David A McIntee**)
1998/06/01, BBC Worldwide Ltd, UK
Dr 6. Cover by Black Sheep.
REF: ISBN 0-563-40592-9 OP: £4.99 p/b NM: £7

BBP-013 *Doctor Who: Zeta Major* (**Simon Messingham**)
1998/07/06, BBC Worldwide Ltd, UK
Dr 5. Cover by Black Sheep.
REF: ISBN 0-563-40597-X OP: £4.99 p/b NM: £7

BBP-014 *Doctor Who: Dreams of Empire* (**Justin Richards**)
1998/08/03, BBC Worldwide Ltd, UK
Dr 2. Cover by Black Sheep.
REF: ISBN 0-563-40598-8 OP: £4.99 p/b NM: £7

BBP-007

BBP-008

BBP-009

BBP-010

BBP-011

BBP-012

BBP-013

BBP-014

BBP-015   **BBP-016**

BBP-015 *Doctor Who: Last Man Running* **(Chris Boucher)**
1998/09/07, BBC Worldwide Ltd, UK
Dr 4. Cover by Black Sheep.
REF: ISBN 0-563-40594-5 OP: £4.99 p/b NM: £7

BBP-016 *Doctor Who: Matrix* **(Robert Perry & Mike Tucker)**
1998/10/05, BBC Worldwide Ltd, UK
Dr 7. Cover by Black Sheep.
REF: ISBN 0-563-40596-1 OP: £4.99 p/b NM: £7

BBP-017 *Doctor Who: The Infinity Doctors* **(Lance Parkin)**
1998/11/16, BBC Worldwide Ltd, UK
Book features an 'alternate' Doctor. Cover by Colin Howard.
REF: ISBN 0-563-40591-0 OP: £4.99 p/b NM: £7

BBP-018 *Doctor Who: Salvation* **(Steve Lyons)**
1999/01/04, BBC Worldwide Ltd, UK
Dr 1. Cover by Black Sheep.
REF: ISBN 0-563-55566-1 OP: £4.99 p/b NM: £7

BBP-019 *Doctor Who: The Wages of Sin* **(David A McIntee)**
1999/02/01, BBC Worldwide Ltd, UK
Dr 3. Cover by Black Sheep.
REF: ISBN 0-563-55572-6 OP: £4.99 p/b NM: £7

BBP-020 *Doctor Who: Deep Blue* **(Mark Morris)**
1999/03/01, BBC Worldwide Ltd, UK
Dr 5. Cover by Black Sheep. Alien by Colin Howard.
REF: ISBN 0-563-55571-8 OP: £4.99 p/b NM: £7

BBP-017   **BBP-018**

BBP-019   **BBP-020**   **BBP-021**   **BBP-022**

BBP-021 *Doctor Who: Players* **(Terrance Dicks)**
1999/04/26, BBC Worldwide Ltd, UK
Dr 6. Cover by Black Sheep.
REF: ISBN 0-563-55573-4 OP: £4.99 p/b NM: £7

BBP-022 *Doctor Who: Millennium Shock* **(Justin Richards)**
1999/05/24, BBC Worldwide Ltd, UK
Dr 4. Cover by Black Sheep.
REF: ISBN 0-563-55586-5 OP: £4.99 p/b NM: £7

BBP-023 *Doctor Who: Storm Harvest* **(Robert Perry & Mike Tucker)**
1999/06/07, BBC Worldwide Ltd, UK
Dr 2. Cover by Black Sheep. Alien by Mike Tucker.
REF: ISBN 0-563-55577-7 OP: £5.99 p/b

BBP-024 *Doctor Who: Divided Loyalties* **(Gary Russell)**
1999/07/05, BBC Worldwide Ltd, UK
Dr 5. Cover by Black Sheep.
REF: ISBN 0-563-55578-0 OP: £5.99 p/b

BBP-025 *Doctor Who: City At Worlds End* **(Christopher Bulis)**
1999/09/06, BBC Worldwide Ltd, UK
Dr 1. Cover by Black Sheep.
REF: ISBN 0-563-55579-7 OP: £5.99 p/b

BBP-026 *Doctor Who: The Final Sanction* **(Steve Lyons)**
1999/10/05, BBC Worldwide Ltd, UK
Dr 7. Cover by Black Sheep.
REF: ISBN 0-563-55584-1 OP: £5.99 p/b

BBP-027 *Doctor Who: Corpse Marker* **(Chris Boucher)**
1999/11/01, BBC Worldwide Ltd, UK
Dr 4. Cover by Black Sheep.
REF: ISBN 0-563-55575-9 OP: £5.99 p/b

BBP-028 *Doctor Who: Last of the Gaderene* **(Mark Gatiss)**
2000/01/03, BBC Worldwide Ltd, UK
Dr 3. Cover by Black Sheep.
REF: ISBN 0-563-55587-4 OP: £5.99 p/b

BBP-029 *Doctor Who: Tomb of Valdemar* **(Simon Messingham)**
2000/02/07, BBC Worldwide Ltd, UK
Dr 4. Cover by Black Sheep.
REF: ISBN 0-563-55591-2 OP: £5.99 p/b

BBP-023   BBP-024

BBP-025   BBP-026

BBP-027   BBP-028

BBP-029

BBP-030

BBP-031

BBP-032

BBP-033

BBP-034

BBP-030 *Doctor Who: Verdigris* (Paul Magrs)
2000/04/03, BBC Worldwide Ltd, UK
Dr 4. Cover by Black Sheep.
REF: ISBN 0-563-55591-2 OP: £5.99 p/b

BBP-031 *Doctor Who: Grave Matter* (Justin Richards)
2000/05/01, BBC Worldwide Ltd, UK
Dr 4. Cover by Black Sheep.
REF: ISBN 0-563-55591-2 OP: £5.99 p/b

BBP-032 *Doctor Who: Heart of TARDIS* (Dave Stone)
2000/06/05, BBC Worldwide Ltd, UK
Drs 2 and 4. Cover by Black Sheep.
REF: ISBN 0-563-55596-3 OP: £5.99 p/b

BBP-033 *Doctor Who: Prime Time* (Mike Tucker)
2000/07/03, BBC Worldwide Ltd, UK
Dr 7. Cover by Black Sheep.
REF: ISBN 0-563-55597-1 OP: £5.99 p/b

BBP-034 *Doctor Who: Imperial Moon* (Christopher Bulis)
2000/08/07, BBC Worldwide Ltd, UK
Dr 5. Cover by Black Sheep.
REF: ISBN 0-563-53801-5 OP: £5.99 p/b

BBP-035 *Doctor Who: Festival of Death* (Jonathan Morris)
2000/09/04, BBC Worldwide Ltd, UK
Dr 4. Cover by Black Sheep.
REF: ISBN 0-563-53803-1 OP: £5.99 p/b

BBP-036 *Doctor Who: Independence Day* (Peter Darvill-Evans)
2000/10/02, BBC Worldwide Ltd, UK
Dr 7. Cover by Black Sheep.
REF: ISBN 0-563-53804-X OP: £5.99 p/b

BBP-037 *Doctor Who: The King of Terror* (Keith Topping)
2000/11/06, BBC Worldwide Ltd, UK
Dr 5. Cover by Black Sheep.
REF: ISBN 0-563-53802-3 OP: £5.99 p/b

BBP-038 *Doctor Who: The Quantum Archangel* (Craig Hinton)
2001/01/08, BBC Worldwide Ltd, UK
Dr 6. Cover by Black Sheep.
REF: ISBN 0-563-53824-4 OP: £5.99 p/b

BBP-035   **BBP-036**   **BBP-037**   **BBP-038**

BBP-039 *Doctor Who: Bunker Soldiers* (Martin Day)
2001/02/05, BBC Worldwide Ltd, UK
Dr 1. Cover by Black Sheep.
REF: ISBN 0-563-53819-8 OP: £5.99 p/b

BBP-040 *Doctor Who: Rags* (Mick Lewis)
2001/03/05, BBC Worldwide Ltd, UK
Dr 3.
REF: ISBN 0-563-53826-0 OP: £5.99 p/b

BBP-041 *Doctor Who: The Shadow In the Glass*
(Justin Richards and Stephen Cole)
2001/04/01, BBC Worldwide Ltd, UK
Dr 6.
REF: ISBN 0-563-53838-4 OP: £5.99 p/b

BBP-042 *Doctor Who: Asylum* (Peter Darvill-Evans)
2001/05/07, BBC Worldwide Ltd, UK
Dr 4.
REF: ISBN 0-563-53833-3 OP: £5.99 p/b

BBP-043 *Doctor Who: Superior Beings* (Nick Walters)
2001/06/04, BBC Worldwide Ltd, UK
Dr 5.
REF: ISBN 0-563-53830-9 OP: £5.99 p/b

BBP-044 *Doctor Who: Byzantium!* (Keith Topping)
2001/07/02, BBC Worldwide Ltd, UK
Dr 1.
REF: ISBN 0-563-53836-8 OP: £5.99 p/b

BBP-039   **BBP-040**

BBP-041   **BBP-042**

BBP-043   **BBP-044**

BBP-045 *Doctor Who: Bullet Time* (David A. McIntee)
2001/08/06, BBC Worldwide Ltd, UK
Dr 7.
REF: ISBN 0-563-53834-1 OP: £5.99 p/b

BBP-046 *Doctor Who: Psi-Ence Fiction* (Chris Boucher)
2001/09/03, BBC Worldwide Ltd, UK
Dr 4.
REF: ISBN 0-563-53814-7 OP: £5.99 p/b

BBP-047 *Doctor Who: Dying in the Sun* (Jon de Burgh Miller)
2001/10/01, BBC Worldwide Ltd, UK
Dr 2.
REF: ISBN 0-563-53840-6 OP: £5.99 p/b

BBP-048 *Doctor Who: Instruments of Darkness* (Gary Russell)
2001/11/05, BBC Worldwide Ltd, UK
Dr 6.
REF: ISBN 0-563-53828-7 OP: £5.99 p/b

BBP-049 *Doctor Who: Relative Dimentias* (Mark Michalowski)
2002/01/07, BBC Worldwide Ltd, UK
Dr 7.
REF: ISBN 0-563-53844-9 OP: £5.99 p/b

BBP-050 *Doctor Who: Drift* (Simon A Forward)
2002/02/04, BBC Worldwide Ltd, UK
Dr 4.
REF: ISBN 0-563-53843-0 OP: £5.99 p/b

BBP-051 *Doctor Who: Palace of the Red Sun* (Christopher Bulis)
2002/03/04, BBC Worldwide Ltd, UK
Dr 6.
REF: ISBN 0-563-53849-X OP: £5.99 p/b

BBP-045   **BBP-046**

BBP-047   **BBP-048**   **BBP-049**   **BBP-050**

BBP-052 *Doctor Who: Amorality Tale* (**David Bishop**)
2002/04/08, BBC Worldwide Ltd, UK
Dr 3.
REF: ISBN 0-563-53850-3 OP: £5.99 p/b

BBP-053 *Doctor Who: Warmonger* (**Terrance Dicks**)
2002/05/06, BBC Worldwide Ltd, UK
Dr 5.
REF: ISBN 0-563-53852-X OP: £5.99 p/b

BBP-054 *Doctor Who: Ten Little Aliens* (**Steve Cole**)
2002/06/03, BBC Worldwide Ltd, UK
Dr 1.
REF: ISBN 0-563-53853-8 OP: £5.99 p/b

BBP-055 *Doctor Who: Combat Rock* (**Mick Lewis**)
2002/07/01, BBC Worldwide Ltd, UK
Dr 2.
REF: ISBN 0-563-53855-4 OP: £5.99 p/b

BBP-056 *Doctor Who: The Suns of Caresh* (**Paul Saint**)
2002/08/05, BBC Worldwide Ltd, UK
Dr 3.
REF: ISBN 0-563-53858-9 OP: £5.99 p/b

BBP-057 *Doctor Who: Heritage* (**Dale Smith**)
2002/10/07, BBC Worldwide Ltd, UK
Dr 7.
REF: ISBN 0-563-53864-3 OP: £5.99 p/b

BBP-051

BBP-052

BBP-053

BBP-054

BBP-055

BBP-056

BBP-057

BCO-001

BBS-002 (front view and side view)

BCO-002

BCO-003

BCO-004

BCO-005

BOOKS, BOOKENDS

BBS-001 TARDIS Book ends
1990, Friends of Doctor Who, USA
No further information available.

BBS-002 Police Box Bookends
2002/01, Courtney Collectors, UK
Measuring approx. 5x4x6 inches.
OP: £34 pair

BOOKS, COLLECTIONS

BCO-001 *Doctor Who Omnibus, The* (Terrance Dicks/Malcolm Hulke)
1977, Book Club Associates (BCA), UK
Grey flecked dust jacket. Contains: *The Space War*; *The Web of Fear*; *The Revenge of the Cybermen*.
REF: CN 4054 OP: £4.95 h/b NM: £17-£27

BCO-002 *Adventures of Doctor Who, The* (Terrance Dicks)
1979, Nelson Doubleday Inc, USA
Jacket illustration by Gary Viskupic (dated 1979). Book club edition. Contains *Doctor Who and the Genesis of the Daleks*; *Doctor Who and the Revenge of the Cybermen*; *Doctor Who and the Loch Ness Monster*. There are two different editions known to exist of this title. One has a yellow cloth binding to the book, the dust jacket has no marking on the back cover, and the numbers '5208' are printed at the bottom of the inside back flap. The other has a dark grey cloth binding, with a scarlet spine portion, the number '5208' is printed in a small white box at the bottom of the back cover, and not on the inside back flap.
REF: 5208 OP: h/b NM: £27.50

BCO-003 *Further Adventures of Doctor Who, The* (Terrance Dicks)
1986, Nelson Doubleday Inc, USA
Jacket illustration by Daniel R Horne (dated 1985). Book club edition. Contains *Doctor Who and the Deadly Assassin*, *Doctor Who and the Face of Evil* and *Doctor Who and the Robots of Death*.
REF: 01067 OP: h/b NM: £33

BCO-004 *Doctor Who – Dalek Omnibus* (Terrance Dicks)
1983/06/23, W. H. Allen & Co. Ltd, UK
Cover by Andrew Skilleter. No dust jacket. Contains *The Dalek Invasion of Earth*, *Day of the Daleks* and *Planet of the Daleks*.
REF: ISBN 0-491-03420-2
OP: £8.95 h/b NM: £12-£22

BCO-005 Doctor Who Classics – The Dalek Invasion of Earth and The Crusaders
1988/08/18, Star/W. H. Allen & Co. PLC, UK
The *Doctor Who Classics* series was an attempt by the publishers to reduce warehouse stocks of selected titles. Cover by Andrew Skilleter (from *The Dalek Omnibus*).
REF: ISBN 0-352-32264-0 OP: £2.95 p/b NM: £5.50

BCO-006 Doctor Who Classics – The Myth Makers and The Gunfighters
1988/08/18, Star/W. H. Allen & Co. PLC, UK
Cover by Andrew Skilleter (from *The Gunfighters*).
REF: ISBN 0-352-32263-2 OP: £2.95 p/b NM: £4-£6

BCO-007 Doctor Who Classics – The Dominators and The Krotons
1988/09/15, Star/W. H. Allen & Co. PLC, UK
Cover by Andrew Skilleter (from *The Dominators*).
REF: ISBN 0-352-32265-9 OP: £2.95 p/b NM: £4-£6

BCO-008 Doctor Who Classics – The Dæmons and The Time Monster
1989/03/16, Star/W. H. Allen & Co. PLC, UK
Cover by Andrew Skilleter (from *The Dæmons*).
REF: ISBN 0-352-32382-5 OP: £2.95 p/b NM: £4-£6

BCO-009 Doctor Who Classics – The Mind of Evil and The Claws of Axos
1989/03/16, Star/W. H. Allen & Co. PLC, UK
Cover by Andrew Skilleter (from *The Mind of Evil*).
REF: ISBN 0-352-32381-7 OP: £2.95 p/b NM: £4-£6

BCO-010 Doctor Who Classics – The Face of Evil and The Sunmakers
1989/05/18, Star/W. H. Allen & Co. PLC, UK
Cover by Jeff Cummins (from *The Face of Evil*).
REF: ISBN 0-352-32417-1 OP: £2.95 p/b NM: £4-£6

BCO-011 Doctor Who Classics – The Seeds of Doom and The Deadly Assassin
1989/05/18, Star/W. H. Allen & Co. PLC, UK
Cover by Chris Achilleos (from *The Seeds of Doom*).
REF: ISBN 0-352-32416-3 OP: £2.95 p/b NM: £4-£6

BCO-012 First Doctor Who Gift Set
1982, W. H. Allen & Co. Ltd (Target), UK
Box Cover: Bill Donohoe from the 1st edition of *The Doctor Who Programme Guide*. Red logo and text.
Contains: *An Unearthly Child*; *Enemy of the World*; *State of Decay*; *The Keeper of Traken*.
REF: ISBN 0-426-19270-2 OP: £5.25 p/b NM: £12

BCO-006

BCO-007

BCO-008

BCO-009

BCO-010

BCO-011

BCO-012 to BCO-015

BCO-16 & BCO-017

BCO-18 to BCO-020

BCO-013 Second Doctor Who Gift Set
1982, W. H. Allen & Co. Ltd (Target), UK
Box Cover: Bill Donohoe from the 1st edition of *The Doctor Who Programme Guide*. Blue logo and text.
Contains: *The Leisure Hive*; *Full Circle*; *The Visitation*; *Warriors' Gate*.
REF: ISBN 0-426-19289-3 OP: £5.25 p/b NM: £12

BCO-014 Third Doctor Who Gift Set
1983, W. H. Allen & Co. Ltd (Target), UK
Red box with blue logo and Peter Davison photograph. Contains: *Castrovalva*; *Four to Doomsday*; *Earthshock*; *Terminus*.
REF: ISBN 0-426-19422-5 OP: £5.75 p/b NM: £12

BCO-015 Fourth Doctor Who Gift Set
1983, W. H. Allen & Co. Ltd (Target), UK
Blue box with red logo and Peter Davison photograph. Contains: *The Giant Robot*; *State of Decay*; *Logopolis*; *Time-Flight*.
REF: ISBN 0-426-19430-6 OP: £5.75 p/b NM: £12

BCO-016 Fifth Doctor Who Gift Set
1984, W. H. Allen & Co. PLC (Target), UK
Black box with blue logo and Colin Baker photograph. Contains: *Kinda*; *Arc of Infinity*; *Snakedance*; *Warriors of the Deep*.
REF: ISBN 0-426-19596-5 OP: £6.50 p/b NM: £12

BCO-017 Sixth Doctor Who Gift Set
1984, W. H. Allen & Co. PLC (Target), UK
Orange box with red logo and 'Five Doctors' photograph. Contains: *The Dominators*; *Mawdryn Undead*; *Enlightenment*; *The Five Doctors*. Picture shows different books but this was a pre-release shoot.
REF: ISBN 0-426-19609-0 OP: £6.50 p/b NM: £12

BCO-018 Seventh Doctor Who Gift Set
1985, W. H. Allen & Co. PLC (Target), UK
Box Cover: Graham Potts from *Doctor Who: A Celebration*.
Contains: *The Highlanders*; *Inferno*; *Frontios*; *Planet of Fire*.
REF: ISBN 0-426-20206-6 OP: p/b NM: £12

BCO-019 Eighth Doctor Who Gift Set
1985, W. H. Allen & Co. PLC (Target), UK
Box Cover: Andrew Skilleter from *The Awakening* and *The Caves of Androzani*. Contains: *Marco Polo*; *The Mind of Evil*; *The Awakening*; *The Caves of Androzani*.
REF: ISBN 0-426-20207-4 OP: p/b NM: £12

BCO-020 Doctor Who Gift Set
1986, W. H. Allen & Co. PLC (Target), UK
Colin Baker photograph on box. Contains: *The Keys of Marinus*; *The Mind of Evil*; *Meglos*; *The Keeper of Traken*.
REF: ISBN 0-426-32410-8 OP: p/b NM: £12

BOOKS, FACTUAL

BFA-001a *Making of Doctor Who, The* **(Malcolm Hulke & Terrance Dicks)**
1972/04/20, Piccolo/Pan Books Ltd, UK
A fairly detailed look at the background to the TV show written by Hulke (one of the show's writers) and Dicks (the show's script editor). This book was suggested to Pan by Hulke who did the bulk of the writing for the first edition. Features a script-to-screen section on *The Sea Devils*. Photographic cover: Third Doctor and Sea Devil.
REF: ISBN 0-330-23203-7 OP: 25p p/b NM: £27.50

BFA-001b *Making of Doctor Who, The* **(Terrance Dicks & Malcolm Hulke)**
1976/12/16, Target/Tandem Publishing Ltd, UK
Cover by Chris Achilleos. This was not a straight reprint of the 1972 book. Terrance Dicks virtually re-wrote the entire content and added several new chapters. Features a script-to-screen section on *Robot*. Print run: 50,000 copies.
REF: ISBN 0-426-11615-1 OP: 60p p/b NM: £3.50

BFA-001c *Making of Doctor Who, The* **(Terrance Dicks & Malcolm Hulke)**
1980/03/20, Target/W H Allen & Co Ltd, UK
Print run: 15,000 copies. Reprint of the 1976 edition.
REF: ISBN 0-426-11615-1 OP: £1.80 p/b NM: £2.25

BFA-002a *Doctor Who Monster Book, The* **(Terrance Dicks)**
1975/11/20, Target/Tandem Publishing Ltd, UK
Large photos, Target cover artwork and minimal text on selected *Doctor Who* monsters. Cover by Chris Achilleos. First edition had a print run of 100,000 copies. Contained a stapled in poster of the cover artwork.
REF: ISBN 0-426-11447-7
OP: 50p lfp/b NM: £15-£23

BFA-002b *Doctor Who Monster Book, The* **(Terrance Dicks)**
1985/05/16, W. H. Allen & Co. PLC (Target), UK
Re-issue. Print run: 30,000 copies. No poster.
REF: ISBN 0-426-11447-7 OP: £1.95 lfp/b NM: £3.50

BFA-003 *Second Doctor Who Monster Book, The* **(Terrance Dicks)**
1977/10/20, W. H. Allen & Co. Ltd, UK
Cover by Chris Achilleos. Featured monsters from *Robot* to *The Talons of Weng-Chiang*.
REF: ISBN 0-426-20001-2 OP: 70p p/b NM: £17-£25

BFA-001a

BFA-001b

BFA-002a

BFA-002b

BFA-003

BFA-004

BFA-004 *A Day With A TV Producer* (Graham Rickard)
1980/11, Wayland Publishers Ltd, UK
Photographic cover. One of a series of 'A Day with…' books. Follows the making of *The Leisure Hive*.
REF: ISBN 0-85340-793-2 OP: £3.25 h/b NM: £16.50

BFA-005a *Doctor Who Programme Guide Vol 1, The* (Jean-Marc Lofficier)
1981/05/21, W. H. Allen & Co. Ltd, UK
Cover by Bill Donohoe. Frenchman Jean-Marc Lofficier had been writing about science fiction and fantasy for many years for the French magazine *L'Ecran Fantastique*, and, in the course of writing a dossier on *Doctor Who* – eventually published in issues 23 & 24 – had corresponded with Terrance Dicks. On seeing the final dossier, Dicks felt that it was worth bringing to a wider audience and spoke to W. H. Allen. Editor Christine Donougher liked the idea and the updated dossier was split by W. H. Allen into a two-volume guide collectively called *The Doctor Who Programme Guide*. The first volume was a story-by-story look at the series up to *Logopolis*, with cast lists, synopses and transmission dates. The second volume was an encyclopaedic view of the characters, places, monsters and other things mentioned in the context of *Doctor Who*'s fictional history. The books sold well and, provided for the first time an extensive guide to *Doctor Who*. Some copies of the hardback edition contained an insert errata sheet for Season 18.
REF: ISBN 0-491-02804-0 OP: £4.50 h/b NM: £8

BFA-005a

BFA-005b

BFA-005b *Doctor Who Programme Guide Vol 1, The* (Jean-Marc Lofficier)
1981/10/15, Target/W. H. Allen & Co. Ltd, UK
Cover by Bill Donohoe. Covers series up to *Logopolis*. Revised from hardback edition. Print run: 25,000 copies.
REF: ISBN 0-426-20139-6 OP: £1.25 p/b NM: £7

BFA-005c *Doctor Who The Programme Guide* (Jean-Marc Lofficier)
1989/12/21, Target/W. H. Allen & Co. PLC, UK
'New Edition Updated Revised' flash on cover. New cover artwork by Alistair Pearson.
REF: ISBN 0-426-20342-9 OP: £1.99 p/b NM: £3

BFA-005d *Doctor Who Programme Guide* (Jean-Marc Lofficier)
1994/06/16, Virgin Publishing Ltd, UK
Revised and corrected reissue. Cover by Alistair Pearson as for 1989 edition, but contained in a box on the cover rather than being full-bleed.
REF: ISBN 0-426-20342-9 OP: £4.99 p/b NM: £6

BFA-005c

BFA-005d

BFA-006a *Doctor Who Programme Guide Vol 2, The* (Jean-Marc Lofficier)
1981/05/21, W. H. Allen & Co. Ltd, UK
Cover by Bill Donohoe. Covers series up to *Logopolis*.
REF: ISBN 0-491-02885-7 OP: £4.50 h/b NM: £8

BFA-006b *Doctor Who Programme Guide Vol 2, The* (Jean-Marc Lofficier)
1981/10/15, Target/W. H. Allen & Co. Ltd, UK
Cover by Bill Donohoe. Covers series up to *Logopolis*.
Revised from hardback edition. Print run: 25,000 copies.
REF: ISBN 0-426-20142-6 OP: £1.25 p/b NM: £7

BFA-006a

BFA-006b

BFA-007a *Doctor Who – The Making of a Television Series* (Alan Road)
1982/07, André Deutsch Ltd, UK
Photographic cover. Covers the production of the 1982 story *The Visitation*.
REF: ISBN 0233-97444-X OP: £4.95 h/b NM: £16.50

BFA-007b *Doctor Who – The Making of a Television Series* (Alan Road)
1983, Puffin, UK
REF: ISBN 0-1403-1687-6 OP: £1.95 lfp/b NM: £9

BFA-008a *Doctor Who Technical Manual, The* (Mark Harris)
1983/03, Severn House Publishers Ltd, UK
Basic and not entirely accurate designs of numerous *Doctor Who* robots and other items that can be constructed, including Daleks, Cybermen and the TARDIS.
REF: ISBN 0-7278-2034-6 OP: £4.95 h/b NM: £16.50

BFA-007b

BFA-008a

BFA-008b *Doctor Who Technical Manual, The* (Mark Harris)
1983, Sphere Books Ltd, UK
REF: ISBN 0-7221-4825-9 OP: £2.50 lfp/b NM: £11

BFA-008c *Doctor Who Technical Manual, The* (Mark Harris)
1983, JM Dent Pty Ltd/ABC/Severn House, AUS
ABC (then the Australian Broadcasting Commission) logo on front and back cover.
REF: ISBN 0-86770-022-X OP: $8.95 NM: £11

BFA-009a *Doctor Who – The TARDIS Inside Out* (John Nathan-Turner)
1985/05, Piccadilly Press Ltd, UK
Illustrated by Andrew Skilleter. Producer John Nathan-Turner's reminiscences about the actors who played the Doctor.
REF: ISBN 0-946826-71-4 OP: £7.50 h/b NM: £11

BFA-009a

BFA-010a

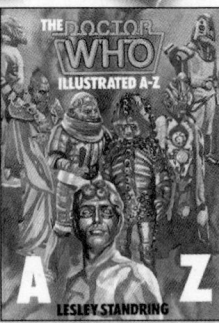

BFA-011a

BFA-012a

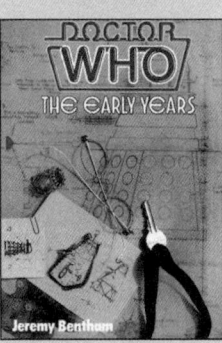

BFA-013b

BFA-014b

BFA-014c

BFA-009b *Doctor Who – The TARDIS Inside Out*
(John Nathan-Turner)
1985/05, Piccadilly Press Ltd, UK
REF: ISBN 0-946826-65-X OP: £4.95 lfp/b NM: £8

BFA-009c *Doctor Who – The TARDIS Inside Out*
(John Nathan-Turner)
1985, Random House, New York, USA
REF: ISBN 0-394-97415-8 OP: h/b NM: £16.50

BFA-009d *Doctor Who – The TARDIS Inside Out*
(John Nathan-Turner)
1985, Random House, New York, USA
Paperback edition went to a second printing.
REF: ISBN 0-394-87415-3 OP: $6.95 lfp/b NM: £11

BFA-010a *Doctor Who – The Companions* **(John Nathan-Turner)**
1986/11, Piccadilly Press Ltd, UK
Illustrated by Stuart Hughes. Producer John Nathan-Turner's reminiscences about the actors who played the Doctor's companions.
REF: ISBN 0-946826-62-5 OP: £7.95 h/b NM: £16.50

BFA-010b *Doctor Who – The Companions* **(John Nathan-Turner)**
1986/11, Piccadilly Press Ltd, UK
REF: ISBN 0-946826-29-5 OP: £4.95 lfp/b NM: £11

BFA-010c *Doctor Who – The Companions* **(John Nathan-Turner)**
1986, Random House, New York, USA
REF: ISBN 0-394-98291-6 OP: h/b NM: £22

BFA-010d *Doctor Who – The Companions* **(John Nathan-Turner)**
1986, Random House, New York, USA
REF: ISBN 0-394-88291-1 OP: lfp/b NM: £13.20

BFA-011a *Doctor Who The Illustrated A – Z*
(Lesley Standring)
1985/09/12, W. H. Allen & Co. PLC, UK
Cover and illustrations by Lesley Standring. Initial print run was 12,000 copies. A selective A-Z of *Doctor Who*.
REF: ISBN 0-491-03484-9 OP: £8.95 h/b NM: £13.20

BFA-011b *Doctor Who The Illustrated A – Z*
(Lesley Standring)
1987/03/19, W. H. Allen & Co. PLC, UK
REF: ISBN 0-426-20299-6 OP: £3.50 lfp/b NM: £7

BFA-012a *Doctor Who: Timeview – The Complete Doctor Who Illustrations of Frank Bellamy* **(David Bellamy)**

1985/10, Who Dares Publishing, UK
Cover by Frank Bellamy. A collection of all of artist
Frank Bellamy's *Doctor Who* pieces for *Radio Times*.
Written by Frank Bellamy's son.
REF: ISBN 0-948487-02-X OP: £5.95 h/b NM: £13.20

BFA-012b *Doctor Who: Timeview – The
Complete Doctor Who Illustrations of Frank
Bellamy* **(David Bellamy)**
1985/10, Who Dares Publishing, UK
REF: ISBN 0-948487-03-8 OP: £3.95 lfp/b NM: £9

BFA-013a *Doctor Who – The Early Years*
(Jeremy Bentham)
1986/05/15, W. H. Allen & Co. PLC, UK
200 copy limitation. Signed by the author and by
Raymond P Cusick, the BBC designer responsible for
the Daleks. ISBN does not appear in the leather-
bound edition. Slipcased.
REF: ISBN 0-491-03863-1 OP: £75 l/b NM: £82.50

BFA-013b *Doctor Who – The Early Years*
1986/05/15, W. H. Allen & Co. PLC, UK
Photographic cover. Initial print run of 15,000 copies.
Jeremy Bentham ran the DWAS' Reference
Department from its formation in 1976 until 1979.
The book concentrates mainly on the sixties stories
designed by Raymond P Cusick.
REF: ISBN 0-491-03612-4 OP: £13.50 h/b NM: £38.50

BFA-013c *Doctor Who – The Early Years*
1988/02/18, W. H. Allen & Co. PLC/Comet, UK
REF: ISBN 0-86379-170-0 OP: £6.95 lfp/b NM: £13.20

BFA-014a *Doctor Who – A Celebration* **(Peter
Haining)**
1983/09/15, W. H. Allen & Co. Ltd, UK
Limited edition. Slipcased.
REF: ISBN 0-491-03351-6 OP: £30 l/b NM: £66 l/b

BFA-014b *Doctor Who – A Celebration*
1983/09/15, W. H. Allen & Co. Ltd, UK
Cover by Graham Potts. This is the first major factual
overview of the background to the series. The book
went on to be one of W H Allen's best-ever sellers
with over 100,000 copies sold in hardback. A limited
leather bound edition was also produced.
REF: ISBN 0-491-03351-6
OP: £10.95 h/b NM: £22 h/b

BFA-014c *Doctor Who – A Celebration*
1995/07/20, Virgin Publishing Ltd, UK
REF: ISBN 0-86369-932-4 OP: £14.99 lfp/b

BFA-015a *Doctor Who – The Key to Time* **(Peter
Haining)**
1984/09/20, W. H. Allen & Co. PLC, UK
1000 copy limited edition. Signed by the author. ISBN
does not appear in the leather-bound edition. Slipcased.
REF: ISBN 0-491-03014-2 OP: £50 l/b NM: £82.50

BFA-015b *Doctor Who – The Key to Time* **(Peter
Haining)**
1984/09/20, W. H. Allen & Co. PLC, UK
Cover by Andrew Skilleter. A fairly innaccurate day-by-
day account of *Doctor Who*'s creation and surrounding
activities. Illustrated by fan artists who had been request-
ed to send work in by W. H. Allen for a 'mystery project'.
The initial print run on this title was 15,000 copies.
REF: ISBN 0-491-03283-8 OP: £12.50 h/b NM: £20

BFA-015c *Doctor Who – The Key to Time* **(Peter
Haining)**
1987/10/15, W. H. Allen & Co. PLC/Comet, UK
Paperback edition. Cover by Andrew Skilleter. A proposed Virgin paperback edition in 1995 was never
released.
REF: ISBN 0-863790153-0 OP: £5.95 lfp/b NM: £13.20

BFA-015a (leather bound edition)

BFA-015b

BFA-016a

BFA-017a

THE
TIME-TRAVELLERS'
GUIDE

PETER HAINING
BFA-017c

BFA-018a

BFA-016a *Doctor Who File, The* **(Peter Haining)**
1986/09/18, W. H. Allen & Co. PLC, UK
Cover by Tony Masero. Interviews with various *Doctor Who* personalities. A proposed leather-bound edition was never released.
REF: ISBN 0-491-03813-5   OP: £14.95 h/b   NM: £22

BFA-016b *Doctor Who File, The* **(Peter Haining)**
1989/01/19, W. H. Allen & Co. PLC, UK
REF: ISBN 0-863-79169-7   OP: £9.99 lfp/b   NM: £13.20

BFA-017a *Doctor Who – The Time-Travellers' Guide* **(Peter Haining)**
1987/09/17, W. H. Allen & Co. PLC, UK
Cover by Tony Masero. Initial print run of 10,000 copies. An overview of different elements in the *Doctor Who* universe: planets, aliens, spaceships and so on.
REF: ISBN 0-491-03497-0   OP: £14.95 h/b   NM: £22

BFA-017b *Doctor Who – The Time-Travellers' Guide* **(Peter Haining)**
1987, W. H. Allen & Co. PLC, UK
Paperback edition.
OP: p/b   NM: £11

BFA-017c *Doctor Who – The Time-Traveller's Guide* **(Peter Haining)**
1995/08/17, Virgin Publishing Ltd, UK
REF: ISBN 0-86369-927-8   OP: £14.99 lfp/b   NM: £13.20

BFA-018a *Doctor Who – 25 Glorious Years* **(Peter Haining)**
1988/11/17, W. H. Allen & Co. PLC/Planet, UK
Initial print run of 12,000 copies. Effectively an updated and more accurate version of *Doctor Who: A*

Celebration. Allegedly, almost the entire number went to America, and consequently only the reprinted edition (in November 1988) was available in the UK.
REF: ISBN 1-85227-021-7   OP: £14.95 h/b   NM: £22

BFA-018b *Doctor Who – 25 Glorious Years* **(Peter Haining)**
1990/09/20, Virgin Publishing Ltd, UK
REF: ISBN 0-86369-324-5   OP: £8.99 lfp/b   NM: £13.20

BFA-019a *Doctor Who Special Effects* **(Mat Irvine)**
1986/08/22, Hutchinson, UK
Photographic cover. Mat Irvine was a BBC Visual Effects Department designer who worked on many *Doctor Who* stories. This book looks in detail at the stories he worked on.
REF: ISBN 0-09-167920-6   OP: £8.95 h/b   NM: £22

BFA-019b *Doctor Who Special Effects* **(Mat Irvine)**
1986/08/22, Arrow Books Ltd (Beaver Books), UK
REF: ISBN 0-09-942630-7   OP: £5.95 lfp/b   NM: £11

BFA-020 *Travel Without the TARDIS* **(Jean Airey and Laurie Haldeman)**
1986/07/17, Target/W. H. Allen & Co. PLC, UK
Photographic cover. A fairly inaccurate guide to *Doctor Who* locations in England, written by two American fans from the point of view of Americans visiting England for the first time.
REF: ISBN 0-426-20240-6   OP: £1.60 p/b   NM: £11

BFA-021a *Doctor Who – Cybermen* **(David Banks)**
1988/11, Who Dares Publishing / Silver Fist, UK
Each volume of this special edition was individually bound and finished by hand by French artist Cathy Robert with two initials (specified by the purchaser) incorporated into an embossed Cybermark design on the front cover. The book was bound in a silver material, developed by NASA, as thin as cellophane but immensely strong and durable. It came in a black slipcase with a limited edition certificate pasted in, was signed and numbered by Banks, Skilleter and Robert, and had a black satin marker and silvered graphite page edges. The books were created as they were ordered. It is not known how many were finally produced.
REF: No ISBN OP: £100

BFA-019a

BFA-020

BFA-021b *Doctor Who – Cybermen* **(David Banks)**
1988/11, Who Dares Publishing / Silver Fist, UK
Cover and illustrations by Andrew Skilleter. Additional Material by Adrian Rigelsford. Consultant for 'Archive' Jan Vincent-Rudzki. A complete history of the Cybermen expanded and extrapolated from what was seen on television.
REF: No ISBN OP: £14.95 h/b

BFA-021c *Cybermen* **(David Banks)**
1990/09/20, Virgin Publishing Ltd, UK
Revised paperback, includes a photographic feature on the latest (at the time) Cyberman adventure *Silver Nemesis*.
REF: ISBN 0-352-32738-3 OP: £8.99 lfp/b

BFA-021b

BFA-021c

BFA-022 *Doctor Who Magazine Master Index*
1988/12, Asquith Publishing, UK
Covers the first 142 issues of *Doctor Who Magazine*. This was compiled by a fan named Murray Easedale.
OP: £7.50 p/b

BFA-023a *Encyclopedia of The Worlds of Doctor Who (A-D)* **(David Saunders)**
1987/11/23, Piccadilly Press Ltd, UK
Cover by Dr Jean Lorre/Science Photo Library. Illustrated by Tony Clark. An attempt to create a complete listing of all the elements in the *Doctor Who* universe. David Saunders was the co-ordinator of the DWAS for several years in the eighties.
REF: ISBN 0-946826-54-4 OP: £5.95 h/b NM: £5

BFA-023b *Encyclopedia of The Worlds of Doctor Who (A-D)* **(David Saunders)**
1988/10, Hodder & Stoughton Ltd (Knight Books), UK
Photographic cover of Bok from *The Dæmons*. Illustrated by Tony Clark.
REF: ISBN 0-340-42842-2 OP: £2.99 p/b NM: £3

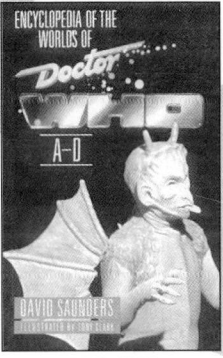

BFA-023a

BFA-023b

BFA-024a

BFA-024b

BFA-025

BFA-026

BFA-027

BFA-028

BFA-024a *Encyclopedia of The Worlds of Doctor Who* (E-K) (David Saunders)
1989/03, Piccadilly Press Ltd, UK
Cover and illustrations by Tony Clark.
REF: ISBN 1-85340-036-X OP: £7.95 h/b NM: £5

BFA-024b *Encyclopedia of The Worlds of Doctor Who* (E-K) (David Saunders)
1989/11/16, Knight Books/Hodder & Stoughton Ltd, UK
Photographic cover of the Guardian from *Colony in Space*. Illustrated by Tony Clark.
REF: ISBN 0-340-51106-0 OP: £3.50 p/b NM: £3

BFA-025 *Encyclopedia of the Worlds of Doctor Who L-R* (David Saunders)
1990/07, Piccadilly Press Ltd, UK
Cover and illustrations by Tony Clark. The Encyclopedia was never completed and this was the last volume published. There was no paperback edition of this volume.
REF: ISBN 1-85340-081-5 OP: £10.95 h/b NM: £11

BFA-026 *Doctor Who: The Terrestrial Index* (Jean-Marc Lofficier)
1991/11/21, Virgin Publishing Ltd, UK
Cover by Alistair Pearson. Greatly expanded version of a portion of the original 'Volume 2' of *The Doctor Who Programme Guide*. Indicies of actors, technicians, writers, plus details of all non-televised *Doctor Who* stories.
REF: ISBN 0-426-20361-5 OP: £3.50 p/b NM: £6

BFA-027 *Doctor Who: The Universal Databank* (Jean-Marc Lofficier)
1992/11/19, Virgin Publishing Ltd, UK
Cover by Alistair Pearson. Greatly expanded version of the original 'Volume 2' of *The Doctor Who Programme Guide*. A comprehensive A-Z of *Doctor Who* using references both from the TV stories and from the Target novelisations.
REF: ISBN 0-426-20370-4 OP: £4.99 p/b

BFA-028 *Files Magazine Spotlight on Doctor Who – The Pertwee Years* (John Peel)
1985, Schuster & Schuster Inc., USA
Guide to season 7 only.
The 'Files Magazine' format was developed by Hal Schuster as a spin-off from his magazine *Fantasy Empire*. Writer John Peel was the editor of *Fantasy Empire* and suggested episode guides to classic TV (which started with *The Man From UNCLE* and *Star Trek*) produced as magazines. The range was always produced in a paperback format, despite the 'magazine' title, and ran from 1984 to 1988, when Peel

stopped contributing. Other writers included James Van Hise (*Batman*, *Star Trek*, *Green Hornet* among others) and Doug Murray (*Outer Limits*), but Peel wrote around 110 of the volumes, including all of the *Doctor Who* ones. Each book contained character outlines, actor biographies, synopses of the relevant stories, plus some limited behind the scenes information and critical commentary.
REF: No ISBN OP: $4.95 lfp/b NM: £11

BFA-029 *Files Magazine Spotlight on Doctor Who – The Fourteenth Season* (John Peel)
1985, Schuster & Schuster Inc., USA
This book was reprinted and the reprint was ISBN 1-55698-037-X
REF: No ISBN OP: $4.95 lfp/b NM: £6

BFA-029

BFA-030 *Files Magazine Spotlight on Doctor Who – The Fifteenth Season* (John Peel)
1985, Schuster & Schuster Inc., USA
REF: No ISBN OP: $4.95 lfp/b NM: £6

BFA-031 *Files Magazine Spotlight on Doctor Who – Season Sixteen* (John Peel)
1985, Schuster & Schuster Inc., USA
REF: No ISBN OP: $4.95 lfp/b NM: £6

BFA-030

BFA-032 *Files Magazine Spotlight on Doctor Who – Season Seventeen* (John Peel)
1985, Schuster & Schuster Inc., USA
REF: No ISBN OP: $4.95 lfp/b NM: £6

BFA-033 *Files Magazine Spotlight on Doctor Who – Season Eighteen* (John Peel)
1985, Schuster & Schuster Inc., USA
REF: No ISBN OP: $4.95 lfp/b NM: £6

BFA-031

BFA-034a *Files Magazine Spotlight on Doctor Who – The First Baker Years* (John Peel)
1985, Schuster & Schuster Inc., USA
REF: No ISBN OP: $9.95 lfp/b NM: £6

BFA-034b *A Classic Files Magazine Spotlight on Doctor Who : The First Baker Years Part One* (John Peel)
1986, Schuster & Schuster Inc., USA
Reprint of material from *The First Baker Years*
REF: No ISBN OP: $6.95 lfp/b NM: £6

BFA-034a

BFA-034c *A Classic Files Magazine Spotlight on Doctor Who : The First Baker Years Part Two* (John Peel)
1986, Schuster & Schuster Inc., USA
Reprint of material from *The First Baker Years*.
REF: No ISBN OP: $6.95 lfp/b NM: £6

BFA-035

BFA-036

BFA-038

BFA-043

BFA-035 *Doctors File Magazine Spotlight On Patrick Troughton* (John Peel)
1986, Schuster & Schuster Inc., USA
REF: ISBN 1-55698-091-4 OP: $6.95 lfp/b NM: £6

BFA-036 *Files Magazine Spotlight on Doctor Who Season One: Part I* (John Peel)
1986, Schuster & Schuster Inc., USA
REF: No ISBN OP: $5.95 lfp/b NM: £6

BFA-037 *Files Magazine Spotlight on Doctor Who Season One: Part II* (John Peel)
1986, Schuster & Schuster Inc., USA
REF: No ISBN OP: $5.95 lfp/b NM: £56

BFA-038 *Files Magazine Spotlight on Doctor Who Season Two: Part I* (John Peel)
1986, Schuster & Schuster Inc., USA
REF: No ISBN OP: $5.95 lfp/b NM: £6

BFA-039 *Files Magazine Spotlight on Doctor Who Season Two: Part II* (John Peel)
1986, Schuster & Schuster Inc., USA
REF: No ISBN OP: $5.95 lfp/b NM: £6

BFA-040 *Files Magazine Spotlight on Doctor Who Season Three: Part I* (John Peel)
1986, Schuster & Schuster Inc., USA
REF: ISBN 1-55698-001-9 OP: $5.95 lfp/b NM: £6

BFA-041 *Files Magazine Spotlight on Doctor Who Season Three: Part II* (John Peel)
1986, Schuster & Schuster Inc., USA
REF: No ISBN OP: $5.95 lfp/b NM: £6

BFA-042 *Files Magazine Spotlight on Doctor Who Season Four: Part I* (John Peel)
1986, Schuster & Schuster Inc., USA
REF: No ISBN OP: $5.95 lfp/b NM: £6

BFA-043 *Files Magazine Spotlight on Doctor Who Season Four: Part II* (John Peel)
1986, Schuster & Schuster Inc., USA
REF: No ISBN OP: $5.95 lfp/b NM: £6

BFA-044 *Files Magazine Spotlight on Doctor Who The Ice Warriors Season Five: Part I*(John Peel)
1986, Schuster & Schuster Inc., USA
Listed on the spine as *The Ice Warrior*.
REF: ISBN 1-55698-042-6 OP: $5.95 lfp/b NM: £6

BFA-044

BFA-045

BFA-046

BFA-047

BFA-045 *Files Magazine Spotlight on Doctor Who The Wheel In Space Season Five: Part II* (John Peel)
1986, Schuster & Schuster Inc., USA
REF: ISBN 1-55698-031-0 OP: $6.95 lfp/b NM: £6

BFA-046 *Files Magazine Spotlight on Doctor Who Season Six Part One* (John Peel)
1986, Schuster & Schuster Inc., USA
REF: ISBN 1-55698-079-5 OP: $6.95 lfp/b NM: £6

BFA-047 *Files Magazine Spotlight on Doctor Who The War Games* (John Peel)
1986, Schuster & Schuster Inc., USA
This book was 'Season Six Part Two'.
REF: ISBN 1-55698-080-9 OP: $6.95 lfp/b NM: £6

BFA-048

BFA-048 *Files Magazine Spotlight on Doctor Who Season Eight* (John Peel)
1986, Schuster & Schuster Inc., USA
REF: No ISBN OP: $4.95 lfp/b NM: £6

BFA-049 *Files Magazine Spotlight on Doctor Who Season Nine* (John Peel)
1986, Schuster & Schuster Inc., USA
REF: No ISBN OP: $4.95 lfp/b NM: £6

BFA-050 *Files Magazine Spotlight on Doctor Who The Tenth Season* (John Peel)
1986, Schuster & Schuster Inc., USA
REF: No ISBN OP: $5.95 lfp/b NM: £6

BFA-050

BFA-051 *Files Magazine Spotlight on Doctor Who The Eleventh Season* (John Peel)
1986, Schuster & Schuster Inc., USA
REF: No ISBN OP: $5.95 lfp/b NM: £6

BFA-052 *Doctor Who The Complete Baker Years* (John Peel)
1987, Schuster & Schuster Inc., USA
Compilation of the Tom Baker *Files* magazines
REF: ISBN 1-55698-147-3 OP: $19.95 lfp/b NM: £20

BFA-052

BFA-054

BFA-055

BFA-057

BFA-059

BFA-060

BFA-053 *Files Magazine Focus On The Davison Years Book One* (John Peel)
1987, Schuster & Schuster Inc., USA
REF: No ISBN OP: $6.95 lfp/b NM: £6

BFA-054 *Doctors File Magazine Focus On Colin Baker* (John Peel)
1987, Schuster & Schuster Inc., USA
REF: No ISBN OP: $6.95 lfp/b NM: £6

BFA-055 *Files Magazine Focus On Doctor Who Movies* (John Peel)
1987, Schuster & Schuster Inc., USA
REF: ISBN 1-55698-130-9 OP: $6.95 lfp/b NM: £6

BFA-056 *Doctors File Magazine Spotlight On Tom Baker* (John Peel)
1987, Schuster & Schuster Inc., USA
REF: ISBN 1-55698-028-0 OP: $5.95 lfp/b NM: £6

BFA-057 *Doctors File Spotlight On Jon Pertwee* (John Peel)
1987, Schuster & Schuster Inc., USA
REF: ISBN 1-55698-029-9 OP: $5.95 lfp/b NM: £6

BFA-058 *The Doctors* (John Peel)
1987, Schuster & Schuster Inc., USA
Compilation of the individual Doctors' *Files* magazines.
OP: $17.95 lfp/b NM: £6

BFA-059 *Files Magazine Spotlight on Doctor Who: The Pertwee Years* (John Peel)
1988, Schuster & Schuster Inc., USA
Compilation of the individual Jon Pertwee *Files* magazines.
REF: ISBN 1-55698-212-7 OP: $19.95 lfp/b NM: £6

BFA-060 *The Doctor Who Encyclopedia The Baker Years* (John Peel)
1988, Schuster & Schuster Inc., USA
A to Z listings of both the fictional and factual aspects of *Doctor Who* during the era of the Fourth Doctor.
REF: No ISBN OP: $19.95 lfp/b NM: £6

BFA-061 *The Official Doctor Who & the Daleks Book* (John Peel & Terry Nation)
1989, St Martin's Press, USA
Information on every TV Dalek story, plus the stage plays, exhibitions, films and other media in which Nation's creations have appeared. Include the original outline for the first Dalek story, and a plot breakdown for a projected (but unmade) American TV

series featuring the Daleks. This book was not widely available in the UK.
REF: ISBN 0-312-02264-6
OP: $12.95 lfp/b NM: £17-£27

BFA-062 *The Gallifrey Chronicles* (John Peel)
1991/10/17, Virgin Publishing Ltd, UK
Cover by Andrew Skilleter. Information on every Time Lord to have appeared in *Doctor Who*, plus a fictional history of the Doctor's home planet, Gallifrey.
REF: ISBN 1-85227-329-1 OP: £14.99 h/b NM: £8

BFA-061   BFA-062

BFA-063a *The DWB Compendium* (Ed. Gary Leigh)
1993, Dream Watch Publishing, UK
Compendium of material from the *Doctor Who* and SF television fan magazine *DWB* (*Doctor Who Bulletin*).
REF: ISBN 0-9522307-0-4 OP: £16.99 h/b NM: £11

BFA-063b *The DWB Compendium* (Ed. Gary Leigh)
1993, Dream Watch Publishing, UK
REF: ISBN 0-9522307-0-4 OP: £12.99 lfp/b NM: £6

BFA-064a *The DWB Interview File* (Ed Gary Leigh)
1994, Dream Watch Publishing, UK
Compendium of material from the *Doctor Who* and SF television fan magazine *DWB* (*Doctor Who Bulletin*).
REF: ISBN 0-9522307-1-2 OP: £18.99 h/b NM: £11

BFA-064b *The DWB Interview File* (Ed Gary Leigh)
1994, Dream Watch Publishing, UK
REF: ISBN 0-9522307-1-2 OP: £14.99 lfp/b NM: £6

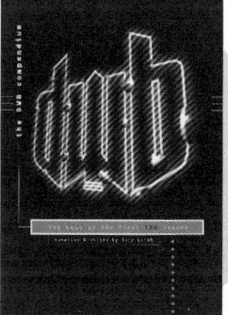

BFA-063b   BFA-064b

BFA-065 *Doctor Who: The Handbook: The Fourth Doctor* (David J Howe, Mark Stammers & Stephen James Walker)
1992/12/04, Virgin Publishing Ltd, UK
Cover by Alistair Pearson. A book looking at all aspects of the Fourth Doctor's era. Special feature on the making of *The Brain of Morbius*. Some minor textual corrections were made in the second printing of this book.
REF: ISBN 0-426-20369-0
OP: £3.99 p/b NM: £23

BFA-066 *Doctor Who: The Handbook: The Sixth Doctor* (David J Howe, Mark Stammers & Stephen James Walker)
1993/11/18, Virgin Publishing Ltd, UK
Cover by Alistair Pearson. A book looking at all aspects of the Sixth Doctor's era. Special feature on the making of *Revelation of the Daleks*. Some minor

BFA-065   BFA-066

BFA-067

BFA-068

BFA-069

BFA-070

BFA-071

BFA-072a

textual corrections were made in the second printing of this book.
REF: ISBN 0-426-20400-X OP: £4.99 p/b NM: £15

BFA-067 ***Doctor Who: The Handbook: The First Doctor*** **(David J Howe, Mark Stammers & Stephen James Walker)**
1994/11/17, Virgin Publishing Ltd, UK
Cover by Alistair Pearson. A book looking at all aspects of the First Doctor's era. Special feature on the making of *The Ark*, and a day-by-day guide to the development of the show over the first three years.
REF: ISBN 0-426-20430-1 OP: £4.99 p/b NM: £15

BFA-068 ***Doctor Who: The Handbook: The Fifth Doctor*** **(David J Howe and Stephen James Walker)**
1995/12/07, Virgin Publishing Ltd , UK
Cover by Alistair Pearson. A book looking at all aspects of the Fifth Doctor's era. Special feature on the making of *The Five Doctors*.
REF: ISBN 0-426-20458-1 OP: £4.99 p/b NM: £15

BFA-069 ***Doctor Who: The Handbook: The Third Doctor*** **(David J Howe & Stephen James Walker)**
1996/11/21, Virgin Publishing Ltd, UK
Cover by Alistair Pearson. A book looking at all aspects of the Third Doctor's era. Special feature on the making of *Day of the Daleks*.
REF: ISBN 0-426-20486-7 OP: £4.99 p/b NM: £12

BFA-070 ***Doctor Who: The Handbook: The Second Doctor*** **(David J Howe, Mark Stammers & Stephen James Walker)**
1997/11/20, Virgin Publishing Ltd, UK
Cover by Alistair Pearson. A book looking at all aspects of the Second Doctor's era. Special feature on the making of *The Mind Robber*.
REF: ISBN 0-426-20516-2 OP: £5.99 p/b NM: £12

BFA-071 ***Doctor Who: The Handbook: The Seventh Doctor*** **(David J Howe and Stephen James Walker)**
1998/11/19, Virgin Publishing Ltd , UK
Cover by Alistair Pearson. A book looking at all aspects of the Seventh Doctor's era. Special feature on the making of *Dragonfire*. Also contains details of the Eighth Doctor, and a complete index to all the Handbooks.
REF: ISBN 0-426-20527-8 OP: £6.99 p/b NM: £10

BFA-072a ***Doctor Who: The Sixties*** **(David J Howe, Mark Stammers & Stephen James Walker)**
1992/10/22, Virgin Publishing Ltd, UK
Photographic cover. Detailed look at the development

of *Doctor Who* in the sixties. Print run: 10,000 copies.
REF: ISBN 1-85227-420-4 OP: £14.99 h/b NM: £25

BFA-072b *Doctor Who: The Sixties* (David J Howe, Mark Stammers & Stephen James Walker)
1993/09/16, Virgin Publishing Ltd, UK
Photographic cover
REF: ISBN 0-86369-707-0 OP: £9.99 lfp/b NM: £20

BFA-073a *Doctor Who: The Seventies* (David J Howe, Mark Stammers & Stephen James Walker)
1994/11/03, Virgin Publishing Ltd, UK
Photographic cover. Detailed look at the development of *Doctor Who* in the seventies. Book was delayed from its scheduled date of 20/10/1994. Print run: 16,000 copies.
REF: ISBN 1-85227-444-1 OP: £15.99 h/b NM: £25

BFA-072b   **BFA-073a**

BFA-073b *Doctor Who: The Seventies* (David J Howe, Mark Stammers & Stephen James Walker)
1995/08/17, Virgin Publishing Ltd, UK
Photographic cover. Revised from h/b
REF: ISBN 0-86369-871-9 OP: £12.99 lfp/b NM: £20

BFA-074a *Doctor Who: The Eighties* (David J Howe, Mark Stammers & Stephen James Walker)
1996/10/03, Virgin Publishing Ltd, UK
Photographic cover. Detailed look at the development of *Doctor Who* in the eighties.
REF: ISBN 1-85227-680-0 OP: £17.99 h/b NM: £20

BFA-073b   **BFA-074a**

BFA-074b *Doctor Who: The Eighties* (David J Howe, Mark Stammers & Stephen James Walker)
1997/11/20, Virgin Publishing Ltd, UK
Photographic cover. Revised from h/b
REF: ISBN 0-7535-0128-7 OP: £14.99 lfp/b NM: £15

BFA-074b

BFA-075a *Doctor Who: Timeframe: The Illustrated History* (David J Howe)
1993/10/21, Virgin Publishing Ltd, UK
Photographic cover. Book released to celebrate the thirtieth anniversary of the show. Two editions with a single page of artwork reversed (corrected) in the second edition. This is the piece for Nigel Robinson's book *Birthright* on page 121. The second edition was published in 1994. Print run of first edition: 20,000 copies.
REF: ISBN 1-85227-427-1 OP: £15.99 h/b NM: £20

BFA-075a

BFA-075b

BFA-076

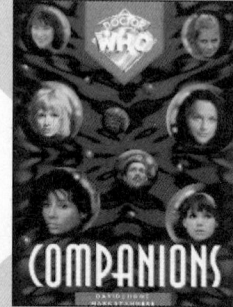

BFA-077a

BFA-077b

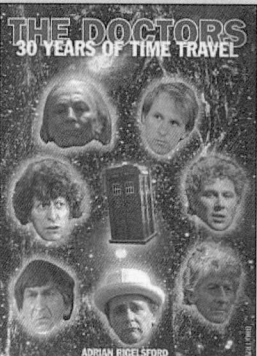

BFA-078

BFA-079

BFA-080

BFA-081

BFA-075b *Doctor Who: Timeframe: The Illustrated History* **(David J Howe)**
1994/08, Virgin Publishing Ltd, UK
Photographic cover. Revised from h/b
REF: ISBN 0-86369-861-1 OP: £9.99 lfp/b NM: £15

BFA-076 *Blacklight* **(Andrew Skilleter)**
1995/11/16, Virgin Publishing Ltd, UK
Cover by Andrew Skilleter. A collection of Andrew Skilleter's *Doctor Who* artwork.
REF: ISBN 1-85227-415-8 OP: £17.99 h/b

BFA-077a *Doctor Who: Companions* **(David J Howe & Mark Stammers)**
1995/10/06, Virgin Publishing Ltd , UK
Photographic cover. A celebration of all the Doctor's companions.
REF: ISBN 1-85227-582-0 OP: £15.99 h/b

BFA-077b *Doctor Who: Companions* **(David J Howe & Mark Stammers)**
1996/09/19, Virgin Publishing Ltd , UK
Photographic cover. Revised from h/b
REF: ISBN 0-86369-921-9 OP: £12.99 lfp/b

BFA-078 *Doctor Who: The Discontinuity Guide* **(Paul Cornell, Martin Day & Keith Topping)**
1995/05/18, Virgin Publishing Ltd, UK
Cover by Colin Howard. An irreverant look at *Doctor Who*, including all the goofs, continuity errors and painful lines of dialogue.
REF: ISBN 0-426-20442-5 OP: £4.99 p/b

BFA-079 *The Doctors: 30 Years of Time Travel* **(Adrian Rigelsford)**
1995/02, Boxtree, UK
Photographic composite cover. A largely innaccurate look at the history of *Doctor Who*. Misses out Season 18 altogether. Scheduled 25/11/1994, delayed publication. Reports suggest that 15,000 copies of this book were sold.
REF: ISBN 0-7522-0959-0 OP: £14.99 h/b

BFA-080 *Classic Who: The Hinchcliffe Years* **(Adrian Rigelsford)**
1996, Boxtree, UK
Photographic cover. A look at the *Doctor Who* stories produced by Philip Hinchcliffe. Scheduled 10/1995, delayed publication.
REF: ISBN 0-7522-0749-0 OP: £14.99 h/b NM: £8

BFA-081 *Classic Who: The Harper Classics* **(Adrian Rigelsford)**
1996/11/22, Boxtree, UK

Photographic cover. A look at the two *Doctor Who* stories directed by Graeme Harper.
REF: ISBN 0-7522-0188-3 OP: £14.99 h/b NM: £10

BFA-082 *Ace!* (Sophie Aldred & Mike Tucker)
1996/03/21, Virgin Publishing Ltd , UK
Photographic cover. Book looking at the Sylvester McCoy era of *Doctor Who*. Sophie Aldred played the Doctor's companion Ace, and Mike Tucker was a BBC Visual Effects designer who worked on the show.
REF: ISBN 1-85227-574-X OP: £17.99 h/b NM: £10

BFA-083 *Doctor Who: A History of the Universe* (Lance Parkin)
1996/05/16, Virgin Publishing Ltd , UK
Cover by Alistair Pearson. An attempt to put all of *Doctor Who*'s events and dates into a single chronological pattern. Previously available as a fan-produced item: *The Doctor Who Chronology*, autumn 1994, Seventh Door Fanzines. Introduction to the fan edition by Andrew Pixley.
REF: ISBN 0-426-20471-9 OP: £7.99 p/b

BFA-084 *Doctor Who: A Book of Monsters* (David J Howe)
1997/10/06, BBC Worldwide Ltd, UK
Photographic cover. A celebration of *Doctor Who*'s monsters. Print run: 6000 copies.
REF: ISBN 0-563-40562-7 OP: £16.99 h/b

BFA-085 *Doctor Who: The Book of Lists* (Justin Richards & Andrew Martin)
1997/10/06, BBC Worldwide Ltd, UK
Book of *Doctor Who* trivia in list form.
REF: ISBN 0-563-40569-4 OP: £5.99 p/b

BFA-086 *Doctor Who: The Nth Doctor* (Jean-Marc Lofficier)
1997/01/16, Virgin Publishing Ltd, UK
Cover by Colin Howard. Book explores all the unmade versions of a *Doctor Who* film from when the show ended in 1989, up until the TV Movie of 1996.
REF: ISBN 0-426-20499-9 OP: £4.99 p/b NM: £11

BFA-087 *Licence Denied* (ed. Paul Cornell)
1997/10/16, Virgin Publishing Ltd, UK
Cover by Slatter/Anderson. Unlicensed. A collection of articles, interviews and other material from *Doctor Who* fanzines.
REF: ISBN 0-7535-0104-X OP: £6.99 p/b

BFA-082

BFA-083

BFA-084

BFA-085

BFA-086

BFA-087

BFA-088

BFA-089

BFA-088 *Doctor Who: From A to Z* **(Gary Gillatt)**
1998/11/16, BBC Worldwide Ltd, UK
Book contains 26 articles about the show, each spinning off of a different letter of the alphabet. Gary Gillatt was editor of *Doctor Who Magazine*.
REF: ISBN 0-563-40589-0 OP: £17.99 h/b

BFA-089 *Doctor Who: The Television Companion* **(David J Howe and Stephen James Walker)**
1998/10/05, BBC Worldwide Ltd, UK
Photographic cover. A complete and authorised programme guide to the series. Delayed from its scheduled date of 07/09/98 by binding and printing problems.
REF: ISBN 0-563-40588-0 OP: £8.99 p/b

BFA-090

BFA-091

BFA-090 *The Doctor's Affect* **(Stephen Cambden)**
1999/08, FX Fanzines, UK
Photographic cover. A fan-produced paperback memoir of Stephen Cambden's experiences of working on *Doctor Who* in the late eighties as Assistant K9 Operator. Originally priced at £10.99, it was later reduced to £7.99.
REF: No ISBN OP: £10.99 p/b NM: £8

BFA-091 *The Nine Lives of Doctor Who* **(Peter Haining)**
1999/10, Hodder Headline, UK
Photographic composite cover. Interviews with the actors who played the Doctor. Originally scheduled for 1998, the book was put back a year following copyright issues.
REF: ISBN 0-7472-2243-6 OP: £16.99 h/b

BFA-092 *I, Who: The Unauthorised Guide to Doctor Who Novels* **(Lars Pearson)**
1999/08, Sidewinder Press, USA
Cover by Alan Evans. Edited by Matthew Saunders. A complete guide to *Doctor Who* fiction in original novels.
REF: ISBN 0-9673746-0-X
OP: $14.95 p/b NM: £17

BFA-093a *The Doctor Who Production Guide Volume One: The Locations* **(Keith A Armstrong)**
1996/06, Nine Travellers Publishing/Global Productions, UK
Spiral bound edition. A complete but flawed guide to all the locations used in *Doctor Who*, with photographs and access directions.
REF: No ISBN OP: £7.50 lfp/b

BFA-092

BFA-093b *The Doctor Who Production Guide Volume One: The Locations* **(Keith A Armstrong, David Brunt and Andrew Pixley)**
1998/08, Nine Travellers Publishing/Global

Productions, UK
Perfect Bound edition. Revised and updated with information from *The Doctor Who Production Guide Volume 2: Reference Journal*. Brunt and Pixley had no direct imput into this book, but are credited as co-authors.
REF: No ISBN OP: £7.50 lfp/b

BFA-094 *The Doctor Who Production Guide Volume Two: Reference Journal* **(David Brunt and Andrew Pixley with Keith A Armstrong)**
1997/07, Nine Travellers Publishing/Global Productions, UK
Perfect Bound edition. Limited to 500 copies, numbered. Details of all recording dates and times for all *Doctor Who* shows. The *Doctor Who* production guides were researched and released in an attempt to collect together all the techinical information known about the programme in one place. The books are meticulous in their detail.
REF: No ISBN OP: £7.50 lfp/b NM: £46.50

BFA-093b   **BFA-094**

BFA-095 *The Doctor Who Production Guide Volume Three: Cast and Crew* **(David Brunt and Andrew Pixley)**
1998/04/18, The Doctor Who Appreciation Society, UK
A5 Perfect Bound edition. Details of all cast and crew who worked on *Doctor Who*.
REF: No ISBN OP: £5.00 p/b

BFA-096 *The Doctor Who Chronicles: Season One* **(David Brunt and Andrew Pixley)**
1998/06, The Doctor Who Appreciation Society, UK
Perfect Bound edition. The *Doctor Who* Chronicles series is an attempt to produce as definitive a background study to the stories of a given season as possible. The books are illustrated with stills from the stories and contain very detailed plot synopses as well as factual behind the scenes material on the original scripts and their development.
REF: No ISBN OP: £5.50 lfp/b

BFA-095   **BFA-096**

BFA-097 *The Doctor Who Chronicles: Season Six* **(David Brunt and Andrew Pixley)**
1998/12, The Doctor Who Appreciation Society, UK
Perfect Bound edition.
REF: No ISBN OP: £6.50 lfp/b

BFA-098 *The Doctor Who Chronicles: Season Two* **(David Brunt and Andrew Pixley)**
1999/08, The Doctor Who Appreciation Society, UK.
Perfect Bound edition.
REF: No ISBN OP: £7.50 lfp/b

BFA-097   **BFA-098**

BFA-099

BFA-100

BFA-099 *A Bibliography of Doctor Who* (Graham Groom)
1999/07, Little Darren Books, UK
Perfect Bound edition. A basic listing of books and other printed materials published in the UK from 1964 to 1998.
REF: ISBN 0-9532481-1-9 OP: £4.50 p/b

BFA-100 *The Pocket Essential: Doctor Who* (Mark Campbell)
2000/06, Pocket Essentials, UK
A slim 96 page overview guide of all 26 years of television *Doctor Who*. 'A completely and utterly unauthorised guide'.
REF: ISBN 1-903047-19-6 OP: £2.99 p/b

BFA-101 *Timelink* (Jon Preddle)
2000/07, TSV Books, NZ
A complete analysis of *Doctor Who* dating and timelines. Independently produced by fan Jon Preddle. A4 sized. Second edition was loose leaves bound in a black spine-grip with clear perspex covers.
REF: ISBN 0 473 06853 2 OP: NZ$30 lfp/b

BFA-102 *The Doctor Who Chronicles: Season Five* (David Brunt and Andrew Pixley)
2000/09, DWAS, UK
Guide to Season Five. Edited by David Brunt and Andrew Pixley.
REF: No ISBN OP: £13.99 lfp/b

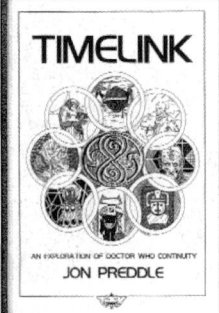

BFA-101

BFA-102

BFA-103a *Doctor Who – Regeneration* (Philip Segal with Gary Russell)
2000/10/25, HarperCollins, UK
This book was originally to have been published by Virgin Publishing, but they cancelled the title following the departure of editor Peter Darvil-Evans. The book was then picked up by HarperCollins, and delayed from its original release date of March to September, and then to October. Covers the background and making of the 1996 Paul McGann television movie. Philip Segal was executive producer on the film.
REF: ISBN 0-00-710591-6 OP: £17.99 h/b

BFA-103b *Doctor Who – Regeneration* (Philip Segal with Gary Russell)
2001/08/20, HarperCollins, UK
Paperback edition.
REF: ISBN 0-00-712025-7 OP: £12.99 p/b

BFA-103a

BFA-104 *Howe's Transcendental Toybox* (**David J Howe and Arnold T Blumberg**)
2000/11/23, Telos Publishing/ATB Publishing, UK
The first edition of the book you are now holding! A complete guide to all *Doctor Who* merchandise ever released. First edition was 1000 copies; second printing was 500 copies, third printing was 1000 copies.
REF: ISBN 0-9538681-0-9 OP: £25 p/b

BFA-105 *The Doctor's Effects* (**Steve Cambden**)
2001/02, FX Fanzines, UK
Photo montage cover. A collection of interviews and notes on the BBC Visual effects department through the years.
REF: No ISBN OP: £10 p/b

BFA-104

BFA-105

BFA-106 *The Doctor Who Chronicles: SeasonFour* (**David Brunt and Andrew Pixley**)
2001/04, DWAS, UK
Guide to Season Four. Edited by David Brunt and Andrew Pixley.
REF: No ISBN OP: £13.99 lfp/b

BFA-107 *Doctor Who: On Location* (**Richard Bignell**)
2001/10/26, Reynolds and Hearn, UK
Foreword by Sylvester McCoy. The book details all the location work done on *Doctor Who*, plus photographs and schedule. Cover design by Paul Vyse.
REF: ISBN 1-903111-22-6 OP: £17.95 lfp/b

BFA-108 *I, Who 2* (**Lars Pearson**)
2001/11, Mad Norwegian Press, USA
Second volume of this reference work to the original novels. Includes the Bernice Summerfield novels plus other items. Introduction by Peter David. Cover by Bryan Hitch.
REF: ISBN 1-57032-900-1 OP: $19.95 lfp/b

BFA-109 *The Doctor Who Chronicles: Season Three* (**David Brunt and Andrew Pixley**)
2002, DWAS, UK
Guide to Season Three. Edited by David Brunt and Andrew Pixley.
REF: No ISBN OP: £13.99 lfp/b

BFA-106

BFA-107

BFA-108

BFA-109

BGA-001   BGA-002

BGA-003a

BGA-003b

BGA-004a

BGA-004b

BOOKS, GAME

THESE books feature solo role-playing adventures or "choose your own adventure" style stories with *Doctor Who* characters.

BGA-001 *Doctor Who and the Rebel's Gamble; A Solo-Play Adventure Game* (**William H. Keith Jr**)
1986, FASA Corporation, USA
Cover by Harry Quinn. Maps by Todd F. Marsh. Incorrectly listed as #8902 on FASA product order forms dated through October 1 (1986), which also called it a 'Plot-Your-Own-Adventure' book. Sixth Doctor.
REF: ISBN 0-931787-68-8 #8901
OP: $3.95 p/b NM: £12

BGA-002 *Doctor Who and the Vortex Crystal: A Solo-Play Adventure Game* (**William H. Keith Jr**)
1986, FASA Corporation, USA
Cover by Harry Quinn. Maps by Dana Knutson. Incorrectly listed as #8901 on FASA product order forms dated through October 1 (1986), which also called it a 'Plot-Your-Own-Adventure' book. Fourth Doctor.
REF: ISBN 0-931787-67-X #8902
OP: $3.95 p/b NM: £12

BGA-003a *Make Your Own Adventure With Doctor Who – Search for the Doctor* (**David Martin**)
1986/06, Severn House Publishers Ltd, UK
Cover and illustrations by Gail Bennett. Features K9 and Drax. These books were also available in packs, each containing two titles. The UK editions were not numbered. A promotional poster was also available for £4.00. Sixth Doctor.
REF: ISBN 0-7278-2087-7 OP: £1.95 p/b NM: £6

BGA-003b *Find Your Fate: Doctor Who #1 – Search for the Doctor* (**David Martin**)
1986/08, Ballantine Books, USA
Cover by Romas. Interior illustrations by Gail Bennett. The US editions of these books were published (and numbered on the covers) in a different order to the UK editions.
REF: ISBN 0-345-33224-5 OP: $2.50 p/b NM: £7

BGA-004a *Make Your Own Adventure With Doctor Who – Crisis in Space* (**Michael Holt**)
1986/06, Severn House Publishers Ltd, UK
Cover and illustrations by Gail Bennett. Sixth Doctor.
REF: ISBN 0-7278-2093-1 OP: £1.95 p/b NM: £6

BGA-004b *Find Your Fate: Doctor Who #2 –
Crisis in Space* **(Michael Holt)**
1986/08, Ballantine Books, USA
Cover by Romas. Interior illustrations by Gail Bennett.
REF: ISBN 0-345-33225-3 OP: $2.50 p/b NM: £7

BGA-005a *Make Your Own Adventure With
Doctor Who –The Garden of Evil* **(David Martin)**
1986/08, Severn House Publishers Ltd, UK
Cover and illustrations by Gail Bennett. Based on an
idea by Bob Baker. Sixth Doctor.
REF: ISBN 0-7278-2113-X OP: £1.95 p/b NM: £6

BGA-005a   **BGA-005b**

BGA-005b *Find Your Fate: Doctor Who #3 –
Garden of Evil* **(David Martin)**
1986/09, Ballantine Books, USA
Cover by Romas. Interior illustrations by Gail Bennett.
REF: ISBN 0-345-33226-1 OP: $2.50 p/b NM: £7

BGA-006a *Make Your Own Adventure With
Doctor Who – Race Against Time* **(Pip and Jane
Baker)**
1986/08, Severn House Publishers Ltd, UK
Cover and illustrations by Gail Bennett. Features the
Rani. Sixth Doctor.
REF: ISBN 0-7278-2116-4 OP: £1.95 p/b NM: £6

BGA-006b *Find Your Fate: Doctor Who #6 –
Race Against Time* **(Pip and Jane Baker)**
1986/12, Ballantine Books, USA
Cover by Romas. Interior illustrations by Gail Bennett.
REF: ISBN 0-345-33228-8 OP: $2.50 p/b NM: £7

BGA-006a   **BGA-006b**

BGA-007a *Make Your Own Adventure With
Doctor Who – Mission to Venus* **(William Emms)**
1986/10, Severn House Publishers Ltd, UK
Cover and illustrations by Gail Bennett. This title was
based on an unused TV story, *The Imps*, that had at
one point been considered for inclusion in the series'
fourth season in 1966. Book originally titled *The Space
Pirates*. Sixth Doctor.
REF: ISBN 0-7278-2122-9 OP: £1.95 p/b NM: £6

BGA-007b *Find Your Fate: Doctor Who #4 –
Mission to Venus* **(William Emms)**
1986/10, Ballantine Books, USA
Cover by Romas. Interior illustrations by Gail Bennett.
REF: ISBN 0-345-33229-6 OP: $2.95 p/b NM: £7

BGA-007a   **BGA-007b**

BGA-008a　　　　　　BGA-008b

BGA-009

BGE-001

BGA-008a *Make Your Own Adventure With Doctor Who – Invasion of the Ormazoids* **(Philip Martin)**
1986/10, Severn House Publishers Ltd, UK
Cover and illustrations by Gail Bennett. Book originally titled *The Dominators*. Sixth Doctor.
REF: ISBN 0-7278-2100-8　OP: £1.95 p/b　NM: £6

BGA-008b *Find Your Fate: Doctor Who #5 – Invasion of the Ormazoids* **(Philip Martin)**
1986/11, Ballantine Books, USA
Cover by Romas. Interior illustrations by Gail Bennett.
REF: ISBN 0-345-33231-8　OP: $2.95 p/b　NM: £7

BGA-009 *Time Lord* **(Peter Darvill-Evans & Ian Marsh)**
1991/12, Virgin Publishing Ltd, UK
A role-playing game book. Cover and illustrations by Colin Howard.
REF: ISBN 0-426-20362-3　OP: £6.99 p/b　NM: £20

BOOKS, GENERAL

THIS section features general books about *Doctor Who* and different aspects of it.

BGE-001 *Dalek Book, The* **(David Whitaker & Terry Nation)**
1964/06/30, Souvenir Press & Panther Books, UK
One of the first items of *Doctor Who*-related merchandise ever to be produced. An annual-like collection of comic strips, features and text stories. Written by Terry Nation and David Whitaker and illustrated by Richard Jennings, John Woods and A. B. Cornwell (better known as Bruce Cornwell from Frank Hampson's studio, where *Dan Dare* was produced).
Stories: Invasion of the Daleks (s), Red for Danger, The Oil Wheel (s), The Message of Mystery (p), The, Secret of the Mountain , City of the Daleks (s), The Humanoids (s), The Small Defender, Monsters of Gurnian (s), Break-Through!, Battle for the Moon (s). The story 'The Message of Mystery' was an eight-page photo section of stills from *The Daleks*, arranged to form an original story in which Susan arrives on Skaro and helps the Daleks to decipher a message they have found. She manages to escape when her laughter frightens off her Dalek captors.
REF: No ISBN　OP: 9s 6d h/b　NM: £60

BGE-002 *Dalek Pocketbook and Space Travellers Guide, The* **(compiled and presented by Terry Nation)**
1965/10/07, Souvenir Press & Panther Books, UK
A paperback collection of articles and features treat-

ing Daleks as though they really exist. Photo cover
from first Dalek film. Print run: 350,000 copies.
REF: No ISBN. 1934 OP: 2s 6d p/b NM: £50-£55

BGE-003 *Dalek World, The* (**Terry Nation &
David Whitaker**)
1965/10/11, Souvenir Press & Panther Books, UK
Similar to *The Dalek Book*, a collection of comic strips,
articles and text stories. Written by Terry Nation and
David Whitaker and illustrated by Richard Jennings,
John Woods, A. B. Cornwell and W. Wiggins.
Stories: The Mechanical Planet (s), The Secret Struggle,
Treasure of the Daleks (s), The Five-Leaf Clover, The
Invisible Invaders (s), The Log of the 'Gypsy Joe', The
Orbitus (s), The World that Waits (s), Manhunt,
Masters of the World (s).
The book contained a photo section based around
the first Dalek film, *Dr. Who and the Daleks*, the reader
being invited to caption a series of 35 stills. Some of
the stories featured the Mechanoids from *The Chase*.
Initial print run of 300,000 copies.
REF: No ISBN OP: 10s 6d h/b NM: £55

BGE-004 *Doctor Who and the Invasion From Space*
1966, World Distributors, UK
A single text story gift book by J L Morrissey. This
was only issued in a hardbacked version, however if
the hard covers are missing, then the book can appear
to be a paperback version.
REF: No ISBN OP: 5s h/b NM: £55

BGE-005 *Dalek Outer Space Book, The* (**Terry
Nation & Brad Ashton**)
1966/09/08, Souvenir Press & Panther Books, UK
A third annual-like collection of comic strips, articles
and text stories. Written by Nation and Brad Ashton
(with one non-Dalek story by Russ Winterbotham)
and illustrated by Richard Jennings, John Woods, Leslie
Waller and Art Sansom.
Stories: The Dalek Trap (s), The Outlaw Planet, Sara
Kingdom: Space Security Agent (s), The Living Death,
The Super Sub (s), The Secret of the Emperor (s), The
Sea Monsters (s), The Unwilling Traveller (s and text),
Chris Welkin: Planeteer (s), Diamond Dust, The Brain
Tappers (s).
Several of the stories featured Sara Kingdom from the
TV story *The Daleks' Master Plan*, along with other
agents of the Space Security Service (SSS).
REF: No ISBN OP: 10s 6d h/b NM: £60

BGE-002

BGE-003

BGE-004

BGE-005

BGE-006

BGE-007

BGE-008

BGE-009

BGE-006 *Doctor Who and the Daleks Omnibus*
1976/09, Artus Publishing Ltd (for Marks and Spencer Ltd), UK
A large format book featuring factual behind the scenes articles and photographs, as well as the abridged text of two novelisations: *Genesis of the Daleks* and *Planet of the Daleks*. Illustrations © General Illustration Company.
REF: 1425/1051 OP: £1.99 h/b NM: £22

BGE-007 *Amazing World Of Doctor Who, The* (h/b)
1976, P.B.S. Limited, UK
15,000 copies of the book were produced for the Sales Promotion Triangle by World Distributors. It cost £1 and featured reprinted comic strips primarily from the 1976 *Doctor Who* annual and *TV Century 21*, together with black and white and colour photo-features on the series and its more popular monsters. Part of the Ty-Phoo tea promotion and also subsequently available for sale through W H Smiths. See also STR-003 and SPP-004.
Stories: The Sinister Sponge, The Psychic Jungle (s), The Vampires of Crellium, The Daleks in a Fresh Start [Eve of the War] (s), Neuronic Nightmare (s), On the Slippery Trail, The Mission.
REF: NO ISBN OP: £1.00 NM: £13.20

BGE-008 *Doctor Who Dinosaur Book, The* (Terrance Dicks)
1976/12/16, W. H. Allen & Co. Ltd, UK
A non-fiction look at Dinosaurs with the Doctor as your guide. Cover and illustrations by George Underwood. Print run: 75,000 copies.
REF: ISBN 0-426-11842-1 OP: 75p lfp/b NM: £2

BGE-009 *Doctor Who Discovers Early Man*
1977/02/16, W. H. Allen & Co. Ltd, UK
A non-fiction look at the subject with the Doctor as your guide. Cover by Jeff Cummins. Series edited by Fred Newman and designed by Frank Ainscough. According to W H Allen's publicity at the time, these books marked total sales of the *Doctor Who* books passing the two million mark. The series was originally intended to build into a range of 24 titles but was curtailed due to poor sales. Each book had a print run of 40,000 copies. Three books were underway when the series was pulled: *The Miners*, for which cover artwork exists; *The Inventors*, for which a cover proof exists; and *The Pirates*, for which interior layouts exist.
REF: ISBN 0-426-20008-X OP: 75p lfp/b NM: £5-£7

BGE-010 *Doctor Who Discovers Prehistoric Animals*
1977/11/17, Target/W. H. Allen & Co. Ltd, UK
A non-fiction look at the subject with the Doctor as
your guide. Cover by Jeff Cummins.
REF: ISBN 0-426-20002-0 OP: 75p lfp/b NM: £5-£7

BGE-011 *Doctor Who Discovers Space Travel*
1977/11/17, Target/W. H. Allen & Co. Ltd, UK
A non-fiction look at the subject with the Doctor as
your guide. Cover by Jeff Cummins.
REF: ISBN 0-426-20003-9 OP: 75p lfp/b NM: £5-£7

BGE-012 *Doctor Who Discovers the Conquerors*
1978/02/16, Target/W. H. Allen & Co. Ltd, UK
A non-fiction look at the subject with the Doctor as
your guide. Cover by Jeff Cummins. Book © 1977.
REF: ISBN 0-426-20013-6 OP: 75p lfp/b NM: £5-£7

BGE-013 *Doctor Who Discovers Strange And
Mysterious Creatures*
1978/04/20, Target/W. H. Allen & Co. Ltd, UK
A non-fiction look at the subject with the Doctor as
your guide. Cover by Jeff Cummins. Book © 1977.
Sold 10,140 units worldwide.
REF: ISBN 0-426-20004-7 OP: 75p lfp/b NM: £5-£7

BGE-014a *Jon Pertwee Book of Monsters, The*
1978, Methuen, UK
Nothing to do with *Doctor Who*, Pertwee lent his
name to this collection of short stories featuring
monsters. Edited by Richard Davis.
REF: ISBN 0-416-87190-9 OP: h/b NM: £9

BGE-014b *Jon Pertwee Book of Monsters, The*
1979, Magnet/Methuen Children's Books, UK
Paperback editon.
REF: ISBN 0-416-87200-X OP: 65p p/b NM: £5

BGE-015 *Doctor Who – Adventures in Time and
Space*
1981, World International Publishing Ltd, UK
Cover by Paul Crompton and Mel Powell. Collection
of material from various Annuals, including the
Amazing World of Doctor Who book.
Stories: Ten Fathom Pirates, Mission for Duh (s), Peril
in Mechanistra, Death to Mufl, The Vampire Plants (s),
Mastermind of Space, Hunt to the Death, Dead on
Arrival (s), Fugitives from Chance, The Claw, Saucer of
Fate, The Sleeping Beast, A New Life, Double Trouble!,
The Time Snatch, Menace on, Metalupiter (s), War on
Aquatica, The Sinister Sponge, The Traitor (s), The
Vampires of Crellium, On the Slippery Trail, A New
Life, Flashback, The Power (s), Emsone's Castle (s), The
Planet of Dust.
REF: SBN 7235-0968-0 OP: £2.25 h/b NM: £12

BGE-010

BGE-011

BGE-012

BGE-013

BGE-014b

BGE-015

BGE-016

BGE-018a

BGE-018b

BGE-016 Peter Davison's Book of Alien Monsters
1982, Sparrow/Arrow Books Ltd, UK
Nothing to do with *Doctor Who*, Davison lent his name
to this collection of short stories featuring monsters.
REF: ISBN 0-09-928300-X OP: 95p p/b NM: £2

BGE-017a Peter Davison's Book of Alien Planets
1983, Century Hutchinson, UK
Nothing to do with *Doctor Who*, Davison lent his name
to this collection of short stories featuring alien planets.
REF: ISBN 0-091-51430-4 OP: h/b NM: £3

BGE-017b Peter Davison's Book of Alien Planets
1983, Sparrow/Arrow Books Ltd, UK
Paperback editon.
REF: ISBN 0-099-30880-0 OP: 95p p/b NM: £2

**BGE-018a Doctor Who Special (ed. Brenda
Apsley)**
1985, W. H. Smith & Sons/Galley Press, UK
Collection of material from various Annuals, including
the *Amazing World of Doctor Who* book. Subtitled
'Journey through Time'. Edited by Brenda Apsley. SBN
number inside book is: 0-86136-728-6. This had an initial
print run of 20,000 copies. The publishers were repri-
manded by the BBC for using the BBC's own logo on
the cover, which they were not permitted to do.
Stories: Mission for Duh (s), Death to Mufl, Dead on
Arrival (s), The Vampires of Crellium, Flashback, The
Power (s), War on Aquatica, On the Slippery Trail, A
New Life, Emsone's Castle (s), Danger Down Below, The
Penalty, The God Machine, The Armageddon Crysalis,
On the Planet Isopterus (s), The Haven, Night Flight to
Nowhere, The Oxaqua Incident, Winter on Mesique,
The Creation of Camelot, Class 4 Renegade, The
Volcanis Deal, The Nemertines, Day of the Dragon, The
Real Hereward, The Deadly Weed, Vorton's Revenge,
The Time Savers, The Mystery of the Rings
REF: SBN 7235-7099-X OP: £7.95 h/b NM: £8

**BGE-018b Doctor Who – Journey Through Time
(ed. Brenda Apsley)**
1986, Crescent Books, USA
Edition came with a slip-cover identical to the printed
cover of the book. The back-flap on this edition indicates that the stories in the book were by Brenda
Apsley, Charles Pemberton and Lesley Scott. A version
of this edition is known to exist with a 1985 date but
the same ISBN number; the inside cover of this variant says 'BBC TV Doctor Who Special' instead of 'BBC
TV Doctor Who Journey Through Time', as per the
first edition listed above.
REF: ISBN 0-517-479818 OP: $5.98 h/b NM: £16.50

BGE-019 *The Monsters* (Adrian Rigelsford & Andrew Skilleter)
1992/09/11, Virgin Publishing Ltd, UK
Fictional stories about the origins of several popular *Doctor Who* monsters. Illustrated by Andrew Skilleter.
REF: ISBN 1-85227-283-X OP: £14.99 h/b

BOOKS, GRAPHIC NOVELS

WE have taken a graphic novel to be a one-off edition of a single comic-strip story. Other comic-related items can be found under 'Magazines' (MAG, MAO, MAP, MAS). All of these titles are perfect bound except where noted.

BGR-001 Doctor Who – 1985 Summer Special Classic
1985/06, Marvel Comics, UK
Reprint of *The Iron Legion* and *K9's Finest Hour*. Ed. Cefn Ridout. Same item as MAS-017.
REF: No ISSN OP: £1.20 lfp/b NM: £5.50

BGR-002 *Doctor Who Collected Comics*
1986/09/29, Marvel Comics, UK
By Steve Parkhouse (script) and John Ridgway (art). Ed. Sheila Cranna. Contains *The Shape-Shifter* and *Polly the Glot*.
REF: No ISBN OP: £1.75 lfp/b NM: £5.50

BGR-003 *Doctor Who Voyager*
1989/05/26, Marvel Comics, UK
By Steve Parkhouse (script) and John Ridgway (art). Some editions mis-printed with a section printed upside down inside (pp 33-48).
REF: ISBN 1-85400-045-4 OP: £4.95 lfp/b NM: £11

BGR-004 *Abslom Daak – Dalek Killer*
1990/04/27, Marvel Comics, UK
By Steve Moore, Steve Dillon, David Lloyd, Richard Alan, Steve Alan and Lee Sullivan. Cover by Steve Dillon and John Higgins.
REF: ISBN 1-85400-113-2 OP: £5.95 lfp/b NM: £5.50

BGR-005 *Doktor Who's Reisen Durch Raum Und Zeit*
1991, Conpart Verlag, Germany
3-volume German edition of *Polly The Glot*, *Voyager* and others.
REF: No ISBN OP: DM 6,80 lfp/b

BGE-019

BGR-001

BGR-002

BGR-003

BGR-004

BGR-005 (all three shown)

BGR-006   BGR-007

BGR-006 *The Mark of Mandragora*
1993/04/15, Virgin Publishing Ltd, UK
Cover by Alistair Pearson. Graphic novel of a strip
originally published in *Doctor Who Magazine*.
REF: ISBN 0-426-2039608 OP: £6.99 lfp/b NM: £5.50

BGR-007 Doctor Who Classic Comics: *Evening's Empire*
1993/09, Marvel Comics, UK
Written by Andrew Cartmel. Ed. Gary Russell. Art by
Richard Piers Rayner. Autumn Holiday Special. This is a
graphic novel in a stitched magazine format.
REF: ISSN 1350-0279 OP: £2.50 NM: £3

BGR-008 *Doctor Who – The Age of Chaos*
1994/10/06, Marvel Comics, UK
Written by Colin Baker. Ed. Gary Russell. Art by John
M Burns and Barrie Mitchell. This is a graphic novel in
a stitched magazine format.
REF: ISSN 1353-7636 OP: £3.99 NM: £5.50

BGR-008   BHU-001

BOOKS, HUMOUR

BHU-001 *Doctor Who Fun Book, The* (Tim Quinn & Dicky Howett)
1987/05, W. H. Allen & Co. PLC (Target), UK
A selection of cartoons and humourous takes on
Doctor Who. Tim Quinn and Dicky Howitt wrote and
drew the short humorous *Doctor Who?* strip in *Doctor
Who Magazine* through the eighties.
REF: ISBN 0-426-20300-3 OP: £1.95 lfp/b NM: £3.50

BHU-002 *Doctor Who: It's Bigger on the Inside* (Tim Quinn and Dicky Howett)
1988/11, Marvel Comics, UK
A second collection of cartoons and comic strips.
REF: ISBN 1-85400-025-X OP: £1.95 lfp/b NM: £4.40

BHU-003 *Doctor Who: The Completely Useless Encyclopedia* (Chris Howarth & Steve Lyons)
1996/12/05, Virgin Publishing Ltd, UK
Cover by Andrew Skilleter with graffiti by Colin
Howard. An encyclopedia of trivia and gossip.
REF: ISBN 0-426-20485-9 OP: £4.99 p/b

BHU-004 *Dalek Survival Guide*
2002/10/10, BBC Worldwide Ltd, UK
Paperback pastiche on a popular range of 'Survival
Guides' published by another publisher.
Commissioning editor: Ben Dunn; Project editors:
April Warman and Rebecca Kincaid; Designer: Martin
Hendry; Illustrator: Alan Burton; Cover illustration:

BHU-002   BHU-003

Emma Judd; Production Controller: Kenneth McKay;
Contributors: Justin Richards, Nicholas Briggs, Stephen
Cole, Jacqueline Rayner, Mike Tucker.
REF: ISBN 0-563-48600-7 OP: £9.99

BOOKS, JUNIOR

BJU-001a *Junior Doctor Who and the Giant
Robot* **(Terrance Dicks)**
1979/05/24, W. H. Allen & Co. Ltd, UK
Cover by Harry Hants. Illustrated by Peter Edwards.
Dicks' Target novelisation re-written for young children.
REF: ISBN 0-491-02497-5 OP: £2.50 h/b NM: £5

BJU-001b *Junior Doctor Who and the Giant
Robot* **(Terrance Dicks)**
1980, Target/W. H. Allen & Co. Ltd, UK
Cover by Harry Hants. Illustrated by Peter Edwards.
Print run: 15,000 copies.
REF: ISBN 0-426-20064-0 OP: 75p p/b NM: £3

BJU-002a *Junior Doctor Who and the Brain of
Morbius* **(Terrance Dicks)**
1980/06/26, W. H. Allen & Co. Ltd, UK
Cover by Harry Hants. Illustrated by Peter Edwards.
Dicks' Target novelisation re-written for young children.
REF: ISBN 0-491-02417-7 OP: £2.95 h/b NM: £5

BJU-002b *Junior Doctor Who and the Brain of
Morbius* **(Terrance Dicks)**
1980, Target/W. H. Allen & Co. Ltd, UK
Cover by Harry Hants. Illustrated by Peter Edwards.
First edition has a green spine and back and a white
background to the cover image. Print run: 12,500 copies.
REF: ISBN 0-426-20063-2 OP: 85p p/b NM: £3

BJU-002c *Junior Doctor Who and the Brain of
Morbius* **(Terrance Dicks)**
1987/06/15, Target/W. H. Allen & Co. Ltd, UK
Cover by Harry Hants. Illustrated by Peter Edwards. Blue
spine, back cover and background to the cover image.
REF: ISBN 0-426-20063-2 OP: £1.60 p/b NM: £3

BJU-003 *The Adventures of K9 – 1: K9 and the
Time Trap* **(David Martin)**
1980, Sparrow/Arrow Books Ltd, UK
Artwork RCS Graphics Ltd Set of four books featur-
ing K-9 in his own adventures. Firmly aimed at the
pre-school market. David Martin was (with Bob
Baker) one of the creators of K-9 for the TV series.
At least two of these books, possibly all four, may
have also been released in hardback editions.
REF: ISBN 09-924480-2 OP: 65p p/b NM: £9

BHU-004

BJU-001b

BJU-002b

BJU-003

BJU-002c

BJU-004   BJU-005

BJU-006

BJU-007

BJU-004 *The Adventures of K9 – 2: K9 and the Beasts of Vega* **(David Martin)**
1980, Sparrow/Arrow Books Ltd, UK
Artwork RCS Graphics Ltd
REF: ISBN 09-924470-5 OP: 65p p/b NM: £9

BJU-005 *The Adventures of K9 – 3: K9 and the Zeta Rescue* **(David Martin)**
1980, Sparrow/Arrow Books Ltd , UK
Artwork RCS Graphics Ltd
REF: ISBN 09-924460-8 OP: 65p p/b NM: £9

BJU-006 *The Adventures of K9 – 4: K9 and the Missing Planet* **(David Martin)**
1980, Sparrow/Arrow Books Ltd , UK
Artwork RCS Graphics Ltd
REF: ISBN 09-924490-X OP: 65p p/b NM: £9

BJU-007 *TX File: Doctor Who* **(David J Howe)**
1996/10/07, BBC Books, UK
A simple filofax book containing basic information about each Doctor, the TARDIS and the Master. Part of a series of television-related filofax books in the TX- range. There was also a generic TX-Filofax binder.
REF: ISBN 0-563-38009-8 OP: £2.50 p/b

BOOKS, MEDIA STUDIES

MEDIA studies books are usually written by academics in a language which can be understood by anyone studying media...supposedly.

BME-001a *Doctor Who – The Unfolding Text* **(John Tulloch & Manuel Alvarado)**
1983/11, Macmillan Books, UK
Includes a detailed academic analysis of *Kinda*.
REF: ISBN 0-333-34847-8 OP: £20.00 h/b

BME-001b *Doctor Who – The Unfolding Text* **(John Tulloch & Manuel Alvarado)**
1983/11, Macmillan Books, UK
REF: ISBN 0-333-34848-6 OP: £6.95 lfp/b NM: £16.50

BME-001c *Doctor Who – The Unfolding Text* **(John Tulloch & Manuel Alvarado)**
1983, St. Martin's Press, USA
REF: ISBN 0-312-21480-4 OP: $9.95 lfp/b NM: £16.50

BME-002a *Science Fiction Audiences: Watching Doctor Who and Star Trek* **(John Tulloch & Henry Jenkins)**
1995, Routledge, UK
Tulloch analyses *Doctor Who* and Jenkins looks at *Star Trek*. Some research material from *The Unfolding Text* is re-used here, however the text is new.
REF: ISBN 0-415-06140-7 OP: h/b

BME-001b

BME-001c

BME-002b

BME-002b *Science Fiction Audiences: Watching Doctor Who and Star Trek* **(John Tulloch & Henry Jenkins)**
1995, Routledge, UK
REF: ISBN 0-415-06141-5 OP: £12.99 lfp/b

BME-003 *A Critical History of Doctor Who on Television* **(John Kenneth Muir)**
1999/11, McFarland & Company, Inc, USA
No dust jacket. A guide to *Doctor Who* from an American viewpoint. Written for the American media studies market.
REF: ISBN 0-7864-0442-6 OP: $65.00 h/b NM: £55

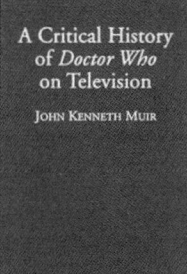

BME-003

BOOKS, NOVELLAS

TELOS Publishing Ltd began publishing a series of novella-length original *Doctor Who* stories in 2001. The intention was to provide a different look at the mythos by inviting authors from other genres and the greater science fiction/fantasy/horror community to try their hand at *Who*.

BNO-001 *Time and Relative* **(Kim Newman)**
2001/11/23, Telos Publishing Ltd, UK
First in a range of original *Doctor Who* novellas (short novels). Neither edition had dust jackets. Featuring the 1st Doctor and Susan. The deluxe edition is signed and numbered and limited to 1400 copies, featuring an art plate by Bryan Talbot. Introduction by Justin Richards.
REF: ISBN 1-903889-02-2 std; 1-903889-03-0 del
OP: £10 std h/b; £25 deluxe h/b

BNO-002 *Citadel of Dreams* **(Dave Stone)**
2002/03/28, Telos Publishing Ltd, UK
Featuring the 7th Doctor and Ace. The deluxe edition is signed and numbered and limited to 1400 copies, featuring an art plate by Lee Sullivan. Introduction by Andrew Cartmel.
REF: ISBN 1-903889-04-9 std; ISBN 1-903889-05-7 del
OP: £10 std h/b; £25 deluxe h/b

BNO-003 *Nightdreamers* **(Tom Arden)**
2002/05/15, Telos Publishing Ltd, UK
Featuring the 3rd Doctor and Jo. The deluxe edition is signed and numbered and limited to 1400 copies, featuring an art plate by Martin McKenna. Introduction by Katy Manning.
REF: ISBN 1-903889-06-5 std; ISBN 1-903889-07-3 del
OP: £10 std h/b; £25 deluxe h/b

BNO-001

BNO-002

BNO-003

BNO-004   BNO-005

BNO-004 *Ghost Ship* **(Keith Topping)**
2002/08/22, Telos Publishing Ltd, UK
Featuring the 4th Doctor. The deluxe edition is signed
and numbered and limited to 800 copies, featuring an art
plate by Dariusz Jasiczak. Introduction by Hugh Lamb.
REF: ISBN 1-903889-08-1 std; ISBN 1-903889-09-X del
OP: £10 std h/b; £25 deluxe h/b

BNO-005 *Foreign Devils* **(Andrew Cartmel)**
2002/11/23, Telos Publishing Ltd, UK
Featuring the 2nd Doctor, Jamie and Zoe. The deluxe
edition is signed and numbered and limited to 800
copies, featuring an art plate by Mike Collins.
Introduction by Mike Ashley.
REF: ISBN 1-903889-10-3 std; ISBN 1-903889-11-1 del
OP: £10 std h/b; £25 deluxe h/b

BOOKS, OTHER

NOVELS which are not a part of the established series.

BOT-001 *Turlough and the Earthlink Dilemma*
(Tony Attwood)
1986/05/15, Target/W. H. Allen & Co. PLC, UK
A one-off novel featuring the adventures of the
Doctor's companion Turlough. Actor Mark Strickson,
who played Turlough on television, was consulted by
author Tony Attwood as to the development of the
character in the book. 'The Companions of Doctor
Who'. Cover by Tony Masero. Interior of book has
ISBN 0-426-20236-8. Print run: 25,000 copies.
REF: ISBN 0-426-20224-4   OP: £1.80 p/b   NM: £16.50

BOT-002 *Harry Sullivan's War* **(Ian Marter)**
1986/09/11, Target/W. H. Allen & Co. PLC, UK
A one-off novel featuring the adventures of the
Doctor's companion Harry Sullivan, written by the
actor who played him on television. Plans for a follow-
up novel were abandoned when Marter died in 1987.
'The Companions of Doctor Who'. Cover by Tony
Masero. Print run: 25,000 copies.
REF: ISBN 0-426-20250-3   OP: £1.60 p/b   NM: £16.50

BOT-001   BOT-002

BOT-003 *Who Killed Kennedy* **(James Stevens &**
David Bishop)
1996/04/18, Virgin Publishing Ltd, UK
A one-off novel describing the Doctor and UNIT's
involvement in the assassination of President Kennedy
in 1963. Cover by Slatter-Anderson. Photograph:
Range Pictures Ltd. James Stevens does not exist.
REF: ISBN 0-426-20467-0   OP: £4.99 p/b   NM: £9

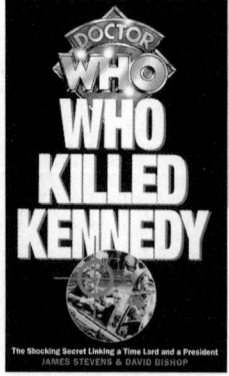

BOT-003

BOT-004 *Campaign* **(Jim Mortimore)**
2000/10, Published by Pyrrhic Pressure in the twenty
first century, UK

Cover artwork by Jim Mortimore. Illustrated by Tim Keable. Hardback has a dust jacket. *Campaign* was originally written by Mortimore for the BBC's 8th Doctor range of books, however they ultimately declined to publish the book. Mortimore subsequently published it himself. Book contains a date of May 2000. Originally advertised November 2000, not available until 2001/01. According to Mortimore, first copies despatched October 2000.
REF: No ISBN OP: £5.99 p/b £12.99 h/b

BOOKS, SCRIPT

ALTHOUGH scripts and other BBC documentation – in themselves highly collectible – are not listed in this book as they were never made commercially available, there have been some *Doctor Who* scripts available to buy.

BSC-001 *Doctor Who The Scripts – The Tribe of Gum* **(Anthony Coburn, ed. John McElroy)**
1988/01, Titan Books Ltd, UK
Cover by Dave McKean. Each script book contained a transcript of the story in question rather than the actual scripts, with McElroy correcting the content to what was actually seen on screen. The books also each featured a factual introduction. Factual material by John McElroy. First edition has neon logo; second edition has triangular logo.
REF: ISBN 1-85286-012-X OP: £2.95 p/b NM: £7

BSC-002 *Doctor Who The Scripts – The Tomb of the Cybermen* **(Gerry Davis & Kit Pedler, ed. John McElroy)**
1989/08/29, Titan Books Ltd, UK
Cover by Tony Clark. Factual material by John McElroy. First edition has McCoy logo; second edition has triangular logo.
REF: ISBN 1-85286-146-0 OP: £3.95 p/b NM: £9

BSC-003 *Doctor Who The Scripts – The Talons of Weng-Chiang* **(Robert Holmes, ed. John McElroy)**
1989/11, Titan Books Ltd, UK
Cover by Duncan Fegredo. Factual material by John McElroy. First edition has McCoy logo; second edition has triangular logo.
REF: ISBN 1-85286-144-4 OP: £3.95 p/b NM: £7

BSC-004 *Doctor Who The Scripts – The Daleks* **(Terry Nation, ed. John McElroy)**
1989/12, Titan Books Ltd, UK
Cover by Tony Clark. Factual material by John McElroy. First edition has McCoy logo; second edition has triangular logo.
REF: ISBN 1-85286-145-2 OP: £3.95 p/b NM: £9

BOT-004

BSC-001

BSC-002

BSC-003

BSC-004

BSC-005   **BSC-006**

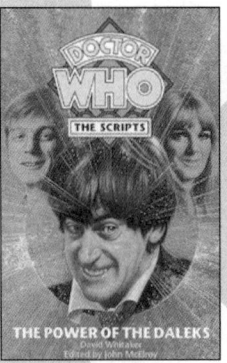

BSC-007   **BSC-008**

BSC-009   **BSC-010**

BSC-005 *Doctor Who The Scripts: The Masters of Luxor* **(Anthony Coburn, ed John McElroy)**
1992/09/24, Titan Books Ltd, UK
Cover by Alistair Pearson. Factual material by John McElroy. As this story had never been made, the scripts were presented as originally written.
REF: ISBN 1-85286-321-8 OP: £4.99 p/b NM: £11

BSC-006 *Doctor Who The Scripts: The Dæmons* **(Robert Sloman & Barry Letts, ed John McElroy)**
1992/11/05, Titan Books Ltd, UK
Cover by Alistair Pearson. Factual material by Stephen James Walker.
REF: ISBN 1-85286-324-2 OP: £4.99 p/b NM: £9

BSC-007 *Doctor Who The Scripts: The Power of the Daleks* **(David Whitaker, ed John McElroy)**
1993/03/18, Titan Books Ltd, UK
Cover by Alistair Pearson. Factual material by Stephen James Walker.
REF: ISBN 1-85286-327-7 OP: £4.99 p/b NM: £9

BSC-008 *Doctor Who The Scripts: Ghost Light* **(Marc Platt, ed John McElroy)**
1993/07/29, Titan Books Ltd, UK
Cover by Alistair Pearson. Factual material by Stephen James Walker, with an article on the creation of the story by Marc Platt.
REF: ISBN 1-85286-477-X OP: £4.99 p/b NM: £7

BSC-009 *Doctor Who The Scripts: Galaxy 4* **(William Emms, ed John McElroy)**
1994/07/15, Titan Books Ltd, UK
Cover by Alistair Pearson. Factual material by Stephen James Walker. At the time this book was released, no video or audio reference were known to exist for episodes 1, 3 and 4 of the story, and so the scripts were presented as originally written.
REF: ISBN 1-85286-566-0 OP: £4.99 p/b NM: £7

BSC-010 *Doctor Who The Scripts: The Crusade* **(David Whitaker, ed John McElroy)**
1994/11/17, Titan Books Ltd, UK
Cover by Alistair Pearson. Factual material by Stephen James Walker. At the time this book was released, no video or audio reference were known to exist for episodes 1, 2 and 4 of the story, and so the scripts were presented as originally written.
REF: ISBN 1-85286-564-4 OP: £4.99 p/b NM: £7

BSC-011 *Doctor Who: The Script of the Film* **(Matthew Jacobs)**
1996/05/17, BBC Worldwide Ltd, UK
Photo cover. Contains the finalised script used during

filming. Introduction by Philip Segal.
REF: ISBN 0-563-40499-X OP: £5.99 p/b

BSC-012 *Doctor Who: The Movie* **(Johnny Byrne)**
1995, USA
In the USA it is possible to buy copies of scripts from
agencies which are set up to handle this type of item.
In the mid-eighties, a copy of the Johnny Byrne script
for one of the ultimately aborted *Doctor Who* film
treatments was generally available for sale from dealers at conventions in the USA. This item is included
here by way of example, but it is possible that other
scripts are also available from US dealers.

BSC-011

BSC-013 *Doctor Who: The Scripts: Tom Baker
1974/5*
2001/10/18, BBC Worldwide Ltd, UK
Hardback compilation of scripts from Season 12.
Commissioning Editor: Ben Dunn; Content Editor:
Justin Richards; Associate Editor: Barnaby Harsent;
Contributing Editor: Andrew Pixley; Project Editor:
April Warman; Art Director: Linda Blakemore.
Additional contribution from Martin Wiggins. The
book features heavily annotated versions of the
scripts which highlight changes from the rehearsal to
transmitted versions, comprehensive background
notes, as well as details on other stories intended for
this season and photographs.
REF: ISBN 0-563-53815-5 OP: £16.99 h/b

BSC-014 *Doctor Who: The Audio Scripts*
2002/12, Big Finish, UK
Four scripts from the Big Finish *Doctor Who* audio
adventures. Cover by Clayton Hickman. Edited by Ian
Farrington. Project editors: Gary Russell and
Jacqueline Rayner. Managing editor: Jason Haigh-Ellery.
Contains: *Loups-Garoux* by Mark Platt, *The Holy Terror*
by Robert Shearman, *The Fires of Vulcan* by Steve Lyons
and *Neverland* by Alan Barnes. Also contains director
commentaries by Nick Pegg and Gary Russell, and an
alternative version of part one of *The Fires of Vulcan*.
REF: ISBN 1-84435-005-3 OP: £15.99 h/b

BSC-013

BSC-014

BOOKS, SPECIAL NOVELS

NOVELISATIONS of specials, one-off productions,
unmade stories and so on.

BSN-001 *K9 and Company* **(Terence Dudley)**
1987/10/15, Target/W. H. Allen & Co. PLC, UK
Novelisation of the one-off 1981 TV special. 'The
Companions of Doctor Who'. Cover by Andrew
Skilleter. Print run: 20,000 copies.
REF: ISBN 0-426-20309-7 OP: £1.95 p/b NM: £13.20

BSN-001

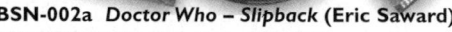

BSN-002b

BSN-003a

BSN-002a *Doctor Who – Slipback* **(Eric Saward)**
1986/08/14, W. H. Allen & Co. PLC, UK
Novelisation of the 1985 radio series. Cover by Paul
Mark Tams.
REF: ISBN 0-491-03793-7 OP: £6.95 h/b NM: £13.20

BSN-002b *Doctor Who – Slipback* **(Eric Saward)**
1987/01/15, Target/W. H. Allen & Co. PLC, UK
Cover by Paul Mark Tams
REF: ISBN 0-426-20263-5 OP: £1.75 p/b NM: £11

BSN-003a *Doctor Who – The Nightmare Fair*
(Graham Williams)
1989/05/18, Target/W. H. Allen & Co. PLC, UK
Novelisation of an unused script intended for the
23rd season. Cover by Alistair Pearson and Graeme
Wey. 'The Missing Episodes'. Print run: 21,000 copies.
REF: ISBN 0-426-20334-8 OP: £1.99 p/b NM: £13.20

BSN-003b *Doctor Who – The Nightmare Fair*
(Graham Williams)
1992/01/23, Target/Virgin Publishing Ltd, UK
Cover by Alistair Pearson and Graeme Wey. Blue spine.
REF: ISBN 0-426-20334-8 OP: £2.99 p/b NM: £7

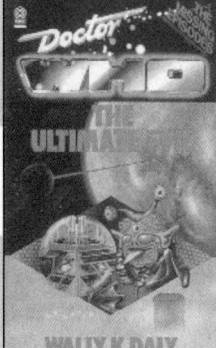

BSN-004

BSN-005

BSN-004 *Doctor Who – The Ultimate Evil*
(Wally K. Daly)
1989/08/17, Target/W. H. Allen & Co. PLC, UK
Novelisation of an unused script intended for the
23rd season. Cover by Alistair Pearson and Graeme
Wey. 'The Missing Episodes'. Print run: 21,000 copies.
REF: ISBN 0-426-20338-0 OP: £1.99 p/b NM: £16.50

BSN-005 *Doctor Who – Mission to Magnus*
(Philip Martin)
1990/07/19, Target/W. H. Allen & Co. PLC, UK
Novelisation of an unused script intended for the
23rd season. Cover by Alistair Pearson. 'The Missing
Episodes'. Print run: 24,000 copies.
REF: ISBN 0-426-20347-X OP: £2.50 p/b NM: £9

BSN-006

BSN-007

BSN-006 *Doctor Who – The Pescatons* **(Victor
Pemberton)**
1991/09/19, Target/Virgin Publishing Ltd, UK
Novelisation of the Argo Record (see ADR-001) Cover
by Pete Wallbank. Number 153. Print run: 22,000 copies.
REF: ISBN 0-426-20353-4 OP: £2.50 p/b NM: £4

BSN-007 *Doctor Who – The Paradise of Death*
(Barry Letts)
1994/04/21, Virgin Publishing Ltd, UK
Novelisation of the 1993 radio series. Cover by
Alistair Pearson. Number 156.
REF: ISBN 0-426-20413-1 OP: £4.99 p/b NM: £6

BOOKS, TALKING

BTA-001 Talking Book (*Carnival of Monsters, The Three Doctors, The Loch Ness Monster*)
1981, RNIB, UK
Read by Gabriel Woolf. 9 hours duration. May also have included sections from the Alan Road *Making of a Television Series* book (see BFA-007). This item was produced for the Royal National Institute for the Blind and was not (as far as is known) commercially available to buy, but it could be borrowed from libraries.
NM: £22

BOOKS, TARGET NOVELISATIONS

IN 1972, the Universal-Tandem Publishing Company was starting up a new children's imprint called Target and the editor of the range, Richard Henwood, was looking for suitable titles to publish. He came across the three *Doctor Who* novelizations put out by Frederick Muller in the sixties and enquiries revealed that these titles – *Doctor Who in an exciting adventure with the Daleks* and *Doctor Who and the Crusaders* by David Whitaker and *Doctor Who and the Zarbi* by Bill Strutton – were available for sale, so he negotiated the rights. The three titles were eventually published under the Target imprint both as hardbacks and paperbacks in May 1973.

Henwood left Target in May of 1974, and his successor as editor was Michael Glover. Universal-Tandem had during this period been taken over by W.H. Allen & Co Ltd, and Glover was been succeeded as editor by Elizabeth Godfray. Godfray oversaw the books from January 1975 until she left in January 1977. No replacement was then appointed until May 1978, when Brenda Gardner took over until she was made redundant from W. H. Allen late in 1979 and her place taken by Christine Donougher. Donougher stopped editing the *Doctor Who* range in 1984 when Nigel Robinson took over. Robinson, stayed with the company for 3 years and moved on in April 1987 passing editorship of the Target range to Sara Barnes for a short while before being taken on briefly by Tim Byrne before finally being taken over by Jo Thurm. Thurm moved on early in 1989, when Peter Darvill-Evans took over the range.

By this time, W H Allen had bought Virgin Publishing, and in 1991, the Virgin side of the operation was brought to the fore and W H Allen

ceased to exist.

By the end of 1989, the majority of *Doctor Who* stories had been novelised, and those that remained were scheduled for the future, *The Power of the Daleks* and *The Evil of the Daleks* appeared in 1992, leaving just four televised stories un-novelised: Douglas Adams' *Doctor Who* work, *The Pirate Planet* and *City of Death*; and Eric Saward's Dalek stories *Resurrection of the Daleks* and *Remembrance of the Daleks*. The Dalek stories were held up because Terry Nation and his agents were in dispute with W. H. Allen and Saward over the royalty for allowing these stories to be novelised, and Adams had by now found fame and fortune with his *Hitch-Hiker's Guide to the Galaxy* series and was unwilling to pen the titles for the fee that the publishers could afford, he had also used plot elements from both *Shada* and *City of Death* as the basis for his 1987 novel *Dirk Gently's Holistic Detective Agency*.

Although the books had always been reprinted, during the early nineties, Darvill-Evans instigated a programme of reprints, and two novelisations were re-issued a month in attractive 'blue spined' editions and mostly featuring new covers by Alistair Pearson. Where possible the publication and covers for these books were tied in with the release of the story on video by the BBC. The reprints were stopped in 1994 when demand for them fell below a level that the company was prepared to accept.

The following listing includes details of all the re-prints and print runs of the books, where these are known. In addition, details have been given of any distinguishing features (usually the price) which will differentiate one edition from another. Because of the sheer number of books and re-issues published, it is possible that some details may be missing.

The following terms are used (examples are pictured on the next page): BLOCK LOGO, CURVE LOGO, NEON LOGO, McCOY LOGO, and TVM LOGO refer to the various versions of the series logo that were used at the top of the Target novelisation covers. COLOUR DECAL, OUTLINE DECAL, and McCOY DECAL refer to the various spine emblems used. These variations help to visually distinguish between different editions of the same novelisation.

In compiling the listing of Target books, information has been included where it has been verified from an actual copy. We have tried not to assume things. Therefore certain ISBN numbers and prices are missing, as are cover and logo details simply because we

BLOCK LOGO

CURVE LOGO

NEON LOGO

COLOUR DECAL

McCOY LOGO

OUTLINE DECAL

McCOY DECAL

TVM LOGO

BTR-001a

BTR-001c

have been unable to verify them. With the reprints, information about their existence has been gleaned from the books themselves, as well as publishers catalogues and internal paperwork. It is very possible that editions have been missed and the authors would like to hear from anyone with reprint editions not listed, or different from those listed.

The books occasionally included information like 'second impression' and so on. We have included this here even though it is obvious that the editions are not those stated on the inside pages.

The manner in which reprints were done also muddies the waters. In some cases, a book would be completely reprinted, whereas sometimes a paperback would have its cover stripped off and re-jacketed with a new cover. These latter books generally show a higher cover price to that generally being used at the time of the printing date on the book's internal pages.

On the pricing aspect, the vast majority of the books today sell for between £1 to £5 depending on condition. There are a few exceptions to this, however, and these are noted where appropriate.

In general terms a mint condition first edition paperback will be worth around £5 to £10. The hardbacks are all generally worth between £12 – £25 each for mint condition copies. Again, exceptions are noted.

BTR-001a *Doctor Who in an exciting adventure with the Daleks* (David Whitaker)
1964/11/12, Frederick Muller Ltd, UK
Cover and illustrations by Arnold Schwartzman. First edition has a pink slip-cover. Novelisation of *The Mutants* (aka *The Daleks*)
REF: No ISBN OP: 12s 6d h/b NM: £60

BTR-001b *Doctor Who in an exciting adventure with the Daleks* (David Whitaker)
1964/12 c., Frederick Muller Ltd, UK
Cover and illustrations by Arnold Schwartzman. Second edition has a green/grey slip cover (and the edition is noted in the book).
REF: No ISBN OP: 12s 6d h/b NM: £49.50

BTR-001c *Dr Who in an exciting adventure with the Daleks* (David Whitaker)
1965/10/04, Armada Paperbacks/Mayfair Books Ltd, UK
Cover and illustrations by Peter Archer.
REF: C130 OP: 2s 6d p/b NM: £13.20

BTR-001d *Dr. Who en de Daleks* (David Whitaker)
1966, U. -M. 'West-Friesland' – Hoorn, Holland
Dust jacket (different from the Muller one) and internal illustrations (essentially the same as the Muller ones, but redrawn) by Herson. Translated by Tuuk Buijtenhuijs.
REF: No ISBN   OP: No Cover Price h/b

BTR-001e *Doctor Who and the Daleks* (David Whitaker)
Saunders SJR, Canada
OP: $2.75

BTR-001f *Doctor Who and the Daleks* (David Whitaker)
1966 c., Soccer, USA
OP: $3.75

BTR-001d

BTR-001g *Doctor Who in an exciting adventure with the Daleks* (David Whitaker)
1967/07, Avon/Stein & Day, USA
Photographic cover by P Weller.
REF: G1322, 50c p/b, £40

BTR-001h *Doctor Who and the Daleks* (David Whitaker)
1973/05/02, Allan Wingate (Publishers) Ltd, UK
Cover by Chris Achilleos. Illustrated by Arnold Schwartzman. Print run: 63,000 copies.
OP: h/b   NM: £44

BTR-001i *Doctor Who and the Daleks* (David Whitaker)
1973/05/02, Target/Universal-Tandem Publishing Co. Ltd, UK
Cover by Chris Achilleos. Illustrated by Arnold Schwartzman. Block logo. Mauve spine. Code number 10110 on spine. Colour decal. Reprinted in Oct/Nov 1973 and again in January/February 1974.
REF: ISBN 0-426-10110-3   OP: 25p p/b   NM: £4.95

BTR-001g

BTR-001i

BTR-001j *Doctor Who en de Daleks* (David Whitaker)
1974, Unieboek B V – Bussum, the Netherlands
Cover by Chris Achilleos (from *Doctor Who and the Daleks*). Translated by Ronald Cohen.
REF: ISBN 90-269-8102-3   OP: F 3,95 p/b   NM: £5.50

BTR-001k *Doctor Who and the Daleks* (David Whitaker)
1974, Target/Tandem Publishing Ltd, UK
Cover by Chris Achilleos. "Second Impression". Full title on inside.
REF: ISBN 0-426-10612-1   OP: 30p p/b   NM: £3.95

BTR-001j

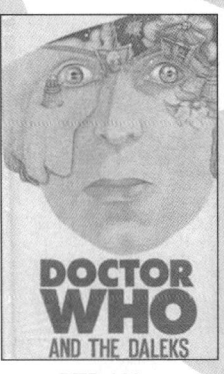

BTR-001p

BTR-001z **BTR-001ab**

BTR-001ac **BTR-001ad**

BTR-002a **BTR-002d**

BTR-001l *Doctor Who and the Daleks* (David Whitaker)
1974/10, Target/Tandem Publishing Ltd, UK
Cover by Chris Achilleos.
REF: ISBN 0-426-11287-3 OP: 30p p/b NM: £3.95

BTR-001m *Doctor Who and the Daleks* (David Whitaker)
1975, Target/Tandem Publishing Ltd, UK
Cover by Chris Achilleos. 2nd Impression. Block logo. Mauve spine.
REF: ISBN 0-426-11287-3 OP: 40p p/b NM: £3.95

BTR-001n *Doctor Who and the Daleks* (David Whitaker)
1975, Target/Tandem Publishing Ltd, UK
Cover by Chris Achilleos. Block logo. Mauve spine.
REF: ISBN 0-426-10110-3 OP: 60p p/b NM: £3.95

BTR-001o *Doktor Kim ve Dalekler* (David Whitaker)
1975/04, Remzi Kitabevi, Turkey
Cover by Chris Achilleos (from *Doctor Who and the Daleks*). Translated by Reha Pinar.
REF: No ISBN OP: 10 Lira p/b

BTR-001p *Doctor Who and the Daleks* (David Whitaker)
1975/06, White Lion, UK
Illustrated by Arnold Schwartzman. Cover shows Fourth Doctor.
REF: ISBN 85686-172-3 OP: £2.10 h/b NM: £49.50

BTR-001q *Doctor Who and the Daleks* (David Whitaker)
1976/01, Target/Wyndham Publications Ltd, UK
REF: ISBN 0-426-10110-3 OP: 40p p/b NM: £3.95

BTR-001r *Doctor Who and the Daleks* (David Whitaker)
1977, Target/Wyndham Publications Ltd, UK
Full title on inside. Cover by Chris Achilleos. Block logo. Purple spine. Colour decal. Wyndham W on back.
REF: ISBN 0-426-10110-3 OP: 60p p/b NM: £3.95

BTR-001s *Doctor Who and the Daleks* (David Whitaker)
1977, Target/Wyndham Publications Ltd, UK
3rd Impression. Blue Curve logo. White spine. Print run: 20,000 copies.
REF: ISBN 0-426-10110-3 OP: 70p p/b NM: £3.95

BTR-001t *Doctor Who and the Daleks* (David Whitaker)
1978/08/17, Target/W. H. Allen & Co. Ltd, UK
4th Impression. Blue Curve logo. White spine. Print run: 6,000 copies.
REF: ISBN 0-426-10110-3 OP: 85p p/b NM: £3.95

BTR-001u *Doctor Who and the Daleks* (David Whitaker)
1979, Target/W. H. Allen & Co. Ltd, UK
Says "Third Impression." Achilleos cover. Blue curve logo. White spine. Wyndham W on back. Print run: 12,000 copies.
REF: ISBN 0-426-10110-3 OP: 70p p/b NM: £3.95

BTR-001v *Doctor Who and the Daleks* (David Whitaker)
1980, Target/W. H. Allen & Co. Ltd, UK
4th impression. Blue curve logo. White spine. Colour decal. Print run: 15,000 copies.
REF: ISBN 0-426-10110-3 OP: 85p p/b NM: £3.95

BTR-001w *[Jikau Dai Chi Tataka!]* (David Whitaker)
1980/03/31, Hayakawa Publishing Inc, Japan
Cover by Michiaki Sato. Translated by Yukio Sekiguchi. Published by Hayakawa Bunko Publishing. Novels published under the series title 'Doctor Who Series'. Title translates as *'Space-Time Big Bloody Battle!'*
REF: SF 381 OP: Y 300 p/b NM: £110

BTR-001x *Doctor Who and the Daleks* (David Whitaker)
1982, Target/W. H. Allen & Co. Ltd, UK
Abbreviated title on inside. Cover by Chris Achilleos. Illustrated by Arnold Schwartzman. Blue curve logo. White spine. Colour decal.
REF: ISBN 0-426-10110-3 OP: £1.50 p/b NM: £3.95

BTR-001y *Doctor Who and the Daleks* (David Whitaker)
1983, Target/W. H. Allen & Co. Ltd, UK
Cover by Chris Achilleos. Illustrated by Arnold Schwartzman. Blue curve logo. White spine. Colour decal.
REF: ISBN 0-426-10110-3 OP: £1.50 p/b NM: £3.95

BTR-001z *Doutor Who E Os Daleks (7)* (David Whitaker)
1983, Editorial Presenca, Portugal
Cover by Rui Ligeiro. Illustrations by Arnold Schwartzman. Translated by Conceicao Jardim and Eduardo Nogueira.
REF: No ISBN OP: p/b

BTR-001aa *Doctor Who and the Daleks* (David Whitaker)
1984, Target/W. H. Allen & Co. Ltd, UK
Cover by Chris Achilleos. Illustrations by Arnold Schwartzman. Blue curve logo. White spine. Outline decal.
REF: ISBN 0-426-10110-3 OP: £1.50 p/b NM: £3.95

BTR-001ab *Docteur Who: Les Daleks (3)* (David Whitaker)
1987/05, Editions Garanciere, France
Artwork cover. Translated by Gilles Bergal then adapted by Corine Derblum.
REF: ISBN 2-7340-0204-3 OP: p/b

BTR-001ac *Doctor Who Und die Invasion der Daleks* (David Whitaker)
1989, Goldmann Verlag, Germany
Cover by Andrew Skilleter (from *Destiny of the Daleks*). Translated by Peter Tuscher.
REF: ISBN 3-442-23611-8 OP: DM 7,80 p/b

BTR-001ad *Doctor Who – The Daleks* (David Whitaker)
1992/01/16, Target/Virgin Publishing Ltd, UK
Cover by Alistair Pearson. Blue spine. Outline decal. Numbered 16.
REF: ISBN 0-426-10110-3 OP: £2.99 p/b NM: £5.50

BTR-002a *Doctor Who and the Zarbi* (Bill Strutton)
1965/10, Frederick Muller Ltd, UK
Jacket design by J Woods. Illustrated by John Wood. Novelisation of *The Web Planet*.
REF: No ISBN OP: 12s 6d h/b NM: £55

BTR-002b *Doctor Who and the Zarbi* (Bill Strutton)
1966 c., Soccer, USA
OP: $3.75

BTR-002c *Doctor Who and the Zarbi* (Bill Strutton)
1973/05/02, Allan Wingate (Publishers) Ltd, UK
Cover by Chris Achilleos. Illustrated by John Wood. Print run: 49,000 copies.
OP: h/b NM: £44

BTR-002d *Doctor Who and the Zarbi* (Bill Strutton)
1973/05/02, Target/Universal-Tandem Publishing Co. Ltd, UK
Cover by Chris Achilleos. Illustrated by John Wood. Block logo. Orange spine. Colour decal. Code number 10129 on spine. Reprinted in October/November 1973 and again in January/February 1974.
REF: ISBN 0-426-10129-4 OP: 25p p/b NM: £4.95

BTR-002e *Doctor Who en de Zarbi's* **(Bill Strutton)**
1974, Unieboek B V – Bussum, the Netherlands
Cover by Chris Achilleos (from *Doctor Who and the Zarbi*). Translated by M Hohage.
REF: ISBN 90-269-8103-1 OP: F 3,95 p/b NM: £5.50

BTR-002f *Doctor Who and the Zarbi* **(Bill Strutton)**
1974/11, Target/Tandem Publishing Ltd, UK
Cover by Chris Achilleos.
REF: ISBN 0-426-11324-1 OP: 30p p/b NM: £3.95

BTR-002g *Doctor Who and the Zarbi* **(Bill Strutton)**
1975, Target/Tandem Publishing Ltd, UK
Cover by Chris Achilleos. Illustrated by John Wood. 2nd impression. Block logo. Orange spine. No code number on spine. A version also exists with an ISBN of 0-426-10663-6 and a price of 30p.
REF: ISBN 0-426-11324-1 OP: 40p p/b NM: £3.95

BTR-002h *Doctor Who and the Zarbi* **(Bill Strutton)**
1975, Target/Tandem Publishing Ltd, UK
Cover by Chris Achilleos. Illustrated by John Wood. Reprinted Autumn 1975. Block logo. Orange spine. It is possible that this edition was published after BTR-002i despite the fact that it has a lower cover price.
REF: ISBN 0-426-11324-1 OP: 40p p/b NM: £3.95

BTR-002i *Doctor Who and the Zarbi* **(Bill Strutton)**
1975/12, White Lion, UK
Cover painting features the Fourth Doctor.
REF: ISBN 0-85686-167-7 OP: £2.25 h/b NM: £38.50

BTR-002j *Doctor Who and the Zarbi* **(Bill Strutton)**
1976/01, Target/W H Allen & Co Ltd, UK
REF: ISBN 0-426-11324-1 OP: 40p p/b NM: £3.95

BTR-002k *Doctor Who and the Zarbi* **(Bill Strutton)**
1978, Target/W H Allen & Co Ltd, UK
Cover by Chris Achilleos. Black curve logo. White spine. Colour decal. Print run: 10,000 copies.
REF: ISBN 0-426-11324-1 OP: 60p p/b NM: £3.95

BTR-002l *Doctor Who and the Zarbi* **(Bill Strutton)**
1978/08/17, Target/W H Allen & Co Ltd, UK
Cover by Chris Achilleos. Illustrated by John Wood. 3rd impression. Black curve logo. White spine. Print run: 4,000 copies.
REF: ISBN 0-426-11324-1 OP: 70p p/b NM: £3.95

BTR-002m *Doctor Who and the Zarbi* **(Bill Strutton)**
1979, Target/W H Allen & Co Ltd, UK
Print run: 12,000 copies.
REF: ISBN 0-426-11324-1 OP: 70p p/b NM: £3.95

BTR-002n *Doctor Who and the Zarbi* **(Bill Strutton)**
1981, Target/W H Allen & Co Ltd, UK
Cover by Chris Achilleos. 'Fourth Impression'. Black curve logo. White spine. Colour decal. Print run: 15,000 copies.
REF: ISBN 0-426-11324-1 OP: 90p p/b NM: £3.95

BTR-002o *Doctor Who and the Zarbi* **(Bill Strutton)**
1982, Target/W H Allen & Co Ltd, UK
Cover by Chris Achilleos. Black curve logo. White spine. Colour decal. Interior ISBN: 0-426-10129-4.
REF: ISBN 0-426-11324-1 OP: £1.50 p/b NM: £3.95

BTR-002p *Doutor Who E Os Zarbi* (10) **(Bill Strutton)**
1983, Editorial Presenca, Portugal
Cover by Rui Ligeiro. Illustrations by John Wood. Translated by Conceicao Jardim and Eduardo Nogueira.
REF: No ISBN OP: p/b

BTR-002q *Doctor Who and the Zarbi* **(Bill Strutton)**
1984, Target/W H Allen & Co Ltd, UK
Cover by Chris Achilleos. Illustrated by John Wood. Black curve logo. White spine. Colour decal. Interior ISBN: 0-426-10129-4. Number 73.
REF: ISBN 0-426-11324-1 OP: £1.50 p/b NM: £3.95

BTR-002r *Doctor Who and the Zarbi* **(Bill Strutton)**
1990/11, Target/Virgin Publishing Ltd, UK
Print run: 5,000 copies.
REF: ISBN 0-426-11324-1 OP: p/b NM: £3.95

BTR-002s *Doctor Who – The Web Planet* **(Bill Strutton)**
1991/01/17, Target/Virgin Publishing Ltd, UK
Cover by Alistair Pearson (as on Video). Blue spine. Print run: 3,000 copies.
REF: ISBN 0-426-20356-9 OP: £2.50 p/b NM: £5.50

BTR-002e

BTR-002i

BTR-002p

BTR-002s

BTR-003a *Doctor Who and the Crusaders*
(David Whitaker)
1966/03, Frederick Muller Ltd, UK
Novelisation of *The Crusade*.
REF: No ISBN OP: 12s 6d h/b NM: £49.50

BTR-003b *Doctor Who and the Crusaders*
(David Whitaker)
1967, Green Dragon/Atlantic Book Publishing Co Ltd, UK
Artwork cover. The interior illustrations are different
to the Muller edition.
REF: D67 ISBN 411-80670-X OP: 2s 6d p/b NM: £22

BTR-003c *Doctor Who and the Crusaders*
(David Whitaker)
1973/05/02, Allan Wingate (Publishers) Ltd, UK
Cover by Chris Achilleos. Illustrated by Henry Fox.
Print run: 51,500 copies.
OP: h/b NM: £44

BTR-003a

BTR-003b

BTR-003d *Doctor Who and the Crusaders*
(David Whitaker)
1973/05/02, Target/Universal-Tandem Publishing Co.
Ltd, UK
Cover by Chris Achilleos. Illustrated by Henry Fox.
Block logo. Red spine. Colour decal. Code number
10137 on spine. Reprinted in October/November
1973 and again in January/February 1974.
REF: ISBN 0-426-10137-5 OP: 25p p/b NM: £4.95

BTR-003e *Doctor Who en de Kruisvaarders*
(David Whitaker)
1974, Unieboek B V – Bussum, the Netherlands
Cover by Chris Achilleos (from *Doctor Who and the
Crusaders*). Translated by J J v d Hulst-Brander.
REF: ISBN 90-269-8101-5 OP: F 3,95 p/b NM: £5.50

BTR-003d

BTR-003e

BTR-003i

BTR-003o

BTR-003r

BTR-003u

BTR-004b

BTR-004d

BTR-003f *Doctor Who and the Crusaders* (David Whitaker)
1974/11, Target/Tandem Publishing Ltd, UK
Cover by Chris Achilleos.
REF: ISBN 0-426-10671-7 OP: 30p p/b NM: £3.95

BTR-003g *Doctor Who and the Crusaders* (David Whitaker)
1975, Target/Universal-Tandem Publishing Co. Ltd, UK
"Second Impression". Cover by Chris Achilleos.
Illustrated by Henry Fox. Block logo. Red Spine.
Colour decal. No code number on spine.
REF: ISBN 0-426-10671-7 OP: 30p p/b NM: £3.95

BTR-003h *Doctor Who and the Crusaders* (David Whitaker)
1975, Target/Tandem Publishing Ltd, UK
"Reprinted in Autumn". Cover by Chris Achilleos.
Illustrated by Henry Fox. Block logo. Red Spine.
Colour decal. No code number on spine.
REF: ISBN 0-426-11316-0 OP: 40p p/b NM: £3.95

BTR-003i *Doctor Who and the Crusaders* (David Whitaker)
1975/12, White Lion, UK
Illustrated by Henry Fox. Cover shows Fourth Doctor.
Interior states that edition was published in 1965.
REF: ISBN 85686-162-6 OP: £2.25 h/b NM: £38.50

BTR-003j *Doctor Who and the Crusaders* (David Whitaker)
1976/01, Target/W H Allen & Co Ltd, UK
Cover by Chris Achilleos. Illustrated by Henry Fox.
REF: ISBN 0-426-11316-0 OP: 40p p/b NM: £3.95

BTR-003k *Doctor Who and the Crusaders* (David Whitaker)
1978, Target/W H Allen & Co Ltd, UK
Cover by Chris Achilleos. Illustrated by Henry Fox.
Block logo. Red Spine. Print run: 5,500 copies.
REF: ISBN 0-426-11316-0 OP: 70p p/b NM: £3.95

BTR-003l *Doctor Who and the Crusaders* (David Whitaker)
1979/05/24, Target/W H Allen & Co Ltd, UK
Cover by Chris Achilleos. Illustrated by Henry Fox.
Red curve logo. White spine. Colour decal. Print run:
15,000 copies.
REF: ISBN 0-426-11316-0 OP: 70p p/b NM: £3.95

BTR-003m *Doctor Who and the Crusaders* (David Whitaker)
1980, Target/W H Allen & Co Ltd, UK
Cover by Chris Achilleos. Illustrated by Henry Fox.

Red curve logo. White spine. Colour decal. Print run: 12,000 copies.
REF: ISBN 0-426-11316-0 OP: 75p p/b NM: £3.95

BTR-003n *Doctor Who and the Crusaders* **(David Whitaker)**
1982, Target/W H Allen & Co Ltd, UK
Cover by Andrew Skilleter. Illustrated by Henry Fox.
Brown curve logo. White spine.
REF: ISBN 0-426-11316-0 OP: £1.35 p/b NM: £3.95

BTR-003o *Doctor Who and the Crusaders* **(David Whitaker)**
1982, Target/W H Allen & Co Ltd, UK
Cover by Andrew Skilleter. Illustrated by Henry Fox.
Red neon logo. White spine. Print run: 19,000 copies.
REF: ISBN 0-426-11316-0 OP: £1.50 p/b NM: £3.95

BTR-003p *Doctor Who and the Crusaders* **(David Whitaker)**
1983, Target/W H Allen & Co Ltd, UK
Cover by Andrew Skilleter. Illustrated by Henry Fox.
Red neon logo. White spine. Edition also available with a light blue spine. Interior ISBN: 0-426-10137-5.
REF: ISBN 0-426-11316-0 OP: £1.50 p/b NM: £3.95

BTR-003q *Doctor Who and the Crusaders* **(David Whitaker)**
1983, Target/W H Allen & Co Ltd, UK
Cover by Chris Achilleos. Illustrated by Henry Fox.
Dark red/brown curve logo. White spine. Colour decal. Interior ISBN: 0-426-10137-5.
REF: ISBN 0-426-11316-0 OP: £1.50 p/b NM: £3.95

BTR-003r *Doutor Who E Os Cruzados* **(8) (David Whitaker)**
1983, Editorial Presenca, Portugal
Cover by Shanti. Illustrations by Henry Fox. Translated by Conceicao Jardim and Eduardo Nogueira.
REF: No ISBN OP: p/b

BTR-003s *Doctor Who and the Crusaders* **(David Whitaker)**
1984, Target/W H Allen & Co Ltd, UK
Cover by Andrew Skilleter. Red neon logo. Blue spine.
Colour decal. Interior ISBN: 0-426-10137-5.
REF: ISBN 0-426-11316-0 OP: £1.50 p/b NM: £3.95

BTR-003t *Doctor Who and the Crusaders* **(David Whitaker)**
1985/01/17, W. H. Allen & Co. PLC, UK
Cover by Andrew Skilleter.
REF: ISBN 0-491-03670-1 OP: £5.95 h/b NM: £13.20

BTR-003u *Docteur Who: Les Croises* **(2) (David Whitaker)**
1987/02, Editions Garanciere, France
Artwork cover. Translated by Andre Ruaud.
REF: ISBN 2-7340-0202-7 OP: p/b

BTR-003v *Doctor Who and the Crusaders* **(David Whitaker)**
1988, Target/W H Allen & Co Ltd, UK
Print run: 2,500 copies.
REF: ISBN 0-426-11316-0 OP: £1.50 p/b NM: £3.95

BTR-004a *Doctor Who and the Auton Invasion* **(Terrance Dicks)**
1974/01/17, Allan Wingate (Publishers) Ltd, UK
Cover and illustrations by Chris Achilleos.
Novelisation of *Spearhead from Space*.
REF: ISBN 85523-035-5 OP: £1.75 h/b NM: £33

BTR-004b *Doctor Who and the Auton Invasion* **(Terrance Dicks)**
1974/01/17, Target/Universal-Tandem Publishing Co. Ltd, UK
Cover and illustrations by Chris Achilleos. Block logo.
Brown spine. Colour decal.
REF: ISBN 0-426-10313-0 OP: 25p p/b NM: £5.50

BTR-004c *Doctor Who and the Auton Invasion* **(Terrance Dicks)**
1974/10, Target/Universal-Tandem Publishing Co. Ltd, UK
Cover and illustrations by Chris Achilleos. Block logo.
Brown spine. Colour decal.
REF: ISBN 0-426-10313-0 OP: 30p p/b NM: £4.50

BTR-004d *Doctor Who en de Invasie van de Autonen* **(Terrance Dicks)**
1974, Unieboek B V – Bussum, the Netherlands
Cover by Chris Achilleos (from *Doctor Who and the Auton Invasion*). Translated by J J v d Hulst-Brander.
REF: ISBN 90-269-8105-8 OP: F 3,95 p/b NM: £5.50

BTR-004e *Doctor Who and the Auton Invasion* **(Terrance Dicks)**
1975, Target/Tandem Publishing Co. Ltd, UK
Cover and illustrations by Chris Achilleos. Block logo.
Brown spine. Colour decal.
REF: ISBN 0-426-11295-4 OP: 40p p/b NM: £4.50

BTR-004f *Doktor Kim ve Otonlar* **(Terrance Dicks)**
1975, Remzi Kitabevi, Turkey
Cover by Chris Achilleos (from *Doctor Who and the Auton Invasion*). Translated by Reha Pinar.
REF: No ISBN OP: 10 Lira p/b

BTR-004g *Doctor Who and the Auton Invasion*
(Terrance Dicks)
1976/01, Target/Universal-Tandem Publishing Co. Ltd, UK
Cover and illustrations by Chris Achilleos. Block logo.
Brown spine.
REF: ISBN 0-426-11295-4 OP: 40p p/b NM: £4.50

BTR-004h *Tohtori Kuka ja autonien hyökkäys*
(Terrance Dicks)
1976, Weilin+Göös, Finland
Translated by Renne Nikupaavola. Hardback. No further information available.

BTR-004i *Doctor Who and the Auton Invasion*
(Terrance Dicks)
1978/08/17, Target/W H Allen & Co Ltd, UK
Cover and illustrations by Chris Achilleos. Green
curve logo. White spine. Colour decal. Print run:
10,000 copies.
REF: ISBN 0-426-11295-4 OP: 60p p/b NM: £3.95

BTR-004j *Doctor Who and the Auton Invasion*
(Terrance Dicks)
1980/02/21, Target/W H Allen & Co Ltd, UK
Cover by Chris Achilleos. 'Third impression'. Green
curve logo. White spine. Colour decal. Wyndham W
on back. Print run: 12,000 copies.
REF: ISBN 0-426-11295-4 OP: 75p p/b NM: £4.50

BTR-004k *[Oh-ton gundan no shuurai]*
(Terrance Dicks)
1980/04/30, Hayakawa Publishing Inc, Japan
Cover by Michiaki Sato. Translated by Yukio Sekiguchi.
Title translates as 'The Auton Army Invasion.'
REF: SF 388 OP: Y 300 p/b NM: £110

BTR-004l *Doctor Who and the Auton Invasion*
(Terrance Dicks)
1981/11/19, W. H. Allen & Co. Ltd, UK
Cover by Andrew Skilleter. Print run: 3,000 copies.
REF: ISBN 0-491-02895-4 OP: £4.95 h/b NM: £11

BTR-004m *Doctor Who and the Auton Invasion*
(Terrance Dicks)
1982, Target/W. H. Allen & Co. Ltd, UK
Cover and illustrations by Chris Achilleos. Green
curve logo. White spine. Colour decal.
REF: ISBN 0-426-11295-4 OP: £1.50 p/b NM: £4.50

BTR-004n *Doctor Who and the Auton Invasion*
(Terrance Dicks)
1982, Target/W. H. Allen & Co. Ltd, UK
Cover by Andrew Skilleter. Blue neon logo. Blue spine.
REF: ISBN 0-426-11295-4 OP: p/b NM: £3.95

BTR-004o *Doutor Who E A Invasao Dos Autones*
(1) (Terrance Dicks)
1982, Editorial Presenca, Portugal
Cover by Rui Ligeiro. Illustrations by Chris Achilleos.
Translated by Eduardo Nogueira and Conceicao Jardim.
REF: No ISBN OP: p/b

BTR-004p *Doctor Who and the Auton Invasion*
(Terrance Dicks)
1983/12/08, Target/W. H. Allen & Co. Ltd, UK
Cover by Andrew Skilleter. Illustrated by Chris
Achilleos. Blue neon logo. Blue spine. Colour decal.
Print run: 20,000 copies.
REF: ISBN 0-426-11295-4 OP: £1.50 p/b NM: £3.95

BTR-004q *Doctor Who and the Auton Invasion*
(Terrance Dicks)
1984, Target/W. H. Allen & Co. Ltd, UK
Cover by Andrew Skilleter. Illustrated by Chris
Achilleos. Blue neon logo. Blue spine. Colour decal.
Interior ISBN: 0-426-10313-0.
REF: ISBN 0-426-11295-4 OP: £1.50 p/b NM: £3.95

BTR-004r *Doctor Who and the Auton Invasion*
(Terrance Dicks)
1984, Target/W. H. Allen & Co. Ltd, UK
Cover by Andrew Skilleter. Illustrated by Chris
Achilleos. Blue neon logo. Blue spine. Outline decal.
Interior ISBN: 0-426-10313-0.
REF: ISBN 0-426-11295-4 OP: £1.50 p/b NM: £3.95

BTR-004s *Doctor Who – The Auton Invasion*
(Terrance Dicks)
1991/03/21, Target/Virgin Publishing Ltd, UK
Cover by Alistair Pearson. Blue spine. Print run: 8,000
copies.
REF: ISBN 0-426-11295-4 OP: £2.50 p/b NM: £5.50

BTR-005a *Doctor Who and the Cave-Monsters*
(Malcolm Hulke)
1974/01/17, Allan Wingate (Publishers) Ltd, UK
Cover and illustrations by Chris Achilleos.
Novelisation of *Doctor Who and the Silurians*.
REF: ISBN 85523-036-3 OP: £1.75 h/b NM: £33

BTR-005b *Doctor Who and the Cave-Monsters*
(Malcolm Hulke)
1974/01/17, Target/Universal-Tandem Publishing Co.
Ltd, UK
Cover and illustrations by Chris Achilleos. Block logo.
Green spine. Colour decal.
REF: ISBN 0-426-10292-4 OP: 25p p/b NM: £4.95

BTR-005c *Doctor Who en de Holenmonsters* (Malcolm Hulke)
1974, Unieboek B V – Bussum, the Netherlands
Cover by Chris Achilleos (from *Doctor Who and the Cave Monsters*). Translated by J J v d Hulst-Brander.
REF: ISBN 90-269-8106-6 OP: F 3,95 p/b NM: £5.50

BTR-005d *Doctor Who and the Cave-Monsters* (Malcolm Hulke)
1975/02, Target/Universal-Tandem Publishing Co. Ltd, UK
Cover and illustrations by Chris Achilleos. '2nd impression'. Block logo. Green spine. Colour decal.
REF: ISBN 0-426-10292-4 OP: 35p p/b NM: £3.95

BTR-005e *Doctor Who and the Cave-Monsters* (Malcolm Hulke)
1975, Target/Universal-Tandem Publishing Co. Ltd, UK
Cover and illustrations by Chris Achilleos. '2nd impression'. Block logo. Green spine. Colour decal.
REF: ISBN 0-426-10292-4 OP: 40p p/b NM: £3.95

BTR-005f *Doctor Who and the Cave-Monsters* (Malcolm Hulke)
1976/03, Target/Tandem Publishing Co. Ltd, UK
Cover and illustrations by Chris Achilleos. Block logo. Green spine. Colour decal.
REF: ISBN 0-426-11471-X OP: 40p p/b NM: £3.95

BTR-005g *Tohtori Kuka ja luolahirviöt* (Malcolm Hulke)
1976, Weilin+Göös, Finland
Translated by Renne Nikupaavola. Hardback. No further information available.

BTR-004f

BTR-004h

BTR-004k

BTR-004n

BTR-004o

BTR-004s

BTR-005b

BTR-005c

MALCOLM HULKE

TOHTORI KUKA JA LUOLAHIRVIÖT

BTR-005g

BTR-005k

BTR-005n

BTR-005p

BTR-005h *Doctor Who and the Cave-Monsters*
(Malcolm Hulke)
1978, Target/W H Allen & Co Ltd, UK
Cover and illustrations by Chris Achilleos. Block logo.
Green spine. Print run: 4,000 copies.
REF: ISBN 0-426-11471-X OP: 40p p/b NM: £3.95

BTR-005i *Doctor Who and the Cave-Monsters*
(Malcolm Hulke)
1979, Target/W H Allen & Co Ltd, UK
Cover and illustrations by Chris Achilleos. 2nd
impression. Green curve logo. White spine. Print run:
15,000 copies.
REF: ISBN 0-426-11471-X OP: 70p p/b NM: £3.95

BTR-005j *Doctor Who and the Cave-Monsters*
(Malcolm Hulke)
1980, Target/W H Allen & Co Ltd, UK
Cover and illustrations by Chris Achilleos. Green
curve logo. White spine. Colour decal. Print run:
12,000 copies.
REF: ISBN 0-426-11471-X OP: 75p p/b NM: £3.95

BTR-006a

BTR-006c

BTR-005k {*Senritsu! Chitei Monsutaa*}
(Malcolm Hulke)
1980/05/31, Hayakawa Publishing Inc, Japan
Cover by Michiaki Sato. Translated by Yukio Sekiguchi.
Title translates as 'Shuddering! The Underground Monsters.'
REF: SF 390 OP: Y 320 p/b NM: £110

BTR-005l *Doctor Who and the Cave-Monsters*
(Malcolm Hulke)
1982, Target/W H Allen & Co Ltd, UK
Cover and illustrations by Chris Achilleos. Green
curve logo. White spine. Colour decal. Interior ISBN:
0-426-10292-4.
REF: ISBN 0-426-11471-X OP: £1.35 p/b NM: £3.95

DOKTOR KİM VE DALEK BASKINI
TERRANCE DICKS

BTR-006e

BTR-006j

BTR-005m *Doctor Who and the Cave-Monsters* (Malcolm Hulke)
1983, Target/W H Allen & Co Ltd, UK
Cover and illustrations by Chris Achilleos. Green curve logo. White spine. Colour decal. Print run: 13,000 copies.
REF: ISBN 0-426-11471-X OP: £1.50 p/b NM: £3.95

BTR-005n *Doutor Who E Os Monstros Das Cavernas (2)* (Malcolm Hulke)
1983, Editorial Presenca, Portugal
Cover by Rui Ligeiro. Translated by Conceicao Jardim and Eduardo Nogueira.
REF: No ISBN OP: p/b

BTR-005o *Doctor Who and the Cave-Monsters* (Malcolm Hulke)
1984, Target/W H Allen & Co Ltd, UK
Cover by Chris Achilleos. Illustrated by Chris Achilleos. Green curve logo. White spine. Colour decal. Interior ISBN: 0-426-10292-4.
REF: ISBN 0-426-11471-X OP: £1.50 p/b NM: £3.95

BTR-005p *Doctor Who – The Silurians* (Malcolm Hulke)
1992/08/20, Target/Virgin Publishing, UK
Cover by Allister Pearson. Blue spine.
REF: ISBN 0-426-20382-8 OP: £2.99 p/b NM: £4.50

BTR-006a *Doctor Who and the Day of the Daleks* (Terrance Dicks)
1974/04, Target/Universal-Tandem Publishing Co. Ltd, UK
Cover and illustrations by Chris Achilleos. Block logo. Orange spine. Colour decal.
REF: ISBN 0-426-10380-7 OP: 30p p/b NM: £5.95

BTR-006b *Doctor Who and the Day of the Daleks* (Terrance Dicks)
1974, Target/Universal-Tandem Publishing Co. Ltd, UK
Cover and illustrations by Chris Achilleos. '2nd impression'. Block logo. Orange spine.
REF: ISBN 0-426-10380-7 OP: 30p p/b NM: £4.95

BTR-006c *Doctor Who en de dag van de Daleks* (Terrance Dicks)
1974, Unieboek B V – Bussum, the Netherlands
Cover by Chris Achilleos (from *Doctor Who and the Day of the Daleks*). Translated by J J v d Hulst-Brander.
REF: ISBN 90 269 8108 2 OP: F 3,95 NM: £5.50

BTR-006d *Doutor Who e a Mudanca da Historia* (Terrance Dicks)
1974, Global, Brazil
Cover by Darlon (poor copy of Chris Achilleos' cover

for *Doctor Who and the Daleks*). Translated by Marcio Pugliesi and Norberto de Paula Lima. Cover art is dated 1975.
REF: No ISBN. Catalogue no: 1019 OP: p/b NM: £110

BTR-006e *Doktor Kim ve Dalek Baskini* (Terrance Dicks)
1975, Remzi Kitabevi, Turkey
Cover by Chris Achilleos (from *Doctor Who and the Day of the Daleks*). Translated by Reha Pinar
REF: No ISBN OP: 10 Lira p/b

BTR-006f *Doctor Who and the Day of the Daleks* (Terrance Dicks)
1975/04, Target/Universal-Tandem Publishing Co. Ltd, UK
Cover and illustrations by Chris Achilleos.
REF: ISBN 0-426-10380-7 OP: 30p p/b NM: £4.95

BTR-006g *Doctor Who and the Day of the Daleks* (Terrance Dicks)
1976, Target/Universal-Tandem Publishing Co. Ltd, UK
Cover and illustrations by Chris Achilleos. 'Second Impression'. Black curve logo. White spine.
REF: ISBN 0-426-10380-7 OP: 40p p/b NM: £4.95

BTR-006h *Doctor Who and the Day of the Daleks* (Terrance Dicks)
1978, Target/W. H. Allen & Co. Ltd, UK
Cover and illustrations by Chris Achilleos. 'Third Impression'. Black curve logo. White spine. Colour decal. Wyndham W on back. Print run: 15,000 copies.
REF: ISBN 0-426-10380-7 OP: 60p p/b NM: £4.95

BTR-006i *Doctor Who and the Day of the Daleks* (Terrance Dicks)
1979, Target/W. H. Allen & Co. Ltd, UK
'Fourth Impression'. Print run: 12,000 copies. Two printings in 1979; the first printing cost 70p.
REF: ISBN 0-426-10380-7 OP: 75p p/b NM: £4.95

BTR-006j *Doctor Who and the Day of the Daleks #1* (Terrance Dicks)
1979/04, Pinnacle Books, USA
Cover by David Mann. Red logo.
REF: ISBN 0-523-40565-0 OP: $1.75 p/b NM: £5.50

BTR-006k *[Dareku Joku-no Kyakushyuu!]* (Terrance Dicks)
1980, Hayakawa Publishing Inc, Japan
Cover by Michiaki Sato. Translated by Yukio Sekiguchi. Title translates as 'The Dalek Race's Counterattack!'
REF: SF 402 OP: Y 320 p/b NM: £110

BTR-006l *Doctor Who and the Day of the Daleks* (Terrance Dicks)
1980/08/15, Target/W. H. Allen & Co. Ltd, UK
Cover and illustrations by Chris Achilleos. 'Fourth Impression'. Black curve logo. White spine. Colour decal. Print run: 12,000 copies.
REF: ISBN 0-426-10380-7 OP: 75p p/b NM: £4.95

BTR-006m *Doctor Who and the Day of the Daleks* (Terrance Dicks)
1981/08/21, W. H. Allen & Co. Ltd, UK
Cover by Andrew Skilleter. Yellow neon logo. Print run: 3,000 copies. This is a reprint of the *Daleks Omnibus* version with no interior illustrations.
REF: ISBN 0-491-02975-6 OP: £4.50 h/b NM: £11

BTR-006n *Doctor Who and the Day of the Daleks* (Terrance Dicks)
1982, Target/W. H. Allen & Co. Ltd, UK
Cover by Chris Achilleos, no interior illustrations. Black curve logo. White spine. Colour decal.
REF: ISBN 0-426-10380-7 OP: £1.35 p/b NM: £2.75

BTR-006o *Doctor Who and the Day of the Daleks* (Terrance Dicks)
1982, Target/W. H. Allen & Co. Ltd, UK
Cover by Andrew Skilleter. Red neon logo. White spine.
REF: ISBN 0-426-10380-7 OP: p/b NM: £2.75

BTR-006p *Doctor Who and the Day of the Daleks* #1 (Terrance Dicks)
1982/06, Pinnacle Books, USA
Cover by David Mann. 'Second printing'. Orange logo.
REF: ISBN 0-523-41986-4 OP: $1.95 p/b NM: £5.50

BTR-006q *Doutor Who E O Dia Dos Daleks* (6) (Terrance Dicks)
1983, Editorial Presença, Portugal
Cover by Rui Ligeiro. Illustrations by Chris Achilleos. Translated by Conceicao Jardim and Eduardo Nogueira.
REF: No ISBN OP: p/b

BTR-006r *Doctor Who and the Day of the Daleks* (Terrance Dicks)
1984, Target/W. H. Allen & Co. Ltd, UK
Cover by Andrew Skilleter. Red neon logo. White spine. Colour decal. Number 18.
REF: ISBN 0-426-10380-7 OP: £1.35 p/b NM: £2.75

BTR-006s *Doctor Who and the Day of the Daleks* #1 (Terrance Dicks)
1984, Pinnacle Books, USA
Cover by David Mann. Yellow logo.
REF: ISBN 0-523-42496-5 OP: $2.95 p/b NM: £5.50

BTR-006t *Doctor Who and the Day of the Daleks* (Terrance Dicks)
1985/06, Amereon/Aeonian, USA
American published hardback edition. No slip-cover. Limited edition of 300 copies. Copyright date inside book is 1978. 1985 date from Barnes and Noble online.
REF: ISBN 0-8488-0151-2 OP: $18.95 h/b

BTR-006u *Doctor Who and the Day of the Daleks* (Terrance Dicks)
1987, Target/W. H. Allen & Co. Ltd, UK
Outline decal. Print run: 9,000 copies. Might be rejacketed 1984 Target reprint.
REF: ISBN 0-426-10380-7 OP: £1.95 p/b NM: £2.75

BTR-006v *Doctor Who and the Day of the Daleks* #1 (Terrance Dicks)
1989/01, Pinnacle Books, USA
Cover by David Mann. 'Sixth printing'. Yellow logo.
REF: ISBN 1-55817-188-6 OP: $3.50 p/b NM: £7.95

BTR-006w *Doctor Who – The Day of the Daleks* (Terrance Dicks)
1991/04/18, Target/Virgin Publishing Ltd, UK
Cover by Alistair Pearson. Blue spine. Print run: 8,000 copies. Although the book says it is 'illustrated by Chris Achilleos' it is not illustrated.
REF: ISBN 0-426-10380-7 OP: £2.50 p/b NM: £4.50

BTR-006x *Doctor Who – The Day of the Daleks* (Terrance Dicks)
1994/01/20, Target/Virgin Publishing Ltd, UK
Cover by Alistair Pearson. McCoy logo. Blue spine. Outline decal. No illustrations. Two printings in 1994; the first printing cost £2.50.
REF: ISBN 0-426-10380-7 OP: £3.50 p/b NM: £4.50

BTR-006y *Doctor Who – Dzień Daleków* (Terrance Dicks)
1994, Oficyna Wydawnicza "Empire", Poland
Translator: Andrzej Solny.
REF: ISBN 83-86126-04-3

BTR-007a *Doctor Who and the Doomsday Weapon* (Malcolm Hulke)
1974/04, Target/Universal-Tandem Publishing Co. Ltd, UK
Cover and illustrations by Chris Achilleos. Block logo. Mauve spine. Colour decal. Novelisation of *Colony in Space*.
REF: ISBN 0-426-10372-6 OP: 30p p/b NM: £6.50

BTR-007b *Doctor Who and the Doomsday Weapon* (Malcolm Hulke)
1974, Target/Universal-Tandem Publishing Co. Ltd, UK

Cover and illustrations by Chris Achilleos. 'Second impression'. Block logo. Mauve spine. Colour decal.
REF: ISBN 0-426-10372-6 OP: 30p p/b NM: £5.50

BTR-007c *Doctor Who en het Dodelijke Wapen* (Malcolm Hulke)
1974, Unieboek B V – Bussum, the Netherlands
Cover by Chris Achilleos (from *Doctor Who and the Doomsday Weapon*). Translated by Wim Hohage.
REF: ISBN 90-269-8107-4 OP: F 3,95 p/b NM: £5.50

BTR-007d *Doctor Who and the Doomsday Weapon* (Malcolm Hulke)
1975/03, Target/Universal-Tandem Publishing Co. Ltd, UK
Cover and illustrations by Chris Achilleos.
REF: ISBN 0-426-10372-6 OP: 30p p/b NM: £5.50

BTR-007e *Doktor Kim ve Gizli Silah* (Malcolm Hulke)
1975/06, Remzi Kitabevi, Turkey
Cover by Chris Achilleos (from *Doctor Who and the Doomsday Weapon*). Translated by Reha Pinar.
REF: No ISBN OP: 10 Lira p/b

BTR-007f *Doctor Who and the Doomsday Weapon* (Malcolm Hulke)
1976, Target/Universal-Tandem Publishing Co. Ltd, UK
Cover and illustrations by Chris Achilleos. 2nd impression. Block logo. Mauve spine.
REF: ISBN 0-426-10372-6 OP: 40p p/b NM: £5.50

BTR-006k

BTR-006o

BTR-006q

BTR-006x

BTR-006y

BTR-007a

BTR-007c

BTR-007e

BTR-007h

BTR-007i

BTR-007p

BTR-008a

BTR-008e

BTR-008i

BTR-007g *Doctor Who and the Doomsday Weapon* **(Malcolm Hulke)**
1979/08/16, Target/W. H. Allen & Co. Ltd, UK
Cover by Jeff Cummins. 2nd impression. Black curve logo. White spine. Colour decal. Wyndham W on back. Print run: 12,000 copies.
REF: ISBN 0-426-10372-6   OP: 70p p/b   NM: £5.50

BTR-007h *Doctor Who and the Doomsday Weapon* **(Malcolm Hulke)**
1979, Target/W. H. Allen & Co. Ltd, UK
"Second Impression." Cover by Jeff Cummins. Illustrated by Chris Achilleos. Black curve logo. White spine. Colour decal.
REF: ISBN 0-426-10372-6   OP: 85p p/b   NM: £5.50

BTR-007i *Doctor Who and the Doomsday Weapon #2* **(Malcolm Hulke)**
1979/04, Pinnacle Books, USA
Cover by David Mann. Orange logo.
REF: ISBN 0-523-40566-9   OP: $1.75 p/b   NM: £5.50

BTR-007j *Doctor Who and the Doomsday Weapon* **(Malcolm Hulke)**
1980, Target/W. H. Allen & Co. Ltd, UK
Print run: 15,000 copies. Some books packaged with 1979 interiors.
REF: ISBN 0-426-10372-6   OP: 85p p/b   NM: £5.50

BTR-007k *[Kowaru Beki Saishyuu Heiki!]* **(Malcolm Hulke)**
1980/07/15, Hayakawa Publishing Inc, Japan
Cover by Michiaki Sato. Translated by Yukio Sekiguchi. Title translates as 'The Frightening Ultimate Weapon' or '(Must) be Fearful of the Final (Ultimate) Weapon.'
REF: SF 398   OP: Y 340 p/b   NM: £110

BTR-007l *Doctor Who and the Doomsday Weapon #2* **(Malcolm Hulke)**
1981, Pinnacle Books, USA
Cover by David Mann. Green logo.
REF: ISBN 0-523-42005-6 OP: $1.95 p/b NM: £5.50

BTR-007m *Doctor Who and the Doomsday Weapon* **(Malcolm Hulke)**
1982, Target/W. H. Allen & Co. Ltd, UK
Cover by Jeff Cummins. Black curve logo. White spine.
Colour decal. Print run: 10,000 copies.
REF: ISBN 0-426-10372-6 OP: £1.35 p/b NM: £5.50

BTR-007n *Doctor Who and the Doomsday Weapon* **(Malcolm Hulke)**
1982/03/18, W. H. Allen & Co. Ltd, UK
Cover by Jeff Cummins. Purple neon logo. Print run: 2,500 copies.
REF: ISBN 0-491-02707-9 OP: £4.95 h/b NM: £11

BTR-007o *Doctor Who and the Doomsday Weapon* **(Malcolm Hulke)**
1983, Target/W. H. Allen & Co. Ltd, UK
Cover by Jeff Cummins. Illustrated by Chris Achilleos.
Black curve logo. White spine. Colour decal. Number 23.
REF: ISBN 0-426-10372-6 OP: £1.50 p/b NM: £5.50

BTR-007p *Doutor Who E A Arma Total* **(4)** **(Malcolm Hulke)**
1983, Editorial Presenca, Portugal
Cover by Shanti. Illustrations by Alan Willow. Translated by Eduardo Nogueira and Conceicao Jardim.
REF: No ISBN OP: p/b

BTR-007q *Doctor Who and the Doomsday Weapon #2* **(Malcolm Hulke)**
1989/01, Pinnacle Books, USA
Cover by David Mann. 'Sixth Printing'. Red logo.
REF: ISBN 1-55817-189-4 OP: $3.50 p/b NM: £7.95

BTR-008a *Doctor Who and the Dæmons* **(Barry Letts)**
1974/10/17, Target/Universal-Tandem Publishing Co. Ltd, UK
Cover by Chris Achilleos. Illustrated by Alan Willow. Block logo. Mauve spine. Colour decal.
REF: ISBN 0-426-10444-7 OP: 30p p/b NM: £5.50

BTR-008b *Doctor Who en de Demonen* **(Barry Letts)**
1974, Unieboek B V – Bussum, the Netherlands
Cover by Chris Achilleos (from *Doctor Who and the Dæmons*). Translated by Wim Hohage.
REF: ISBN 90 269 8109 0 OP: F 3,95 p/b NM: £5.50

BTR-008c *Doctor Who and the Dæmons* **(Barry Letts)**
1975, Target/Tandem Publishing Co. Ltd, UK
Cover by Chris Achilleos. Illustrated by Alan Willow. Block logo. Mauve spine. Two printings in 1975.
REF: ISBN 0-426-10444-7 OP: 40p p/b NM: £4.50

BTR-008d *Doctor Who and the Dæmons* **(Barry Letts)**
1976/01, Target/Universal-Tandem Publishing Co. Ltd, UK
Cover by Chris Achilleos. Illustrated by Alan Willow. Block logo. Mauve spine.
REF: ISBN 0-426-11332-2 OP: 40p p/b NM: £4.50

BTR-008e *Doctor Who and the Dæmons* **(Barry Letts)**
1980/01/24, Target/W. H. Allen & Co. Ltd, UK
Cover by Andrew Skilleter. '2nd impression'. Green curve logo. White spine. Print run: 12,000 copies. Copies also available with an 85p cover price.
REF: ISBN 0-426-11332-2 OP: 75p p/b NM: £4.50

BTR-008f *Doctor Who and the Dæmons* **(Barry Letts)**
1982, Target/W. H. Allen & Co. Ltd, UK
Cover by Andrew Skilleter. Illustrated by Alan Willow. Green curve logo. White spine. Colour decal. Two printings in 1982.
REF: ISBN 0-426-11332-2 OP: £1.50 p/b NM: £4.50

BTR-008g *Doctor Who Doctor Who and the Dæmons* **(Barry Letts)**
1982/01/14, W. H. Allen & Co. Ltd, UK
Cover by Andrew Skilleter. Red neon logo. The title does include the words 'Doctor Who' twice. Print run: 3,000 copies.
REF: ISBN 0-491-02687-0 OP: £4.95 h/b NM: £11

BTR-008h *Doctor Who and the Dæmons* **(Barry Letts)**
1983, Target/W. H. Allen & Co. Ltd, UK
Cover by Andrew Skilleter. Illustrated by Alan Willow. Green curve logo. White spine. Colour decal. Print run: 20,000 copies.
REF: ISBN 0-426-11332-2 OP: £1.50 p/b NM: £4.50

BTR-008i *Doutor Who E Os Demonios* **(3)** **(Barry Letts)**
1983, Editorial Presenca, Portugal
Cover by Rui Ligeiro. Illustrations by Alan Willow. Translated by Lucio Nogueira and Conceicao Jardim.
REF: No ISBN OP: p/b

BTR-008j *Doctor Who and the Dæmons*
1984, Target/W. H. Allen & Co. Ltd, UK
Cover by Andrew Skilleter. Illustrated by Alan Willow.
Green curve logo. White spine. Colour decal. Two
printings in 1984. Numbered 15 on the spine of the
second printing.
REF: ISBN 0-426-11332-2 OP: £1.50 p/b NM: £4.50

BTR-008k *Doctor Who – The Dæmons*
1993/10/21, Target/Virgin Publishing Ltd, UK
Cover by Alistair Pearson. Blue spine.
REF: ISBN 0-426-11332-2 OP: £3.50 p/b NM: £4.50

BTR-009a *Doctor Who and the Sea-Devils*
(Malcolm Hulke)
1974/10/17, Target/Universal-Tandem Publishing Co.
Ltd, UK
Cover by Chris Achilleos. Illustrated by Alan Willow.
Block logo. Green spine. Colour decal. Early title:
Doctor Who and the Sea Monsters.
REF: ISBN 0-426-10516-8 OP: 30p p/b NM: £5.95

BTR-009b *Doctor Who and the Sea-Devils*
(Malcolm Hulke)
1975, Target/Tandem Publishing Co. Ltd, UK
Cover by Chris Achilleos. Illustrated by Alan Willow.
'Second impression'. Block logo. Green spine. Colour
decal. Some copies have an interior ISBN 0-426-11308-X.
Two printings in 1975.
REF: ISBN 0-426-10516-8 OP: 40p p/b NM: £4.95

BTR-009c *Doctor Who and the Sea-Devils*
(Malcolm Hulke)
1976/01, Target/Universal-Tandem Publishing Co. Ltd, UK
Cover by Chris Achilleos. Illustrated by Alan Willow.
Block logo. Green spine.
REF: ISBN 0-426-11308-X OP: 40p p/b NM: £4.95

BTR-009d *Doctor Who and the Sea Devils*
(Malcolm Hulke)
1979/04/19, Target/W. H. Allen & Co. Ltd, UK
Cover by John Geary. 2nd impression. Green curve
logo. White spine. Print run: 12,000 copies.
REF: ISBN 0-426-11308-X OP: 60p p/b NM: £3.50

BTR-009e *Doctor Who and the Sea Devils*
(Malcolm Hulke)
1981/01/15, Target/W. H. Allen & Co. Ltd, UK
Cover by John Geary. Illustrations by Alan Willow.
Third impression. Green curve logo. White spine.
Dated 1980 on the inside. Print run: 15,000 copies.
REF: ISBN 0-426-11308-X OP: 90p p/b NM: £3.50

BTR-009f *Doctor Who and the Sea Devils*
(Malcolm Hulke)
1981/06/18, W. H. Allen & Co. Ltd, UK
Cover by John Geary. Print run: 3,000 copies.
REF: ISBN 0-491-02954-3 OP: £4.25 h/b NM: £11

BTR-009g *Doctor Who and the Sea Devils*
(Malcolm Hulke)
1982, Target/W. H. Allen & Co. Ltd, UK
Cover by John Geary. Illustrated by Alan Willow.
Green curve logo. White spine. Colour decal.
REF: ISBN 0-426-11308-X OP: £1.35 p/b NM: £3.50

BTR-009h *Doutor Who E Os Demonios*
Marinhos (5) **(Malcolm Hulke)**
1983, Editorial Presenca, Portugal
Cover by Rui Ligeiro. Illustrations by Alan Willow.
Translated by Lucio Nogueira and Conceicao Jardim.
REF: No ISBN OP: p/b

BTR-009i *Doctor Who and the Sea Devils*
(Malcolm Hulke)
1984, Target/W. H. Allen & Co. Ltd, UK
Cover by John Geary. Illustrated by Alan Willow.
Green curve logo. White spine. Colour decal.
Number 54.
REF: ISBN 0-426-11308-X OP: £1.35 p/b NM: £3.50

BTR-009j *Doctor Who and the Sea Devils*
(Malcolm Hulke)
1984, Target/W. H. Allen & Co. Ltd, UK
Cover by John Geary. Green curve logo. White spine.
Outline decal. Book numbered '54' on spine. 1987
reprint run: 4,000 copies.
REF: ISBN 0-426-11308-X OP: £1.95 p/b NM: £3.50

BTR-010a *Doctor Who and the Abominable*
Snowmen **(Terrance Dicks)**
1974/11/21, Target/Universal-Tandem Publishing, UK
Cover by Chris Achilleos. Illustrated by Alan Willow.
Block logo. Light blue spine. Colour decal. Early title:
Doctor Who and the Yeti.
REF: ISBN 0-426-10583-4 OP: 30p p/b NM: £8.95

BTR-010b *Doktor Kim ve Korkunc Karadamlari*
(Terrance Dicks)
1975, Remzi Kitabevi, Turkey
Cover by Chris Achilleos (from *Doctor Who and the
Abominable Snowmen*). Translated by Reha Pinar.
REF: No ISBN OP: 10 Lira p/b

BTR-010c *Doctor Who and the Abominable*
Snowmen **(Terrance Dicks)**
1976/03, Target/Tandem Publishing Co. Ltd, UK
Cover by Chris Achilleos. Illustrated by Alan Willow.

Light blue spine. Block logo. Colour decal.
REF: ISBN 0-426-11455-8 OP: 40p p/b NM: £7.95

BTR-010d *Doctor Who and the Abominable
Snowmen* (**Terrance Dicks**)
1978/03/30, Target/W H Allen & Co Ltd, UK
"Second Impression." Cover by Chris Achilleos.
Illustrated by Alan Willow. Blue curve logo. White
spine. Colour decal. Print run: 10,000 copies.
REF: ISBN 0-426-11455-8 OP: 60p p/b NM: £7.95

BTR-010e *Doctor Who and the Abominable
Snowmen* (**Terrance Dicks**)
1979, Target/W H Allen & Co Ltd, UK
Cover by Chris Achilleos. Illustrated by Alan Willow.
'Third impression'. Blue curve logo. White spine.
Colour decal. Wyndham W on back. Print run: 12,000
copies.
REF: ISBN 0-426-11455-8 OP: 70p p/b NM: £7.95

BTR-010f *Doctor Who and the Abominable
Snowmen* (**Terrance Dicks**)
1982, Target/W H Allen & Co Ltd, UK
Cover by Chris Achilleos. Illustrated by Alan Willow.
Blue curve logo. White spine. Colour decal.
REF: ISBN 0-426-11455-8 OP: £1.35 p/b NM: £7.95

BTR-010g *Doctor Who and the Abominable
Snowmen* (**Terrance Dicks**)
1983, Target/W H Allen & Co Ltd, UK
Cover by Andrew Skilleter. Illustrated by Alan Willow.
Orange neon logo. Blue spine. Colour decal. No ISBN
on cover, inside ISBN: 0-426-01583-4.
REF: No ISBN OP: £1.35 p/b NM: £6.50

BTR-008k

BTR-009a

BTR-009d

BTR-009h

BTR-010a

BTR-010b

BTR-010g

BTR-010h

BTR-010k

BTR-011a

BTR-11f

BTR-011j

BTR-012a

BTR-012g

BTR-010h *Doutor Who E Os Abominaveis Homens Das Neves (9)* **(Terrance Dicks)**
1983, Editorial Presenca, Portugal
Cover by Rui Ligeiro. Illustrations as for Target edition. No translator given.
REF: No ISBN OP: p/b

BTR-010i *Doctor Who and the Abominable Snowmen* **(Terrance Dicks)**
1984, Target/W. H. Allen & Co. Ltd, UK
Cover by Andrew Skilleter. Orange neon logo. Blue spine.
REF: ISBN 0-426-10583-4 OP: £1.35 p/b NM: £6.50

BTR-010j *Doctor Who and the Abominable Snowmen* **(Terrance Dicks)**
1985/01/17, W. H. Allen & Co. PLC, UK
Cover by Andrew Skilleter.
REF: ISBN 0-491-03660-4 OP: £5.95 h/b NM: £13.20

BTR-010k *Docteur Who: L'Abominable Homme des Neiges (7)* **(Terrance Dicks)**
1987/08/20, Editions Garanciere, France
Artwork cover. Translated by Corine Derblum.
REF: ISBN 2-7340-0226-4 OP: p/b

BTR-011a *Doctor Who and the Curse of Peladon* **(Brian Hayles)**
1975/01, Target/Universal-Tandem Publishing Co. Ltd, UK
Cover by Chris Achilleos. Illustrated by Alan Willow.
Block logo. Brown spine. Colour decal. Says
'1974' inside.
REF: ISBN 0-426-10452-8 OP: 30p p/b NM: £5.50

BTR-011b *Doktor Kim ve Peledon Gezegeni* **(Brian Hayles)**
1975, Remzi Kitbevi, Turkey
Cover by Chris Achilleos (from *Doctor Who and the Curse of Peladon*). Translated by Reha Pinar. Scheduled but never actually printed?
REF: No ISBN OP: 10 Lira p/b

BTR-011c *Doctor Who and the Curse of Peladon* **(Brian Hayles)**
1976/03, Target/Tandem Publishing Co. Ltd, UK
Cover by Chris Achilleos. Illustrated by Alan Willow.
Block logo. Brown spine. Colour decal.
REF: ISBN 0-426-11498-1 OP: 40p p/b NM: £4.50

BTR-011d *Doctor Who and the Curse of Peladon* **(Brian Hayles)**
1977, Target/Tandem Publishing Co. Ltd, UK
Cover by Chris Achilleos. Illustrated by Alan Willow.
Block logo. Brown spine.
REF: ISBN 0-426-11498-1 OP: 40p p/b NM: £4.50

BTR-011e *Doctor Who and the Curse of Peladon* **(Brian Hayles)**
1979/07, Target/Tandem Publishing Co. Ltd, UK
Cover by Chris Achilleos. Illustrated by Alan Willow. '3rd impression'. Outline curve logo. Brown spine. Colour decal. Print run: 12,000 copies.
REF: ISBN 0-426-20061-6 OP: 70p p/b NM: £4.50

BTR-011f *Doctor Who and the Curse of Peladon* **(Brian Hayles)**
1980/07/17, W. H. Allen & Co. Ltd, UK
Cover by Bill Donohoe. Green curve logo. Print run: 3,000 copies.
REF: ISBN 0-491-02783-4 OP: £3.95 h/b NM: £22

BTR-011g *Doctor Who and the Curse of Peladon* **(Brian Hayles)**
1980/07/17, Target/W H Allen & Co. Ltd, UK
Cover by Chris Achilleos. Brown curve logo. Brown spine. Two printings in 1980, 12,000 copies each.
REF: ISBN 0-426-20061-6 OP: 75p p/b NM: £4.50

BTR-011h *Doctor Who and the Curse of Peladon* **(Brian Hayles)**
1982, Target/Universal-Tandem Publishing Co. Ltd, UK
Cover by Chris Achilleos. Brown curve logo. Brown spine. Colour decal. Illustrated by Alan Willow. Print run: 6,000 copies. Interior ISBN: 0-426-11498-1. Copies are known to exist with stickers on cover listing the interior ISBN and a price of $2.50. Since this is obviously a modification introduced in the US to resolve the ISBN conflict, there may be other Target books featuring two different ISBNs with similar stickers.
REF: ISBN 0-426-20061-6 OP: £1.50 p/b NM: £3.50

BTR-011i *Doctor Who and the Curse of Peladon* **(Brian Hayles)**
1984, Target/W H Allen & Co. Ltd, UK
Cover by Chris Achilleos. Illustrated by Alan Willow. Brown curve logo. Brown spine. Colour decal.
REF: ISBN 0-426-11498-1 OP: £1.35 p/b NM: £3.50

BTR-011j *Doctor Who – The Curse of Peladon* **(Brian Hayles)**
1992/06/18, Target/Virgin Publishing Ltd, UK
Cover by Alistair Pearson. Blue spine.
REF: ISBN 0-426-11498-1 OP: £2.99 p/b NM: £3.95

BTR-012a *Doctor Who and the Cybermen* **(Gerry Davis)**
1975/02/20, Target/Universal-Tandem Publishing Co. Ltd, UK
Cover by Chris Achilleos. Illustrated by Alan Willow. Block logo. Black spine. Colour decal. Novelisation of

The Moonbase. Dated 1974 on the inside.
REF: ISBN 0-426-10575-3 OP: 35p p/b NM: £5.50

BTR-012b *Doktor Kim ve Sibermenler* **(Gerry Davis)**
1975, Remzi Kitabevi, Turkey
Cover by Chris Achilleos (from *Doctor Who and the Cybermen*). Translated by Reha Pinar.
REF: No ISBN OP: 10 Lira p/b

BTR-012c *Doctor Who and the Cybermen* **(Gerry Davis)**
1976/03, Target/Tandem Publishing Co. Ltd, UK
Cover by Chris Achilleos. Block logo. Black spine. Colour decal.
REF: ISBN 0-426-11463-9 OP: 40p p/b NM: £4.50

BTR-012d *Doctor Who and the Cybermen* **(Gerry Davis)**
1978/08/17, Target/W. H. Allen & Co. Ltd, UK
Cover by Chris Achilleos. '2nd Impression'. Red curve logo. White spine. Colour decal. Print run: 10,000 copies.
REF: ISBN 0-426-10575-3 OP: 60p p/b NM: £4.50

BTR-012e *Doctor Who and the Cybermen* **(Gerry Davis)**
1979/08/16, Target/W. H. Allen & Co. Ltd, UK
Cover by Chris Achilleos. 3rd impression. Red curve logo. White spine. Print run: 12,000 copies.
REF: ISBN 0-426-10575-3 OP: 70p p/b NM: £4.50

BTR-012f *Doctor Who and the Cybermen* **(Gerry Davis)**
1980, Target/W. H. Allen & Co. Ltd, UK
Cover by Chris Achilleos. Illustrated by Alan Willow. 4th impression. Red curve logo. White spine. Colour decal.
REF: ISBN 0-426-10575-3 OP: 85p p/b NM: £4.50

BTR-012g *Doctor Who and the Cybermen* **(Gerry Davis)**
1981, Target/W. H. Allen & Co. Ltd, UK
Cover by Bill Donohoe. Illustrated by Alan Willow. Red neon logo. Red spine. Colour decal.
REF: ISBN 0-426-11463-9 OP: 95p p/b NM: £3.50

BTR-012h *Doctor Who and the Cybermen* **(Gerry Davis)**
1981/07/16, W. H. Allen & Co. Ltd, UK
Cover by Bill Donohoe. Red neon logo. Print run: 3,000 copies.
REF: ISBN 0-491-02915-2 OP: £4.50 h/b NM: £13.20

BTR-012i *Doctor Who and the Cybermen*
(Gerry Davis)
1982, Target/W. H. Allen & Co. Ltd, UK
Cover by Bill Donohoe. Red spine. Red neon logo.
Colour Decal. Print run: 15,000 copies.
REF: ISBN 0-426-11463-9 OP: 95p p/b NM: £3.50

BTR-012j *Doctor Who and the Cybermen*
(Gerry Davis)
1982, Target/W. H. Allen & Co. Ltd, UK
Cover by Bill Donohoe. Illustrated by Alan Willow.
Red spine. Red neon logo. Colour decal.
REF: ISBN 0-426-11463-9 OP: £1.50 p/b NM: £3.50

BTR-012k *Doctor Who and the Cybermen*
(Gerry Davis)
1984, Target/W. H. Allen & Co. Ltd, UK
Cover by Bill Donohoe. Red spine. Red neon logo.
Outline decal. Number 14 on the spine. Book reprint-
ed twice in 1984. Print run: 20,000 copies.
REF: ISBN 0-426-11463-9 OP: £1.50 p/b NM: £3.50

BTR-013a *Doctor Who and the Giant Robot*
(Terrance Dicks)
1975/03/13, Target/Universal-Tandem Publishing Co.
Ltd, UK
Cover by Peter Brookes. Red curve logo. White spine.
Colour decal. Art on back cover. Art of Tom Baker's
head within the 'O' of 'WHO' on the front cover.
Novelisation of *Robot*.
REF: ISBN 0-426-10858-2 OP: 35p p/b NM: £5.95

BTR-013b *Doctor Who and the Giant Robot*
(Terrance Dicks)
1975, Target/Tandem Publishing Co. Ltd, UK
Cover by Peter Brookes. Red curve logo. White spine.
Colour decal. Art on back cover. "Reprinted Autumn
1975" inside.
REF: ISBN 0-426-11279-2 OP: 40p p/b NM: £5.95

BTR-013c *Doctor Who and the Giant Robot*
(Terrance Dicks)
1976/01, Target/Universal-Tandem Publishing Co. Ltd, UK
Cover by Peter Brookes. Red curve logo. White spine.
Colour decal.
REF: ISBN 0-426-11279-2 OP: 40p p/b NM: £4.95

BTR-013d *Doctor Who and the Giant Robot*
(Terrance Dicks)
1979/04/19, Target/W. H. Allen & Co. Ltd, UK
Cover by Jeff Cummins. Blue curve logo. White spine.
Colour decal.
REF: ISBN 0-426-11279-2 OP: 60p p/b NM: £3.95

BTR-013e *Doctor Who and the Giant Robot*
(Terrance Dicks)
1979, Target/W. H. Allen & Co. Ltd, UK
"Second Impression." Cover by Jeff Cummins. Blue
curve logo. White spine. Colour decal.
REF: ISBN 0-426-11279-2 OP: 70p p/b NM: £3.95

BTR-013f *Doctor Who and the Giant Robot*
(Terrance Dicks)
1980/06, Amereon/Aeonian, USA
No slip-cover. Limited edition of 300 copies. Date inside
book is 1978. 1980 date from Barnes and Noble online.
REF: ISBN 0-8488-0153-9 OP: $17.95 h/b

BTR-013g *Doctor Who and the Giant Robot*
(Terrance Dicks)
1980/07/17, Target/W. H. Allen & Co. Ltd, UK
"Third Impression." Cover by Jeff Cummins. Blue
curve logo. White spine. Colour decal.
REF: ISBN 0-426-11279-2 OP: 85p p/b NM: £3.95

BTR-013h *Doctor Who and the Giant Robot*
(Terrance Dicks)
1981, Target/W. H. Allen & Co. Ltd, UK
Cover by Jeff Cummins. 'Fourth Impression'. Blue
curve logo. White spine. Colour decal.
REF: ISBN 0-426-11279-2 OP: 95p p/b NM: £3.95

BTR-013i *Doctor Who and the Giant Robot*
(Terrance Dicks)
1982, Target/W. H. Allen & Co. Ltd, UK
Cover by Jeff Cummins. Blue curve logo. White spine.
Colour decal.
REF: ISBN 0-426-11279-2 OP: £1.25 p/b NM: £3.95

BTR-013j *Doctor Who and the Giant Robot*
(Terrance Dicks)
1984, Target/W. H. Allen & Co. Ltd, UK
Cover by Jeff Cummins. Blue curve logo. White spine.
Colour decal. Number on spine.
REF: ISBN 0-426-11279-2 OP: £1.35 p/b NM: £3.95

BTR-013k *Doctor Who and the Giant Robot*
(Terrance Dicks)
1986/04/17, W. H. Allen & Co. PLC, UK
Cover by Jeff Cummins. Red neon logo. Print run:
3,000 copies.
REF: ISBN 0-491-03663-9 OP: £6.95 h/b NM: £11

BTR-013l *Doctor Who and the Giant Robot*
(Terrance Dicks)
1988, Target/W. H. Allen & Co. Ltd, UK
Cover by Jeff Cummins. Blue curve logo. White spine.
Outline decal. Number on spine. Print run: 10,000 copies.
REF: ISBN 0-426-11279-2 OP: £1.95 p/b NM: £3.95

BTR-013m *Doctor Who – Robot* **(Terrance Dicks)**
1992/05/21, Target/Virgin Publishing Ltd, UK
Cover by Alistair Pearson. Blue spine.
REF: ISBN 0-426-20371-2 OP: £2.99 p/b NM: £4.50

BTR-014a *Doctor Who and the Terror of the Autons* **(Terrance Dicks)**
1975/05/15, Target/Universal-Tandem Publishing, UK
Cover by Peter Brookes. Illustrated by Alan Willow.
Blue curve logo. White spine. Colour decal. Art on
back cover.
REF: ISBN 0-426-10639-3 OP: 35p p/b NM: £5.50

BTR-014b *Doctor Who and the Terror of the Autons* **(Terrance Dicks)**
1976/03, Target/Tandem Publishing Co. Ltd, UK
Cover by Peter Brookes. Illustrated by Alan Willow.
Blue curve logo. White spine. Colour decal.
REF: ISBN 0-426-11500-7 OP: 40p p/b NM: £4.50

BTR-014c *Doctor Who and the Terror of the Autons* **(Terrance Dicks)**
1977/03/24, Target/Universal-Tandem Publishing, UK
Cover by Peter Brookes. Illustrated by Alan Willow.
REF: ISBN 0-426-10639-3 OP: 40p p/b NM: £4.50

BTR-014d *Doctor Who and the Terror of the Autons* **(Terrance Dicks)**
1979/03/29, Target/W. H. Allen & Co Ltd, UK
Cover by Peter Brookes. Illustrated by Alan Willow.
Blue curve logo. White spine. Print run: 12,000 copies.
Priced as 60p in contemporary Target catalogue.
REF: ISBN 0-426-11500-7 OP: 40p p/b NM: £4.50

BTR-014e *Doctor Who and the Terror of the Autons* **(Terrance Dicks)**
1979, Target/W. H. Allen & Co Ltd, UK
"Second Impression." Cover by Alun Hood. Orange
curve logo. White spine. Colour decal.
REF: ISBN 0-426-11500-7 OP: 60p p/b NM: £3.50

BTR-014f *Doctor Who and the Terror of the Autons* **(Terrance Dicks)**
1980, Target/W. H. Allen & Co. Ltd, UK
Cover by Alun Hood. Orange curve logo. White spine.
Print run: 12,000 copies.
REF: ISBN 0-426-11500-7 OP: 60p p/b NM: £3.50

BTR-014g *Doctor Who and the Terror of the Autons* **(Terrance Dicks)**
1981/02/19, W. H. Allen & Co. Ltd, UK
Cover by Alun Hood. Print run: 2,500 copies.
REF: ISBN 0-491-02864-4 OP: £4.25 h/b NM: £11

BTR-013a BTR-013d

BTR-013m

BTR-014a BTR-014e

BTR-015a

BTR-015d

BTR-016a

BTR016d

BTR-016i

BTR-017b

BTR-014h *Doctor Who and the Terror of the Autons* **(Terrance Dicks)**
1982, Target/W. H. Allen & Co. Ltd, UK
Cover by Alun Hood. Illustrated by Alan Willow.
Yellow curve logo. White spine. Colour decal.
REF: ISBN 0-426-11500-7 OP: £1.25 p/b NM: £3.50

BTR-014i *Doctor Who and the Terror of the Autons* **(Terrance Dicks)**
1984, Target/W. H. Allen & Co. Ltd, UK
Cover by Alun Hood. Orange curve logo. White spine.
Colour decal. Number 63.
REF: ISBN 0-426-11500-7 OP: £1.35 p/b NM: £3.50

BTR-014j *Doctor Who and the Terror of the Autons* **(Terrance Dicks)**
1984, Target/W. H. Allen & Co. Ltd, UK
Cover by Alun Hood. Illustrated by Alan Willow.
Orange curve logo. White spine. Outline decal. 1987
reprint run: 5,000 copies.
REF: ISBN 0-426-11500-7 OP: £1.95 p/b NM: £3.50

BTR-015a *Doctor Who and the Green Death* **(Malcolm Hulke)**
1975/08/21, Target/Tandem Publishing Ltd, UK
Cover by Peter Brookes. Illustrated by Alan Willow.
Green curve logo. White spine. Colour decal.
REF: ISBN 0-426-10647-4 OP: 35p p/b NM: £5.95

BTR-015b *Doctor Who and the Green Death* **(Malcolm Hulke)**
1976/04, Target/Tandem Publishing Ltd, UK
Cover by Peter Brookes. Illustrated by Alan Willow.
Green curve logo. White spine. Colour decal. Art on
back cover.
REF: ISBN 0-426-11543-0 OP: 40p p/b NM: £4.95

BTR-015c *Doctor Who and the Green Death* **(Malcolm Hulke)**
1977/03/24, Target/Tandem Publishing Ltd, UK
REF: ISBN 0-426-11543-0 OP: 40p p/b NM: £4.95

BTR-015d *Doctor Who and the Green Death* **(Malcolm Hulke)**
1979/03/29, Target/W. H. Allen & Co. Ltd, UK
Cover by Alun Hood. Illustrated by Alan Willow. 2nd
impression. Green curve logo. Colour decal. White
spine. Print run: 12,000 copies.
REF: ISBN 0-426-11543-0 OP: 60p p/b NM: £3.50

BTR-015e *Doctor Who and the Green Death* **(Malcolm Hulke)**
1980/04/24, Target/W. H. Allen & Co. Ltd, UK
Print run: 12,000 copies
REF: ISBN 0-426-11543-0 OP: p/b NM: £3.50

BTR-015f *Doctor Who and the Green Death*
(Malcolm Hulke)
1981/04/16, W. H. Allen & Co. Ltd, UK
Cover by Alun Hood. Print run: 2,750 copies.
REF: ISBN 0-491-02874-1 OP: £4.25 h/b NM: £11

BTR-015g *Doctor Who and the Green Death*
(Malcolm Hulke)
1982, Target/W. H. Allen & Co. Ltd, UK
Print run: 20,000 copies.
REF: ISBN 0-426-11543-0 OP: £1.50 p/b NM: £3.50

BTR-015h *Doctor Who and the Green Death*
(Malcolm Hulke)
1983, Target/W. H. Allen & Co. Ltd, UK
Cover by Alun Hood. Illustrated by Alan Willow.
Green curve logo. White spine. Colour decal. Also
packaged with 1982 internal pages.
REF: ISBN 0-426-11543-0 OP: £1.35 p/b NM: £3.50

BTR-015i *Doctor Who and the Green Death*
(Malcolm Hulke)
1985, Target/W. H. Allen & Co. PLC., UK
Cover by Alun Hood. Illustrated by Alan Willow.
Green curve logo. White spine. Outline decal.
REF: ISBN 0-426-11543-0 OP: £1.50 p/b NM: £3.50

BTR-016a *Doctor Who and the Planet of the
Spiders* **(Terrance Dicks)**
1975/10/16, Target/Tandem Publishing Ltd, UK
Cover by Peter Brookes. Orange curve logo. White
spine. Colour decal. Art on back cover.
REF: ISBN 0-426-10655-5 OP: 35p p/b NM: £6.50

BTR-016b *Doctor Who and the Planet of the
Spiders* **(Terrance Dicks)**
1975/11/20, Allan Wingate (Publishers) Ltd, UK
Cover by Peter Brookes.
REF: ISBN 0-85523-052-5 OP: £2.25 h/b NM: £27.50

BTR-016c *Doctor Who and the Planet of the
Spiders* **(Terrance Dicks)**
1977, Allan Wingate (Publishers) Ltd, UK
Cover by Peter Brookes. 'Second Impression'. Print
run: 1,500 copies.
REF: ISBN 0-85523-052-5 OP: h/b NM: £5.50

BTR-016d *Doctor Who and the Planet of the
Spiders* **(Terrance Dicks)**
1978/09/28, Target/Tandem Publishing Ltd, UK
Cover by Alun Hood. Blue curve logo. White spine.
Print run: 10,000 copies.
REF: ISBN 0-426-10655-5 OP: 60p p/b NM: £4.50

BTR-016e *Doctor Who and the Planet of the
Spiders* **(Terrance Dicks)**
1979, Target/W. H. Allen & Co. Ltd, UK
Cover by Alun Hood. 'Third Impression'. Blue curve
logo. White spine. Colour decal. Wyndham W on back.
Print run: 12,000 copies.
REF: ISBN 0-426-10655-5 OP: 70p p/b NM: £4.50

BTR-016f *Doctor Who and the Planet of the
Spiders* **(Terrance Dicks)**
1980, Target/Tandem Publishing Ltd, UK
Cover by Alun Hood. Blue curve logo. White spine.
Colour decal. Print run: 15,000 copies.
REF: ISBN 0-426-10655-5 OP: 85p p/b NM: £4.50

BTR-016g *Doctor Who and the Planet of the
Spiders* **(Terrance Dicks)**
1982, Target/Tandem Publishing Ltd, UK
OP: p/b NM: £4.50

BTR-016h *Doctor Who and the Planet of the
Spiders* **(Terrance Dicks)**
1984, Target/Tandem Publishing Ltd, UK
Cover by Alun Hood. Blue curve logo. White spine.
Colour decal.
REF: ISBN 0-426-10655-5 OP: £1.35 p/b NM: £4.50

BTR-016i *Doctor Who – Planet of the Spiders*
(Terrance Dicks)
1991/08/22, Target/Virgin Publishing Ltd, UK
Cover by Alistair Pearson. Blue spine. Print run: 9,000
copies.
REF: ISBN 0-426-10655-5 OP: £2.50 p/b NM: £5.50

BTR-017a *Doctor Who – The Three Doctors*
(Terrance Dicks)
1975, Allan Wingate (Publishers) Ltd, UK
Cover by Chris Achilleos.
REF: ISBN 85523-053-3 OP: £2.25 h/b NM: £27.50

BTR-017b *Doctor Who – The Three Doctors*
(Terrance Dicks)
1975/11/20, Target/Tandem Publishing Ltd, UK
Cover by Chris Achilleos. Black curve logo. White
spine. Colour decal. Art on back cover. Another version was released in 1976 with a price of 40p.
REF: ISBN 0-426-10938-4 OP: 35p p/b NM: £6.50

BTR-017c *Doctor Who – The Three Doctors*
(Terrance Dicks)
1976, Target/Tandem Publishing Ltd, UK
Cover by Jeff Cummins. 'Second Impression'. Retitled
Doctor Who and the Three Doctors on the cover only.
Red curve logo. White spine. Colour decal. Wyndham
W on back.
REF: ISBN 0-426-11578-3 OP: 60p p/b NM: £5.50

BTR-017d *Doctor Who – The Three Doctors*
(Terrance Dicks)
1977, Allan Wingate (Publishers) Ltd, UK
Cover by Chris Achilleos. Print run: 1,500 copies.
REF: ISBN 85523-053-3 OP: h/b NM: £16.50

BTR-017e *Doctor Who – The Three Doctors*
(Terrance Dicks)
1978/04/20, Target/W H Allen & Co Ltd, UK
Cover by Jeff Cummins. Red curve logo. White spine.
Print run: 14,500 copies. Some copies packaged with
1976 interiors.
REF: ISBN 0-426-11578-3 OP: 60p p/b NM: £4.50

BTR-017f *Doctor Who – The Three Doctors*
(Terrance Dicks)
1979/10/25, Target/W H Allen & Co Ltd, UK
Print run: 12,000 copies. Copies also available with a
75p price.
REF: ISBN 0-426-11578-3 OP: 60p p/b NM: £4.50

BTR-017g *Doctor Who – The Three Doctors*
(Terrance Dicks)
1980, Target/W H Allen & Co Ltd, UK
OP: 85p p/b NM: £4.50

BTR-017h *Doctor Who – The Three Doctors*
(Terrance Dicks)
1982, Target/W H Allen & Co Ltd, UK
Cover by Jeff Cummins. Retitled *Doctor Who and the
Three Doctors* on the cover only. Red curve logo.
White spine. Colour decal.
REF: ISBN 0-426-11578-3 OP: £1.35 p/b NM: £4.50

BTR-017i *Doctor Who – The Three Doctors*
(Terrance Dicks)
1983, Target/W H Allen & Co Ltd, UK
Cover by Jeff Cummins. Red curve logo. Colour decal.
REF: ISBN 0-426-11578-3 OP: £1.35 p/b NM: £4.50

BTR-017j *Doctor Who – The Three Doctors*
(Terrance Dicks)
1984, Target/W H Allen & Co Ltd, UK
Cover by Jeff Cummins. Red curve logo. White spine.
Outline decal. Print run: 6,000 copies.
REF: ISBN 0-426-11578-3 OP: £1.50 p/b NM: £4.50

BTR-017k *Doctor Who – The Three Doctors*
(Terrance Dicks)
1991/08/22, Target/Virgin Publishing Ltd, UK
Cover by Alistair Pearson. Blue spine. Print run: 9,000
copies.
REF: ISBN 0-426-11578-3 OP: £2.50 p/b NM: £5.50

BTR-017l *Doctor Who – Wladcy Czasu*
(Terrance Dicks)
1994, Oficyna Wydawnicza "Empire", Poland
Translator: Juliusz Garztecki
REF: ISBN 83-86126-01-9

BTR-018a *Doctor Who and the Loch Ness
Monster* **(Terrance Dicks)**
1976/01/15, Allan Wingate (Publishers) Ltd, UK
Cover by Chris Achilleos. Print run: 3,000 copies.
Novelisation of *Terror of the Zygons*.
REF: ISBN 0-85523-054-1 OP: £2.25 h/b NM: £27.50

BTR-018b *Doctor Who and the Loch Ness
Monster* **(Terrance Dicks)**
1976/01/15, Target/Tandem Publishing Ltd, UK
Cover by Chris Achilleos. Blue curve logo. White
spine. Colour decal. Two printings in 1976.
REF: ISBN 0-426-11041-2 OP: 40p p/b NM: £4.50

BTR-018c *Doctor Who and the Loch Ness
Monster* **(Terrance Dicks)**
1976, Target/Tandem Publishing Ltd, UK
Cover by Chris Achilleos. Blue curve logo. White
spine. Colour decal. Wyndham W on back.
REF: ISBN 0-426-11041-2 OP: 50p p/b NM: £3.50

BTR-018d *Doctor Who and the Loch Ness
Monster* **(Terrance Dicks)**
1977, Allan Wingate (Publishers) Ltd, UK
Cover by Chris Achilleos. Print run: 1,500 copies.
REF: ISBN 0-85523-054-1 OP: £2.95 h/b NM: £13.20

BTR-018e *Doctor Who and the Loch Ness
Monster* **(Terrance Dicks)**
1978/08/17, Target/Tandem Publishing Ltd, UK
Cover by Chris Achilleos. 2nd impression. Green
curve logo. White spine. Two editions in 1978. First
Print run: 3,000 copies; second print run: 10,000
copies. Copies of this 1978 edition exist with 'Fourth
Impression' inside and a cost of 60p.
REF: ISBN 0-426-11041-2 OP: 75p p/b NM: £3.50

BTR-018f *Doctor Who and the Loch Ness
Monster* **(Terrance Dicks)**
1979/11/20, Target/Tandem Publishing Ltd, UK
Print run: 12,000 copies.
REF: ISBN 0-426-11041-2 OP: 75p p/b NM: £3.50

BTR-018g *Doctor Who and the Loch Ness
Monster #6* **(Terrance Dicks)**
1979/06, Pinnacle Books, USA
Cover by David Mann. Orange logo.
REF: ISBN 0-523-40609-6 OP: $1.75 p/b NM: £5.50

BTR-018h *Doctor Who and the Loch Ness Monster* (Terrance Dicks)
1980, Target/Tandem Publishing Ltd, UK
Print run: 15,000 copies.
REF: ISBN 0-426-11041-2 OP: 85p p/b NM: £3.50

BTR-018i *Doctor Who and the Loch Ness Monster #6* (Terrance Dicks)
1981, Pinnacle Books, USA
Cover by David Mann. Blue logo.
REF: ISBN 0-523-41791-8 OP: $1.95 p/b NM: £5.50

BTR-018j *Doctor Who and the Loch Ness Monster* (Terrance Dicks)
1982, Target/Tandem Publishing Ltd, UK
Cover by Chris Achilleos. Lime green curve logo.
White spine. Colour decal. Print run: 15,000 copies.
REF: ISBN 0-426-11041-2 OP: £1.25 p/b NM: £3.50

BTR-017e

BTR-017k

BTR-018k *Doctor Who and the Loch Ness Monster* (Terrance Dicks)
1983, Target/Tandem Publishing Ltd, UK
Print run: 20,000 copies.
REF: ISBN 0-426-11041-2 OP: p/b NM: £3.50

BTR-018l *Doctor Who and the Loch Ness Monster* (Terrance Dicks)
1986, Target/Tandem Publishing Ltd, UK
Cover by Chris Achilleos. Green curve logo. Outline decal. Print run: 10,000 copies.
REF: ISBN 0-426-11041-2 OP: £1.60 p/b NM: £3.50

BTR-017l

BTR-018b

BTR-018m *Doctor Who and the Loch Ness Monster #6* (Terrance Dicks)
1989/01, Pinnacle Books, USA
Cover by David Mann. 'Seventh printing'. Yellow/tan logo.
REF: 1-55817-193-2 OP: $3.50 p/b NM: £7.95

BTR-018n *Doctor Who – Terror of the Zygons* (Terrance Dicks)
1993/03/18, Target/Virgin Publishing Ltd, UK
Cover by Alistair Pearson (cover marked Pearson's 75th *Doctor Who* commission). Blue spine. Interior ISBN 0-426-11041-2.
REF: ISBN 0-426-20391-7 OP: £3.50 p/b NM: £5.50

BTR-019a *Doctor Who and the Dinosaur Invasion* (Malcolm Hulke)
1976/02/19, Allan Wingate (Publishers) Ltd, UK
Cover by Chris Achilleos. Print run: 3,000 copies.
Novelisation of *Invasion of the Dinosaurs*.
REF: ISBN 0-85523-061-4 OP: £2.25 h/b NM: £27.50

BTR-018g

BTR-018n

BTR-019b   BTR-019d

BTR-019e   BTR-019m

BTR-020b

BTR-019b *Doctor Who and the Dinosaur Invasion* **(Malcolm Hulke)**
1976/02/19, Target/Tandem Publishing Ltd, UK
Cover by Chris Achilleos. Orange curve logo. White
spine. Colour decal.
REF: ISBN 0-426-10874-4 OP: 40p p/b NM: £6.50

BTR-019c *Doctor Who and the Dinosaur Invasion* **(Malcolm Hulke)**
1977, Allan Wingate (Publishers) Ltd, UK
Cover by Chris Achilleos. Print run: 1,500 copies.
REF: ISBN 0-85523-061-4 OP: h/b NM: £16.50

BTR-019d *Doctor Who and the Dinosaur Invasion* **(Malcolm Hulke)**
1978/06/29, Target/W H Allen & Co Ltd, UK
"Second Impression." Cover by Jeff Cummins. Red
curve logo. White spine. Wyndham W on back. Print
run: 25,000 copies.
REF: ISBN 0-426-10874-4 OP: 60p p/b NM: £2.75

BTR-019e *Doctor Who and the Dinosaur Invasion #3* **(Malcolm Hulke)**
1979/05, Pinnacle Books, USA
Cover by David Mann. Blue logo.
REF: ISBN 0-523-40606-1 OP: $1.75 p/b NM: £5.50

BTR-019f *Doctor Who and the Dinosaur Invasion* **(Malcolm Hulke)**
1979/12/13, Target/W H Allen & Co Ltd, UK
Cover by Jeff Cummins. Red curve logo. White spine.
Colour decal. Print run: 12,000 copies. 'Third impression'.
REF: ISBN 0-426-10874-4 OP: 75p p/b NM: £2.75

BTR-019g *Doctor Who and the Dinosaur Invasion #3* **(Malcolm Hulke)**
1981/05, Pinnacle Books, USA
Cover by David Mann. 'Second printing'. Green logo.
REF: ISBN 0-523-41613-X OP: $1.95 p/b NM: £5.50

BTR-019h *Doctor Who and the Dinosaur Invasion* **(Malcolm Hulke)**
1982, Target/W H Allen & Co Ltd, UK
Cover by Jeff Cummins. Red curve logo. White spine.
Colour decal.
REF: ISBN 0-426-10874-4 OP: £1.35 p/b NM: £2.75

BTR-019i *Doctor Who and the Dinosaur Invasion* **(Malcolm Hulke)**
1983, Target/W H Allen & Co Ltd, UK
REF: ISBN 0-426-10874-4 OP: £1.35 p/b NM: £2.75

BTR-019j *Doctor Who and the Dinosaur Invasion #3* **(Malcolm Hulke)**
1983/02, Pinnacle Books, USA
Cover by David Mann. 'Third printing'. Green logo.
REF: ISBN 0-523-41613-X OP: $1.95 p/b NM: £5.50

BTR-019k *Doctor Who and the Dinosaur Invasion* **(Malcolm Hulke)**
1984, Target/W H Allen & Co Ltd, UK
Cover by Jeff Cummins. Red curve logo. White spine. Colour decal.
REF: ISBN 0-426-10874-4 OP: £1.35 p/b NM: £2.75

BTR-019l *Doctor Who and the Dinosaur Invasion #3* **(Malcolm Hulke)**
1989/01, Pinnacle Books, USA
Cover by David Mann. 'Sixth Printing'. Blue logo.
REF: ISBN 1-55817-190-8 OP: $3.50 p/b NM: £7.95

BTR-019m *Doctor Who – Invasion of the Dinosaurs* **(Malcolm Hulke)**
1993/11/18, Target/Virgin Publishing Ltd, UK
Cover by Alistair Pearson. Blue spine. Interior ISBN 0-426-10374-4.
REF: ISBN 0-426-10874-4 OP: £3.50 p/b NM: £5.50

BTR-020a *Doctor Who and the Tenth Planet* **(Gerry Davis)**
1976/02/19, Allan Wingate (Publishers) Ltd, UK
Cover by Chris Achilleos. Print run: 3,000 copies.
REF: ISBN 0-85523-062-2 OP: £2.25 h/b NM: £27.50

BTR-020b *Doctor Who and the Tenth Planet* **(Gerry Davis)**
1976/02/19, Target/Tandem Publishing Ltd, UK
Cover by Chris Achilleos. Mauve curve logo. White spine. Colour decal. Back cover illustration.
REF: ISBN 0-426-11068-4 OP: 40p p/b NM: £5.50

BTR-020c *Doctor Who and the Tenth Planet* **(Gerry Davis)**
1977, Allan Wingate (Publishers) Ltd, UK
Cover by Chris Achilleos. Print run: 1,500 copies.
REF: ISBN 0-85523-062-2 OP: h/b NM: £16.50

BTR-020d *Doctor Who and the Tenth Planet* **(Gerry Davis)**
1978, Target/W. H. Allen & Co. Ltd, UK
Cover by Chris Achilleos. 'Second Impression'. Blue curve logo. White spine. Colour decal.
REF: ISBN 0-426-11068-4 OP: 60p p/b NM: £4.50

BTR-020e *Doctor Who and the Tenth Planet* **(Gerry Davis)**
1978/08/17, Target/W. H. Allen & Co. Ltd, UK
Cover by Chris Achilleos. Blue curve logo. White spine. Colour decal. Print run: 10,000 copies.
REF: ISBN 0-426-11068-4 OP: 65p p/b NM: £4.50

BTR-020f *Doctor Who and the Tenth Planet* **(Gerry Davis)**
1979/09/27, Target/W. H. Allen & Co. Ltd, UK
Cover by Chris Achilleos. Light blue curve logo. White spine. No back cover illustration. Print run: 12,000 copies.
REF: ISBN 0-426-11068-4 OP: 75p p/b NM: £4.50

BTR-020g *Doctor Who and the Tenth Planet* **(Gerry Davis)**
1980, Target/W. H. Allen & Co. Ltd, UK
Cover by Chris Achilleos. Light blue curve logo. White spine. No back cover illustration.
REF: ISBN 0-426-11068-4 OP: 85p p/b NM: £4.50

BTR-020h *Doctor Who and the Tenth Planet* **(Gerry Davis)**
1982, Target/W. H. Allen & Co. Ltd, UK
Cover by Chris Achilleos. Light blue curve logo. White spine. No back cover illustration. Print run: 20,000 copies.
REF: ISBN 0-426-11068-4 OP: p/b NM: £4.50

BTR-020i *Doctor Who and the Tenth Planet* **(Gerry Davis)**
1984, Target/W. H. Allen & Co. Ltd, UK
Cover by Chris Achilleos. Light blue curve logo. White spine. Colour decal. No back cover illustration.
REF: ISBN 0-426-11068-4 OP: £1.35 p/b NM: £4.50

BTR-020j *Doctor Who and the Tenth Planet* **(Gerry Davis)**
1984, Target/W. H. Allen & Co. Ltd, UK
Print run: 20,000 copies.
REF: ISBN 0-426-11068-4 OP: £1.50 p/b NM: £4.50

BTR-020k *Doctor Who and the Tenth Planet* **(Gerry Davis)**
1985, Target/W. H. Allen & Co. Ltd UK
Cover by Chris Achilleos. Light blue curve logo. White spine. Outline decal.
REF: ISBN 0-426-11068-4 OP: £1.50 p/b NM: £4.50

BTR-0201 *Doctor Who – The Tenth Planet*
(Gerry Davis)
1993/02/18, Target/Virgin Publishing Ltd, UK
Cover by Alistair Pearson. Blue spine.
REF: ISBN 0-426-11068-4 OP: £3.50 p/b NM: £5.50

BTR-021a *Doctor Who and the Ice Warriors*
(Brian Hayles)
1976/03/18, Allan Wingate (Publishers) Ltd, UK
Cover by Chris Achilleos. Print run: 3,000 copies.
REF: ISBN 0-85523-066-5 OP: £2.25 h/b NM: £27.50

BTR-021b *Doctor Who and the Ice Warriors*
(Brian Hayles)
1976/03/18, Target/Tandem Publishing Ltd, UK
Cover by Chris Achilleos. Green curve logo. White
spine. Colour decal.
REF: ISBN 0-426-10866-3 OP: 40p p/b NM: £7.95

BTR-021c *Doctor Who and the Ice Warriors*
(Brian Hayles)
1977, Target/W H Allen & Co Ltd, UK
OP: p/b NM: £6.50

BTR-021d *Doctor Who and the Ice Warriors*
(Brian Hayles)
1978, Target/W H Allen & Co Ltd, UK
'Second impression'. Cover by Chris Achilleos. Red
curve logo. White spine. Colour decal. Wyndham W
on back.
REF: ISBN 0-426-10866-3 OP: 60p p/b NM: £6.50

BTR-021e *Doctor Who and the Ice Warriors*
(Brian Hayles)
1978/07/20, Allan Wingate (Publishers) Ltd, UK
Cover by Chris Achilleos. Print run: 1,500 copies.
REF: ISBN 0-85523-066-X OP: h/b NM: £16.50

BTR-021f *Doctor Who and the Ice Warriors*
(Brian Hayles)
1979, Target/W H Allen & Co Ltd, UK
Cover by Chris Achilleos. 2nd impression. Blue curve
logo. White spine. Colour decal. Wyndham W on back.
Print run: 12,000 copies.
REF: ISBN 0-426-10866-3 OP: 70p p/b NM: £6.50

BTR-021g *Doctor Who and the Ice Warriors*
(Brian Hayles)
1980, Target/W H Allen & Co Ltd, UK
Cover by Chris Achilleos. 3rd impression. Blue curve
logo. White spine. Colour decal.
REF: ISBN 0-426-10866-3 OP: 85p p/b NM: £6.50

BTR-021h *Doctor Who and the Ice Warriors*
(Brian Hayles)
1981, Target/W H Allen & Co Ltd, UK
Cover by Chris Achilleos. Blue curve logo. White
spine. Print run: 13,000 copies.
REF: ISBN 0-426-10866-3 OP: 85p p/b NM: £6.50

BTR-021i *Doctor Who and the Ice Warriors*
(Brian Hayles)
1982, Target/W H Allen & Co Ltd, UK
Cover by Chris Achilleos. Blue curve logo. White
spine. Colour decal.
REF: ISBN 0-426-10866-3 OP: £1.35 p/b NM: £6.50

BTR-021j *Doctor Who and the Ice Warriors*
(Brian Hayles)
1983, Target/W H Allen & Co Ltd, UK
Cover by Chris Achilleos. Blue curve logo. White
spine. Outline decal.
REF: ISBN 0-426-10866-3 OP: £1.95 p/b NM: £6.50

BTR-021k *Doctor Who and the Ice Warriors*
(Brian Hayles)
1984, Target/W H Allen & Co Ltd, UK
Cover by Chris Achilleos. Blue curve logo. White
spine. Colour decal.
REF: ISBN 0-426-10866-3 OP: £1.35 p/b NM: £6.50

BTR-021l *Doctor Who and the Ice Warriors*
(Brian Hayles)
1984, Target/W H Allen & Co Ltd, UK
Cover by Chris Achilleos. Blue curve logo. White
spine. outline decal. 1987 reprint run: 10,000 copies.
REF: ISBN 0-426-10866-3 OP: £1.95 p/b NM: £6.50

BTR-022a *Doctor Who and the Revenge of the*
Cybermen **(Terrance Dicks)**
1976/05/20, Allan Wingate (Publishers) Ltd, UK
Cover by Chris Achilleos. Print run: 3,400 copies.
REF: ISBN 85523-071-1 OP: £2.25 h/b NM: £27.50

BTR-022b *Doctor Who and the Revenge of the*
Cybermen **(Terrance Dicks)**
1976/05/20, Target/Tandem Publishing Ltd, UK
Cover by Chris Achilleos. Orange curve logo. White
spine. Colour decal.
REF: ISBN 0-426-10997-X OP: 40p p/b NM: £5.50

BTR-022c *Doctor Who and the Revenge of the*
Cybermen **(Terrance Dicks)**
1978/08/17, Target/W H Allen & Co Ltd, UK
Cover by Chris Achilleos. 'Second Impression'. Red
curve logo. White spine. Colour decal. Wyndham W
on back. Print run: 10,000 copies.
REF: ISBN 0-426-10997-X OP: 60p p/b NM: £4.50

BTR-022d *Doctor Who and the Revenge of the Cybermen* **(Terrance Dicks)**
1979/10/25, Target/W H Allen & Co Ltd, UK
Cover by Chris Achilleos. 3rd impression. Red curve logo. White spine. Print run: 12,000 copies.
REF: ISBN 0-426-10997-X OP: 75p p/b NM: £4.50

BTR-022e *Doctor Who and the Revenge of the Cybermen #5* **(Terrance Dicks)**
1979/06, Pinnacle Books, USA
Cover by David Mann. Dark pink logo.
REF: ISBN 0-523-40611-8 OP: $1.75 p/b NM: £5.50

BTR-022f *Doctor Who and the Revenge of the Cybermen* **(Terrance Dicks)**
1981, Target/W H Allen & Co Ltd, UK
Cover by Chris Achilleos. 'Fourth Impression'. Red curve logo. White spine. Colour decal. Print run: 15,000 copies.
REF: ISBN 0-426-10997-X OP: 95p p/b NM: £4.50

BTR-022g *Doctor Who and the Revenge of the Cybermen #5* **(Terrance Dicks)**
1981, Pinnacle Books, USA
Cover by David Mann. Orange logo.
REF: ISBN 0-523-41615-6 OP: $1.95 p/b NM: £5.50

BTR-022h *Doctor Who and the Revenge of the Cybermen* **(Terrance Dicks)**
1983, Target/W H Allen & Co Ltd, UK
Cover by Chris Achilleos. Red curve logo. White spine. Colour decal.
REF: ISBN 0-426-10997-X OP: £1.25 p/b NM: £4.50

BTR-022i *Doctor Who and the Revenge of the Cybermen* **(Terrance Dicks)**
1987, Target/W H Allen & Co Ltd, UK
Print run: 2,400 copies.
REF: ISBN 0-426-10997-X OP: £1.95 p/b NM: £4.50

BTR-022j *Doctor Who and the Revenge of the Cybermen #5* **(Terrance Dicks)**
1989/01, Pinnacle Books, USA
Cover by David Mann. 'Seventh printing'. Red logo.
REF: ISBN 1-55817-192-4 OP: $3.50 p/b NM: £7.95

BTR-022k *Doctor Who – Revenge of the Cybermen* **(Terrance Dicks)**
1991/05/16, Target/Virgin Publishing Ltd, UK
Cover by Alistair Pearson. Blue spine. Print run: 10,000 copies.
REF: ISBN 0-426-10997-X OP: £2.50 p/b NM: £4.50

BTR-020l   BTR-021b

BTR-022b

BTR-022e

BTR-022k

BTR-022l

BTR-023b

BTR-022l *Doctor Who – Zemsta Cyborgów*
(**Terrance Dicks**)
1994, Oficyna Wydawnicza "Empire", Poland
Translator: Grzegorz Wozniak.
REF: ISBN 83-86126-05-1

BTR-023a *Doctor Who and the Genesis of the
Daleks* (**Terrance Dicks**)
1976, Allan Wingate (Publishers) Ltd, UK
Cover by Chris Achilleos. Print run: 2,500 copies.
REF: ISBN 0-85523-072-X OP: £2.25 h/b NM: £27.50

BTR-023b *Doctor Who and the Genesis of the
Daleks* (**Terrance Dicks**)
1976/07/22, Target/Tandem Publishing Ltd, UK
Cover by Chris Achilleos. Red curve logo. Red spine.
Colour decal. Print run: 40,000 copies. Two printings
in 1976.
REF: ISBN 0-426-11260-1 OP: 45p p/b NM: £5.95

BTR-023c *Doctor Who and the Genesis of the
Daleks* (**Terrance Dicks**)
1977/07/21, Target/W H Allen & Co Ltd, UK
Cover by Chris Achilleos. Red curve logo. Red spine.
Colour decal. Print run: 15,000 copies.
REF: ISBN 0-426-11260-1 OP: 60p p/b NM: £4.95

BTR-023d *Doctor Who and the Genesis of the
Daleks* (**Terrance Dicks**)
1978, Target/W H Allen & Co Ltd, UK
Cover by Chris Achilleos. 'Second Impression'.
Blue/purple curve logo. White spine. Colour decal.
Wyndham W on back. Print run: 15,000 copies.
REF: ISBN 0-426-11260-1 OP: 60p p/b NM: £4.95

BTR-023e *Doctor Who and the Genesis of the
Daleks* (**Terrance Dicks**)
1978/08/17, Target/W H Allen & Co Ltd, UK
Cover by Chris Achilleos. '3rd edition'. Purple curve
logo. White spine. Print run: 10,000 copies.
REF: ISBN 0-426-11260-1 OP: 75p p/b NM: £4.95

BTR-023f *Doctor Who and the Genesis of the
Daleks #4* (**Terrance Dicks**)
1979/05, Pinnacle Books, USA
Cover by David Mann. Green logo.
REF: ISBN 0-523-40608-8 OP: $1.75 p/b NM: £5.50

BTR-023g *Doctor Who and the Genesis of the
Daleks* (**Terrance Dicks**)
1980/01/24, Target/W H Allen & Co Ltd, UK
Print run: 12,000 copies.
REF: ISBN 0-426-11260-1 OP: 75p p/b NM: £4.95

BTR-023h *Doctor Who and the Genesis of the Daleks* **(Terrance Dicks)**
1981, Target/W H Allen & Co Ltd, UK
'Fourth Impression'. Cover by Chris Achilleos. Purple curve logo. White spine. Print run: 15,000 copies.
REF: ISBN 0-426-11260-1 OP: 95p p/b NM: £4.95

BTR-023i *Doctor Who and the Genesis of the Daleks #4* **(Terrance Dicks)**
1981, Pinnacle Books, USA
Cover by David Mann. Orange logo.
REF: ISBN 0-523-41973-2 OP: $1.95 p/b NM: £5.50

BTR-023j *Doctor Who and the Genesis of the Daleks* **(Terrance Dicks)**
1982, Target/W H Allen & Co Ltd, UK
Cover by Chris Achilleos. Purple curve logo. White spine. Colour decal.
REF: ISBN 0-426-11260-1 OP: £1.35 p/b NM: £4.95

BTR-023k *Doctor Who and the Genesis of the Daleks #4* **(Terrance Dicks)**
1989/01, Pinnacle Books, USA
Cover by David Mann. 'Sixth printing'. Green logo.
REF: ISBN 1-55817-191-6 OP: $3.50 p/b NM: £5.50

BTR-023l *Doctor Who – Genesis of the Daleks* **(Terrance Dicks)**
1991/09/19, Target/Virgin Publishing Ltd, UK
Cover by Alistair Pearson. Blue spine. Print run: 9,000 copies.
REF: ISBN 0-426-11260-1 OP: £2.50 p/b NM: £4.95

BTR-024a *Doctor Who and the Web of Fear* **(Terrance Dicks)**
1976/08/19, Allan Wingate (Publishers) Ltd, UK
Cover by Chris Achilleos. Print run: 3,000 copies.
REF: ISBN 0-85523-073-8 OP: £2.25 h/b NM: £27.50

BTR-024b *Doctor Who and the Web of Fear* **(Terrance Dicks)**
1976/08/19, Target/Wyndham Publications Ltd, UK
Cover by Chris Achilleos. Mauve curve logo. Mauve spine. Colour decal. Print run: 40,000 copies.
REF: ISBN 0-426-11084-6 OP: 45p p/b NM: £7.95

BTR-024c *Doctor Who and the Web of Fear* **(Terrance Dicks)**
1978, Allan Wingate (Publishers) Ltd, UK
Cover by Chris Achilleos. 'Second impression'. Print run: 1,500 copies.
REF: ISBN 0-491-02184-4 OP: £2.95 h/b NM: £16.50

BTR-023f

BTR-023l

BTR-024b

BTR-024f   **BTR-024i**

BTR-025b

BTR-024d *Doctor Who and the Web of Fear*
(Terrance Dicks)
1978/08/17, Target/W H Allen & Co Ltd, UK
Cover by Chris Achilleos. Light blue curve logo. Two
editions in 1978. First Print run: 4,500 copies; second
Print run: 10,000 copies.
REF: ISBN 0-426-11084-6   OP: 60p p/b   NM: £6.50

BTR-024e *Doctor Who and the Web of Fear*
(Terrance Dicks)
1979/12/13, Target/W H Allen & Co Ltd, UK
Cover by Chris Achilleos. Light blue curve logo. White
spine. Print run: 12,000 copies.
REF: ISBN 0-426-11084-6   OP: 75p p/b   NM: £6.50

BTR-024f *Doctor Who and the Web of Fear*
(Terrance Dicks)
1983, Target/W H Allen & Co Ltd, UK
Cover by Andrew Skilleter. Orange neon logo. White
spine. Colour decal. Print run: 20,000 copies. Edition
also available with black spine.
REF: ISBN 0-426-11084-6   OP: £1.25 p/b   NM: £5.50

BTR-024g *Doctor Who and the Web of Fear*
(Terrance Dicks)
1984, Target/W H Allen & Co Ltd, UK
Cover by Andrew Skilleter. Orange neon logo. White
spine. Colour decal. Print run: 20,000 copies. Edition
also available with black spine.
REF: ISBN 0-426-11084-6   OP: £1.35 p/b   NM: £5.50

BTR-024h *Doctor Who and the Web of Fear*
(Terrance Dicks)
1984, Target/W H Allen & Co Ltd, UK
Cover by Andrew Skilleter. Orange neon logo. White
spine. Outline decal. 1987 reprint run: 7,500 copies.
REF: ISBN 0-426-11084-6   OP: £1.95 p/b   NM: £5.50

BTR-024i *Doctor Who – The Web of Fear*
(Terrance Dicks)
1993/12/02, Target/Virgin Publishing Ltd, UK
Cover by Alistair Pearson. Blue spine.
REF: ISBN 0-426-11084-6   OP: £3.50 p/b   NM: £6.50

BTR-025a *Doctor Who and the Space War*
(Malcolm Hulke)
1976/09/23, Allan Wingate (Publishers) Ltd, UK
Cover by Chris Achilleos. Print run: 3,000 copies.
Novelisation of *Frontier in Space*.
REF: ISBN 0-85523-077-0   OP: £2.50 h/b   NM: £27.50

BTR-025b *Doctor Who and the Space War*
(Malcolm Hulke)
1976/09/23, Target/Wyndham Publications Ltd, UK
Cover by Chris Achilleos. Green curve logo. White

BTR-026b   **BTR-026f**

spine. Colour decal. Print run: 40,000 copies.
REF: ISBN 0-426-11033-1 OP: 45p p/b NM: £3.95

BTR-025c *Doctor Who and the Space War*
(Malcolm Hulke)
1978, Allan Wingate (Publishers) Ltd, UK
Cover by Chris Achilleos. Print run: 1,500 copies.
REF: ISBN 0-85523-077-0 OP: h/b NM: £16.50

BTR-025d *Doctor Who and the Space War*
(Malcolm Hulke)
1979/01/18, Target/W H Allen & Co Ltd, UK
Cover by Chris Achilleos. 'Second Impression'. Blue
curve logo. White spine. Colour decal. Wyndham W
on back. Print run: 10,000 copies.
REF: ISBN 0-426-11033-1 OP: 60p p/b NM: £2.75

BTR-025e *Doctor Who and the Space War*
(Malcolm Hulke)
1980/02/21, Target/W H Allen & Co Ltd, UK
Cover by Chris Achilleos. 3rd impression. Blue curve
logo. White spine. Colour decal. Print run: 15,000 copies.
REF: ISBN 0-426-11033-1 OP: 85p p/b NM: £2.75

BTR-025f *Doctor Who and the Space War*
(Malcolm Hulke)
1982, Target/W H Allen & Co Ltd, UK
Cover by Chris Achilleos. Blue curve logo. White
spine. Colour decal.
REF: ISBN 0-426-11033-1 OP: £1.25 p/b NM: £2.75

BTR-025g *Doctor Who and the Space War*
(Malcolm Hulke)
1983, Target/W H Allen & Co Ltd, UK
Cover by Chris Achilleos. Blue curve logo. White
spine. Colour decal.
REF: ISBN 0-426-11033-1 OP: £1.35 p/b NM: £2.75

BTR-025h *Doctor Who and the Space War*
(Malcolm Hulke)
1984, Target/W H Allen & Co Ltd, UK
Cover by Chris Achilleos. Blue curve logo. White
spine. Colour decal.
REF: ISBN 0-426-11033-1 OP: £1.35 p/b NM. £2.75

BTR-025i *Doctor Who and the Space War*
(Malcolm Hulke)
1984, Target/W H Allen & Co Ltd, UK
Cover by Chris Achilleos. Blue curve logo. White
spine. Outline decal. 1987 reprint run: 14,500 copies.
REF: ISBN 0-426-11033-1 OP: £1.95 p/b NM: £2.75

BTR-026a *Doctor Who and the Planet of the*
Daleks **(Terrance Dicks)**
1976/10/21, Allan Wingate (Publishers) Ltd, UK

Cover by Chris Achilleos. Print run: 3,000 copies.
REF: ISBN 0-85523-076-2 OP: £2.50 h/b NM: £27.50

BTR-026b *Doctor Who and the Planet of the*
Daleks **(Terrance Dicks)**
1976/10/21, Target/Wyndham Publications Ltd, UK
Cover by Chris Achilleos. Red curve logo. White
spine. Colour decal. Print run: 40,000 copies.
REF: ISBN 0-426-11252-0 OP: 45p p/b NM: £4.50

BTR-026c *Doctor Who and the Planet of the*
Daleks **(Terrance Dicks)**
1977/07/21, Target/Wyndham Publications Ltd, UK
Cover by Chris Achilleos. Red curve logo. White
spine. Print run: 10,000 copies.
REF: ISBN 0-426-11252-0 OP: 60p p/b NM: £3.50

BTR-026d *Doctor Who and the Planet of the*
Daleks **(Terrance Dicks)**
1978, Target/W H Allen & Co Ltd, UK
Cover by Chris Achilleos. 2nd impression. Green curve
logo. White spine. Colour decal. Print run: 4,000 copies.
REF: ISBN 0-426-11252-0 OP: 60p p/b NM: £3.50

BTR-026e *Doctor Who and the Planet of the*
Daleks **(Terrance Dicks)**
1980, Target/W H Allen & Co Ltd, UK
Cover by Chris Achilleos. 'Third impression'. Red
curve logo. White spine. Colour decal. Print run:
12,000 copies. Copies also available with an 85p price.
REF: ISBN 0-426-11252-0 OP: 75p p/b NM: £3.50

BTR-026f *Dr. Who: Der Planet Der Daleks*
(Terrance Dicks)
1980, Schneider-Buch, Germany
Cover by David Hardy. Illustrations by Herbert Horn.
Edited by Angela Djuren and translated by Ulla
Neckenauer.
REF: ISBN 3-505-07254-0 OP: DM 3,95 p/b

BTR-026g *Doctor Who and the Planet of the*
Daleks **(Terrance Dicks)**
1982, Target/W H Allen & Co Ltd, UK
Printed twice in 1982.
REF: ISBN 0-426-11252-0 OP: £1.25 p/b NM: £3.50

BTR-026h *Doctor Who and the Planet of the*
Daleks **(Terrance Dicks)**
1983, Target/W H Allen & Co Ltd, UK
Print run: 20,000 copies.
REF: ISBN 0-426-11252-0 OP: p/b NM: £3.50

BTR-026i *Doctor Who and the Planet of the Daleks* **(Terrance Dicks)**
1984, Target/W H Allen & Co Ltd, UK
Cover by Chris Achilleos. Red curve logo. White spine. Colour decal.
REF: ISBN 0-426-11252-0 OP: £1.35 p/b NM: £3.50

BTR-026j *Doctor Who and the Planet of the Daleks* **(Terrance Dicks)**
1984, Target/W H Allen & Co Ltd, UK
Cover by Chris Achilleos. Red curve logo. White spine. Outline decal. 1987 reprint run: 8,400 copies.
REF: ISBN 0-426-11252-0 OP: £1.95 p/b NM: £3.50

BTR-026k *Doctor Who Und der Planet der Daleks* **(Terrance Dicks)**
1989, Goldmann Verlag, Germany
Cover by Chris Achilleos (from *Planet of the Daleks*). Translated by Bettina Zeller.
REF: ISBN 3-442-23622-3 OP: DM 7,80 p/b

BTR-026l *Doctor Who – Planet of the Daleks* **(Terrance Dicks)**
1992/07/16, Target/Virgin Publishing Ltd, UK
Cover by Alistair Pearson. Blue spine.
REF: ISBN 0-426-11252-0 OP: £2.99 p/b NM: £5.50

BTR-027a *Doctor Who and the Pyramids of Mars* **(Terrance Dicks)**
1976/12/16, Allan Wingate (Publishers) Ltd, UK
Cover by Chris Achilleos. Print run: 3,000 copies.
REF: ISBN 85523-141-6 OP: £2.50 h/b NM: £27.50

BTR-027b *Doctor Who and the Pyramids of Mars* **(Terrance Dicks)**
1976/12/16, Target/Wyndham Publications Ltd, UK
Cover by Chris Achilleos. Mauve curve logo. White spine. Colour decal. Print run: 40,000 copies.
REF: ISBN 0-426-11666-6 OP: 45p p/b NM: £6.50

BTR-027c *Doctor Who and the Pyramids of Mars* **(Terrance Dicks)**
1978, Allan Wingate (Publishers) Ltd, UK
Print run: 1,500 copies.
REF: ISBN 85523-141-6 OP: £2.95 h/b NM: £16.50

BTR-027d *Doctor Who and the Pyramids of Mars* **(Terrance Dicks)**
1979, Target/W H Allen & Co Ltd, UK
Cover by Chris Achilleos. Purple curve logo. Colour decal. Print run: 12,000 copies.
REF: ISBN 0-426-11666-6 OP: 75p p/b NM: £5.50

BTR-027e *Doctor Who and the Pyramids of Mars* **(Terrance Dicks)**
1982, Target/W H Allen & Co Ltd, UK
Cover by Andrew Skilleter. Blue neon logo. Brown spine. Colour decal. Print run: 20,000 copies.
REF: ISBN 0-426-11666-6 OP: £1.25 p/b NM: £4.50

BTR-027f *Doctor Who and the Pyramids of Mars* **(Terrance Dicks)**
1983, Target/W H Allen & Co Ltd, UK
Cover by Andrew Skilleter. Blue neon logo. Brown spine. Colour decal.
REF: ISBN 0-426-11666-6 OP: £1.35 p/b NM: £4.50

BTR-027g *Doctor Who – Pyramids of Mars* **(Terrance Dicks)**
1993/03/18, Target/Virgin Publishing Ltd, UK
Cover by Alistair Pearson. Blue spine. Art also used for the CD release *Pyramids of Mars*.
REF: ISBN 0-426-11666-6 OP: £3.50 p/b NM: £5.50

BTR-028a *Doctor Who and the Carnival of Monsters* **(Terrance Dicks)**
1977/01/20, Allan Wingate (Publishers) Ltd, UK
Cover by Chris Achilleos. Print run: 3,000 copies.
REF: ISBN 0-85523-151-3 OP: £2.50 h/b NM: £27.50

BTR-028b *Doctor Who and the Carnival of Monsters* **(Terrance Dicks)**
1977/01/20, Target/Tandem Publishing Ltd, UK
Cover by Chris Achilleos. Green curve logo. Yellow spine. Colour decal. Print run: 35,000 copies.
REF: ISBN 0-426-11025-0 OP: 50p p/b NM: £4.95

BTR-028c *Doctor Who and the Carnival of Monsters* **(Terrance Dicks)**
1978, Allan Wingate (Publishers) Ltd, UK
Cover by Chris Achilleos. Print run: 1,500 copies.
REF: ISBN 0-491-02114-0 OP: £2.95 h/b NM: £16.50

BTR-028d *Doctor Who and the Carnival of Monsters* **(Terrance Dicks)**
1979/04/19, Target/W H Allen & Co Ltd, UK
Cover by Chris Achilleos. 3rd impression. Green curve logo. Yellow spine. Print run: 12,000 copies. Some copies priced at 70p.
REF: ISBN 0-426-11025-0 OP: 85p p/b NM: £3.95

BTR-028e *Doctor Who and the Carnival of Monsters* **(Terrance Dicks)**
1980, Target/W H Allen & Co Ltd, UK
OP: p/b NM: £3.95

BTR-028f *Doctor Who and the Carnival of Monsters* (Terrance Dicks)
1982, Target/W H Allen & Co Ltd, UK
Cover by Chris Achilleos. Green curve logo. Yellow spine. Colour decal.
REF: ISBN 0-426-11025-0 OP: £1.25 p/b NM: £3.95

BTR-028g *Doctor Who and the Carnival of Monsters* (Terrance Dicks)
1984, Target/W H Allen & Co Ltd, UK
Cover by Chris Achilleos. Green curve logo. Yellow spine. Colour decal.
REF: ISBN 0-426-11025-0 OP: £1.35 p/b NM: £3.95

BTR-028h *Doctor Who and the Carnival of Monsters* (Terrance Dicks)
1985, Target/W H Allen & Co Ltd, UK
Cover by Chris Achilleos. Green curve logo. Yellow spine. Outline decal. Print run: 10,000 copies.
REF: ISBN 0-426-11025-0 OP: £1.50 p/b NM: £3.95

BTR-028i *Doctor Who – Carnival of Monsters* (Terrance Dicks)
1993/05/20, Target/Virgin Publishing Ltd, UK
Cover by Alistair Pearson. Blue spine. Released to tie in with the BBC repeat. Rejacketed 1985 Target reprint.
REF: ISBN 0-426-11025-0 OP: £3.50 p/b NM: £4.50

BTR-029a *Doctor Who and the Seeds of Doom* (Philip Hinchcliffe)
1977/02/17, Allan Wingate (Publishers) Ltd, UK
Cover by Chris Achilleos. Two editions in 1977. First Print run: 3,000 copies, second print run: 1,500 copies.
REF: ISBN 0-85523-161-0 OP: £2.50 h/b NM: £27.50

BTR-029b *Doctor Who and the Seeds of Doom* (Philip Hinchcliffe)
1977/02/17, Target/Tandem Publishing Ltd, UK
Cover by Chris Achilleos. Red curve logo. White spine. Colour decal. Print run: 35,000 copies.
REF: ISBN 0-426-11658-5 OP: 50p p/b NM: £4.50

BTR-029c *Doctor Who and the Seeds of Doom* (Philip Hinchcliffe)
1979/02/15, Target/W H Allen & Co Ltd, UK
Print run: 12,000 copies.
REF: ISBN 0-426-11658-5 OP: 60p p/b NM: £3.50

BTR-029d *Doctor Who and the Seeds of Doom* #10 (Philip Hinchcliffe)
1980/03, Pinnacle Books, USA
Cover by David Mann. Green logo.
REF: ISBN 0-523-40639-8 OP: $1.75 p/b NM: £5.50

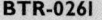

BTR-026l

BTR-027b

BTR-027e

BTR-027g

BTR-028b

BTR-028i

BTR-029b   BTR-029d

BTR-030b   BTR-030g

BTR-030m

BTR-030l

BTR-029e *Doctor Who and the Seeds of Doom*
(Philip Hinchcliffe)
1980, Target/W H Allen & Co Ltd, UK
'Third Impression'. Cover by Chris Achilleos. Red curve
logo. White spine. Colour decal. Print run: 12,000 copies.
Two printings in 1980; the first printing cost 75p.
REF: ISBN 0-426-11658-5 OP: 85p p/b NM: £3.50

BTR-029f *Doctor Who and the Seeds of Doom*
#10 (Philip Hinchcliffe)
1981, Pinnacle Books, USA
Cover by David Mann. Blue logo. A later printing, year
unknown, had a cover price of $2.95 and ISBN 0-523-
42507-4.
REF: ISBN 0-523-41620-2 OP: $1.95 p/b NM: £5.50

BTR-029g *Doctor Who and the Seeds of Doom*
(Philip Hinchcliffe)
1982, Target/W H Allen & Co Ltd, UK
Cover by Chris Achilleos. Red curve logo. White
spine. Colour decal.
REF: ISBN 0-426-11658-5 OP: £1.25 p/b NM: £3.50

BTR-029h *Doctor Who and the Seeds of Doom*
(Philip Hinchcliffe)
1984, Target/W H Allen & Co Ltd, UK
Cover by Chris Achilleos. Red curve logo. White
spine. Colour decal.
REF: ISBN 0-426-11658-5 OP: £1.35 p/b NM: £3.50

BTR-029i *Doctor Who and the Seeds of Doom*
(Philip Hinchcliffe)
1987, Target/W H Allen & Co Ltd, UK
Cover by Chris Achilleos. Print run: 17,300 copies.
REF: ISBN 0-426-11658-5 OP: £1.95 p/b NM: £3.50

BTR-029j *Doctor Who and the Seeds of Doom*
#10 (Philip Hinchcliffe)
1989/12, Pinnacle Books, USA
Cover by David Mann. 'Sixth printing'. Blue logo.
REF: ISBN 1-55817-297-1 OP: $3.50 p/b NM: £7.95

BTR-030a *Doctor Who and the Dalek Invasion
of Earth* **(Terrance Dicks)**
1977/03/24, Allan Wingate (Publishers) Ltd, UK
Cover by Chris Achilleos. Print run: 3,000 copies. Title
page says 'Based on the BBC television serial *Doctor
Who and the World's End*'. This notation appears in
subsequent editions through to at least 1984.
REF: ISBN 0-85523-171-8 OP: £2.50 h/b NM: £27.50

BTR-030b *Doctor Who and the Dalek Invasion
of Earth* **(Terrance Dicks)**
1977/03/24, Target/W. H. Allen & Co. Ltd, UK

Cover by Chris Achilleos. Orange curve logo. White spine. Colour decal. Print run: 30,000 copies. Reprinted in 1977.
REF: ISBN 0-426-11244-X OP: 50p p/b NM: £4.50

BTR-030c *Doctor Who and the Dalek Invasion of Earth* (**Terrance Dicks**)
1978, Allan Wingate (Publishers) Ltd, UK
Cover by Chris Achilleos. Print run: 1,500 copies.
REF: ISBN 0-491-02124-0 OP: £2.95 h/b NM: £16.50

BTR-030d *Doctor Who and the Dalek Invasion of Earth* (**Terrance Dicks**)
1978/08/17, Target/W. H. Allen & Co. Ltd, UK
Cover by Chris Achilleos. 2nd Impression. Blue curve logo. Print run: 5,800 copies.
REF: ISBN 0-426-11244-X OP: 70p p/b NM: £3.50

BTR-030e *Doctor Who and the Dalek Invasion of Earth* (**Terrance Dicks**)
1979, Target/W. H. Allen & Co. Ltd, UK
Cover by Chris Achilleos. 2nd Impression. Blue curve logo. White spine. Colour decal. Wyndham W on back. Print run: 15,000 copies.
REF: ISBN 0-426-11244-X OP: 70p p/b NM: £3.50

BTR-030f *Doctor Who and the Dalek Invasion of Earth* (**Terrance Dicks**)
1980, Target/W. H. Allen & Co. Ltd, UK
Print run: 12,000 copies.
REF: ISBN 0-426-11244-X OP: p/b NM: £3.50

BTR-030g *Dr. Who: Kampf um die Erde* (**Terrance Dicks**)
1981, Schneider-Buch, Germany
Cover by David Hardy. Edited by Angela Djuren and translated by Ulla Neckenauer.
REF: ISBN 3-505-07302-4 OP: DM 4,80 p/b

BTR-030h *Doctor Who and the Dalek Invasion of Earth* (**Terrance Dicks**)
1982, Target/W. H. Allen & Co. Ltd, UK
Cover by Chris Achilleos. Blue curve logo. White spine. Colour decal. Reprinted twice in 1982.
REF: ISBN 0-426-11244-X OP: £1.25 p/b NM: £3.50

BTR-030i *Doctor Who and the Dalek Invasion of Earth* (**Terrance Dicks**)
1983, Target/W. H. Allen & Co. Ltd, UK
Print run: 20,000 copies.
REF: ISBN 0-426-11244-X OP: p/b NM: £3.50

BTR-030j *Doctor Who and the Dalek Invasion of Earth* (**Terrance Dicks**)
1984, Target/W. H. Allen & Co. PLC, UK
Cover by Chris Achilleos. Red curve logo. White spine. Colour decal.
REF: ISBN 0-426-11244-X OP: £1.35 p/b NM: £3.50

BTR-030k *Doctor Who and the Dalek Invasion of Earth* (**Terrance Dicks**)
1984, Target/W. H. Allen & Co. PLC, UK
Cover by Chris Achilleos. Blue curve logo. White spine. Colour decal.
REF: ISBN 0-426-11244-X OP: £1.50 p/b NM: £3.50

BTR-030l *Docteur Who: Les Daleks Envahissent La Terre (4)* (**Terrance Dicks**)
1987/05, Editions Garanciere, France
Artwork cover. Translated by Roland C Wagner. Adapted by Corine Derblum.
REF: ISBN 2-7340-0203-5 OP: p/b NM: £8.95

BTR-030m *Doctor Who Und das Komplott der Daleks* (**Terrance Dicks**)
1989, Goldmann Verlag, Germany
Cover by Chris Achilleos (from *The Dalek Invasion of Earth*). Translated by Bettina Zeller.
REF: ISBN 3-442-23612-6 OP: DM 8,80 p/b

BTR-030n *Doctor Who – The Dalek Invasion of Earth* (**Terrance Dicks**)
1990/08, Target/Virgin Publishing Ltd, UK
Cover by Alistair Pearson (as on Video). Blue spine. Print run: 5,000 copies.
REF: ISBN 0-426-11244-X OP: £2.50 p/b NM: £5.50

BTR-031a *Doctor Who and the Claws of Axos* (**Terrance Dicks**)
1977/04/21, Allan Wingate (Publishers) Ltd, UK
Cover by Chris Achilleos. Print run: 3,000 copies.
REF: ISBN 0-85523-181-5 OP: £2.50 h/b NM: £27.50

BTR-031b *Doctor Who and the Claws of Axos* (**Terrance Dicks**)
1977/04/21, Target/Wyndham Publications Ltd, UK
Cover by Chris Achilleos. Blue curve logo. White spine. Colour decal. Print run: 30,000 copies.
REF: ISBN 0-426-11703-4 OP: 50p p/b NM: £5.95

BTR-031c *Doctor Who and the Claws of Axos* (**Terrance Dicks**)
1979, Target/W. H. Allen & Co. Ltd, UK
Cover by John Geary. 2nd impression. Red curve logo. White spine. Colour decal.
REF: ISBN 0-426-11703-4 OP: 60p p/b NM: £3.50

BTR-031d *Doctor Who and the Claws of Axos*
(Terrance Dicks)
1979/06/28, Target/W. H. Allen & Co. Ltd, UK
Cover by John Geary. 3rd impression. Red curve logo.
White spine. Print run: 12,000 copies.
REF: ISBN 0-426-11703-4 OP: 75p p/b NM: £3.50

BTR-031e *Doctor Who and the Claws of Axos*
(Terrance Dicks)
1980, Target/W. H. Allen & Co. Ltd, UK
"Third impression." Cover by John Geary cover. Red
curve logo. White spine. Colour decal. Print run:
12,000 copies.
REF: ISBN 0-426-11703-4 OP: 75p p/b NM: £3.50

BTR-031f *Doctor Who and the Claws of Axos*
(Terrance Dicks)
1982, Target/W. H. Allen & Co. Ltd, UK
Red curve logo. White spine. Colour decal. Some
books packaged with 1979 interiors.
REF: ISBN 0-426-11703-4 OP: £1.35 p/b NM: £3.50

BTR-031g *Doctor Who and the Claws of Axos*
(Terrance Dicks)
1984, Target/W. H. Allen & Co. Ltd, UK
Cover by John Geary. Red curve logo. White spine.
Colour decal. Print run: 20,000 copies.
REF: ISBN 0-426-11703-4 OP: £1.35 p/b NM: £3.50

BTR-031h *Doctor Who and the Claws of Axos*
(Terrance Dicks)
1985, Target/W. H. Allen & Co. PLC, UK
Cover by John Geary. Red curve logo. White spine.
Colour decal. Numbered spine. Some books packaged
with 1984 interiors.
REF: ISBN 0-426-11703-4 OP: £1.50 p/b NM: £3.50

BTR-031i *Doctor Who and the Claws of Axos*
(Terrance Dicks)
1985, Target/W. H. Allen & Co. PLC, UK
Cover by John Geary. Red curve logo. White spine.
Outline decal. Numbered spine.
REF: ISBN 0-426-11703-4 OP: £1.50 p/b NM: £3.50

BTR-032a *Doctor Who and the Ark In Space*
(Ian Marter)
1977/04/21, Allan Wingate (Publishers) Ltd, UK
Cover by Chris Achilleos. Print run: 3,000 copies.
REF: ISBN 0-85523-191-2 OP: £2.50 h/b NM: £27.50

BTR-032b *Doctor Who and the Ark In Space*
(Ian Marter)
1977/05/19, Target/Wyndham Publications Ltd, UK
Cover by Chris Achilleos. Orange curve logo. Yellow

spine. Colour decal. Print run: 35,000 copies.
REF: ISBN 0-426-11631-3 OP: 60p p/b NM: £5.50

BTR-032c *Doctor Who and the Ark In Space*
(Ian Marter)
1979, Target/W H Allen & Co Ltd, UK
"Second Impression." Cover by Chris Achilleos.
Orange curve logo. Yellow spine. Colour decal.
Wyndham W on back. Print run: 15,000 copies.
REF: ISBN 0-426-11631-3 OP: 70p p/b NM: £4.50

BTR-032d *Doctor Who and the Ark In Space*
(Ian Marter)
1980, Target/W H Allen & Co Ltd, UK
Print run: 15,000 copies.
REF: ISBN 0-426-11631-3 OP: p/b NM: £4.50

BTR-032e *Doctor Who and the Ark In Space*
(Ian Marter)
1981, Target/W H Allen & Co Ltd, UK
Cover by Chris Achilleos. Orange curve logo. Yellow
spine. Colour decal.
REF: ISBN 0-426-11631-3 OP: 90p p/b NM: £4.50

BTR-032f *Doctor Who and the Ark In Space* **(Ian
Marter)**
1982, Target/W H Allen & Co Ltd, UK
Cover by Chris Achilleos. Print run: 5,000 copies.
REF: ISBN 0-426-11631-3 OP: £1.95 p/b NM: £4.50

BTR-032g *Doctor Who and the Ark In Space*
(Ian Marter)
1984, Target/W H Allen & Co Ltd, UK
Cover by Chris Achilleos. Orange curve logo. Yellow
spine. Colour decal. Print run: 5,000 copies.
REF: ISBN 0-426-11631-3 OP: £1.35 p/b NM: £4.50

BTR-032h *Doctor Who – The Ark in Space* **(Ian
Marter)**
1991/05/16, Target/Virgin Publishing Ltd, UK
Cover by Alistair Pearson. Blue spine. Print run:
10,000 copies.
REF: ISBN 0-426-11631-3 OP: £2.50 p/b NM: £5.50

BTR-033a *Doctor Who and the Brain of Morbius*
(Terrance Dicks)
1977/05/19, Allan Wingate (Publishers) Ltd, UK
Cover by Mike Little. Red background to art. Print
run: 3,000 copies.
REF: ISBN 0-85523-201-3 OP: £2.95 h/b NM: £27.50

BTR-033b *Doctor Who and the Brain of Morbius*
(Terrance Dicks)
1977/06/23, Target/W. H. Allen & Co. Ltd, UK

Cover by Mike Little. Red background to art. Black curve logo. Yellow spine. Colour decal. Print run: 30,000 copies.
REF: ISBN 0-426-11674-7 OP: 60p p/b NM: £4.50

BTR-033c *Doctor Who and the Brain of Morbius* **(Terrance Dicks)**
1978/10/19, Target/W. H. Allen & Co. Ltd, UK
Cover by Mike Little Yellow background to art. Black curve logo. White spine. Colour decal. Print run: 10,000 copies.
REF: ISBN 0-426-11674-7 OP: 60p p/b NM: £3.50

BTR-033d *Doctor Who and the Brain of Morbius* **(Terrance Dicks)**
1979, Allan Wingate (Publishers) Ltd, UK
Print run: 3,000 copies.
REF: ISBN 0-85523-201-3 OP: h/b NM: £3.50

BTR-033e *Doctor Who and the Brain of Morbius* **(Terrance Dicks)**
1979, Target/W. H. Allen & Co. Ltd, UK
REF: ISBN 0-426-11674-7 OP: p/b NM: £3.50

BTR-033f *Doctor Who and the Brain of Morbius* **(Terrance Dicks)**
1980/01/24, Target/W. H. Allen & Co. Ltd, UK
Print run: 12,000 copies.
REF: ISBN 0-426-11674-7 OP: 75p p/b NM: £3.50

BTR-033g *Doctor Who and the Brain of Morbius* **(Terrance Dicks)**
1981, Target/W. H. Allen & Co. Ltd, UK
Cover by Mile Little. Yellow background to art. Black curve logo. White spine. Colour decal. Print run: 15,000 copies.
REF: ISBN 0-426-11674-7 OP: 95p p/b NM: £3.50

BTR-033h *Doctor Who and the Brain of Morbius* **(Terrance Dicks)**
1982, Target/W. H. Allen & Co. Ltd, UK
Cover by Mike Little. Yellow background to art. Black curve logo. White spine. Colour decal.
REF: ISBN 0-426-11674-7 OP: £1.35 p/b NM: £3.50

BTR-033i *Doctor Who and the Brain of Morbius* **(Terrance Dicks)**
1984, Target/W. H. Allen & Co. Ltd, UK
Cover by Mike Little. Yellow background to art. Black curve logo. White spine. Colour decal.
REF: ISBN 0-426-11674-7 OP: £1.35 p/b NM: £3.50

BTR-030n   BTR-031b

BTR-031c   BTR-032b

BTR-032h   BTR-033b

BTR-033k   BTR-033l

BTR-034b   BTR-034d

BTR-035b   BTR-036b

BTR-033j *Doctor Who and the Brain of Morbius*
(Terrance Dicks)
1987, Target/W. H. Allen & Co. Ltd, UK
Outline decal. Print run: 2,700 copies.
REF: ISBN 0-426-11674-7 OP: £1.95 p/b NM: £3.50

BTR-033k *Docteur Who: Le Cerveau de Morbius*
(5) (Terrance Dicks)
1987/06, Editions Garanciere, France
Artwork cover. Translated by Francine Mondolini.
Adapted by Corine Derblum. ISBN inside book is 2-
7340-0218-3.
REF: ISBN 2-7340-0219-1 OP: p/b

BTR-033l *Doctor Who – The Brain of Morbius*
(Terrance Dicks)
1991/01/17, Target/Virgin Publishing Ltd, UK
Cover by Alistair Pearson (as on Video). Blue spine.
Print run: 8,000 copies.
REF: ISBN 0-426-11674-7 OP: £2.50 p/b NM: £5.50

BTR-034a *Doctor Who and the Planet of Evil*
(Terrance Dicks)
1977/07/21, Allan Wingate (Publishers) Ltd, UK
Cover by Mike Little. Print run: 3,000 copies.
REF: ISBN 0-85523-231-5 OP: £2.95 h/b NM: £27.50

BTR-034b *Doctor Who and the Planet of Evil*
(Terrance Dicks)
1977/08/18, Target/W. H. Allen & Co. Ltd, UK
Cover by Mike Little. Black curve logo. White spine.
Colour decal. Print run: 30,000 copies.
REF: ISBN 0-426-11682-8 OP: 60p p/b NM: £5.95

BTR-034c *Doctor Who and the Planet of Evil*
(Terrance Dicks)
1979/09/27, Target/W. H. Allen & Co. Ltd, UK
Cover by Mike Little. 'Second Impression'. Black curve
logo. White spine. Colour decal. Print run: 12,000 copies.
REF: ISBN 0-426-11682-8 OP: 75p p/b NM: £4.95

BTR-034d *Doctor Who and the Planet of Evil*
(Terrance Dicks)
1982, Target/W. H. Allen & Co. Ltd, UK
Cover by Andrew Skilleter. Red neon logo. Dark green
spine. Colour decal.
REF: ISBN 0-426-11682-8 OP: £1.25 p/b NM: £3.50

BTR-034e *Doctor Who and the Planet of Evil*
(Terrance Dicks)
1983, Target/W. H. Allen & Co. Ltd, UK
Print run: 20,000 copies.
REF: ISBN 0-426-11682-8 OP: p/b NM: £3.50

BTR-034f *Doctor Who and the Planet of Evil*
(Terrance Dicks)
1984, Target/W. H. Allen & Co. Ltd, UK
Cover by Andrew Skilleter. Red neon logo. Green
spine. Colour decal.
REF: ISBN 0-426-11682-8 OP: £1.35 p/b NM: £3.50

BTR-034g *Doctor Who and the Planet of Evil*
(Terrance Dicks)
1984, Target/W. H. Allen & Co. Ltd, UK
Cover by Andrew Skilleter. Red neon logo. Green
spine. Outline decal. 1987 reprint run: 3,900 copies.
REF: ISBN 0-426-11682-8 OP: £1.95 p/b NM: £3.50

BTR-035a *Doctor Who and the Mutants*
(Terrance Dicks)
1977/09/29, Allan Wingate (Publishers) Ltd, UK
Cover by Jeff Cummins. Print run: 3,000 copies.
REF: ISBN 0-85523-471-7 OP: £2.95 h/b NM: £27.50

BTR-035b *Doctor Who and the Mutants*
(Terrance Dicks)
1977/09/29, Target/Wyndham Publications Ltd, UK
Cover by Jeff Cummins. Black curve logo. White spine.
Colour decal. Print run: 30,000 copies.
REF: ISBN 0-426-11690-9 OP: 60p p/b NM: £3.95

BTR-035c *Doctor Who and the Mutants*
(Terrance Dicks)
1979/11/20, Target/W H Allen & Co Ltd, UK
Cover by Jeff Cummins. Black curve logo. White spine.
Colour decal. Print run: 12,000 copies.
REF: ISBN 0-426-11690-9 OP: 75p p/b NM: £2.75

BTR-035d *Doctor Who and the Mutants*
(Terrance Dicks)
1982, Target/W H Allen & Co Ltd, UK
Cover by Jeff Cummins. Black curve logo. White spine.
Outline decal. 1987 reprint run: 15,000 copies.
REF: ISBN 0-426-11690-9 OP: £1.95 p/b NM: £2.75

BTR-035e *Doctor Who and the Mutants*
(Terrance Dicks)
1982, Target/W H Allen & Co Ltd, UK
Cover by Jeff Cummins. Black curve logo. White spine.
Colour decal.
REF: ISBN 0-426-11690-9 OP: £1.25 p/b NM: £2.75

BTR-035f *Doctor Who and the Mutants*
(Terrance Dicks)
1984, Target/W H Allen & Co Ltd, UK
Cover by Jeff Cummins. Black curve logo. White spine.
Colour decal. Print run: 15,000 copies.
REF: ISBN 0-426-11690-9 OP: £1.35 p/b NM: £2.75

BTR-035g *Doctor Who and the Mutants*
(Terrance Dicks)
1984, Target/W H Allen & Co Ltd, UK
Cover by Jeff Cummins. Black curve logo. White spine.
Outline decal. Print run: 14,800 copies.
REF: ISBN 0-426-11690-9 OP: £1.95 p/b NM: £2.75

BTR-036a *Doctor Who and the Deadly Assassin*
(Terrance Dicks)
1977/10/20, Allan Wingate (Publishers) Ltd, UK
Cover by Mike Little. Print run: 3,500 copies. This was
the last original hardback published under the Allan
Wingate imprint.
REF: ISBN 0-85523-120-3 OP: £2.95 h/b NM: £27.50

BTR-036b *Doctor Who and the Deadly Assassin*
(Terrance Dicks)
1977/10/20, Target/Wyndham Publications Ltd, UK
Cover by Mike Little. Red curve logo. White spine.
Colour decal. Print run: 30,000 copies.
REF: ISBN 0-426-11965-7 OP: 60p p/b NM: £3.95

BTR-036c *Doctor Who and the Deadly Assassin*
(Terrance Dicks)
1979/02/15, Target/W. H. Allen & Co. Ltd, UK
Cover by Mike Little. Red curve logo. White spine.
Colour decal. Print run: 12,000 copies.
REF: ISBN 0-426-11965-7 OP: 60p p/b NM: £2.75

BTR-036d *Doctor Who and the Deadly Assassin*
(Terrance Dicks)
1980, Target/W. H. Allen & Co. Ltd, UK
Cover by Mike Little. Red curve logo. White spine.
Colour decal. Print run: 12,000 copies.
REF: ISBN 0-426-11965-7 OP: 85p p/b NM: £2.75

BTR-036e *Doctor Who and the Deadly Assassin*
(Terrance Dicks)
1982, Target/W. H. Allen & Co. Ltd, UK
Cover by Mike Little. Red curve logo. White spine.
Colour decal.
REF: ISBN 0-426-11965-7 OP: £1.25 p/b NM: £2.75

BTR-036f *Doctor Who and the Deadly Assassin*
(Terrance Dicks)
1984, Target/W. H. Allen & Co. PLC, UK
Cover by Mike Little. Red curve logo. White spine.
Colour decal.
REF: ISBN 0-426-11965-7 OP: £1.35 p/b NM: £2.75

BTR-036g *Doctor Who and the Deadly Assassin*
(Terrance Dicks)
1984, Target/W. H. Allen & Co. PLC, UK
Cover by Mike Little. Red curve logo. White spine.

Colour decal. Number on spine. Print run: 18,000 copies.
REF: ISBN 0-426-11965-7 OP: £1.50 p/b NM: £2.75

BTR-037a *Doctor Who and the Talons of Weng-Chiang* (**Terrance Dicks**)
1977/11/15, Allan Wingate (Publishers) Ltd, UK
Cover by Jeff Cummins. Print run: 3,500 copies.
REF: ISBN 0-85523-170-X OP: £2.95 h/b NM: £16.50

BTR-037b *Doctor Who and the Talons of Weng-Chiang* (**Terrance Dicks**)
1977/11/15, Target/W. H. Allen & Co. Ltd, UK
Cover by Jeff Cummins. Black curve logo. White spine.
Colour decal. Print run: 30,000 copies.
REF: ISBN 0-426-11973-8 OP: 60p p/b NM: £6.50

BTR-037c *Doctor Who and the Talons of Weng-Chiang* (**Terrance Dicks**)
1979/01/18, Target/W. H. Allen & Co. Ltd, UK
Cover by Jeff Cummins. 'Second Impression'. Black curve logo. White spine. Colour decal. Wyndham W on back. Print run: 10,000 copies.
REF: ISBN 0-426-11973-8 OP: 60p p/b NM: £5.50

BTR-037d *Doctor Who and the Talons of Weng-Chiang #7* (**Terrance Dicks**)
1979/09, Pinnacle Books, USA
Cover by David Mann.
REF: ISBN 0-523-40638-X OP: $1.75 p/b NM: £5.50

BTR-037e *Doctor Who and the Talons of Weng-Chiang #7* (**Terrance Dicks**)
1979/09, Pinnacle Books, USA
Cover by David Mann. 'Second printing'. Red logo.
REF: ISBN 0-523-40638-X OP: $1.75 p/b NM: £5.50

BTR-037f *Doctor Who and the Talons of Weng-Chiang* (**Terrance Dicks**)
1980/02/21, Target/W. H. Allen & Co. Ltd, UK
Cover by Jeff Cummins. Black curve logo. White spine.
Colour decal. Print run: 12,000 copies.
REF: ISBN 0-426-11973-8 OP: 75p p/b NM: £5.50

BTR-037g *Doctor Who and the Talons of Weng-Chiang #7* (**Terrance Dicks**)
1981, Pinnacle Books, USA
Cover by David Mann. Orange logo.
REF: ISBN 0-523-41974-0 OP: $1.95 p/b NM: £5.50

BTR-037h *Doctor Who and the Talons of Weng-Chiang* (**Terrance Dicks**)
1982, Target/W. H. Allen & Co. Ltd, UK
Cover by Jeff Cummins. Black curve logo. White spine.

Colour decal.
REF: ISBN 0-426-11973-8 OP: £1.25 p/b NM: £5.50

BTR-037i *Doctor Who and the Talons of Weng-Chiang* (**Terrance Dicks**)
1982, Target/W. H. Allen & Co. Ltd, UK
Cover by Jeff Cummins. Black curve logo. Yellow spine.
Colour decal. Print run: 12,000 copies.
REF: ISBN 0-426-11973-8 OP: £1.35 p/b NM: £5.50

BTR-037j *Doctor Who and the Talons of Weng-Chiang #7* (**Terrance Dicks**)
1982/05, Pinnacle Books, USA
Cover by David Mann. 'Third printing'. Orange logo.
REF: ISBN 0-523-41974-0 OP: $1.95 p/b NM: £5.50

BTR-037k *Doctor Who and the Talons of Weng-Chiang* (**Terrance Dicks**)
1987, Target/W. H. Allen & Co. Ltd, UK
Outline decal. Print run: 2,000 copies.
REF: ISBN 0-426-11973-8 OP: £1.95 p/b NM: £5.50

BTR-037l *Doctor Who and the Talons of Weng-Chiang #7* (**Terrance Dicks**)
1989/04, Pinnacle Books, USA
Cover by David Mann. 'Seventh printing'. Green logo.
REF: ISBN 1-55817-209-2 OP: $3.50 p/b NM: £7.95

BTR-037m *Doctor Who – The Talons of Weng-Chiang* (**Terrance Dicks**)
1994/03/17, Target/Virgin Publishing Ltd, UK
Cover by Alistair Pearson. Blue spine.
REF: ISBN 0-426-11973-8 OP: £3.99 p/b NM: £5.50

BTR-038a *Doctor Who and the Masque of Mandragora* (**Philip Hinchcliffe**)
1977/12/08, Target/W. H. Allen & Co. Ltd, UK
Cover by Mike Little. Red curve logo. White spine.
Colour decal. Print run: 27,000 copies.
REF: ISBN 0-426-11893-6 OP: 60p p/b NM: £4.50

BTR-038b *Doctor Who and the Masque of Mandragora* (**Philip Hinchcliffe**)
1978/01/19, Longbow/W. H. Allen & Co. Ltd, UK
Cover by Mike Little. Print run: 4,000 copies.
REF: ISBN 0-491-02272-7 OP: £2.95 h/b NM: £16.50

BTR-038c *Doctor Who and the Masque of Mandragora* (**Philip Hinchcliffe**)
1979/07/26, Target/W. H. Allen & Co. Ltd, UK
Cover by Mike Little. 'Second Impression'. Red curve logo. White spine. Colour decal. Wyndham W on back.
Print run: 12,000 copies.
REF: ISBN 0-426-11893-6 OP: 70p p/b NM: £3.50

BTR-038d *Doctor Who and the Masque of Mandragora #8* **(Philip Hinchcliffe)**
1979/11, Pinnacle Books, USA
Cover by David Mann. Purple logo.
REF: ISBN 0-523-40640-1 OP: $1.75 p/b NM: £5.50

BTR-038e *Doctor Who and the Masque of Mandragora* **(Philip Hinchcliffe)**
1980, Target/W. H. Allen & Co. Ltd, UK
Cover by Mike Little. Red curve logo. White spine.
Colour decal. Two editions in 1980. Print run: 12,000 copies.
REF: ISBN 0-426-11893-6 OP: 75p p/b NM: £3.50

BTR-038f *Doctor Who and the Masque of Mandragora* **(Philip Hinchcliffe)**
1980, Target/W. H. Allen & Co. Ltd, UK
Cover by Mike Little. '4th Impression'. Red curve logo.
White spine. Colour decal. Print run: 15,000 copies.
REF: ISBN 0-426-11893-6 OP: 85p p/b NM: £3.50

BTR-038g *Doctor Who and the Masque of Mandragora #8* **(Philip Hinchcliffe)**
1981, Pinnacle Books, USA
Cover by David Mann. Orange logo.
REF: ISBN 0-523-41975-9 OP: $1.95 p/b NM: £5.50

BTR-038h *Doctor Who and the Masque of Mandragora* **(Philip Hinchcliffe)**
1982, Target/W. H. Allen & Co. Ltd, UK
Cover by Mike Little. Red curve logo. White spine.
Colour decal.
REF: ISBN 0-426-11893-6 OP: £1.25 p/b NM: £3.50

BTR-038i *Doctor Who and the Masque of Mandragora* **(Philip Hinchcliffe)**
1987, Target/W. H. Allen & Co. Ltd, UK
Outline decal. Print run: 3,000 copies.
REF: ISBN 0-426-11893-6 OP: £1.95 p/b NM: £3.50

BTR-038j *Docteur Who: Le Masque de Mandragore (6)* **(Philip Hinchcliffe)**
1987/08, Editions Garanciere, France
Artwork cover. Translated by Richard D Nolane.
Adapted by Corine Derblum. ISBN inside book is 2-7340-0219-1.
REF: ISBN 2-7340-0218-3 OP: p/b

BTR-038k *Doctor Who and the Masque of Mandragora #8* **(Philip Hinchcliffe)**
1989/06, Pinnacle Books, USA
Cover by David Mann. 'Fifth printing'. Violet logo.
REF: ISBN 1-55817-224-6 OP: $3.50 p/b NM: £7.95

BTR-037b

BTR-037d

BTR-037m

BTR-038a

BTR-038d

BTR-038j

BTR-038l

BTR-39b

BTR-039h

BTR-040b

BTR-041b

BTR-038l *Doctor Who – The Masque of Mandragora* (Philip Hinchcliffe)
1991/09/19, Target/Virgin Publishing Ltd, UK
Cover by Alistair Pearson. Blue spine. Print run: 9,000 copies.
REF: ISBN 0-426-11893-6 OP: £2.99 p/b NM: £5.50

BTR-039a *Doctor Who and the Face of Evil* (Terrance Dicks)
1978/01/19, Longbow/W. H. Allen & Co. Ltd, UK
Cover by Jeff Cummins. Print run: 4,000 copies.
REF: ISBN 0-491-02214-X OP: £2.95 h/b NM: £16.50

BTR-039b *Doctor Who and the Face of Evil* (Terrance Dicks)
1978/01/19, Target/W. H. Allen & Co. Ltd, UK
Cover by Jeff Cummins. Green curve logo. White spine. Colour decal. Print run: 25,000 copies.
REF: ISBN 0-426-20006-3 OP: 60p p/b NM: £3.95

BTR-039c *Doctor Who and the Face of Evil* (Terrance Dicks)
1979/07/29, Target/W. H. Allen & Co. Ltd, UK
Cover by Jeff Cummins. 'Second Impression'. Green curve logo. White spine. Colour decal. Wyndham W on back. Print run: 12,000 copies.
REF: ISBN 0-426-20006-3 OP: 70p p/b NM: £2.75

BTR-039d *Doctor Who and the Face of Evil* (Terrance Dicks)
1980, Target/W. H. Allen & Co. Ltd, UK
Cover by Jeff Cummins. Green curve logo. White spine. Colour decal. Print run: 12,000 copies.
REF: ISBN 0-426-20006-3 OP: 85p p/b NM: £2.75

BTR-039e *Doctor Who and the Face of Evil* (Terrance Dicks)
1982, Target/W. H. Allen & Co. Ltd, UK
Cover by Jeff Cummins. Green curve logo. White spine. Colour decal.
REF: ISBN 0-426-20006-3 OP: £1.25 p/b NM: £2.75

BTR-039f *Doctor Who and the Face of Evil* (Terrance Dicks)
1983, Target/W. H. Allen & Co. Ltd, UK
Cover by Jeff Cummins. Green curve logo. White spine. Colour decal.
REF: ISBN 0-426-20006-3 OP: £1.35 p/b NM: £2.75

BTR-039g *Doctor Who and the Face of Evil* (Terrance Dicks)
1984, Target/W. H. Allen & Co. Ltd, UK
Cover by Jeff Cummins. Green curve logo. White spine. Outline decal. Print run: 20,000 copies.
REF: ISBN 0-426-20006-3 OP: £1.50 p/b NM: £2.75

BTR-039h *Doctor Who – The Face of Evil*
(Terrance Dicks)
1993/04/15, Target/Virgin Publishing Ltd, UK
Cover by Alistair Pearson. Blue spine.
REF: ISBN 0-426-20006-3 OP: £3.50 p/b NM: £5.50

BTR-040a *Doctor Who and the Horror of Fang*
Rock (Terrance Dicks)
1978, Longbow/W. H. Allen & Co. Ltd, UK
Cover by Jeff Cummins. Print run: 4,000 copies.
REF: ISBN 0-491-02252-2 OP: £2.95 h/b NM: £16.50

BTR-040b *Doctor Who and the Horror of Fang*
Rock (Terrance Dicks)
1978/03/30, Target/W. H. Allen & Co. Ltd, UK
Cover by Jeff Cummins. Red curve logo. White spine.
Colour decal. Print run: 27,000 copies. Two printings
in 1978.
REF: ISBN 0-426-20009-8 OP: 60p p/b NM: £5.95

BTR-040c *Doctor Who and the Horror of Fang*
Rock (Terrance Dicks)
1979, Target/W. H. Allen & Co. Ltd, UK
Cover by Jeff Cummins. Red curve logo. White Spine.
Colour decal. Print run: 12,000 copies.
REF: ISBN 0-426-20009-8 OP: 70p p/b NM: £4.95

BTR-040d *Doctor Who and the Horror of Fang*
Rock (Terrance Dicks)
1981, Target/W. H. Allen & Co. Ltd, UK
Cover by Jeff Cummins. Red curve logo. White Spine.
Colour decal. Print run: 15,000 copies.
REF: ISBN 0-426-20009-8 OP: 95p p/b NM: £4.95

BTR-040e *Doctor Who and the Horror of Fang*
Rock (Terrance Dicks)
1982, Target/W. H. Allen & Co. Ltd, UK
REF: ISBN 0-426-20009-8 OP: p/b NM: £4.95

BTR-040f *Doctor Who and the Horror of Fang*
Rock (Terrance Dicks)
1984, Target/W. H. Allen & Co. Ltd, UK
Cover by Jeff Cummins. Red curve logo. White spine.
Colour decal.
REF: ISBN 0-426-20009-8 OP: £1.35 p/b NM: £4.95

BTR-040g *Doctor Who and the Horror of Fang*
Rock (Terrance Dicks)
1988, Target/W. H. Allen & Co. Ltd, UK
Print run: 4,000 copies.
REF: ISBN 0-426-20009-8 OP: £1.95 p/b NM: £4.95

BTR-041a *Doctor Who and the Tomb of the*
Cybermen (Gerry Davis)
1978, Longbow/W. H. Allen & Co. Ltd, UK
Cover by Jeff Cummins. Print run: 4,000 copies.
REF: ISBN 0-491-02262-X OP: £2.95 h/b NM: £16.50

BTR-041b *Doctor Who and the Tomb of the*
Cybermen (Gerry Davis)
1978/05/18, Target/W. H. Allen & Co. Ltd, UK
Cover by Jeff Cummins. Orange curve logo. White
spine. Colour decal. Print run: 25,000 copies.
REF: ISBN 0-426-11076-5 OP: 60p p/b NM: £6.50

BTR-041c *Doctor Who and the Tomb of the*
Cybermen (Gerry Davis)
1979/10/25, Target/W. H. Allen & Co. Ltd, UK
Cover by Jeff Cummins. '2nd impression'. Orange
curve logo. White spine. Colour decal. Print run:
12,000 copies.
REF: ISBN 0-426-11076-5 OP: 75p p/b NM: £5.50

BTR-041d *Doctor Who and the Tomb of the*
Cybermen (Gerry Davis)
1981, Target/W. H. Allen & Co. Ltd, UK
Cover by Jeff Cummins. Orange curve logo. White
spine. Colour decal. Print run: 15,000 copies.
REF: ISBN 0-426-11076-5 OP: 95p p/b NM: £5.50

BTR-041e *Doctor Who and the Tomb of the*
Cybermen (Gerry Davis)
1982, Target/W. H. Allen & Co. Ltd, UK
Cover by Jeff Cummins cover. Orange curve logo.
White spine. Colour decal.
REF: ISBN 0-426-11076-5 OP: £1.25 p/b NM: £5.50

BTR-041f *Doctor Who and the Tomb of the*
Cybermen (Gerry Davis)
1983, Target/W. H. Allen & Co. Ltd, UK
Print run: 20,000 copies.
REF: ISBN 0-426-11076-5 OP: p/b NM: £5.50

BTR-041g *Doctor Who and the Tomb of the*
Cybermen (Gerry Davis)
1984, Target/W. H. Allen & Co. Ltd, UK
Cover by Jeff Cummins. Orange curve logo. White
spine. Colour decal.
REF: ISBN 0-426-11076-5 OP: £1.35 p/b NM: £5.50

BTR-041h *Doctor Who and the Tomb of the*
Cybermen (Gerry Davis)
1984, Target/W. H. Allen & Co. Ltd, UK
Cover by Jeff Cummins. Orange curve logo. White
spine. Outline decal.
REF: ISBN 0-426-11076-5 OP: £1.95 p/b NM: £5.50

BTR-041j   BTR-042b

BTR-041i *Doctor Who and the Tomb of the Cybermen* **(Gerry Davis)**
1987, Target/W. H. Allen & Co. Ltd, UK
Print run: 8,000 copies.
REF: ISBN 0-426-11076-5 OP: £1.95 p/b NM: £5.50

BTR-041j *Doctor Who – The Tomb of the Cybermen* **(Gerry Davis)**
1992/10/15, Target/Virgin Publishing Ltd, UK
Cover by Alistair Pearson (as on video). Blue spine.
REF: ISBN 0-426-11076-5 OP: £2.99 p/b NM: £5.50

BTR-042a *Doctor Who and the Time Warrior* **(Terrance Dicks)**
1978/05/18, Longbow/W. H. Allen & Co. Ltd, UK
Cover by Roy Knipe. Robert Holmes wrote the book's prologue. Print run: 4,000 copies.
REF: ISBN 0-491-02413-4 OP: £2.95 h/b NM: £16.50

BTR-042g   BTR-043b

BTR-042b *Doctor Who and the Time Warrior* **(Terrance Dicks)**
1978/06/29, Target/W. H. Allen & Co. Ltd, UK
Cover by Roy Knipe. Burgundy curve logo. White spine. Colour decal. Print run: 25,000 copies.
REF: ISBN 0-426-20023-3 OP: 60p p/b NM: £3.95

BTR-042c *Doctor Who and the Time Warrior* **(Terrance Dicks)**
1980/02/21, Target/W. H. Allen & Co. Ltd, UK
Cover by Roy Knipe. Red curve logo. White spine. Colour decal. Print run: 12,000 copies.
REF: ISBN 0-426-20023-3 OP: 75p p/b NM: £2.75

BTR-042d *Doctor Who and the Time Warrior* **(Terrance Dicks)**
1982, Target/W. H. Allen & Co. Ltd, UK
REF: ISBN 0-426-20023-3 OP: p/b NM: £2.75

BTR-042e *Doctor Who and the Time Warrior* **(Terrance Dicks)**
1983, Target/W. H. Allen & Co. Ltd, UK
Cover by Roy Knipe. Red curve logo. White spine. Colour decal.
REF: ISBN 0-426-20023-3 OP: £1.35 p/b NM: £2.75

BTR-043j   BTR-044b

BTR-042f *Doctor Who and the Time Warrior* **(Terrance Dicks)**
1984, Target/W. H. Allen & Co. Ltd, UK
Cover by Roy Knipe. Red curve logo. White spine. Colour decal. Print run: 15,000 copies.
REF: ISBN 0-426-20023-3 OP: £1.50 p/b NM: £2.75

BTR-042g *Doctor Who – The Time Warrior*
(Terrance Dicks)
1993/06/17, Target/Virgin Publishing Ltd, UK
Cover by Alistair Pearson. Blue spine. This is a rejacketed 1984 Target reprint.
REF: ISBN 0-426-20023-3 OP: £3.50 p/b NM: £4.50

BTR-043a *Doctor Who – Death to the Daleks*
(Terrance Dicks)
1978, Longbow/W. H. Allen & Co. Ltd, UK
Cover by Roy Knipe. Print run: 3,500 copies.
REF: ISBN 0-491-02433-9 OP: £3.25 h/b NM: £16.50

BTR-043b *Doctor Who – Death to the Daleks*
(Terrance Dicks)
1978/07/20, Target/W. H. Allen & Co. Ltd, UK
Cover by Roy Knipe. Black curve logo. White spine.
Colour decal. Print run: 25,000 copies.
REF: ISBN 0-426-20042-X OP: 60p p/b NM: £5.50

BTR-043c *Doctor Who – Death to the Daleks*
(Terrance Dicks)
1979/11/20, Target/W. H. Allen & Co. Ltd, UK
'Second Impression'. Cover by Roy Knipe. Black curve logo. White spine. Colour decal. Wyndham W on back. Print run: 12,000 copies.
REF: ISBN 0-426-20042-X OP: 75p p/b NM: £4.50

BTR-043d *Doctor Who – Death to the Daleks*
(Terrance Dicks)
1980, Target/W. H. Allen & Co. Ltd, UK
'Third Impression'. Cover by Roy Knipe. Black curve logo. White spine. Colour decal.
REF: ISBN 0-426-20042-X OP: 75p p/b NM: £4.50

BTR-043e *Doctor Who – Death to the Daleks*
(Terrance Dicks)
1982, Target/W. H. Allen & Co. Ltd, UK
Cover by Roy Knipe. Black curve logo. White spine. Colour decal. Two printings in 1982.
REF: ISBN 0-426-20042-X OP: £1.35 p/b NM: £4.50

BTR-043f *Doctor Who – Death to the Daleks*
(Terrance Dicks)
1984, Target/W. H. Allen & Co. Ltd, UK
Cover by Roy Knipe. Black curve logo. White spine. Colour decal.
REF: ISBN 0-426-20042-X OP: £1.35 p/b NM: £4.50

BTR-043g *Doctor Who – Death to the Daleks*
(Terrance Dicks)
1984, Target/W. H. Allen & Co. Ltd, UK
Cover by Roy Knipe. Black curve logo. White spine. Colour decal.
REF: ISBN 0-426-20042-X OP: £1.50 p/b NM: £4.50

BTR-043h *Doctor Who – Death to the Daleks*
(Terrance Dicks)
1985, Target/W. H. Allen & Co. Ltd, UK
Cover by Roy Knipe. Black curve logo. White numbered spine. Outline decal. Print run: 10,000 copies.
REF: ISBN 0-426-20042-X OP: £1.50 p/b NM: £4.50

BTR-043i *Doctor Who tod den Daleks!*
(Terrance Dicks)
1990, Goldmann Verlag, Germany
Cover by Roy Knipe (from *Death to the Daleks*).
Translated by Bettina Zeller.
REF: ISBN 3-442-23623-1 OP: DM 7,80 p/b

BTR-043j *Doctor Who – Death to the Daleks*
(Terrance Dicks)
1991/04/18, Target/Virgin Publishing Ltd, UK
Cover by Alistair Pearson. Blue spine. Print run: 8,000 copies.
REF: ISBN 0-426-20042-X OP: £2.50 p/b NM: £5.50

BTR-044a *Doctor Who and the Android Invasion*
(Terrance Dicks)
1978/11/16, W. H. Allen & Co. Ltd, UK
Cover by Roy Knipe. Print run: 3,500 copies.
REF: ISBN 0-491-02026-0 OP: £3.25 h/b NM: £16.50

BTR-044b *Doctor Who and the Android Invasion*
(Terrance Dicks)
1978/11/16, Target/W. H. Allen & Co. Ltd, UK
Cover by Roy Knipe. Red curve logo. White spine.
Colour decal. Print run: 25,000 copies.
REF: ISBN 0-426-20037-3 OP: 60p p/b NM: £7.95

BTR-044c *Doctor Who and the Android Invasion*
(Terrance Dicks)
1979/12/13, Target/W. H. Allen & Co. Ltd, UK
Print run: 12,000 copies.
REF: ISBN 0-426-20037-3 OP: 75p p/b NM: £6.50

BTR-044d *Doctor Who and the Android Invasion*
#9 **(Terrance Dicks)**
1980/01, Pinnacle Books, USA
Cover by David Mann. Blue logo.
REF: ISBN 0-523-40641-X OP: $1.75 p/b NM: £5.50

BTR-044e *Doctor Who and the Android Invasion*
(Terrance Dicks)
1981/01/15, Target/W. H. Allen & Co. Ltd, UK
Cover by Roy Knipe. Red curve logo. White spine.
Colour decal. Print run: 15,000 copies.
REF: ISBN 0-426-20037-3 OP: 90p p/b NM: £6.50

BTR-044f *Doctor Who and the Android Invasion* **#9 (Terrance Dicks)**
1981/05, Pinnacle Books, USA
Cover by David Mann. 'Second printing'. Orange logo.
Identical third and fourth printings in April and July 1983.
REF: ISBN 0-523-41619-9   OP: $1.95 p/b   NM: £5.50

BTR-044g *Doctor Who and the Android Invasion* **(Terrance Dicks)**
1982/11/16, Target/W. H. Allen & Co. Ltd, UK
Cover by Roy Knipe. Red curve logo. White spine.
Colour decal.
REF: ISBN 0-426-20037-3   OP: £1.25 p/b   NM: £6.50

BTR-044h *Doctor Who and the Android Invasion* **#9 (Terrance Dicks)**
1989/11, Pinnacle Books, USA
Cover by David Mann. 'Seventh printing'. Green logo.
REF: ISBN 1-55817-287-4   OP: $3.50 p/b   NM: £7.95

BTR-045a *Doctor Who and the Sontaran Experiment* **(Ian Marter)**
1978, W. H. Allen & Co. Ltd, UK
Cover by Roy Knipe. Print run: 3,500 copies.
REF: ISBN 0-491-02046-5   OP: £3.25 h/b   NM: £16.50

BTR-045b *Doctor Who and the Sontaran Experiment* **(Ian Marter)**
1978/12/07, Target/W. H. Allen & Co. Ltd, UK
Cover by Roy Knipe. Blue curve logo. White spine.
Colour decal. Print run: 25,000 copies.
REF: ISBN 0-426-20049-7   OP: 60p p/b   NM: £5.50

BTR-045c *Doctor Who and the Sontaran Experiment* **(Ian Marter)**
1981, Target/W. H. Allen & Co. Ltd, UK
Print run: 20,000 copies.
REF: ISBN 0-426-20049-7   OP: p/b   NM: £4.50

BTR-045d *Doctor Who and the Sontaran Experiment* **(Ian Marter)**
1982, Target/W. H. Allen & Co. Ltd, UK
Cover by Roy Knipe. Blue curve logo. White spine.
Colour decal. Two printings in 1982.
REF: ISBN 0-426-20049-7   OP: £1.25 p/b   NM: £4.50

BTR-045e *Doctor Who and the Sontaran Experiment* **(Ian Marter)**
1984, Target/W. H. Allen & Co. Ltd, UK
Cover by Roy Knipe. Blue curve logo. White spine.
Colour decal. Print run: 20,000 copies.
REF: ISBN 0-426-20049-7   OP: £1.35 p/b   NM: £4.50

BTR-045f *Doctor Who and the Sontaran Experiment* **(Ian Marter)**
1984, Target/W. H. Allen & Co. Ltd, UK
Cover by Roy Knipe. Blue curve logo. White spine.
Outline decal. 1987 reprint run: 14,000 copies.
REF: ISBN 0-426-20049-7   OP: £1.95 p/b   NM: £4.50

BTR-046a *Doctor Who and the Hand of Fear* **(Terrance Dicks)**
1979/01/18, W. H. Allen & Co. Ltd, UK
Cover by Roy Knipe. Print run: 3,500 copies.
REF: ISBN 0-491-02256-5   OP: £3.25 h/b   NM: £16.50

BTR-046b *Doctor Who and the Hand of Fear* **(Terrance Dicks)**
1979/01/18, Target/W. H. Allen & Co. Ltd, UK
Cover by Roy Knipe. Red curve logo. White spine.
Colour decal. Print run: 27,000 copies.
REF: ISBN 0-426-20033-0   OP: 60p p/b   NM: £4.50

BTR-046c *Doctor Who and the Hand of Fear* **(Terrance Dicks)**
1980/01/24, Target/W. H. Allen & Co. Ltd, UK
Cover by Roy Knipe. Red curve logo. White spine.
Colour decal. Print run: 12,000 copies.
REF: ISBN 0-426-20033-0   OP: 75p p/b   NM: £3.50

BTR-046d *Doctor Who and the Hand of Fear* **(Terrance Dicks)**
1983, Target/W. H. Allen & Co. Ltd, UK
Cover by Roy Knipe. Red curve logo. White spine.
Colour decal. Print run: 20,000 copies.
REF: ISBN 0-426-20033-0   OP: £1.25 p/b   NM: £3.50

BTR-046e *Doctor Who and the Hand of Fear* **(Terrance Dicks)**
1984, Target/W. H. Allen & Co. Ltd, UK
Cover by Roy Knipe. Red curve logo. White spine.
Colour decal.
REF: ISBN 0-426-20033-0   OP: £1.35 p/b   NM: £3.50

BTR-046f *Doctor Who and the Hand of Fear* **(Terrance Dicks)**
1984, Target/W. H. Allen & Co. Ltd, UK
Cover by Roy Knipe. Red curve logo. White spine.
Outline decal.
REF: ISBN 0-426-20033-0   OP: £1.95 p/b   NM: £3.50

BTR-046g *Doctor Who and the Hand of Fear* **(Terrance Dicks)**
1986, Target/W. H. Allen & Co. Ltd, UK
Print run: 20,000 copies.
REF: ISBN 0-426-20033-0   OP: £1.95 p/b   NM: £3.50

BTR-046h *Doctor Who and the Hand of Fear*
(Terrance Dicks)
1988, Target/W. H. Allen & Co. Ltd, UK
Print run: 7,000 copies.
REF: ISBN 0-426-20033-0 OP: p/b NM: £3.50

BTR-047a *Doctor Who and the Invisible Enemy*
(Terrance Dicks)
1979/03/29, W. H. Allen & Co. Ltd, UK
Cover by Roy Knipe. Print run: 3,500 copies.
REF: ISBN 0-491-02437-1 OP: £3.25 h/b NM: £16.50

BTR-047b *Doctor Who and the Invisible Enemy*
(Terrance Dicks)
1979/03/29, Target/W. H. Allen & Co. Ltd, UK
Cover by Roy Knipe. Red curve logo. White spine.
Colour decal. Print run: 27,000 copies.
REF: ISBN 0-426-20054-3 OP: 60p p/b NM: £3.95

BTR-044d

BTR-047c *Doctor Who and the Invisible Enemy*
(Terrance Dicks)
1979, Target/W. H. Allen & Co. Ltd, UK
REF: ISBN 0-426-20054-3 OP: 75p p/b NM: £2.75

BTR-047d *Doctor Who and the Invisible Enemy*
(Terrance Dicks)
1980, Target/W. H. Allen & Co. Ltd, UK
Print run: 12,000 copies.
REF: ISBN 0-426-20054-3 OP: p/b NM: £2.75

BTR-047e *Doctor Who and the Invisible Enemy*
(Terrance Dicks)
1982, Target/W. H. Allen & Co. Ltd, UK
Cover by Roy Knipe. Red curve logo. White spine.
Colour decal. Two printings in 1982.
REF: ISBN 0-426-20054-3 OP: £1.25 p/b NM: £2.75

BTR-045b   BTR-046b

BTR-047f *Doctor Who and the Invisible Enemy*
(Terrance Dicks)
1984, Target/W. H. Allen & Co. Ltd, UK
Cover by Roy Knipe. Red curve logo. White spine.
Colour decal
REF: ISBN 0-426-20054-3 OP: £1.35 p/b NM: £2.75

BTR-047g *Doctor Who and the Invisible Enemy*
(Terrance Dicks)
1987, Target/W. H. Allen & Co. Ltd, UK
Outline decal. Print run: 13,500 copies.
REF: ISBN 0-426-20054-3 OP: £1.95 p/b NM: £2.75

BTR-047b

BTR-048b   BTR-048h

BTR-049b

BTR-050b

BTR-048a *Doctor Who and the Robots of Death*
(Terrance Dicks)
1979/05/24, W. H. Allen & Co. Ltd, UK
Cover by John Geary. Orange spine. Print run: 3,500
copies.
REF: ISBN 0-491-02436-3 OP: £3.50 h/b NM: £16.50

BTR-048b *Doctor Who and the Robots of Death*
(Terrance Dicks)
1979/05/24, Target/W. H. Allen & Co. Ltd, UK
Cover by John Geary. Orange curve logo. White
spine. Colour decal. Print run: 27,000 copies.
REF: ISBN 0-426-20061-6 OP: 70p p/b NM: £4.95

BTR-048c *Doctor Who and the Robots of Death*
(Terrance Dicks)
1981/01/15, Target/W. H. Allen & Co. Ltd, UK
Cover by John Geary. Gold curve logo. White spine.
Colour decal. Print run: 15,000 copies.
REF: ISBN 0-426-20061-6 OP: 90p p/b NM: £3.95

BTR-048d *Doctor Who and the Robots of Death*
(Terrance Dicks)
1982, Target/W. H. Allen & Co. Ltd, UK
REF: ISBN 0-426-20061-6 OP: p/b NM: £3.95

BTR-048e *Doctor Who and the Robots of Death*
(Terrance Dicks)
1984, Target/W. H. Allen & Co. Ltd, UK
Cover by John Geary. Orange curve logo. White
spine. Colour decal.
REF: ISBN 0-426-20061-6 OP: £1.35 p/b NM: £3.95

BTR-048f *Doctor Who and the Robots of Death*
(Terrance Dicks)
1984, Target/W. H. Allen & Co. Ltd, UK
Cover by John Geary. Orange curve logo. White
spine. Outline decal.
REF: ISBN 0-426-20061-6 OP: £1.95 p/b NM: £3.95

BTR-048g *Doctor Who and the Robots of Death*
(Terrance Dicks)
1988, Target/W. H. Allen & Co. Ltd, UK
Print run: 5,000 copies.
REF: ISBN 0-426-20061-6 OP: £1.95 p/b NM: £3.95

BTR-048h *Doctor Who – The Robots of Death*
(Terrance Dicks)
1994/02/17, Target/Virgin Publishing Ltd, UK
Cover by Alistair Pearson. Blue spine.
REF: ISBN 0-426-20061-6 OP: £3.99 p/b NM: £5.50

BTR-049a *Doctor Who and the Image of the Fendahl* (Terrance Dicks)
1979/07/26, W. H. Allen & Co. Ltd, UK
Cover by John Geary. Print run: 3,500 copies. Red curve logo.
REF: ISBN 0-491-02127-5 OP: £3.50 h/b NM: £16.50

BTR-049b *Doctor Who and the Image of the Fendahl* (Terrance Dicks)
1979/07/26, Target/W. H. Allen & Co. Ltd, UK
Cover by John Geary. Yellow curve logo. White spine. Colour decal. Print run: 30,000 copies. Two printings in 1979.
REF: ISBN 0-426-20077-2 OP: 70p p/b NM: £5.95

BTR-049c *Doctor Who and the Image of the Fendahl* (Terrance Dicks)
1980, Target/W. H. Allen & Co. Ltd, UK
Cover by John Geary. Yellow curve logo. White spine. Colour decal. Print run: 12,000 copies.
REF: ISBN 0-426-20077-2 OP: 75p p/b NM: £4.95

BTR-049d *Doctor Who and the Image of the Fendahl* (Terrance Dicks)
1982, Target/W. H. Allen & Co. Ltd, UK
REF: ISBN 0-426-20077-2 OP: p/b NM: £4.95

BTR-049e *Doctor Who and the Image of the Fendahl* (Terrance Dicks)
1983, Target/W. H. Allen & Co. Ltd, UK
Cover by John Geary. Yellow curve logo. White spine. Colour decal.
REF: ISBN 0-426-20077-2 OP: £1.35 p/b NM: £4.95

BTR-049f *Doctor Who and the Image of the Fendahl* (Terrance Dicks)
1987, Target/W. H. Allen & Co. Ltd, UK
Print run: 4,500 copies. Some editions had internal pages from 1983 edition. Outline decal.
REF: ISBN 0-426-20077-2 OP: £1.95 p/b NM: £4.95

BTR-050a *Doctor Who and the War Games* (Malcolm Hulke)
1979/10/25, W. H. Allen & Co. Ltd, UK
Cover by John Geary. Blue spine. Print run: 3,000 copies.
REF: ISBN 0-491-02428-2 OP: £3.75 h/b NM: £16.50

BTR-050b *Doctor Who and the War Games* (Malcolm Hulke)
1979/10/25, Target/W. H. Allen & Co. Ltd, UK
Cover by John Geary. Yellow curve logo. White spine. Colour decal. Print run: 30,000 copies.
REF: ISBN 0-426-20082-9 OP: 75p p/b NM: £4.95

BTR-050c *Doctor Who and the War Games* (Malcolm Hulke)
1980, Target/W. H. Allen & Co. Ltd, UK
"Second impression." Cover by John Geary. Yellow curve logo. White spine. Colour decal.
REF: ISBN 0-426-20082-9 OP: 85p p/b NM: £3.95

BTR-050d *Doctor Who and the War Games* (Malcolm Hulke)
1982, Target/W. H. Allen & Co. Ltd, UK
Cover by John Geary. Yellow curve logo. White spine. Colour decal.
REF: ISBN 0-426-20082-9 OP: £1.35 p/b NM: £3.95

BTR-050e *Doctor Who and the War Games* (Malcolm Hulke)
1983, Target/W. H. Allen & Co. Ltd, UK
Cover by John Geary. Yellow curve logo. White numbered spine. Colour decal.
REF: ISBN 0-426-20082-9 OP: £1.35 p/b NM: £3.95

BTR-050f *Doctor Who and the War Games* (Malcolm Hulke)
1984, Target/W. H. Allen & Co. PLC., UK
Cover by John Geary. Yellow curve logo. White spine. Colour decal. Print run: 12,000 copies.
REF: ISBN 0-426-20082-9 OP: £1.50 p/b NM: £3.95

BTR-050g *Doctor Who – The War Games* (Malcolm Hulke)
1990/02/15, Target/Virgin Publishing Ltd, UK
Cover by Alistair Pearson (as on Video). Blue spine. Print run: 6,000 copies.
REF: ISBN 0-426-20082-9 OP: £2.50 p/b NM: £3.95

BTR-051a *Doctor Who and the Destiny of the Daleks* (Terrance Dicks)
1979/11/20, W. H. Allen & Co. Ltd, UK
Cover by Andrew Skilleter. Deep red spine. Print run: 4,000 copies.
REF: ISBN 0-491-02640-4 OP: £3.50 h/b NM: £16.50

BTR-051b *Doctor Who and the Destiny of the Daleks* (Terrance Dicks)
1979/11/20, Target/W. H. Allen & Co. Ltd, UK
Cover by Andrew Skilleter. Burgundy curve logo. White spine. Colour decal. Print run: 39,000 copies.
REF: ISBN 0-426-20096-9 OP: 75p p/b NM: £5.50

BTR-051c *Doctor Who and the Destiny of the Daleks* (Terrance Dicks)
1981, Target/W. H. Allen & Co. Ltd, UK
Cover by Andrew Skilleter. Red curve logo. Colour decal. Print run: 15,000 copies.
REF: ISBN 0-426-20096-9 OP: 90p p/b NM: £4.50

BTR-050g

BTR-051b

BTR-051g

BTR-051d *Doctor Who and the Destiny of the Daleks* (Terrance Dicks)
1982, Target/W. H. Allen & Co. Ltd, UK
Cover by Andrew Skilleter. Red curve logo. White spine. Colour decal.
REF: ISBN 0-426-20096-9   OP: £1.35 p/b   NM: £4.50

BTR-051e *Doctor Who and the Destiny of the Daleks* (Terrance Dicks)
1983, Target/W. H. Allen & Co. Ltd, UK
Cover by Andrew Skilleter. Red curve logo. White spine. Colour decal. Print run: 20,000 copies.
REF: ISBN 0-426-20096-9   OP: £1.35 p/b   NM: £4.50

BTR-051f *Doctor Who and the Destiny of the Daleks* (Terrance Dicks)
1985, Target/W. H. Allen & Co. Ltd, UK
Cover by Andrew Skilleter. Red curve logo. White numbered spine. Outline decal. Print run: 10,000 copies.
REF: ISBN 0-426-20096-9   OP: £1.50 p/b   NM: £4.50

BTR-051g *Doctor Who und der Schopfer der Daleks* (Terrance Dicks)
1990/07, Goldmann Verlag, Germany
Cover by Chris Achilleos (from *Doctor Who and the Daleks*). Translated by Peter Tuscher.
REF: ISBN 3-442-23625-8   OP: DM 7,80 p/b

BTR-051h *Doctor Who – Destiny of the Daleks* (Terrance Dicks)
1992/07/16, Target/Virgin Publishing Ltd, UK
Cover by Alistair Pearson. Blue spine.
REF: ISBN 0-426-20096-9   OP: £2.99 p/b   NM: £5.50

BTR-052a *Doctor Who and the Ribos Operation* (Ian Marter)
1979/12/13, W. H. Allen & Co. Ltd, UK
Cover by John Geary. Orange spine. Print run: 3,000 copies.
REF: ISBN 0-491-02429-0   OP: £3.75 h/b   NM: £16.50

BTR-052b *Doctor Who and the Ribos Operation* (Ian Marter)
1979/12/13, Target/W. H. Allen & Co. Ltd, UK
Cover by John Geary. Red curve logo. White spine. Colour decal. Print run: 27,000 copies.
REF: ISBN 0-426-20092-6   OP: 75p p/b   NM: £5.50

BTR-052c *Doctor Who and the Ribos Operation* (Ian Marter)
1980, Target/W. H. Allen & Co. Ltd, UK
Cover by John Geary. '2nd impression'. Red curve logo. White spine. Colour decal. Print run: 15,000 copies.
REF: ISBN 0-426-20092-6   OP: 85p p/b   NM: £4.50

BTR-052d *Doctor Who and the Ribos Operation*
(Ian Marter)
1982, Target/W. H. Allen & Co. Ltd, UK
Cover by John Geary. Red curve logo. White spine.
Colour decal.
REF: ISBN 0-426-20092-6 OP: £1.35 p/b NM: £4.50

BTR-052e *Doctor Who and the Ribos Operation*
(Ian Marter)
1983, Target/W. H. Allen & Co. Ltd, UK
Cover by John Geary. Red curve logo. White spine.
Colour decal.
REF: ISBN 0-426-20092-6 OP: £1.35 p/b NM: £4.50

BTR-052f *Doctor Who and the Ribos Operation*
(Ian Marter)
1984, Target/W. H. Allen & Co. Ltd, UK
Cover by John Geary. Red curve logo. White num-
bered spine. Outline decal. Print run: 15,000 copies.
REF: ISBN 0-426-20092-6 OP: £1.50 p/b NM: £4.50

BTR-053a *Doctor Who and the Underworld*
(Terrance Dicks)
1980/01/24, W. H. Allen & Co. Ltd, UK
Cover by Bill Donohoe. Blue spine. Print run: 3,500 copies.
REF: ISBN 0-491-02229-8 OP: £3.75 h/b NM: £13.20

BTR-053b *Doctor Who and the Underworld*
(Terrance Dicks)
1980/01/24, Target/W. H. Allen & Co. Ltd, UK
Cover by Bill Donohoe. Blue curve logo. White spine.
Colour decal. Print run: 25,000 copies. Two printings
in 1980; the first printing cost 75p.
REF: ISBN 0-426-20068-3 OP: 85p p/b NM: £3.95

BTR-053c *Doctor Who and the Underworld*
(Terrance Dicks)
1982/02/21, Target/W. H. Allen & Co. Ltd, UK
Cover by Bill Donohoe. Blue curve logo. White spine.
Colour decal.
REF: ISBN 0-426-20068-3 OP: £1.25 p/b NM: £2.75

BTR-053d *Doctor Who and the Underworld*
(Terrance Dicks)
1984, Target/W. H. Allen & Co. Ltd, UK
Cover by Bill Donohoe. Blue curve logo. White spine.
Colour decal.
REF: ISBN 0-426-20068-3 OP: £1.35 p/b NM: £2.75

BTR-053e *Doctor Who and the Underworld*
(Terrance Dicks)
1984, Target/W. H. Allen & Co. Ltd, UK
Print run: 12,000 copies.
REF: ISBN 0-426-20068-3 OP: £1.50 p/b NM: £2.75

BTR-051h

BTR-052b

BTR-053b

BTR-053f *Doctor Who and the Underworld*
(Terrance Dicks)
1985, Target/W. H. Allen & Co. Ltd, UK
Cover by Bill Donohoe. Blue curve logo. Outline
decal. Print run: 12,000 copies.
REF: ISBN 0-426-20068-3 OP: £1.50 p/b NM: £2.75

BTR-054a *Doctor Who and the Invasion of Time*
(Terrance Dicks)
1980/02/21, W. H. Allen & Co. Ltd, UK
Cover by Andrew Skilleter. Red spine. Print run: 4,000
copies.
REF: ISBN 0-491-02439-8 OP: £3.75 h/b NM: £13.20

BTR-054b *Doctor Who and the Invasion of Time*
(Terrance Dicks)
1980/02/21, Target/W. H. Allen & Co. Ltd, UK
Cover by Andrew Skilleter. Red curve logo. White
spine. Print run: 30,000 copies.
REF: ISBN 0-426-20093-4 OP: 75p p/b NM: £9.95

BTR-054c *Doctor Who and the Invasion of Time*
(Terrance Dicks)
1981, Target/W. H. Allen & Co. Ltd, UK
Cover by Andrew Skilleter. Red curve logo. White
spine. Colour decal. Print run: 15,000 copies.
REF: ISBN 0-426-20093-4 OP: 95p p/b NM: £8.95

BTR-054d *Doctor Who and the Invasion of Time*
(Terrance Dicks)
1982, Target/W. H. Allen & Co. Ltd, UK
Cover by Andrew Skilleter. Red curve logo. White
spine. Colour decal.
REF: ISBN 0-426-20093-4 OP: £1.35 p/b NM: £8.95

BTR-054e *Doctor Who and the Invasion of Time*
(Terrance Dicks)
1984, Target/W. H. Allen & Co. Ltd, UK
Cover by Andrew Skilleter. Red curve logo. White
spine. Colour decal.
REF: ISBN 0-426-20093-4 OP: £1.35 p/b NM: £8.95

BTR-055a *Doctor Who and the Stones of Blood*
(Terrance Dicks)
1980/03/20, W. H. Allen & Co. Ltd, UK
Cover by Andrew Skilleter. Red spine. Print run: 3,500
copies.
REF: ISBN 0-491-02680-3 OP: £3.75 h/b NM: £13.20

BTR-055b *Doctor Who and the Stones of Blood*
(Terrance Dicks)
1980/03/20, Target/W. H. Allen & Co. Ltd, UK
Cover by Andrew Skilleter. Red curve logo. White
spine. Colour decal. Print run: 30,000 copies.
REF: ISBN 0-426-20099-3 OP: 75p p/b NM: £5.50

BTR-055c *Doctor Who and the Stones of Blood*
(Terrance Dicks)
1981, Target/W. H. Allen & Co. Ltd, UK
Cover by Andrew Skilleter. Red curve logo. Colour
decal. Print run: 15,000 copies.
REF: ISBN 0-426-20099-3 OP: 95p p/b NM: £4.50

BTR-055d *Doctor Who and the Stones of Blood*
(Terrance Dicks)
1982, Target/W. H. Allen & Co. Ltd, UK
REF: ISBN 0-426-20099-3 OP: £1.25 p/b NM: £4.50

BTR-055e *Doctor Who and the Stones of Blood*
(Terrance Dicks)
1984, Target/W. H. Allen & Co. Ltd, UK
Cover by Andrew Skilleter. Red curve logo. White
spine. Colour decal.
REF: ISBN 0-426-20099-3 OP: £1.35 p/b NM: £4.50

BTR-055f *Doctor Who and the Stones of Blood*
(Terrance Dicks)
1984, Target/W. H. Allen & Co. Ltd, UK
Cover by Andrew Shilleter. Red curve logo. White
spine. Outline decal.
REF: ISBN 0-426-20099-3 OP: £1.95 p/b NM: £4.50

BTR-055g *Doctor Who and the Stones of Blood*
(Terrance Dicks)
1988, Target/W. H. Allen & Co. Ltd, UK
Print run: 10,500 copies.
REF: ISBN 0-426-20099-3 OP: £1.95 p/b NM: £4.50

BTR-056a *Doctor Who and the Androids of Tara*
(Terrance Dicks)
1980/04/24, W. H. Allen & Co. Ltd, UK
Cover by Andrew Skilleter. Print run: 3,500 copies.
REF: ISBN 0-491-02651-X OP: £3.95 h/b NM: £13.20

BTR-056b *Doctor Who and the Androids of Tara*
(Terrance Dicks)
1980/04/24, Target/W. H. Allen & Co. Ltd, UK
Cover by Andrew Skilleter. Orange curve logo. White
spine. Colour decal. Print run: 30,000 copies.
REF: ISBN 0-426-21108-6 OP: 75p p/b NM: £4.50

BTR-056c *Doctor Who and the Androids of Tara*
(Terrance Dicks)
1982, Target/W. H. Allen & Co. Ltd, UK
Cover by Andrew Skilleter. Orange curve logo. White
spine. Colour decal.
REF: ISBN 0-426-21108-6 OP: £1.25 p/b NM: £3.50

BTR-056d *Doctor Who and the Androids of Tara*
(Terrance Dicks)

1984, Target/W. H. Allen & Co. Ltd, UK
Cover by Andrew Skilleter. Orange curve logo. White spine. Colour decal.
REF: ISBN 0-426-21108-6 OP: £1.35 p/b NM: £3.50

BTR-056e *Doctor Who and the Androids of Tara* **(Terrance Dicks)**
1987, Target/W. H. Allen & Co. Ltd, UK
Print run: 4,700 copies.
REF: ISBN 0-426-21108-6 OP: £1.95 p/b NM: £3.50

BTR-057a *Doctor Who and the Power of Kroll* **(Terrance Dicks)**
1980/05/29, W. H. Allen & Co. Ltd, UK
Cover by Andrew Skilleter. Burgundy spine. Print run: 3,500 copies.
REF: ISBN 0-491-02721-4 OP: £3.95 h/b NM: £13.20

BTR-057b *Doctor Who and the Power of Kroll* **(Terrance Dicks)**
1980/05/29, Target/W. H. Allen & Co. Ltd, UK
Cover by Andrew Skilleter. Red curve logo. White spine. Colour decal. Print run: 30,000 copies.
REF: ISBN 0-426-20101-9 OP: 85p p/b NM: £3.95

BTR-057c *Doctor Who and the Power of Kroll* **(Terrance Dicks)**
1982, Target/W. H. Allen & Co. Ltd, UK
Cover by Andrew Skilleter. Red curve logo. White spine. Colour decal.
REF: ISBN 0-426-20101-9 OP: £1.25 p/b NM: £2.75

BTR-057d *Doctor Who and the Power of Kroll* **(Terrance Dicks)**
1983, Target/W. H. Allen & Co. Ltd, UK
Cover by Andrew Skilleter. Red curve logo. White spine. Colour decal.
REF: ISBN 0-426-20101-9 OP: £1.35 p/b NM: £2.75

BTR-057e *Doctor Who and the Power of Kroll* **(Terrance Dicks)**
1984, Target/W. H. Allen & Co. PLC., UK
Cover by Andrew Skilleter. Red curve logo. White spine. Outline decal. Print run: 17,000 copies.
REF: ISBN 0-426-20101-9 OP: £1.50 p/b NM: £2.75

BTR-058a *Doctor Who and the Armageddon Factor* **(Terrance Dicks)**
1980/06/26, W. H. Allen & Co. Ltd, UK
Cover by Bill Donohoe. Light blue spine. Print run: 3,250 copies. This was the last hardback book to have a separate dust jacket. After this the books had the cover image laminated onto the hard cover of the book.
REF: ISBN 0-491-02660-9 OP: £3.95 h/b NM: £13.20

BTR-054b   BTR-055b

BTR-056b   BTR-057b

BTR-058b   BTR-059b

BTR-060a

BTR-061b

BTR-062b

BTR-062d

BTR-062e

BTR-058b *Doctor Who and the Armageddon Factor* (Terrance Dicks)
1980/06/26, Target/W. H. Allen & Co. Ltd, UK
Cover by Bill Donohoe. Blue curve logo. White spine.
Colour decal. Print run: 40,000 copies.
REF: ISBN 0-426-20104-3   OP: 85p p/b   NM: £3.95

BTR-058c *Doctor Who and the Armageddon Factor* (Terrance Dicks)
1982, Target/W. H. Allen & Co. Ltd, UK
Blue curve logo. White spine. Colour decal. Interior ISBN 0-426-20103-5.
REF: ISBN 0-426-20104-3   OP: p/b   NM: £2.75

BTR-058d *Doctor Who and the Armageddon Factor* (Terrance Dicks)
1984, Target/W. H. Allen & Co. PLC., UK
Cover by Bill Donohoe. Blue curve logo. White spine.
Colour decal. Print run: 17,000 copies. Two printings in 1984; the first printing cost £1.35.
REF: ISBN 0-426-20104-3   OP: £1.50 p/b   NM: £2.75

BTR-059a *Doctor Who and the Keys of Marinus* (Philip Hinchcliffe)
1980/08/21, W. H. Allen & Co. Ltd, UK
Cover by David McAllister. Print run: 3,250 copies.
REF: ISBN 0-491-02921-7   OP: £3.95 h/b   NM: £13.20

BTR-059b *Doctor Who and the Keys of Marinus* (Philip Hinchcliffe)
1980/08/21, Target/W. H. Allen & Co. Ltd, UK
Cover by David McAllister. Brown curve logo. Brown spine. Colour decal. Print run: 40,000 copies.
REF: ISBN 0-426-20125-6   OP: 85p p/b   NM: £5.50

BTR-059c *Doctor Who and the Keys of Marinus* (Philip Hinchcliffe)
1980, Target/W. H. Allen & Co. Ltd, UK
Cover by David McAllister. Orange curve logo.
Orange spine. Colour decal. ISBN on page 2, not on cover. Title page says 'Based on the BBC television serial *Doctor Who and the Sea of Death*'!
REF: ISBN 0-426-20125-6   OP: £1.25 p/b   NM: £5.50

BTR-059d *Doctor Who and the Keys of Marinus* (Philip Hinchcliffe)
1984, Target/W. H. Allen & Co. Ltd, UK
Cover by David McAllister. Orange curve logo.
Orange spine. Colour decal.
REF: ISBN 0-426-20125-6   OP: £1.35 p/b   NM: £4.50

BTR-059e *Doctor Who and the Keys of Marinus* (Philip Hinchcliffe)
1987, Target/W. H. Allen & Co. Ltd, UK
1984 contents. Cover by David McAllister. Orange

curve logo. Orange numbered spine. Outline decal.
Print run: 4,700 copies.
REF: ISBN 0-426-20125-6 OP: £1.95 p/b NM: £4.50

BTR-060a *Doctor Who and the Nightmare of Eden* **(Terrance Dicks)**
1980/08/21, Target/W. H. Allen & Co. Ltd, UK
Cover by Andrew Skilleter. Green curve logo. Green spine. Colour decal. Print run: 35,000 copies.
REF: ISBN 0-426-20130-2 OP: 85p p/b NM: £4.50

BTR-060b *Doctor Who and the Nightmare of Eden* **(Terrance Dicks)**
1980/09/18, W. H. Allen & Co. Ltd, UK
Cover by Andrew Skilleter. Print run: 3,250 copies.
REF: ISBN 0-491-02118-6 OP: £3.95 h/b NM: £13.20

BTR-060c *Doctor Who and the Nightmare of Eden* **(Terrance Dicks)**
1982, Target/W. H. Allen & Co. Ltd, UK
REF: ISBN 0-426-20130-2 OP: p/b NM: £3.50

BTR-060d *Doctor Who and the Nightmare of Eden* **(Terrance Dicks)**
1983, Target/W. H. Allen & Co. Ltd, UK
Cover by Andrew Skilleter. Green curve logo. Green spine. Colour decal.
REF: ISBN 0-426-20130-2 OP: £1.35 p/b NM: £3.50

BTR-060e *Doctor Who and the Nightmare of Eden* **(Terrance Dicks)**
1988, Target/W. H. Allen & Co. Ltd, UK
Cover by Andrew Skilleter. Green curve logo. Green spine. Outline decal. Print run: 4,000 copies.
REF: ISBN 0-426-20130-2 OP: £1.95 p/b NM: £3.50

BTR-061a *Doctor Who and the Horns of Nimon* **(Terrance Dicks)**
1980/10/16, W. H. Allen & Co. Ltd, UK
Cover by Steve Kyte. Print run: 3,250 copies.
REF: ISBN 0-491-02278-6 OP: £3.95 h/b NM: £13.20

BTR-061b *Doctor Who and the Horns of Nimon* **(Terrance Dicks)**
1980/10/16, Target/W. H. Allen & Co. Ltd, UK
Cover by Steve Kyte. Red curve logo. Blue spine. Colour decal. Print run: 35,000 copies.
REF: ISBN 0-426-20131-0 OP: 85p p/b NM: £5.50

BTR-061c *Doctor Who and the Horns of Nimon* **(Terrance Dicks)**
1982, Target/W. H. Allen & Co. Ltd, UK
Cover by Steve Kyte. Red curve logo. Blue spine. Colour decal.
REF: ISBN 0-426-20131-0 OP: £1.25 p/b NM: £5.50

BTR-061d *Doctor Who and the Horns of Nimon* **(Terrance Dicks)**
1984, Target/W. H. Allen & Co. Ltd, UK
Cover by Steve Kyte. Red curve logo. Blue spine. Colour decal.
REF: ISBN 0-426-20131-0 OP: £1.35 p/b NM: £4.50

BTR-061e *Doctor Who and the Horns of Nimon* **(Terrance Dicks)**
1987, Target/W. H. Allen & Co. Ltd, UK
Print run: 12,000 copies.
REF: ISBN 0-426-20131-0 OP: £1.95 p/b NM: £4.50

BTR-062a *Doctor Who and the Monster of Peladon* **(Terrance Dicks)**
1980/11/20, W. H. Allen & Co. Ltd, UK
Cover by Steve Kyte. Print run: 3,250 copies.
REF: ISBN 0-491-02823-7 OP: £3.95 h/b NM: £13.20

BTR-062b *Doctor Who and the Monster of Peladon* **(Terrance Dicks)**
1980/12/04, Target/W. H. Allen & Co. Ltd, UK
Cover by Steve Kyte. Green curve logo. Green spine. Colour decal. Print run: 35,000 copies.
REF: ISBN 0-426-20132-9 OP: 85p p/b NM: £5.50

BTR-062c *Doctor Who and the Monster of Peladon* **(Terrance Dicks)**
1982 c., Target/W. H. Allen & Co. Ltd, UK
Cover by Steve Kyte. Green curve logo. Green spine. Colour decal. No reprint information in book. Probably a rejacket.
REF: ISBN 0-426-20132-9 OP: £1.25 p/b NM: £4.50

BTR-062d *Beyond The Stars*
1983, St Michael (Octopus books for Marks and Spencer), UK
A hardback 286 page children's SF anthology, featured 'Return to Peladon', the first 22 pages of *The Monster of Peladon*. Illustrations of a Trevor Martin-esque Doctor, a butch Sarah Jane and Alpha Centauri boasting tentacles like a Jules Verne creature by Peter Dennis (Linda Rogers Associates). The book was withdrawn after the publishers allegedly ran into copyright problems over using an excerpt from the first *Star Wars* novel.
REF: ISBN 0-86273-094-5 OP: £1.75 h/b

BTR-062e *Beyond The Stars*
1986, Marylebone Books (Octopus Books Limited), UK
Re-release with a different cover by an unknown artist. Apparently available from Woolworths.
REF: ISBN 0-86178-294-1 OP: £1.75 h/b

BTR-062f *Doctor Who and the Monster of Peladon* **(Terrance Dicks)**
1984, Target/W. H. Allen & Co. Ltd, UK
Cover by Steve Kyte. Green curve logo. Green spine. Colour decal.
REF: ISBN 0-426-20132-9 OP: £1.35 p/b NM: £4.50

BTR-062g *Doctor Who and the Monster of Peladon* **(Terrance Dicks)**
1984, Target/W. H. Allen & Co. Ltd, UK
Cover by Steve Kyte. Green curve logo. Green spine. Outline decal. 1987 reprint run: 8,300 copies.
REF: ISBN 0-426-20132-9 OP: £1.95 p/b NM: £4.50

BTR-062h *Doctor Who – The Monster of Peladon* **(Terrance Dicks)**
1992/06/18, Target/Virgin Publishing Ltd, UK
Cover by Alistair Pearson. Blue spine.
REF: ISBN 0-426-20132-9 OP: £2.99 p/b NM: £5.50

BTR-063a *Doctor Who and the Creature from the Pit* **(David Fisher)**
1981/01/15, W. H. Allen & Co. Ltd, UK
Cover by Brian Dennington. Print run: 3,250 copies.
REF: ISBN 0-491-02991-8 OP: £4.25 h/b NM: £13.20

BTR-063b *Doctor Who and the Creature from the Pit* **(David Fisher)**
1981/01/15, Target/W. H. Allen & Co. Ltd, UK
Cover by Brian Dennington. Red curve logo. Red spine. Colour decal. Print run: 35,000 copies.
REF: ISBN 0-426-20123-X OP: 90p p/b NM: £4.50

BTR-063c *Doctor Who and the Creature from the Pit* **(David Fisher)**
1982, Target/W. H. Allen & Co. Ltd, UK
Cover by Brian Dennington. Red curve logo. Red spine. Colour decal.
REF: ISBN 0-426-20123-X OP: £1.25 p/b NM: £3.50

BTR-063d *Doctor Who and the Creature from the Pit* **(David Fisher)**
1984, Target/W. H. Allen & Co. Ltd, UK
Cover by Brian Dennington. Red curve logo. Red spine. Colour decal.
REF: ISBN 0-426-20123-X OP: £1.35 p/b NM: £3.50

BTR-063e *Doctor Who and the Creature from the Pit* **(David Fisher)**
1984, Target/W. H. Allen & Co. Ltd, UK
Cover by Brian Dennington. Red curve logo. Red spine. Outline decal. 1987 reprint run: 11,600 copies.
REF: ISBN 0-426-20123-X OP: £1.95 p/b NM: £3.50

BTR-064a *Doctor Who and the Enemy of the World* **(Ian Marter)**
1981/04/16, W. H. Allen & Co. Ltd, UK
Cover by Bill Donohoe. Print run: 3,250 copies.
REF: ISBN 0-491-02972-1 OP: £4.25 h/b NM: £13.20

BTR-064b *Doctor Who and the Enemy of the World* **(Ian Marter)**
1981/04/16, Target/W. H. Allen & Co. Ltd, UK
Cover by Bill Donohoe. Brown curve logo. White spine. Colour decal. Print run: 30,000 copies.
REF: ISBN 0-426-20126-4 OP: 95p p/b NM: £5.50

BTR-064c *Doctor Who and the Enemy of the World* **(Ian Marter)**
1982, Target/W. H. Allen & Co. Ltd, UK
Cover by Bill Donohoe. Red curve logo. White spine. Colour decal.
REF: ISBN 0-426-20126-4 OP: £1.25 p/b NM: £4.50

BTR-064d *Doctor Who and the Enemy of the World* **(Ian Marter)**
1983, Target/W. H. Allen & Co. Ltd, UK
Cover by Bill Donohoe. Brown curve logo. White spine. Colour decal.
REF: ISBN 0-426-20126-4 OP: £1.35 p/b NM: £4.50

BTR-064e *Doctor Who and the Enemy of the World* **(Ian Marter)**
1983, Target/W. H. Allen & Co. Ltd, UK
Print run: 30,000 copies.
REF: ISBN 0-426-20126-4 OP: £1.50 p/b NM: £4.50

BTR-064f *Doctor Who and the Enemy of the World* **(Ian Marter)**
1984, Target/W. H. Allen & Co. Ltd, UK
Cover by Bill Donohoe. Red curve logo. White spine. Outline decal. Edition also available with a cover price of 95p.
REF: ISBN 0-426-20126-4 OP: £1.50 p/b NM: £4.50

BTR-064g *Doctor Who – Enemy of the World* **(Ian Marter)**
1993/05/20, Target/Virgin Publishing Ltd, UK
Cover by Alistair Pearson. Blue spine.
REF: ISBN 0-426-20126-4 OP: £3.50 p/b NM: £4.50

BTR-065a *Doctor Who and the State of Decay* **(Terrance Dicks)**
1981/09/17, W. H. Allen & Co. Ltd, UK
Cover by Andrew Skilleter. Print run: 3,000 copies.
REF: ISBN 0-491-02953-5 OP: £4.50 h/b NM: £13.20

BTR-065b *Doctor Who and the State of Decay*
(Terrance Dicks)
1982/01/14, Target/W. H. Allen & Co. Ltd, UK
Cover by Andrew Skilleter. Pink neon logo. Cyan
spine. Colour decal. Print run: 25,000 copies. Two
printings in 1982, The second printing cost £1.25.
REF: ISBN 0-426-20133-7 OP: £1.00 p/b NM: £4.50

BTR-065c *Doctor Who and the State of Decay*
(Terrance Dicks)
1983, Target/W. H. Allen & Co. Ltd, UK
Cover by Andrew Skilleter. Pink neon logo. Blue spine.
Colour decal.
REF: ISBN 0-426-20133-7 OP: £1.35 p/b NM: £3.50

BTR-065d *Doctor Who and the State of Decay*
(Terrance Dicks)
1984, Target/W. H. Allen & Co. Ltd, UK
Cover by Andrew Skilleter. Pink neon logo. Blue spine.
Colour decal.
REF: ISBN 0-426-20133-7 OP: p/b NM: £3.50

BTR-065e *Doctor Who and the State of Decay*
(Terrance Dicks)
1987, Target/W. H. Allen & Co. Ltd, UK
Print run: 10,000 copies.
REF: ISBN 0-426-20133-7 OP: £1.95 p/b NM: £3.50

BTR-066a *Doctor Who and An Unearthly Child*
(Terrance Dicks)
1981, W. H. Allen & Co. Ltd, UK
Cover by Andrew Skilleter. Print run: 2,500 copies.
REF: ISBN 0-491-02748-6 OP: £4.95 h/b NM: £16.50

BTR-066b *Doctor Who and An Unearthly Child*
(Terrance Dicks)
1981/10/15, Target/W. H. Allen & Co. Ltd, UK
Cover by Andrew Skilleter. Red foil neon logo. Cover
Flash: 'First publication of the very first *Doctor Who*
story.' Red spine. Colour decal. Print run: 30,000 copies.
REF: ISBN 0-426-20144-2 OP: £1.25 p/b NM: £7.95

BTR-066c *Doctor Who and An Unearthly Child*
(Terrance Dicks)
1982, Target/W. H. Allen & Co. Ltd, UK
Cover by Andrew Skilleter. Red neon logo (not foil).
Cover Flash: 'First publication of the very first *Doctor
Who* story.' Red spine. Colour decal.
REF: ISBN 0-426-20144-2 OP: £1.25 p/b NM: £5.50

BTR-066d *Doctor Who and An Unearthly Child*
(Terrance Dicks)
1983, Target/W. H. Allen & Co. Ltd, UK
Cover by Andrew Skilleter. with 'First Publication'

BTR-062h

BTR-063b

BTR-064b

BTR-064g

BTR-065b

BTR-066b

BTR-066g **BTR-066i**

BTR-067b **BTR-068b**

BTR-068f **BTR-069b**

flash. Red neon logo. Red spine. Colour decal.
REF: ISBN 0-426-20144-2 OP: £1.25 p/b NM: £5.50

**BTR-066e Doctor Who and An Unearthly Child
(Terrance Dicks)**
1984, Target/W. H. Allen & Co. Ltd, UK
Red neon logo. Red spine. Colour decal. Cover flash
reads 'First publication of the very first Doctor Who story'.
REF: ISBN 0-426-20144-2 OP: £1.35 p/b NM: £5.50

**BTR-066f Doctor Who and An Unearthly Child
(Terrance Dicks)**
1985, Target/W. H. Allen & Co. PLC., UK
Cover by Andrew Skilleter. Red neon logo. Red spine.
Outline decal.
REF: ISBN 0-426-20144-2 OP: £1.50 p/b NM: £5.50

**BTR-066g Docteur Who: Entre En Scène (1)
(Terrance Dicks)**
1987/02, Editions Garanciere, France
Artwork cover. Translated by Jean-Daniel Breque.
REF: ISBN 2-7340-0201-9 OP: p/b

**BTR-066h Doctor Who und das Kind von den
Sternen (Terrance Dicks)**
1990, Goldmann Verlag, Germany
Cover by David McAllister (from Doctor Who and the
Keys of Marinus). Translated by Bettina Zeller.
REF: ISBN 3-442-23626-6 OP: DM 7,80 p/b

**BTR-066i Doctor Who – An Unearthly Child
(Terrance Dicks)**
1990/02/15, Target/Virgin Publishing Ltd, UK
Cover by Alistair Pearson (as on Video). Blue spine.
Print run: 5,000 copies.
REF: ISBN 0-426-20144-2 OP: £2.50 p/b NM: £5.50

**BTR-067a Doctor Who and Warriors' Gate (John
Lydecker)**
1982/04/15, W. H. Allen & Co. Ltd, UK
Cover by Andrew Skilleter. John Lydecker is a pseudo-
nym for Stephen Gallagher.
REF: ISBN 0-491-02746-X OP: £4.95 h/b NM: £20

**BTR-067b Doctor Who and Warriors' Gate (John
Lydecker)**
1982/04/15, Target/W. H. Allen & Co. Ltd, UK
Cover by Andrew Skilleter. Red neon logo. Cyan
spine. Colour decal. Print run: 25,000 copies. Two
printings in 1982.
REF: ISBN 0-426-20146-9 OP: £1.25 p/b NM: £9.95

BTR-067c *Doctor Who and Warriors' Gate* (John Lydecker)
1983, Target/W. H. Allen & Co. Ltd, UK
ISBN on back cover. Colour decal.
REF: ISBN 0-426-20146-9 OP: £1.35 p/b NM: £8.95

BTR-067d *Doctor Who and Warriors' Gate* (John Lydecker)
1983, Target/W. H. Allen & Co. Ltd, UK
Red neon logo. Blue spine. Colour decal. Print run: 20,000 copies.
REF: ISBN 0-426-20146-9 OP: £1.95 p/b NM: £8.95

BTR-067e *Doctor Who and Warriors' Gate* (John Lydecker)
1984, Target/W. H. Allen & Co. Ltd, UK
Cover by Andrew Skilleter. Red neon logo. Cyan spine. Outline decal. No ISBN on back cover.
REF: No ISBN OP: £1.35 p/b NM: £8.95

BTR-068a *Doctor Who and the Keeper of Traken* (Terrance Dicks)
1982/05/20, W. H. Allen & Co. Ltd, UK
Cover by Andrew Skilleter. Print run: 3,000 copies.
REF: ISBN 0-491-02717-6 OP: £4.95 h/b NM: £13.20

BTR-068b *Doctor Who and the Keeper of Traken* (Terrance Dicks)
1982/05/20, Target/W. H. Allen & Co. Ltd, UK
Cover by Andrew Skilleter. Blue neon logo. Red spine. Colour decal. Print run: 20,000 copies. Three printings in 1982; the first two printings cost £1.25.
REF: ISBN 0-426-20148-5 OP: £1.35 p/b NM: £5.50

BTR-068c *Doctor Who and the Keeper of Traken* (Terrance Dicks)
1983, Target/W. H. Allen & Co. Ltd, UK
Cover by Andrew Skilleter. Blue neon logo. Red spine. Colour decal.
REF: ISBN 0-426-20148-5 OP: £1.35 p/b NM: £4.50

BTR-068d *Doctor Who and the Keeper of Traken* (Terrance Dicks)
1984, Target/W H. Allen & Co. PLC., UK
Cover by Andrew Skilleter. Blue neon logo. Red spine. Ouline decal.
REF: ISBN 0-426-20148-5 OP: £1.35 p/b NM: £4.50

BTR-068e *Doctor Who and the Keeper of Traken* (Terrance Dicks)
1984, Target/W. H. Allen & Co. PLC., UK
Cover by Andrew Skilleter. Blue neon logo. Red spine. Ouline decal. 1987 reprint run: 8,000 copies.
REF: ISBN 0-426-20148-5 OP: £1.95 p/b NM: £4.50

BTR-068f *Doctor Who – The Keeper of Traken* (Terrance Dicks)
1993/06/17, Target/Virgin Publishing Ltd, UK
Cover by Alistair Pearson. Blue spine. This is a rejacketed 1984 Target reprint.
REF: ISBN 0-426-20148-5 OP: £3.50 p/b NM: £5.50

BTR-069a *Doctor Who and the Leisure Hive* (David Fisher)
1982/07/22, W. H. Allen & Co. Ltd, UK
Cover by Andrew Skilleter.
REF: ISBN 0-491-02727-3 OP: £4.95 h/b NM: £13.20

BTR-069b *Doctor Who and the Leisure Hive* (David Fisher)
1982/07/22, Target/W. H. Allen & Co. Ltd, UK
Cover by Andrew Skilleter. Orange neon logo. Orange spine. Colour decal. Title page has 'A Star Book' and Star logo in place of the usual Target logo; appears to have been corrected in all subsequent editions. Print run: 35,000 copies. Two printings in 1982.
REF: ISBN 0-426-20147-7 OP: £1.25 p/b NM: £4.50

BTR-069c *Doctor Who and the Leisure Hive* (David Fisher)
1983, Target/W. H. Allen & Co. Ltd, UK
Print run: 20,000 copies.
REF: ISBN 0-426-20147-7 OP: p/b NM: £3.50

BTR-069d *Doctor Who and the Leisure Hive* (David Fisher)
1984, Target/W. H. Allen & Co. Ltd, UK
Cover by Andrew Skilleter. Orange neon logo. Orange spine. Colour logo.
REF: ISBN 0-426-20147-7 OP: £1.35 p/b NM: £3.50

BTR-069e *Doctor Who and the Leisure Hive* (David Fisher)
1984, Target/W. H. Allen & Co. Ltd, UK
Cover by Andrew Skilleter. Orange neon logo. Orange spine. Outline logo. 1987 reprint run: 14,000 copies.
REF: ISBN 0-426-20147-7 OP: £1.95 p/b NM: £3.50

BTR-069f *Doctor Who – The Leisure Hive* (David Fisher)
1993/10/21, Target/Virgin Publishing Ltd, UK
Cover by Alistair Pearson. Blue spine.
REF: ISBN 0-426-20147-7 OP: £3.50 p/b NM: £5.50

BTR-070a *Doctor Who and the Visitation* (Eric Saward)
1982/08/19, W. H. Allen & Co. Ltd, UK
Photographic cover.
REF: ISBN 0-491-02847-4 OP: £4.95 h/b NM: £13.20

BTR-070b *Doctor Who and the Visitation* **(Eric Saward)**
1982/08/19, Target/W. H. Allen & Co. Ltd, UK
Photographic cover. Orange neon logo. Blue spine.
Colour decal. Print run: 35,000 copies. Two printings in 1982.
REF: ISBN 0-426-20135-3 OP: £1.25 p/b NM: £3.95

BTR-070c *Doctor Who and the Visitation* **(Eric Saward)**
1984, Target/W. H. Allen & Co. Ltd, UK
Photographic cover. Orange neon logo. Blue spine.
Colour decal. Print run: 35,000 copies.
REF: ISBN 0-426-20135-3 OP: £1.35 p/b NM: £2.75

BTR-070d *Doctor Who and the Visitation* **(Eric Saward)**
1987, Target/W. H. Allen & Co. Ltd, UK
1984 contents. Photographic cover. Orange neon logo.
Blue spine. Outline decal. Print run: 12,000 copies.
REF: ISBN 0-426-20135-3 OP: £1.95 p/b NM: £2.75

BTR-070e *Doctor Who – The Visitation* **(Eric Saward)**
1992/02/20, Target/Virgin Publishing Ltd, UK
Cover by Alistair Pearson. Blue spine.
REF: ISBN 0-426-20135-3 OP: £2.99 p/b NM: £4.50

BTR-071a *Doctor Who – Full Circle* **(Andrew Smith)**
1982/09/16, W. H. Allen & Co. Ltd, UK
Cover by Andrew Skilleter. Print run: 2,500 copies.
REF: ISBN 0-491-02738-9 OP: £5.25 h/b NM: £13.20

BTR-071b *Doctor Who – Full Circle* **(Andrew Smith)**
1982/09/16, Target/W. H. Allen & Co. Ltd, UK
Cover by Andrew Skilleter. Orange neon logo. Orange spine. Colour decal. Print run: 35,000 copies.
REF: ISBN 0-426-20150-7 OP: £1.25 p/b NM: £5.50

BTR-071c *Doctor Who – Full Circle* **(Andrew Smith)**
1983, Target/W. H. Allen & Co. Ltd, UK
Cover by Andrew Skilleter. Orange neon logo. Orange spine. Colour decal.
REF: ISBN 0-426-20150-7 OP: £1.35 p/b NM: £4.50

BTR-071d *Doctor Who – Full Circle* **(Andrew Smith)**
1984, Target/W. H. Allen & Co. Ltd, UK
Cover by Andrew Skilleter. Brown neon logo. Brown spine. Colour decal.
REF: ISBN 0-426-20150-7 OP: £1.35 p/b NM: £4.50

BTR-071e *Doctor Who – Full Circle* **(Andrew Smith)**
1987, Target/W. H. Allen & Co. Ltd, UK
Outline decal. Print run: 10,000 copies.
REF: ISBN 0-426-20150-7 OP: £1.95 p/b NM: £4.50

BTR-072a *Doctor Who – Logopolis* **(Christopher H Bidmead)**
1982/10/21, W. H. Allen & Co. Ltd, UK
Cover by Andrew Skilleter. Print run: 2,500 copies.
REF: ISBN 0-491-02857-1 OP: £5.25 h/b NM: £13.20

BTR-072b *Doctor Who – Logopolis* **(Christopher H Bidmead)**
1982/10/21, Target/W. H. Allen & Co. Ltd, UK
Cover by Andrew Skilleter. Orange neon logo. Blue spine. Colour decal. Print run: 30,000 copies.
REF: ISBN 0-426-20149-3 OP: £1.25 p/b NM: £6.50

BTR-072c *Doctor Who – Logopolis* **(Christopher H Bidmead)**
1983, Target/W. H. Allen & Co. Ltd, UK
Cover by Andrew Skilleter. Orange neon logo. Blue spine. Colour decal.
REF: ISBN 0-426-20149-3 OP: £1.25 p/b NM: £5.50

BTR-072d *Doctor Who – Logopolis* **(Christopher H Bidmead)**
1984, Target/W. H. Allen & Co. Ltd, UK
Cover by Andrew Skilleter. Orange neon logo. Blue spine. Colour decal.
REF: ISBN 0-426-20149-3 OP: £1.35 p/b NM: £5.50

BTR-072e *Doctor Who – Logopolis* **(Christopher H Bidmead)**
1987, Target/W. H. Allen & Co. Ltd, UK
1984 contents. Cover by Andrew Skilleter. Orange neon logo. Blue spine. Outline decal.
REF: ISBN 0-426-20149-3 OP: £1.95 p/b NM: £5.50

BTR-072f *Doctor Who – Logopolis* **(Christopher H Bidmead)**
1991/12/19, Target/Virgin Publishing Ltd, UK
Cover by Alistair Pearson. Blue spine.
REF: ISBN 0-426-20149-3 OP: £2.99 p/b NM: £5.50

BTR-073a *Doctor Who and the Sunmakers* **(Terrance Dicks)**
1982/11/18, W. H. Allen & Co. Ltd, UK
Cover by Andrew Skilleter.
REF: ISBN 0-491-02758-3 OP: £5.25 h/b NM: £13.20

BTR-073b *Doctor Who and the Sunmakers*
(Terrance Dicks)
1982/11/18, Target/W. H. Allen & Co. Ltd, UK
Cover by Andrew Skilleter. Orange neon logo. Orange
spine. Colour decal. Print run: 30,000 copies.
REF: ISBN 0-426-20059-4 OP: £1.25 p/b NM: £3.95

BTR-073c *Doctor Who and the Sunmakers*
(Terrance Dicks)
1983, Target/W. H. Allen & Co. Ltd, UK
Cover by Andrew Skilleter. Orange neon logo. Orange
spine. Colour decal.
REF: ISBN 0-426-20059-4 OP: £1.25 p/b NM: £2.75

BTR-073d *Doctor Who and the Sunmakers*
(Terrance Dicks)
1984, Target/W. H. Allen & Co. Ltd, UK
Cover by Andrew Skilleter. Orange neon logo. Orange
spine. Colour decal. No ISBN on cover. Print run:
20,000 copies.
REF: ISBN 0-426-20059-4 OP: £1.50 p/b NM: £2.75

BTR-074a *Doctor Who – Time-Flight* **(Peter
Grimwade)**
1983/01/20, W. H. Allen & Co. Ltd, UK
Photographic cover. Print run: 4,500 copies.
REF: ISBN 0-491-03140-8 OP: £5.25 h/b NM: £13.20

BTR-074b *Doctor Who – Time-Flight* **(Peter
Grimwade)**
1983/04/14, Target/W. H. Allen & Co. Ltd, UK
Photographic cover. Orange neon logo. Pale blue
spine. Colour decal. Print run: 40,000 copies. Two
printings in 1983.
REF: ISBN 0-426-19297-4 OP: £1.35 p/b NM: £4.50

BTR-069f

BTR-070b

BTR-070e

BTR-071b

BTR-072b

BTR-072f

BTR-073b

BTR-074b

BTR-075b

BTR-075e

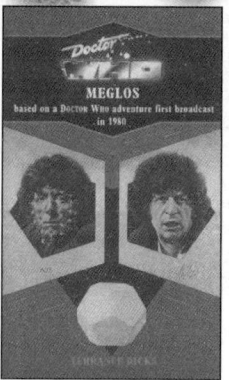

BTR-075f

BTR-076b

BTR-076d

BTR-077b

BTR-074c *Doctor Who – Time-Flight* **(Peter Grimwade)**
1984, Target/W. H. Allen & Co. PLC., UK
Photographic cover. Orange neon logo. Blue spine.
Outline decal. No ISBN on cover.
REF: ISBN 0-426-19297-4 OP: £1.50 p/b NM: £3.50

BTR-075a *Doctor Who – Meglos* **(Terrance Dicks)**
1983/02/17, W. H. Allen & Co. Ltd, UK
Cover by Andrew Skilleter. Print run: 3,000 copies.
REF: ISBN 0-491-03150-5 OP: £5.25 h/b NM: £13.20

BTR-075b *Doctor Who – Meglos* **(Terrance Dicks)**
1983/05/19, Target/W. H. Allen & Co. Ltd, UK
Cover by Andrew Skilleter. Blue neon logo. Blue spine.
Colour decal. Print run: 40,000 copies.
REF: ISBN 0-426-20136-1 OP: £1.35 p/b NM: £3.95

BTR-075c *Doctor Who – Meglos* **(Terrance Dicks)**
1984, Target/W. H. Allen & Co. Ltd, UK
Cover by Andrew Skilleter. Blue neon logo. Blue spine.
Colour decal
REF: ISBN 0-426-20136-1 OP: £1.35 p/b NM: £2.75

BTR-075d *Doctor Who – Meglos* **(Terrance Dicks)**
1984, Target/W. H. Allen & Co. Ltd, UK
Cover by Andrew Skilleter. Blue neon logo. Blue spine.
Interior ISBN is still 0-426-20136-1. 1987 reprint run:
6,000 copies.
REF: ISBN 0-426-20136-X OP: £1.95 p/b NM: £2.75

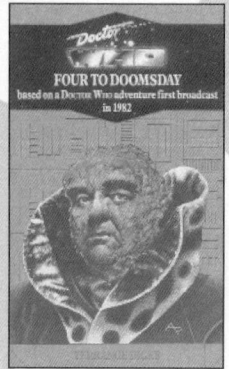

BTR-077e

BTR-078b

BTR-075e *Docteur Who: Meglos (8)* **(Terrance Dicks)**
1987/08, Editions Garanciere, France
Artwork cover. Translated by Corine Derblum.
REF: ISBN 2-7340-0227-2 OP: p/b

BTR-075f *Doctor Who – Meglos* **(Terrance Dicks)**
1993/04/15, Target/Virgin Publishing Ltd, UK
Cover by Alistair Pearson. Blue spine.
REF: ISBN 0-426-20136-1 OP: £3.50 p/b NM: £5.50

BTR-076a *Doctor Who – Castrovalva* **(Christopher H Bidmead)**
1983/03/17, W. H. Allen & Co. Ltd, UK
Photographic cover. Print run: 3,000 copies.
REF: ISBN 0-491-03330-3 OP: £5.25 h/b NM: £13.20

BTR-076b *Doctor Who – Castrovalva* **(Christopher H Bidmead)**
1983/06/16, Target/W. H. Allen & Co. Ltd, UK
Photographic cover. Red neon logo. Black spine.
Colour decal. Print run: 40,000 copies.
REF: ISBN 0-426-19326-1 OP: £1.35 p/b NM: £4.50

BTR-076c *Doctor Who – Castrovalva* **(Christopher H Bidmead)**
1984, Target/W. H. Allen & Co. PLC., UK
Photographic cover. Red neon logo. Black numbered spine. Colour decal. Two printings in 1984; the first printing cost £1.35.
REF: ISBN 0-426-19326-1 OP: £1.50 p/b NM: £3.50

BTR-076d *Doctor Who – Castrovalva* **(Christopher H Bidmead)**
1991/06/20, Target/Virgin Publishing Ltd, UK
Cover by Alistair Pearson. Blue spine.
REF: ISBN 0-426-19326-1 OP: £2.50 p/b NM: £5.50

BTR-077a *Doctor Who – Four to Doomsday* **(Terrance Dicks)**
1983/04/14, W. H. Allen & Co. Ltd, UK
Photographic cover. Print run: 3,000 copies
REF: ISBN 0-491-03450-4 OP: £5.25 h/b NM: £13.20

BTR-077b *Doctor Who – Four to Doomsday* **(Terrance Dicks)**
1983/07/21, Target/W. H. Allen & Co. Ltd, UK
Photographic cover. Blue neon logo. Red spine. Colour decal. Print run: 40,000 copies.
REF: ISBN 0-426-19334-2 OP: £1.35 p/b NM: £4.95

BTR-077c *Doctor Who – Four to Doomsday* **(Terrance Dicks)**
1984, Target/W. H. Allen & Co. Ltd, UK
Photographic cover. Blue neon logo. Red spine.
Outline decal.
REF: ISBN 0-426-19334-2 OP: £1.95 p/b NM: £3.95

BTR-077d *Doctor Who – Four to Doomsday* **(Terrance Dicks)**
1987, Target/W. H. Allen & Co. Ltd, UK
Photographic cover. Print run: 2,500 copies.
REF: ISBN 0-426-19334-2 OP: £1.95 p/b NM: £3.95

BTR-077e *Doctor Who – Four to Doomsday* **(Terrance Dicks)**
1991/06/20, Target/Virgin Publishing Ltd, UK
Cover by Alistair Pearson. Blue spine. Print run: 10,000 copies.
REF: ISBN 0-426-19334-2 OP: £2.50 p/b NM: £5.50

BTR-078a *Doctor Who – Earthshock* **(Ian Marter)**
1983/05/19, W. H. Allen & Co. Ltd, UK
Photographic cover. Print run: 3,000 copies.
REF: ISBN 0-491 03181-5 OP: £5.25 h/b NM: £13.20

BTR-078b *Doctor Who – Earthshock* **(Ian Marter)**
1983/08/18, Target/W. H. Allen & Co. Ltd, UK
Photographic cover. Red neon logo. Blue spine.
Colour decal. Print run: 40,000 copies. Two printings in 1983.
REF: ISBN 0-426-19377-6 OP: £1.35 p/b NM: £4.95

BTR-078c *Doctor Who – Earthshock* **(Ian Marter)**
1992/04/16, Target/Virgin Publishing Ltd, UK
Cover by Alistair Pearson. Blue spine.
REF: ISBN 0-426-19377-6 OP: £2.99 p/b NM: £5.50

BTR-079a *Doctor Who – Terminus* **(John Lydecker)**
1983/06/16, W. H. Allen & Co. Ltd, UK
Photographic cover. John Lydecker is a pseudonym for Stephen Gallagher. Print run: 3,000 copies.
REF: ISBN 0-491-03131-9 OP: £5.50 h/b NM: £13.20

BTR-079b *Doctor Who – Terminus* **(John Lydecker)**
1983/09/15, Target/W. H. Allen & Co. Ltd, UK
Photographic cover. Red neon logo. Pinky/Orange spine. Colour decal. First paperback book to be numbered as a part of the Target *Doctor Who* library on first release on the spine. Number 79. On first

BTR-078c

BTR-079b

BTR-080b

release, *Four to Doomsday* and *Earthshock* had been numbered 77 and 78, respectively, on the interior title page but not the spine. From this point all books (bar *Arc of Infinity*) were numbered. The number of each book corresponds with our BTR- coding (up to and including BTR-152). The first 73 titles were simply numbered alphabetically (not including *Time-Flight, Meglos* and *Castrovalva*) and the numbers appeared on re-issues from 1983 onwards. Print run: 40,000 copies.
REF: ISBN 0-426-19385-7 OP: £1.50 p/b NM: £6.50

BTR-079c Doctor Who – *Terminus* (John Lydecker)
1984, Target/W. H. Allen & Co. Ltd, UK
Photographic cover. Red neon logo. Pink/orange spine. Colour decal.
REF: ISBN 0-426-19385-7 OP: £1.50 p/b NM: £5.50

BTR-080a *Doctor Who – Arc of Infinity* (Terrance Dicks)
1983/07/21, W. H. Allen & Co. Ltd, UK
Photographic cover. Print run: 3,000 copies.
REF: ISBN 0-491-03061-4 OP: £6.50 h/b NM: £13.20

BTR-080b *Doctor Who – Arc of Infinity* (Terrance Dicks)
1983/10/20, Target/W. H. Allen & Co. Ltd, UK
Photographic cover. Red neon logo. Orange spine. Colour decal. Print run: 40,000 copies.
REF: ISBN 0-426-19342-3 OP: £1.35 p/b NM: £5.95

BTR-080c *Doctor Who – Arc of Infinity* (Terrance Dicks)
1984, Target/W. H. Allen & Co. Ltd, UK
Photographic cover. Red neon logo. Orange spine. Colour decal.
REF: ISBN 0-426-19342-3 OP: £1.35 p/b NM: £4.95

BTR-080d *Doctor Who – Arc of Infinity* (Terrance Dicks)
1992/03/19, Target/Virgin Publishing Ltd, UK
Cover by Alistair Pearson. Blue spine.
REF: ISBN 0-426-19342-3 OP: £2.99 p/b NM: £5.50

BTR-081a *Doctor Who – The Five Doctors* (Terrance Dicks)
1983/11/.24, W. H. Allen & Co. Ltd, UK
Cover by Andrew Skilleter. Print run: 3,000 copies.
REF: ISBN 0-491-03052-5 OP: £5.95 h/b NM: £16.50

BTR-081b *Doctor Who – The Five Doctors*
(Terrance Dicks)
1983/11/24, Target/W. H. Allen & Co. Ltd, UK
Cover by Andrew Skilleter. Red neon logo. Red spine.
Colour decal. Number 81. 'First edition' flash on
cover. Silver foil background to cover art. Print run:
50,000 copies.
REF: ISBN 0-426-19510-8 OP: £1.50 p/b NM: £7.95

BTR-081c *Doctor Who – The Five Doctors*
(Terrance Dicks)
1983, Target/W. H. Allen & Co. Ltd, UK
Cover by Andrew Skilleter. Red neon logo. Red spine.
Colour decal. Number 81. 'Second edition' flash on
cover. Silver foil background to cover art. 'Second
Impression'.
REF: ISBN 0-426-19510-8 OP: £1.50 p/b NM: £7.95

BTR-080d

BTR-081d *Doctor Who – The Five Doctors*
(Terrance Dicks)
1984, Target/W. H. Allen & Co. Ltd, UK
Cover by Andrew Skilleter. Red neon logo. Red spine.
Colour decal. 'Third Impression'. 'Second edition' flash
on cover.
REF: ISBN 0-426-19510-8 OP: £1.50 p/b NM: £6.50

BTR-081e *Doctor Who – The Five Doctors*
(Terrance Dicks)
1984, Target/W. H. Allen & Co. Ltd, UK
Cover by Andrew Skilleter. Red neon logo. Red spine.
Outline decal. 'Fourth Impression'.
REF: ISBN 0-426-19510-8 OP: £1.50 p/b NM: £6.50

BTR-081f *Doctor Who – The Five Doctors*
(Terrance Dicks)
1986, Target/W. H. Allen & Co. Ltd, UK
Cover by Andrew Skilleter. Red neon logo. Red spine.
Outline decal.
REF: ISBN 0-426-19510-8 OP: £1.75 p/b NM: £6.50

BTR-081b

BTR-081g *Doctor Who – The Five Doctors*
(Terrance Dicks)
1991/02/21, Target/Virgin Publishing Ltd, UK
Cover by Alistair Pearson. Blue spine. Print run: 8,500
copies.
REF: ISBN 0-426-19510-8 OP: £2.50 p/b NM: £6.50

BTR-082a *Doctor Who – Mawdryn Undead*
(Peter Grimwade)
1983/08/18, W. H. Allen & Co. Ltd, UK
Photographic cover. Print run: 3,000 copies.
REF: ISBN 0-491-03091-6 OP: £5.50 h/b NM: £13.20

BTR-081g

BTR-082b

BTR-082b *Doctor Who – Mawdryn Undead* **(Peter Grimwade)**
1984, Target/W. H. Allen & Co. PLC., UK
Photographic cover. Orange neon logo. Grey/Brown
spine. Colour decal. Number 82.
REF: ISBN 0-426-19393-8 OP: £1.35 p/b NM: £5.50

BTR-082c *Doctor Who – Mawdryn Undead* **(Peter Grimwade)**
1984, Target/W. H. Allen & Co. Ltd, UK
Photographic cover. Orange neon logo. Grey/Brown
spine. Outline decal. 1987 reprint run: 3,500 copies.
REF: ISBN 0-426-19393-8 OP: £1.95 p/b NM: £4.50

BTR-082d *Doctor Who – Mawdryn Undead* **(Peter Grimwade)**
1984/01/12, Target/W. H. Allen & Co. Ltd, UK
Photographic cover. Print run: 40,000 copies.
REF: ISBN 0-426-19393-8 OP: £1.35 p/b NM: £4.50

BTR-082e *Doctor Who – Mawdryn Undead* **(Peter Grimwade)**
1992/03/19, Target/Virgin Publishing Ltd, UK
Cover by Alistair Pearson. Blue spine.
REF: ISBN 0-426-19393-8 OP: £2.99 p/b NM: £4.50

BTR-082e

BTR-083a *Doctor Who – Snakedance* **(Terrance Dicks)**
1984/01/12, W. H. Allen & Co. PLC, UK
Cover by Andrew Skilleter. Photograph of Davison
behind logo. Print run: 3,000 copies.
REF: ISBN 0-491-03151-3 OP: £5.95 h/b NM: £13.20

BTR-083b *Doctor Who – Snakedance* **(Terrance Dicks)**
1984/04/19, Target/W. H. Allen & Co. PLC, UK
Cover by Andrew Skilleter. Photograph of Davison
behind logo. Red neon logo. Purple spine. Colour decal.
Number 83. Print run: 40,000 copies. Reprinted in 1984.
REF: ISBN 0-426-19457-8 OP: £1.35 p/b NM: £4.50

BTR-083c *Doctor Who – Snakedance* **(Terrance Dicks)**
1984, Target/W. H. Allen & Co. PLC, UK
Cover by Andrew Skilleter. Photograph of Davison
behind logo. Red neon logo. Purple spine. Outline
decal. This is a rejacketed first edition. 1987 reprint
run: 4,600 copies.
REF: ISBN 0-426-19457-8 OP: £1.95 p/b NM: £3.50

BTR-083b

BTR-084a *Doctor Who – Kinda* **(Terrance Dicks)**
1983/12/08, W. H. Allen & Co. Ltd, UK
Photographic cover. Print run: 3,000 copies.
REF: ISBN 0-491-03121-1 OP: £5.95 h/b NM: £13.20

BTR-084b *Doctor Who – Kinda* **(Terrance Dicks)**
1984/03/15, Target/W. H. Allen & Co. Ltd, UK
Photographic cover. Red neon logo. Red spine. Colour logo. Number 84. Print run: 40,000 copies.
REF: ISBN 0-426-19529-9 OP: £1.35 p/b NM: £5.50

BTR-084c *Doctor Who – Kinda* **(Terrance Dicks)**
1984, Target/W. H. Allen & Co. Ltd, UK
Photographic cover. Red neon logo. Red spine. Outline logo. 1987 reprint run: 4,200 copies.
REF: ISBN 0-426-19529-9 OP: £1.95 p/b NM: £4.50

BTR-084d *Doctor Who – Kinda* **(Terrance Dicks)**
1992/02/20, Target/Virgin Publishing Ltd, UK
Cover by Alistair Pearson. Blue spine.
REF: ISBN 0-426-19529-9 OP: £2.99 p/b NM: £4.50

BTR-084b BTR-084d

BTR-085a *Doctor Who – Enlightenment* **(Barbara Clegg)**
1984/02/16, W. H. Allen & Co. PLC, UK
Cover by Andrew Skilleter. Photograph of Davison behind logo. Print run: 3,000 copies.
REF: ISBN 0-491-03132-7 OP: £5.95 h/b NM: £13.20

BTR-085b *Doctor Who – Enlightenment* **(Barbara Clegg)**
1984/05/24, Target/W. H. Allen & Co. PLC, UK
Cover by Andrew Skilleter. Photograph of Davison behind logo. Blue neon logo. Black spine. Colour decal. Number 85. Print run: 40,000 copies.
REF: ISBN 0-426-19537-X OP: £1.35 p/b NM: £8.95

BTR-085c *Doctor Who – Enlightenment* **(Barbara Clegg)**
1984, Target/W. H. Allen & Co. PLC, UK
Cover by Andrew Skilleter. Photograph of Davison behind logo. Blue neon logo. Black spine. Outline decal.
REF: ISBN 0-426-19537-X OP: £1.50 p/b NM: £7.95

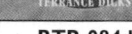

BTR-085b

BTR-086a *Doctor Who – The Dominators* **(Ian Marter)**
1984/04/19, W. H. Allen & Co. PLC, UK
Cover by Andrew Skilleter. Print run: 3,000 copies.
REF: ISBN 0-491-03292-7 OP: £5.95 h/b NM: £11

BTR-086b *Doctor Who – The Dominators* **(Ian Marter)**
1984/07/19, Target/W. H. Allen & Co. PLC, UK
Cover by Andrew Skilleter. Purple neon logo. Blue spine. Colour decal. Number 86. Print run: 50,000 copies. Two printings in 1984; the second printing features the outline decal.
REF: ISBN 0-426-19553-1 OP: £1.50 p/b NM: £5.50

BTR-086b

BTR-086c

BTR-087b

BTR-087d

BTR-088b

BTR-086c *Doctor Who – The Dominators* (Ian Marter)
1991/02/21, Target/Virgin Publishing Ltd, UK
Cover by Alistair Pearson. Blue spine. (as on Video).
Print run: 8,000 copies.
REF: ISBN 0-426-19553-1 OP: £2.50 p/b NM: £4.50

BTR-087a *Doctor Who – Warriors of the Deep* (Terrance Dicks)
1984/05/24, W. H. Allen & Co. PLC, UK
Cover by Andrew Skilleter. Print run: 3,000 copies.
REF: ISBN 0-491-03302-8 OP: £5.95 h/b NM: £13.20

BTR-087b *Doctor Who – Warriors of the Deep* (Terrance Dicks)
1984/08/16, Target/W. H. Allen & Co. PLC, UK
Cover by Andrew Skilleter. Lime green neon logo. Blue spine. Outline logo. Number 87. Print run: 50,000 copies.
REF: ISBN 0-426-19561-2 OP: £1.50 p/b NM: £3.95

BTR-087c *Doctor Who – Warriors of the Deep* (Terrance Dicks)
1985, Target/W. H. Allen & Co. PLC, UK
Cover by Andrew Skilleter. Green neon logo. Blue spine. Outline decal. Print run: 15,000 copies.
REF: ISBN 0-426-19561-2 OP: £1.50 p/b NM: £2.75

BTR-087d *Doctor Who – Warriors of the Deep* (Terrance Dicks)
1992/08/20, Target/Virgin Publishing Ltd, UK
Cover by Alistair Pearson. Blue spine.
REF: ISBN 0-426-19561-2 OP: £2.99 p/b NM: £4.50

BTR-088a *Doctor Who – The Aztecs* (John Lucarotti)
1984/06/21, W. H. Allen & Co. PLC, UK
Cover by Nick Spender. Print run: 3,000 copies.
REF: ISBN 0-491-03462-8 OP: £5.95 h/b NM: £13.20

BTR-088b *Doctor Who – The Aztecs* (John Lucarotti)
1984/09/20, Target/W. H. Allen & Co. PLC, UK
Cover by Nick Spender. Red neon logo. Blue spine. Colour decal. Number 88. Print run: 60,000 copies.
REF: ISBN 0-426-19588-4 OP: £1.50 p/b NM: £5.50

BTR-088c *Doctor Who – The Aztecs* (John Lucarotti)
1992/09/17, Target/Virgin Publishing Ltd, UK
Blue spine. Cover by Andrew Skilleter (as on Video).
REF: ISBN 0-426-19588-4 OP: £2.99 p/b NM: £5.50

BTR-089a *Doctor Who – Inferno* (**Terrance Dicks**)
1984/07/19, W. H. Allen & Co. PLC, UK
Cover by Nick Spender. Print run: 3,000 copies.
REF: ISBN 0-491-03143-2 OP: £5.95 h/b NM: £16.50

BTR-089b *Doctor Who – Inferno* (**Terrance Dicks**)
1984/10/18, Target/W. H. Allen & Co. PLC, UK
Cover by Nick Spender. Red neon logo. Orange spine. Outline decal. Number 89. Print run: 60,000 copies.
REF: ISBN 0-426-19617-1 OP: £1.50 p/b NM: £11

BTR-090a *Doctor Who – The Highlanders* (**Gerry Davis**)
1984/08/16, W. H. Allen & Co. PLC, UK
Cover by Nick Spender. Print run: 3,000 copies.
REF: ISBN 0-491-03193-9 OP: £5.95 h/b NM: £22

BTR-090b *Doctor Who – The Highlanders* (**Gerry Davis**)
1984/11/15, Target/W. H. Allen & Co. PLC, UK
Cover by Nick Spender. Red neon logo. Red spine. Outline decal. Number 90. Print run: 60,000 copies.
REF: ISBN 0-426-19676-7 OP: £1.50 p/b NM: £16.50

BTR-091a *Doctor Who – Frontios* (**Christopher H Bidmead**)
1984/09/20, W. H. Allen & Co. PLC, UK
Cover by Andrew Skilleter. Print run: 3,000 copies.
REF: ISBN 0-491-03253-6 OP: £5.95 h/b NM: £13.20

BTR-091b *Doctor Who – Frontios* (**Christopher H Bidmead**)
1984/12/10, Target/W. H. Allen & Co. PLC, UK
Cover by Andrew Skilleter. Red neon logo. Blue spine. Outline decal. Number 91. Print run: 60,000 copies.
REF: ISBN 0-426-19780-1 OP: £1.50 p/b NM: £3.50

BTR-092a *Doctor Who – The Caves of Androzani* (**Terrance Dicks**)
1984/11/15, W. H. Allen & Co. PLC, UK
Cover by Andrew Skilleter. Print run: 3,000 copies.
REF: ISBN 0-491-03483-0 OP: £5.95 h/b NM: £13.20

BTR-092b *Doctor Who – The Caves of Androzani* (**Terrance Dicks**)
1985/02/14, Target/W. H. Allen & Co. PLC, UK
Cover by Andrew Skilleter. Orange neon logo. Blue spine. Outline decal. Number 92. Print run: 60,000 copies. Title page credits author as 'Robert Holmes'.
REF: ISBN 0-426-19959-6 OP: £1.50 p/b NM: £5.50

BTR-088c

BTR-089b

BTR-090b

BTR-091b

BTR-092b

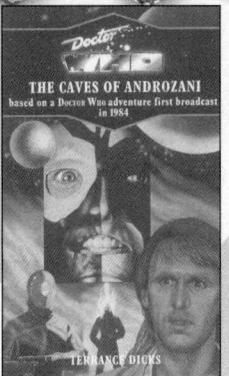

BTR-092c *Doctor Who – The Caves of Androzani*
(Terrance Dicks)
1992/05/21, Target/Virgin Publishing Ltd, UK
Blue spine. Cover by Andrew Skilleter (as on Video).
REF: ISBN 0-426-19959-6 OP: £2.99 p/b NM: £5.50

BTR-093a *Doctor Who – Planet of Fire* **(Peter**
Grimwade)
1984/10/18, W. H. Allen & Co. PLC, UK
Cover by Andrew Skilleter. Print run: 3,000 copies.
REF: ISBN 0-491-03323-0 OP: £5.95 h/b NM: £13.20

BTR-093b *Doctor Who – Planet of Fire* **(Peter**
Grimwade)
1985/01/17, Target/W. H. Allen & Co. PLC, UK
Cover by Andrew Skilleter. Red neon logo. Blue spine.
Outline decal. Number 93. Print run: 60,000 copies.
Interior ISBN 0-426-19908-1.
REF: ISBN 0-426-19940-5 OP: £1.50 p/b NM: £3.50

BTR-092c   **BTR-093b**

BTR-094a *Doctor Who – Marco Polo* **(John**
Lucarotti)
1984/12/10, W. H. Allen & Co. PLC, UK
Cover by David McAllister. Print run: 3,000 copies.
REF: ISBN 0-491-03493-8 OP: £5.95 h/b NM: £13.20

BTR-094b *Doctor Who – Marco Polo* **(John**
Lucarotti)
1985/04/11, Target/W. H. Allen & Co. PLC, UK
Cover by David McAllister. Pink neon logo. Pale
orange spine. Outline decal. Number 94. Print run:
65,000 copies.
REF: ISBN 0-426-19967-7 OP: £1.50 p/b NM: £5.50

BTR-094b

BTR-095a *Doctor Who – The Awakening* **(Eric**
Pringle)
1985/02/14, W. H. Allen & Co. PLC, UK
Cover by Andrew Skilleter.
REF: ISBN 0-491-03194-7 OP: £5.95 h/b NM: £13.20

BTR-095b *Doctor Who – The Awakening* **(Eric**
Pringle)
1985/06/13, Target/W. H. Allen & Co. PLC, UK
Cover by Andrew Skilleter. Orange neon logo. Blue
spine. Outline decal. Number 95. Print run: 40,000
copies. Two printings in 1985. Print run: 5,000 copies
of second printing.
REF: ISBN 0-426-20158-2 OP: £1.50 p/b NM: £5.50

BTR-095c *Doctor Who – The Awakening* **(Eric**
Pringle)
1992/04/16, Target/Virgin Publishing Ltd, UK
Cover by Alistair Pearson. Blue spine.
REF: ISBN 0-426-20158-2 OP: £2.99 p/b NM: £5.50

BTR-095b

BTR-096a *Doctor Who – The Mind of Evil*
(Terrance Dicks)
1985/03/21, W. H. Allen & Co. PLC, UK
Cover by Andrew Skilleter.
REF: ISBN 0-491-03333-8 OP: £5.95 h/b NM: £16.50

BTR-096b *Doctor Who – The Mind of Evil*
(Terrance Dicks)
1985/07/11, Target/W. H. Allen & Co. PLC, UK
Cover by Andrew Skilleter. Red neon logo. Light
brown spine. Outline decal. Number 96. Print run:
40,000 copies. Reprinted in 1985.
REF: ISBN 0-426-20166-3 OP: £1.50 p/b NM: £11

BTR-097a *Doctor Who – The Myth Makers*
(Donald Cotton)
1985/04/11, W. H. Allen & Co. PLC, UK
Cover by Andrew Skilleter.
REF: ISBN 0-491-03580-2 OP: £6.25 h/b NM: £13.20

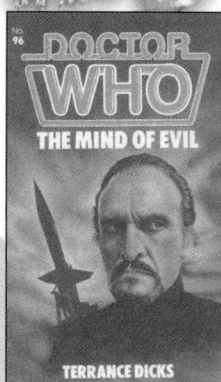

BTR-095c   BTR-096b

BTR-097b *Doctor Who – The Myth Makers*
(Donald Cotton)
1985/09/12, Target/W. H. Allen & Co. PLC, UK
Cover by Andrew Skilleter. Blue neon logo. Pale yellow spine. Outline decal. Number 97. Print run:
65,000 copies.
REF: ISBN 0-426-20170-1 OP: £1.50 p/b NM: £3.50

BTR-098a *Doctor Who – The Invasion* **(Ian
Marter)**
1985/05/16, W. H. Allen & Co. PLC, UK
Cover by Andrew Skilleter.
REF: ISBN 0-491-03324-9 OP: £6.25 h/b NM: £16.50

BTR-098b *Doctor Who – The Invasion* **(Ian
Marter)**
1985/10/10, Target/W. H. Allen & Co. PLC, UK
Cover by Andrew Skilleter. Orange neon logo. Black
spine. Outline decal. Number 98. Print run: 55,000 copies.
REF: ISBN 0-426-20169-8 OP: £1.50 p/b NM: £11

BTR-097b   BTR-098b

BTR-098c *Doctor Who – The Invasion* **(Ian
Marter)**
1993/09/16, Target/Virgin Publishing Ltd, UK
Cover by Alistair Pearson. Blue spine.
REF: ISBN 0-426-20169-8 OP: £3.50 p/b NM: £11

BTR-099a *Doctor Who – The Krotons* **(Terrance
Dicks)**
1985/06/13, W. H. Allen & Co. PLC, UK
Cover by Andrew Skilleter.
REF: ISBN 0-491-03550-0 OP: £6.25 h/b NM: £11

BTR-098c

BTR-099b   **BTR-099c**

BTR-100b

BTR-101b

BTR-099b *Doctor Who – The Krotons* (Terrance Dicks)
1985/11/14, Target/W. H. Allen & Co. PLC, UK
Cover by Andrew Skilleter. Purple neon logo. Purple spine. Outline decal. Number 99. Print run: 50,000 copies.
REF: ISBN 0-426-20189-2 OP: £1.50 p/b NM: £4.50

BTR-099c *Doctor Who – The Krotons* (Terrance Dicks)
1991/07/18, Target/Virgin Publishing Ltd, UK
Cover by Alistair Pearson. Blue spine. (as on Video). Print run: 9,000 copies.
REF: ISBN 0-426-20189-2 OP: £2.50 p/b NM: £4.50

BTR-100a *Doctor Who – The Two Doctors* (Robert Holmes)
1985/08/15, W. H. Allen & Co. PLC, UK
Cover by Andrew Skilleter. Inside cover is a high quality blue paper unlike the other hardbacks.
REF: ISBN 0-491-03500-4 OP: £6.95 h/b NM: £16.50

BTR-100b *Doctor Who – The Two Doctors* (Robert Holmes)
1985/12/05, Target/W. H. Allen & Co. PLC, UK
Cover by Andrew Skilleter. Gold foil neon logo. Blue spine. Outline decal. Number 100. 'First edition' star on cover. Print run: 60,000 copies.
REF: ISBN 0-426-20201-5 OP: £1.75 p/b NM: £8.95

BTR-100c *Doctor Who – The Two Doctors* (Robert Holmes)
1985/12, Target/W. H. Allen & Co. PLC, UK
Cover by Andrew Skilleter. Gold foil neon logo. Blue spine. Outline decal. 'Second edition' star on cover.
REF: ISBN 0-426-20201-5 OP: £1.75 p/b NM: £6.50

BTR-101a *Doctor Who – The Gunfighters* (Donald Cotton)
1985/07/11, W. H. Allen & Co. PLC, UK
Cover by Andrew Skilleter.
REF: ISBN 0-491-03721-X OP: £6.25 h/b NM: £13.20

BTR-101b *Doctor Who – The Gunfighters* (Donald Cotton)
1986/01/09, Target/W. H. Allen & Co. PLC, UK
Cover by Andrew Skilleter. Blue neon logo. Blue spine. Outline decal. Number 101. Print run: 55,000 copies.
REF: ISBN 0-426-20195-7 OP: £1.60 p/b NM: £5.50

BTR-102a *Doctor Who – The Time Monster* (Terrance Dicks)
1985/09/12, W. H. Allen & Co. PLC, UK
Cover by Andrew Skilleter.
REF: ISBN 0-491-03870-4 OP: £6.25 h/b NM: £16.50

BTR-102b *Doctor Who – The Time Monster*
(Terrance Dicks)
1986/02/13, Target/W. H. Allen & Co. PLC, UK
Cover by Andrew Skilleter. Red neon logo. Blue spine.
Outline decal. Number 102. Print run: 55,000 copies.
Interior ISBN 0-426-20213-9.
REF: ISBN 0-426-20221-X OP: £1.60 p/b NM: £11

BTR-103a *Doctor Who – The Twin Dilemma*
(Eric Saward)
1985/10/10, W. H. Allen & Co. PLC, UK
Cover by Andrew Skilleter.
REF: ISBN 0-491-03124-6 OP: £6.25 h/b NM: £13.20

BTR-103b *Doctor Who – The Twin Dilemma*
(Eric Saward)
1986/03/13, Target/W. H. Allen & Co. PLC, UK
Cover by Andrew Skilleter. Blue neon logo. Green spine.
Outline decal. Number 103. Print run: 55,000 copies.
REF: ISBN 0-426-20155-8 OP: £1.60 p/b NM: £3.50

BTR-103c *Doctor Who – The Twin Dilemma*
(Eric Saward)
1993/01/21, Target/Virgin Publishing Ltd, UK
Blue spine. Cover by Andrew Skilleter (as on video).
REF: ISBN 0-426-20155-8 OP: £2.99 p/b NM: £5.50

BTR-104a *Doctor Who – Galaxy Four* **(William**
Emms)
1985/11/14, W. H. Allen & Co. PLC, UK
Cover by Andrew Skilleter.
REF: ISBN 0-491-03691-4 OP: £6.50 h/b NM: £13.20

BTR-104b *Doctor Who – Galaxy Four* **(William**
Emms)
1986/04/10, Target/W. H. Allen & Co. PLC, UK
Cover by Andrew Skilleter. Orange neon logo. Red spine.
Outline decal. Number 104. Print run: 55,000 copies.
REF: ISBN 0-426-20202-3 OP: £1.60 p/b NM: £5.50

BTR-105a *Doctor Who – Timelash* **(Glen**
McCoy)
1985/12/12, W. H. Allen & Co. PLC, UK
Cover by David McAllister.
REF: ISBN 0-491-03851-8 OP: £6.50 h/b NM: £13.20

BTR-105b *Doctor Who – Timelash* **(Glen**
McCoy)
1986/05/15, Target/W. H. Allen & Co. PLC, UK
Cover by David McAllister. Yellow neon logo. Purple spine.
Outline decal. Number 105. Print run: 40,000 copies.
REF: ISBN 0-426-20229-5 OP: £1.60 p/b NM: £3.50

BTR-102b

BTR-103b

BTR-103c

BTR-104b

BTR-105b

BTR-106b

BTR-106c

BTR-107b

BTR-108b

BTR-106a *Doctor Who – Vengeance on Varos*
(Philip Martin)
1988/01/21, W. H. Allen & Co. PLC, UK
Cover by David McAllister.
REF: ISBN 0-491-03502-0 OP: £7.95 h/b NM: £13.20

BTR-106b *Doctor Who – Vengeance on Varos*
(Philip Martin)
1988/06/16, Target/W. H. Allen & Co. PLC, UK
Cover by David McAllister. Red neon logo. Pale blue
spine. Outline decal. Number 106. Print run: 23,000
copies. Book delayed but the original *Doctor Who*
library number was retained.
REF: ISBN 0-426-20291-0 OP: £1.99 p/b NM: £4.95

BTR-106c *Doctor Who – Vengeance on Varos*
(Philip Martin)
1993/01/21, Target/Virgin Publishing Ltd, UK
Cover by Alistair Pearson. Blue spine.
REF: ISBN 0-426-20291-0 OP: £2.99 p/b NM: £5.50

BTR-107a *Doctor Who – The Mark of the Rani*
(Pip and Jane Baker)
1986/01/16, W. H. Allen & Co. PLC, UK
Cover by Andrew Skilleter.
REF: ISBN 0-491-03532-2 OP: £6.50 h/b NM: £16.50

BTR-107b *Doctor Who – The Mark of the Rani*
(Pip and Jane Baker)
1986/06/12, Target/W. H. Allen & Co. PLC, UK
Cover by Andrew Skilleter. Violet neon logo. Violet
spine. Outline decal. Number 107. Print run: 40,000
copies.
REF: ISBN 0-426-20232-5 OP: £1.60 p/b NM: £11

BTR-107c *Doctor Who – The Mark of the Rani*
(Pip and Jane Baker)
1988, Target/W. H. Allen & Co. PLC, UK
Cover by Andrew Skilleter. Print run: 10,000 copies.
REF: ISBN 0-426-20232-5 OP: £1.60 p/b NM: £11

BTR-108a *Doctor Who – The King's Demons*
(Terence Dudley)
1986/02/20, W. H. Allen & Co. PLC, UK
Cover by David McAllister.
REF: ISBN 0-491-03642-6 OP: £6.50 h/b NM: £22

BTR-108b *Doctor Who – The King's Demons*
(Terence Dudley)
1986/07/10, Target/W. H. Allen & Co. PLC, UK
Cover by David McAllister. Green/blue neon logo.
Light blue spine. Outline decal. Number 108. Print
run: 40,000 copies.
REF: ISBN 0-426-20227-9 OP: £1.60 p/b NM: £16.50

BTR-109a *Doctor Who – The Savages* **(Ian Stuart Black)**
1986/03/20, W. H. Allen & Co. PLC, UK
Cover by David McAllister.
REF: ISBN 0-491-03602-7 OP: £6.95 h/b NM: £22

BTR-109b *Doctor Who – The Savages* **(Ian Stuart Black)**
1986/09/11, Target/W. H. Allen & Co. PLC, UK
Cover by David McAllister. Red neon logo. Black spine. Outline decal. Number 109. Print run: 35,000 copies. Interior ISBN 0-426-20330-9.
REF: ISBN 0-426-20230-9 OP: £1.60 p/b NM: £11

BTR-109c *Doctor Who – The Savages* **(Ian Stuart Black)**
1992/11/19, Target/Virgin Publishing Ltd, UK
Cover by Alistair Pearson. Blue spine.
REF: ISBN 0-426-20230-9 OP: £2.99 p/b NM: £11

BTR-110a *Doctor Who – Fury from the Deep* **(Victor Pemberton)**
1986/05/22, W. H. Allen & Co. PLC, UK
Cover by David McAllister.
REF: ISBN 0-491-03652-3 OP: £7.95 h/b NM: £27.50

BTR-110b *Doctor Who – Fury from the Deep* **(Victor Pemberton)**
1986/10/16, Target/W. H. Allen & Co. PLC, UK
Cover by David McAllister. Cyan neon logo. Pale blue spine. Outline decal. Number 110. Print run: 32,500 copies.
REF: ISBN 0-426-20259-7 OP: £1.95 p/b NM: £22

BTR-111a *Doctor Who – The Celestial Toymaker* **(Gerry Davis and Alison Bingeman)**
1986/06/19, W. H. Allen & Co. PLC, UK
Cover by Graeme Potts.
REF: ISBN 0-491-03232-3 OP: £6.95 p/b NM: £16.50

BTR-111b *Doctor Who – The Celestial Toymaker* **(Gerry Davis and Alison Bingeman)**
1986/11/20, Target/W. H. Allen & Co. PLC, UK
Cover by Graeme Potts. Mauve neon logo. Peach spine. Outline decal. Number 111. Print run: 30,000 copies.
REF: ISBN 0-426-20251-1 OP: £1.60 p/b NM: £11

BTR-111c *Doctor Who – The Celestial Toymaker* **(Gerry Davis and Alison Bingeman)**
1992/12/03, Target/Virgin Publishing Ltd, UK
Cover by Alistair Pearson. Blue spine.
REF: ISBN 0-426-20251-1 OP: £2.99 p/b NM: £11

BTR-109b

BTR-109c

BTR-110b

BTR-111b

BTR-111c

BTR-112b

BTR-113b

BTR-114b

BTR-114c

BTR-112a *Doctor Who – The Seeds of Death*
(Terrance Dicks)
1986/07/17, W. H. Allen & Co. PLC, UK
Cover by Tony Masero. Interior ISBN 0-491-02104-0.
REF: ISBN 0-491-03662-0 OP: £6.95 h/b NM: £27.50

BTR-112b *Doctor Who – The Seeds of Death*
(Terrance Dicks)
1986/12/04, Target/W. H. Allen & Co. PLC, UK
Cover by Tony Masero. Grey blue neon logo. Dark
blue spine. Outline decal. Number 112. Print run:
32,500 copies.
REF: ISBN 0-426-20252-X OP: £1.60 p/b NM: £22

BTR-113a *Doctor Who – Black Orchid* (Terence
Dudley)
1986/09/11, W. H. Allen & Co. PLC, UK
Cover by Tony Masero.
REF: ISBN 0-491-03823-2 OP: £6.95 h/b NM: £22

BTR-113b *Doctor Who – Black Orchid* (Terence
Dudley)
1987/02/19, Target/W. H. Allen & Co. PLC, UK
Cover by Tony Masero. Red neon logo. Red spine.
Outline decal. Number 113. Print run: 32,500 copies.
REF: ISBN 0-426-20254-6 OP: £1.75 p/b NM: £16.50

BTR-114a *Doctor Who – The Ark* (Paul
Erickson)
1986/10/09, W. H. Allen & Co. PLC, UK
Cover by David McAllister.
REF: ISBN 0-491-03963-8 OP: £7.25 h/b NM: £22

BTR-114b *Doctor Who – The Ark* (Paul
Erickson)
1987/03/19, Target/W. H. Allen & Co. PLC, UK
Cover by David McAllister. Red neon logo. Blue spine.
Outline decal. Number 114. Print run: 32,500 copies.
Two printings in 1987. 3,500 copies of second printing.
REF: ISBN 0-426-20253-8 OP: £1.75 p/b NM: £11

BTR-114c *Doctor Who – The Ark* (Paul
Erickson)
1992/12/03, Target/Virgin Publishing Ltd, UK
Cover by Alistair Pearson. Blue spine.
REF: ISBN 0-426-20253-8 OP: £2.99 p/b NM: £11

BTR-115a *Doctor Who – The Mind Robber*
(Peter Ling)
1986/11/20, W. H. Allen & Co. PLC, UK
Cover by David McAllister.
REF: ISBN 0-491-03682-5 OP: £7.25 h/b NM: £16.50

BTR-115b *Doctor Who – The Mind Robber*
(Peter Ling)
1987/04/16, Target/W. H. Allen & Co. PLC, UK
Cover by David McAllister. Pale orange neon logo.
Burgundy spine. Outline decal. Number 115. Print run:
32,500 copies.
REF: ISBN 0-426-20286-4 OP: £1.75 p/b NM: £4.50

BTR-115c *Doctor Who – The Mind Robber*
(Peter Ling)
1990/08, Target/Virgin Publishing Ltd, UK
Cover by Alistair Pearson. Blue spine. (as on video)
REF: ISBN 0-426-20286-4 OP: £2.50 p/b NM: £4.50

BTR-116a *Doctor Who – The Faceless Ones*
(Terrance Dicks)
1986/12/11, W. H. Allen & Co. PLC, UK
Cover by Tony Masero.
REF: ISBN 0-491-03692-2 OP: £7.25 h/b NM: £22

BTR-116b *Doctor Who – The Faceless Ones*
(Terrance Dicks)
1987/05/21, Target/W. H. Allen & Co. PLC, UK
Cover by Tony Masero. Red neon logo. Blue spine.
Outline decal. Number 116. Print run: 32,500 copies.
REF: ISBN 0-426-20294-5 OP: £1.75 p/b NM: £11

BTR-117a *Doctor Who – The Space Museum*
(Glyn Jones)
1987/01/15, W. H. Allen & Co. PLC, UK
Cover by David McAllister.
REF: ISBN 0-491-03295-1 OP: £7.25 h/b NM: £22

BTR-117b *Doctor Who – The Space Museum*
(Glyn Jones)
1987/06/18, Target/W. H. Allen & Co. PLC, UK
Cover by David McAllister. Red neon logo. Black
spine. Outline decal. Number 117. Print run: 32,500
copies. Interior states ISBN as: 0-426-20253-8.
REF: ISBN 0-426-20289-9 OP: £1.80 p/b NM: £11

BTR-118a *Doctor Who – The Sensorites* **(Nigel
Robinson)**
1987/02/19, W. H. Allen & Co. PLC, UK
Cover by Nick Spender.
REF: ISBN 0-491-03455-5 OP: £7.50 h/b NM: £13.20

BTR-118b *Doctor Who – The Sensorites* **(Nigel
Robinson)**
1987/07/16, Target/W. H. Allen & Co. PLC, UK
Cover by Nick Spender. Blue neon logo. Burgundy spine.
Outline decal. Number 118. Print run: 32,500 copies.
REF: ISBN 0-426-20295-3 OP: £1.95 p/b NM: £5.50

BTR-115b

BTR-115c

BTR-116b

BTR-117b

BTR-118b

BTR-119b   BTR-120b

BTR-121b

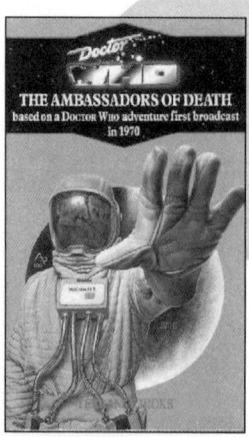

BTR-121c

BTR-119a *Doctor Who – The Reign of Terror* (Ian Marter)
1987/03/19, W. H. Allen & Co. PLC, UK
Cover by Tony Masero.
REF: ISBN 0-491-03702-3 OP: £7.50 h/b NM: £13.20

BTR-119b *Doctor Who – The Reign of Terror* (Ian Marter)
1987/08/20, Target/W. H. Allen & Co. PLC, UK
Cover by Tony Masero. Dark blue neon logo. Orange spine. Outline decal. Number 119. Print run: 32,500 copies.
REF: ISBN 0-426-20264-3 OP: £1.95 p/b NM: £5.50

BTR-120a *Doctor Who – The Romans* (Donald Cotton)
1987/04/16, W. H. Allen & Co. PLC, UK
Cover by Tony Masero.
REF: ISBN 0-491-03833-X OP: £7.50 h/b NM: £22

BTR-120b *Doctor Who – The Romans* (Donald Cotton)
1987/09/19, Target/W. H. Allen & Co. PLC, UK
Cover by Tony Masero. Purple neon logo. Dark pink spine. Outline decal. Number 120. Print run: 30,000 copies.
REF: ISBN 0-426-20288-0 OP: £1.95 p/b NM: £11

BTR-121a *Doctor Who – The Ambassadors of Death* (Terrance Dicks)
1987/05/21, W. H. Allen & Co. PLC, UK
Cover by Tony Masero.
REF: ISBN 0-491-03712-0 OP: £7.50 h/b NM: £22

BTR-121b *Doctor Who – The Ambassadors of Death* (Terrance Dicks)
1987/10/01, Target/W. H. Allen & Co. PLC, UK
Cover by Tony Masero. Blue neon logo. Purple spine. Outline decal. Number 121. Print run: 27,500 copies.
REF: ISBN 0-426-20305-4 OP: £1.95 p/b NM: £11

BTR-121c *Doctor Who – The Ambassadors of Death* (Terrance Dicks)
1991/03/21, Target/Virgin Publishing Ltd, UK
Cover by Alistair Pearson. Blue spine. Print run: 5,000 copies.
REF: ISBN 0-426-20305-4 OP: £2.50 p/b NM: £11

BTR-122a *Doctor Who – The Massacre* (John Lucarotti)
1987/06/18, W. H. Allen & Co. PLC, UK
Cover by Tony Masero.
REF: ISBN 0-491-03423-7 OP: £7.50 h/b NM: £22

BTR-122b *Doctor Who – The Massacre* (John Lucarotti)
1987/11/19, Target/W. H. Allen & Co. PLC, UK
Cover by Tony Masero. Yellow neon logo. Yellow spine.
Outline decal. Number 122. Print run: 25,300 copies.
REF: ISBN 0-426-20297-X OP: £1.95 p/b NM: £11

BTR-122c *Doctor Who – The Massacre* (John Lucarotti)
1992/10/15, Target/Virgin Publishing Ltd, UK
Cover by Alistair Pearson. Blue spine.
REF: ISBN 0-426-20297-X OP: £2.99 p/b NM: £11

BTR-123a *Doctor Who – The Macra Terror* (Ian Stuart Black)
1987/07/16, W. H. Allen & Co. PLC, UK
Cover by Tony Masero.
REF: ISBN 0-491-03227-7 OP: £7.95 h/b NM: £27.50

BTR-123b *Doctor Who – The Macra Terror* (Ian Stuart Black)
1987/12/10, Target/W. H. Allen & Co. PLC, UK
Cover by Tony Masero. Blue neon logo. Orange spine.
Outline decal. Number 123. Print run: 25,500 copies.
Two editions in 1987. Interior ISBN 0-426-20253-8.
REF: ISBN 0-426-20307-0 OP: £1.95 p/b NM: £22

BTR-124a *Doctor Who – The Rescue* (Ian Marter)
1987/08/20, W. H. Allen & Co. PLC, UK
Cover by Tony Clark.
REF: ISBN 0-491-03317-6 OP: £7.95 h/b NM: £27.50

BTR-124b *Doctor Who – The Rescue* (Ian Marter)
1988/01/21, Target/W. H. Allen & Co. PLC, UK
Cover by Tony Clark. Red neon logo. Green spine.
Outline decal. Number 124. Novel completed by range editor Nigel Robinson after Marter's death in October 1986. Print run: 25,000 copies.
REF: ISBN 0-426-20308-9 OP: £1.95 p/b NM: £27.50

BTR-125a *Doctor Who – Terror of the Vervoids* (Pip and Jane Baker)
1987/09/17, W. H. Allen & Co. PLC, UK
Cover by Tony Masero. Print run: 1,750 copies.
REF: ISBN 0-491-03056-8 OP: £7.95 h/b NM: £27.50

BTR-125b *Doctor Who – Terror of the Vervoids* (Pip and Jane Baker)
1988/02/18, Target/W. H. Allen & Co. PLC, UK
Cover by Tony Masero. Purple neon logo. Blue spine.
Outline decal. Number 125. Print run: 25,000 copies.
Interior ISBN 0-426-20309-7-X.
REF: ISBN 0-426-20313-5 OP: £1.95 p/b NM: £22

BTR-122b   BTR-122c

BTR-123b   BTR-124b

BTR-125b

BTR-126b

BTR-127b

BTR-128b

BTR-126a *Doctor Who – The Time Meddler*
(Nigel Robinson)
1987/10/15, W. H. Allen & Co. PLC, UK
Cover by Jeff Cummins.
REF: ISBN 0-491-03337-0 OP: £7.95 h/b NM: £16.50

BTR-126b *Doctor Who – The Time Meddler*
(Nigel Robinson)
1988/03/17, Target/W. H. Allen & Co. PLC, UK
Cover by Jeff Cummins. Red neon logo. Blue spine.
Outline decal. Number 126. Print run: 22,500 copies.
REF: ISBN 0-426-20312-7 OP: £1.99 p/b NM: £8.95

BTR-126c *Doctor Who – The Time Meddler*
(Nigel Robinson)
1992/05, Target/Virgin Publishing Ltd, UK
Blue spine. Cover by Jeff Cummins (original reversed).
Rush-release to tie in with the BBC repeat.
REF: ISBN 0-426-20312-7 OP: £2.99 p/b NM: £8.95

BTR-127a *Doctor Who – The Mysterious Planet*
(Terrance Dicks)
1987/11/19, W. H. Allen & Co. PLC, UK
Cover by Tony Masero.
REF: ISBN 0-491-03096-7 OP: £7.95 h/b NM: £27.50

BTR-127b *Doctor Who – The Mysterious Planet*
(Terrance Dicks)
1988/04/21, Target/W. H. Allen & Co. PLC, UK
Cover by Tony Masero. Orange neon logo. Light blue
spine. Outline decal. Number 127. Title page says the
book is number 126. Print run: 22,500 copies.
REF: ISBN 0-426-20319-4 OP: £1.99 p/b NM: £22

BTR-128a *Doctor Who – Time and the Rani* **(Pip
and Jane Baker)**
1987/12/17, W. H. Allen & Co. PLC, UK
Photographic cover by Chris Capstick. Originally, the
book was to have a Tony Masero artwork cover of the
Tetraps, and the artwork appeared on a draft cover
proof, but with the Tetraps standing on the floor rather
than hanging from the ceiling. The artwork image was
ultimately replaced with a specially taken photograph of
the creatures.
REF: ISBN 0-491-03186-6 OP: £7.95 h/b NM: £22

BTR-128b *Doctor Who – Time and the Rani* **(Pip
and Jane Baker)**
1988/05/05, Target/W. H. Allen & Co. PLC, UK
Photographic cover by Chris Capstick. McCoy logo.
Violet spine. Outline decal. Although this is book number 128, the cover, spine and title page states 'No.
127'. 'First edition' flash, as well as a flash reading 'The
First Adventure of the Seventh Doctor!'. Print run:

23,000 copies. Some copies had a sticker over the barcode on the back cover with a different ISBN on: 0-426-20331-3. Proof covers exist for the unused Masero version of the cover.
REF: ISBN 0-426-20232-5 OP: £1.99 p/b NM: £11

BTR-128c *Doctor Who – Time and the Rani* (**Pip and Jane Baker**)
1991/10/17, Target/Virgin Publishing Ltd, UK
Cover by Alistair Pearson. Blue spine. The cover, spine and title page states 'No. 127'. Print run: 10,000 copies. Interior ISBN 0-426-20232-5.
REF: ISBN 0-426-20331-3 OP: £2.50 p/b NM: £5.50

BTR-128c

BTR-129a *Doctor Who – The Underwater Menace* (**Nigel Robinson**)
1988/02/18, W. H. Allen & Co. PLC, UK
Cover by Alistair Pearson.
REF: ISBN 0-491-03496-2 OP: £7.95 h/b NM: £27.50

BTR-129b *Doctor Who – The Underwater Menace* (**Nigel Robinson**)
1988/07/21, Target/W. H. Allen & Co. PLC, UK
Cover by Alistair Pearson. McCoy logo. Green spine. Outline decal. Number 129. Print run: 22,500 copies. Interior states ISBN as: 0-426-20336-7.
REF: ISBN 0-426-20326-7 OP: £1.99 p/b NM: £22

BTR-129b

BTR-130a *Doctor Who – The Wheel in Space* (**Terrance Dicks**)
1988/03/17, W. H. Allen & Co. PLC, UK
Cover by Ian Burgess. Burgess went on to produce a range of photograph-based merchandise designed for actors and actresses who had appeared in *Doctor Who* to sign at conventions. These were released under his Cineffigy label and feature current photographs of the artistes concerned. See AAP-001.
REF: ISBN 0-491-03356-7 OP: £7.95 h/b NM: £44

BTR-130b *Doctor Who – The Wheel in Space* (**Terrance Dicks**)
1988/08/18, Target/W. H. Allen & Co. PLC, UK
Cover by Ian Burgess. Purple neon logo. Black spine. Outline decal. Number 130. Print run: 23,000 copies.
REF: ISBN 0-426-20321-6 OP: £1.99 p/b NM: £33

BTR-131a *Doctor Who – The Ultimate Foe* (**Pip and Jane Baker**)
1988/04/21, W. H. Allen & Co. PLC, UK
Cover by Alistair Pearson.
REF: ISBN 0-491-03106-8 OP: £7.95 h/b NM: £27.50

BTR-130b

BTR-131b

BTR-132b

BTR-133b   **BTR-134a**

BTR-131b *Doctor Who – The Ultimate Foe* (**Pip and Jane Baker**)
1988/09/15, Target/W. H. Allen & Co. PLC, UK
Cover by Alistair Pearson. McCoy logo. Blue spine.
Outline decal. Number 131. Print run: 23,000 copies.
REF: ISBN 0-426-20329-1 OP: £1.99 p/b NM: £22

BTR-132a *Doctor Who – The Edge of Destruction* (**Nigel Robinson**)
1988/05/19, W. H. Allen & Co. PLC, UK
Cover by Alistair Pearson.
REF: ISBN 0-491-03138-6 OP: £7.95 h/b NM: £27.50

BTR-132b *Doctor Who – The Edge of Destruction* (**Nigel Robinson**)
1988/10/20, Target/W. H. Allen & Co. PLC, UK
Cover by Alistair Pearson. McCoy Logo. Pale orange spine.
Outline decal. Number 132. Print run: 23,000 copies.
REF: ISBN 0-426-20327-5 OP: £1.99 p/b NM: £22

BTR-133a *Doctor Who – The Smugglers* (**Terrance Dicks**)
1988/06/16, W. H. Allen & Co. PLC, UK
Cover by Alistair Pearson. McCoy logo. Blue spine.
Outline decal. Number 133. Print run: 1,000 copies.
This was the last Target book to have a hardback edition produced at time of first publication. The hardbacks were discontinued due to poor sales.
REF: ISBN 0-491-03148-3 OP: £7.95 h/b NM: £22

BTR-133b *Doctor Who – The Smugglers* (**Terrance Dicks**)
1988/11/17, Target/W. H. Allen & Co. PLC, UK
Cover by Alistair Pearson. McCoy logo. Blue spine.
Outline decal. Print run: 23,000 copies.
REF: ISBN 0-426-20328-3 OP: £1.99 p/b NM: £11

BTR-133c *Doctor Who – The Smugglers* (**Terrance Dicks**)
1993/02/18, Target/Virgin Publishing Ltd, UK
Cover by Alistair Pearson as on original. Blue spine.
REF: ISBN 0-426-20328-3 OP: £3.50 p/b NM: £11

BTR-134a *Doctor Who – Paradise Towers* (**Stephen Wyatt**)
1988/12/01, Target/W. H. Allen & Co. PLC, UK
Cover by Alistair Pearson. McCoy logo. Orange spine.
Outline decal. Number 134. Print run: 25,000 copies.
The scheduled hardback for *Paradise Towers* (21/07/1988) was never released.
REF: ISBN 0-426-20330-5 OP: £1.99 p/b NM: £6.50

BTR-134b *Doctor Who – Paradise Towers*
(Stephen Wyatt)
1991, Target/Virgin Publishing Ltd, UK
Cover by Alistair Pearson as on original. Blue spine.
Print run: 9,000 copies.
REF: ISBN 0-426-20330-5 OP: £2.50 p/b NM: £6.50

BTR-135a *Doctor Who – Delta and the*
Bannermen **(Malcolm Kohll)**
1989/01/19, Target/W. H. Allen & Co. PLC, UK
Cover by Alistair Pearson. McCoy logo. Blue spine.
Outline decal. Number 135. Print run: 21,000 copies.
The scheduled hardback for *Delta and the Bannermen*
(01/1989) was never released. The spine reads *Delta*
and the Bannerman.
REF: ISBN 0-426-20333-X OP: £1.99 p/b NM: £6.50

BTR-135a

BTR-135b *Doctor Who – Delta and the*
Bannermen **(Malcolm Kohll)**
1991/11/21, Target/Virgin Publishing Ltd, UK
Cover by Alistair Pearson as on original. Blue spine.
Print run: 9,000 copies.
REF: ISBN 0-426-20333-X OP: £2.99 p/b NM: £6.50

BTR-136a *Doctor Who – The War Machines* **(Ian**
Stuart Black)
1989/02/16, Target/W. H. Allen & Co. PLC, UK
Cover by Alistair Pearson and Graeme Wey. McCoy
logo. Grey spine. Outline decal. Number 136. Print
run: 21,000 copies.
REF: ISBN 0-426-20332-1 OP: £1.99 p/b NM: £11

BTR-136b *Doctor Who – The War Machines* **(Ian**
Stuart Black)
1992/11/19, Target/Virgin Publishing Ltd, UK
Cover by Alistair Pearson and Graeme Wey as on
original. Blue spine.
REF: ISBN 0-426-20332-1 OP: £2.99 p/b NM: £11

BTR-136a

BTR-137a *Doctor Who – Dragonfire* **(Ian Briggs)**
1989/03/16, Target/W. H. Allen & Co. PLC, UK
Cover by Alistair Pearson. McCoy logo. Black spine.
Outline decal. Number 137. Print run: 21,000 copies.
REF: ISBN 0-426-20322-4 OP: £1.99 p/b NM: £6.50

BTR-137b *Doctor Who – Dragonfire* **(Ian**
Briggs)
1991/10/17, Target/Virgin Publishing Ltd, UK
Cover by Alistair Pearson as on original. Blue spine.
Print run: 9,000 copies.
REF: ISBN 0-426-20322-4 OP: £2.99 p/b NM: £6.50

BTR-137a

BTR-138a

BTR-138b

BTR-139a

BTR-140a

BTR-141a

BTR-142a

BTR-138a *Doctor Who – Attack of the Cybermen* **(Eric Saward)**
1989/04/20, Target/W. H. Allen & Co. PLC, UK
Cover by Colin Howard. McCoy logo. White spine.
Outline decal. Number 138. Print run: 21,000 copies.
REF: ISBN 0-426-20290-2 OP: £1.99 p/b NM: £11

BTR-138b *Doctor Who – Attack of the Cybermen* **(Eric Saward)**
1992/10/15, Target/Virgin Publishing Ltd, UK
Cover by Alistair Pearson. Blue spine.
REF: ISBN 0-426-20290-2 OP: £2.99 p/b NM: £11

BTR-139 *Doctor Who – Mindwarp* **(Philip Martin)**
1989/06/15, Target/W. H. Allen & Co. PLC, UK
Cover by Alistair Pearson. McCoy logo. White spine.
Outline decal. Number 139. Print run: 23,000 copies.
Reprinted in September 1989.
REF: ISBN 0-426-20335-6 OP: £1.99 p/b NM: £22

BTR-140a *Doctor Who – The Chase* **(John Peel)**
1989/07/20, Target/W. H. Allen & Co. PLC, UK
Cover by Alistair Pearson. McCoy logo. White spine.
Outline decal. Number 140. Print run: 24,000 copies.
Two printings in 1989; the first printing cost £1.99.
REF: ISBN 0-426-20336-4 OP: £2.50 p/b NM: £16.50

BTR-140b *Doctor Who – The Chase* **(John Peel)**
1991/07/18, Target/Virgin Publishing Ltd, UK
Cover by Alistair Pearson as on original. Blue spine.
Print run: 5,000 copies.
REF: ISBN 0-426- OP: £2.50 p/b NM: £16.50

BTR-141a *Doctor Who – The Daleks' Master Plan: Part I: Mission to the Unknown* **(John Peel)**
1989/09/21, Target/W. H. Allen & Co. PLC, UK
Cover by Alistair Pearson. McCoy logo. Black spine.
Outline decal. Number 141. Print run: 22,000 copies.
REF: ISBN 0-426-20343-7 OP: £1.99 p/b NM: £7.95

BTR-141b *Doctor Who – The Daleks' Master Plan: Part I: Mission to the Unknown* **(John Peel)**
1990, Target/W. H. Allen & Co. PLC, UK
Cover by Alistair Pearson. McCoy logo. Black spine.
Outline decal. Print run: 6,000 copies.
REF: ISBN 0-426-20343-7 OP: £2.50 p/b NM: £7.95

BTR-142a *Doctor Who – The Daleks' Master Plan: Part II: The Mutation of Time* **(John Peel)**
1989/10/19, Target/W. H. Allen & Co. PLC, UK
Cover by Alistair Pearson. McCoy logo. White spine.
Outline decal. Number 142. Print run: 22,000 copies.
REF: ISBN 0-426-20344-5 OP: £1.99 p/b NM: £7.95

BTR-142b *Doctor Who – The Daleks' Master Plan: Part II: The Mutation of Time* (John Peel)
1990, Target/W. H. Allen & Co. PLC, UK
Cover by Alistair Pearson. McCoy logo. White spine.
Outline decal. Print run: 5,000 copies.
REF: ISBN 0-426-20344-5 OP: £2.50 p/b NM: £7.95

BTR-143a *Doctor Who – Silver Nemesis* (Kevin Clarke)
1989/11/16, Target/W. H. Allen & Co. PLC, UK
Cover by Alistair Pearson. McCoy logo. Blue spine.
Outline decal. Number 143. Print run: 22,000 copies.
REF: ISBN 0-426-20340-2 OP: £1.99 p/b NM: £11

BTR-143b *Doctor Who – Silver Nemesis* (Kevin Clarke)
1993/09/16, Target/Virgin Publishing Ltd, UK
With a different cover, also by Alistair Pearson. Blue spine.
REF: ISBN 0-426-20340-2 OP: £3.50 p/b NM: £11

BTR-144a *Doctor Who – The Greatest Show in the Galaxy* (Stephen Wyatt)
1989/12/21, Target/W. H. Allen & Co. PLC, UK
Cover by Alistair Pearson. McCoy logo. Blue spine.
Outline decal. Number 144. Print run: 22,000 copies.
REF: ISBN 0-426-20341-0 OP: £1.99 p/b NM: £6.50

BTR-144b *Doctor Who – The Greatest Show in the Galaxy* (Stephen Wyatt)
1991/12/12, Target/Virgin Publishing Ltd, UK
Cover by Alistair Pearson (as on original). Blue spine.
REF: ISBN 0-426-20341-0 OP: £2.99 p/b NM: £6.50

BTR-145 *Doctor Who – Planet of Giants* (Terrance Dicks)
1990/01/18, Target/Virgin Publishing Ltd, UK
Cover by Alistair Pearson. McCoy logo. Grey spine.
Outline decal. Number 145. Print run: 22,000 copies.
REF: ISBN 0-426-20345-3 OP: £1.99 p/b NM: £22

BTR-146 *Doctor Who – The Happiness Patrol* (Graeme Curry)
1990/02/15, Target/Virgin Publishing Ltd, UK
Cover by Alistair Pearson. McCoy logo. White spine.
Outline decal. Number 146. Print run: 25,000 copies.
REF: ISBN 0-426-20339-9 OP: £2.50 p/b NM: £11

BTR-147 *Doctor Who – The Space Pirates* (Terrance Dicks)
1990/03/15, Target/Virgin Publishing Ltd, UK
Cover by Tony Clark. McCoy logo. Pale blue spine.
Outline decal. Number 147. Print run: 24,000 copies.
REF: ISBN 0-426-20346-1 OP: £2.50 p/b NM: £11

BTR-143a   BTR-143b

BTR-144a   BTR-145

BTR-146   BTR-147

BTR-148   BTR-149

BTR-150   BTR-151

BTR-152   BTR-153

BTR-148 *Doctor Who – Remembrance of the Daleks* (Ben Aaronovitch)
1990/06/21, Target/Virgin Publishing Ltd, UK
Cover by Alistair Pearson. McCoy logo. Grey spine.
Outline decal. Number 148. Print run: 25,000 copies.
Reissued in 1990. Print run: 5,000 copies.
REF: ISBN 0-426-20337-2 OP: £2.50 p/b NM: £16.50

BTR-149 *Doctor Who – Ghost Light* (Marc Platt)
1990/09/20, Target/Virgin Publishing Ltd, UK
Cover by Alistair Pearson. McCoy logo. White spine.
Outline decal. Number 149. Print run: 25,000 copies.
REF: ISBN 0-426-20351-8 OP: £2.50 p/b NM: £6.50

BTR-150 *Doctor Who – Survival* (Rona Munro)
1990/10/18, Target/Virgin Publishing Ltd, UK
Cover by Alistair Pearson. McCoy logo. White spine.
Outline decal. Number 150. Print run: 25,000 copies.
REF: ISBN 0-426-20352-6 OP: £2.50 p/b NM: £6.50

BTR-151 *Doctor Who – The Curse of Fenric* (Ian Briggs)
1990/11/15, Target/Virgin Publishing Ltd, UK
Cover by Alistair Pearson. McCoy logo. White spine.
Outline decal. Number 151. Print run: 29,000 copies.
Map featured on page 5.
REF: ISBN 0-426-20348-8 OP: £2.50 p/b NM: £6.50

BTR-152 *Doctor Who – Battlefield* (Marc Platt)
1991/07/18, Target/Virgin Publishing Ltd, UK
Cover by Alistair Pearson. McCoy logo. White spine.
Outline decal. Number 152. Print run: 22,000 copies.
REF: ISBN 0-426-20350-X OP: £2.50 p/b NM: £8.95

BTR-153 *Doctor Who – The Power of the Daleks* (John Peel)
1993/07/15, Virgin Publishing Ltd, UK
Cover by Alistair Pearson. McCoy logo. Black spine.
McCoy decal. Number 154. Originally scheduled for
17 June 1993. Book number 153 is *Doctor Who and the Pescatons*, which is not a television novelisation.
REF: ISBN 0-426-20390-9 OP: £4.50 p/b NM: £11

BTR-154 *Doctor Who – The Evil of the Daleks* (John Peel)
1993/08/19, Virgin Publishing Ltd, UK
Cover by Alistair Pearson. McCoy logo. Black spine.
McCoy decal. Number 155.
REF: ISBN 0-426-20389-5 OP: £4.50 p/b NM: £11

BTR-155 *Doctor Who* (Gary Russell)
1996/05/15, BBC Worldwide Ltd, UK
Photographic cover. Novelisation of the 1996 TV-movie.
REF: ISBN 0-563-38000-4 OP: £3.99 p/b NM: £5.50

BTR-154

BTR-155

BVM-001

BVM-002

BVM-003

BVM-004

BOOKS, VIRGIN MISSING ADVENTURES

'THE Missing Adventures' were introduced by Virgin Publishing as demand for the books showed that novels featuring past Doctors would be as popular as the range of 'New Adventures' featuring the Seventh Doctor.

BVM-001 *The Missing Adventures: Goth Opera* (Paul Cornell)
1994/07/21, Virgin Publishing Ltd, UK
Cover by Alistair Pearson. Dr 5. Cover does not have 'The' on it.
REF: ISBN 0-426-20418-2 OP: £4.99 p/b NM: £8

BVM-002 *The Missing Adventures: Evolution* (John Peel)
1994/09/15, Virgin Publishing Ltd, UK
Cover by Alistair Pearson. Dr 4.
REF: ISBN 0-426-20422-0 OP: £4.99 p/b NM: £8

BVM-003 *The Missing Adventures: Venusian Lullaby* (Paul Leonard)
1994/10/20, Virgin Publishing Ltd, UK
Cover by Alistair Pearson. Dr 1.
REF: ISBN 0-426-20424-7 OP: £4.99 p/b NM: £6

BVM-004 *The Missing Adventures: The Crystal Bucephalus* (Craig Hinton)
1994/11/17, Virgin Publishing Ltd, UK
Cover by Alistair Pearson. Dr 5.
REF: ISBN 0-426-20429-8 OP: £4.99 p/b NM: £7

BVM-005 *The Missing Adventures: State of Change* (Christopher Bulis)
1994/12/01, Virgin Publishing Ltd, UK
Cover by Alistair Pearson. Dr 6.
REF: ISBN 0-426-20431-X OP: £4.99 p/b NM: £8

BVM-005

BVM-006

BVM-006 *The Missing Adventures: The Romance of Crime* (Gareth Roberts)
1995/01/19, Virgin Publishing Ltd, UK
Cover by Alistair Pearson. Dr 4.
REF: ISBN 0-426-20435-2 OP: £4.99 p/b NM: £8

BVM-007 *The Missing Adventures: The Ghosts of N-Space* (Barry Letts)
1995/02/16, Virgin Publishing Ltd, UK
Cover by Alistair Pearson. Dr 3.
REF: ISBN 0-426-20434-4 OP: £4.99 p/b NM: £7

BVM-007

BVM-008

BVM-009

BVM-010

BVM-011

BVM-012

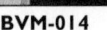

BVM-013

BVM-014

BVM-015

BVM-016

BVM-008 *The Missing Adventures: Time Of Your Life* **(Steve Lyons)**
1995/03/16, Virgin Publishing Ltd, UK
Cover by Paul Campbell. Dr 6.
REF: ISBN 0-426-20438-7 OP: £4.99 p/b NM: £8

BVM-009 *The Missing Adventures: Dancing The Code* **(Paul Leonard)**
1995/04/20, Virgin Publishing Ltd, UK
Cover by Paul Campbell. Dr 3.
REF: ISBN 0-426-20441-7 OP: £4.99 p/b NM: £8

BVM-010 *The Missing Adventures: The Menagerie* **(Martin Day)**
1995/05/18, Virgin Publishing Ltd, UK
Cover by Paul Campbell. Dr 2.
REF: ISBN 0-426-20449-2 OP: £4.99 p/b NM: £8

BVM-011 *The Missing Adventures: System Shock* **(Justin Richards)**
1995/06/15, Virgin Publishing Ltd, UK
Cover by Martin Rawle. Dr 4.
REF: ISBN 0-426-20445-X OP: £4.99 p/b NM: £8

BVM-012 *The Missing Adventures: The Sorcerer's Apprentice* **(Christopher Bulis)**
1995/07/20, Virgin Publishing Ltd, UK
Cover by Paul Campbell. Dr 1.
REF: ISBN 0-426-20447-6 OP: £4.99 p/b NM: £8

BVM-013 *The Missing Adventures: Invasion of the Cat-People* **(Gary Russell)**
1995/08/17, Virgin Publishing Ltd, UK
Cover by Colin Howard. Dr 2.
REF: ISBN 0-426-20440-9 OP: £4.99 p/b NM: £8

BVM-014 *The Missing Adventures: Managra* **(Stephen Marley)**
1995/09/21, Virgin Publishing Ltd, UK
Cover by Paul Campbell. Dr 4.
REF: ISBN 0-426-20453-0 OP: £4.99 p/b NM: £8

BVM-015 *The Missing Adventures: Millennial Rites* **(Craig Hinton)**
1995/10/19, Virgin Publishing Ltd, UK
Cover by Alistair Pearson. Dr 6.
REF: ISBN 0-426-20455-7 OP: £4.99 p/b NM: £8

BVM-016 *The Missing Adventures: The Empire of Glass* **(Andy Lane)**
1995/11/16, Virgin Publishing Ltd, UK
Cover by Paul Campbell. Dr 1.
REF: ISBN 0-426-20457-3 OP: £4.99 p/b NM: £8

BVM-017 *The Missing Adventures: Lords of the Storm* **(David A McIntee)**
1995/12/07, Virgin Publishing Ltd, UK
Cover by Alistair Pearson. Dr 5.
REF: ISBN 0-426-20460-3 OP: £4.99 p/b NM: £6

BVM-018 *The Missing Adventures: Downtime* **(Marc Platt)**
1996/01/18, Virgin Publishing Ltd, UK
Cover by Paul Campbell. No Doctor. Video tie-in.
Features a photo section. See VID-002a.
REF: ISBN 0-426-20462-X OP: £4.99 p/b NM: £8

BVM-019 *The Missing Adventures: The Man in the Velvet Mask* **(Daniel O'Mahony)**
1996/02/15, Virgin Publishing Ltd, UK
Cover by Alistair Pearson. Dr 1.
REF: ISBN 0-426-20461-1 OP: £4.99 p/b NM: £7

BVM-020 *The Missing Adventures: The English Way of Death* **(Gareth Roberts)**
1996/03/21, Virgin Publishing Ltd, UK
Cover by Alistair Pearson. Dr 4.
REF: ISBN 0-426-20466-2 OP: £4.99 p/b NM: £11

BVM-021 *The Missing Adventures: The Eye of the Giant* **(Christopher Bulis)**
1996/04/18, Virgin Publishing Ltd, UK
Cover by Paul Campbell. Dr 3.
REF: ISBN 0-426-20469-7 OP: £4.99 p/b NM: £11

BVM-022 *The Missing Adventures: The Sands of Time* **(Justin Richards)**
1996/05/16, Virgin Publishing Ltd, UK
Cover by Alistair Pearson. Dr 5.
REF: ISBN 0-426-20472-7 OP: £4.99 p/b NM: £14

BVM-023 *The Missing Adventures: Killing Ground* **(Steve Lyons)**
1996/06/20, Virgin Publishing Ltd, UK
Cover by Alistair Pearson. Dr 6.
REF: ISBN 0-426-20474-3 OP: £4.99 p/b NM: £11

BVM-017   BVM-018

BVM-019   BVM-020

BVM-021   BVM-022

BVM-023

BVM-024

BVM-025

BVM-026

BVM-027

BVM-028

BVM-029

BVM-030

BVM-024 *The Missing Adventures: The Scales of Injustice* **(Gary Russell)**
1996/07/18, Virgin Publishing Ltd, UK
Cover by Andrew Skilleter. Sea Devil/Silurian hybrid by Paul Vyse. Dr 3.
REF: ISBN 0-426-20477-8 OP: £4.99 p/b NM: £11

BVM-025 *The Missing Adventures: The Shadow of Weng-Chiang* **(David A McIntee)**
1996/08/15, Virgin Publishing Ltd, UK
Cover by Alistair Pearson. Dr 4.
REF: ISBN 0-426-20479-4 OP: £4.99 p/b NM: £14

BVM-026 *The Missing Adventures: Twilight of the Gods* **(Christopher Bulis)**
1996/09/19, Virgin Publishing Ltd, UK
Cover by Alistair Pearson. Dr 2.
REF: ISBN 0-426-20480-8 OP: £4.99 p/b NM: £11

BVM-027 *The Missing Adventures: Speed of Flight* **(Paul Leonard)**
1996/10/17, Virgin Publishing Ltd, UK
Cover by Alistair Pearson. Dr 3.
REF: ISBN 0-426-20487-5 OP: £4.99 p/b NM: £11

BVM-028 *The Missing Adventures: The Plotters* **(Gareth Roberts)**
1996/11/21, Virgin Publishing Ltd, UK
Cover by Alistair Pearson. Dr 1.
REF: ISBN 0-426-20488-3 OP: £4.99 p/b NM: £11

BVM-029 *The Missing Adventures: Cold Fusion* **(Lance Parkin)**
1996/12/05, Virgin Publishing Ltd, UK
Cover by Alistair Pearson. Dr 5.
REF: ISBN 0-426-20489-1 OP: £4.99 p/b NM: £25

BVM-030 *The Missing Adventures: Burning Heart* **(Dave Stone)**
1997/01/16, Virgin Publishing Ltd, UK
Cover by Alistair Pearson. Dr 6.
REF: ISBN 0-426-20498-0 OP: £4.99 p/b NM: £14

BVM-031 *The Missing Adventures: A Device of Death* **(Christopher Bulis)**
1997/02/20, Virgin Publishing Ltd, UK
Cover by Alistair Pearson. Dr 4.
REF: ISBN 0-426-20501-4 OP: £4.99 p/b NM: £9

BVM-032 *The Missing Adventures: The Dark Path* **(David A McIntee)**
1997/03/20, Virgin Publishing Ltd, UK
Cover by Alistair Pearson. Dr 2.
REF: ISBN 0-426-20503-0 OP: £4.99 p/b NM: £15

BVM-033 *The Missing Adventures: The Well-Mannered War* **(Gareth Roberts)**
1997/04/17, Virgin Publishing Ltd, UK
Cover by Alistair Pearson. Dr 4.
REF: ISBN 0-426-20506-5 OP: £4.99 p/b NM: £30

BVM-031 **BVM-032**

BVM-033

BOOKS, VIRGIN NEW ADVENTURES

IN 1989, editor Peter Darvill-Evans finally gained permission from the BBC to develop a range of original novels featuring the Seventh Doctor and his companion Ace. These were launched in 1991 to much acclaim, and carried on until the BBC opted not to renew their licence in 1997. The initial editor on the range was Peter Darvill-Evans and he was joined by Rebecca Levene who eventually took over editing the range (around the release of *Tragedy Day*), while assistant Simon Winstone joined towards the end of the range's life.

BVN-001 *The New Adventures: Timewyrm: Genesys* **(John Peel)**
1991/06/20, Virgin Publishing Ltd, UK
Cover by Andrew Skilleter.
REF: ISBN 0-426-20355-0 OP: £3.50 p/b NM: £15

BVN-002 *The New Adventures: Timewyrm: Exodus* **(Terrance Dicks)**
1991/08/15, Virgin Publishing Ltd, UK
Cover by Andrew Skilleter.
REF: ISBN 0-426-20357-7 OP: £3.50 p/b NM: £15

BVN-003 *The New Adventures: Timewyrm: Apocalypse* **(Nigel Robinson)**
1991/10/17, Virgin Publishing Ltd, UK
Cover by Andrew Skilleter.
REF: ISBN 0-426-20359-3 OP: £3.50 p/b NM: £15

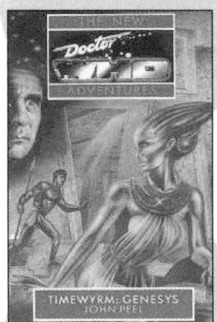

BVN-001 **BVN-002**

BVN-003

BVN-004

BVN-005a

BVN-004 The New Adventures: Timewyrm: Revelation (Paul Cornell)
1991/12/05, Virgin Publishing Ltd, UK
Cover by Andrew Skilleter.
REF: ISBN 0-426-20360-7 OP: £3.50 p/b NM: £15

BVN-005a The New Adventures: Cat's Cradle: Time's Crucible (Marc Platt)
1992/02/20, Virgin Publishing Ltd, UK
Cover by Peter Elson.
REF: ISBN 0-426-20365-8 OP: £3.50 p/b NM: £7

BVN-005b Doctor Who: Uj Kalandok: Az Idö Fogságában (Marc Platt)
1993, Uj Venusz Lap – Es Konyvkiado, Hungary
Cover by Gál László. Translated by Bihari György.
Only foreign edition of a NA. Released under the Android imprint. Title translates to 'Captured in Time' or 'In Time's Captivity'.
REF: ISBN 963-7755-810 ISSN 1217-6923
OP: 298 ft p/b NM: £20

BVN-005b

BVN-006

BVN-006 The New Adventures: Cat's Cradle: Warhead (Andrew Cartmel)
1992/04/16, Virgin Publishing Ltd, UK
Cover by Peter Elson.
REF: ISBN 0-426-20367-4 OP: £3.50 p/b NM: £9

BVN-007 The New Adventures: Cat's Cradle: Witch Mark (Andrew Hunt)
1992/06/18, Virgin Publishing Ltd, UK
Cover by Peter Elson.
REF: ISBN 0-426-20368-2 OP: £3.99 p/b NM: £6

BVN-008 The New Adventures: Nightshade (Mark Gatiss)
1992/08/20, Virgin Publishing Ltd, UK
Cover by Peter Elson.
REF: ISBN 0-426-20376-3 OP: £3.99 p/b NM: £6

BVN-007

BVN-008

BVN-009 The New Adventures: Love and War (Paul Cornell)
1992/10/15, Virgin Publishing Ltd, UK
Cover by Lee Sullivan.
REF: ISBN 0-426-20385-2 OP: £3.99 p/b NM: £6

BVN-010 The New Adventures: Transit (Ben Aaronovitch)
1992/12/03, Virgin Publishing Ltd, UK
Cover by Peter Elson.
REF: ISBN 0-426-20384-4 OP: £3.99 p/b NM: £6

BVN-009

BVN-010

BVN-011 *The New Adventures: The Highest Science* **(Gareth Roberts)**
1993/02/18, Virgin Publishing Ltd, UK
Cover by Peter Elson.
REF: ISBN 0-426-20377-1 OP: £3.99 p/b NM: £6

BVN-012 *The New Adventures: The Pit* **(Neil Penswick)**
1993/03/18, Virgin Publishing Ltd, UK
Cover by Peter Elson.
REF: ISBN 0-426-20378-X OP: £3.99 p/b NM: £6

BVN-013 *The New Adventures: Deceit* **(Peter Darvill-Evans)**
1993/04/15, Virgin Publishing Ltd, UK
Cover by Luis Rey.
REF: ISBN 0-426-20387-9 OP: £3.99 p/b NM: £6

BVN-014 *The New Adventures: Lucifer Rising* **(Andy Lane & Jim Mortimore)**
1993/05/20, Virgin Publishing Ltd, UK
Cover by Jim Mortimore. Illustrated by Lee Brimmicombe-Wood.
REF: ISBN 0-426-20388-7 OP: £4.50 p/b NM: £6

BVN-015 *The New Adventures: White Darkness* **(David A McIntee)**
1993/06/17, Virgin Publishing Ltd, UK
Cover by Peter Elson.
REF: ISBN 0-426-20395-X OP: £4.50 p/b NM: £6

BVN-016 *The New Adventures: Shadowmind* **(Christopher Bulis)**
1993/07/15, Virgin Publishing Ltd, UK
Cover by Christopher Bulis.
REF: ISBN 0-426-20394-1 OP: £4.50 p/b NM: £6

BVN-017a *The New Adventures: Birthright* **(Nigel Robinson)**
1993/08/19, Virgin Publishing Ltd, UK
Cover by Peter Elson.
REF: ISBN 0-426-20393-3 OP: £4.50 p/b NM: £6

BVN-017b *Birthright* **(Nigel Robinson)**
1999, Big Finish, UK
Audio adaptation of Robinson's novel, removing all BBC copyright characters and including Bernice Summerfield from the Virgin range. Audio adapted by Jac Rayner.
REF: BFPCD4 OP: £12.99 CD

BVN-011

BVN-012

BVN-013

BVN-014

BVN-015

BVN-016

BVN-017b

BVN-017a

BVN-018

BVN-019

BVN-020

BVN-021

BVN-022

BVN-023

BVN-024

BVN-025

BVN-018 *The New Adventures: Iceberg* (**David Banks**)
1993/09/16, Virgin Publishing Ltd, UK
Cover by Andrew Skilleter.
REF: ISBN 0-426-20392-5 OP: £4.50 p/b NM: £6

BVN-019 *The New Adventures: Blood Heat* (**Jim Mortimore**)
1993/10/21, Virgin Publishing Ltd, UK
Cover by Jeff Cummins.
REF: ISBN 0-426-20399-2 OP: £4.50 p/b NM: £6

BVN-020 *The New Adventures: The Dimension Riders* (**Daniel Blythe**)
1993/11/18, Virgin Publishing Ltd, UK
Cover by Jeff Cummins.
REF: ISBN 0-426-20397-6 OP: £4.50 p/b NM: £6

BVN-021 *The New Adventures: The Left-Handed Hummingbird* (**Kate Orman**)
1993/12/02, Virgin Publishing Ltd, UK
Cover by Pete Wallbank.
REF: ISBN 0-426-20404-2 OP: £4.50 p/b NM: £6

BVN-022 *The New Adventures: Conundrum* (**Steve Lyons**)
1994/01/20, Virgin Publishing Ltd, UK
Cover by Jeff Cummins.
REF: ISBN 0-426-20408-5 OP: £4.99 p/b NM: £6

BVN-023 *The New Adventures: No Future* (**Paul Cornell**)
1994/02/17, Virgin Publishing Ltd, UK
Cover by Pete Wallbank.
REF: ISBN 0-426-20409-3 OP: £4.99 p/b NM: £6

BVN-024 *The New Adventures: Tragedy Day* (**Gareth Roberts**)
1994/03/17, Virgin Publishing Ltd, UK
Cover by Jeff Cummins.
REF: ISBN 0-426-20410-7 OP: £4.99 p/b NM: £6

BVN-025 *The New Adventures: Legacy* (**Gary Russell**)
1994/04/21, Virgin Publishing Ltd, UK
Cover by Peter Elson.
REF: ISBN 0-426-20412-3 OP: £4.99 p/b NM: £9

BVN-026 *The New Adventures: Theatre of War* (**Justin Richards**)
1994/05/19, Virgin Publishing Ltd, UK
Cover by Jeff Cummins.
REF: ISBN 0-426-20414-X OP: £4.99 p/b NM: £6

BVN-026

BVN-027

BVN-028

BVN-029

BVN-027 *The New Adventures: All-Consuming Fire* **(Andy Lane)**
1994/06/16, Virgin Publishing Ltd, UK
Cover by Jeff Cummins.
REF: ISBN 0-426-20415-8 OP: £4.99 p/b NM: £6

BVN-028 *The New Adventures: Blood Harvest* **(Terrance Dicks)**
1994/07/21, Virgin Publishing Ltd, UK
Cover by Bill Donohoe.
REF: ISBN 0-426-20417-4 OP: £4.99 p/b NM: £6

BVN-029 *The New Adventures: Strange England* **(Simon Messingham)**
1994/08/18, Virgin Publishing Ltd, UK
Cover by Paul Campbell.
REF: ISBN 0-426-20419-0 OP: £4.99 p/b NM: £6

BVN-030

BVN-030 *The New Adventures: First Frontier* **(David A McIntee)**
1994/09/15, Virgin Publishing Ltd, UK
Cover by Tony Masero.
REF: ISBN 0-426-20421-2 OP: £4.99 p/b NM: £6

BVN-031 *The New Adventures: St Anthony's Fire* **(Mark Gatiss)**
1994/10/20, Virgin Publishing Ltd, UK
Cover by Paul Campbell.
REF: ISBN 0-426-20423-9 OP: £4.99 p/b NM: £6

BVN-031

BVN-032 *The New Adventures: Falls The Shadow* **(Daniel O'Mahoney)**
1994/11/17, Virgin Publishing Ltd, UK
Cover by Kevin Jenkins.
REF: ISBN 0-426-20427-1 OP: £4.99 p/b NM: £6

BVN-033 *The New Adventures: Parasite* **(Jim Mortimore)**
1994/12/01, Virgin Publishing Ltd, UK
Cover by Paul Campbell.
REF: ISBN 0-426-20425-5 OP: £4.99 p/b NM: £6

BVN-032

BVN-033

BVN-034

BVN-035

BVN-034 *The New Adventures: Warlock*
(Andrew Cartmel)
1995/01/19, Virgin Publishing Ltd, UK
Cover by Tony Masero.
REF: ISBN 0-426-20433-6 OP: £4.99 p/b NM: £6

BVN-035 *The New Adventures: Set Piece* **(Kate Orman)**
1995/02/16, Virgin Publishing Ltd, UK
Cover by Tony Masero.
REF: ISBN 0-426-20436-0 OP: £4.99 p/b NM: £6

BVN-036

BVN-037

BVN-036 *The New Adventures: Infinite Requiem*
(Daniel Blythe)
1995/03/16, Virgin Publishing Ltd, UK
Cover by Barry Jones.
REF: ISBN 0-426-20437-9 OP: £4.99 p/b NM: £6

BVN-037 *The New Adventures: Sanctuary*
(David A McIntee)
1995/04/20, Virgin Publishing Ltd, UK
Cover by Peter Elson.
REF: ISBN 0-426-20439-5 OP: £4.99 p/b NM: £6

BVN-038

BVN-039

BVN-038 *The New Adventures: Human Nature*
(Paul Cornell)
1995/05/18, Virgin Publishing Ltd, UK
Cover by Bill Donohoe.
REF: ISBN 0-426-20443-3 OP: £4.99 p/b NM: £10

BVN-039 *The New Adventures: Original Sin*
(Andy Lane)
1995/06/15, Virgin Publishing Ltd, UK
Cover and illustrations by Tony Masero.
REF: ISBN 0-426-20444-1 OP: £4.99 p/b NM: £7

BVN-040 *The New Adventures: Sky Pirates!*
(Dave Stone)
1995/07/20, Virgin Publishing Ltd, UK
Cover by Jeff Cummins.
REF: ISBN 0-426-20446-8 OP: £4.99 p/b NM: £6

BVN-040

BVN-041

BVN-042

BVN-043

BVN-041 *The New Adventures: Zamper* **(Gareth Roberts)**
1995/08/17, Virgin Publishing Ltd, UK
Cover by Tony Masero.
REF: ISBN 0-426-20450-6 OP: £4.99 p/b NM: £6

BVN-042 *The New Adventures: Toy Soldiers* **(Paul Leonard)**
1995/09/21, Virgin Publishing Ltd, UK
Cover by Peter Elson.
REF: ISBN 0-426-20452-2 OP: £4.99 p/b NM: £6

BVN-043 *The New Adventures: Head Games* **(Steve Lyons)**
1995/10/19, Virgin Publishing Ltd, UK
Cover by Bill Donohoe.
REF: ISBN 0-426-20454-9 OP: £4.99 p/b NM: £6

BVN-044 *The New Adventures: The Also People* **(Ben Aaronovitch)**
1995/11/16, Virgin Publishing Ltd, UK
Cover by Tony Masero.
REF: ISBN 0-426-20456-5 OP: £4.99 p/b NM: £6

BVN-045 *The New Adventures: Shakedown* **(Terrance Dicks)**
1995/12/07, Virgin Publishing Ltd, UK
Cover by Peter Elson. Novelisation of video. Book includes photo section. See VID-004a.
REF: ISBN 0-426-20459-X OP: £4.99 p/b NM: £7

BVN-046a *The New Adventures: Just War* **(Lance Parkin)**
1996/01/18, Virgin Publishing Ltd, UK
Cover by Nik Spender.
REF: ISBN 0-426-20463-8 OP: £4.99 p/b NM: £11

BVN-046b *Just War* **(Lance Parkin)**
1999/06, Big Finish, UK
Audio adaptation of Parkin's novel, removing all BBC copyright characters and including Bernice Summerfield from the Virgin range. Audio adapted by Jac Rayner.
REF: BFPCD5 OP: £12.99 CD

BVN-047 *The New Adventures: Warchild* **(Andrew Cartmel)**
1996/02/15, Virgin Publishing Ltd, UK
Cover by Jeff Cummins.
REF: ISBN 0-426-20464-6 OP: £4.99 p/b NM: £11

BVN-044   BVN-045

BVN-046a

BVN-046b

BVN-047

BVN-048   **BVN-049**

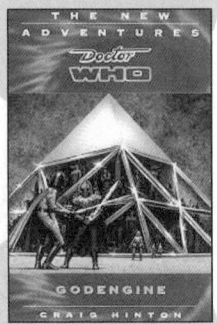

BVN-050   **BVN-051**

BVN-052   **BVN-053**

BVN-054

BVN-048 *The New Adventures: Sleepy* **(Kate Orman)**
1996/03/21, Virgin Publishing Ltd, UK
Cover by Mark Wilkinson. Illustrated by Jason Towers.
REF: ISBN 0-426-20465-4   OP: £4.99 p/b   NM: £9

BVN-049 *The New Adventures: Death and Diplomacy* **(Dave Stone)**
1996/04/18, Virgin Publishing Ltd, UK
Cover by Bill Donohoe.
REF: ISBN 0-426-20468-9   OP: £4.99 p/b   NM: £9

BVN-050 *The New Adventures: Happy Endings* **(Paul Cornell)**
1996/05/16, Virgin Publishing Ltd, UK
Cover by Paul Campbell. Poster Offer of the cover artwork to mark the 50th New Adventure.
REF: ISBN 0-426-20470-0   OP: £4.99 p/b   NM: £10

BVN-051 *The New Adventures: GodEngine* **(Craig Hinton)**
1996/06/20, Virgin Publishing Ltd, UK
Cover by Peter Elson.
REF: ISBN 0-426-20473-5   OP: £4.99 p/b   NM: £9

BVN-052 *The New Adventures: Christmas On A Rational Planet* **(Lawrence Miles)**
1996/07/18, Virgin Publishing Ltd, UK
Cover by Mike Posen.
REF: ISBN 0-426-20476-X   OP: £4.99 p/b   NM: £12

BVN-053 *The New Adventures: Return of the Living Dad* **(Kate Orman)**
1996/08/15, Virgin Publishing Ltd, UK
Cover by Mark Wilkinson.
REF: ISBN 0-426-20482-4   OP: £4.99 p/b   NM: £12

BVN-054 *The New Adventures: The Death of Art* **(Simon Bucher-Jones)**
1996/09/19, Virgin Publishing Ltd, UK
Cover by Jon Sullivan.
REF: ISBN 0-426-20481-6   OP: £4.99 p/b   NM: £12

BVN-055 *The New Adventures: Damaged Goods* **(Russell T Davies)**
1996/10/17, Virgin Publishing Ltd, UK
Cover by Bill Donohoe.
REF: ISBN 0-426-20483-2   OP: £4.99 p/b   NM: £9

BVN-056 *The New Adventures: So Vile A Sin* **(Ben Aaronovitch and Kate Orman)**
1997/04/24, Virgin Publishing Ltd, UK
Cover by Jon Sullivan. Publication originally scheduled for 21/11/1996.
REF: ISBN 0-426-20484-0   OP: £4.99 p/b   NM: £25

BVN-057 *The New Adventures: Bad Therapy*
(Matthew Jones)
1996/12/05, Virgin Publishing Ltd, UK
Cover by Mark Salwowski.
REF: ISBN 0-426-20490-5 OP: £4.99 p/b NM: £12

BVN-058 *The New Adventures: Eternity Weeps*
(Jim Mortimore)
1997/01/16, Virgin Publishing Ltd, UK
Cover by Peter Elson. *Doctor Who* logo dropped from
books.
REF: ISBN 0-426-20497-2 OP: £4.99 p/b NM: £12

BVN-059 *The New Adventures: The Room With*
No Doors **(Kate Orman)**
1997/02/20, Virgin Publishing Ltd, UK
Cover by Jon Sullivan.
REF: ISBN 0-426-20500-6 OP: £4.99 p/b NM: £12

BVN-060 *The New Adventures: Lungbarrow*
(Marc Platt)
1997/03/20, Virgin Publishing Ltd, UK
Cover by Fred Gambino.
REF: ISBN 0-426-20502-2 OP: £4.99 p/b NM: £35

BVN-061 *The New Adventures: The Dying Days*
(Lance Parkin)
1997/04/17, Virgin Publishing Ltd, UK
Cover by Fred Gambino. Eighth Doctor novel. Final
Virgin *Doctor Who* novel.
REF: ISBN 0-426-20504-9 OP: £4.99 p/b NM: £40

BVN-055   BVN-056

BVN-057   BVN-058

BVN-059   BVN-060   BVN-061

CBA-001

CBA-002

CBA-003

CBA-004

CBA-005

CBA-006

CLOTHING ETC., BADGES

BADGES are one of the staple products issued to tie-in with a popular event. They are also easy and cheap to produce thus making it very hard to determine if such an item was officially sanctioned or not. We have not attempted to document every fan-produced badge here – for example almost every fan convention issues a badge of some sort to attendees – but have sought to list those official items which have been released, and those which tied in with public events associated with the show.

CBA-001 Dalek Badge (large)
1964, Plastoid Ltd, UK
A black plastic badge with gold highlights. The plastoid badges sold more than a million units overall. The badge came mounted on a card. A recent replica made in black and silver is known to exist.
OP: 1s 3d NM: £40

CBA-002 Dalek Badge (small)
1964, Plastoid Ltd, UK
A black plastic badge with gold highlights.
OP: 9d NM: £45

CBA-003 Menoptra Badge
1965, Plastoid Ltd, UK
A black plastic badge with gold highlights.
OP: 1s 3d NM: £55

CBA-004 Zarbi and Venom Gun Badge
1965, Plastoid Ltd, UK
A black plastic badge with gold highlights.
OP: 1s 3d NM: £60

CBA-005 Doctor Who Badges, Sugar Smacks
1971/10, Kelloggs, UK
Six different 31mm badges to collect in packs of Sugar Smacks, featuring artwork depictions of: the Doctor, Bessie, Jo Grant, the Brigadier, the Master and a UNIT symbol. See also PRO-002.
OP: free NM: £12 each

CBA-006 TARDIS Commander BBC TV Special Effects Badge (two types)
1972, BBC Enterprises, UK
Badge released to tie in with a BBC exhibition at London's Science Museum in 1972. The exhibition featured several Doctor Who monsters and props, including the Draconians who had not at that time been seen on television.
NM: £5.50

CBA-007 Doctor Who Badge
1973, BBC Enterprises, UK
Orange logo on blue background. 55mm.
NM: £8

CBA-008 Doctor Who Badges
1975, BBC Enterprises, UK
Blue/red on white, 1" diameter
NM: £9

**CBA-009 John Menzies Monster Painting
Competition Badge**
1976, John Menzies, UK
A badge was sent to every entrant to this competition run by the John Menzies newsagent chain.
OP: free NM: £11

CBA-010 Dalek Button Badges
1980, S. Weiner Ltd, USA
NM: £5.50

CBA-011 K-9 Button Badges
1980, S. Weiner Ltd, USA
NM: £5.50

CBA-012 Badges
1980, S Weiner Ltd, UK
Three badges: Tom Baker & K9 (22581); Dalek firing (22582); K9 (22583); all against a plain background. Offered for sale though Denis Alan Print as (DB09/DB10 and DB08)
REF: 22581-22583 OP: 35p each NM: £5.50

CBA-013 Badges- Assorted Photographic (7 diff)
1980, Denis Alan Print, UK
2" diameter full colour badges. One diamond Doctor Who logo badge, the remainder are pictures of Tom Baker.
REF: DB01 – DB07 OP: 35p each NM: £5.50

CBA-014 Diamond Logo Badge
1980, NADWAS, USA
White badge with blue diamond logo and 'WHO' in red with flags of Canada, UK, USA above. 'NADWAS' on the bottom left and 'North American Doctor Who Appreciation Society' on the bottom right. Individual membership numbers written with felt tip pen on the very bottom.

CBA-015 Tom Baker Badges- (7 diff)
1980, Ian Nicoll Enterprises, AUS
No other information.

CBA-016 Badges – Assorted Doctor Who
1981/03, Image Screencraft, UK
Day-glo, blue/green, prismatic, black/blue. 50mm.
OP: 50p each NM: £5.50

CBA-007 CBA-008

CBA-009 CBA-010?

CBA-014

CBA-016 (three examples)

CBA-017

CBA-018

CBA-020

CBA-021 (two variations)

CBA-023

CBA-017 Doctor Who Logo Badge
1982?
Neon logo.

CBA-018 Doctor Who Logo Badge
1987
McCoy logo.

CBA-019 'The How, Why and Where of Doctor Who' Badge
1982, André Deutsch Ltd, UK
Produced to tie in with the book *Doctor Who: The Making of a Television Series.*
OP: free   NM: £5.50

CBA-020 Resin badges
1982, Susan Moore, UK
Ice Warrior head, Robot of Death head, Cybermat, Cyber-logo. Produced commercially by fan Susan Moore.
OP: £1.00 NM: £9

CBA-021 Badges – Assorted Cyberman
1982/03, Image Screencraft, UK
Day-glo, blue/green, prismatic, black/blue. 50mm.
OP: 50p each NM: £5.50-£6.50

CBA-022 Button Badge
1983, Fantasy Traders, USA
Fourth Doctor.

CBA-023 Button Badges
1983, Glenwood Distributors Inc., USA
17+ designs. Most of these have 'BBC Enterprises LTD. Barb Elder Corp. Glenwood Dist. Inc.' printed on their edge and depict Doctors from standard publicity stills.
OP: $1.00 each

CBA-024 'I am A Doctor Who Reader' Badge
1983, W. H. Allen & Co. Ltd, UK
Blue and white. Red and white version issued in 1987. 38mm.
OP: free NM: £3.50

CBA-025 Doctor Who Celebration Longleat Badge
1983, BBC Enterprises, UK
55mm. Red neon logo.
NM: £3.50

CBA-026 Doctor Who Exhibition Badge
1983, BBC Enterprises, UK
55mm. Blue neon logo.
OP: 30p NM: £5.50

CBA-024   **CBA-025**

CBA-026   **CBA-029**

CBA-029   **CBA-033**

CBA-027 'TARDIS Access' Badge: clip on
1984, USA
NM: £5.50

CBA-028 Flicker Pin Badge
1984, USA
Diamond logo.

CBA-029 Button Badges
1984, DWFCA, USA
5 designs. One is a white diamond logo on a black
badge with 'Fan Club Of America' underneath. An
enamel badge is also known.
NM: £5.50

CBA-030 Button Badges
USA
7 designs.
OP: $1.50 each   NM: £5.50

CBA-031 Full colour diamond logo badge
USA
OP: $2.00   NM: £5.50

CBA-032 Full colour neon logo badge
USA
OP: $2.00   NM: £5.50

CBA-033 'I love Doctor Who badge'
DWFCA, USA
Black, square badge w/ 2 hearts, neon logo. See also
SST-008.
OP: $1.50   NM: £5.50

CBA-034 Enamel Badges
1984, DWFCA, USA
Fifth Doctor (2 designs), Fourth Doctor (2 designs?),
Sixth Doctor (2 designs), Third Doctor and Bessie.
OP: $6.00 (£5.95 import) each   NM: £9

CBA-035 Enamel Badges
1984, DWFCA, USA
Logo, TARDIS, K-9, Question Mark.
OP: $4.00 (£5.95 import) each   NM: £9

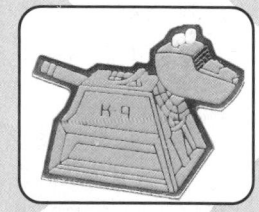

CBA-034   **CBA-035**

CBA-038

CBA-039

CBA-041

CBA-040

CBA-047

CBA-048

CBA-049

CBA-050

CBA-036 Second Doctor square badge
1984, DWFCA, USA
NM: £5.50

CBA-037 Thermal dynamic 'I Love Doctor Who' Badge
1984, DWFCA, USA
NM: £5.50

CBA-038 Thermal dynamic diamond logo Badge
1984, DWFCA, USA
Badge itself is in a diamond shape.
OP: $3.00 NM: £5.50

CBA-039 Thermal dynamic K-9 Badge
1984, DWFCA, USA
Badge is square in shape.
OP: $3.00 NM: £5.50

CBA-040 Thermal dynamic neon logo Badge
1984, DWFCA, USA
OP: $3.00 NM: £5.50

CBA-041 Thermal dynamic TARDIS Badge
1984, DWFCA, USA
OP: $3.00 NM: £5.50

CBA-042 Time Lord Hearts
1984, DWFCA, USA
Gold rim and red heart.
OP: $6.00 NM: £5.50

CBA-043 Button Badges
1984, Fantasy Traders, USA
5 designs.
NM: £5.50

CBA-044 Button Badges
1984, Star Tech, USA
2-1/4" diam, 25 designs.
OP: $1.00 each, 10 or more 75¢ each NM: £5.50

CBA-045 ID Badges
1984, Star Tech, USA
Various colours, 5 designs.
OP: $1.00 each, 6 for $5.00 NM: £5.50

CBA-046 Love Buttons
1984, Star Tech, USA
20 designs.
OP: $1.00 each, 10 or more 75¢ each NM: £5.50

CBA-047 Dalek Enamel Badge
1985, DWFCA, USA
OP: $4.00 (£5.95 import) each NM: £9

CBA-048 'I'm On Target with Doctor Who' Badge
1985, W. H. Allen & Co. PLC, UK
OP: free NM: £5.50

CBA-049 Cat Badges
1985, Susie Trevor, UK
Suzie Trevor supplied the cat badge worn by Colin
Baker on his lapel in *The Twin Dilemma*. The DWAS
later contacted her and arranged for the badge to be
made available for sale.
OP: £3.50 each NM: £12

CBA-050 Unofficial Doctor Who Badges (5 diff.?)
1980s, Imagebond, AUS
Coloured plastic laminate front glued onto a shaped
black plastic pinback. The *Doctor Who* badges in this
unauthorised range included a Dalek, a TARDIS, a
neon logo, a Cyberman, and possibly a K9.

CBA-051

CBA-051 USA Tour Button Badges
1986, Silverscreen UK, USA
Two badges blisterpacked on cardboard. Both are black
badges with starfields. The first is an angled TARDIS with
the roof forming the diamond of a full colour logo. The
TARDIS is standing in a diamond shaped pool of yellow
and orange with 'USA' and 'TOUR' printed in a rainbow
of colors. The second features a full colour diamond
logo with 'USA' underneath. Also see CKE-009.

CBA-052 Enamel Badges
1987, DWFCA, USA
Giant Robot, Second Doctor, Cyberman (2 designs),
First Doctor (2 designs), Leela, Seventh Doctor,
TARDIS Console.
OP: $6.00 (£5.95 import) each NM: £9

CBA-053 Doctor/TARDIS Badge
1987
Doctor with TARDIS. Part of set above?

CBA-054 'I ♥ the Doctor' Badge 'Fly with me' w/ TARDIS
1987, Lionheart, USA
OP: $1.50

CBA-055 'I ♥ the Doctor' Badge
1987, Lionheart, USA
Diamond logo.
OP: $1.25

CBA-052

CBA-060

CBA-062a

CBA-062b

CBA-064

CBA-066

CBA-067

CBA-070

CBA-071

CBA-073

CBA-056 'I ♥ the Doctor' Badge
1987, Lionheart, USA
Neon logo.
OP: $1.00

CBA-057 Cat Badges
1987, Maggy's Moggies, UK
These badges were commissioned by Colin Baker and based on his own cats, 'Eric' and 'Weeble'. He wore the badges in the show, and the manufacturer also made them available for sale.
OP: £3.25 each

CBA-058 Lapel Pin: circular, 'Celebration and Tour '87–'88'
1988, Lionheart, USA
OP: $6.00

CBA-059 Doctor Who – 25 Years Badge
1988, BBC Enterprises, UK
OP: 50p NM: £5.50

CBA-060 Metal Logo Badge
1988/08, John Fitton, UK
A plastic McCoy logo badge is also known.
OP: £3.99 NM: £5.50

CBA-061 BBC/Doctor Who Badge
1988, Sydney Royal Easter show, AUS
The theme of that year's show was 'Britain'. A BBC Exhibition Dalek appeared at the show near a stand where a specially produced badge was available. The badge featured the BBC logo above the neon logo with a starfield background in white, pink and black. Thousands were made.

CBA-076a

CBA-080

CBA-062a *The Ultimate Adventure* **Badge**
1989, UK
Tie-in with the stage play. Circular badge.
OP: 60p

CBA-062b *The Ultimate Adventure* **Badge**
1989, UK
Tie-in with the stage play. Oblong badge.
OP: 60p

CBA-063 Doctor Who Question Mark badges
1990, John Fitton, UK
Five Colours (Yellow, Red, Green, Blue, Black).
OP: £2.50 each NM: £5.50

CBA-064 Dalek MOMI Badge
1991, MOMI, UK
NM: £3.50

CBA-065 'Seal of Rassilon' pin badge
1991, Dominitemporal Services, UK
Small metal badge. Blue on gold. 2.5cm across.

CBA-066 Cyber-tomb pin badge
1993, Dominitemporal Services, UK
Small metal badge. Silver/black, silver/blue, gold/black
colour combinations.

CBA-067 *Classic Comics* **Badge**
1993, Marvel/Panini, UK
Green plastic badge with Classic Comics magazine
logo. Came taped onto issue as a giveaway.
OP: free NM: £3.50

CBA-068 Dalek Badge
1993, Alpha Marketing, UK
Dalek-shaped badge. No further information available.

CBA-069 30th anniversary pin badge
1993, Alpha Marketing, UK
Badge has an enamel-less line crossing the WHO.
Came with mug (see HCR-035).
OP: £3.50 NM: £5.50

CBA-070 30th anniversary pin badge
1993, Pinpoint Merchandising Ltd, UK
Badge has a yellow enamel line crossing the WHO.
OP: £2.99 NM: £5.50

CBA-071 Dalek Pin Badges
1994, The Ultimate Buckle Company, UK
Plain/Blue/Red.
REF: BP02P/BP02EBU/BP02ER
OP: £2.95 (plain) £3.95 (colour)

CBA-072 Logo Pin Badges
1994, The Ultimate Buckle Company, UK
Plain/Colour.
REF: BP01P/BP01E
OP: £2.95 (plain) £3.95 (colour)

CBA-073 Tardis Pin Badges
1994, The Ultimate Buckle Company, UK
Plain/Coloured.
REF: BP03P/BP03E
OP: £2.95 (plain) £3.95 (colour)

CBA-074 '21 Years at Longleat' Badges
1994, BBC Enterprises, UK
Commemorative badge with same slogan as related T-
shirt
OP: 25p

CBA-075 TARDIS Badge
1994, Who Shop International, UK
White background. No further information available.

CBA-076a Enamel Badges
1994, Alpha Marketing, UK
Boxed set of 7. Cyberman, Question Mark (with
Doctors' faces on), Diamond logo, Davros, Emperor
Dalek, Ice Warrior, Dalek.
OP: £9.99

CBA-076b Enamel Badges
1996, Downpace, UK
As previously released by Alpha Marketing.
OP: £2.99 each

CBA-077 'Seal of Rassilon' pin badge
1996, Dominitemporal Services, UK
Small metal badge. Gold/Black, silver/blue, red/gold,
green/silver colour combinations. 2cm.

CBA-078 Question Mark Umbrella Badges
1999, Dapol, UK
Multiple colours available, green and gold known.
OP: 50p

**CBA-079 'National Association of Daleks
Against Stairs'**
Emotional Rescue Ltd, UK
OP: 70p

CBA-080 'Have TARDIS Will Travel' Badge
Unknown origin.

CCH-013

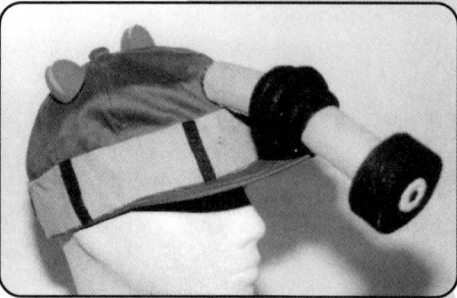

CCH-014

CCH-015

CCH-019

CLOTHING ETC., HATS

CCH-001 Painters Cap
USA
Neon logo: red on white.

CCH-002 Cap
DWFCA, USA
Full colour diamond logo: royal blue, red, green, black, gold, navy.
OP: $8.00

CCH-003 Baseball Cap
DWFCA, USA
Full colour diamond logo.
OP: $8.00

CCH-004 Hat
DWFCA, USA
Full colour: diamond logo.
OP: $10.00

CCH-005 Hats
DWFCA, USA
Neon or diamond logo: made with puff-up ink.
OP: $10.00 each

CCH-006 Visor
USA
Full colour diamond logo, assorted colours.
OP: $7.00

CCH-007 Baseball Cap
1980, Nightstar Corp., USA
Diamond logo (blue, black, red).
OP: $7.00

CCH-008 Baseball Cap
1980, Nightstar Corp., USA
Neon logo (blue, black, red).
OP: $7.00

CCH-009 Cap
1985, UK

CCH-010 *Doctor Who* USA Tour Baseball Cap
1986, Silverscreen, UK
Dark blue cap with a design including the TARDIS and diamond logo. The words 'USA Tour' surround the design against a red background. The cap came in a clear plastic bag sealed by a piece of black card reading 'Doctor Who USA Tour Baseball cap'.

CCM-020?

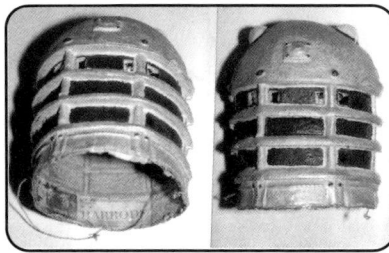

CCM-001

CCM-002

CCH-011 Black mesh glow in the dark cap
1988, Lionheart, USA
25th Anniversary.
OP: $7.00

CCH-012 Cap: Police Box
1989, DWFCA, USA
OP: $7.00

**CCH-013 *The Ultimate Adventure* Baseball
Hats**
1989, UK
Featuring the logo from the stage play.
NM: £16.50

CCH-014 Dalek Hat, The
1985, Deanem Ltd, UK
A baseball cap headpiece with a Dalek eye-stalk
mounted on the front and attached to the top of
the hat by a length of 'invisible' plastic cotton so
that it bounced as the wearer moved. The eye-stalk
is made from felt filled with an expanded foam
material.
OP: £6.99 NM: £22

CCH-015 Dalek Hat
1991, Visionstyle Ltd, UK
Available through the Museum of the Moving Image
exhibition in London. A similar idea, but different
design, to the Deanem Hat.
OP: £12.99 NM: £22

CCH-016 Baseball Caps
1993/02/06, GUDI, UK
These were a limited edition of 200, one featuring
Sylvester McCoy and one featuring Sophie Aldred,
signed by the actors at a one-off event.
OP: £9.00 NM: £6.50

CCH-017 Tombwatch Baseball Cap
1993, Dominitemporal Services Ltd, UK
Tombwatch logo.

CCH-018 Doctor Who Diamond Logo Cap
1994, Morestyle, UK
Black with diamond logo. No further information available.

CCH-019 Doctor Who Movie Baseball Cap
1996, BBC Worldwide, UK
No manufacturers mark.
OP: £6.99 NM: £9

CCH-020 Baseball Cap
1998, The Ultimate Embroidery Company, UK
OP: £2

CLOTHING ETC., MISC.

CCM-001 Dalek Mask
1965, A. Bangham & Co. Ltd, UK
9" by 7" papier-mâché mask in the shape of a Dalek's
head.
OP: 1s 6d NM: £165

CCM-002 Dalek Slippers
1965, Furness Footwear Ltd, UK
Made in hard-wearing red needlecord with Dalek
motifs flocked on and with a sponge rubber sole.
Available in sizes 7 to 2. The slippers were later reissued without the flocked Dalek and logo, but with a
plastic Dalek 'pocket' on one side.
NM: £400

CCM-004

CCM-005

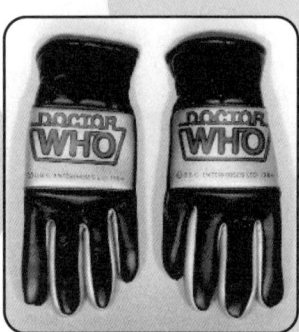

CCM-011 (small)

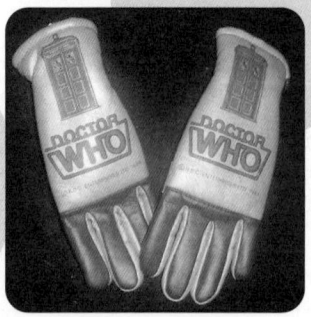

CCM-011 (large)

CCM-003 TARDIS Tie
1966, Ergon Tie, UK
No further information available.
NM: £90

CCM-004 Doctor Who Scarf
1976, Today Promotions Ltd, UK
A replica of the Fourth Doctor's scarf with an authen-
ticating patch.
OP: £5.50 (8') £6.50 (10') NM: £55

CCM-005 Underpants
1980, British Home Stores, UK
Blue underpants with an image of the Fourth Doctor's
face on the crotch. Around 46,000 units sold.
OP: 85p NM: £27.50

CCM-006 Cotton Scarf
1981, Aristocrat Textiles Ltd, UK
No further information available.

CCM-007 Jacket
DWFCA, USA
Diamond logo, nylon sateen: gold, red, royal, or navy,
logo on back.
OP: $45.00

CCM-008 Jacket
1984, DWFCA, USA
Neon or diamond, black satin finish, silver neon logo
in starfield on back.
OP: $60.00

CCM-009 Scarf
1984, Spirit of Light Enterprises Ltd, USA
12 foot long, 7 colours.
OP: $35.00

CCM-010 Chef's Apron
1985, DWFCA, USA
Navy denim, silver diamond logo. Also assorted
colours with diamond logo.
OP: $12.00

CCM-011 Gloves
1984/04, Peshawear UK Ltd, UK
Black and silver gloves with a blue neon logo on the
back of the hand (small sizes). The larger sizes also
included an image of the TARDIS.
OP: £4.99 (sizes 4,5,6) £6.99 (sizes 7-10) NM: £16.50

CCM-012 Suspenders
1987, Lionheart, USA
Red or green.
OP: $12.95

CCM-013 Sun Visor
1987, UK
OP: £1.99

CCM-014 Doctor Who Outfit
1988/02, Dapol, UK
Includes a fawn jacket, green checked trousers, a
question-mark pullover and paisley scarf.
OP: £19.99 sizes 3-8 NM: £66

CCM-013

CCM-015 Melanie Outfit
1988/02, Dapol, UK
A pink and white top and a pair of white trousers.
OP: £15.99 sizes 3-8 NM: £45

CCM-016 Doctor Who Pullover
1988, Dapol, UK
The Seventh Doctor's distinctive question mark
pullover. Early version had the pocket as shown, later
version had no pocket. Available in five sizes: 28"-30"
(child); 32"-34" (small); 36"-38" (medium); 40"-42"
(large); 44"-46" (x.large).
REF: W017-0/1/2/3/4 OP: £25.00 NM: £33

CCM-016

CCM-017 Pyjamas
1988/12, Mothercare, UK
Blue and white with black collar and cuffs, featuring an
image of the TARDIS and a Dalek and the words 'The
Time Lord Doctor Who' on the front.
OP: £9.50 (l) £8.50 (s) NM: £45

CCM-018 Slippers
1988/12, Mothercare, UK
Grey plush slippers with the McCoy logo set into the
top. The slippers were in the 'Footstep' range.
NM: £27.50

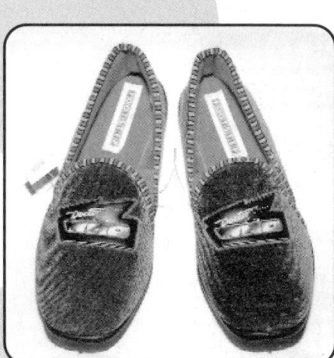

CCM-018

CCM-019 Nite Shirt
1989, DWFCA, USA
OP: $15.00

CCM-020 Sweatpants
1989, DWFCA, USA
Full colour diamond logo.
OP: $20.00

**CCM-021 Doctor Who 30th Anniversary
Official Jacket**
1993, Peartree, UK
A puffer jacket with the *Doctor Who* logo embroidered
on the back and front.
OP: £69.95 NM: £75

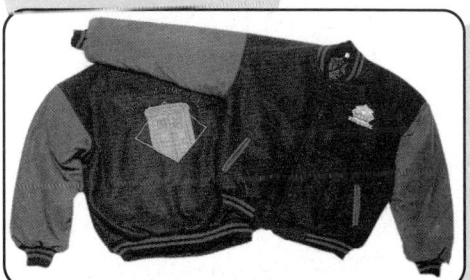

CCM-021

CCM-022 30th Anniversary Tie
1993, Alpha Marketing, UK
No further information available.

CCM-023 Doctor Who Boxer Shorts
1996, St. Tropez, AUS
Made of a silky satin polyester material and featured the diamond logo, the Police Box, Red Daleks, silver Cybermen on a background of black, interspersed with purple question marks.
OP: $20.00 NM: £16.50

CCM-024 Doctor Who Pyjamas
1996, St. Tropez, AUS
Available in two sizes. Short and Long. Made of a silky satin polyester material and featured the diamond logo, the Police Box, Red Daleks, silver Cybermen on a background of black, interspersed with purple question marks.
OP: $59.95 short NM: £35

CCM-025 Doctor Who Socks
1996, St. Tropez, AUS
Blue or grey socks with a *Doctor Who* logo and question marks embroidered on.
OP: $12.95

CCM-026 Doctor Who Kimono Style Dressing Gown
1996, St. Tropez, AUS
Made of a silky satin polyester material and featured the diamond logo, the Police Box, Red Daleks, silver Cybermen on a background of black, interspersed with purple question marks.
OP: $59.95 NM: £35

CCM-027 Doctor Who Waistcoat
1996, St. Tropez, AUS
Made of a silky satin polyester material and featured the diamond logo, the Police Box, Red Daleks, silver Cybermen on a background of black, interspersed with purple question marks.
OP: $59.95

CCM-028 TARDIS Ties
1997, Who Shop International, UK
OP: £9.95 NM: £3.50

CCM-029 Flying Jackets
1998, The Ultimate Embroidery Company, UK
Reversible flying jacket. Black/Orange; Petrol/Orange. Size 44". Colour logo.
OP: £47.99

CCM-030 Winter Fleece Jackets
1998, The Ultimate Embroidery Company, UK
Reversible jacket. Black/Navy/Grey. Size 44". Colour logo.
OP: £46.99

CCM-031 Doctor Who Tie Tack
1998, Ultimate Buckle Ltd, UK
Doctor Who logo.
OP: £9.99

CCM-032 Doctor Who Cufflinks
1998, Ultimate Buckle Ltd, UK
Doctor Who logo.
OP: £13.99

CLOTHING ETC., POLO SHIRTS

CCP-001 Polo Shirt
DWFCA, USA
2-colour logo on burgundy, green, or red.
OP: $18.00

CCP-002 Polo Shirt
DWFCA, USA
Full colour diamond logo on white.
OP: $20.00

CCP-003 Polo Shirt
DWFCA, USA
Neon logo on royal or black.
OP: $17.00

CCP-004 Polo Shirts
1996, Dapol, UK
Cyberman/Dalek/plain.
OP: £14.99

CCP-005 *Doctor Who* Experience Polo Shirt
1997, Screen Stars/Fruit of the Loom, UK
Maroon shirt with K9 logo, "The Doctor Who Experience Llangollen".

CCP-006 Polo Shirts
1998, The Ultimate Embroidery Company, UK
Pique Polo short sleeved shirt. Black/White/Burgundy/Yellow. Size 44". Choice of logo: Dalek/Cyberman/Tardis/logo.
OP: £16.99

CLOTHING ETC., RUGBY SHIRTS

CCR-001 Long Sleeve Shirt
DWFCA, USA
Royal blue w/ silver TARDIS. Also Official DWFCA:
3/4 sleeve, diamond logo in colour.
OP: $12.00

CCR-002 Baseball Jersey: Fourth Doctor and Dalek
1982, Nightstar Corp., USA
Royal blue, red, black.
OP: $14.00

CCR-003 Baseball Jersey
1982, Nightstar Corp., USA
Diamond logo (royal blue, red, black). Neon Logo
(royal blue, red, black).
OP: $12.00

CCR-004 Rugby Shirt
1998, The Ultimate Embroidery Company, UK
Long sleeved. 100% cotton. Black/White/Gold. Size
44". Choice of logo: Dalek/Cyberman/Tardis/logo.
OP: £27.99

CCR-005 Rugby Shirt
1998, The Ultimate Embroidery Company, UK
Short sleeved. 100% cotton. Denim/Moss/Rust. Size
44". Choice of logo: Dalek/Cyberman/Tardis/logo.
OP: £28.99

CLOTHING ETC., SWEATSHIRTS

CCS-001 Sweatshirt
DWFCA, USA
Full colour diamond logo.
OP: $20.00 or $16.00 children's sizes

CCS-002 Sweatshirt: TARDIS
DWFCA, USA
OP: $20.00

CCS-003 Sweat Shirt – K-9
1980, Miles Bros., UK
Available in S, M, L.
OP: £5.25 (s) £6.75 (l)

CCS-004 Sweat Shirt – Cyberman
1982, Image Screencraft, UK
OP: £5.95 (s) £7.95 (l)

CCM-023

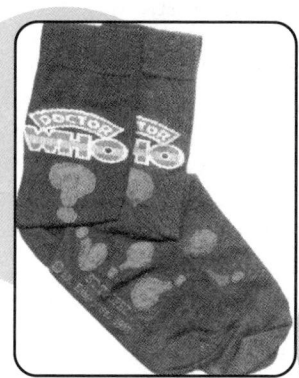

CCM-025

CCM-026

CCM-027

CCS-005 Sweat Shirts
BBC Enterprises, UK

CCS-006 Sweat Shirt – Doctor Who
1982/01, Image Screencraft, UK
Pocket Phosphor on Navy. S, M, L.
OP: £5.95 (s) £7.95 (l)

CCS-007 Sweat Shirt – 20 Years – A Celebration
1983/11, Image Screencraft, UK
Adult S, M, L. Child 26", 28", 30".
OP: £5.95 (s) £7.95 (l)

CCS-008 Sweat Shirt – Doctor Who
1987, Image Merchandising Ltd, UK
Colour on Black.
OP: £9.99 (S,M,L) £10.99 (XL)

CCS-009 Sweatshirt: 'TARDIS EXPRESS – When it absolutely, positively, has to be there BEFORE you mailed it...'
1988, Mere Dragons, USA
Sweatshirt has a variation of the Federal Express logo.
OP: $15.00

CCS-010 Police Box Sweatshirt
1993, Dominitemporal Services Ltd, UK
Police box design by Mark Freshney on pocket in white. Navy shirt.

CCS-011 Sweatshirt
1998, The Ultimate Embroidery Company, UK
Long sleeved. Cotton fleece. White/Black/Sky. Size 44".
Choice of logo: Dalek/Cyberman/Tardis/logo.
OP: £17.99

CLOTHING ETC., T-SHIRTS

THE T-shirt is probably one of the most popular items of merchandise to be produced. The problem from a cataloguing point of view is that they are so easy and cheap to make that unlicensed versions and limited-run shirts can be produced for just about any event or situation. The shirts we have listed here are, most likely, just a few of those that were issued, and we are sure that there are others around. However this list gives some idea of the sheer number of *Doctor Who* related T-shirts that have been issued over the years.

CCT-001 Tee Shirts
BBC Enterprises, UK

CCT-002 Doctor Who and the Daleks T-shirt
1975, Silly Things (Aha Ltd), UK
Red, black & yellow on white.
OP: £1.55 (adult 34"-40") £1.10 (junior 26"-32")

CCT-003 Doctor Who Logo T-shirt
1975, Rumpelstiltskin, UK
Black diamond logo on mustard. S, M, L.
OP: £1.75 (l) £1.35 (s)

CCT-004 Doctor Who T-shirt
1976, BBC Enterprises (Portugal), UK
Glitter logo on black. S, M, L.
OP: £2.00

CCT-005 Tee Shirt – K-9
1980, Miles Bros., UK
Grey/Red/Black on white. S, M, L.
OP: £2.50 (s) £2.75 (l)

CCT-006 T-shirt: Hard Rock Cafe Gallifrey
1980s, USA
When these T-shirts, available in a variety of colour schemes, were first released, the Hard Rock Cafe found out about the unlicensed use of their name and ended their distribution. Around 1996, John McElroy put out newly made versions. A sweatshirt also exists in purple with pink writing.

CCT-007 T-shirt: Master
USA
White on black.
OP: $10.00

CCT-008 T-shirt
USA
Two colour diamond logo: assorted colours.
OP: $12.00

CCT-009 T-shirts
USA
New Jersey Network pledge gifts.
OP: free

CCT-010 T-shirt: Dalek
DWFCA, USA
Short sleeve, black, scarlet and silver Dalek, DWFCA logo on sleeve.
OP: $10.00 NM: £16.50

CCT-011 T-shirt
DWFCA, USA
Diamond logo full colour: white.
OP: $13.00 or $11.00 children's sizes NM: £16.50

CCT-012 T-shirt: Five Doctors
DWFCA, USA
Long sleeve, assorted colours, (same as hooded).
OP: $15.00 NM: £16.50

CCT-013 T-shirt
DWFCA, USA
Full colour diamond logo: long sleeve, DWFCA logo
on front, British Broadcasting Corporation on sleeve.
OP: $15.00 NM: £16.50

CCT-014 T-shirt: Glow-in-the-Dark
DWFCA, USA
Silver neon DWFCA logo in starfield, glows yellow.
OP: $11.00

CCT-015 T-shirt: K-9
DWFCA, USA
Short sleeve, red with silver K-9, royal trim, DWFCA
on sleeve.
OP: $10.00; adult: s, m, l, xl $9.00; childrens: xs, s, m, l

CCT-016 T-shirt
DWFCA, USA
Neon logo glow in the dark: black shirt. Came with
free glow neon badge.
OP: $11.00

CCT-017 T-shirt
DWFCA, USA
Neon logo: 3/4 sleeve, one sleeve royal, one red, gold
neck band, white body.
OP: $12.00

CCT-018 T-shirt
DWFCA, USA
Neon logo: black w/ hot pink logo, white starfield.
OP: $11.00

CCT-019 T-shirt
DWFCA, USA
Neon logo: white w/ royal, red, or green neck and
sleeve trim.
OP: $8.50

CCT-020 T-shirt: Official Whovian
DWFCA, USA
Short sleeve, purple, WHOVIAN in red & gold.
OP: $10.00

CCT-021 T-shirt: TARDIS
DWFCA, USA
New design, short sleeve, TARDIS on front, logo on
sleeve.
OP: $11.00

CCT-022 T-shirt: TARDIS
DWFCA, USA
Short sleeve, silver shirt, TARDIS in royal, DWFCA on
sleeve.
OP: $10.00

CCT-023 T-shirt: TARDIS
DWFCA, USA
White w/ full colour TARDIS, new logo on back.
OP: $13.95

CCT-024 T-shirt: Time Lord
DWFCA, USA
3/4 sleeve, one sleeve green, one red, red & gold neck
band, white body, full colour TIMELORD.
OP: $12.00

CCT-025 T-shirt: Timelord
DWFCA, USA
Full colour, short sleeve.
OP: $12.00

CCT-026 T-shirt
1982, Nightstar Corp., USA
Light blue, tan, yellow, white.
OP: $12.00

CCT-027 T-shirt: Fourth Doctor and Daleks
1982, Nightstar Corp., USA
Light blue, tan, yellow, white.
OP: $12.50

**CCT-028 T-shirt: Fourth Doctor and Daleks
ladies**
1982, Nightstar Corp., USA
Light blue, tan, yellow, white.
OP: $12.00

CCT-029 T-shirt: K-9
1982, Nightstar Corp., USA
Light blue, tan, yellow, white.
OP: $12.50

CCT-030 T-shirt: ladies
1982, Nightstar Corp., USA
Light blue, tan, yellow, white.
OP: $12.00

CCT-034

CCT-031 T-shirt: neon logo
1982, Nightstar Corp., USA
Light blue, tan, yellow, white.
OP: $10.00

CCT-032 T-shirt: neon logo ladies
1982, Nightstar Corp., USA
Light blue, tan, yellow, white.
OP: $10.00

CCT-033 Tee Shirt – Doctor Who
1982/01, Image Screencraft, UK
Red & Yellow on White or Phosphor on Navy.
OP: £3.25 (s) £3.95 (l)

CCT-034 Tee Shirt – Cyberman
1982/09, Image Screencraft, UK
Green & Black on White. S, M, L, XL, 26, 28, 30.
OP: £3.25 (s) £3.95 (l)

CCT-035 Hooded Shirt, Five Doctors
1983, DWFCA, USA
Assorted colours, draw-string hood, 5 Drs on front,
neon logo on back, British Broadcasting Corporation
on sleeve.
OP: $20.00

CCT-036 Tee Shirt – The Fifth Doctor
1983/04, Image Screencraft, UK
Colour art on White. S, M, L, XL, 26, 28, 30, 32.
OP: £3.25 (s) £3.95 (l)

CCT-037 T-shirt: Sixth Doctor
1984, USA
Royal on ecru.
OP: $10.00

CCT-038 T-shirt: 'I Love Doctor Who'
1984, DWFCA, USA
Royal neon logo, 2 red hearts, short sleeve. Came
with matching bumper sticker.
OP: $11.00

CCT-039 T-shirt: 'I love Tom Baker'
1984, DWFCA, USA
Short sleeve.
OP: $11.00

CCT-040 T-shirt: Five Doctors
1984, DWFCA, USA
Short sleeve (like hooded).
OP: $13.00

CCT-041 T-shirt: Jelly Babies
1984, DWFCA, USA
Full colour reproduction of box, white w/ red trim.
OP: $13.00

CCT-042 T-shirt: Romana
1984, DWFCA, USA
Short sleeve, wine shirt, Romana's full name royal &
gold, DWFCA logo on sleeve.
OP: $10.00

CCT-043 T-shirt: Six Doctors
1984, DWFCA, USA
Black w/ white ink, logo on back.
OP: $15.00

CCT-044 T-shirt: TARDIS 21
1984, Spirit of Light Enterprises Ltd, USA
OP: $21.00

CCT-045 T-shirts
1984, Spirit of Light Enterprises Ltd, USA
Sixth Doctor, Baker Logo, Baker double logo, The
Master, Davison/TARDIS, Davison/Master.
OP: $10.00 each

CCT-046 T-shirt: Zygon
1984 c., DWFCA, USA
White (advertised as their worst selling T-shirt).
OP: $10.00

CCT-047 Tee Shirt – Daleks
1984/01, Image Merchandising Ltd, UK
3 colour screenprint by Rod Vass. S, M, L, XL, 26, 28,
30, 32.
OP: £3.25 (s) £3.95 (l)

CCT-048 T-shirt: Cyberman
1985, DWFCA, USA
Short sleeve, silver Cyberman & Cyber logo on back,
Who logo on back.
OP: $11.00

CCT-049 Neon Logo Shirt
1985, Southern Star, AUS
Featured the neon logo in red above the Southern Cross in white all on a blue background; designed to look something like the diamond logo.

CCT-050 T-shirt: Doctor Who festival
1986, DWFCA, USA
Neon logo zooming out, white on black.
OP: $10.00

CCT-051 Tee Shirt – Doctor Who Across The Universe
1986/09, Image Merchandising Ltd, UK
Limited hand-printed background. S, M, L.
OP: £5.99

CCT-052 Tee Shirt – Doctor Who Across The Universe
1986/09, Image Merchandising Ltd, UK
4 colour screenprint. S, M, L, 26, 28, 30.
OP: £3.99

CCT-053 T-shirt
1987, DWFCA, USA
White w/ McCoy logo in full colour.
OP: $13.95

CCT-054 T-shirt: 'TARDIS EXPRESS – When it absolutely, positively, has to be there BEFORE you mailed it...'
1988, Mere Dragons, USA
T-shirt has a variation of the Federal Express logo.
OP: $8.00

CCT-055 T-shirt: 25th Anniversary
1988, DWFCA, USA
W/ diamond logo (made with special printing process) black.
OP: $18.00 long sleeve; $15.00 short sleeve

CCT-056 T-shirt
1988, Lionheart, USA
Black glow in the dark neon logo 25th Anniversary.
OP: $13.00

CCT-057 Tee Shirt – Cyberman
1988, Acme Ltd, UK

CCT-058 Tee Shirt – Daleks
1988, Acme Ltd, UK

CCT-059 T-shirt: DWFCA
1989, DWFCA, USA
OP: $15.00

CCT-060 T-shirt: Gallifrey Beach and Body Club
1989, DWFCA, USA
OP: $14.00 NM: £12

CCT-061 T-shirt: Seven Doctors
1989, DWFCA, USA
White with Doctors (in one colour or full colour) in diamond shapes Seven Doctors also featured on sweatshirt ($21.95).
OP: $13.95 NM: £12

CCT-062 T-shirt: University of Gallifrey
1989, DWFCA, USA
OP: $14.00 NM: £12

CCT-063 Tee Shirts
1989, Levendis Enterprises Ltd, UK
Four designs: 1) Logo, TARDIS and K9; 2) Logo, TARDIS flying, K9; 3) Logo, Cyberman; 4) Doctor Who and the Daleks.

CCT-064 Tee Shirt – *The Ultimate Adventure*
1989, UK
OP: £5.00

CCT-065 T-shirt (Diamond Logo)
1990, Friends of Doctor Who, USA
NM: £12

CCT-066 T-shirt (Materialising TARDIS)
1990, Friends of Doctor Who, USA

CCT-067 Absalom Daak T-shirt
1990/04, Levendis Enterprises Ltd, UK
Limited edition.

CCT-068 Doctor Who T-shirts
1990/09, Skansen, AUS
Two varieties. One featured a black and white diamond logo on white/black shirt. The other was a Dalek shirt with 'EX-TER-MIN-ATE' printed in four lines on the front.
OP: $24.95

CCT-069 T-shirt: Hirschfeld Litho
1990 c., USA
Offered on PBS pledge drives, white T-shirt with 'Seven Faces' litho on front; also available as a black long-sleeved turtleneck with litho art in white. See COL-007.

CCT-070 DSL T-shirts
1990, Dominitemporal Services Ltd, UK
Produced for the annual UK convention, Panopticon, organised by Dominitemporal Services for the *Doctor Who* Appreciation Society. Black or blue print on white T-shirts. 'Seal of Rassilon' design.

CCT-071 T-shirt: Dematerialising TARDIS
1991, USA
OP: $18.00

CCT-072 DSL T-shirts
1991, Dominitemporal Services Ltd, UK
Produced for the annual UK convention, Panopticon, organised by Dominitemporal Services for the *Doctor Who* Appreciation Society. Black or blue print on white T-shirts. 'DSL Timelord Head' design.

CCT-073 MOMI T-shirts
1991, MOMI, UK
Diddly Dum; Head Set, The Original Full Metal jacket, X-terminate.
OP: £9.99 each   NM: £22

CCT-074 T-shirt: 'TARDIS CREW'
1992, USA
Light gray colour with a TARDIS on the chest and the words 'TARDIS CREW' at shoulder height in electronic lettering.
OP: $8.00

CCT-075 Character T-shirts
1992/01, GUDI /The Black T-shirt Design Company, UK
Colin Baker, Sylvester McCoy, Sophie Aldred. McCoy shirt known to have actor signatures.
OP: £10.50

CCT-076 Character T-shirts
1992/09, GUDI/The Black T-shirt Design Company, UK
New versions of McCoy, Baker and Aldred ('Wickec') shirts, plus Nicholas Courtney ('Five Rounds Rapid') and Patrick Troughton ('When I Say Run...'). A Nicholas Courtney shirt with 'Liberty Hall' and an Aldred shirt with 'Serious Hardware' (considered the last black shirt in the line) are also known.

CCT-077 T-shirts
1992, LPI, UK
Two designs.

CCT-078 T-shirts
1992/93, BBC Enterprises?, UK
Dalek "Out of Control", seven Doctors, K9 & TARDIS designs. Possibly more.
OP: £5.99

CCT-078 DSL T-shirts
1992, Dominitemporal Services Ltd, UK
Produced for the annual UK convention, Panopticon, organised by Dominitemporal Services for the *Doctor Who* Appreciation Society. Black or blue print on white T-shirts. 'figure 8' design incorporating 'seal of Rassilon' and 'DSL Timelord Head'.

CCT-079 30th Anniversary T-shirts
1993, Alpha Marketing, UK
3 designs: Dalek, Davros, 'Dalek War Zone'
OP: £6.99

CCT-080 'Tombwatch' T-Shirt
1993, Dominitemporal Services Ltd, UK
Grey/black T shirt with the Cybermen head design from *Tomb of the Cybermen*. Originally produced for DSL's 'Tombwatch' event, also reprinted for the Panopticon '93 event.

CCT-081 Panopticon '93 T-shirt – Title Sequence
1993, Dominitemporal Services Ltd, UK
Black and red on white shirt. Design by Mark Freshney. Same design on yellow T-shirts for stewards only.

CCT-082 Panopticon '93 T-shirt – Console
1993, Dominitemporal Services Ltd, UK
White and red on black shirt. Design by Mark Freshney.

CCT-083 Character T-shirts
1993/09, GUDI/The Black T-shirt Design Company, UK
New Colin Baker ('The Cat That Walks Alone'), Nicola Bryant ('All These Corridors Look The Same').
OP: £10.50

CCT-084 '21 Years at Longleat' T-shirts
1994, BBC Enterprises, UK
Commemorative T-shirt with same slogan as related badge.

CCT-085 Character T-shirts
1994/03, GUDI/The Black T-shirt Design Company, UK
Deborah Watling ('Aaaaaaaaarrhhh!'), Jon Pertwee ('Reverse The Polarity Of The Neutron Flow'), William Hartnell ('HMMM').
OP: £10.50

CCT-086 T-shirts
1995, It's Classic, UK
Four designs: Davros ('Pathetic earthlings you must obey the will of Davros'), Dalek ('Exterminate!'), TARDIS, Cybermen ('Silver Nemesis').
OP: £9.99 (L, XL)

CCT-087 TARDIS/K9 T-Shirts
2000, Aardvark Screenprinting, USA
TARDIS shirt plays off the idea that *Doctor Who* has its main US home on PBS. Linking it with the PBS home improvement show *This Old House*, the shirt features the words 'This Old Tardis' in blue letters and an illustration of the TARDIS, both on the front of the shirt. The K9 shirt has a line drawing of K9 and the slogan 'TARDIS-Broken' in '80s-style computer lettering.
OP: $20

CCT-088 *Cybertech Pharos* T-Shirt
1995, Jump Cut Records?, UK
Image same as the album cover.

CCT-089 Adric T-shirt
1995, GUDI/The Black T-shirt Design Company, UK
An unlikely addition to the GUDI line, it is reported that they also produced a shirt with the legend 'Fu*k off Adric', with Adric's broken star in place of the 'c'. These were almost certainly not offered for general sale.

CCT-090 Character T-shirts
1996/01, GUDI/The Black T-shirt Design Company, UK
New Hartnell ('HMMM'), Courtney ('Liberty Hall, Liberty Hall'). The phrases were on the backs of the shirts with the faces on the front.
OP: £10.50

CCT-091 Sarah Jane T-shirt
1996, GUDI/The Black T-shirt Design Company, UK
A limited edition of 75 of these white t-shirts were produced for the 1996 Sydney Whovention in Australia, commissioned by Richard Nolan. Sarah Jane's face appears on the front, while on the back is a spider, the phrase 'Give Me the Crystal', and a signature. These were probably never offered for general sale.

CCT-092 Doctor Who T-shirt
1996, St. Tropez, AUS
Featured a big red and blue question mark.
OP: $24.95

CCT-093 Doctor Who Movie T-shirts
1996, It's Classic, UK
Three designs: Doctor and 'Seal of Rassilon', small colour Doctor and Movie logo, large b/w Doctor and Movie logo.
OP: £9.99 (L, XL) $15.00

CCT-094 Leonardo's TARDIS T-shirt
1996, Dapol, UK
A sketch of the TARDIS in the style of Leonardo da Vinci.
OP: £13.95

CCT-076

CCT-079

CCT-087

CCT-091

CCT-093

CCT-100

CCT-103

CCT-104

CCT-095 Panopticon '96 T-Shirt
1996, Dominitemporal Services Ltd, UK
4 colour print on oatmeal shirt. 3-D image of DSL logo. Also available on tangerine shirt for stewards.

CCT-096 'The Re-Generation' T-shirt
1997, BBC Worldwide, UK
T-shirt to promote the launch of the BBC's range of books.
OP: free

CCT-097 'Who On Earth is Tom Baker' T-shirt
1998, HarperCollins, UK
T-shirt to promote the launch of Tom Baker's autobiography.
OP: free

CCT-098 Panopticon '98 T-Shirt – Logo
1998, Dominitemporal Services Ltd, UK
Panopticon logo in red on oatmeal shirt, breast pocket position. Also available on green shirt for stewards.

CCT-099 Panopticon '98 T-Shirt – Police Box
1998, Dominitemporal Services Ltd, UK
Police Box on white shirt.

CCT-100 T-Shirts
1990s?, SilverScreen Leisurewear, UK?
At least three different designs. Black shirt with diamond logo and words 'Dalek Warzone' accompanying a Dalek and explosions; black shirt with diamond logo, Davros and Dalek images; 30th anniversary diamond logo.

CCT-101 T-Shirts
2000/05, 10th Planet, UK
Two designs: The Daleks and The Cybermen. Images are paintings by Duncan Gutteridge. Available in M, L and XL.
OP: £15.99

CCT-102 T-Shirts
2000/09, 10th Planet, UK
TARDIS design. Available in M, L and XL.
OP: £15.99

CCT-103 T-Shirts
2001/08, 10th Planet, UK
4th Doctor Design. Available in M, L and XL.
OP: £15.99/XXL at £16.99

CCT-104 T-Shirts
2002/05, 10th Planet, UK
Three different monster montage designs 'sixties', 'seventies' and 'eighties'. Available in M, L and XL.
OP: £15.99/XXL at £16.99

CLOTHING ETC., JEWELRY

CJE-001a Doctor Who Medallion and Chain (copper finish)
1974, A.P. Services & Co., UK
OP: 36p

CJE-001b Doctor Who Medallion and Chain (gold plated finish)
1974, A.P. Services & Co., UK
OP: 39p

CJE-001c Doctor Who Medallion and Chain (satin finish)
1974, A.P. Services & Co., UK
OP: 35p

CJE-001d Doctor Who Medallion and Chain (silver finish)
1974, A.P. Services & Co., UK
OP: 37p

CJE-002 Dalek Enamel Brooch
1979, S. Weiner Ltd, UK
REF: 22349 OP: 75p

CJE-003 Dalek Enamel Pendant
1979, S. Weiner Ltd, UK
REF: 13950 OP: 75p

CJE-004 Dalek Enamel Ring
1979, S. Weiner Ltd, UK
REF: 22352 OP: 50p

CJE-005 K-9 Enamel Brooch
1979, S. Weiner Ltd, UK
REF: 22350 OP: 75p

CJE-006 K-9 Enamel Pendant
1979, S. Weiner Ltd, UK
REF: 13951 OP: 75p

CJE-007 K-9 Enamel Ring
1979, S. Weiner Ltd, UK
REF: 22352 OP: 50p

CJE-008 Necklace: Miniature TARDIS
USA
OP: $3.00

CJE-009 Necklace: TARDIS Key
1984, Spirit of Light Enterprises Ltd, USA
OP: $8.00 NM: £5.50

CJE-002

CJE-004

CJE-005

CJE-003

CJE-006

CJE-007

CJE-009

CJE-013 (front and back)

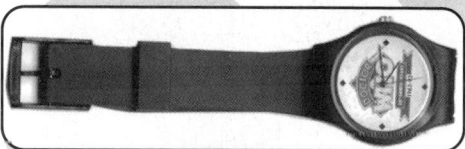
CJE-015

CJE-016

CJE-017

CJE-019

CJE-020

CJE-021

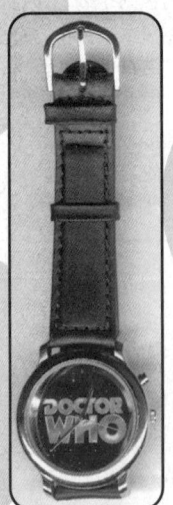

CJE-023

CJE-023 (tin)

CJE-010 Belt buckles
1985, DWFCA, USA
Pure German silver, neon logo (numbered & registered).
OP: $60.00 (small) $75.00 (large)

CJE-011 Digital Watch
1987, Lionheart, USA
Blue w/ neon logo.
OP: $12.50

CJE-012 Watch
1988, DWFCA, USA
Full colour diamond logo.
OP: $24.95 NM: £20

CJE-013 Doctor Who Buckle
1990, English Accents, US
A Copper belt buckle with the diamond *Doctor Who* logo in relief on the front.

CJE-014 Sunglasses: Gallifrey Beach Club
1992, USA
OP: $14.95

CJE-015 30th anniversary watches
1993, Who Shop International, UK
30th Anniversary logo on face.
OP: £19.99

CJE-016 Cyberman buckle
1994, The Ultimate Buckle Company, UK
REF: UL89E OP: £20.95

CJE-017 Dalek buckle
1994, The Ultimate Buckle Company, UK
Blue and black/Red and black.
REF: UL326EBU/UL326ER OP: £12.95

CJE-018 Dalek pendant thong
1994, The Ultimate Buckle Company, UK
Plain/Blue/Red.
REF: BT02P/BT02EBU/BT02ER
OP: £3.95 (plain) £4.55 (colour)

CJE-019 Logo buckle
1994, The Ultimate Buckle Company, UK
REF: UL76P/UL76E
OP: £10.95 (plain) £12.95 (colour)

CJE-020 Logo pendant thong
1994, The Ultimate Buckle Company, UK
REF: BT01P/BT01E
OP: £3.95 (plain) £4.55 (colour)

CJE-021 'Seal of Rassilon' buckle
1994, The Ultimate Buckle Company, UK
Red/Black/Plain/Blue.
REF: UL89ER/UL89EBL/UL113P/UL89EBU
OP: £10.95 (plain) £12.95 (colour)

CJE-022 Tardis pendant thong
1994, The Ultimate Buckle Company, UK
Coloured/Plain.
REF: BT03E/BT03P
OP: £3.95 (plain) £4.55 (colour)

CJE-023 Doctor Who Movie Watch
1996, Wesco Limited, UK
Doctor Who logo on face and 'Electro-Luminescence' –
it lights up blue! Sold in a 'Limited Edition' tin.
OP: £29.95 ($75)

CJE-024 'Seal of Rassilon' Pendant
1996, The Ultimate Buckle Company, UK
Green/red/blue/yellow.
OP: £6.99

CJE-025 'Seal of Rassilon' pewter buckle
1996, The Ultimate Buckle Company, UK
'Seal of Rassilon' (plain/red/blue/black).
OP: £10.99 (plain) £12.99 (colour)

CJE-026 TARDIS Necklet
1996, The Ultimate Buckle Company, UK
OP: £12.95

CJE-027 TARDIS Watch
1997/09, Aqua Janeiro, UK
TARDIS appears and vanishes with each minute.
Special presentation box stamped with the TVM logo.
OP: £29.99

CJE-028a 35th Anniversary Fob Watch – Gold
1998/03, Aqua Janeiro, UK
Limited to 200 gold casing. Came with a numbered
certificate of authenticity. Face listed the 8 actors to
have played the Doctor. No numerals.
OP: £35.99 NM: £90-£110

CJE-028b 35th Anniversary Fob Watch –
Chrome
1998, Aqua Janeiro, UK
Limited to 250 chrome casing. Came with a numbered certificate of authenticity. This edition produced
as the gold edition sold out almost immediately. Face
contained the 'Seal of Rassilon' in silver and red, plus
roman numerals.
OP: £34.95 NM: £75

CJE-027

CJE-028a

CJE-028b

CJE-029

CJE-030

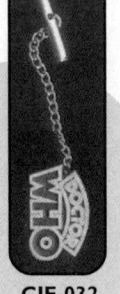

CJE-032

CJE-031

CJE-034

CJE-035

CJE-036

CJE-029 Doctor Who Bubble Watch
1998/10, Aqua Janeiro, UK
Bubble face with a 3D TARDIS in. Clock face is digital.
OP: £9.99

CJE-030 Gilt clip on belt buckles
1998/06, The Ultimate Buckle Company, UK
Assorted photographic designs. Master, McCoy, Davison,
Troughton, Pertwee, Hartnell, C Baker, Diamond logo,
K9, 'Seal of Rassilon' (red/blue/yellow /green).
REF: BITAL10/J - BITAL 20J OP: £12.99 each

CJE-031 Logo cuff links
1998, The Ultimate Buckle Company, UK
OP: £13.99

CJE-032 Logo tie tack
1998, The Ultimate Buckle Company, UK
9 designs/colours.
OP: £9.99

CJE-033 Pendants
1998, The Ultimate Buckle Company, UK
Assorted photographic designs. Master, McCoy, Davison,
Troughton, Pertwee, Hartnell, Diamond logo, K9.
OP: £6.99

CJE-034 Rassilon Watch
1998/03, Aqua Janeiro, UK
Analog watch has the 'Seal of Rassilon' design in the
centre of the face. Also has the design continued on
the straps.
OP: £16.95

CJE-035 Ring Watch
1998, Aqua Janeiro, UK
Watch set into a ring. Two colours available. Limited
edition of 500. Available in boxed pairs (£34.99) or
individually (£19.99).
OP: £19.99 each

CJE-036 K9 Anniversary Pendant
1998/08, UK
Pendant celebrating the 21st anniversary of K9.
OP: £14.99

CJE-037 TARDIS Key
1998, The Ultimate Buckle Company, UK
Limited edition. 5000 made. Cast from pewter.
OP: £14.99

CLOTHING ETC., KEY RINGS

CKE-001 Doctor Who Keyring (leather)
1976, UK
OP: 35p

CKE-002 Doctor Who Leather Key Rings (green, black, blue, red, brown)
1980, BBC Enterprises, UK
OP: 35p each

CKE-003 Doctor Who Exhibition/TARDIS Key Ring
1982, BBC Enterprises, UK

CKE-004 Key Fob: Glow in the Dark
1982, Nightstar Corp., USA
Diamond or neon logo.
OP: $1.50

CKE-005 Key Chain: Light TARDIS
1984, USA
OP: $4.00

CKE-006 Key Fob
1984, DWFCA, USA
Diamond or neon logo: assorted colours.
OP: $1.00   NM: £2

CKE-007 Key Rings
1984, Susan Moore, UK
Photographs cased in clear perspex.
OP: £1.00

CKE-008 Key Chain: TARDIS Key
1984, Spirit of Light Enterprises Ltd, USA
OP: $8.00   NM: £5.50

CKE-009 USA Tour Key Ring
1986, Silverscreen UK, USA
Features the same full colour diamond logo with
'USA' underneath as on one of the USA Tour button
badges (see CBA-051).
OP: $2.50

CKE-010 Key Chain Penlight:
1987, Lionheart, USA
Diamond logo.
OP: $2.00

CKE-011 Key Fob
1987, Lionheart, USA
White, shaped like an owl, 'Who gives a hoot!', diamond logo on back.
OP: $1.50

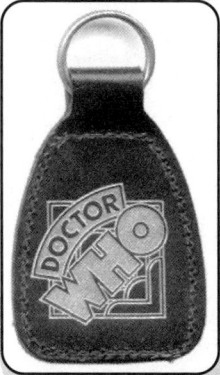

CKE-001

CKE-004

CKE-005

CKE-008

CKE-009

CKE-012

CKE-015

CKE-014

CKE-016

CKE-017

CKE-019

CKE-020

CKE-012 Doctor Who Exhibition Key Ring
1987, BBC Enterprises, UK
McCoy logo with TARDIS.

CKE-013 Key Chain: TARDIS Squeez-o-light
1988, USA
A plastic cylinder printed with a TARDIS design which lights up when squeezed.
OP: $5.00

CKE-014 Dalek Key Ring
1994, The Ultimate Buckle Company, UK
Plain/Blue/Red.
REF: BK02P/BK02EBU/BK02ER
OP: £3.55 (plain) £4.55 (colour)

CKE-015 Logo Key Ring
1994, The Ultimate Buckle Company, UK
REF: BK01P/BK01E   OP: £3.55 (plain) £4.55 (colour)

CKE-016 Tardis Key Ring
1994, The Ultimate Buckle Company, UK
REF: BK03E/BK03P
OP: £3.55 (plain) £4.55 (colour)

CKE-017 Key Rings
1996, Downpace
Metal. Dr Who logo /'Seal of Rassilon'/Movie logo.
OP: £3.99 each

CKE-018 'Seal of Rassilon' Key ring
1996, The Ultimate Buckle Company, UK
Green/red/blue/yellow. Diamond logo with 'Exhibition' underneath.
OP: £4.99

CKE-019 Key Fobs
1996, Dapol, UK
Diamond logo. White/Black/Blue/Red.
REF: W026-001/2/3/4   OP: £1.35

CKE-020 Keyrings
1998, The Ultimate Buckle Company, UK
Assorted photographic designs. Master, McCoy, Davison, Troughton, Pertwee, Hartnell, Diamond logo, K9, Cyberman. Each photograph is set into a pewter and enamel display, with the 'Seal of Rassilon' logo at the bottom.
REF: BK 10/H - BK 20/H OP: £4.99 each

CKE-021 Key Rings
1999, Bally/Midway Amusement Games, USA
Set of 7 small plastic 1" key rings featuring the Doctors from Hartnell to McCoy and made available at the Llangollen Exhibition. The plastic discs were originally pro-

motional items manufactured by Bally for dealers to use as promotion for the pinball machine (see GAR-003b).
OP: £1.99 each

CKE-022 Tardis Key Ring
2000?, UK
Plastic white police box on ring.

CLOTHING ETC., KNITTING PATTERNS

CKN-001 Doctor Who-Style Slipover and Scarf Knitting Pattern
1976, Mayfield Knitting Wools, UK
Photo on front features a child in clothes and a cardboard Dalek. 4 page pattern.
REF: No 1237 D/K OP: 12p NM: £12

CKN-002 Scarf Knitting Pattern
1976, BBC TV, UK
The Doctor Who production office sent out a single-sheet pattern for the scarf along with a number of other information sheets during the late seventies and early eighties. It is unclear from where this pattern originated.
OP: free

CKN-003 Knitted Tom Baker doll pattern
1979 c., BBC TV, UK
An A3-sized knitting pattern for a Tom Baker doll, complete with scarf. Origin unknown, but it was among a package of information sheets sent out by the Production Office in the late seventies.
OP: free

CKN-004a Doctor Who Pattern Book, The (Joy Gammon)
1984/10, W. H. Allen & Co. PLC, UK
A selection of knitting patterns all with a Doctor Who theme. Joy Gammon was the author of several other books of knitting patterns.
REF: ISBN 0-491-03403-2 OP: £7.95 h/b NM: £12

CKN-004b Doctor Who Pattern Book, The (Joy Gammon)
1986/10, W. H. Allen & Co. PLC, UK
Print run: 9,500 copies. The interior pages appear to be directly from the hardback edition, with 1984 date and matching ISBN number.
REF: ISBN 0-426-20287-2 OP: £3.50 lfp/b NM: £5

CKN-005 Doctor Who: 6 Intarsia Designs
1990, Hard Graphed, UK
By Denise Jones and Mike Barber based on the artwork of Andrew Skilleter.
REF: No ISBN OP: £3.45

CKE-022

CKN-004a

CKN-005

CKN-005 (interior examples)

CLP-001

CLP-002

CLOTHING ETC., PATCHES

CLP-001 Patches
1984, Glenwood Distributors Inc., USA
TARDIS, K-9, diamond Logo, neon Logo. All patches
read 'BBC Enterprises LTD. Barb Elder Corp.
Glenwood Dist. Inc.' along the edge.
OP: $3.00 each

CLP-002 Cloth Patch
1988, John Fitton, UK
McCoy logo.
OP: £3.99

CLP-003 DSL Patches
1991, Dominitemporal Services Ltd
Embroidered patches: circular with 'seal of Rassilon';
circular with DSL logo (both in assorted colours).

CLP-004 UNIT patches
1996, UK
Cloth patches of the oval UNIT logo.
OP: £2.00

COLLECTIBLES

THE phenomenon of a 'collectible limited
edition' item specially manufactured and expressly
intended for collecting is a fairly recent one. In
terms of *Doctor Who*, it was in the eighties, when
fans of the show were getting older, and had jobs
and therefore more money to spend, that 'limited
edition' items started to appear. These are usually of
a display only nature, and usually cost a lot of
money. In some cases, the nature of the 'limited edition' is in question: being limited to as many people wanted to buy it, for example, or by setting
unrealistic upper limits on the production runs, or
even not declaring what the limitation is. In general, items which are produced as 'collectible limited
editions' are rarely an investment for the future, and
most are so overpriced initially that their re-sale
value is less than their original price.

COL-001

COL-003 & COL-004

COL-001 Sonic Screwdriver
1984, Spirit of Light Enterprises Ltd, USA
A non-working replica of the Doctor's sonic screwdriver.
OP: $15.00 (£11.50 import) NM: £27.50

COL-005

COL-002 Stained Glass Window
1985, DWFCA, USA
Diamond logo: 16'x16'.
OP: $125.00   NM: £125

COL-003 'Six Doctors' Bust Set
1985, Fine Art Castings, UK
First six Doctors represented. Set came with a certificate
of authenticity and a display stand. 2000 sets world wide.
OP: £9.44 each bust / £75 set ($250)

COL-004 'Villains' Bust Set
1986/01, Fine Art Castings, UK
Featured: Celestial Toymaker, Ice Warrior, The Master,
Mining Robot (from *The Robots of Death*), Cyberman,
Sil. Set came with a certificate of authenticity and a
display stand. 2000 sets world wide.
OP: £12.30 each bust / £75 set

COL-005 Latex Masks
1987/08, Imagineering Ltd, UK
Imagineering Ltd provided many of the visual effects
props and monster costumes for the Davison era. Full
head latex masks. Davros (1) , Davros (2), Draconian,
Silurian (1), Silurian (2), Sontaran. Available exclusively
through The Movie Store (a UK *Doctor Who* dealer).
OP: £39.95   NM: £27.50

COL-006 Doctor Who 'Time Travellers' watch
1988, USA
5' giant watch.
OP: $29.95

COL-007 Limited edition Hirschfeld litho-graph: 'The Seven Faces of DOCTOR WHO'
1990, Margo Field Galleries, New York, USA
Featuring the seven Doctors in Hirschfeld's inimitable
style (with three 'Ninas' hidden in the artwork, refer-
ring to Hirschfeld's running gag of including his daugh-
ter's name in the intricate lines of his caricatures).
OP: $1,500

COL-008 Doctor Who Tankards
1992-4, The Lustleigh Pottery/Aidee International Ltd, UK
750 of each produced. Mail order only. One tankard
was issued for each Doctor, and came with an accompanying certificate of authentication. Subscribers
received the same edition number of each one. After
the initial series of tankards was complete, there were
plans to produce further tankards (including the
Master) but these came to nothing.
OP: £59.95 each   NM: £75 each

COL-007

COL-008

COL-009

COL-009 Full size Daleks

1995/05, This Planet Earth Ltd, UK

Full size, fully operational Daleks. Initially available in 'Renegade Dalek' (grey/black) and 'Supreme Dalek' (black/silver) versions. In later years, the company added a movie-style Dalek, a white/gold Imperial Dalek, and '60s/'70s style colour variations. A Special Weapons Dalek was also planned.

OP: £1595 (Renegade) / £1695 (Supreme) / £1795 (Imperial) / £1995 (Movie)

COL-010 Doctor Who Chess Set

1992, MBI Inc, UK

Each figure cost £15.45. There were 38 pieces in the initial set. The wooden chess board itself came free, within which the initial set could be stored. There was an additional expansion set issued, which came with a TARDIS-shaped wooden display carousel. The figures were:

Initial Set: The First Doctor (King), The Second Doctor (King), The Third Doctor (King), The Fourth Doctor (King), The Fifth Doctor (King), The Sixth Doctor (King), The Seventh Doctor (King), Leela (Queen), Kameleon (Bishop), The Brigadier (Bishop), James McCrimmon (Knight), Adric (Knight), TARDIS (Rook), K9 (Pawn); The Master (King), The Rani (Queen), Cyberman (Bishop), Draconian (Bishop), Ice Warrior (Knight), Sea Devil (Knight), Sontaran (Rook), Dalek (Pawn)

Expansion Set: Susan Foreman (Queen), Zoe Heriot (Queen), Jo Grant (Queen), Tegan Jovanka (Queen), Peri Brown (Queen), Ace (Queen), The Castellan (Bishop), Alpha Centauri (Bishop), Captain Yates (Bishop), Sergeant Benton (Bishop), Harry Sullivan (Knight), Turlough (Knight), Davros (Bishop), Morbius (Bishop), Omega (Bishop), Sharaz Jek (Bishop), Silurian (Knight), Terileptil (Knight), Zygon (Knight), Yeti (Knight), Robot of Death (Rook), Master's TARDIS (Rook)

COL-010

COL-010 (detail of pawns)

COL-010 (selected Expansion Set figures)

COL-011

COL-012

COL-013

COL-014

After the 1996 TV Movie was aired, a further set of 4 figures was released. The first two sets of figures came with booklets written by David J Howe. The first was called 'A Mighty Battle Between Good and Evil' and the second 'The Battle Continues'. The four figures from the TV Movie each came with an A6 card, again written by David J Howe, giving information about the character.
OP: £625.10 total cost
NM: £75 each figure

COL-011 Eighth Doctor Figure
1996, MBI Inc, UK
Additional figure for the MBI Chess Set. King.
OP: £16.99 NM: £75

COL-012 Chang Lee Figure
1996, MBI Inc, UK
Additional figure for the MBI Chess Set. Knight.
OP: £16.99 NM: £75

COL-013 Dr Grace Holloway Figure
1996, MBI Inc, UK
Additional figure for the MBI Chess Set. Queen.
OP: £16.99 NM: £75

COL-014 The Master Figure
1996, MBI Inc, UK
Additional figure for the MBI Chess Set. King.
OP: £16.99 NM: £75

COL-015 30th anniversary print
1993, C Woodward, UK
Painted by Andrew Robins in black ink. Limited edition of 1000, size A2.
OP: £35.00 NM: £35

COL-016 Doctor Who Salt and Pepper Daleks
1993, Asmartartz Production, NZ
Designed by Steve Shields. Cast from pewter.
OP: £40.00 NM: £70

COL-015

COL-016

COL-017

COL-018

COL-019

COL-020

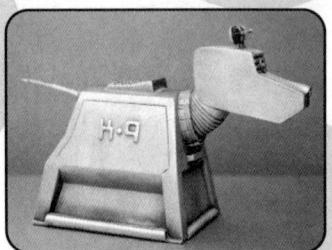

COL-021

COL-022

COL-023

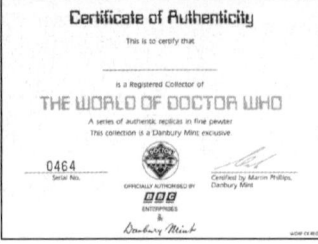

COL-018-023 certificate

COL-017 Doctor Who Dalek lighter case
1998, Asmartartz Production, NZ
Designed by Steve Shields. Cast from pewter. This is similar to the salt and pepper Daleks but the Dalek's head flips back to reveal a space for the lighter.
NM: £45

COL-018 Cyberman large pewter model
1995, Danbury Mint, UK
Following the success of the Chess Set, Danbury mint made available selected figures as large pewter models. Flier in *DWM* #258. After all six releases, collectors received a certificate (pictured).
OP: £73.50

COL-019 Dalek large pewter model
1995, Danbury Mint, UK
The Dalek's head turns.
OP: £73.50   NM: £90

COL-020 TARDIS large pewter model
1995, Danbury Mint, UK
OP: £73.50   NM: £90

COL-021 K-9 large pewter model
1995, Danbury Mint, UK
OP: £73.50   NM: £90

COL-022 Ice Warrior large pewter model
1995/1996, Danbury Mint, UK
OP: £73.50   NM: £90

COL-023 Sea Devil large pewter Model
1995/1996, Danbury Mint, UK
OP: £73.50   NM: £90

COL-024 Jon Pertwee
1995, Lifelike Creatures, UK
Model kit sculpted by Simon Laurens. Kit came with a signed photograph of Pertwee and a certificate. 14" tall. Kit was approved and licensed by Pertwee. Available in resin or a small number of bronzed resin kits.

COL-025 Cyberman Helmet
1988, Sevans Models, UK
Finished in matte black.
OP: £42.50

COL-026 Cyberman Helmet
1996, Sevans Models, UK
OP: £250

COL-027 Cyberman Gun
1996, Sevans Models, UK
OP: £175

COL-028 Cyberman Chest Unit and shoulders
1997, Sevans Models, UK
OP: £225

COL-029 Sonic Screwdriver
1996, Who Shop International, UK
A non-working metal tooled prop. This replica was originally made in Scotland and available as early as 1987 before being offered by the Who Shop in the '90s.
OP: £34.99

COL-030 Jelly Baby filled transparent TARDIS
1999, Dapol, UK
A transparent TARDIS case containing jelly babies. This was the Dapol TARDIS but in clear plastic and without the mechanism for the flashing light.
REF: W05-JB OP: £8.99

COL-031 Fine-art glass sculpture
1999/10, Dapol, UK
A black base with two sheets of etched glass and a blue tinted mirror at the back. Features images of William Hartnell as the Doctor, the TARDIS in flight and the time vortex. Limited to 750 world wide. Each has a serial number and a certificate of authenticity.
OP: £249.00

COL-032 Millennium Daleks
1999/04 – 1999/11, Dapol, UK
Translucent 'glitter' plastic Dalek. Available in different colours and released one every six weeks through 1999: 1: Blue; 2: Green; 3: Red; 4: Purple; 5: Black; 6: Silver. A presentation box for the Daleks was available for £2.99 by sending off vouchers supplied with each Millennium Dalek.
REF: W008-M1/2/3/4/5/6 OP: £6.99

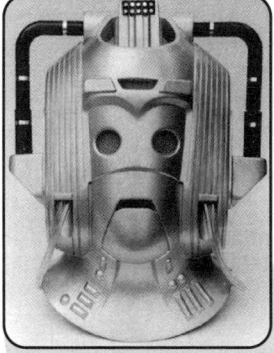
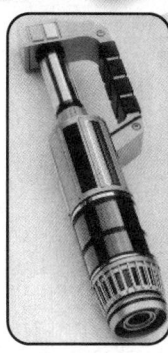

COL-026

COL-027

COL-029

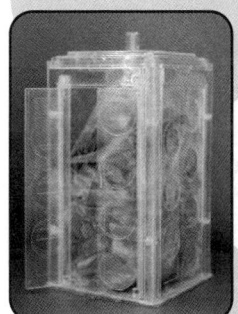

COL-030

COL-031

COL-032 (full set shown in presentation box)

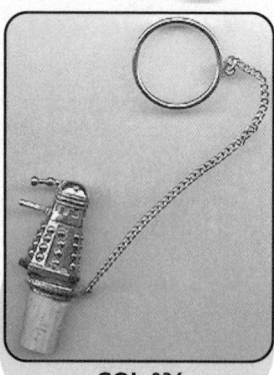

COL-035

COL-036

COL-033 Silver Dalek No 1 Fine Art Statue
1999, Animation Art Gallery, UK
A series of limited edition marble resin statues, hand painted. 500 in edition.
OP: £195

COL-034 TARDIS Fine Art Statue
1999, Animation Art Gallery, UK
A series of limited edition marble resin statues, hand painted. 500 in edition.
OP: £245

COL-035 Dr Who – Peter Cushing Fine Art Statue
1999, Animation Art Gallery, UK
A series of limited edition marble resin statues, hand painted. 500 in edition.
OP: £350

COL-036 Dalek Bottle-stopper
1999, Dapol, UK
Solid Pewter Dalek bottle-stopper. Only has one 'arm'.
OP: £19.95

COL-037 Full size TARDIS
2000, This Planet Earth Ltd, UK
TARDIS prop in three styles: full size (approx. 9 feet tall); 9/10ths version about 7 feet tall; wardrobe version featuring the front half of the 9/10ths TARDIS with closet fittings inside. The TV-style TARDIS was discontinued but a movie-style version was released.
OP: £1895 (full) / £1695 (9/10ths) / £995 (wardrobe)

COL-038 Full size K9
2001?, This Planet Earth Ltd, UK
Accurate full size working reproduction of K9. Discontinued by 2003.
OP: £795

COL-039 Full size Cyberman
2001?, This Planet Earth Ltd, UK
Accurate full size reproduction of 'Earthshock' Cyberman. Also available were a variety of different style full size Cyberhelmets.
OP: £1695 (full size) / £295 (each helmet)

COL-040 The TARDIS
2000/05, ARC Modelmakers/The Green/Burnage Partenership, UK
A 1:10 hand made scale model of the TARDIS with a numbered certificate of authenticity. Limited to 2000 models. Features authentic 'take-off' sound and flashing light. Opening doors. Display base and membership card. 30.5cm/12 inches tall.
OP: £94.50

COL-041

COL-042

COL-043

COL-044

COL-045

COL-041 William Hartnell Porcelain figure
2000/06, Sheercast, UK
8 inch high painted figurine of the first Doctor. This
was the only figure licensed by the BBC. The remaining figures, and the busts (COL-050) were produced
unlicensed. Each figure came with a numbered plaque
on the wooden base, and collectors could obtain all
the figures with the same number.
OP: £79

COL-042 Patrick Troughton Porcelain figure
2000/08, Sheercast, UK
 8 inch high painted figurine of the second Doctor.
OP: £79

COL-046   COL-047   COL-048

COL-043 Jon Pertwee Porcelain figure
2000/09, Sheercast, UK
8 inch high painted figurine of the third Doctor.
OP: £79

COL-044 Tom Baker Porcelain figure
2000/10, Sheercast, UK
8 inch high painted figurine of the fourth Doctor. This
figure was only £79 if bought with other figures.
Otherwise it cost £84.
OP: £79

COL-045 Peter Davison Porcelain figure
2001/01, Sheercast, UK
8 inch high painted figurine of the fifth Doctor.
OP: £84

COL-049

COL-046 Colin Baker Porcelain figure
2001/05, Sheercast, UK
8 inch high painted figurine of the sixth Doctor.
OP: £84

COL-047 Sylvester McCoy Porcelain figure
2001/07, Sheercast, UK
8 inch high painted figurine of the seventh Doctor.
OP: £84

COL-050

COL-048 Paul McGann Porcelain figure
2002/07, Sheercast, UK
8 inch high painted figurine of the eighth Doctor.
OP: £84

COL-049 Half Size Dalek
2001, Daleks Direct Ltd, UK
Accurate half size replica of a Dalek. Fiberglass body
with metal attachments and castors. 8 Colour
schemes available: Black and silver; silver and black;
white and gold; silver and blue; gunmetal and black;
red and black; grey and black; silver and red.
OP: £499.99

COL-050 1st, 2nd, 3rd, 4th Doctor Busts
2001/02, Sheercast, UK
5 inch high bronze-effect busts of the Doctor.
Hartnell and Troughton released first, followed by
Pertwee and T Baker, later in November.
OP: £19.99

COL-051

COL-052

COL-053

COL-054

COL-051 *An Unearthly Child* Classic Moments
2001/10, Product Enterprises Ltd, UK
Small diorama of the Doctor and Susan in the Junkyard.
Originally scheduled for July 2001.
OP: £79.99

COL-052 Salt and Pepper Pot Daleks
2001/11/23, The Stamp Centre, UK
Two antique effect pewter Daleks. Around 8cm tall.
OP: £95 set of two

COL-053 Doctor's Calling Card
2001, Ministry of Sound and Vision, USA
As seen in *Remembrance of the Daleks*.

COL-054 Coal TARDIS
2002
TARDIS model made from coal with limitation certificate.

COL-055 Hartnell Figurine
2002/01, Product Enterprises Ltd, UK
12" Figure of the first Doctor. Only 500 available.
OP: £54.99

COL-056 Troughton Figurine
2002/03, Product Enterprises Ltd, UK
12" Figure of the second Doctor. Only 500 available.
Future figurines were cancelled due to 'unrealistic
demands by third parties.' However production samples
exist of the third Doctor figure.
OP: £54.99

COL-057 *Tomb of the Cybermen* Classic Moments
2002/03, Product Enterprises Ltd, UK
Small diorama of the Cybermen and the Doctor in
the Tombs. Future Dioramas would have included *Day
of the Daleks* however they were cancelled following
the release of the *Tomb* one due to 'unrealistic
demands by third parties'.
OP: £79.99

COL-058 Dalek Bottle Top
2001/08/23, The Stamp Centre, UK
Pewter Dalek mounted on a cork.
OP: £9.95

COL-059 Cyberman Bottle Top
2002/11, The Stamp Centre, UK
Pewter Cyberman head mounted on a cork.
OP: £9.95

COL-060 'The Who Bear'
1987, Ambrosia Designer Collectibles, US
Created and handmade by Diane McClamma, the first

COL-055

COL-056

COL-057

COL-058 & 059

released was the 4th Doctor Bear. Each fully jointed bear was handcrafted with clothing (hat, scarf, trousers, shirt and vest).

4th Doctor bear deluxe edition - $125 (15 units)
4th Doctor bear small edition - $35 (65 units)
1st Doctor bear deluxe edition - $125 (3 units)
2nd Doctor bear deluxe edition - $125 (1 unit)
3rd Doctor bear deluxe edition - $125 (4 units)
5th Doctor bear deluxe edition - $125 (2 units)
6th Doctor bear deluxe edition - $125 (1 unit)
7th Doctor bear small edition - $45 (15 units)

COMPUTER ACCESSORIES

CPA-001 Mousemat
1997, Who Shop International, UK
Image of the TARDIS in flight.
OP: £9.95

CPA-002 Mousemat
1997, Steve Broster, UK
Limited edition. 'The Cloven Hoof' pub sign from *The Dæmons*. Broster was one of a group of fans who bought the actual sign from The Blue Boar– the real life pub in Aldbourne used as a location for *The Dæmons*.
OP: £7.99

CPA-003 Mousemat
1996, Dominitemporal Services Ltd, UK
A 'cyber-mat' featuring the cyber-logo as seen in *The Tomb of the Cybermen*.
OP: £7.00

CPA-004 WhoBase Seven
1990, Who Base International Inc, USA
A hyperlinked rudimentary database program by Roger Stagnaro. Came on a 5-1/4" floppy disk.
OP: $19.95

COL-060

CPA-002

CPA-006

CPA-005

CPA-005 Police Box Mouse Mat
2000, The Who Shop, UK
TARDIS-shaped mouse mat.
OP: £6.99

CPA-006 Cyber-Symbol Mouse Mat
2000, The Who Shop, UK
Symbol from *Tomb of the Cybermen*.
OP: £6.99

CPA-007 Mouse Mats
2001/11/23, The Stamp Centre, UK
Three mousemats: Tardis; Daleks; The Fourth Doctor.
Designed by Ian Burgess.
OP: £7.50 each

CPA-007

CPG-001

COMPUTER GAMES

CPG-001 *First Adventure, The*
1983, BBC Software, UK
BBC Computer only. Cassette. Cover illustration by
Mick Brownfield. Game written by 17 year old Jeremy
Ruston. A very basic four-game package. The first
game, 'The Labyrinth of Death', involved moving a cart
around a mine, avoiding dangerous snakes along the
way. The second, 'The Prison', was a variation on the
game 'frogger' where the TARDIS must be moved
across three hazard areas by either hopping onto or
avoiding objects that moved into the player's path. The
third, 'The Terrordactyls', involved moving up to the
TARDIS while avoiding flying beasts. The fourth, 'The
Box of Tantalus', was a form of electronic 'Battleships'.
REF: ISBN 0-563-16587-1 OP: £10.00 NM: £22-£28

CPG-002 *Key to Time*
1984, Lumpsoft, UK
Unofficial game. This was a text-adventure based
around the hunt for the Key to Time. Several *Doctor
Who* characters appeared.
OP: £5.99 NM: £16.50

CPG-002   **CPG-003**

CPG-003 *Doctor Who and the Warlord*
1985/02, BBC Software, UK
BBC Computer only. Cassette. Program designed by
Pluto inc, written by Chessfield Microgames. A selection of hints could be obtained by sending a SAE to
the BBC. These hints came in code and had to be
typed in as printed for the program to decode them.
This was a two-part text only game and the idea was,
in the first part, to find the Doctor on a strange planet in the distant future, and in the second part to try
and stop the Warlord from interfering with history at
the Battle of Waterloo. There were several rather
devious puzzles and 250 locations in each part.
REF: ISBN 0-563-21074-5 OP: £7.95 NM: £16.50

CPG-004 *Doctor Who and the Mines of Terror*
1985, Micro Power Ltd, UK
Available on 16K ROM Chip and diskette or cassette.
Contents: a decoding card, instructions on distracting
a Madrag, card showing what the icons meant, loading
instructions and game instructions, blue-print of mine
workings. The accompanying documentation was
obscurely worded and the game, a sophisticated plat-
form adventure, gave few hints as to how it should be
played. The version for the Spectrum computer was
not released until 1987.
OP: £18.95 (BBC Cass), £19.95 (BBC Disk/ROM),
£18.95 (Amst Disk), £11.95 (Amst Cass), £13.95
(CBM Disk), £11.95 (CBM Cass) NM: £27.50

CPG-005a *Dalek Attack*
1992/12/17, Alternative Software/ Admiral Software, UK
A platform/shoot-em-up game. Diskette. Poster and
'I've been exterminated' sticker also available. A limited number of games were issued on the first day of
release and these came with a certificate (dated
17/12/92).
OP: £16.99 (Amiga, Atari, IBM PC); £7.99 (CBM 64,
Spectrum, Amstrad) NM: £12

CPG-005b *Dalek Attack*
React, UK
Re-issue.
OP: £5.99

CPG-005c *The Sci-Fi Collection - Dalek Attack /
Suburban Commando / Galactic Warrior Rats*
1994, Alternative Software Ltd, UK
Three game set for the Amiga on four 3" floppy discs.
Discs 1 and 2 were *Dalek Attack*, Disc 3 was *Suburban
Commando*, and Disc 4 was *Galactic Warrior Rats*. The
instruction booklet for *Dalek Attack* had the words
'Admiral Software' blackened out or covered with
stickers in several places.
OP: £5.99

CPG-004

CPG-005a

CPG-007

CSF-001

CSF-002

CSF-008 (display box & bar)

CPG-006 *Doctor Who* **Interactive Floppy Disc**
1994, Hollywood Online Inc., USA
Free 3-1/4" floppy disc offered in either Windows or
Mac format with the purchase of any two of the following CBS-FOX *Doctor Who* video releases: *The
Aztecs, Terminus, Robot, City of Death, Resurrection of the
Daleks,* and/or *Planet of the Spiders.* Only available to
US and Canadian residents by mail. Offer ran from
May 18-October 31, 1994.
OP: free

CPG-007 *Doctor Who: Destiny of the Doctors*
1997/12, BBC Multimedia, UK
A first person quest-type game based around the
TARDIS, guest-starring Anthony Ainley as The Master
in material recorded especially for the game. It also
includes a 'Database' of alien monsters written by
Gary Russell. IBM PC-compatible only.
REF: BBCMM 010 ISBN 0-563-55910-1
OP: £29.99 CD ROM

CONSUMABLES, CONFECTIONERY

DOCTOR Who confectionery can be highly collectible as not many intact items exist. This is true
of most collectibles where, in the normal course of
using the item, they are destroyed...or eaten.

**CSF-001 Dr Who and the Daleks Sweet
Cigarettes**
1964, Cavenham Confectionery Ltd/Paramount Labs
Ltd (Cadet), UK
Candy sticks sold in boxes of ten, each containing a collectible card. The boxes had two different backs, some
featuring a planet while others depicted a rocket. Sales
of the sweet cigarettes ceased on 9 November 1969, by
which date more than 14,000 units had been bought.
OP: 2d NM: £110

CSF-002 Dalek Chocolate Bars
1965, Cavenham Confectionery, UK
Sales topped 22,000 units before the end of 1967.
OP: 1d NM: £55

CSF-003 Dalek Easter Egg
1965, UK
No further information available.
NM: £165

CSF-004 Dalek Jelly Babies (2 sizes)
1965, Bellamy's Ltd, UK
No further information available.
NM: £55

CSF-005 Dalek novelties, foil wrapped chocolate
1965/08, Edward Sharp & Sons Ltd, UK
'Exact scale models' in milk chocolate. Covered in brightly coloured metallic foil, and complete with protruding 'antenna'.
OP: 1s 6d NM: £110

CSF-006 Milk Gum Daleks
1965, UK
No further information available.
NM: £50

CSF-007 TARDIS Toffee
UK
Produced in the sixties. No further information available.

CSF-008 Doctor Who Milk Chocolate
1971, The Nestlé Company Ltd, UK
Fifteen-part story, Doctor Who Fights Masterplan Q on the numbered wrappers, featuring the Doctor and the Master. Bars available singly or in packs of four. There are two variants of the boxes the individual bars came backed in. They are the same except for a different artwork image of the Third Doctor on the box-top. A variant of the wrapper had no '3p' printed on them.
OP: 3p each NM: £11

CSF-008 (wrapper)

CSF-009 Dalek's Death Ray Ice Lolly
1975 – 77, T. Wall & Sons (Ice Cream) Ltd, UK
A chocolate and mint ice cream lolly. Eighteen different wrappers.
Titles: Plain (no feature) 1975, Make A Dalek 1975, Win a Real Life-Size Dalek 1975
From the world of the Daleks... (wrapper is unpriced) 1976: Transmol, The Grenium Invisibility System, Dalek Officer, The Cyclops Z-Ray, Daleks and the Ancient Britons, When the Daleks Flooded the Earth!, The Swamp Creatures of Terroth, A Dalek Deep Space Battle Cruiser
The Incredible Daleks (wrapper is priced) 1977:
A Dalek Raid against the primitive Megapods, How Daleks bend time, A Dalek 'Buggy', The great Dalek workshops on the planet Styros, Venusians attack a small Dalek base, A fleet of Dalek Starships in a meteor storm, The Great Laser 'Destructor' used to conquer the planet Ur.
OP: 5p each NM: £22

CSF-009

CSF-010 Doctor Who Milk Chocolate
1975, The Nestlé Company ltd, UK
Six different wrappers: Brigadier Lethbridge Stewart, Surgeon Lt. Harry Sullivan RN, Sarah Jane Smith, Doctor Who, The Tardis, Sergeant Benton. Bars available singly or in packs of four.
OP: 6p each NM: £22

CSF-010

CSF-012b

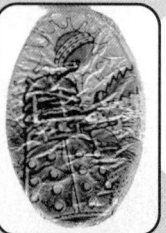

CSF-013

CSF-011 Doctor Who Rock
1975, Regent Confectionery, UK
Produced to tie-in with the opening of a *Doctor Who* exhibition on Blackpool's Golden Mile.
NM: £11

CSF-012a Doctor Who Candy Favourites
1979, Goodies, UK
White chocolate pieces in four different shapes: the TARDIS, K-9, a Dalek and a Cyberman.
OP: 3p each NM: £3.50

CSF-012b Doctor Who Candy Favourites
1980/03, Goodies, UK
White chocolate pieces in four different shapes: the TARDIS, K-9, a Dalek and a Cyberman. Boxed set containing four of each shape.
OP: 60p NM: £40

CSF-013 Christmas Tree Decorations
1981, Goodies/Cavenham Confectionery Ltd, UK
Foil-wrapped oval decorations.
Dalek/Cyberman, TARDIS/K-9. Available individually or in a tub or a box.
OP: 7p each NM: £5.50

CSF-014 Streets Doctor Who Vanilla & Chocolate Ice Lolly
1981, Streets Confectionery, AUS
Fourth Doctor featured on box and wrappers. This product was only marketed in Australia.
NM: £11

CSF-015 Streets Doctor Who Iceblock
1980s?, Streets Confectionery, AUS
Only available in boxes of 8 at supermarkets. Each

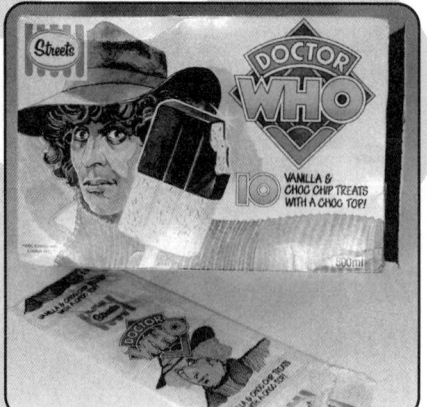

CSF-014

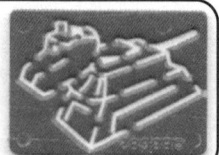

CSF-015 (stencils)

box included a plastic stencil. The exact number of different stencils is not known but three of them were the TARDIS, the *Doctor Who* logo and K9. They were made in various colours.

CSF-016 Favourites Bars
1982, Famous Names, UK
Available in apple, raspberry or orange. These were re-issued in 1983 as tubs of Christmas Candy. The tubs each included one of the 1965 Cadet Sweet Cigarette cards, re-printed by Goodies, but these were hastily withdrawn when the manufacturers realised that the Doctor was no longer played by William Hartnell.
OP: 3p each   NM: £2

CSF-016

CSF-017 Milk Chocolate Novelties
1982, Goodies, UK
Dalek/Cyberman/TARDIS/K-9.
OP: 4p each   NM: £5.50

CSF-018 TARDIS Easter Egg
1982/02, Tobler Suchard Ltd, UK
Featured a cut-out of Peter Davison behind the moveable front doors. It also contained a small book entitled *Doctor Who's Little Book Of Villains* and an accompanying set of rub-down transfers. Sales around 33,000 units.
OP: £2.25   NM: £27.50

CSF-019 Invasion of the Daleks Easter Egg
1983/03, Tobler Suchard Ltd, UK
Featuring a board game on the box. Sales were around 50,000 units.
OP: £2.45   NM: £35

CSF-018

CSF-020 Doctor Who Jelly Babies
1985, Newtime Foods (imported by Sterling Candy Corp.), USA
TARDIS box design.
OP: $3.00

CSF-021 Doctor Who Exhibition Chocolate Bars
1997, Delvaus Chocolatier/R.C. Brady & Co, UK
In dark or milk chocolate varieties. Made with Belgium chocolate and packaged in a white box with TARDIS, Dalek and Exhibition logo graphics. Manufactured by Delvaus and distributed by R.C. Brady. Available from Longleat or Llangollen.
OP. £1.25

CSF-019

CSG-001

GAR-001

GAR-002

CONSUMABLES, GENERAL

EDIBLE items which are not confectionary.

CSG-001 Dalek Cake
1965, Selfridges, UK
Chocolate novelty cake offered through Selfridges'
London store for Christmas 1965.
OP: 10s 6d NM: £35

CSG-002 'Galafrey' Wine
1987, Mount Barker vineyard, AUS
A vineyard near Albany, Western Australia produced
wine with the name 'Gallifrey' deliberately misspelled
to avoid copyright issues. Their 1987 Chardonnay
included a blue TARDIS on its label. Wine boxes also
featured a blue TARDIS printed on one of its sides.

CSG-003 'Who's Thirty' Beer
1993, Chaz Mason, UK
Only 30 bottles produced to celebrate *Doctor Who*'s
30th anniversary. Similar recipe to 'Old Peculiar'.

FIREWORKS

FIR-001 Dalek Fireworks
1965, UK
No further information is available on the Dalek fire-
works and they may never have been produced.
However they are mentioned in contemporary
reports of *Doctor Who* merchandise.
NM: £325

GAMES, ARCADE MACHINES

GAR-001 Dalek Kiddie Ride
1967, Edwin Hall & Co., UK
The Dalek kiddie ride stood about eight feet tall and
followed the basic Dalek shape, but with a number of
modifications to make it less vulnerable to damage by
the thousands of children who would use it. The ride
included a Dalek voice box as well as flashing lights
and a mechanism to produce a rocking movement.
Only about forty of these were made.
OP: unknown NM: £1100

GAR-002 TARDIS Kiddie Ride
1980s, ???, UK
Similar to the Dalek ride, this light blue police box-
shaped ride went up and down when you pulled a lever
and made various noises when you pressed the buttons.
Quite common at seaside resorts in East Anglia.
OP: unknown NM: £1100

GAR-003a

GAR-003a Pinball

1992, Bally-Williams, USA

This was the first and so far only *Doctor Who* pinball game produced. The game has a 'plot' which is described in the pinball's accompanying documentation thus:

'The Doctor is in … but the Master is back – and this time he will not fail. He's recruited Davros and what remains of his desperate Daleks, and they all have but one enemy – the Doctor.

'Armed with his ultimate weapon, the Time Expander, the Master can now manipulate space and time events to interact with an entirely new time stream. He plans to destroy the Doctor by expanding his time stream, but must find him first – all seven of him.

'The key is the Doctor's favourite planet, Earth. All of his regenerations past, present and future have arrived, or will arrive, on Earth. If the Master can expand the Earth's time and push all the Doctors into the final nova of the Earth's Sun, his mission will be complete.

'All does not go as planned. The Doctors, aware of the time expansion, escape (but they are not necessarily safe). They must find the Time Expander to restore Earth's Time to normal. They must confront the Master and the Daleks. And they must destroy Davros in the final battle.'

The initial shipment of the Pinball machines featured a moving Dalek head on the top of the backboard, and 'standard' machines could also be converted to include this feature by purchase of a conversion kit. It is believed that 200 machines were produced with the moving Dalek head. A variety of replacement parts were also commercially available for some time from licenced Bally-Williams and authorised dealers.

REF: 16-20006 OP: £2,500 (+vat)/$3,000 NM: £3250

GAR-003b Pinball Promotional Plastics

1992, Bally/Midway Amusement Games, USA

Set of 7 small plastic 1" discs featuring the Doctors from Hartnell to McCoy. A larger set of 3 2" discs feature the diamond logo, a Dalek and the TARDIS. These were promotional items manufactured by Bally for dealers to use as promotion for the pinball machine. The 7 small discs were also available as keyrings (see CKE-021).

OP: $2.00 each NM: £1.50

GAR-003c Pinball Promotional Plastic: Dalek Scene Cut-Out

1992, Bally/Midway Amusement Games, USA

6" wide x 2" high. This was another premium made to promote Bally's pinball machine. A two-sided full colour promotional flyer is another peripheral pinball item that frequently turns up for sale.

OP: $5.00 NM: £5.50

GAR-004 Fruit Machine

1994/10, Bell-Fruit Manufacturing Co, UK

Fairly standard electronic fruit machine game called 'The Timelord'. Released October 1994 and sold up to early December. Just over 2000 units sold. At least three different prize jackpots are available: £6, £8, and £10. 3 versions of the game were created, but only 'The Timelord' survived the test procedures before mass production.

REF: 92-207-563 OP: £1900 NM: £2250

GAR-003b (seven large and three small disks)

GAR-003c

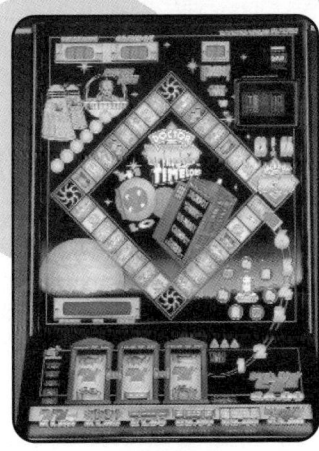

GAR-004

GAMES, JIGSAWS

GJI-001 Dalek Jigsaws
1965, Thomas Hope & Sankey Hudson Ltd, UK
Produced for F W Woolworth. Artwork by Walter
Howarth. 17" x 11" 187-piece artwork puzzles. Five
in series: *Daleks Attack, In the Laboratory, Daleks in
Westminster, Peace Talks* and *In The TARDIS*. The latter
title was withdrawn and *In the Laboratory* substituted
as it was felt that the TARDIS should not be seen to
be an unsafe place to be. As a further indication of the
swap, some of the puzzles in the set are known to
have different backs as well.
OP: 2s 9d   NM: £35

GJI-002 Dr. Who and the Daleks Wooden Stand-up Jigsaws
1965, Thomas Hope & Sankey Hudson Ltd, UK
Produced for F W Woolworths. Artwork by Walter
Howarth. 9" x 13" 29-piece plywood-backed puzzles.
The artwork, reproduced on the box fronts, depicted
scenes from a Dalek invasion of London. An added
bonus was that the Doctor, the Daleks and the
TARDIS were all separate jigsaw pieces and could be
erected on small wooden stands within the picture to
give a three dimensional effect. Also of note is the fact
these puzzles were amongst the few items of sixties
Doctor Who merchandise actually to include the
Doctor!
OP: 5s 11d   NM: £135

GJI-003a Dr Who Jigsaws (set of two)
1971, Michael Stanfield Holdings, UK
Photographic. 11"x9". 100 piece puzzles. *Dr Who and
Bessie* (Third Doctor in Bessie), *Dr Who at work* (Third
Doctor in lab).
OP: 20p each   NM: £40

GJI-003b Dr Who Jigsaws (two-in-one set)
1971, Michael Stanfield Holdings, UK
Photographic. 11"x9". 100 piece puzzles. *Dr Who and Bessie* (Third Doctor in Bessie), *Dr Who at work* (Third Doctor in lab).
NM: £45

GJI-003c Dr Who Jigsaws (two re-issues)
1972, Michael Stanfield Holdings, UK
Photographic. 11"x9". 100 piece puzzles. *Dr Who and Bessie* (Third Doctor in Bessie), *Dr Who at work* (Third Doctor in lab).
OP: 25p each NM: £38

GJI-004 Dr Who Jigsaws (two new)
1972, Michael Stanfield Holdings, UK
Photographic. 11"x9". 100 piece puzzles. *Dr Who and the Daleks* (Third Doctor, Daleks and Ogrons); *Odds against Dr Who* (Third Doctor and Ogrons). In total, the Michael Stanfield Holdings jigsaws sold in excess of 215,000 units.
OP: 25p each NM: £38

GJI-005 Dr Who Jigsaws (set of four)
1973, Whitman Publishing (UK) Ltd, UK
125 piece jigsaws. 15"x11". Photographic: Pertwee & Troughton (*The Three Doctors*); Pertwee at desk (*The Green Death*); Pertwee with Daleks and Ogrons (*Day of the Daleks*); Pertwee holding mushroom (*The Green Death*)
REF: Series 7408 OP: 35p each NM: £16.50

GJI-006 Dr Who Jigsaws (set of four)
1975/01, Whitman Publishing (UK) Ltd, UK
224 piece jigsaws. 47x33cm. Photographic. All from the story *Robot*. Fourth Doctor in Bessie (front view), Brigadier, Harry and Fourth Doctor in jeep, Fourth Doctor in Bessie (side view), Giant Robot facing troops. This set sold in excess of 60,000 units.
REF: Series 7511 OP: 50p each NM: £16.50

GJI-007 Doctor Who Jigsaws (set of four)
1977, Whitman Publishing (UK) Ltd, UK
224 piece puzzles. 47x33cm. Artwork by Paul Crompton. Fourth Doctor on planet with robed blue-faced men, collage: Fourth Doctor, Fourth Doctor by lake with savages, Fourth Doctor and Time Lords facing a monster in the Panopticon.
REF: Series 7836 OP: 99p each NM: £16.50

GJI-008 Enemies of Doctor Who Jigsaws (set of four)
1978, Whitman Publishing (UK) Ltd, UK
224 piece jigsaws. 47x33cm. The four artwork jigsaws were individually titled: *The enormously powerful Giant Robots*, *Sontarans the war-obsessed space travellers*, *The evil Kraals planning to conquer Earth* and *The Zygons emerging from their crippled spaceship beneath Loch Ness*.
REF: Series 7915 OP: 99p each NM: £16.50

GJI-003a

GJI-002

GJI-004 (one example)

GJI-005 (three of four)

GJI-006 (two of four)

GJI-007 (one of four)

GJI-008

GJI-009 (one of four)

GJI-009 Amazing World Of Doctor Who Jigsaws, The (set of four)
1979, World International Publishing Ltd, UK
180 piece puzzles. 27x33cm. Artwork. K9 and robots, K9 blasting warriors, Daleks on parade, Dalek Emperor and Daleks on battlefield.
REF: Series 8015   OP: 99p each   NM: £16.50

GJI-010 Jigsaws (Set of 4)
1982, Waddingtons, UK
200 piece puzzles. 17" x 11" in size. Composite photographs: 5th Doctor holding gun on Dalek (A), 5th Doctor outside TARDIS (not composite) (B), 5th Doctor and two Cybermen (C), Master and 5th Dr in TARDIS (D).
REF: Series 051   OP: £1.50 each   NM: £13.20

GJI-010 & GJI-012

GJI-011 (all four shown)

GJI-011 Doctor Who Jigsaws (set of four)
1984, Waddingtons, CAN
Artwork by Andrew Skilleter. 500 piece puzzles.
Omega, Davros and Daleks, Sontarans, K9. Artwork
previously released as Who Dares' Profile Prints.
REF: No 154 OP: £6.95 import NM: £16.50

GJI-012 Doctor Who Jigsaws (set of two)
1984, Arrow, UK
Artwork. 200 piece puzzles. 10" x 8" in size. Sixth
Doctor and robot by TARDIS; Daleks and Davros
with Peri and Sixth Doctor.
REF: Series 5333.20/21 OP: £1.99 each NM: £11

GJI-013 Doctor Who double sided jigsaw
1994, Alpha Marketing, UK
1000 piece puzzle. Anniversary poster on one side,
reverse lists all *Doctor Who* stories, writers, episode
numbers and transmission dates.
OP: £9.99 NM: £11

GJI-013

GRP-001a

GAMES, ROLE-PLAYING

**GRP-001a *The Doctor Who Role-Playing Game*
(boxed with 3 books; Wm. John Wheeler,
Michael P. Bledsoe, Guy W. McLimore Jr. &
Patrick Larkin)**
1985, FASA Corporation, Chicago, USA
Cover was a painting of the Fourth Doctor and Leela
surrounded by a blue cloud-like mist. Box set contained: two dice (one white, one red), FASA product
order form sheet [this helped to determine the date
of manufacture, the earliest sets contained the blue
product form in which prices were effective until
December 1 (1985); and three softcover booklets
titled: 'Doctor Who Role Playing Game: Game
Operations Manual' (written by Wm. John Wheeler
and Guy W. MacLimore Jr.) [80 pages], 'Doctor Who
Role Playing Game: The Player's Manual' (written by
Wm. John Wheeler and Guy W. MacLimore Jr.) [48
pages], 'Doctor Who Role playing Game: A
Sourcebook For Field Agents' (written by Wm. John
Wheeler, Guy W. MacLimore Jr., and Patrick Larkin)
[64 pages]. The three softcover books each had white
covers with blue print on them, and featured a
TARDIS on the front; these three softcover books
also featured photos (from up through season 22) and
stats for the Sixth Doctor in them.
REF: ISBN 0-931787-90-4 #9001
OP: $15.00 (£14.95 import) NM: £16.50-£22

**GRP-001b *The Doctor Who Role-Playing Game*
(boxed with 3 books; Wm. John Wheeler,
Michael P. Bledsoe, Guy W. MacLimore Jr. &
Patrick Larkin)**
1985, FASA Corporation, Chicago, USA
Cover was a photo of the Fourth Doctor and Leela in a
black vortex that included many dates of years among the
white stars. Cover contained a subtitle not on the original

set: 'Adventures in Space and Time.' This subtitle was let-
tered in white on the box cover and in red on the side of
the box. Box set contained: two dice (colours unknown
but one die suspected to be white, the second another
colour), a FASA product order form sheet [this helped to
determine the date of manufacture, the sets contained the
orange product form in which prices were effective until
July 1 (1986), with a mistake on the form that may cause
some confusion as the 'Prices as of' is mis-dated as "April
1, 1985" that should have read "April 1, 1986". The order
sheet also includes more of the additional expansion
module and supplements for the game, and a price
increase for the game to $17]; and three softcover book-
lets titled: 'Doctor Who Role Playing Game: Game
Operations Manual' (written by Wm. John Wheeler and
Guy W. MacLimore Jr.)[80 pages], 'Doctor Who Role
Plying Game: The Player's Manual' (written by Wm. John
Wheeler and Guy W. MacLimore Jr.)[48 page], 'Doctor
Who Role Playing Game: A Sourcebook for Field Agents'
(written by Wm. John Wheeler, Guy W. MacLimore Jr. and
Patrick Larkin) [64 pages]. The three softcover books
were printed on white cardstock with a light brown/tan
print (attempting to make the cover look textured) for
the cover and featured a TARDIS and the name of the
manual (in the same font type as the first edition set) on
the cover. The TARDIS and manual name were printed in
a different colour for each book: red for the 'Game
Operations Manual', blue for 'The Player's Manual', and
green for "A Sourcebook for Field Agents.' These three
softcover books did *not* feature photos and stats for the
Sixth Doctor in them (photos only through Season 21).
Co-author Guy W. MacLimore Jr. was not sure why this
was the case, though he suspected that the license FASA
was granted for the game did not include the Sixth
Doctor so in the reprint all references to the Sixth
Doctor were removed; this often confuses people into
believing this to be an earlier set.
REF: ISBN 0-931787-90-4 #9001
OP: $17.00

**GRP-001c *The Doctor Who Role-Playing Game*
(boxed with 3 books; Wm. John Wheeler,
Michael P. Bledsoe, Guy W. MacLimore Jr. &
Patrick Larkin)**
1985, FASA Corporation, Chicago, USA
Cover same as the second edition. Box set contained: two
dice (one white, one black), FASA product order form
sheet [this helped to determine the date of manufacture,
the form contained in this set was the white product
form for which prices were effective until October 1
(1986)]; and three softcover booklets titled: 'Doctor Who
Role Playing Game: Game Operations Manual' (written by
Wm. John Wheeler and Guy W. MacLimore Jr.)[80 pages],
'Doctor Who Role Plying Game: The Player's Manual'

(written by Wm. John Wheeler and Guy W. MacLimore Jr.)[48 page], 'Doctor Who Role Playing Game: A Sourcebook for Field Agents' (written by Wm. John Wheeler, Guy W. MacLimore Jr. and Patrick Larkin) [64 pages]. The three softcover books were printed on tan coloured textured cardstock for the cover and featured a very Victorian design with a TARDIS on the cover. The manuals each featured a different colour background around the title of the manual: yellow for the 'Game Operations Manual', purple for 'The Player's Manual', and lime green for "A Sourcebook for Field Agents.'; As with the second edition, these three softcover books did *not* feature photos and stats for the Sixth Doctor in them (photos only through Season 21). See explanation for GRP-001b.
REF: ISBN 0-931787-90-4 #9001
OP: $17.00

GRP-001b

GRP-001c

GRP-002 *The Daleks* (2 books; written by Fantasimulation Associates; cover art for 'The Daleks' by Jim Halloway)
1985, Fantasimulations Associates (FASA Corporation), USA
This and the following modules were shrink-wrapped with a cardboard insert larger than the booklet with a punched hole at the top for hanging on a display rack. It featured a photo of the Dalek booklet cover on one side and a photo of the photographic cover of the box game on the other side; all modules also had a copy of the FASA product order sheet. There were two booklets in this set:
1) 'The Daleks' (Written by Fantasimulation Associates) [38 pages]
2) 'The Dalek Problem: A Symposium' (Written by Fantasimulation Associates) [24 pages]
REF: ISBN 0-931787-93-9 #9101
OP: $10.00 p/b [This was the original price, listed next to the UPC symbol of 'The Daleks' booklet. It later sold for $11.00 and is listed as such on the white product form dated effective through October 1 (1986).] (£9.95 import)
NM: £16.50

GRP-002

GRP-003 *The Master* (2 books; J. Andrew Keith; front cover art for 'The Master' by Lucy A. Synk; back cover art for 'The Master' by Todd F. Marsh)
1985, FASA Corporation, USA
There were two booklets in this set: 1) 'The Master' (Written by J. Andrew Keith) [63 pages]; 2) 'The Master: CIA File Extracts (CIA File No. 197,648,200/7 A)' (Written by J. Andrew Keith) [16 pages]
REF: ISBN 0-931787-94-7 #9102
OP: $11.00 p/b (£9.95 import) NM: £13.20

GRP-003

GRP-004   **GRP-005**

GRP-006   **GRP-007**

GRP-008

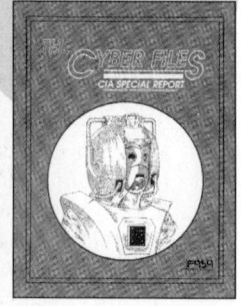

GRP-009

GRP-004 *The Iytean Menace* **(Game module; J. Andrew Keith), 48 pages**
1985, FASA Corporation, USA
Wrap-around cover art by Gustave Caillebotte, a painting called 'Paris Street; Rainy Day' that hangs in the Art Institute of Chicago. The back cover of the booklet (which is the left half of the painting) had the Third Doctor and two unspecific companions (one male one female) added to it.
REF: ISBN 0-931787-91-2 #9201
OP: $7.00 p/b (£4.95 import) NM: £12

GRP-005 *The Lords of Destiny* **(Game module; written by and featuring wrap-around cover art by William H. Keith, Jr.), 48 pages**
1985, FASA Corporation, USA
REF: USA ISBN 0-931787-92-0 #9202
OP: $7.00 p/b (£4.95 import) NM: £12

GRP-006 *Countdown* **(Game module; Ray Winninger; wrap-around cover art by David Deitrick), 48 pages**
1985, FASA Corporation, USA
REF: ISBN 0-931787-95-5 #9203
OP: $7.00 p/b (£4.95 import) NM: £12

GRP-007 *The Hartlewick Horror* **(Game module; Ray Winninger; wrap-around cover art by David Deitrick), 40 pages**
1985, FASA Corporation, USA
REF: ISBN 0-931787-75-0 #9204
OP: $7.00 p/b (£4.95 import) NM: £12

GRP-008 *The Legions of Death* **(Game module; J. Andrew Keith; wrap-around cover art by Harry Quinn), 52 pages**
1985, FASA Corporation, USA
REF: ISBN 0-931787-26-2 #9205
OP: $8.00 p/b (£5.50 import) NM: £12

GRP-009 *The Cybermen* **(2 books; Ray Winninger; cover art for 'The Cybermen' booklet by Jeff Laubenstein)**
1986, FASA Corporation, USA
There were two booklets in this set:
1) 'The Cybermen' (Written by Ray Winninger)
2) 'Cyber Files: CIA Special Report' (Written by Ray Winninger)
REF: ISBN 0-931787-73-4 #9103
OP: $11.00 p/b (£4.95 import) NM: £16.50

GRP-010 *City of Gold* (Game module; J. Andrew Keith; wrap-around cover art by Harry Quinn), 52 pages
1986, FASA Corporation, USA
REF: ISBN 0-931787-49-1 #9206
OP: $8.00 p/b (£5.50 import) NM: £12

GRP-011 *The Warrior's Code* (Game module; J. Andrew Keith; cover art by Jim Halloway), 56 pages (52 for module, 4 page players handout)
1986, FASA Corporation, USA
This is the only FASA booklet to have a somewhat flat spine with the name of the booklet printed on it
REF: ISBN 0-931787-36-X #9207
OP: $8.00 p/b (£5.50 import) NM: £12

GRP-010   GRP-011

HOUSEHOLD ITEMS, BATHROOM

HBA-001 Dalek Sponge (fist)
1965, UK

HBA-002 Dalek Sponge (shaped)
1965, UK

HBA-003 Dalek Toilet Soap
1965, Northamptonshire (Town and Country) Association for the Blind, UK
Set of three coloured Dalek soaps in a presentation box. Made for Scorpion Universal Toys Ltd.
OP: 5s 11d NM: £125

HBA-003

HBA-004 Dalek Bubble Bath
1976, The Water Margin, UK
This came in a box, and the 250ml of liquid soap was contained within a black moulded Dalek with a bright yellow dome and removable arm section. Sold over 26,000 units.
OP: £1.59 NM: £55

HBA-005 Wall Tiles
1982, Pictiles, UK
When assembled, the nine tiles show a picture of Tom Baker with the Daleks. Image supplied by an American *Doctor Who* fan organisation.
OP: £18.00 set of 9 NM: £50

HBA-006 Beach Towel
USA

HBA-004

HBA-005

HBA-007 (detail)

HBA-008 (in box)

HBA-007 TARDIS beach towel
1986, DWFCA, USA
Towel: 30"x60".
OP: $17.50

HBA-008 TARDIS Bubble Bath
1988, DMS Toiletries, UK
Bubble bath in a TARDIS-shaped plastic container.
Came in a box.
OP: 59p NM: £12

HBA-009 TARDIS Bubble Bath
1980s, Aidee International Ltd, UK
Bubble bath in a TARDIS-shaped plastic container. Only
one police box sticker on front. Black screw top.
NM: £12

HBA-010 TARDIS Beach Towel
1992, USA
2 colour.
OP: $29.95

HOUSEHOLD ITEMS, CROCKERY

HBA-008 (bottle)

Advertisement for HCR-001 to HCR-006 (HCR-005 & HCR-001 shown at front)

HCR-001 Dalek Baby Plate
1965, J. H. Weatherby & Sons Ltd, UK
NM: £90

HCR-002 Dalek Cup
1965, J. H. Weatherby & Sons Ltd, UK
NM: £110

HCR-003 Dalek Mug
1965, J. H. Weatherby & Sons Ltd, UK
NM: £110

HCR-004 Dalek Porridge Bowl
1965, J. H. Weatherby & Sons Ltd, UK
NM: £110

HCR-005 Dalek Saucer
1965, J. H. Weatherby & Sons Ltd, UK
NM: £110

HCR-006 Dalek Tilly-Tray
1965, J. H. Weatherby & Sons Ltd, UK
NM: £110

HCR-007 Dalek Wall Plaque
1965, J. H. Weatherby & Sons Ltd, UK
NM: £110

HCR-005

HCR-008 Mug
USA
Full colour diamond or neon logo: silver on navy blue.
OP: $10.00

HCR-009 Mug
1980, Nightstar Corp., USA
Diamond logo on white frosted china.
OP: $6.00

HCR-010 Mug
1980, A. B. & Son, UK
Diamond logo & TARDIS on white china. Two diff.
OP: £1.50

HCR-011 Mug
1982, A. B. & Son?, UK
Full colour diamond logo on white china.

HCR-012 Mug
1983, A. B. & Son, UK
Neon logo & star pattern on white china.
OP: £1.25

HCR-013 Mug
1984, Glenwood Distributors Inc., USA
Diamond logo & T.Baker pic in plastic. Has 'BBC
Enterprises LTD. Barb Elder Corp. Glenwood Dist.
Inc.' printed on it.
OP: $10.00 NM: £5.50

HCR-014 Mug
1984, Lionheart/BBC Enterprises, UK
Neon logo on blue china.

HCR-015 Mug
1985, DWFCA, USA
Full colour neon logo.
OP: $9.95 NM: £5.50

HCR-016 Mug
1985, Ettinger Bros./Spirit of Light Enterprises Ltd, USA
Neon logo on dark blue china. Reads '©1985 BBC
Ent. LTD. ©1986 / The Excalibur Corporation LTD.' on
the bottom.

HCR-017 Plates
1985, Royal Doulton/Bona-Plus Ltd, UK
Five 21cm diameter plates issued. Featuring the first three
Doctors (Jan 1985), the Master (Roger Delgado) and
Davros with a Dalek (June 1985). The plates featured
black outline sketches of the characters against the white
porcelain of the plate and an eight carat gold rim.
OP: £9.95 each NM: £25-£35 each

HCR-009   HCR-010

HCR-012

HCR-013

HCR-014   HCR-016

HCR-017

HCR-018 (with and without vanishing TARDIS)

HCR-018 Mug: Disappearing TARDIS
1987, Image Design Concepts Ltd/DHI-Friends of
Doctor Who, USA
Two different versions by different manufacturers. The
TARDIS looks different and one has the diamond logo
on the back.
OP: $12.00 NM: £13.20

HCR-019 Glass: Vanishing TARDIS
1987, Image Design Concepts Ltd, USA
Glass tumbler (10 ounces?). Came in set of four? Two
variations are known.
OP: $10.00 NM: £9

HCR-020 Glass: K9
1987, Image Design Concepts Ltd, USA
Grey K9 with red collar. Same size as Vanishing
TARDIS glass above.
OP: $10.00 NM: £9

HCR-021 Mug
1987, A. B. & Son (?), UK
Block logo & TARDIS on white china.

HCR-022 *Trial of a Time Lord* Commemorative Plate
1987, Gladstone Pottery, UK
Plate commemorating the filming of parts of *The Trial
of a Time Lord* at the Gladstone Pottery.
OP: £6.00 NM: £27.50

HCR-023 Mug
1987, UK
OP: £1.75

HCR-024 Mug
1988, Lionheart, USA
Black plastic rounded mug with silver diamond logo
and '25th Anniversary' on the other side.
OP: $12.00

HCR-019

HCR-021

HCR-030

HCR-032

HCR-034

HCR-035 (examples seen with pin badges)

HCR-025 Stadium cup
1988, Lionheart, USA
White plastic, blue with silver neon logo also exists
with red diamond logo.
OP: $1.50

**HCR-026 Patrick Troughton Commemorative
Plate**
1988/11, Seabridge Ceramics, UK
Fine bone china plate marking Patrick Troughton's
death in 1987. Featured a quote from *The Moonbase*
and a signature. Designed by B. Marshall. 1500 Limited
edition.
OP: £16.00 NM: £27.50

HCR-027 Mug: K-9
1989, DWFCA, USA
OP: $10.00

HCR-028 Mug
1990, Friends of Doctor Who, USA
Chrome logo.

HCR-029 Mug
1990, Friends of Doctor Who, USA
Materialising TARDIS.

HCR-030 Glass: Vanishing TARDIS
1990, BBC Enterprises, UK
Glass tumbler with heat-sensitive TARDIS on a
starfield and the McCoy logo on the other side.
NM: £11

HCR-031 TARDIS piggy bank
1990, Friends of Doctor Who, USA

HCR-032 MOMI Exhibition Mug
1991, MOMI, UK
Features the 'words' to the Doctor Who theme. Same
design as the 'Diddly Dum' T-shirt.
OP: £2.99

HCR-033 TARDIS Iced Tea glasses
1992 c., USA
15oz.
OP: $14.95 (set of 2)

HCR-034 Fake Egg Cups
1992 c., UK
A rare example of faked *Doctor Who* merchandise. These
egg cups were available singly from market-stall dealers
in London's Covent Garden Market in 1992. They
appear to be 1965 William Hartnell egg cups, with
images of the Doctor and a Dalek on them. They are
also yellowed and dirty inside. There is a badly printed
stamp on the bottom reading '© BBC 1965'. There was
no such item produced, and these are modern fakes,
made to look like an authentic product. The stall hold-
ers were charging around £50 each for these items.

HCR-035 30th anniversary mug
1993, Alpha Marketing, UK
Includes free pin badge (see CBA-069).
OP: £4.99

HCR-036 (set shown with 2 Dalek badges)

HCR-038

HCR-039 (both sides shown)

HCR-040

HCR-036 Commemorative Mugs
1993, Aidee International, UK
7 mugs each featuring artwork of a different Doctor, plus 8th mug free (all Doctors), and a free Alpha Marketing Dalek badge.
OP: £24.99

HCR-037 Seal design Mugs
1993, Dominitemporal Services Ltd, UK
'Seal of Rassilon' in gold on black.

HCR-038 Magic Mugs
1994, Alpha Marketing, UK
7 Doctors, logo and TARDIS design on one mug. When filled with hot liquid, the TARDIS appears. Although all the Doctors are present, the Fifth Doctor looks more like UK TV personality Noel Edmonds (he has a beard!) than Peter Davison.
OP: £5.99

HCR-039 Mug
1996, USA
New TV-Movie Logo black mug with gold *Doctor Who* logo on one side and gold 'Seal of Rassilon' on the back.
OP: $6.00

HCR-040 Mugs
1996/06, Downpace, UK
Three designs: 'Seal of Rassilon', Diamond logo, Movie Logo..
OP: £4.99

HCR-041 Seal of Rassilon Coasters
1996
Set of six cork coasters with Seal of Rassilon printed in gold on blue.

HCR-042 *The Day of the Daleks* Plate
1999/09, Danbury Mint, UK
Artwork by Colin Howard. The first in a proposed series of 7" diameter plates. Initial take-up of the offer was poor, however, and so only sufficient copies of the initial plate were produced for those who had ordered it (around 50).
OP: £19.95 NM: £35

HCR-043 Doctor Who Thimbles
2002, Birchcroft Fine Bone China, UK
During 2002 a number of *Doctor Who* thimbles appeared on eBay for sale. Further investigation revealed that Birchcroft China had purchased from a liquidated china company a number of transfers for *Doctor Who* thimbles produced around 1980 but never manufactured. There were also a number of test thim-

HCR-042

HCR-043

HCR-043 (additional merchandise)

HGE-002 (front & back)

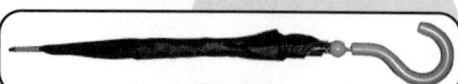

HGE-009b

HGE-017

HGE-019　　　　　**HGE-020**

HGE-025

bles from the time produced. These were made available for sale on eBay. However some thimbles were fired with the transfers in 2002 – these have 'Birchcroft China' printed inside them – the original 1980 tests did not. There were four thimbles produced in the test batch: Dr. Who; K9; TARDIS and Dalek. However there are a further two transfers: Adric and Leela. These latter two were never produced as test thimbles. At press-time, further merchandise utilising the transfers has come to light. See the accompanying photograph.
OP: £30 (eBay)

HOUSEHOLD ITEMS, GENERAL

HGE-001 Dalek Candle
1965, Candle Art Ltd, UK
NM: £165

HGE-002 Dalek Plastic Jar
1965, H & B Plastics Ltd, UK
A beaker decorated with transfers.
NM: £80

HGE-003 Dalek PVC Sheeting
1965, Storey's Bros Ltd, UK
NM: £55

HGE-004 TARDIS Climbing Frame and Playhouse
1968, Furnitubes Associated Products, UK
Only twelve of these items are known to have been supplied to shops (six to Hamleys in London's Regent Street and six to Raggity Anne's in Blackheath village, South London).
OP: £5 5s NM: £550

HGE-005 Chequebook Cover: 'Gallifrey Diplomatic Service'
TK Graphics, USA
OP: $3 NM: £3.50

HGE-006 Chequebook Cover: 'Panoptikon Library Gallifrey'
TK Graphics, USA
OP: $3 NM: £3.50

HGE-007 Pouch: 'Time Lords Academy'
TK Graphics, USA
OP: $6 NM: £5.50

HGE-008 Sign: 'Caution – Tardis in Dematerialization Phase'
USA

HGE-009a Umbrella
1983, BBC Enterprises, UK
Dark blue and white alternating panels with neon logo in white on the blue panels.
OP: £6.00 (s) £7.00 (l)

HGE-009b Question Mark Umbrella
Who Shop, UK
Hand-made replicas based on the Seventh Doctor's umbrella. Painted wooden handle.
OP: £65.00

HGE-009c Question Mark Umbrellas
2001, UK
Red, Grey and White striped umbrella with a red question mark handle.

HGE-010 Diamond Logo Pillow
1983, USA?
12 inches on a side in dark blue with a white diamond logo. A limited run of 500.

HGE-011 Window Decal
1984, DWFCA, USA
Full colour
OP: $3.00

HGE-012 Wallet
1984, DWFCA, USA
Assorted colours, diamond logo.
OP: $10.00

HGE-013 Wallet
1984, DWFCA, USA
Neon logo
OP: $5.00

HGE-014 Easel clock
1988, USA
With silver diamond logo and 25th anniversary plaque.
OP: $24.00

HGE-015 Dalek Clock
1988/11, K.B.W., UK
OP: £26.50 NM: £100

HGE-016 TARDIS Clock
1988/11, K.B.W., UK
OP: £26.50 NM: £100

HGE-017 TARDIS Telephone
1988/09, Holdcourt Ltd, UK
A lightweight plywood TARDIS with a telephone handset inside.
OP: £99.95 NM: £165

HGE-018 *The Ultimate Adventure* Clock
1989, UK
OP: £10.00

HGE-019 Doctor Who Character Shades – Cybermen
1995, Gibson Lighting, AUS
Polypropalene lamp shade in Luma Character Shades range. Artwork.
REF: Design Ref 2031714 OP: £3.99 NM: £5.50

HGE-020 Doctor Who Character Shades – Dalek
1995, Gibson Lighting, AUS
Polypropalene lamp shade in Luma Character Shades range. Artwork.
REF: Design Ref 2031714 OP: £3.99 NM: £5.50

HGE-021 Credit Card Holder
1996, Dapol, UK
Diamond logo, blue leather.
REF: W029 OP: £4.50

HGE-022 Key-Wallet
1996, Dapol, UK
Diamond logo. White/Black/Red/Maroon.
REF: W026-020/21/22/23 OP: £2.99

HGE-023 Cheque Book Holder
1996, Dapol, UK
Diamond logo. Black/White/Blue/Red/Green.
REF: W028-001/2/3/4/5 OP: £2.99

HGE-024 Comb in Leather case
1996, Dapol, UK
Diamond Logo. Black/Blue/Red/Green.
REF: W030-001/2/3/4 OP: £1.45

HGE-025 Drink Mats
1996, Dapol, UK
Diamond logo. Set of seven coasters.
White/Black/Blue/Red/Mixed. Also available individually at 75 pence each.
REF: W024-001/2/3/4/5 (011/2/3/4/5 for individuals)
OP: £4.50

HGE-029 (TARDIS)

HGE-030

HGE-032

HGE-033

HGE-026 Leather Neck Purse
1996, Dapol, UK
Diamond logo. Black/Blue/Red/Green.
REF: W027-001/2/3/4 OP: £2.49

HGE-027 Doctor Who Wall Clock
1997/07, Mister O Art and Design Workshop, UK
Three designs: The Seal, The TARDIS, The Eighth
Doctor and TARDIS. Large wall clocks around 18"
diameter.
OP: £59.95 NM: £45

HGE-028 Purses
1997, Who Shop International, UK
OP: £3.50 NM: £6.50

HGE-029 Doctor Who Wall Clock
1998, Mister O Art and Design Workshop, UK
Two new designs: TARDIS in flight; 'Seal of Rassilon'.
OP: £39.99

HGE-030 Credit card holder
1998, The Ultimate Buckle Company, UK
Holder with metal *Doctor Who* logo. Includes a
Gallifrey symbol card inside.
OP: £11.99

HGE-031 TARDIS Mirror
1998, John Fitton, UK
Limited edition engraved mirror. Limited to 100.
Approx 20 x 24" in walnut.
OP: £89.99

HGE-032 Dalek Wallplaques
1999, Product Enterprise Ltd, UK
Set of three hand polished metalised resin Daleks. The
Daleks are intended to be hung on a wall and are in
three sizes: 19cm, 14cm and 10cm thus being the
Doctor Who equivalent of a traditional 'flying ducks'
display. Limited to 700 copies.
OP: £29.99

HGE-033 Glass Coaster
1999, Dapol, UK
A sand-blasted and etched (with a question mark)
glass coaster.
REF: WG-08 OP: £9.99

HGE-034 Doorknob Hanger
1990s?
Laminated card stock. Black with TARDIS in blue and
yellow lettering on bottom reading 'TARDIS In Use -
Do Not Enter'.

HGE-035 Coasters
2001/04/12, The Stamp Centre, UK
Set of four photo collage coasters. Images: Cybermen; Zygons; Cailleach; Sontarans. Designed by Ian Burgess.
OP: £12.95 per set

HGE-036a Doctor Who CD Clocks
2001, Ministry of Sound and Vision, USA
Produced from the Big Finish CD releases.

HGE-036b Doctor Who CD Clocks
2002, UK
Amongst many unlicensed items are several which have appeared, fuelled by the rise in popularity of eBay, the online auction house. CD Clocks seem to have sprung up featuring all manner of images, among them some *Doctor Who* related ones. The starting bid for these items tends to be around the £5.99 price bracket.

HGE-035

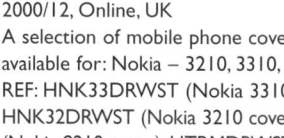

HMA-001 Doctor Who Collectors Fridge Magnet
1998/03, KP Classic Collectables, UK
12 designs: First Dr, Second Dr, Third Dr, Fourth Dr, Fifth Dr, Sixth Dr, Seventh Dr, Eighth Dr, Daleks, Cybermen, Yeti/Sea Devils, K9.
OP: £1.99 each / £15.00 set

HOUSEHOLD ITEMS, PHONE

HPH-001 Doctor Who Mobile Phone accessories - covers
2000/12, Online, UK
A selection of mobile phone covers and cases. Covers available for: Nokia – 3210, 3310, 8210; Trium Mars.
REF: HNK33DRWST (Nokia 3310 cover); HNK32DRWST (Nokia 3210 cover); HNK82DRWST (Nokia 8210 cover); HTRMDRWST (Trium Mars cover)
OP: £12.99 (Nokia 3310 covers)

HPH-002 Doctor Who Mobile Phone accessories - 'Fone Buddie'
2001, Online, UK
A small plastic Dalek about one inch tall with a plastic clip to attach it to the ariel on a mobile phone.
REF: FBDRW (Dalek Buddie) OP: £3.47

HMA-001

HPH-001

HOUSEHOLD ITEMS, VEHICLE ITEMS

HVE-001 License Plate: TARDIS
1985, Lionheart, USA
OP: $6.00

HVE-002 Car Window Sign (like the 'Baby on Board' signs) 'Who's on Board'
1987, Lionheart, USA
Yellow sign with suction cup and the diamond logo above the slogan 'Who's on Board.'
OP: $2.50

HVE-003 TARDIS car window heat shield
1990, Friends of Doctor Who, USA

HVE-004 TARDIS Heat Shield (automobile sun shade)
1991 c., USA
McCoy logo & TARDIS 'TARDIS Heat Shield' in silver & blue.
OP: $14.95

MAGAZINE ACCESSORIES

MAA-001a Doctor Who Magazine Binder
1983/11, Napier & Son Ltd, UK
Holds 12 issues.
OP: £3.50

MAA-001b Doctor Who Magazine Binder
1988/11, John Fitton, UK
Dark blue leather-look binder. Holds 24 copies. Logo blocked in gold on the cover.
OP: £5.95

MAA-001c Doctor Who Binders
1990, John Fitton, UK
OP: £5.95

HPH-002

HVE-001

HVE-002

MAA-001b

MAGAZINES, MARVEL

DOCTOR *Who Weekly* was the brainchild of editor and publisher Des Skinn who launched the publication in 1979 after Marvel Comics had bought his own magazine *Starburst* in 1978.

Doctor Who Weekly became a monthly magazine from issue 44 onwards and changed its name accordingly to *Doctor Who Monthly*. The magazine's name was to change several times during the eighties as the publication changed editors and styles. Dez Skinn, who had originated the title, stayed as editor until issue 23 when Paul Neary took over. Alan McKenzie was at the helm from issue 49 until issue 97 when Sheila Cranna took over for one issue. Cefn Ridout was in charge from issue 98 until issue 107 when Cranna became editor on a permanent basis. John Freeman took over as editor from issue 137 and saw the magazine through until issue 185 when he handed over to Gary Russell. Russell was editor from issue 186 to 220 and was joined on issue 200 by Marcus Hearn as assistant editor, and who became joint editor from issue 201 onwards. From issue 219, Hearn was credited ahead of Russell, and Warwick Gray joined as assistant editor from issue 220. For issue 221, Russell was editor and Hearn was associate editor. For issue 222, Russell was editor and Hearn and Gary Gillatt were associate editors. From issue 223, Gillatt took over as editor, with Hearn as associate editor and Gray as assistant editor. From issue 226, Hearn was credited as 'Magazine Group' rather than associate editor. From issue 236 Alan Barnes joined as editorial assistant, though he was not credited in issue 238 and stopped with issue 239. Gray left with issue 246 and from issue 247, Barnes took over the assistant editor post. For issue 255 actress Sophie Aldred handled the editorial duties. Barnes and Gillatt swapped roles for issue 262 and from issue 272 until the end of the nineties they were credited as joint editors.

Gillatt dropped out from issue 293 and for issue 294, Barnes was joined by Ed Salt as Editorial Assistant. Issue 295 was handled by Barnes alone, and from issue 296 Clayton Hickman joined as Assistant Editor. Issue 313 saw Barnes and Hickman credited as joint editors while Benjamin Cook joined as Editorial Assistant. Issue 314 saw Barnes credited as 'Captain Oates,' and from issue 315 onwards, Hickman was the sole editor. For issues 319, 322 and 323, Ed Salt was credited as Editorial Assistant as well as Cook, and from issue 324 (the December 2002 edition), the Assistant post was filled by Conrad Westmaas.

In 1981 the publication won the Eagle Award for Best Comic Magazine.

Although the monthly publication still retained its comic strip, the publication moved away from the somewhat childish approach of the weekly issues and towards a more adult and analytical approach spearheaded by McKenzie and Jeremy Bentham, the title's regular writer. There were more factual interviews and features, the archives section became steadily more comprehensive and the number of photographs printed also increased. There were features on merchandise and on those who produced it, a regular question/answer column and numerous other features and fillers. The emphasis on factual material was continued following Bentham's departure by Richard Landen, Gary Russell, Richard Marson, David J. Howe, Andrew Pixley, Marcus Hearn, Richard Bignell, Peter Griffiths and Benjamin Cook among many others.

In 1999 the magazine celebrated twenty years of publication, no mean feat in a marketplace renowned for short lived and one-off publications.

Magazine pricing is generally well documented, and we would recommend that anyone interested seek out a current edition of either *The Overstreet Comic Book Price Guide* or the *McAlpine Comic Book Price Guide*. The prices given below are generalisations.

MAG-001 Doctor Who Weekly (Issue 1 – 43)
1979/10/17 – 1980/08/07, Marvel Comics, UK
Issues 1-4 are worth around £10 each with transfers.
OP: 12p each NM: £4-£6

MAG-002 Doctor Who A Marvel Monthly (Issue 44 – 60)
1980/09 – 1982/01, Marvel Comics, UK
OP: 30p – 40p each NM: £4

MAG-003 Doctor Who Monthly (Issue 61 – 84)
1982/02 – 1984/01, Marvel Comics, UK
OP: 45p – 60p each NM: £2.50-£4

MAG-004 Official Doctor Who Magazine, The (Issue 85 – 98)
1984/02 – 1985/03, Marvel Comics, UK
OP: 60p – 65p each NM: £2.50-£4

MAG-005 Doctor Who Magazine, The (Issue 99 – 106)
1985/04 – 1985/11, Marvel Comics, UK
OP: 65p – 75p each NM: £2.50-£4

MAG-006 Doctor Who Magazine (Issue 107 –)
1985/12– , Marvel Comics, UK
The final issue of *Doctor Who* magazine in 2002 was issue 324, dated 8 January 2003 and released in December 2002.
OP: 75p – £3.20 each NM: £5-£7

DOCTOR WHO MAGAZINE PREMIUMS

Occasionally *Doctor Who Magazine* would include an 'extra' for readers. This list features those issues which came with a free gift or other notable give-away:

ISSUE/PREMIUM

1-4   #1 featured a transfer sheet on cover; the other issues included a transfer sheet inside

73   Free sticker inside

105   Free 'Who Dares' card bookmark mounted on cover

167   Flexidisk on cover. DWM-1. Contains: Terror in Totter's Lane (Mark Ayres); The Trial (excerpt) (Dominic Glynn); Theme from Abslom Daak– Dalek Killer (The Slaves of Kane)

184   Photographic Postcards attached to cover (C Baker, McCoy, Davison, TARDIS 'Greetings from Gallifrey')

185   Photographic Postcards attached to cover (T Baker, Troughton, Hartnell, Pertwee)

186   Photographic Postcards attached to cover (K9, Dalek, The Master, Cybermen)

187   Photographic Postcards attached to cover (Omega, Brigadier, Valeyard, The Master)

188   Photographic Postcards attached to cover (Silurian, Sea Devil, Ice Warrior, Zygon)

189   Photographic Postcards attached to cover (Lynx, The Master, Omega, Voc Robot)

194   Photographic Postcards attached to cover (Victoria, Jo, Sarah, Leela)

195   Photographic Postcards attached to cover (Romana 1, Romana 2, Tegan, Nyssa)

196   Photographic Postcards attached to cover (Turlough, Peri, Mel, Ace)

201   Script Book art postcards inside magazine (*Power of the Daleks, Masters of Luxor, Ghost Light, The Dæmons*)

202   Target book cover art postcards inside magazine (*The War Machines, Mission to the Unknown, Battlefield, The Ambassadors of Death*)

203   Target book cover art postcards inside magazine (*The Face of Evil, Arc of Infinity, The Tenth Planet, The Web of Fear*)

204   Target book cover art postcards inside magazine (*Warriors of the Deep, Remembrance of the Daleks, The Smugglers, The Underwater Menace*)

205   Target book cover art postcards inside magazine (*Silver Nemesis, Robot, Vengeance on Varos, The Daleks*)

206   Target book cover art postcards inside magazine (*Pyramids of Mars, The Visitation, Enemy of the World, The Curse of Peladon*)

208   Free collector's card from CCC's Anniversary card collection on cover

209   Target book cover art postcards inside magazine (*The Awakening, The Keeper of Traken, The Monster of Peladon, Planet of Giants*)

210   Target book cover art postcards inside magazine (*Horror of Fang Rock, The Talons of Weng-Chiang, Paradise of Death, The Robots of Death*)

211   Target book cover art postcards inside magazine (*Power of the Daleks, Evil of the Daleks, Destiny of the Daleks, Planet of the Daleks*)

212   Cover mounted set of Cornerstone *Doctor Who* trading cards series 1 promotional cards.

213   Target book cover art postcards inside magazine (*Dragonfire, Attack of the Cybermen, Mawdryn Undead, The Edge of Destruction*)

214   Target book cover art postcards inside magazine (*The Massacre, The Three Doctors, The Ultimate Foe, Terror of the Zygons*)

215   Target book cover art postcards inside magazine (*The War Machines, 'Gallifrey's Finest', The Tomb of the Cybermen, 'The Roving Reporter'*)

218   *Doctor Who* Magazine part 1 index on cover

219   *Doctor Who* Magazine part 2 index on cover

279   Promotional CD for Big Finish's *Doctor Who* audios on cover

298 Free trading card
299 Free trading card
300 Free Big Finish CD: *Last of the Titans/Storm Warning* Part 1
313 Free Big Finish CD: *The Ratings War/Invaders From Mars* Part 1

Note: Issue 272 celebrated *Doctor Who*'s 35th anniversary and a limited number of copies were produced printed on a thinner than normal paper stock for an event in London. This print run was actually in error and the copies that eventually hit the news-stands were on the standard paper stock.

Issue 283 celebrated 20 years of publishing *Doctor Who Magazine* and had two variant covers: one of Paul McGann and one of Tom Baker.

MAGAZINES, MARVEL ((ONT'D)

MAG-007 Marvel Premiere (57–60)
1980/12 – 1981/06, Marvel Comics, USA
UK editions (with a UK price) also available. These four issues were intended as a taster to see if American audiences would buy a *Doctor Who* comic.
OP: 50¢ each (15p) NM: £2.50

MAG-008 *Doctor Who* (23 issues)
1984/10 – 1986/08, Marvel Comics, USA
As a result of good feedback from the Marvel Premiere, a monthly *Doctor Who* comic was released from October 1984 to August 1986. Issue 9 is scarce in the UK.
OP: $1.50 each NM: £2

MAG-009 Doctor Who Classic Comics (27 issues)
1992/12/09 – 1994/12/07, Marvel Comics, UK
Ed. Gary Russell. Ran to 27 issues. Issue 13 featured a free cover-mounted badge. **NOTE:** See the colour section for a gallery of all the *Classic Comics* covers.
OP: £2.50 each NM: £3 each. £65 set inc. gift

MAG-010 Doctor Who Marvel Adventure Comics
1986/11, Golden Wonder / Marvel Comics, UK
Free mini-comics given away in a specially produced package including the "Odduns" range of crisps, multi-packs of Crisps, Wotsits and Ringos. Comics: 1 – *Revelation*; 2 – *Fun House*; 3 – *War Game*; 4 – *Once Upon A Time Lord*; 5 – *The Shape Shifter*; 6 – *Voyager Dreams of Eternity*. Coloured and re-laid out/redrawn versions of strips from DWM, with Peri removed from all the frames. See PRO-008.
OP: free NM: £4 each

MAG-011 Doctor Who Magazine Giveaways
1987, Marvel Comics, UK
DWM issues (#122 and #125) given free at Berni Inns. The covers featured a 'Berni Funtime' flash on the bottom corner, and the price was amended to 'free'. See PRO-009.
OP: free

MAG-007 (#57)

MAG-007 (#58)

MAG-007 (#59)

MAG-007 (#60)

MAG-008 (#1)

MAG-008 (#2)

MAG-008 (#3)

MAG-008 (#4)

MAG-008 (#5)

MAG-008 (#6)

MAG-008 (#7)

MAG-008 (#8)

MAG-008 (#9)

MAG-008 (#10)

MAG-008 (#11)

MAG-008 (#12)

MAG-008 (#13)

MAG-008 (#14)

MAG-008 (#15)

MAG-008 (#16)

MAG-008 (#17)

MAG-008 (#18)

MAG-008 (#19)

MAG-008 (#20)

MAG-008 (#21)

MAG-008 (#22)

MAG-008 (#23)

MAG-010 (#1)

MAG-010 (#2)

MAG-010 (#3)

MAG-010 (#4)

MAG-010 (#5)

MAG-010 (#6)

MAG-011 (#122)

MAG-011 (#125)

MAO-001 (#712)

MAO-003 (2/72)

MAO-005 (#62)

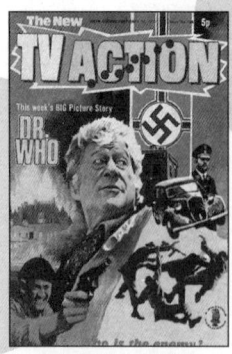

MAO-006 (#104)

MAO-006 (#131)

MAGAZINES, OTHER

EVERY magazine issue listed here featured a *Doctor Who* comic strip. For detailed information on all the strips noted below, see the appendix.

MAO-001 TV Comic (issues 674-999)
1964/11/14 – 1971/02/06, TV Publications Ltd (to issue 850)/Polystyle Publications Ltd, UK

MAO-002 Countdown (issues 1-45)
1971/02/20 – 1971/12/25, Polystyle Publications Ltd, UK

MAO-003 Countdown for TV Action (issues 46-57)
1972/01/01 – 1972/03/18, Polystyle Publications Ltd, UK

MAO-004 TV Action in Countdown (issue 58)
1972/03/25, Polystyle Publications Ltd, UK

MAO-005 TV Action + Countdown (issues 59-100)
1972/04/01 – 1973/01/13, Polystyle Publications Ltd, UK

MAO-006 TV Action (issues 101-131)
1973/01/20 – 1973/08/18, Polystyle Publications Ltd, UK

MAO-007 TV Comic plus TV Action (issues 1133-1291)
1973/09/01 – 1976/09/11, Polystyle Publications Ltd, UK

MAO-008 Mighty TV Comic (issues 1292-1352)
1976/09/18 – 1977/11/12, Polystyle Publications Ltd, UK

MAO-009 TV Comic (issues 1353-1392)
1977/11/19 – 1978/08/18, Polystyle Publications Ltd, UK

MAO-010 TV Comic with Target (issues 1393-1400)
1978/08/25 – 1978/10/13, Polystyle Publications Ltd, UK

MAO-011 TV Comic (issues 1401-1430)
1978/10/20 – 1979/05/12, Polystyle Publications Ltd, UK

MAGAZINES, POSTER

MAP-001 Doctor Who (Poster Magazine)
1975/05, Legend Publishing, UK
Ed. Gent Shaw. Print run was around 65,000.
REF: No ISBN OP: 25p NM: £16.50-£22

MAP-002 Doctor Who – A Special Monster Packed Issue (Poster Magazine)
1976/04, Harpdown Publishing Ltd, UK
Compiled by John Barraclough.
REF: No ISBN OP: 30p NM: £16.50-£22

MAP-001   MAP-002

MAP-003 *Zig Zag* Poster Magazine
1986/11, BBC Education/BBC Information, UK
Poster magazine produced by the educational department of the BBC following the behind the scenes aspects of the making of *The Trial of a Time Lord*. *Zig Zag* was the name of the BBC educational program for which this was prepared.
OP: free NM: £16.50

MAP-003

MAP-004 Doctor Who Poster Magazine
1994/12 – 1996/01, Marvel Comics, UK
Eds. Gary Russell, Marcus Hearn, Gary Gillatt. 8 issues. The final two featured specific stories in an attempt to increase sales. Subjects: 1: Daleks; 2: Cybermen; 3: Silurians/Sea Devils; 4: UNIT; 5: Time Lords; 6: Sontarans; 7: *Remembrance of the Daleks*; 8: *Pyramids of Mars*.
OP: £1.50 NM: £2.75

MAP-004 (all eight issues shown)

RADIO TIMES: DOCTOR WHO FEATURES/STORIES

THE BBC's listings magazine has been a long and staunch supporter of *Doctor Who*. Aside from the regular programme listings for each week's episode, between 1963 and 1970, the magazine regularly featured articles and features about the show, usually marking the start of each story in some way. After this time, the coverage lessened to once per season through the early Seventies, and then only sporadic through the latter part of the Seventies and Eighties. Those issues which featured *Doctor Who* on the cover are the most sought after by fans and these editions are detailed here:

ISSUE	COVER DATE	FEATURE/STORY
2102	22 – 28 February 1964	*Marco Polo*
2141	21 – 27 November 1964	*The Dalek Invasion of Earth*
2153	13 – 19 February 1965	*The Web Planet*
2243	5 – 11 November 1966	*The Power of the Daleks*
2286	2 – 8 September 1967	*The Tomb of the Cybermen*
2306	20 – 27 January 1968	The Monstrous World of *Doctor Who*
2408	3 – 9 January 1970	*Spearhead from Space*
2460	2 – 8 January 1971	*Terror of the Autons*
2512	2 – 7 January 1972	*The Day of the Daleks*
2564	30 December – 5 January 1973	*The Three Doctors*
2614	15 – 21 December 1973	*The Time Warrior*
3132	19 – 25 November 1983	*The Five Doctors*
3646	20 – 26 November 1993	Thirtieth Anniversary
3774	25 – 31 May 1996	Paul McGann TV Movie
3952	13 – 19 November 1999	*Doctor Who* Night

Four other issues contained features of particular note:

2474	10 – 16 April 1971	Frank Bellamy *Colony in Space* strip
2703	30 August – 5 September 1975	*Terror of the Zygons* – Bellamy Art
3764	16 – 22 March 1996	Behind the scenes preview of the McGann movie
3775	1 – 7 June, 1996	Cover banner advertising new weekly Eighth Doctor comic strip

RT #2102

RT #2141

RT #2153

RT #2243

RT #2286

RT #2306

RT #2408

RT #2460

RT #2512

RT #2564

RT #2614

RT #3132

RT #3646

RT #3774

RT #3952

MAS-001

MAS-002

MAS-003

MAS-004

MAS-005

MAS-006

MAS-013a

MAGAZINES, SPECIALS & ONE-SHOTS

THE content is ony noted when it is of particular relevance: the various Marvel Comics specials all tended to contain a mix of comic strips and text features, and we have noted when there was an apparent or stated theme running through the edition. NOTE: See the colour section for a gallery of all Marvel/Panini specials.

MAS-001 *Dr. Who and the Daleks*
1966/12, Dell Publishing Co Inc, USA
Comic version of the film. Art by Dick Giordano, inked by Sal Trapani.
REF: 12-190-612 OP: 12 cents NM: £70

MAS-002 *Doctor Who*
1973, Radio Times, UK
Eds. David Driver, Jack London. 10th Anniversary Special. Contained a listing of stories to date, original fiction by Terry Nation and interviews/features on Doctors, companions and technical staff.
REF: ISBN 0-563-12577-2 OP: 30p NM: £75

MAS-003 Doctor Who Holiday Special
1973/05, Polystyle Publications Ltd, UK
Ed. Dennis Hooper. Lots of photos. Photo feature on *Frontier in Space.*
OP: 10p NM: £27.50

MAS-004 Doctor Who Holiday Special
1974/05, Polystyle Publications Ltd, UK
Ed. Dennis Hooper. Photo cover of Pertwee by TARDIS.
REF: No ISBN OP: 13p NM: £27.50

MAS-005 Doctor Who – Mighty Midget Comic
1976/09/18, Polystyle Publications Ltd, UK
Dated 18th September 1976. Free with Mighty TV Comic #1. Contains: 'Doomcloud' and a re-laid out black and white version of 'Power Play' from *TV Century 21.*
REF: No ISBN OP: free NM: £22

MAS-006 Doctor Who Winter Special
1977/11, Polystyle Publications Ltd, UK
Photographic cover of Leela and the Doctor in the sewers from *The Talons of Weng-Chiang.*
REF: No ISBN OP: 35p NM: £16.50

MAS-007 Doctor Who Summer Special
1980/06, Marvel Comics, UK
Ed. Paul Neary. Reprint of *The Iron Legion.*
REF: No ISBN OP: 40p NM: £3.50

MAS-008 Very Best of Doctor Who, The (Marvel Summer Special)
1981/06, Marvel Comics, UK
Ed. Alan McKenzie.
REF: No ISBN OP: 45p NM: £3.50

MAS-009 Doctor Who – A Marvel Winter Special
1981/11, Marvel Comics, UK
Ed. Alan McKenzie.
REF: No ISBN OP: 45p NM: £2.75

MAS-010 Doctor Who Summer Special
1982/06, Marvel Comics, UK
Ed. Alan McKenzie.
REF: No ISBN OP: 55p NM: £2.75

MAS-011 Doctor Who Winter Special
1982/12, Marvel Comics, UK
No editor credited (Alan McKenzie).
REF: No ISBN OP: 60p NM: £2.50

MAS-012 Doctor Who – A Summer Special
1983/06, Marvel Comics, UK
No editor credited (Alan McKenzie). Contains reprints of *Junk Yard Demon/Absalom Daak… Dalek-Killer* plus a linking narrative.
REF: No ISBN OP: 60p NM: £2.50

MAS-013a Radio Times Doctor Who 20th Anniversary Special
1983/11/03, Radio Times / BBC, UK
Ed. Brian Gearing. Similar to the 10th anniversary special, this was a mix of articles, interviews and features on all aspects of *Doctor Who*.
REF: No ISBN OP: £1.50 NM: £22

MAS-013b Radio Times Doctor Who 20th Anniversary Special
1983/11, Starlog Communications, USA
USA edition. Only cover differs from UK edition.
REF: 0-931064-64-3 OP: $4.95 NM: £22

MAS-013c BBC Doctor Who 20th Anniversary Special
1983/12, AUS
Australasian edition of the *Radio Times* special. Only cover text differs slightly from that on the UK and US editions.
REF: 0-563-20265-3 OP: NZ $6.95

MAS-014 Doctor Who Winter Special
1983/12, Marvel Comics, UK
Ed. Alan McKenzie. Interviews with all *Doctor Who*'s Producers. Written by Jeremy Bentham.
REF: No ISBN OP: 95p NM: £2.50

MAS-015 Doctor Who Summer Special
1984/05, Marvel Comics, UK
Ed. Alan McKenzie. Merchandise special. Written by Gary Russell.
REF: No ISBN OP: 95p NM: £2.50

MAS-016 Doctor Who Winter Special
1984/12, Marvel Comics, UK
Ed. Alan McKenzie. Archives special. Written by Richard Marson and Jeremy Bentham.
REF: No ISBN OP: 95p NM: £2.50

MAS-017 Doctor Who Summer Special Classic
1985/06, Marvel Comics, UK
Reprints of *The Iron Legion* and *K9's Finest Hour*. Same item as BGR-001.
REF: No ISBN OP: £1.20 NM: £5.50

MAS-018 Doctor Who Magazine Winter Special, The
1985/11, Marvel Comics, UK
Ed. Sheila Cranna. Pertwee Special. Written by Richard Marson and Patrick Mulkern.
REF: No ISBN OP: £1.00 NM: £2

MAS-019 Doctor Who Magazine Summer Special
1986/06/12, Marvel Comics, UK
Ed. Sheila Cranna. Features on historical stories.
REF: No ISBN OP: £1.10 NM: £1.75

MAS-020 Doctor Who Magazine Winter Special
1986/11/13, Marvel Comics, UK
Ed. Sheila Cranna. The Tom Baker years.
REF: No ISBN OP: £1.10 NM: £1.75

MAS-021 Doctor Who Magazine Autumn Special
1987/09/10, Marvel Comics, UK
Ed. Sheila Cranna. Designers special. Written by Patrick Mulkern.
REF: No ISBN OP: £1.95 NM: £1.50

MAS-022 Doctor Who 25th Anniversary Special
1988/11/10, Marvel Comics, UK
Ed. Louise Cassell.
REF: No ISBN OP: £2.25 NM: £2.75

MAS-023 Doctor Who Magazine 1979–1989 (10th Anniversary Special)
1989/10/19, Marvel Comics, UK
Ed. John Freeman.
REF: ISBN 1-85400-170-1 OP: £2.50 NM: £2.50

MAS-024 The Bash Street Kids: Dr. Wotsit
1990, D C Thompson & Co Ltd, UK
A magazine-length parody of *Doctor Who* in which Dr
Wotsit picks up the kids' screams as teacher scrapes
chalk on a blackboard as punishment. The Doctor
then takes all the kids back in time. This story was
also printed in 1990's *Bash Street Kids* Annual.
REF: Beano Special No 24 OP: 95p

MAS-025 Doctor Who Magazine Summer Special
1991/07/25, Marvel Comics, UK
Ed. Harry Papadopoulos. Locations special. ISSN on
cover is the same as the UNIT special.
REF: ISSN 0963-12700-7 OP: £2.25 NM: £2.50

MAS-026 Doctor Who Magazine Winter Special: UNIT Exposed
1991/11/28, Marvel Comics, UK
Ed. John Freeman. ISSN printed in magazine is 0963-1275.
ISSN on cover is the same as the Locations Special.
REF: ISSN 0963-12700-7 OP: £2.25 NM: £2.50

MAS-027 Doctor Who Magazine Holiday Special: Who is Sarah Jane Smith?
1992/08/27, Marvel Comics, UK
Ed. Gary Russell. Sarah Jane Smith special. ISSN printed in magazine is 0963-1275.
REF: ISSN 0963-12701-4 OP: £2.50 NM: £2.50

MAS-028 Doctor Who Magazine Winter Special: The Definitive Guide to the Time Lords of Gallifrey
1992/12/03, Marvel Comics, UK
Ed. Gary Russell. ISSN printed in magazine is 0963-1275. ISSN on cover is the same as the Sarah Jane Smith Special.
REF: ISSN 0963-12701-4 OP: £2.50 NM: £2.50

MAS-029 Doctor Who Magazine Summer Special: The Definitive Guide to Thirty Years of the Daleks
1993/06/24, Marvel Comics, UK
Ed. Gary Russell. ISSN printed in magazine is 0963-1275. ISSN on cover is the same as the Time Lords Special.
REF: ISSN 0963-12701-4 OP: £2.50 NM: £2.50

MAS-030 Doctor Who 30th Anniversary 1963-93
1993/11/18, Marvel Comics, UK
Ed. Gary Russell. Design and content based on the 10th Anniversary *Radio Times* special. ISSN printed in magazine is 0963-1275.
REF: ISSN 0963-12702-1 OP: £3.25 NM: £12

MAS-031 Doctor Who Magazine Summer Special: The Genesis of Doctor Who/The Destiny of Doctor Who
1994/07/14, Marvel Comics, UK
Ed. Gary Russell. Double-fronted magazine. ISSN printed in magazine is 0963-1275.
REF: ISSN 0963-12703-8 OP: £2.99 NM: £2.75

MAS-032 The Dalek Chronicles
1994/08/04, Marvel Comics, UK
Collects together all of the Dalek comic strips from *TV Century 21*.
REF: ISSN 1353-7628 OP: £3.99 NM: £13.20

MAS-033 Doctor Who Winter Special
1994/12/08, Marvel Comics, UK
Ed. Marcus Hearn. *Doctor Who* writer and script editor Robert Holmes special. ISSN printed in magazine is 0963-1275.
REF: ISSN 0963-12703-8 OP: £2.99

MAS-034 Doctor Who Summer Special
1995/07/13, Marvel Comics, UK
Ed. Gary Russell. Season 16 special. ISSN printed in magazine is 0963-1275.
REF: ISSN 0963-12703-8 OP: £2.99

MAS-035 Doctor Who Magazine Spring Special: The Sixties Dalek Movies
1996/02/29, Marvel Comics, UK
Ed. Gary Gillatt. Written by Marcus Hearn. Cover by Paul Campbell. ISSN printed in magazine is 0963-1275.
REF: ISSN 0963- 12703-8 OP: £2.99

MAS-036 Doctor Who Movie Special
1996/05/15, Marvel Comics, UK
Ed. Gary Gillatt. ISSN printed in magazine is 0963-1275.
REF: ISSN 0963-12704-5 OP: £1.99

MAS-037 Radio Times: Doctor Who: Return of the Time Lord
1996/05/23, Radio Times, UK
Free insert with issue dated 25-31 May 1996.
OP: free NM: £5.50

MAS-038 *Doctor Who Magazine Special Edition #1: The Complete Fifth Doctor*
2002/01/24, Panini, UK
A Special magazine containing facts and figures about the Fifth Doctor.
REF: ISSN 0957-9818 OP: £3.99

DOCTOR WHO MAGAZINE: THE COMPLETE COVER GALLERY

FOR a large percentage of *Doctor Who* fans, the many incarnations of *Doctor Who Magazine* have served as the principal conduit for news, behind-the-scenes information, personality interviews, and entertainment – especially via the long-running comic strip and occasional prose fiction – for almost twenty-five years. From its early days as a black-and-white Marvel weekly to its current full colour monthly format published by Panini, *Doctor Who Magazine* has been a fixture of *Who* fandom. For the first time ever, we proudly present a colour gallery of every *DWM* cover from the very first issue in October 1979 to #325, the last issue to be released in 2002 (cover-dated January 2003), including all the seasonal and anniversary specials released by Marvel and/or Panini to date.

#1 (17/10/1979) #2 (24/10/1979) #3 (31/10/1979) #4 (7/11/1979) #5 (14/11/1979)

#6 (21/11/1979) #7 (28/11/1979) #8 (8/12/1979) #9 (12/12/1979) #10 (19/12/1979)

#11 (26/12/1979) #12 (2/1/1980) #13 (9/1/1980) #14 (16/1/1980) #15 (23/1/1980)

#16 (30/1/1980) #17 (6/2/1980) #18 (13/2/1980) #19 (20/2/1980) #20 (27/2/1980)

#21 (5/3/1980)

#22 (12/3/1980)

#23 (19/3/1980)

#24 (26/3/1980)

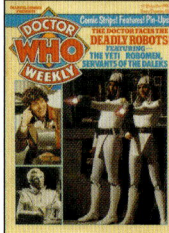
#25 (2/4/1980)

#26 (9/4/1980)

#27 (16/4/1980)

#28 (23/4/1980)

#29 (30/4/1980)

#30 (7/5/1980)

#31 (14/5/1980)

#32 (21/5/1980)

#33 (28/5/1980)

#34 (5/6/1980)

#35 (12/6/1980)

#36 (19/6/1980)

#37 (26/6/1980)

#38 (3/7/1980)

#39 (10/7/1980)

#40 (17/7/1980)

#41 (23/7/1980)

#42 (31/7/1980)

#43 (7/8/1980)

#44 (9/1980)

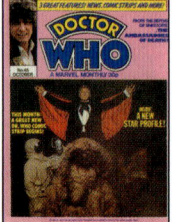
#45 (10/1980)

#46 (11/1980)

#47 (12/1980)

#48 (1/1981)

#49 (2/1981)

#50 (3/1981)

#51 (4/1981)

#52 (5/1981)

#53 (6/1981)

#54 (7/1981)

#55 (8/1981)

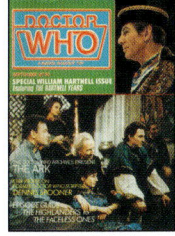
#56 (9/1981)

#57 (10/1981)

#58 (11/1981)

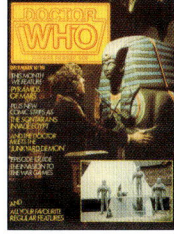
#59 (12/1981)

#60 (1/1982)

#61 (2/1982)

#62 (3/1982)

#63 (4/1982)

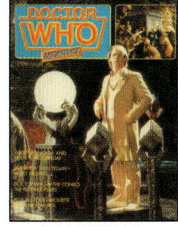
#64 (5/1982)

#65 (6/1982)

#66 (7/1982)

#67 (8/1982)

#68 (9/1982)

#69 (10/1982)

#70 (11/1982)

#71 (12/1982)

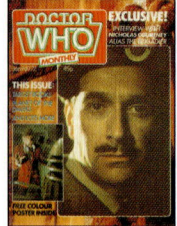
#72 (1/1983)

#73 (2/1983)

#74 (3/1983)

#75 (4/1983)

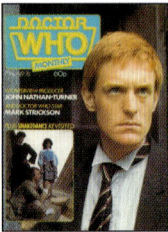
#76 (5/1983)

#77 (6/1983)

#78 (7/1983)

#79 (8/1983)

#80 (9/1983)

#81 (10/1983)

#82 (11/1983)

#83 (12/1983)

#84 (1/1984)

#85 (2/1984)

#86 (3/1984)

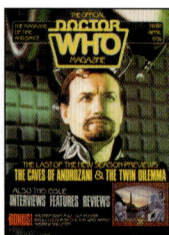
#87 (4/1984)

#88 (5/1984)

#89 (6/1984)

#90 (7/1984)

#91 (8/1984)

#92 (9/1984)

#93 (10/1984)

#94 (11/1984)

#95 (12/1984)

#96 (1/1985)

#97 (2/1985)

#98 (3/1985)

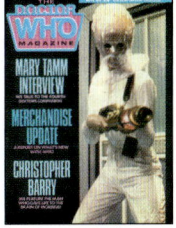
#99 (4/1985)

#100 (5/1985)

#101 (6/1985)

#102 (7/1985)

#103 (8/1985)

#104 (9/1985)

#105 (10/1985)

#106 (11/1985)

#107 (12/1985)

#108 (1/1986)

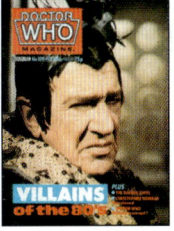
#109 (2/1986)

#110 (3/1986)

#111 (4/1986)

#112 (5/1986)

#113 (6/1986)

#114 (7/1986)

#115 (8/1986)

#116 (9/1986)

#117 (10/1986)

#118 (11/1986)

#119 (12/1986)

#120 (1/1987)

#121 (2/1987)

#122 (3/1987)

#123 (4/1987)

#124 (5/1987)

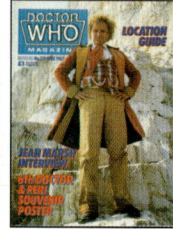
#125 (6/1987)

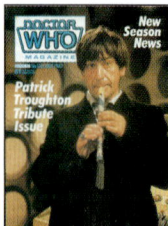
#126 (7/1987)

#127 (8/1987)

#128 (9/1987)

#129 (10/1987)

#130 (11/1987)

#131 (12/1987)

#132 (1/1988)

#133 (2/1988)

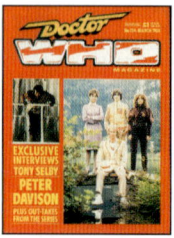
#134 (3/1988)

#135 (4/1988)

#136 (5/1988)

#137 (6/1988)

#138 (7/1988)

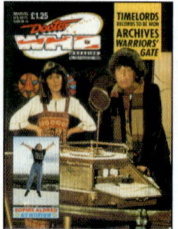
#139 (8/1988)

#140 (9/1988)

#141 (10/1988)

#142 (11/1988)

#143 (12/1988)

#144 (1/1989)

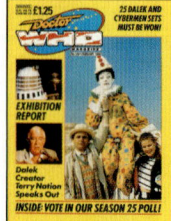
#145 (2/1989)

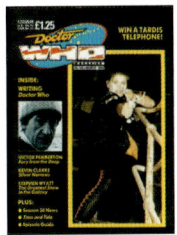
#146 (3/1989)

#147 (4/1989)

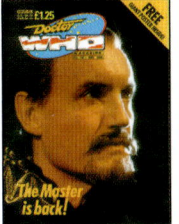
#148 (5/1989)

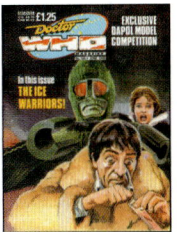
#149 (6/1989)

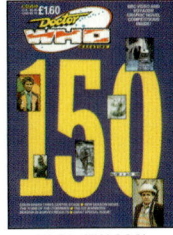
#150 (7/1989)

#151 (8/1989)

#152 (9/1989)

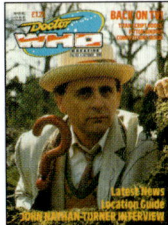
#153 (10/1989)

#154 (11/1989)

#155 (12/1989)

#156 (1/1990)

#157 (2/1990)

#158 (3/1990)

#159 (4/1990)

#160 (5/1990)

#161 (6/1990)

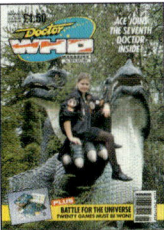
#162 (7/1990)

#163 (8/1990)

#164 (8/9/1990)

#165 (3/10/1990)

#166 (31/10/1990)

#167 (28/11/1990)

#168 (26/12/1990)

#169 (23/1/1991)

#170 (20/2/1991)

#171 (13/3/1991)

#172 (17/4/1991)

#173 (15/5/1991)

#174 (12/6/1991)

#175 (10/7/1991)

#176 (7/8/1991)

#177 (4/9/1991)

#178 (2/10/1991)

#179 (30/10/1991)

#180 (27/11/1991)

#181 (25/12/1991)

#182 (22/1/1992)

#183 (19/2/1992)

#184 (18/3/1992)

#185 (15/4/1992)

#186 (13/5/1992)

#187 (10/6/1992)

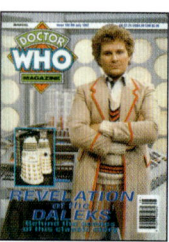
#188 (8/7/1992)

#189 (5/8/1992)

#190 (2/9/1992)

#191 (30/9/1992)

#192 (28/10/1992)

#193 (25/11/1992)

#194 (23/12/1992)

#195 (20/1/1993)

#196 (17/2/1993)

#197 (17/3/1993)

#198 (14/4/1993)

#199 (12/5/1993)

#200 (9/6/1993)

#201 (7/7/1993)

#202 (4/8/1993)

#203 (1/9/1993)

#204 (29/9/1993)

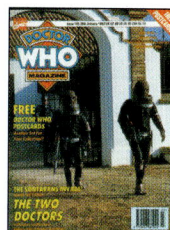
#205 (27/10/1993)

#206 (24/11/1993)

#207 (22/12/1993)

#208 (19/1/1994)

#209 (16/2/1994)

#210 (16/3/1994)

#211 (13/4/1994)

#212 (11/5/1994)

#213 (8/6/1994)

#214 (6/7/1994)

#215 (3/8/1994)

#216 (31/8/1994)

#217 (28/9/1994)

#218 (26/10/1994)

#219 (23/11/1994)

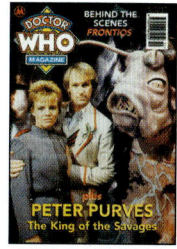
#220 (21/12/1994)

#221 (18/1/1995)

#222 (15/2/1995)

#223 (15/3/1995)

#224 (12/4/1995)

#225 (10/5/1995)

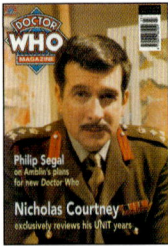

#226 (7/6/1995)

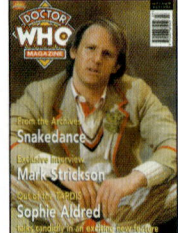

#227 (5/7/1995)

#228 (2/8/1995)

#229 (30/8/1995)

#230 (27/9/1995)

#231 (25/10/1995)

#232 (22/11/1995)

#233 (20/12/1995)

#234 (17/1/1996)

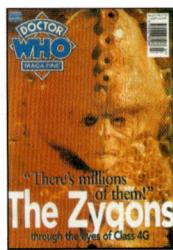

#235 (14/2/1996)

#236 (13/3/1996)

#237 (10/4/1996)

#238 (8/5/1996)

#239 (5/6/1996)

#240 (3/7/1996)

#241 (31/7/1996)

#242 (28/8/1996)

#243 (25/9/1996)

#244 (23/10/1996)

#245 (20/11/1996)

So, Doctor... which way now?
#246 (18/12/1996)

Who's fooling Who?
#247 (15/1/1997)

Graham Williams
#248 (12/2/1997)

CLIFFHANGER!
#249 (12/3/1997)

ELISABETH SLADEN
#250 (9/4/1997)

THE DOCTOR
#251 (7/5/1997)

THE DALEKS
#252 (4/6/1997)

RESULT!
#253 (2/7/1997)

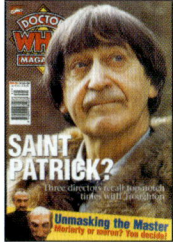
SAINT PATRICK?
#254 (30/7/1997)

SOPHIE ALDRED
#255 (27/8/1997)

HIPPY CHICK
#256 (24/9/1997)

THE END OF AN ERA
#257 (22/10/1997)

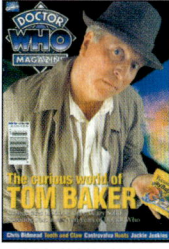
TOM BAKER
#258 (19/11/1997)

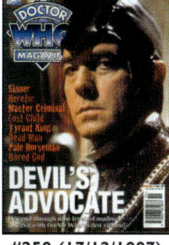
DEVIL'S ADVOCATE
#259 (17/12/1997)

BONNIE LANGFORD
#260 (14/1/1998)

WILD THING!
#261 (11/2/1998)

Class of '78
#262 (11/3/1998)

SCARY MONSTERS!
#263 (8/4/1998)

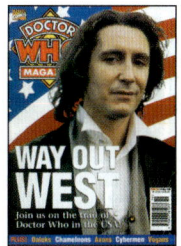
WAY OUT WEST
#264 (6/5/1998)

Doctor Who stories of all time!
#265 (3/6/1998)

DAZED AND CONFUSED?
#266 (1/7/1998)

CANON FODDER!
#267 (29/7/1998)

NO SEX PLEASE ...he's British!
#268 (26/8/1998)

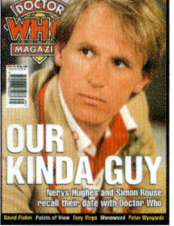
OUR KINDA GUY
#269 (23/9/1998)

DO NOT ADJUST YOUR SET
#270 (21/10/1998)

#271 (18/11/1998)

#272 (16/12/1998)

#273 (13/1/1999)

#274 (10/2/1999)

#275 (10/3/1999)

#276 (7/4/1999)

#277 (5/5/1999)

#278 (2/6/1999)

#279 (30/6/1999)

#280 (28/7/1999)

#281 (25/8/1999)

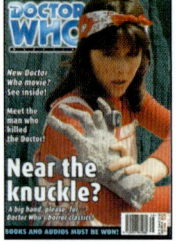

#282 (22/9/1999)

#283a (20/10/1999)

#283b (20/10/1999)

#284 (17/11/1999)

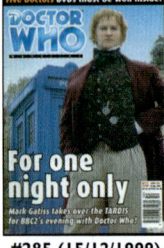

#285 (15/12/1999)

#286 (12/1/2000)

#287 (9/2/2000)

#288 (8/3/2000)

#289 (5/4/2000)

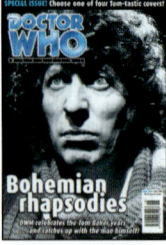

#290a (3/5/2000)

#290b (3/5/2000)

#290c (3/5/2000)

#290d (3/5/2000)

#291 (31/5/2000)

#292 (28/6/2000)

#293 (26/7/2000)

#294 (23/8/2000)

#295 (20/9/2000)

#296 (18/10/2000)

#297 (15/11/2000)

#298 (13/12/2000)

#299 (10/1/2001)

#300 (7/2/2001)

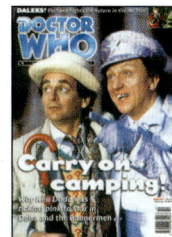
#301 (7/3/2001)

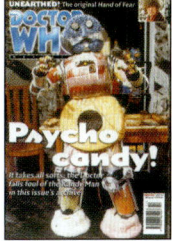
#302 (4/4/2001)

#303 (2/5/2001)

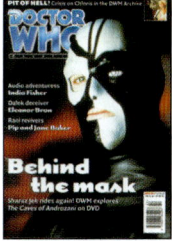
#304 (30/5/2001)

#305 (27/6/2001)

#306 (25/7/2001)

#307 (22/8/2001)

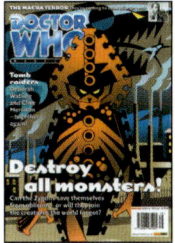
#308 (19/9/2001)

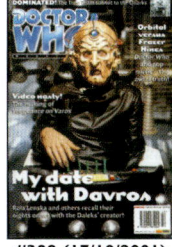
#309 (17/10/2001)

#310 (14/11/2001)

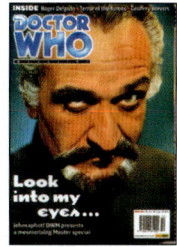
#311 (12/12/2001)

#312 (9/1/2002)

#313 (6/2/2002)

#314 (6/3/2002)

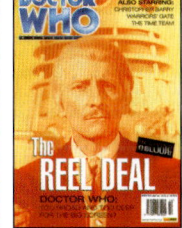
#315 (3/4/2002)

#316 (1/5/2002)

#317 (29/5/2002)

#318 (26/6/2002)

#319 (24/7/2002)

#320 (21/8/2002)

#321 (18/9/2002)

#322 (16/10/2002)

#323 (13/11/2002)

#324 (11/12/2002)

#325 (8/1/2003)

Summer 1980

Summer 1981

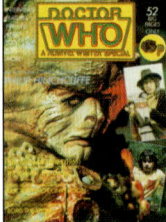
Winter 1981

Summer 1982

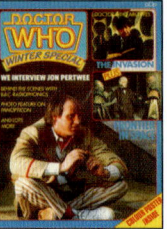
Winter 1982

Summer 1983

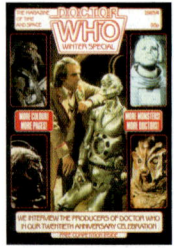
Winter 1983

Summer 1984

Winter 1984

Summer 1985

Winter 1985

Summer 1986

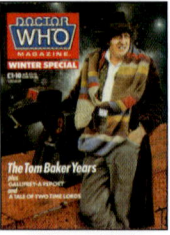
Winter 1986

Autumn 1987

25th Ann. Special

DWM 1979-1989

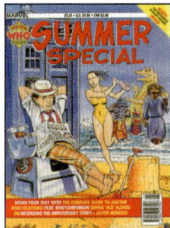
Summer 1991

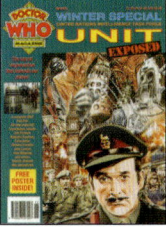
Winter 1991

Holiday Spec. 1992

Winter 1992

Summer 1993

30th Ann. Special

Summer 1994 (flip cover)

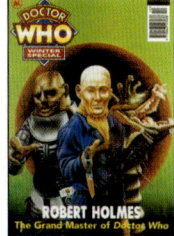
Dalek Chronicles

Winter 1994

Summer 1995

Spring 1996

Movie Special 1996

Complete Fifth
Doctor Sp. Ed. '02

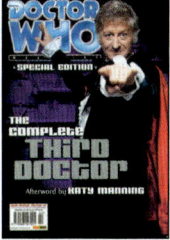
Complete Third
Doctor Sp. Ed. '02

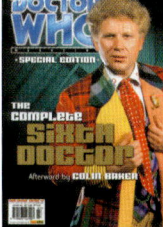
Complete Sixth
Doctor Sp. Ed. '02

DOCTOR WHO CLASSIC COMICS GALLERY

IN addition to the regular *DWM*, there was a relatively short-lived companion series dubbed *Doctor Who Classic Comics* which reprinted previously hard-to-find comic book exploits of the various Doctors from older magazines like *TV Action*. The series ran for 27 issues, with one special presenting a complete version of the Seventh Doctor *DWM* strip, "Evening's Empire," which had only been partially printed in *DWM*. The series featured some stunning full-colour artwork covers, all of which are presented here together for the first time.

CC #1 (9/12/1992)

CC #2 (6/1/1993)

CC #3 (3/2/1993)

CC #4 (3/3/1993)

CC #5 (31/3/1993)

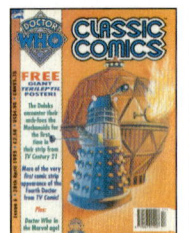
CC #6 (28/4/1993)

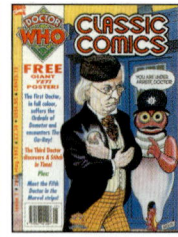
CC #7 (26/5/1993)

CC #8 (23/6/1993)

CC #9 (21/7/1993)

CC #10 (18/8/1993)

CC #11 (15/9/1993)

CC #12 (13/10/1993)

CC #13 (10/11/1993)

CC #14 (8/12/1993)

CC #15 (15/1/1994)

CC #16 (2/2/1994)

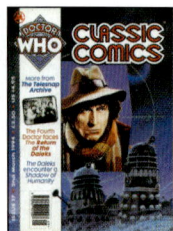
CC #17 (2/3/1994)

CC #18 (30/3/1994)

CC #19 (27/4/1994)

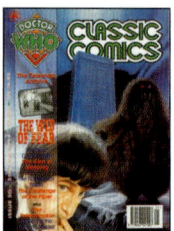
CC #20 (25/5/1994)

CC #21 (22/6/1994)

CC #22 (20/7/1994)

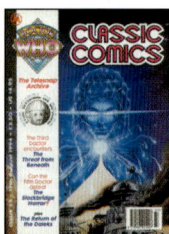
CC #23 (17/8/1994)

CC #24 (14/9/1994)

CC #25 (12/10/1994)

CC #26 (9/11/1994)

CC #27 (7/12/1994)

Autumn Holiday
Spec. 1993

MAS-039 Doctor Who Magazine Special Edition #2: The Complete Third Doctor
2002/07/11, Panini, UK
A Special magazine containing facts and figures about the Third Doctor. Cover dated 5 September 2002.
REF: ISSN 0963-1275 OP: £4.99

MAS-040 Doctor Who Magazine Special Edition #3: The Complete Sixth Doctor
2002/11/28, Panini, UK
A Special magazine containing facts and figures about the Sixth Doctor. Cover dated 22 January 2003.
REF: ISSN 0963-1275 OP: £3.99

MAS-024   MAS-037

MODELS, GARAGE KITS

'GARAGE' kits are so called because they are traditionally produced in someone's garage. These are generally resin kits produced in very low quantities by fans. Because these are unlicensed it is difficult to ascertain whether the list is complete, or anything about their production. In this category we have also included a number of related models and masks that were produced by the same unlicensed companies.

MGA-001 Cybermat
1984/1985, UK
Resin kit.
OP: £22.99

MGA-002 Mark Three Travelling Machine
Enigma Models, UK
1/16 scale Dalek model.
OP: £29.99

MGA-003 Emperor Dalek Model
1995, Comet, UK
OP: £35.00

MGA-004 Giant Robot
1995, Out of this World Models, UK
Sculpted by Graham Nattress. 1.6 scale resin kit.
OP: £60.00

MGA-005 Gunner Dalek
1995, Reshape, UK
Resin kit.
OP: £10.00

MGA-002

MGA-004

MGA-005

IMPERIAL DALEK
EMPEROR
1-8 SCALE GRP RESIN KIT

RESHAPE

MGA-006

MGA-009

MGA-010

MGA-016 (selected)

MGA-011

MGA-013

MGA-006 Cyberman
1996, Mam-Mod/Warp, UK
Sculpted by MAMAS. *Moonbase*-style Cyberman.
OP: £44.99

MGA-007 Dalek flying skiff
1996, Comet, UK
OP: £34.99

MGA-008 Ice Lord
1996, Mam-Mod/Warp, UK
Sculpted by MAMAS. Resin kit.
REF: MAM05 OP: £49.99

MGA-009 Imperial Dalek Emperor
1996, Reshape, UK
Resin kit.
OP: £49.99

MGA-010 K9
1996, Genesis Products, UK
OP: £19.99

MGA-011 Sea Devil
1996, UK
OP: £49.99

MGA-012 Sontaran (Linx)
1996, Invaders, UK
Sculpted by Paul Fay. 13" high. 10 parts.
OP: £35.00

MGA-013 TARDIS exterior
1996, Comet, UK

MGA-014 TARDIS interior
1996, Comet, UK
OP: £50.00

MGA-015 Zygon
1996, UK
OP: £49.99

MGA-016 'MiniTerrors' Figurines
1999, Head-Up Display, UK
Monsters from the series in about 1:20 scale.
Available: Alpha Centauri, Yeti (two styles), Zygon,
Aggedor, Ice Warrior, Service Mummy, Rutan, Monoid,
Mandrell, Gell Guard, Drashig, Macra.
OP: £15.50-29.99 each

MGA-017 Mk 2 Cyberman (*Tomb*)
1999, Head-Up Display, UK
Resin and vac-formed kit. 27.5 cm tall. Available in kit

form or assembled and painted.
OP: £69.99 (kit) / £120 (assembled and painted)

MGA-018 Mk 5 Cyberman (*Revenge*)
1999, Head-Up Display, UK
Resin and vac-formed kit.25.5 cm tall. Available in kit
form or assembled and painted.
OP: £69.99 (kit) / £120 (assembled and painted)

MGA-019 Cyberman helmets
1999, Head-Up Display, UK
Full size fibreglass helmets in kit form or completed.
Available: *Tomb* Controller, *Tomb*, *Wheel in Space*,
Invasion, *Revenge*, *Attack* Controller, and a Mk1 from
Tenth Planet that was only available in finished form.
OP: £150 (each compete kit) / £220-250 (fully painted
and finished) / £265 (*Tomb* Controller with dome
lighting) / £299 (Mk1 Cyberman)

MGA-020 CyberSuits
1999, Head-Up Display, UK
Full size costumes with helmets. Available in Mk 1
(*Tenth Planet*), Mk 2 (*Tomb*), and Mk 5 (*Revenge*) styles.
OP: £1599.99 (*Tenth Planet*) / £799.99 (*Tomb*) /
£899.99 (*Revenge*)

MGA-021 Cybermats
1999, Head-Up Display, UK
1:3 scale Cybermats in 3 versions: *Tomb*, *Wheel*, and
Revenge. Also available in a full size resin and vac-
formed, articulated kit representing the *Tomb* style.
OP: £20.50-23.50 (1:3 models) / £39.50 (*Tomb* kit)

MGA-022 Sontaran Costume
1999, Head-Up Display, UK
Full size costume with head, resembling Linx from *The
Time Warrior*.
OP: £999.99

MGA-017

MGA-018

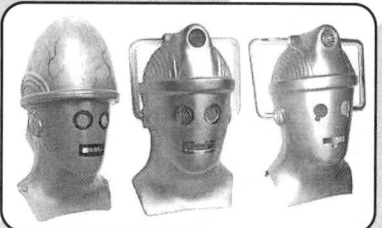

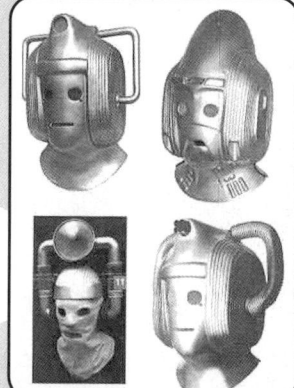

MGA-019 (all styles shown)

MGA-020 (*Tomb*)   MGA-021 (3 styles and kit shown)   MGA-022

MGA-023

MGA-024

MGA-023 Giant Robot
1999, Head-Up Display, UK
Resin and vac-formed kit. 30.5 cm tall. Available in kit form or assembled and painted.
OP: £69.99 (kit) / £120 (assembled and painted)

MGA-024 Morbius Monster
1999, Head-Up Display, UK
Resin and vac-formed kit. 25.5 cm tall. Available in kit form or assembled and painted.
OP: £69.99 (kit) / £130 (assembled and painted)

MGA-025 Davros Mask
1999, Head-Up Display, UK
Latex mask of Davros from *Genesis of the Daleks*.
OP: £55.99

MGA-026 Ice Warrior Mask
1999, Head-Up Display, UK
Latex mask of Ice Warrior soldier with amber lenses.
OP: £299.99

MGA-025-026

MGA-027 'The Doctors' Busts
1999, Head-Up Display, UK
Handcrafted, painted busts of all eight Doctors cast in plaster. Each approximately 7cm tall.
OP: £19.50 each / £21.50 each (Colin Baker & Sylvester McCoy busts only)

MGA-028 'The Masters' Busts
1999, Head-Up Display, UK
Handcrafted, painted busts cast in plaster. 3 incarnations of the Master. Each 7.5cm tall.
OP: £19.50 (Delgado, Ainley) / £23.50 (*Deadly Assassin*)

MGA-027

MGA-029 'Monster Heads'
1999, Head-Up Display, UK
Handcrafted, painted busts of a wide variety of *Doctor Who* monsters. All cast in plaster, some with additional pieces in perspex or cast resin. Ranging from about 7cm to 11cm tall. A specially designed base for the entire series was sold separately for each bust. Available: Sharaz Jek, Koquillon, Ogron, Azal, Ice Lord, ice Warrior, Kraal, Destroyer, Sutekh, Draconian, Scaroth, Ancient Haemovore, Haemovore, Ice Guard, Voord, Terileptil, Auton (2 kinds), Davros, Sontaran (2 kinds), Sea Devil, Silurian, Mister Sin, Bok, Omega, Zygon, Dum Robot, Voc Robot, Super Voc Robot, Vervoid, Mut, Sensorite, Hieronymous, Exxilon, Vogan.
OP: £18.50-£29.50

MGA-028

MGA-029 (assorted)

MGA-030 TARDIS Model kit
2001, Millennia Models International, UK
Kit contains 7 resin parts, styrene rod and self adhesive labels. 1/32 scale.
REF: MMI-1140   OP: $20

MGA-031 1st Doctor Figure
2001, UK
Kit containing parts to make a model of the 1st Doctor.
OP: £60

MGA-032 2nd Doctor Figure
2001, UK
Kit containing parts to make a model of the 2nd Doctor.
OP: £60

MGA-033 3rd Doctor Figure
2001, UK
Kit containing parts to make a model of the 3rd Doctor.
OP: £60

MGA-034 'Hexicondek' TARDIS Console Model Kit
2002/11, Ainsty, UK
Small model of the TARDIS console in three parts: a resin top and base, and a clear perspex rod.
REF: 2766   OP: £2.50

MGA-035 'Fourth Lord of Time'
2002/11, Imar Models, UK
1/32 scale white metal kit of the 4th Doctor. In a proposed 'Time Travellers' series.
REF: TT:1   OP: £6.00

MGA-030 unassembled and assembled (inset)

MGA-034

MGA-035

MGA-036-038

MGA-036 'Genesis of Evil' Bust
2002, Squidz Kitz Studios, USA
Unpainted 6" high resin bust of Davros.

MGA-037 'The 4th Face' Bust
2002, Squidz Kitz Studios, USA
Unpainted 6" high resin bust of the Fourth Doctor.

MGA-038 'The 7th Face' Bust
2002, Squidz Kitz Studios, USA
Unpainted 6" high resin bust of the Seventh Doctor.

MODELS, METAL MINIATURES

METAL miniatures have been produced in various sizes over the years. In general terms, a made-up, mounted and painted figure will cost more than a standard blister pack to buy. The prices and details given are for the standard figures in all cases.

MMM-001

MMM-001 Doctors 1, 2, 3
1985, Citadel Miniatures, UK
REF: DW1 OP: £1.95

MMM-002 Doctors 4, 5 and The Master
1985, Citadel Miniatures, UK
REF: DW2 OP: £1.95

MMM-002

MMM-003 Dalek (2)
1985, Citadel Miniatures, UK
REF: DW3 OP: £1.95

MMM-004 Davros, Dalek & K9
1985, Citadel Miniatures, UK
REF: DW8 OP: £1.95

MMM-005 Time Lord (4)
1985, Citadel Miniatures, UK
REF: DW9 OP: £1.95

MMM-003

MMM-004

MMM-006 Romana, Jo & Turlough
1985, Citadel Miniatures, UK
REF: DW11 OP: £1.95

MMM-007 Doctor Who Miniatures: The Five Doctors
1986, FASA Corporation, USA
Contains Hartnell, Troughton, Pertwee, T. Baker, and Davison figures with oval metal stands. All of the FASA-released *Doctor Who* 25mm white metal miniatures came in a cardboard box shaped like a small TARDIS and were manufactured by RAFM (made in

MMM-005

Canada). They were designed by Citadel Miniatures, a
division of Games Workshop Ltd(of Eastwoods,
Notts, England), and were originally released in the
UK in blister packs.
REF: 9501 OP: $8.00

**MMM-008a Doctor Who Miniatures: Sarah
Jane, Leela, Adric**
1985, Citadel Miniatures, UK
3 white metal miniatures with six-sided plastic
stands.
REF: DW7 OP: £1.95 NM: £16.50

MMM-006

**MMM-008b Doctor Who Miniatures:
Companion Set #1**
1986, FASA Corporation, USA
Contains 3 figures: Sarah Jane, Leela and Adric with
oval metal stands.
REF: 9502 OP: $4.50 NM: £16.50

MMM-009 Doctor Who Miniatures: Daleks
1986, FASA Corporation, USA
Contains 3 identical figures which required assembly
in three parts: the base, middle section with gun and
sucker, and the head with eye stalk and lights. Daleks
were sculpted by Alan Merret. [Sculptor not named
on the box but sculptor name is on the Citadel
'Daleks & Cybermen' box – the original manufacturer
of the figures].
REF: 9503 OP: $6.00 NM: £16.50

MMM-007

**MMM-010a Doctor Who Miniatures:
Cybermen**
1985, Citadel Miniatures, UK
3 white metal miniatures with six-sided plastic stands.
REF: DW4 OP: £1.95 NM: £16.50

**MMM-010b Doctor Who Miniatures:
Cybermen**
1986, FASA Corporation, USA
Contains 3 identical figures with oval metal stands;
Cybermen were sculpted by Michael and Alan Perry.
[Sculptors not named on the box but sculptors names
are on the Citadel 'Daleks & Cybermen' box – the
original manufacturer of the figures].
REF: 9504 OP: $4.50 NM: £16.50

MMM-008b

MMM-011a Doctor Who Miniatures: UNIT
1985, Citadel Miniatures, UK
3 white metal miniatures with six-sided plastic stands.
REF: DW6 OP: £1.95 NM: £16.50

MMM-010a

MMM-011b

MMM-012

MMM-013

MMM-014

MMM-015a

MMM-015b

MMM-011b Doctor Who Miniatures: The Brigadier and UNIT Troopers
1986, FASA Corporation, USA
Contains 3 figures with oval metal stands: The Brigadier with riding crop, a soldier shooting rifle, and a soldier carrying rifle.
REF: 9505 OP: $4.50 NM: £16.50

MMM-012 Doctor Who Miniatures: Sgt. Benton and UNIT Troopers
1986, FASA Corporation, USA
Contains 3 figures with oval metal stands.: Sergeant Benton with pistol, a soldier shooting rifle, and a soldier carrying rifle.
REF: 9506 OP: $4.50 NM: £16.50

MMM-013 Doctor Who Miniatures: Player Character Time Lords
1986, FASA Corporation, USA
Contains 3 male figures with oval metal stands.: one pointing, one with top hat and cane, and one holding a ball; set was called 'Player Character Time Lords, Male' on both the orange FASA product form dated effective through July 1 (1986) and the white FASA product form dated effective through October 1 (1986).
REF: 9507 OP: $4.50 NM: £16.50

MMM-014 Doctor Who Miniatures: Temporal Marauders
1986, FASA Corporation, USA
Contains 3 male figures with oval metal stands. one wearing helmet holding pistol, one holding rifle at port arms, one holding rifle and running. These figures were re-released by Citadel Miniatures as part of their 'Warhammer 40,000' game.
REF: 9508 OP: $4.50 NM: £16.50

MMM-015a Doctor Who Miniatures: Ice Warriors
1985, Citadel Miniatures, UK
3 white metal miniatures with six-sided plastic stands.
REF: DW5 OP: £1.95 NM: £16.50

MMM-015b Doctor Who Miniatures: Ice Warriors
1986, FASA Corporation, USA
Contains 3 figures: 2 identical Ice Warriors, and 1 Ice Lord with oval metal stands.
REF: 9509 OP: $4.50 NM: £16.50

MMM-016 Doctor Who Miniatures: Player Character Time Lords Set #2
1986, FASA Corporation, USA
Contains 3 male figures with oval metal stands: one holding dufflel bag, one resting arm on umbrella, and

one with long hair holding a flower and a pistol.
REF: 9510 OP: $4.50 NM: £16.50

MMM-017 Doctor Who Miniatures: The Master, Davros and a Dalek
1986, FASA Corporation, USA
Contains 3 figures with oval metal stands: The Master, Davros, and a Dalek with a claw arm.
REF: 9511 OP: $4.50 NM: £16.50

MMM-018 Doctor Who Miniatures: Companions Set #2 w/K-9
1986, FASA Corporation, USA
Contains 3 figures with oval metal stands: Romana, K-9, and Sarah Jane; the Sarah Jane figure is the same as found in set #9502 'Companion Set #1'.
REF: 9512 OP: $4.50 NM: £16.50

MMM-016

MMM-019 Doctor Who Miniatures: Player Character Time Lords Set #3
1986, FASA Corporation, USA
Contains 3 male figures with oval metal stands: one holding a teddy bear, one in a marching band costume holding a boom box radio, and one in Renaissance clothes holding a sonic screwdriver in his left hand.
REF: 9513 OP: $4.50 NM: £16.50

MMM-019

MMM-020a Doctor Who Miniatures: Sea Devils
1985, Citadel Miniatures, UK
3 different white metal miniatures with six-sided plastic stands.
REF: DW10 OP: £1.95 NM: £16.50

MMM-020b Doctor Who Miniatures: Sea Devils
1986, FASA Corporation, USA
Contains 3 identical figures with oval metal stands.
REF: 9514 OP: $4.50 NM: £16.50

MMM-020b

MMM-021a Cyberman
1984/11, Fine Art Castings, UK
Fine Art Castings, well known at the time for their range of military pewter models, entered the *Doctor Who* market in 1984 with a range of very accurate and well crafted white pewter figures of the Doctors, companions and enemies. This range expanded through 1985 and 1986 and eventually over 80 different models were issued. Shortly after launching the range with a Fourth Doctor figure, a Cyberman and a Dalek, Fine Art Castings started liaising with fan historians David J Howe and Mark Stammers. This resulted in far greater accuracy in the models and also an expanded production schedule of monsters old and new from the series' history. The 80mm figures were available as plain pewter, antiqued finish or fully painted with varying prices.
OP: £6.25 / £5.80 NM: £12

MMM-021a

MMM-021b (accompanied
by Cybermats MMM-083)

MMM-021b Dead Cyberman
1984/11, Fine Art Castings, UK
OP: £5.80   NM: £12

MMM-022 Dalek
1984, Fine Art Castings, UK
OP: £6.80   NM: £12

MMM-023 Dalek (40mm)
1984, Fine Art Castings, UK
OP: £1.30   NM: £3.50

MMM-024 Davros
1984, Fine Art Castings, UK
OP: £6.80   NM: £12

MMM-025 Draconian
1984, Fine Art Castings, UK
OP: £6.25   NM: £12

MMM-026 Fifth Doctor (40mm)
1984, Fine Art Castings, UK
OP: 80p   NM: £3.50

MMM-027 First Doctor
1984, Fine Art Castings, UK
OP: £6.25   NM: £12

MMM-028 Fourth Doctor
1984, Fine Art Castings, UK
OP: £6.25   NM: £12

MMM-029 K9
1984, Fine Art Castings, UK
OP: £1.50   NM: £2.50

MMM-030 Leela
1984, Fine Art Castings, UK
OP: £5.80   NM: £12

MMM-023

MMM-022

MMM-024

MMM-025

MMM-029

MMM-026

MMM-028

MMM-027

MMM-031 Mk 6 Cyberman
1984, Fine Art Castings, UK
OP: £6.25 NM: £12

MMM-032 Second Doctor
1984, Fine Art Castings, UK
OP: £6.25 NM: £12

MMM-033 Sontaran
1984, Fine Art Castings, UK
OP: £6.25 NM: £12

MMM-034 Third Doctor
1984, Fine Art Castings, UK
OP: £6.50 NM: £12

MMM-035 Turlough (40mm)
1984, Fine Art Castings, UK
OP: 80p NM: £3.50

MMM-036 Zygon
1984, Fine Art Castings, UK
OP: £6.25 NM: £12

MMM-037 Dalek (25mm)
1985, Fine Art Castings, UK
OP: 60p NM: £2.50

MMM-038 Draconian (40mm)
1985, Fine Art Castings, UK
OP: 80p NM: £3.50

MMM-039 Fourth Doctor (mk 2)
1985, Fine Art Castings, UK
OP: £6.80 NM: £12

MMM-030

MMM-031

MMM-032

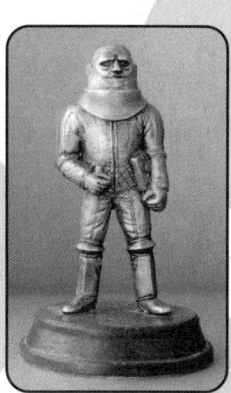

MMM-033

MMM-034

MMM-036

MMM-038

MMM-039

MMM-041

MMM-042

MMM-045

MMM-046

MMM-047

MMM-048

MMM-040 Ice Warrior
1985, Fine Art Castings, UK
OP: £6.80 NM: £12

MMM-041 Jamie
1985, Fine Art Castings, UK
OP: £6.80 NM: £12

MMM-042 Master
1985, Fine Art Castings, UK
OP: £6.50 NM: £12

MMM-043 Master (40 mm)
1985, Fine Art Castings, UK
OP: 80p NM: £3.50

MMM-044 Mk 6 Cyberman (40mm)
1985, Fine Art Castings, UK
OP: 80p NM: £3.50

MMM-045 Peri
1985, Fine Art Castings, UK
OP: £6.25 NM: £12

MMM-046 Raston Robot (40mm)
1985, Fine Art Castings, UK
OP: 80p NM: £3.50

MMM-047 Romana (mk 2)
1985, Fine Art Castings, UK
OP: £6.50 NM: £12

MMM-048 Sea Devil
1985, Fine Art Castings, UK
OP: £6.80 NM: £12

MMM-049

MMM-051

MMM-054

MMM-059

MMM-060

MMM-061

MMM-049 Sea Devil (40mm)
1985, Fine Art Castings, UK
OP: 80p NM: £3.50

MMM-050 Sensorite (40mm)
1985, Fine Art Castings, UK
OP: 80p NM: £3.50

MMM-051 Sixth Doctor
1985, Fine Art Castings, UK
OP: £6.80 NM: £12

MMM-052 Sontaran (25mm)
1985, Fine Art Castings, UK
OP: 50p NM: £2.50

MMM-053 Sontaran (40mm)
1985, Fine Art Castings, UK
OP: 80p NM: £3.50

MMM-054 Sontaran (with helmet)
1985, Fine Art Castings, UK
OP: £6.50 NM: £12

MMM-055 TARDIS (25mm)
1985, Fine Art Castings, UK
OP: 50p NM: £2.50

MMM-056 TARDIS (40mm)
1985, Fine Art Castings, UK
OP: £3.50 NM: £3.50

MMM-057 TARDIS (resin)
1985, Fine Art Castings, UK
OP: £9.50 NM: £12

MMM-062

MMM-058 Third Doctor (25mm)
1985, Fine Art Castings, UK
OP: 50p NM: £2.50

MMM-059 Yeti (40mm)
1985, Fine Art Castings, UK
OP: £1.30 NM: £3.50

MMM-060 Zygon (40mm)
1985, Fine Art Castings, UK
OP: 80p NM: £3.50

MMM-061 Azal
1986, Fine Art Castings, UK
OP: £7.00 NM: £12

MMM-062 Bok
1986, Fine Art Castings, UK
OP: £2.75 NM: £12

MMM-063

MMM-064

MMM-066

MMM-067

MMM-069

MMM-072

MMM-073

MMM-075

MMM-063 Borad
1986, Fine Art Castings, UK
OP: £7.00 NM: £12

MMM-064 Brigadier
1986, Fine Art Castings, UK
OP: £6.80 NM: £12

MMM-065 Brigadier (40mm)
1986, Fine Art Castings, UK
OP: 80p NM: £3.50

MMM-066 Fifth Doctor
1986, Fine Art Castings, UK
OP: £6.80 NM: £12

MMM-067 First Doctor (40mm)
1986, Fine Art Castings, UK
OP: 80p NM: £3.50

MMM-068 Fourth Doctor (25mm)
1986, Fine Art Castings, UK
OP: 50p NM: £2.50

MMM-069 Fourth Doctor (40mm)
1986, Fine Art Castings, UK
OP: 80p NM: £3.50

MMM-070 Leela (25mm)
1986, Fine Art Castings, UK
OP: 50p NM: £2.50

MMM-071 Master (25mm)
1986, Fine Art Castings, UK
OP: 50p NM: £2.50

MMM-072 Mk 3 Cyberman
1986, Fine Art Castings, UK
OP: £6.25 NM: £12

MMM-073 Mk 3 Cyberman (40mm)
1986, Fine Art Castings, UK
OP: 80p NM: £3.50

MMM-074 Mk 6 Cyberman (25mm)
1986, Fine Art Castings, UK
OP: 50p NM: £2.50

MMM-075 Mk 6 Cyberman transforming
1986, Fine Art Castings, UK
Model taken from the *Doctor Who Magazine* comic
strip story 'Genesis!' in issue 110.
OP: £6.25 NM: £12

MMM-076 Mummy
1986, Fine Art Castings, UK
OP: £7.00 NM: £12

MMM-077 Robot of Death
1986, Fine Art Castings, UK
OP: £6.80 NM: £12

MMM-078 Robot of Death (40mm)
1986, Fine Art Castings, UK
OP: £1.15 NM: £3.50

MMM-079 Sarah Jane Smith
1986, Fine Art Castings, UK
OP: £6.50 NM: £12

MMM-080 Second Doctor (40mm)
1986, Fine Art Castings, UK
OP: 80p NM: £3.50

MMM-081 Set of 2 UNIT troops (40mm) 1
1986, Fine Art Castings, UK
OP: £1.50 NM: £6.50

MMM-082 Set of 2 UNIT troops (40mm) 2
1986, Fine Art Castings, UK
OP: £1.50 NM: £6.50

MMM-083 Set of 3 Cybermats
1986, Fine Art Castings, UK
OP: £1.50 NM: £5.50

MMM-084 Set of 3 Cybermen (40mm) 1
1986, Fine Art Castings, UK
OP: £2.25 NM: £10

MMM-085 Set of 3 Cybermen (40mm) 2
1986, Fine Art Castings, UK
OP: £2.25 NM: £10

MMM-086 Set of 3 Sontarans (40mm) 1
1986, Fine Art Castings, UK
OP: £1.25 NM: £10

MMM-087 Set of 3 Sontarans (40mm) 2
1986, Fine Art Castings, UK
OP: £2.25 NM: £10

MMM-088 Set of 6 Cybermen (40mm)
1986, Fine Art Castings, UK
OP: £2.75 NM: £16.50

MMM-089 Set of 6 Sontarans (40mm)
1986, Fine Art Castings, UK
OP: £2.75 NM: £16.50

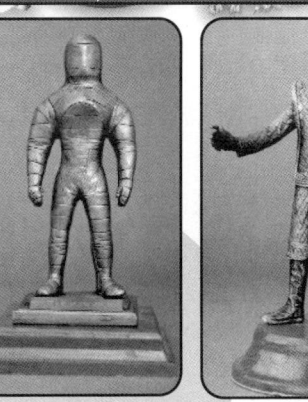

MMM-076   MMM-077

MMM-078

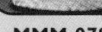

MMM-080

MMM-079

MMM-083 (accompanying
Dead Cyberman MMM-021b)

MMM-091

MMM-090

MMM-092

MMM-093

MMM-095

MMM-096

MMM-100

MMM-110

MMM-090 Silurian
1986, Fine Art Castings, UK
OP: £6.80 NM: £12

MMM-091 Sixth Doctor (40mm)
1986, Fine Art Castings, UK
OP: 80p NM: £3.50

MMM-092 Tegan
1986, Fine Art Castings, UK
OP: £6.50 NM: £12

MMM-093 Third Doctor (40mm)
1986, Fine Art Castings, UK
OP: 80p NM: £3.50

MMM-094 Yates (40mm)
1986, Fine Art Castings, UK
OP: 80p NM: £3.50

MMM-095 Zoe
1986, Fine Art Castings, UK
OP: £6.50 NM: £12

MMM-096 Celestial Toymaker
1987, Fine Art Castings, UK
OP: £6.80 NM: £12

MMM-097 Drathro and Robot L1 (40mm)
1987, Fine Art Castings, UK
OP: £2.75 NM: £3.50

MMM-098 Giant Robot (40mm)
1987, Fine Art Castings, UK
OP: 80p NM: £3.50

MMM-099 Ice Lord (40mm)
1987, Fine Art Castings, UK
OP: 80p NM: £3.50

MMM-100 Ice Warrior (40mm)
1987, Fine Art Castings, UK
OP: 80p NM: £3.50

MMM-101 Inquisitor (40mm)
1987, Fine Art Castings, UK
OP: 80p NM: £3.50

MMM-102 Kiv (40mm)
1987, Fine Art Castings, UK
OP: 80p NM: £3.50

MMM-103 Leela (40mm)
1987, Fine Art Castings, UK
OP: 80p NM: £3.50

MMM-104 Mel (40mm)
1987, Fine Art Castings, UK
OP: 80p NM: £3.50

MMM-105 Mummy
1987, Fine Art Castings, UK
OP: £6.80 NM: £12

MMM-106 Mummy (40mm)
1987, Fine Art Castings, UK
OP: 80p NM: £3.50

MMM-107 Peri (40mm)
1987, Fine Art Castings, UK
OP: 80p NM: £3.50

MMM-108 Romana II (40mm)
1987, Fine Art Castings, UK
OP: 80p NM: £3.50

MMM-109 Sea Devil mk 2 (40mm)
1987, Fine Art Castings, UK
OP: 80p NM: £3.50

MMM-110 Sil
1987, Fine Art Castings, UK
OP: £5.75 NM: £12

MMM-111 Silurian (40mm)
1987, Fine Art Castings, UK
OP: 80p NM: £3.50

MMM-112 Vervoid (40mm)
1987, Fine Art Castings, UK
OP: 80p NM: £3.50

MMM-113 The Second Doctor from *The Power of the Daleks*
1997/11, Harlequin Miniatures, UK
Release 1. At the end of 1997 the Nottingham firm of Harlequin Miniatures launched a range of metal miniatures. They were around 40mm tall and generally good representations of the characters. They released boxed sets to tie in with their *Invasion Earth* tabletop game (see TYG-082). The figures were also available in multipacks.
REF: DW201 OP: £2.00

MMM-114 Zoe from *The Space Pirates*
1997/11, Harlequin Miniatures, UK
Release 1
REF: DW202 OP: £2.00

MMM-115 Jamie from *The Highlanders*
1997/11, Harlequin Miniatures, UK
Release 1
REF: DW203 OP: £2.00

MMM-113   MMM-114   MMM-115

MMM-116   MMM-117   MMM-118

MMM-119   MMM-120

MMM-116 Yeti from *The Abominable Snowmen*
1997/11, Harlequin Miniatures, UK
Release 1
REF: DW204 OP: £2.50

MMM-117 Ice Warrior from *The Ice Warriors*
1997/11, Harlequin Miniatures, UK
Release 1
REF: DW205 OP: £2.00

MMM-118 Cyberman from *Invasion*
1997/11, Harlequin Miniatures, UK
Release 1
REF: DW206 OP: £2.00

MMM-119 Cyberman from *The Tomb of the Cybermen*
1997/11, Harlequin Miniatures, UK
Release 1
REF: DW207 OP: £2.00

MMM-120 Sea Devil from *The Sea Devils*
1997/11, Harlequin Miniatures, UK
Release 1
REF: DW302 OP: £2.00

MMM-121

MMM-122

MMM-123

MMM-124

MMM-125

MMM-126

MMM-127

MMM-128

MMM-129

MMM-130

MMM-121 Dalek from *Death to the Daleks*
1997/11, Harlequin Miniatures, UK
Release 1
REF: DW303 OP: £2.50

MMM-122 UNIT Soldier
1997/11, Harlequin Miniatures, UK
Release 1
REF: DW403 OP: £2.00

MMM-123 UNIT soldier throwing grenade
1997/11, Harlequin Miniatures, UK
Release 1
REF: DW404 OP: £2.00

MMM-124 The Brigadier from *Battlefield*
1997/11, Harlequin Miniatures, UK
Release 1
REF: DW702 OP: £2.00

MMM-125 Blown up Dalek from *Resurrection of the Daleks*
1997/12, Harlequin Miniatures, UK
Release 2
REF: DW550 OP: £2.00

MMM-126 The First Doctor from *The Celestial Toymaker*
1997/12, Harlequin Miniatures, UK
Release 2
REF: DW101 OP: £2.00

MMM-127 Zarbi from *The Web Planet*
1997/12, Harlequin Miniatures, UK
Release 2
REF: DW102 OP: £2.50

MMM-128 Menoptra from *The Web Planet*
1997/12, Harlequin Miniatures, UK
Release 2
REF: DW103 OP: £2.00

MMM-129 Venom Gun from *The Web Planet*
1997/12, Harlequin Miniatures, UK
Release 2
REF: DW104 OP: £2.00

MMM-130 Cyberman firing gun from *The Invasion*
1997/12, Harlequin Miniatures, UK
Release 2
REF: DW208 OP: £2.00

MMM-131 Yeti attacking from *The Abominable Snowmen*
1997/12, Harlequin Miniatures, UK
Release 2
REF: DW209 OP: £2.50

MMM-132 Linx the Sontaran from *The Time Warrior*
1997/12, Harlequin Miniatures, UK
Release 2
REF: DW304 OP: £2.00

MMM-133 Engineer Dalek from *Death to the Daleks*
1997/12, Harlequin Miniatures, UK
Release 2
REF: DW305 OP: £2.50

MMM-134 Zygon from *Terror of the Zygons*
1997/12, Harlequin Miniatures, UK
Release 2
REF: DW405 OP: £2.00

MMM-135 The Sixth Doctor from *The Twin Dilemma*
1997/12, Harlequin Miniatures, UK
Release 2
REF: DW601 OP: £2.00

MMM-136 Peri from *The Twin Dilemma*
1997/12, Harlequin Miniatures, UK
Release 2
REF: DW602 OP: £2.00

MMM-137 The Master (Delgado)
1998, Harlequin Miniatures, UK
Send-off offer. Not available to buy. Tokens were needed from the backing packs of other figures, which meant they had to be bought and cut up to obtain this figure.
OP: free

MMM-138 Doctor Who and the Dinosaurs
1998, Harlequin Miniatures, UK
Boxed set of Third Doctor, Sarah, two UNIT troopers, a Pterodactyl and one giant T-Rex.
REF: DW1002 OP: £50.00

MMM-139 TARDIS
1998, Harlequin Miniatures, UK
Boxed set: First Doctor, Susan, the TARDIS console and the TARDIS.
REF: DW1004 OP: £25.00

MMM-131 MMM-132 MMM-133

MMM-134 MMM-135 MMM-136

MMM-137

MMM-138

MMM-139

MMM-141

MMM-142

MMM-143

MMM-144

MMM-145

MMM-1466

MMM-147

MMM-148

MMM-149

MMM-140 Bessie Box Set
1998, Harlequin Miniatures, UK
Boxed set: Bessie and others. No further information available.
OP: £25.00

MMM-141 Sarah Jane Smith from *Invasion of the Dinosaurs*
1998/01, Harlequin Miniatures, UK
Release 3
REF: DW306 OP: £2.00

MMM-142 Jo Grant from *Day of the Daleks*
1998/01, Harlequin Miniatures, UK
Release 3
REF: DW307 OP: £2.00

MMM-143 Silurian from *Doctor Who and the Silurians*
1998/01, Harlequin Miniatures, UK
Release 3
REF: DW308 OP: £2.00

MMM-144 Davros from *Genesis of the Daleks*
1998/01, Harlequin Miniatures, UK
Release 3
REF: DW406 OP: £2.50

MMM-145 Chumbly from *Galaxy 4*
1998/01, Harlequin Miniatures, UK
Release 3
REF: DW105 OP: £2.00

MMM-146 Susan from *The Daleks*
1998/01, Harlequin Miniatures, UK
Release 3
REF: DW108 OP: £2.00

MMM-147 Toymaker from *The Celestial Toymaker*
1998/01, Harlequin Miniatures, UK
Release 3
REF: DW109 OP: £2.00

MMM-148 The Third Doctor from *Invasion of the Dinosaurs*
1998/01, Harlequin Miniatures, UK
Release 3
REF: DW301 OP: £2.00

MMM-149 The Seventh Doctor from *Battlefield*
1998/01, Harlequin Miniatures, UK
Release 3
REF: DW701 OP: £2.00

MMM-150 Ace from *Battlefield*
1998/01, Harlequin Miniatures, UK
Release 3
REF: DW703 OP: £2.00

MMM-151 Axon monster from *The Claws of Axos*
1998/02, Harlequin Miniatures, UK
Release 4
REF: DW310 OP: £2.00

MMM-152 Marcus Scarman from *Pyramids of Mars*
1998/02, Harlequin Miniatures, UK
Release 4
REF: DW408 OP: £2.00

MMM-153 Namin from *Pyramids of Mars*
1998/02, Harlequin Miniatures, UK
Release 4
REF: DW409 OP: £2.00

MMM-154 The Fifth Doctor from *The Visitation*
1998/02, Harlequin Miniatures, UK
Release 4
REF: DW501 OP: £2.00

MMM-155 Adric from *The Visitation*
1998/02, Harlequin Miniatures, UK
Release 4
REF: DW502 OP: £2.00

MMM-156 Tegan from *The Visitation*
1998/02, Harlequin Miniatures, UK
Release 4
REF: DW503 OP: £2.00

MMM-150   MMM-151   MMM-152

MMM-157 Ian Chesterton
1998/02, Harlequin Miniatures, UK
Release 4
REF: DW106 OP: £2.00

MMM-158 Barbara Wright
1998/02, Harlequin Miniatures, UK
Release 4
REF: DW107 OP: £2.00

MMM-153   MMM-154   MMM-155

MMM-159 Dominator from *The Dominators*
1998/02, Harlequin Miniatures, UK
Release 4
REF: DW210 OP: £2.00

MMM-160 Axon humanoid from *The Claws of Axos*
1998/03, Harlequin Miniatures, UK
Release 5
REF: DW309 OP: £2.00

MMM-156   MMM-157   MMM-158

MMM-161 Romana from *The Armageddon Factor*
1998/03, Harlequin Miniatures, UK
Release 5
REF: DW402 OP: £2.00

MMM-162 Robot Mummy from *Pyramids of Mars*
1998/03, Harlequin Miniatures, UK
Release 5
REF: DW410 OP: £2.00

MMM-159   MMM-160   MMM-161

MMM-163 Robot from *Robot*
1998/03, Harlequin Miniatures, UK
Release 5
REF: DW411 OP: £3.00

MMM-164 Steven Taylor from *The Ark*
1998/03, Harlequin Miniatures, UK
Release 5
REF: DW110 OP: £2.00

MMM-162   MMM-163

MMM-165

MMM-166

MMM-167

MMM-168

MMM-169

MMM-170

MMM-171

MMM-173

MMM-174

MMM-175

MMM-177

MMM-178

MMM-179

MMM-165 Dodo Chaplet from *The Ark*
1998/03, Harlequin Miniatures, UK
Release 5
REF: DW111 OP: £2.00

MMM-166 Monoid from *The Ark*
1998/03, Harlequin Miniatures, UK
Release 5
REF: DW112 OP: £2.00

MMM-167 Rill from *Galaxy 4*
1998, Harlequin Miniatures, UK
REF: DW141 OP: £2.50

MMM-168 Ice Warrior attacking from *The Seeds of Death*
1998, Harlequin Miniatures, UK
REF: DW223 OP: £2.50

MMM-169 Sea Devil attacking from *The Sea Devils*
1998, Harlequin Miniatures, UK
REF: DW316 OP: £2.50

MMM-170 Aggedor from *The Curse of Peladon*
1998, Harlequin Miniatures, UK
REF: DW329 OP: £3.00

MMM-171 K9 from *The Armageddon Factor*
1998, Harlequin Miniatures, UK
REF: DW407 OP: £2.00

MMM-172 Zygon advancing from *Terror of the Zygons*
1998, Harlequin Miniatures, UK
REF: DW424 OP: £2.50

MMM-173 Mandrel from *Nightmare of Eden*
1998, Harlequin Miniatures, UK
REF: DW427 OP: £2.50

MMM-174 Nimon from *The Horns of Nimon*
1998, Harlequin Miniatures, UK
REF: DW428 OP: £3.00

MMM-175 'Death' from *The Visitation*
1998, Harlequin Miniatures, UK
REF: DW505 OP: £2.50

MMM-176 Romulus from *The Twin Dilemma*
1998, Harlequin Miniatures, UK
REF: DW608 OP: £2.00

MMM-177 The Eighth Doctor
1998, Harlequin Miniatures, UK
REF: DW801 OP: £2.50

MMM-178 Seventh Doctor with Dalek Jammer
1998, Harlequin Miniatures, UK
This item is listed in the Harlequin Catalogue as
DW805 although this is an Eighth Doctor code. Also
listed as DW720 (see MMM-215).
REF: DW805 OP: £2.50

MMM-179 Auton Dummy from *Spearhead from*
Space
1998/05, Harlequin Miniatures, UK
Release 7
REF: DW312 OP: £2.00

MMM-180 Sutekh on Throne from *Pyramids of*
Mars
1998/05, Harlequin Miniatures, UK
Release 7
REF: DW412 OP: £4.00

MMM-181 Weng Chiang from *The Talons of*
Weng-Chiang
1998/05, Harlequin Miniatures, UK
Release 7
REF: DW413 OP: £2.00

MMM-182 Mr Sin from *The Talons of Weng-*
Chiang
1998/05, Harlequin Miniatures, UK
Release 7
REF: DW414 OP: £2.00

MMM-183 Victorian Policeman from *The Talons*
of Weng-Chiang
1998/05, Harlequin Miniatures, UK
Release 7
REF: DW415 OP: £2.00

MMM-184 Leela from *The Robots of Death*
1998/05, Harlequin Miniatures, UK
Release 7
REF: DW416 OP: £2.00

MMM-185 Robot of Death from *The Robots of*
Death
1998/05, Harlequin Miniatures, UK
Release 7
REF: DW417 OP: £2.00

MMM-180   MMM-181   MMM-182

MMM-183   MMM-184   MMM-185

MMM-186   MMM-187   MMM-188

MMM-186 Nyssa from *The Visitation*
1998/05, Harlequin Miniatures, UK
Release 7
REF: DW504 OP: £2.00

MMM-187 Haemovore from *The Curse of*
Fenric
1998/05, Harlequin Miniatures, UK
Release 7
REF: DW704 OP: £2.00

MMM-188 The Ancient One from *The Curse of*
Fenric
1998/05, Harlequin Miniatures, UK
Release 7
REF: DW705 OP: £2.00

MMM-189 Li H'sen Chang from *The Talons of*
Weng-Chiang
1998/06, Harlequin Miniatures, UK
Release 8
REF: DW418 OP: £2.00

MMM-189 **MMM-190** **MMM-191**

MMM-193 **MMM-194**

MMM-196 **MMM-197**

MMM-190 Suicide Dalek from *Destiny of the Daleks*
1998/06, Harlequin Miniatures, UK
Release 8
REF: DW419 OP: £2.50

MMM-191 Turlough from *The Awakening*
1998/06, Harlequin Miniatures, UK
Release 8
REF: DW508 OP: £2.00

MMM-192 Captured Menoptra from *The Web Planet*
1998/06, Harlequin Miniatures, UK
Release 8
REF: DW113 OP: £2.00

MMM-193 Kroton from *The Krotons*
1998/06, Harlequin Miniatures, UK
Release 8
REF: DW212 OP: £2.00

MMM-194 Sea Devil from *Warriors of the Deep*
1998/06, Harlequin Miniatures, UK
Release 8
REF: DW510 OP: £2.00

MMM-195 Noma from *The Twin Dilemma*
1998/06, Harlequin Miniatures, UK
Release 8
REF: DW604 OP: £2.00

MMM-196 Mestor from *The Twin Dilemma*
1998/06, Harlequin Miniatures, UK
Release 8
REF: DW605 OP: £2.50

MMM-197 Mel from *The Trial of a Time Lord*
1998/06, Harlequin Miniatures, UK
Release 8
REF: DW606 OP: £2.00

MMM-198 Vervoid from *The Trial of a Time Lord*
1998/06, Harlequin Miniatures, UK
Release 8
REF: DW607 OP: £2.00

MMM-199 Android from *The Visitation*
1998/07, Harlequin Miniatures, UK
Release 9
REF: DW506 OP: £2.00

MMM-200 Terileptil from *The Visitation*
1998/07, Harlequin Miniatures, UK
Release 9
REF: DW507 OP: £2.00

MMM-201 Myrka from *Warriors of the Deep*
1998/07, Harlequin Miniatures, UK
Release 9
REF: DW509 OP: £8.00

MMM-202 Icthar from *Warriors of the Deep*
1998/07, Harlequin Miniatures, UK
Release 9
REF: DW511 OP: £2.00

MMM-203 Raston Warrior from *The Five Doctors*
1998/07, Harlequin Miniatures, UK
Release 9
REF: DW512 OP: £2.00

MMM-204 Drathro from *The Trial of a Time Lord*
1998/07, Harlequin Miniatures, UK
Release 9
REF: DW603 OP: £8.00

MMM-198

MMM-199

MMM-200

MMM-201

MMM-202

MMM-205 Ice Lord from *The Curse of Peladon*
1998/08, Harlequin Miniatures, UK
Release 10
REF: DW326 OP: £2.50

MMM-206 Omega Guard from *The Three Doctors*
1998/08, Harlequin Miniatures, UK
Release 10
REF: DW336 OP: £2.50

MMM-203

MMM-204

MMM-207 Exxilon from *Death to the Daleks*
1998/08, Harlequin Miniatures, UK
Release 10
REF: DW345 OP: £2.50

MMM-208 Professor Kettlewell from *Robot*
1998/08, Harlequin Miniatures, UK
Release 10
REF: DW420 OP: £2.50

MMM-207

MMM-208

MMM-209 Dalek Patrol from *Remembrance of the Daleks*
1998/08, Harlequin Miniatures, UK
Set of 6 Daleks and a Special Weapons Dalek.
REF: DW1001 OP: £16.99

MMM-210 Dalek Roboman from *The Daleks Invasion of Earth*
1998/08, Harlequin Miniatures, UK
Release 10
REF: DW127 OP: £2.50

MMM-209

MMM-211 Slyther from *The Dalek Invasion of Earth*
1998/08, Harlequin Miniatures, UK
Release 10
REF: DW128 OP: £2.50

MMM-212 Ben from *The War Machines*
1998/08, Harlequin Miniatures, UK
Release 10
REF: DW151 OP: £2.50

MMM-210

MMM-211

MMM-212

MMM-213

MMM-214

MMM-215

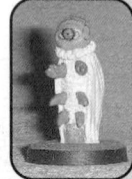

MMM-216

MMM-217

MMM-218

MMM-219

MMM-221

MMM-222

MMM-223

MMM-224

MMM-225

MMM-226

MMM-227

MMM-213 Polly from *The War Machines*
1998/08, Harlequin Miniatures, UK
Release 10
REF: DW152 OP: £2.50

MMM-214 Cyberman from *Earthshock*
1998/08, Harlequin Miniatures, UK
Release 10
REF: DW532 OP: £2.50

**MMM-215 Seventh Doctor with Dalek Jammer
from** *Remembrance of the Daleks*
1998/08, Harlequin Miniatures, UK
Release 10. See also MMM-178.
REF: DW720 OP: £2.50

MMM-216 Sgt Benton from *Day of the Daleks*
1998/09, Harlequin Miniatures, UK
Release 11
REF: DW323 OP: £2.50

MMM-217 Alpha Centauri from *The Curse of
Peladon*
1998/09, Harlequin Miniatures, UK
Release 11
REF: DW328 OP: £3.00

MMM-218 Harry Sullivan from *Genesis of the
Daleks*
1998/09, Harlequin Miniatures, UK
Release 11
REF: DW422 OP: £2.50

MMM-219 Robot Mummy attacking from
Pyramids of Mars
1998/09, Harlequin Miniatures, UK
Release 11
REF: DW474 OP: £3.00

MMM-220 Sontaran Warrior from *The Invasion
of Time*
1998/09, Harlequin Miniatures, UK
Release 11
REF: DW475 OP: £2.50

MMM-221 Optera from *The Web Planet*
1998/09, Harlequin Miniatures, UK
Release 11
REF: DW133 OP: £2.50

MMM-222 Auton dummy firing from
Spearhead from Space
1998/10, Harlequin Miniatures, UK
Release 12
REF: DW313 OP: £2.50

MMM-223 Bok from _The Dæmons_
1998/10, Harlequin Miniatures, UK
Release 12
REF: DW314 OP: £2.50

MMM-224 Draconian from _Frontier in Space_
1998/10, Harlequin Miniatures, UK
Release 12
REF: DW317 OP: £2.50

MMM-225 Captain Mike Yates from _Day of the Daleks_
1998/10, Harlequin Miniatures, UK
Release 12
REF: DW322 OP: £2.50

MMM-226 Ogron from _Day of the Daleks_
1998/10, Harlequin Miniatures, UK
Release 12
REF: DW324 OP: £2.50

MMM-227 Unit Patrol
1998/10, Harlequin Miniatures, UK
Boxed set of 7 UNIT troops.
REF: DW1003 OP: £15.00

MMM-228 Sand Beast from _The Rescue_
1998/10, Harlequin Miniatures, UK
Release 12
REF: DW131 OP: £3.00

MMM-229 Koquillion from _The Rescue_
1998/10, Harlequin Miniatures, UK
Release 12
REF: DW132 OP: £2.50

MMM-230 Vicki from _The Rescue_
1998/10, Harlequin Miniatures, UK
Release 12
REF: DW155 OP: £2.50

MMM-231 Sauvix from _Warriors of the Deep_
1990/10, Harlequin Miniatures, UK
Release 12
REF: DW513 OP: £2.50

MMM-232 Silurian Attacking from _Doctor Who and the Silurians_
1998/11, Harlequin Miniatures, UK
Release 13
REF: DW315 OP: £2.50

MMM-228

MMM-229   MMM-230

MMM-231   MMM-235   MMM-236

MMM-233 Dr Grace Holloway
1998/11, Harlequin Miniatures, UK
Release 13
REF: DW803 OP: £2.50

MMM-234 Chang Lee
1998/11, Harlequin Miniatures, UK
Release 13
REF: DW804 OP: £2.50

MMM-235 Morbius Monster from _The Brain of Morbius_
1998/11, Harlequin Miniatures, UK
Release 13
REF: DW426 OP: £2.50

MMM-236 President of Gallifrey from _The Deadly Assassin_
1998/11, Harlequin Miniatures, UK
Release 13
REF: DW430 OP: £3.00

MMM-237

MMM-238

MMM-239

MMM-240

MMM-241

MMM-242

MMM-243

MMM-244

MMM-245

MMM-247

MMM-237 Cyberman Firing from *Earthshock*
1998/11, Harlequin Miniatures, UK
Release 13
REF: DW533 OP: £2.50

MMM-238 Vervoid Advancing from *The Trial of a Time Lord*
1998/11, Harlequin Miniatures, UK
Release 13
REF: DW609 OP: £2.50

MMM-239 Sensorite from *The Sensorites*
1999/01, Harlequin Miniatures, UK
Release 14
REF: DW114 OP: £2.50

MMM-240 Frankenstein's Monster from *The Chase*
1999/01, Harlequin Miniatures, UK
Release 14
REF: DW126 OP: £4.00

MMM-241 Servo Robot from *The Wheel in Space*
1999/01, Harlequin Miniatures, UK
Release 14
REF: DW218 OP: £3.00

MMM-242 Terror Auton from *Terror of the Autons*
1999/01, Harlequin Miniatures, UK
Release 14
REF: DW318 OP: £2.50

MMM-243 Liz Shaw
1999/01, Harlequin Miniatures, UK
Release 14
REF: DW319 OP: £2.50

MMM-244 Decaying Master from *The Deadly Assassin*
1999/01, Harlequin Miniatures, UK
Release 14
REF: DW431 OP: £2.50

MMM-245 Mandrel Attacking from *Nightmare on Eden*
1999/01, Harlequin Miniatures, UK
Release 14
REF: DW432 OP: £2.50

MMM-246 Haemovore Attacking from *The Curse of Fenric*
1999/01, Harlequin Miniatures, UK
Release 14
REF: DW708 OP: £2.50

MMM-247 Invasion Earth Daleks
1999, Harlequin Miniatures, UK
Boxed Set containing; 7 MKII Daleks.
REF: DW1005 OP: £17.50

MMM-248 UNIT Heavy Weapons Squad
1999, Harlequin Miniatures, UK
Boxed Set containing: 6 miniatures comprising 1
Mortar team, 1 Bazooka team and 1 Bren gun team.
REF: DW1006 OP: £17.50

MMM-248

MMM-249 London Resistance
1999, Harlequin Miniatures, UK
Boxed set containing seven 'resistance' members.
REF: DW1007 OP: £15.00

MMM-250 The Whomobile
1999, Harlequin Miniatures, UK
Boxed set containing: Whomobile, Third Doctor and
Sarah Jane Smith.
REF: DW1008 OP: £15.00

MMM-249

**MMM-251 Mk I Cyberman from *The Tenth
Planet***
1999, Harlequin Miniatures, UK
REF: DW117 OP: £2.50

MMM-252 Alydon the Thal from *The Daleks*
1999, Harlequin Miniatures, UK
REF: DW118 OP: £2.50

MMM-253 Doc Holliday from *The Gunfighters*
1999, Harlequin Miniatures, UK
REF: DW119 OP: £2.50

MMM-250

MMM-254 Mechanoid from *The Chase*
1999, Harlequin Miniatures, UK
REF: DW120 OP: £3.00

**MMM-255 Dortmund from *The Dalek Invasion
of Earth***
1999, Harlequin Miniatures, UK
REF: DW130 OP: £2.50

MMM-251   **MMM-252**

MMM-256 Drahvin from *Galaxy 4*
1999, Harlequin Miniatures, UK
REF: DW142 OP: £2.50

MMM-257 Kroton armed from *The Krotons*
1999, Harlequin Miniatures, UK
REF: DW214 OP: £2.50

MMM-254   **MMM-255**   **MMM-256**

MMM-257   **MMM-258**   **MMM-259**

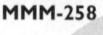

MMM-260   **MMM-262**

MMM-263   **MMM-264**   **MMM-265**

MMM-266   **MMM-267**   **MMM-268**

MMM-269   **MMM-271**

MMM-272   **MMM-275**   **MMM-276**   **MMM-277**   **MMM-278**   **MMM-279**

MMM-258 Clockwork Soldier from *The Mind Robber*
1999, Harlequin Miniatures, UK
REF: DW215 OP: £2.50

MMM-259 Cyber-Laser Cannon Team from *The Moonbase*
1999, Harlequin Miniatures, UK
Contains two Cybermen and a laser cannon.
REF: DW216 OP: £6.00

MMM-260 Primitive from *Colony in Space*
1999, Harlequin Miniatures, UK
REF: DW320 OP: £2.50

MMM-261 Ogron attacking from *Day of the Daleks*
1999, Harlequin Miniatures, UK
REF: DW325 OP: £2.50

MMM-262 Azal the Dæmon from *The Daemons*
1999, Harlequin Miniatures, UK
REF: DW327 OP: £2.50

MMM-263 UNIT Trooper with SMG
1999, Harlequin Miniatures, UK
REF: DW423 OP: £2.50

MMM-264 Scaroth of the Jagaroth from *City of Death*
1999, Harlequin Miniatures, UK
REF: DW425 OP: £2.50

MMM-265 Vorus Vogan Leader from *Revenge of the Cybermen*
1999, Harlequin Miniatures, UK
REF: DW429 OP: £2.50

MMM-266 Kellman from *Revenge of the Cybermen*
1999, Harlequin Miniatures, UK
REF: DW433 OP: £2.50

MMM-267 Romana II
1999, Harlequin Miniatures, UK
REF: DW435 OP: £2.50

MMM-268 Foamasi from *The Leisure Hive*
1999, Harlequin Miniatures, UK
REF: DW436 OP: £2.50

MMM-269 Wirrn from *The Ark in Space*
1999, Harlequin Miniatures, UK
REF: DW437 OP: £3.00

MMM-270 Robot of Death attacking from *The Robots of Death*
1999, Harlequin Miniatures, UK
REF: DW438 OP: £2.50

MMM-271 Katrycia from *The Trial of a Time Lord*
1999, Harlequin Miniatures, UK
REF: DW610 OP: £2.50

MMM-272 Cryon from *Attack of the Cybermen*
1999, Harlequin Miniatures, UK
REF: DW611 OP: £2.50

MMM-273 Urak the Tetrap from *Time and the Rani*
1999, Harlequin Miniatures, UK
REF: DW706 OP: £2.50

MMM-274 Pipe Person from *The Happiness Patrol*
1999, Harlequin Miniatures, UK
REF: DW707 OP: £2.50

MMM-275 Cheetah Person from *Survival*
1999, Harlequin Miniatures, UK
REF: DW709 OP: £2.50

MMM-276 Kandy Man from *The Happiness Patrol*
1999, Harlequin Miniatures, UK
REF: DW710 OP: £3.00

MMM-277 The Destroyer from *Battlefield*
1999, Harlequin Miniatures, UK
REF: DW711 OP: £3.00

MMM-278 Roboman 2151 from *Daleks: Invasion Earth 2150 AD*
1999, Harlequin Miniatures, UK
Model from the film.
REF: DW902 OP: £2.50

MMM-279 Dalek Mk 3 from *Daleks: Invasion Earth 2150 AD*
1999, Harlequin Miniatures, UK
Model from the film.
REF: DW903 OP: £3.00

MMM-280 Tltoxl from *The Aztecs*
1999, Harlequin Miniatures, UK
REF: DW115 OP: £2.50

MMM-281 Sara Kingdom from *The Daleks' Master Plan*
1999, Harlequin Miniatures, UK
REF: DW116 OP: £2.50

MMM-282 Roboman from *The Dalek Invasion of Earth*
1999, Harlequin Miniatures, UK
REF: DW127 OP: £2.50

MMM-283 Roboman Guard from *The Dalek Invasion of Earth*
1999, Harlequin Miniatures, UK
REF: DW129 OP: £2.50

MMM-284 The Emperor Dalek from *The Evil of the Daleks*
1999, Harlequin Miniatures, UK
REF: DW213 OP: £8.00

MMM-285 22nd Century Guerrila from *Day of the Daleks*
1999, Harlequin Miniatures, UK
REF: DW321 OP: £2.50

MMM-280   **MMM-281**   **MMM-282**

MMM-284   **MMM-285**

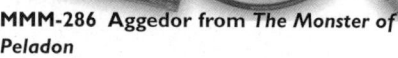

MMM-286

MMM-287

MMM-288

MMM-289

MMM-290

MMM-291

MMM-293

MMM-294

MMM-295

MMM-296

MMM-297

MMM-299

MMM-286 Aggedor from *The Monster of Peladon*
1999, Harlequin Miniatures, UK
REF: DW329 OP: £3.00

MMM-287 Commander Andred from *The Invasion of Time*
1999, Harlequin Miniatures, UK
REF: DW421 OP: £2.50

MMM-288 Vogan Warrior from *Revenge of the Cybermen*
1999, Harlequin Miniatures, UK
REF: DW434 OP: £2.50

MMM-289 Master II (1981)
1999, Harlequin Miniatures, UK
REF: DW449 OP: £2.50

MMM-290 Scibus from *Warriors of the Deep*
1999, Harlequin Miniatures, UK
REF: DW514 OP: £2.50

MMM-291 The Seventh Doctor
1999, Harlequin Miniatures, UK
REF: DW701 OP: £2.50

MMM-292 The Master (1996)
1999, Harlequin Miniatures, UK
REF: DW805 OP: £2.50

MMM-293 Shrivenzale from *The Ribos Operation*
1999, Harlequin Miniatures, UK
REF: DW444 OP: £2.50

MMM-294 Garron from *The Ribos Operation*
1999, Harlequin Miniatures, UK
REF: DW446 OP: £2.50

MMM-295 Vivien Fay from *The Stones of Blood*
1999, Harlequin Miniatures, UK
REF: DW443 OP: £2.50

MMM-296 Tharil from *Warriors' Gate*
1999, Harlequin Miniatures, UK
REF: DW447 OP: £2.50

MMM-297 Cailleach from *The Stones of Blood*
1999, Harlequin Miniatures, UK
REF: DW442 OP: £2.50

MMM-300

MMM-301

MMM-302

MMM-298 Swampie Warrior from *The Power of Kroll*
1999, Harlequin Miniatures, UK
REF: DW445 OP: £2.50

MMM-299 Cyber-Controller (1967) from *The Tomb of the Cybermen*
1999, Harlequin Miniatures, UK
Incorrect body on initial release.
REF: DW217 OP: £2.50

MMM-300 UNIT Land Rover
1999, Harlequin Miniatures, UK
Set includes Land Rover, new Brigadier and UNIT Trooper with SLR.
REF: DW1010 OP: £25.00

MMM-301 Voord Warrior from *The Keys of Marinus*
1999/09, Harlequin Miniatures, UK
Release 22
REF: DW121 OP: £2.50

MMM-302 The Karkus from *The Mind Robber*
1999/09, Harlequin Miniatures, UK
Release 22
REF: DW220 OP: £2.50

MMM-303 Swampie Leader from *The Power of Kroll*
1999/09, Harlequin Miniatures, UK
Release 22
REF: DW448 OP: £2.50

MMM-304 Count Grendel from *The Androids of Tara*
1999/09, Harlequin Miniatures, UK
Release 22
REF: DW450 OP: £2.50

MMM-305 Pirate Guard from *The Pirate Planet*
1999/09, Harlequin Miniatures, UK
Release 22
REF: DW452 OP: £2.50

MMM-306 The Marshall from *The Armageddon Factor*
1999/09, Harlequin Miniatures, UK
Release 22
REF: DW453 OP: £2.50

MMM-307 Autons from *Terror of the Autons*
1999/09, Harlequin Miniatures, UK
Release 22. Set includes a Terror Auton Leader and six Autons.
REF: DW1013 OP: £15.00

MMM-304

MMM-306

MMM-307

MMM-308

MMM-309

MMM-310

MMM-311

MMM-314

MMM-315

MMM-316

MMM-317

MMM-308   Ice Warriors
1999/09, Harlequin Miniatures, UK
Release 22. Set includes Lord Izlyr and 6 new Ice
Warriors.
REF: DW1011   OP: £15.00

MMM-309   White Robot from *The Mind Robber*
1999/10, Harlequin Miniatures, UK
Release 23
REF: DW221   OP: £2.50

MMM-310   Omega 1st from *The Three Doctors*
1999/10, Harlequin Miniatures, UK
Release 23
REF: DW330   OP: £2.50

MMM-311   Melkur from *The Keeper of Traken*
1999/10, Harlequin Miniatures, UK
Release 23
REF: DW455   OP: £3.00

MMM-312   Fendahleen from *Image of the Fendahl*
1999/10, Harlequin Miniatures, UK
Release 23
REF: DW456   OP: £8.00

MMM-313   Rhom Dutt from *The Power of Kroll*
1999/10, Harlequin Miniatures, UK
Release 23
REF: DW457   OP: £2.50

**MMM-314   Sharaz Jek from *The Caves of
Androzani***
1999/10, Harlequin Miniatures, UK
Release 23
REF: DW516   OP: £2.50

**MMM-315   Stike the Sontaran from *The Two
Doctors***
1999/10, Harlequin Miniatures, UK
Release 23
REF: DW613   OP: £2.50

MMM-316   Cyberman Box Set
1999/11, Harlequin Miniatures, UK
Release 23. Contains 6 Cybermen and a Cyber-
Controller. Delayed by a month.
REF: DW1014   OP: £15.00

MMM-317   Second Doctor
1999, Harlequin Miniatures, UK
Send-off offer. Not available to buy.
OP: free

MMM-318 Terror Auton with flowers from
Terror of the Autons
1999/11, Harlequin Miniatures, UK
Release 24
REF: DW331 OP: £2.50

MMM-319 The Captain from *The Pirate Planet*
1999/11, Harlequin Miniatures, UK
Release 24
REF: DW451 OP: £2.50

MMM-320 Professor Chronotis from *Shada*
1999/11, Harlequin Miniatures, UK
Release 24
REF: DW458 OP: £2.50

MMM-321 Sil from *Vengeance on Varos*
1999/11, Harlequin Miniatures, UK
Release 24
REF: DW614 OP: £2.50

MMM-322 Remus from *The Twin Dilemma*
1999/11, Harlequin Miniatures, UK
Release 24
REF: DW615 OP: £2.50

MMM-323 Shockeye from *The Two Doctors*
1999/11, Harlequin Miniatures, UK
Release 24
REF: DW616 OP: £2.50

MMM-324 Gavrok from *Delta and the*
Bannermen
1999/11, Harlequin Miniatures, UK
Release 24
REF: DW712 OP: £2.50

MMM-325 Guards of Gallifrey
1999/11, Harlequin Miniatures, UK
Release 24. Contains 7 new Gallifrey guards.
REF: DW1016 OP: £15.00

MMM-326 Sea Devils
1999/11, Harlequin Miniatures, UK
Release 24. Contains 7 new Sea Devils
REF: DW1015 OP: £15.00

MMM-327 Nero from *The Romans*
1999/12, Harlequin Miniatures, UK
Release 25.
REF: DW122 OP: £2.50

MMM-318   MMM-320

MMM-321   MMM-323

MMM-325

MMM-326

MMM-327

MMM-328   MMM-329   MMM-330

MMM-331   MMM-332   MMM-333

MMM-334

MMM-335   MMM-337

MMM-339   MMM-340

MMM-342

MMM-345

MMM-328 Ambassador from *The Ambassadors of Death*
1999/12, Harlequin Miniatures, UK
Release 25.
REF: DW332 OP: £2.50

MMM-329 Hyperion Passenger from *Nightmare on Eden*
1999/12, Harlequin Miniatures, UK
Release 25.
REF: DW617 OP: £2.50

MMM-330 The Bus Conductor from *The Greatest Show in the Galaxy*
1999/12, Harlequin Miniatures, UK
Release 25.
REF: DW714 OP: £2.50

MMM-331 Morgaine from *Battlefield*
1999/12, Harlequin Miniatures, UK
Release 25.
REF: DW715 OP: £2.50

MMM-332 The Doctor from *Daleks Invasion Earth 2150 AD* film
1999/12, Harlequin Miniatures, UK
Release 25.
REF: DW901 OP: £2.50

MMM-333 Barbara from *Daleks Invasion Earth 2150 AD* film
1999/12, Harlequin Miniatures, UK
Release 25.
REF: DW904 OP: £2.50

MMM-334 Draconians from *Frontier in Space*
1999/12, Harlequin Miniatures, UK
Release 25. Contains 7 new Draconians
REF: DW1012 OP: £15.00

MMM-335 King Peladon from *The Curse of Peladon*
2000/01, Harlequin Miniatures, UK
Release 26.
REF: DW333 OP: £2.50

MMM-336 Servant of Sutekh from *Pyramids of Mars*
2000/01, Harlequin Miniatures, UK
Release 26.
REF: DW459 OP: £2.50

MMM-337 Movellan Warrior from *Destiny of the Daleks*
2000/01, Harlequin Miniatures, UK
Release 26.
REF: DW460 OP: £2.50

MMM-338 Drak from *The Twin Dilemma*
2000/01, Harlequin Miniatures, UK
Release 26.
REF: DW618 OP: £2.50

MMM-339 Bannerman from *Delta and the Bannermen*
2000/01, Harlequin Miniatures, UK
Release 26.
REF: DW713 OP: £2.50

MMM-340 The Dragon from *Dragonfire*
2000/01, Harlequin Miniatures, UK
Release 26.
REF: DW716 OP: £2.50

MMM-341 Mounted Cheetah person from *Survival*
2000/01, Harlequin Miniatures, UK
Release 26.
REF: DW717 OP: £4.00

MMM-342 War Machines
2000/01, Harlequin Miniatures, UK
Release 26. Contains two War Machines.
REF: DW1017 OP: £20.00

MMM-343 Caveman from *100,000 BC*
2000/04, Harlequin Miniatures, UK
Release 27. Scheduled for Feb.
REF: DW123 OP: £2.50

MMM-344 Optra Attacking from *The Web Planet*
2000/04, Harlequin Miniatures, UK
Release 27. Scheduled for Feb.
REF: DW124 OP: £2.50

MMM-345 Voord Leader from *The Keys of Marinus*
2000/04, Harlequin Miniatures, UK
Release 27. Scheduled for Feb.
REF: DW125 OP: £2.50

MMM-346 Sensorite Attacking from *The Sensorites*
2000/04, Harlequin Miniatures, UK
Release 27. Scheduled for Feb.
REF: DW134 OP: £2.50

MMM-349   MMM-352   MMM-355

MMM-347 Cyberleader from *Earthshock*
2000/04, Harlequin Miniatures, UK
Release 27. Scheduled for Feb.
REF: DW517 OP: £2.50

MMM-348 Sharaz Jek Android from *The Caves of Androzani*
2000/04, Harlequin Miniatures, UK
Release 27. Scheduled for Feb.
REF: DW518 OP: £2.50

MMM-349 Lieutenant Scott from *Earthshock*
2000/04, Harlequin Miniatures, UK
Release 27. Scheduled for Feb.
REF: DW519 OP: £2.50

MMM-350 Dalek Troopers
2000/04, Harlequin Miniatures, UK
Release 27. Scheduled for Feb. Contains six Dalek Troopers and one Leader.
REF: DW1018 OP: £15.00

MMM-351 Monoid II from *The Ark*
2000/05, Harlequin Miniatures, UK
Release 28.
REF: DW138 OP: £2.50

MMM-352 Aridian from *The Chase*
2000/05, Harlequin Miniatures, UK
Release 28.
REF: DW139 OP: £2.50

MMM-353 Cowboy from *The Chase*
2000/05, Harlequin Miniatures, UK
Release 28.
REF: DW140 OP: £2.50

MMM-354 Pirate from *The Smugglers*
2000/05, Harlequin Miniatures, UK
Release 28.
REF: DW143 OP: £2.50

MMM-355 The Fourth Doctor II from *The Talons of Weng-Chiang*
2000/05, Harlequin Miniatures, UK
Release 28.
REF: DW462 OP: £2.50

MMM-356

MMM-357

MMM-358

MMM-360

MMM-361

MMM-362

MMM-364

MMM-365

MMM-366

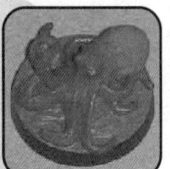
MMM-367

MMM-369
(seen behind
MMM-240)

MMM-371

MMM-373

MMM-375

MMM-356 Hieronymous from *The Masque of Mandragora*
2000/05, Harlequin Miniatures, UK
Release 28.
REF: DW463 OP: £2.50

MMM-357 The Nucleus from *The Invisible Enemy*
2000/05, Harlequin Miniatures, UK
Release 28.
REF: DW464 OP: £2.50

MMM-358 King John from *The King's Demons*
2000/05, Harlequin Miniatures, UK
Release 28.
REF: DW521 OP: £2.50

MMM-359 Rutan from *Horror of Fang Rock*
2000/06, Harlequin Miniatures, UK
Release 29.
REF: DW465 OP: £2.50

MMM-360 The Monitor from *Logopolis*
2000/06, Harlequin Miniatures, UK
Release 29.
REF: DW466 OP: £2.50

MMM-361 The Fifth Doctor II
2000/06, Harlequin Miniatures, UK
Release 29.
REF: DW599 OP: £2.50

MMM-362 Little Susan from *Dr Who and the Daleks*
2000/06, Harlequin Miniatures, UK
Release 29.
REF: DW905 OP: £2.50

MMM-363 Napoleon from *The French Revolution*
2000/06, Harlequin Miniatures, UK
Release 29.
REF: DW144 OP: £2.50

MMM-364 The First Doctor II
2000/06, Harlequin Miniatures, UK
Release 29.
REF: DW199 OP: £2.50

MMM-365 The Fourth Doctor III
2000/06, Harlequin Miniatures, UK
Release 29.
REF: DW499 OP: £2.50

MMM-366 The Third Doctor II
2000/06, Harlequin Miniatures, UK
Release 29.
REF: DW399 OP: £2.50

MMM-367 Mire Beast from *The Chase*
2000/07, Harlequin Miniatures, UK
Release 30.
REF: DW145 OP: £2.50

MMM-368 Abraham Lincoln from *The Chase*
2000/07, Harlequin Miniatures, UK
Release 30.
REF: DW146 OP: £2.50

MMM-369 Count Dracula from *The Chase*
2000/07, Harlequin Miniatures, UK
Release 30.
REF: DW147 OP: £2.50

MMM-370 Algernon ffinch from *The Highlanders*
2000/07, Harlequin Miniatures, UK
Release 30.
REF: DW224 OP: £2.50

MMM-371 Gell Guard II from *The Three Doctors*
2000/07, Harlequin Miniatures, UK
Release 30.
REF: DW347 OP: £2.50

MMM-372 Styggron the Kraal from *The Android Invasion*
2000/07, Harlequin Miniatures, UK
Release 30.
REF: DW467 OP: £2.50

MMM-373 Kameleon from *The King's Demons*
2000/07, Harlequin Miniatures, UK
Release 30.
REF: DW534 OP: £2.50

MMM-374 Sontaran with rifle from *The Two Doctors*
2000/07, Harlequin Miniatures, UK
Release 30.
REF: DW619 OP: £2.50

MMM-375 Mark II Dalek
2001/06, Media Collectables, UK
Resin base and body section. Metal neck and head section. Metal Arms. Small model kit of a Mark II Dalek. The manufacturers termed this Mark II as

Davros' chair was considered Mark I.
REF: D01 OP: £7.50

MMM-376 Emperor Dalek
2001/06, Media Collectables, UK
Resin base and head section. Metal Arms. This is the Emperor from *TV Century 21*.
REF: D02 OP: £7.50

MMM-377 Dalek Flying Disk (Hoverbout)
2001/06, Media Collectables, UK
Resin Disk with metal rin and railing sections.
REF: D03 OP: £6.50

MMM-378 Mark II Dalek Scout Unit
2001/06, Media Collectables, UK
Five of the D01 Daleks.
REF: D04 OP: £30.00

MMM-379 Mark II Dalek Attack Squad
2001/06, Media Collectables, UK
Ten of the D01 Daleks.
REF: D05 OP: £60.00

MMM-376 (shown with Daleks)

MMM-377 (shown with Dalek)

MMM-378

MMM-387

MMM-381

MMM-385

MMM-380 Mark II Dalek Hoverbout Patrol
2001/06, Media Collectables, UK
Three Daleks and Three Hoverbouts.
REF: D06 OP: £35.00

MMM-381 Mark III Dalek
2001/08, Media Collectables, UK
Resin base and body. Metal neck and head section.
Metal Arms. Dalek has shoulder slats added.
REF: D07 OP: £7.50

MMM-382 Mark III Dalek Scout Unit
2001/08, Media Collectables, UK
Five of the D07 Daleks.
REF: D08 OP: £30.00

MMM-383 Mark III Dalek Attack Squad
2001/08, Media Collectables, UK
Ten of the D07 Daleks.
REF: D09 OP: £60.00

MMM-384 Mark II Dalek on Hoverbout
2001/08, Media Collectables, UK
Mark III Dalek and Hoverbout set.
REF: D10 OP: £12.50

MMM-385 Mechanoid
2001/10, Media Collectables, UK
Resin body with metal arms. Taken from *TV Century 21*.
REF: D11 OP: £10.00

MMM-386 Mechanoid Defence unit
2001/10, Media Collectables, UK
Three Mechanoids Taken from *TV Century 21*.
REF: D12 OP: £27.50

MMM-388

MMM-389

MMM-390

MMM-393

**MMM-392 (with
Daleks & Cyberman)**

MMM-394

MMM-395

MMM-396

MMM-397

MMM-398

MMM-399

MMM-400

MMM-401

MMM-402

MMM-387 2K Robot
2001/10, Media Collectables, UK
Taken from the *TV Century 21* comic strip.
REF: D13 OP: £7.50

MMM-388 10th Planet Cyberman Leader
2002/05, Media Collectables, UK
REF: D14 OP: £7.50

MMM-389 10th Planet Cyberman Attacking
2002/05, Media Collectables, UK
REF: D15 OP: £7.50

MMM-390 10th Planet Cyberman Firing
2002/05, Media Collectables, UK
REF: D16 OP: £7.50

MMM-391 Cyberman Unit
2002/05, Media Collectables, UK
Set of D14, D15 and D16.
REF: D17 OP: £20.00

MMM-392 Special Weapons Dalek
2002/08, Media Collectables, UK
REF: D18 OP: £8.50

MMM-393 Davros
2002/08, Media Collectables, UK
REF: D19 OP: £7.50

MMM-394 Yeti
2001/12, Alector, UK
Exclusively available from The Who Shop. The Alector
line of miniatures was available in 35mm painted and
unpainted versions; the first reference number refers
to the painted version.
REF: 71006 / 81006
OP: £3.99 unpainted / £7.99 painted

MMM-395 Zygon
2001/12, Alector, UK
REF: 71004 / 81004
OP: £3.99 unpainted / £7.99 painted

MMM-396 Silurian
2001/12, Alector, UK
REF: 71005 / 81005
OP: £3.99 unpainted / £7.99 painted

MMM-397 Sea Devil
2001/12, Alector, UK
REF: 71011 / 81011
OP: £3.99 unpainted / £7.99 painted

MMM-398 Timelord
2001/12, Alector, UK
REF: 71001 / 81001
OP: £3.99 unpainted / £7.99 painted

MMM-399 Movellan
2001/12, Alector, UK
REF: 71019 / 81019
OP: £3.99 unpainted / £7.99 painted

MMM-400 Davros
2001/12, Alector, UK
REF: 71017 / 81017
OP: £3.99 unpainted / £7.99 painted

MMM-401 Dalek Trooper
2001/12, Alector, UK
REF: 71007 / 81007
OP: £3.99 unpainted / £7.99 painted

MMM-402 Armoured Sea Devil
2001/12, Alector, UK
REF: 71020 / 81020
OP: £3.99 unpainted / £7.99 painted

MMM-403 Ice Warrior
2001/12, Alector, UK
REF: 71013 / 81013
OP: £3.99 unpainted / £7.99 painted

MMM-404 Ice Lord
2001/12, Alector, UK
REF: 71018 / 81018
OP: £3.99 unpainted / £7.99 painted

MMM-405 Draconian
2001/12, Alector, UK
REF: 71009 / 81009
OP: £3.99 unpainted / £7.99 painted

MMM-406 Omega (2)
2001/12, Alector, UK
REF: 71012 / 81012
OP: £3.99 unpainted / £7.99 painted

MMM-407 Aggedor
2001/12, Alector, UK
REF: 71008 / 81008
OP: £3.99 unpainted / £7.99 painted

MMM-408 Alpha Centauri
2001/12, Alector, UK
REF: 71014 / 81014
OP: £3.99 unpainted / £7.99 painted

MMM-403

MMM-404

MMM-405

MMM-406

MMM-407

MMM-408

MMM-409

MMM-410

MMM-411

MMM-412

MMM-413

MMM-414

MMM-409 Cyberman (Silver Nemesis)
2001/12, Alector, UK
REF: 71016 / 81016
OP: £3.99 unpainted / £7.99 painted

MMM-410 Ogron
2001/12, Alector, UK
REF: 71003 / 81003
OP: £3.99 unpainted / £7.99 painted

MMM-411 Sontaran
2001/12, Alector, UK
REF: 71010 / 81010
OP: £3.99 unpainted / £7.99 painted

MMM-412 Voc Robot
2001/12, Alector, UK
REF: 71015 / 81015
OP: £3.99 unpainted / £7.99 painted

MMM-413 Melkur
2001/12, Alector, UK
REF: 71002 / 81002
OP: £3.99 unpainted / £7.99 painted

MMM-414 Sontaran (75mm)
2002, Alector, UK
75mm model.
REF: 91001 / 91002
OP: £8.00 unpainted / £9.99 painted

MMM-415 Daleks
2002, Alector, UK
35mm models. Mark I Black Movie; Mark I Red
Movie; Mark I Silver Movie; Mark II Black Movie; Mark
II Red Movie; Mark II Gold Movie; Mark I Silver TV;
Mark III Black TV; Mark III Grey TV; Mark III Silver TV.
OP: £3.99 unpainted / £7.99 painted

MMM-416 Cyberman (60s)
2002, Alector, UK
35mm models. Mark I Black Movie; Mark I Red
Movie; Mark I Silver Movie; Mark II Black Movie; Mark
II Red Movie; Mark II Gold Movie; Mark I Silver TV;
Mark III Black TV; Mark III Grey TV; Mark III Silver TV.
OP: £3.99 unpainted / £7.99 painted

MMM-417 Cyberman (75mm)
2002, Alector, UK
35mm models. Mark I Black Movie; Mark I Red
Movie; Mark I Silver Movie; Mark II Black Movie; Mark
II Red Movie; Mark II Gold Movie; Mark I Silver TV;
Mark III Black TV; Mark III Grey TV; Mark III Silver TV.
OP: £8.00 unpainted / £9.99 painted

MODELS, GENERAL

GENERAL models are characters fron *Doctor Who* which do not require assembling or painting. This section does not include metal miniatures which can be found in a section of their own.

MOD-001 Fourth Doctor
1983, Susan Moore, UK
Painted resin figure. Susan Moore was a fan of the series and produced a range of resin figures for the fan market during 1982 and 1983. Her initial range consisted of three small resin badges of an Ice Warrior head, a Robot of Death head (which came in silver, green or black) and a Cybermat as well as small resin figures of the Fourth Doctor and the Master. She also produced various designs of 'Cyber-logo' as seen on the door of the CyberController's tomb in *The Tomb of the Cybermen* and a range of photographic stickers and keyrings.
OP: £2.00 – £5.00

MOD-002 Master in cloak
1983, Susan Moore, UK
4" high painted resin figure.
OP: £2.00 – £5.00

MOD-003 Master in suit
1983, Susan Moore, UK
4" high painted resin figure.
OP: £2.00 – £5.00

MOD-004 Menoptra
1983, Susan Moore, UK
4" high painted resin figure with thin and fragile clear resin wings.
OP: £2.00 – £5.00

MOD-005 Robot of Death
1983, Susan Moore, UK
4" high painted resin figure. Came in silver, green or black.
OP: £2.00 – £5.00

MOD-006 Sontaran
1983, Susan Moore, UK
4" high painted resin figure.
OP: £2.00 – £5.00

MOD-007 TARDIS
1983, Susan Moore, UK
Painted resin facsimile of the small metal Dinky police box model first released in the fifties.
OP: £2.00 – £5.00

MOD-001   MOD-002

MOD-003

MOD-004

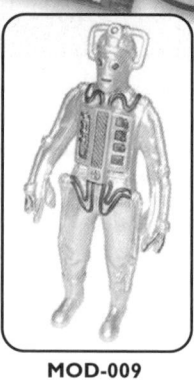

| MOD-005 | MOD-006 | MOD-008 | MOD-009 | MOD-010 |

MOD-008 Time Lord
1983, Susan Moore, UK
4" high painted resin figure in full ceremonial regalia
from *The Deadly Assassin*.
OP: £2.00 – £5.00

MOD-009 Early Cyberman
2001/08, Dapol, UK
Immobile resin figure of a 'Moonbase' style Cyberman.
REF: W026   OP: £7.00

MOD-010 Troughton Figure
2001/11, Dapol, UK
Immobile resin figure of the second Doctor. A figure
of the first Doctor was also planned but never
released. Dapol's *Doctor Who* licence was not renewed
when it ended at the start of 2002 and production of
all their *Doctor Who* ranges stopped thereafter.
OP: £7.00

MOD-011 Sontaran Figure
2002/03, Product Enterprises Ltd, UK

6" tall figure.
OP: £24.99

MOD-012 Zygon Figure
2002/03, Product Enterprises Ltd, UK
6" tall figure.
OP: £24.99

MOD-013 Quark Figure
2002/03, Product Enterprises Ltd, UK
6" tall figure.
OP: £24.99

MOD-014 Sensorite Figure
2002/03, Product Enterprises Ltd, UK
6" tall figure.
OP: £24.99

MOD-015 Draconian Figure
2002/03, Product Enterprises Ltd, UK
6" tall figure.
OP: £24.99

| MOD-011 | MOD-012 | MOD-013 | MOD-014 | MOD-015 |

MODELS, KITS

PLASTIC or resin kits which require assembly and painting.

MOK-001 Dalek
1984/07, Sevans Models, UK
1:5 scale. Accurate but hard to construct scale model.
OP: £11.95 NM: £45

MOK-002 Ice Warrior
1987, Sevans Models, UK
1:5 scale.
OP: £15.95

MOK-003 K9
1987/09, Sevans Models, UK
OP: £13.95

MOK-004 Cyberman
1988, Sevans Models, UK
1:5 scale.
OP: £17.95 NM: £47

MOK-005 Davros #1
1989, Sevans Models, UK
1:5 scale.
OP: £19.95 NM: £47

MOK-006 TV and Movie Type Daleks
1989, Sevans Models, UK
Delayed from 1987.
OP: £17.95 NM: £47

MOK-007 CyberController
1991, Sevans Models, UK
Limited edition.
OP: £45.00 NM: £47

MOK-008 Davros #2
1991, Sevans Models, UK
Limited edition. Head and body sculpted by Peter McKenna.
OP: £45.00 NM: £47

MOK-009 K9
1997/10, Sevans Models, UK
OP: £42.95 NM: £55

MOK-010 TARDIS
1997/10, Sevans Models, UK
OP: £59.95 NM: £55

MOK-001   MOK-002

MOK-004

MOK-005

MOK-007   MOK-008

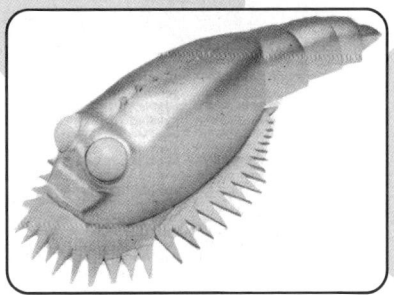

MOK-011 (assembled)

MOK-012

MOK-013

MOK-011 Cybermat
1985/09, BCP Promotions, UK
Actual size. BCP Promotions was set up by fan Barry
Payne. The kit sold around 350 units in the two
months following its launch in April 1985.
OP: £9.80

MOK-012 Mk1 Television Dalek
1992, Comet Miniatures, UK
1:8 scale plastic injection kit. Builds one of two versions.
REF: CM009 OP: £18.95 NM: £26

MOK-013 Jon Pertwee
1993, Amarang/Comet Miniatures, UK
1:8 scale vinyl model kit. Sculpted by David Pamelroy
and Robin. Limited to 250. Kit came with a cape and
sonic screwdriver.
OP: £43.00

MOK-014 Mk3 Movie Dalek
1993, Comet Miniatures, UK
1:8 scale plastic injection kit. Builds one of two versions.
REF: CM010 OP: £19.99 NM: £26

MOK-015 Patrick Troughton
1993, Amarang/Comet Miniatures, UK
1:8 scale vinyl model kit. Sculpted by David Pamelroy.
REF: CM013(V) OP: £29.99

MOK-016 Tom Baker as Doctor Who
1993, Amarang/Comet Miniatures, UK
1:8 scale vinyl model kit. Sculpted by David Pamelroy.
Other promised kits did not appear (Delgado,
Cyberman, Hartnell).
REF: CM014(V) OP: £29.50

MOK-014

MOK-015

MOK-015 (box)

MOK-016

MOK-016 (box)

MODELS, PLASTIC MINIATURES

MPL-001 Daleks & Cybermen Plastic Figures
1987, Citadel Miniatures, UK
Box art by Lee Gibbons. Cyberman model designed
by Michael and Alan Perry, Dalek kit designed by Alan
Merrett. Box contains 20 Cybermen and components
for 20 Daleks. 25mm figures.
REF: 81159-5 OP: £4.95 NM: £11

MODELS, POLICE BOXES

MODELS of the Police Box go back to 1937 when
Corgi released a small die-cast model to go with
their trainsets. Since 1963, however, the Police
Box has become inextricably linked with *Doctor
Who* and the BBC eventually trade-marked the
image. However this has not stopped numerous
companies from releasing Police Box themed
items, both innocently (having no connection
whatsoever with *Doctor Who*) and with an eye on
the *Doctor Who* market. Often a Police Box is produced in a range with other examples of British
street furniture (red telephone boxes, pillar boxes
etc). Listed here are a few non-*Doctor Who* related
Police Box items, but there are doubtless many
more in existence. It should also be noted that in
2002, the BBC won the right to retain the trade-
mark on the police box image (first officially filed
by the corporation in 1996) after a challenge from
the British Metropolitan Police.

MPO-001 Dinky Die-Cast Police Box
1936, Meccano Ltd, UK
Considered rare amongst *Doctor Who* collectors, the original Dinky Police Box is also prized by Dinky collectors.
NM: £27.50

MPO-002 Pottery TARDIS
1978, Melwood, UK
Two versions pictured (A and B).
OP: £2.99 NM: £9

MPO-003 Police Box Telephone Pad
1980, A. B. & Son, UK
OP: £2.50 (two sizes)

MPO-004 Metropolitan Police Box Model Kit
1984, DWFCA, USA
OP: £12.95

MPL-001

MPO-001

MPO-002 (A)

MPO-002 (B)

MPO-004

MPO-005

MPO-006a

MPO-006b (with box)

MPO-007

MPO-009 (closed)

MPO-005 Police Box Models
1984, Langley Model Miniatures, UK
These were kits of hree sizes–1.5cm, 4.5cm and
7.5cm–comprising thin, pre-cut sections of brass which
could be assembled and painted to create the models.
They were intended for railway enthusiasts to complete
realistic scenes for the trains to run through.
OP: £3.50 (4.5cm) £4.75 (7.5cm) NM: £3.50/£5.50

MPO-006a Police Box
1987, Britannia Miniatures, UK
Resin model. Finished and painted. Around 5" tall.
Versions are known to exist with either a blue or
white painted roof light.
OP: £29.99

MPO-006b Tom Baker Police Box
1987, Britannia Miniatures, UK
Resin model. Finished and painted. Around 5" tall. This
limited edition version was painted in a lighter blue
more in keeping with the TARDIS paint scheme after
Tom Baker commented that the original wasn't quite
the proper colour.
OP: £29.99

MPO-007 Police Box Fridge Magnet
1987, UK
OP: £1.99 NM: £2.50

MPO-008 Police Box Phone Index (large – 400 entries)
1988, Anker International PLC, UK
OP: £12

MPO-009 Police Box Phone Index (small – 300 entries)
1988, Anker International PLC, UK
OP: £8

MPO-010 Police Box
1990 c., UK
A detailed approx 1/3 scale model kit of the TARDIS.
OP: £695

MPO-011 Police Box
1990 c., UK
80mm scale. Painted resin model.
OP: £40

MPO-012 Police Box ceramic
1990 c., Anchor Cottage Collectibles, UK
A pottery model of a Police Box standing on a piece
of pavement. Created by Peter Ingham for Anchor
Cottage Collectibles, Cliff Road, Porthleven.

MPO-013 Police Box teapot

1993, Disi Lisi Ceramics, UK
Designed by Jonathan Brookes based on plans from
the Metropolitan Police museum.
OP: £39.50

MPO-014 The Authentic London Police Box

1997, Regal Models, UK
Licensed from the Metropolitan Police.
OP: £26

MPO-015 English Style Police Box

2000, Harburn Hobbies Ltd, UK
42 mm tall. Part of the manufacturer's line of 'Harburn
Hamlet' railroad model accessories. Company literature specifically noted that the police box was 'forever associated with Dr Who' and that this police box
'looks remarkably like a TARDIS'.
REF: SS342 OP: £4.95

MPO-016 Police Box door sign

2000/07, SlowDazzle Worldwide, UK
A tinplate oversized version of the sign from the
TARDIS' front door. 11-3/4 x 15-1/2 inches.
OP: £9.99

MPO-017 Police Box roof sign

2000/07, SlowDazzle Worldwide, UK
A small tinplate version of the 'Police Public Call Box' sign
from the roof of the TARDIS. 3-3/4 x 16 inches in size.
OP: £7.99

MGA-018 Police Box Resin Model

2002, Ainsty, UK
Two versions were available. One was an unpainted
resin police box (seen painted here), while the other
was a limited run in clear resin and half-painted to
suggest the TARDIS materialising...or dematerialising.
OP: £4.50

MPO-008/009

MPO-012

MPO-013

MPO-015

MPO-016

MPO-017

MPO-018

MPO-018
(half-painted clear)

PRO-002

PEN-001   Pennant
1987/10, Who Dares Publishing, UK
A small triangular cloth pennant with the neon *Doctor Who* logo on it.
OP: £4.99

DOCTOR Who has been used as a promotional tool for other companies and goods on several occasions. Where the promotion included an item of merchandise, these are listed under the appropriate heading and are cross referenced here.

PRO-001   Sugar Puffs Promotion
1966, UK
Win a Dalek. As a part of the promotion, the company also provided money for the second *Doctor Who* film in return for prominent placement advertising in the film.
OP: free

PRO-002   Sugar Smacks Promotion
1971/10, Kelloggs, UK
For the duration of the promotion, and beyond, the large and small 'variety' boxes of Sugar Smacks featured an artwork image of Jon Pertwee as the Doctor and the tag-line: 'The Timeless Energy of Dr. Who'. There were six different 31mm metal badges to collect in boxes, featuring artwork depictions of: the Doctor, Bessie, Jo Grant, the Brigadier, the Master and a UNIT symbol. See also CBA-005.
OP: free

PRO-003   Doctor Who Card Figures
1975/04, Weetabix Ltd, UK
April – June 1975 saw *Doctor Who* used in a promotion by Weetabix. Until the end of May, each special '*Doctor Who* And His Enemies' promotional pack contained four stand-up figures from a set of 24. Larger boxes of 48 contained two sets. The figures were very accurate artwork representations of characters from the series. Sets as follows:
Dalek (white/red); Dr Who 1; Cyberman; Ice Warrior
Dalek (white – facing); Aggedor; Giant Robot; Axon Monster
Dalek (white – sideways); Dr Who 2; Ogron; Lynx (or Linx)
Dalek (grey); Yeti; Draconian; White Robot
Dalek (silver); Sea Devil; Sarah Jane; Saarl (or Slaar)
Dalek (black/gold); Silurian; Alpha Centauri; Quark

PRO-003 & PRO-004

To complement the figures, there was usually one of a set of six cut-out 'action settings' (including a TARDIS interior) on the back of the box: a swampy everglade scene; a misty fantasy forest; a stalagtite and stalagmite cave; a lunar vista; inside the TARDIS; cave entrance with futuristic city view outside. Some larger boxes had, instead, a cut-out TARDIS model. Gordon Archer was the artist used for all these promotional items.
OP: free   NM: £6.50 each

PRO-004   Doctor Who Card Figures
1977/03, Weetabix Ltd, UK
Weetabix ran a second *Doctor Who* promotion from March to May 1977. This time each pack of the cereal contained a set of three artwork cards by Gordon Archer, which could be used as playing pieces for a board game printed on the back of the box. There were six different sets of cards to collect, depicting: Bellal, Daleks, Davros (Set 1); Vega Nexos, Aggedor, Blor (Set 2); Daleks, Gellguards, Omega (Set 3); Zygons, Krynoid, Wirrn (Set 4); Vogans, Cybermen, Styggron (Set 5); and TARDIS, Field Major Styre, Hieronymous (Set 6). The cards also featured messages in code ('a secret message from the Time Lords'), the cipher for which was printed on the inside of every box. The sets could be paired up to form continuous pictures as follows: Sets 3 and 2; Sets 6 and 1; and Sets 5 and 4. The were four different board-games: 'Travel through Time', 'Race through Space', 'Escape from the Underworld' and 'Discover the Lost Planet'. All four could be found on the 24-piece 'family size' boxes, but only the first two were available on the smaller 'standard size' 12-piece boxes. The game used small circular cardboard counters with Tom Baker's face on, in at least 4 colours - red, blue, green, and orange. These were not on the box itself, but possibly on a separate card. Archer was not the artist for these board games.
OP: free   NM: £3.75 each

PRO-005   Doctor Who Showbag
1982, Australian Royal Melbourne Show, AUS
Promotional bag containing: make-it-yourself cardboard TARDIS, *Doctor Who* Invisible Ink, *Doctor Who* badge; jigsaw puzzle, *Doctor Who* Game. The game was 'Escape from the Underworld', from the Weetabix promotion of 1977.
OP: $1.00

PRO-006   Doctor Who Bonanza Competition
1985, W. H. Allen & Co. PLC, UK
A competiton to win various prizes including a trip to the BBC to watch *Doctor Who* being recorded.
OP: free

PRO-003 (card figures)

PRO-003 (box back 'action settings')

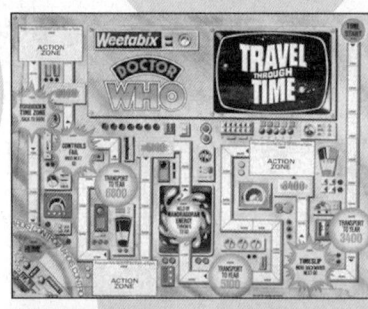 

PRO-004 (board games)

PRO-004 (Card Set 1)

PRO-004 (Card Set 2)

PRO-004 (Card Set 3)

PRO-004 (Card Set 4)

PRO-004 (Card Set 5)

PRO-004 (Card Set 6)

PRO-005 (contents)

PRO-005 (puzzle)

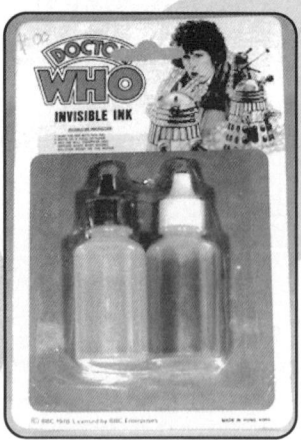

PRO-005 (invisible ink on card)

PRO-007 Save Doctor Who Stickers
1985/03, Sun/Star Newspapers, UK
Stickers were given away by two UK national
Newspapers during a campaign to 'save Doctor Who'
after the show's cancellation was announced in 1985.
See also SST-010.
OP: free   NM: £3.50

PRO-008 Golden Wonder Promotion
1986/11, Golden Wonder / Marvel Comics, UK
Free mini-comics given away within multipacks of Crisps,
Wotsits and Ringos. The individual crisp and snack pack-
ets were emblazoned with the *Doctor Who* logo for the
period of the promotion and advertised copies of the
1987 *Doctor Who* Calendar, a special edition of which was
printed up for this purpose. See MAG-010 for a complete cover gallery.
OP: free

PRO-009 Berni Inns Promotion
1987, Marvel Comics, UK
DWM issues (#122 and #125) given free at Berni Inns. The
covers featured a 'Berni Funtime' flash on the bottom corner, and the price was amended to 'free'. See MAG-011
for cover pictures.
OP: free

PRO-010 New Zealand SuperAnnuation
Services Promotion
1997, NZ
Promotional items released to tie-in with a promotion and series of television advertisements featuring
Tom Baker as the Doctor. Mail Out: an envelope with
Tom Baker's face on it containing the literature for
the SuperAnnuation package. Postcards: Two featuring
Tom Baker as the Doctor. One doubled as a competition entry form. 'Virellian time transformer': a paper
'calculator' to assist in working out inflationary move-
ments over the next 40 years. Poster: Limited run of a
poster featuring Tom Baker as the Doctor.
OP: free

SUNDRIES, BAGS

HOLDALLS, plastic bags and other carrying cases.

SBA-001 Dalek Bag and Picnic Set
1965, Optima Manufacturing Co. Ltd, UK
Hold-all with a single zipper across the top and transfers of Daleks on either side. May have originally been
sold with accompanying picnic items.

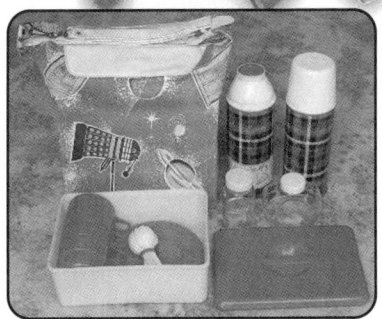

SBA-023

SBA-001 (with original contents?)

SBA-011

SBA-002 Doctor Who 20th Anniversary carrier bag
1983, BBC Enterprises, UK
OP: 10p each NM: £2

SBA-003 Carrier Bags
1983, BBC Enterprises, UK
Blackpool, Longleat, neon logo
OP: 10p each NM: £2

SBA-004 Sydney Royal Easter Show Bag
1984/85, Sydney Royal Easter show, AUS
Paper back with current logo on front. Contained a jigsaw puzzle, a bottle of invisible ink, a ready-to-make cardboard TARDIS and an Ian Nicoll badge. A plastic version of the bag is also known to contain wither a BBC logo or Doctor Who logo sun visor.

SBA-005 Canvas Bag
1985, Peter Black (KLY) Ltd, UK
OP: £5.95 NM: £11

SBA-006 Tote Bag
DWFCA, USA
Canvas Full colour diamond logo.
OP: $12.00 NM: £11

SBA-007 Diamond Logo Duffle Bag
USA

SBA-008 Tote Bag
1982, Nightstar Corp., USA
Denim diamond logo, neon logo, Tom Baker and Daleks, K-9.
OP: $11.00

SBA-009 Duffle Bag
1985, DWFCA, USA
Silver neon logo, navy canvas.
OP: $17.95

SBA-010 Garment Bag
1985, DWFCA, USA
Full colour diamond logo: canvas; neon logo navy: canvas, logo in silver.
OP: $20.00

SBA-011 Paper Carrier Bag
1980s, Gaylord Specialities Corp., New York, USA
Blue paper bag with string handles and red diamond logo.

SBA-012 Bag
1987, USA
McCoy logo

SBA-013 Carrier bags BBC Doctor Who USA Tour
1987, Lionheart, USA
OP: $0.50 each

SBA-014 Duffel Bag
1987, Lionheart, USA
Diamond logo, nylon: blue with white logo.
OP: $11.95

SBA-015 Laundry Bag
1987, Lionheart, USA
Diamond logo, draw string: red w/ white logo.
OP: $8.00

SBA-016 Tote Bag
1987, Lionheart, USA
Natural w/ diamond logo in colour, blue with neon logo in silver.
OP: $9.95 each

SBA-017 Exhibition Carrier Bag
1980s, UK
Silver bag from the Blackpool Exhibition. No further information available.

SBA-018 Hirschfeld Litho Tote Bag
1990 c., USA
Offered on PBS pledge drives, tote bag is off-white with "Seven Faces" litho art on front. See also COL-007.

SBA-019 TARDIS Tote Bag
1992, USA
Tote natural canvas w/ TARDIS in a step & repeat pattern w/ logo in centre
OP: $9.95

SBA-020 Doctor Who Movie record bag
1996, BBC Worldwide, UK
No manufacturers mark
OP: £14.99 NM: £16.50

SBA-021 Document case
1998, The Ultimate Embroidery Company, UK
Black nylon with PVC backing. Colour logo.
OP: £10.99

SBA-022 Record Bag
1998, The Ultimate Embroidery Company, UK
Black nylon with PVC backing. Colour logo.
OP: £16.99

SBA-023 Bum Bag
1998, The Ultimate Embroidery Company, UK
Black nylon. Colour logo.
OP: £9.99

SUNDRIES, BOOKMARKS

SBK-001 Leather Bookmarks
1983, BBC Enterprises, UK
Leather bookmarks. (grey, orange, brown, green, light green)
OP: £1.00 each

SBK-002 Card Bookmarks
1985, Who Dares Publishing, UK
Full colour artwork card bookmarks. Two sets of 9. Art by Andrew Skilleter.
Set A: WM-01: The Cybermen, WM-02: Daleks, WM-03: Daleks, WM-04: Davros, WM-05: William Hartnell, WM-06: Patrick Troughton, WM-07: Jon Pertwee, WM-08: Tom Baker, WM-09: Peter Davison.
Set B: WM-10: Colin Baker, WM-11: Gallifrey, WM-12: K9, WM-13: Sontaran, WM-14: Sea Devils, WM-15: Omega, WM-16: The TARDIS, WM-17: Cyberman, WM-18: Sea Devil.
OP: 40p each, £1.99 set NM: £1.50 each

SBK-003 Leather Bookmarks
1993, Dominitemporal Services Ltd, UK
Leather bookmarks. Red/Green/Blue/Black.
'Panopticon '93 Thirty Years of a Time Lord' in gold.

SBK-004 DWB Bookmarks
1994, DWB, UK
Laminated paper. Eight bookmarks, one for each of the
seven Doctors and two for the Fourth Doctor. Offered
at Visions '94 at DWB's table free with purchase.
OP: free

SBK-005 'Who's Who' Bookmark
1995, Who Shop International, UK
Black bookmark with slogan 'We Show You Who's Who'.

SBK-006 Leather Bookmarks
1996, Dapol, UK
Leather bookmarks. White/Black/Blue/Red. Diamond
Logo, Dalek and TARDIS.
REF: W025-001/2/3/4 OP: £1.20 each

SBK-007 Leather Bookmarks
1996, Dapol, UK
Leather bookmarks. Black/Blue/Red/Green. Diamond
Logo.
REF: W025-020/21/22/23 OP: £1.00 each

SBK-008 Tassled Bookmarks
1999, Bookmarks of Distinction, UK
Set of six plasticised photographic bookmarks with
coloured string tassels: Third Doctor; Dalek; Third Dr
and Jo in the TARDIS; Fourth Dr; TARDIS; McCoy logo.
REF: 5-036590-111388 (TARDIS)
REF: 5-036590-111395 (Dr & Jo)
REF: 5-036590-111401 (Dalek)
REF: 5-036590-111418 (Fourth Doctor)
REF: 5-036590-111425 (Third Dr)
REF: 5-036590-111371 (McCoy logo)
OP: 99p each

SBK-009 Leather Bookmarks
1990s/2000?, UK TV, AUS
Promotional bookmark with all eight Doctors on one
side and details on the other side about "The Tube",
the late-night time slot in which *Doctor Who* aired in
Australiz.

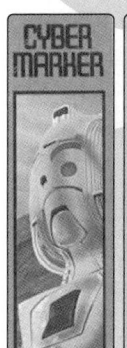

SBK-002 (all 18)

SBK-006   SBK-007

SBK-008 (selected)

SCA-001

SCA-002

SUNDRIES, CALENDARS

SCA-001 Doctor Who 1984 Calendar
1983, Glenwood Distributors Inc., USA
Square photographic calendar. Picture of Fourth
Doctor with K9's innards on front.
OP: $7.95 NM: £8

SCA-002 Doctor Who 1985 Calendar
1984, Glenwood Distributors Inc., USA
Square photographic calendar. Picture of Fourth
Doctor and Leela on front.
OP: $7.95 NM: £8

SCA-003 Doctor Who – The Calendar (1986)
1985/07, Who Dares Publishing, UK
Artwork by Andrew Skilleter. ISBN may be for USA
distribution only.
REF: ISBN 0-8184-9997-4 OP: £5.50 NM: £5.50

SCA-004 Doctor Who – The Calendar (1987)
1986/09, Who Dares Publishing, UK
Artwork by Andrew Skilleter.
OP: £5.95 NM: £8

SCA-005 Doctor Who – The Calendar (1988)
1987/09, Who Dares Publishing, UK
Artwork by Andrew Skilleter (8 pieces) and Stuart
Hughes (4 pieces).
OP: £5.95 NM: £8

SCA-006 Doctor Who – The Calendar 1989
1988/08, Who Dares Publishing, UK
Artwork by Andrew Skilleter.
OP: £5.95 NM: £8

SCA-003

SCA-004

SCA-005

SCA-006

SCA-007

SCA-007 Doctor Who 30th Anniversary Calendar
1992/05, Vision Publications, UK
Artwork by different artists (Colin Howard, Paul Vyse, Alistair Pearson, Les Edwards, Alistair Hughes, Lee Sullivan, Brian Hudd, Pete Wallbank, Mark Oldroyd). Vision Publications was a company set up by authors David J Howe, Stephen James Walker and Mark Stammers specifically for the purpose of releasing a high-quality calendar for *Doctor Who*'s 30th anniversary. The calendar eventually sold around 4,000 copies.
OP: £9.99 NM: £9

SCA-008 Radio Times: Doctor Who 1996 Calendar: 30 Years of Radio Times Covers
1995/09, Slow Dazzle Worldwide, UK
Signed copies. *Radio Times Doctor Who* covers.
REF: 581912 OP: £9.99 NM: £5.50

SCA-009 The Official 1997 Calendar: Doctor Who: Heroes & Villains
1996/09/17, Slow Dazzle Worldwide, UK
Photographic. Comes with one of three audio interview tapes: Elisabeth Sladen (1), Peter Davison (2) or Jon Pertwee (3).
REF: 032863-00001-4 OP: £9.99 NM: £5.50

SCA-010 Doctor Who 35th Anniversary Special Edition. The Official 1998 Calendar
1997, Slow Dazzle Worldwide, UK
Photographic. Free colour cut-out standee with Calendar (Dalek or TARDIS).
REF: 032863-00027-4 OP: £9.99 NM: £5.50

SCA-011 The Official 1998 Calendar: Dr. Who & the Daleks
1997, Slow Dazzle Worldwide, UK
Photographic. Only available mail-order and in selected specialist shops.
REF: 032863-00028-1 OP: £9.99 NM: £5.50

SCA-012 Doctor Who Daleks' Invasion Earth 2150 A.D.: The Official 1999 Calendar
1998/09/14, Slow Dazzle Worldwide, UK
Photographic. The calendar was heavily discounted on issue.
REF: 032863-00122-6 OP: £9.99 NM: £5.50

SCA-013 Doctor Who The Official 1999 Calendar
1998/09/14, Slow Dazzle Worldwide, UK
Artwork by Colin Howard. The calendar was heavily discounted on issue.
REF: 032863-00065-6 OP: £9.99 NM: £5.50

SCA-008

SCA-009

SCA-010

SCA-011

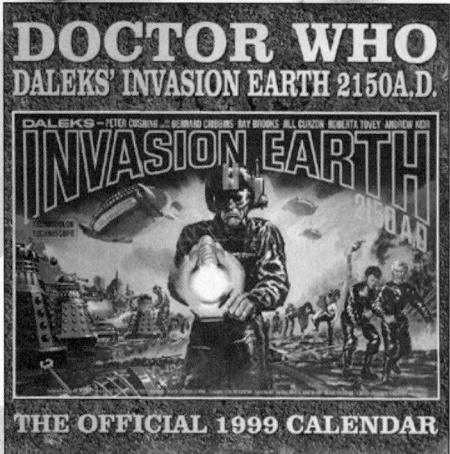

SCA-012

SCA-013

SCA-014

SCA-014 Dr. Who 16 Month 2000 Calendar
1999/09, World of Discovery, UK
Calendar produced as a part of the BBC Millennium
Collection. Runs from October 1999 to January 2001
inclusive.
REF: 038455-500061 OP: £7.99 NM: £5.50

SCA-015 Dr Who & the Daleks Calendar 2000
1999/09, Slow Dazzle Worldwide, UK
A cut-out standee of a Dalek with a calendar with
tear-off pages attached. Artwork by Colin Howard.
REF: 032863-001318 OP: £7.99 NM: £5.50

SCA-016 TARDIS Calendar 2000
1999/09, Slow Dazzle Worldwide, UK
A cut-out standee of the TARDIS with a calendar with
tear-off pages attached. Artwork by Colin Howard.
REF: 032863-001325 OP: £7.99 NM: £5.50

SCA-017 2000 Calendar
1999, Cineffigy, UK
Photographs of *Doctor Who* actors. No further information available.

SCA-018 2001 Calendar
2000/08, Slow Dazzle Worldwide, UK
Calendar comes with one of two free card standees:
Jon Pertwee or Tom Baker.
REF: ISBN 1 903113 20 2 OP: £9.99

SCA-019 2002 Desk Calendar
2001/08, Big Finish Productions, UK
A 15 month desk calendar featuring covers from the
Big Finish range of original *Doctor Who* audio CDs.
OP: £8.99

SCA-015

SCA-016

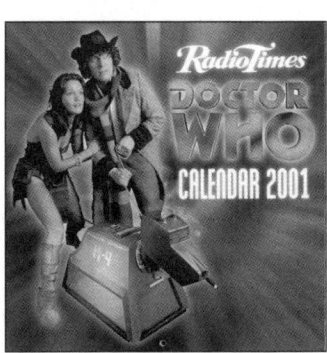

SCA-018

SCA-019

SCA-020 2002 Wall Planner
2001/08, Big Finish Productions, UK
An A2-sized wall planner featuring covers from the
Big Finish range of original *Doctor Who* audio CDs.
OP: £6.99

SCA-021 2002 Calendar
2001/08, Danilo Calendars Ltd, UK
REF: ISBN 1-843-370-417 OP: £9.99

SCA-021

**SCA-022 Dr Who and the Daleks: Dalekmania
Calendar 2003**
2002/06, Street Hassle Ltd, UK
Celebrating 40 years of the Daleks. Art direction, text
and design: Robert Fairclough. Features photographs
from the cinema films, publicity images from the TV
series, Dalek merchandise, and a free poster. Two of
the images are of Julian Vince's Dalek models.
REF: ISBN 1-843-370-697 OP: £9.95

SCA-023 2003/4 Desk Calendar
2002/12, Big Finish Productions, UK
A 15 month desk calendar featuring covers from the
Big Finish range of original *Doctor Who* audio CDs. A
limited edition of 1000.
OP: £9.99

SCA-022

SCA-023

SUNDRIES, GREETINGS CARDS

SGC-001 Dalek Birthday Card
1964, Waldorf Card Company, UK
No further information available.
NM: £55

SGC-002 Dalek Greetings Cards
1965, Newton Mills Ltd, UK
A card with a cut-out cover through which can be seen the first part of each message. When the card is opened, the full message can be seen. Various designs: 'We command you … to have a Happy Birthday'; 'You must come with us … for a birthday that is out of this world'; 'We have the power … to wish you a happy birthday.'
NM: £55

SGC-003 Tom Baker Greetings Card
1976, BBC Enterprises, UK
Photo of Tom Baker as the Doctor.
NM: £5.50

SGC-004 Doctor Who Greetings Cards
(set of 18)
1979, Denis Alan Print, UK
Ten cards showing Tom Baker by the TARDIS with the age written on the TARDIS door with chalk. Three with 'Happy Birthday' printed on the front. One with 'Get Well Soon' written on the TARDIS door in chalk. One with the same message printed on the front. Four generic. 18 total. All cards featured Tom Baker. The cards were also available individually packaged with one of the Blue BBC *Doctor Who* diamond logo badges.
REF: DH2001 – DH2018
OP: 36p each £5.00 set   NM: £3.50 each

SGC-005 Police Box Greetings Card
Valentines of Dundee, UK
TARDIS-shaped card with words 'Time Flies' inside. Card series is 'Icons by Paul Greenwood'.
REF: IGU 5023 NM: £5.50

SGC-002 (two designs shown)

SGC-004 (17 shown on this and facing page)

**SGC-004
(sample packaging
with badge)**

SGC-005

SGC-006   **SGC-007**

SGC-006 "Wrong Again Doctor!" Greetings Card
1983, Great Ideas, UK
Image of Santa emerging from the TARDIS on a beach with words. Image by Peter Ulton.
REF: PU282   NM: £5.50

SGC-007 'Snowbot' Greetings Card
1999, Lightweight Designs, UK
Image of a metal Dalek-inspired robot in the snow with a carrot 'eye', pipe, scarf and twigs for 'arms'.
Image by Max Ellis.
REF: MHX006   OP: £1.40 (£4.99 pack of 5)

SGC-008

SGC-008 Greetings cards set 1
2000/11/23, The Stamp Centre, UK
A pack of four photographic greetings cards. These were initially advertised as featuring speech bubbles, but the final cards are plain photographs. Also, the advertised packs included a picture of Tom Baker with a Dalek (publicity from *Genesis of the Daleks*) but this image was vetoed by the BBC as not being a suitable image. Images featured: Tom Baker with rainbow background (publicity); Sarah Jane Smith and K9 (*K9 and Company*); Cyberman (from *The Five Doctors*); Daleks (from *Rememberance of the Daleks*).
OP: £7.95 pack

SGC-009   **SGC-010**

SGC-009 Greetings cards set 2
2001/04/12, The Stamp Centre, UK
A pack of four photographic collage greetings cards. Images featured: *The Dæmons, The Sensorites; Omega; The Sea Devils*. Designed by Ian Burgess.
OP: £7.95 pack

SGC-010 Greetings cards set 3
2002/05, The Stamp Centre, UK
A pack of four photographic collage greetings cards. Images featured: *Battlefield; City of Death; Earthshock; Terror of the Vervoids*. Designed by Ian Burgess.
OP: £7.95 pack

SGC-011 1964 'I Am A Dalek' DVD Card
2002, Time Bytes, UK
A Greetings Card with a Dapol-like Dalek image on the front (which appears to be artwork rather than a photograph). The Card comes with a one hour DVD of news footage from the BBC and British Pathe. This is one of a range of cards, each for a different year.
OP: £9.99

SGC-011

SUNDRIES, PHOTOGRAPHS

PHOTOGRAPHS from *Doctor Who* come in a great number of types and originate from numerous sources. Foremost are pictures, both colour transparencies and black and white prints, taken by the BBC themselves for use by the photographic library in promoting the series. There are many thousands of these and, for a period in the seventies and eighties, they could be bought from the BBC direct. In the nineties, when the BBC's photographic library was reorganised and combined with other photographic resources within the BBC (like the *Radio Times* photo library) access was restricted to BBC staff and licensed outsiders only. Seeing the potential to exploit the *Doctor Who* range, however, John McElroy was licensed in the mid-eighties to sell copies of some of the BBC's pictures through his Whomobilia company. Other photographs have been taken by newspapers and individuals, both on location and in the studio. These have also been exploited by various magazines and individuals over the years, with sets of pictures being made available to sell, and the photographs themselves being used within magazines and books. This listing covers some of the sales of photographs that have taken place. It is not possible to list every individual image that has been sold, nor can we cover the many instances of private sales of pictures over the years.

SPH-001 Tom Baker Promotional Photo
1979, ABC, AUS
No further information available.

SPH-002 BBC Picture Pack
1980/08, BBC Picture Publicity, UK
Five pictures were issued featuring: K-9 (from *The Invisible Enemy*); the Fourth Doctor and Romana (one from *The Leisure Hive* and another from a publicity shoot for *Destiny of the Daleks*); the Fourth Doctor (publicity from *The Hand of Fear*); and the Fourth Doctor in the TARDIS control room (publicity). This is the first and only time that the BBC directly sold some of its photographs to the public and this offer was carried through the *Radio Times*.
OP: £3.99

SPH-003 BBC Photographs
1984 – 89, Whomobilia / John McElroy, UK
Whomobilia came into being around 1984. Prior to that John McElroy was offering the photographs as a service to the DWAS, and later advertising them through *Doctor Who Magazine* and at conventions.
Feb 1984: 1 – 22 (0.45; £1.20; £1.80; £4.50 all ex.postage), Apr 1984: 23 – 62 (0.50; £1.25; £1.90; £4.60 all inc postage), Jul 1984: 63 – 100 (ex. 69, 72), Sep 1984: 101 – 140, Jan 1985: 141 – 168
At this point the numbering system was re-started.
Nov 1985: 1 – 50 (5x3: 90p; 8x6: £2.00), Jul 1986: 51 – 100, Sep 1986: 101 – 150, Dec 1986: misc 7 – 88 (8x6: £1.30), Mar 1987: 151 – 220 (5x3: 80p; 8x6: £1.60; 10x8: £2.50; 14x11: £4.50), Aug 1987: BW1 – BW40 (8x6:£1.60), Oct 1987: 221 – 260, Jan 1988: 261 – 290 (90p; £1.80; £3.00; £4.50), May 1989: Ray Cusick Collection 1-36 (8x6: £1.80; 10x8: £3.00; 14x11: £5.00), Jun 1989: 27A, 35A, 36A
OP: various NM: 75p – £2.25 each

SPH-004 Doctor Who Photograph Album
1985, Whomobilia, UK
Red, brown, tan
OP: £4.99

SPH-005 Photographs from *The Five Doctors*
1983, Stephen Payne, UK
Set of b/w and colour prints from the photocall and filming for *The Five Doctors*. Stephen Payne went on to set up Visual Imagination, a publishing house which handles magazines like *Starburst*, *TV Zone* and *Film Review*.
OP: £1.25 each

SPH-006 Photos
1984, Spirit of Light Enterprises Ltd, USA
8x10 glossy b/w photos $2.50 (buy 10 get 1 free): Patrick Troughton, Jon Pertwee, Tom Baker, Peter Davison, Anthony Ainley, Nicola Bryant, Nicholas Courtney, Janet Fielding, Carole Ann Ford, Louise Jameson, Ian Marter, Elisabeth Sladen 1, Elisabeth Sladen 2, Mark Strickson, Sarah Sutton, Mary Tamm, Matthew Waterhouse, Colin Baker, John Levene, Lalla Ward, Frazer Hines

SPH-007 Colour Photograph: Peter Davison or Katy Manning
1985, DWFCA, USA
OP: $3.00 each

SPH-008 Photographs from *Power of the Daleks*
1990/05, Visual Imagination Ltd, UK
A set of 29 colour photographs from *Power of the Daleks* owned by the Topham Picture Library. Also included a 30th photo of Barry Letts with Jon Pertwee at the London Planetarium.
OP: 99p – £3.99

SPH-009 The Ultimate Adventure Photographs
1989, Mark Furness Ltd, UK
Two B4 sized colour prints. Daleks in the TARDIS (at start of Act 2); Doctor and cast brought before Emperor (near end of play).
OP: £3.50 each

SPH-010 Steve Cook Photographs
1990, Mediaband, UK
Assorted publicity and set shots. (DWM #160/162). Steve Cook was working for Doctor Who Magazine and attended several Doctor Who location and studio sessions to cover the events for the publication. He retained copyright in his photographs, however, and later made them available to fans through the Mediaband company. Apr 1990: Set 1 SC01-08, Set 2 SC09-16, Set 3 SC17-24; Jun 1990:, Set 4 SC25-32 (5x7), Set 5 SC33-40 (10x8), Set 6 SC41-48 (10x8)
OP: £1.75 each

SPH-011 BBC Photographs
1992, Dominitemporal Services Ltd, UK
Pictures from: Sontaran Experiment (5 pics), Genesis of the Daleks (10 pics), Deadly Assassin (5 pics). After Whomobilia stopped trading, the DWAS made a few official BBC photographs available to fans.
OP: £8.00 per set of 5

SPH-012 Ray Cusick/Day of Daleks Photographs
1994 , TTL, UK
Designer Raymond P Cusick's stills, plus some from actor Rick Lester taken on location for Day of Daleks. See also AAP-003.
OP: £3.50 each

SPH-013 Janet Fielding Photographs
2002/09, 10th Planet, UK
Five different images, signed by Janet Fielding.
OP: £8 each

SPH-014 Paul McGann Photographs
2002/06, 10th Planet, UK
Five different images from the 1996 TVM, signed by Paul McGann.
OP: £15 each

SPH-015 Yee Jee Tso Photographs
2002/06, 10th Planet, UK
Three different images from the 1996 TVM, signed by Yee Jee Tso.
OP: £10 each

SUNDRIES, POSTAL ITEMS

SPI-001 25th Anniversary First Day Cover
1988/11, CoverCraft, UK
Special printed envelope featured a full colour image of the Doctor Who logo and the TARDIS and presented a special 'Gallifrey' postmark over postage stamps from the Post Office's 'Space' collection. Also a signed edition by Sylvester McCoy, Colin Baker, Jon Pertwee. £5.75 each.
OP: £2.50   NM: £11

SPI-002 25th Anniversary First Day Cover
1988, Arlington Supplies Ltd, UK
Only 40 produced. Signed by Tom Baker or Sylvester McCoy. Postmarked with Covercraft's stamp. The envelope was smaller and was stamped with a blue image of the TARDIS and the words 'Special Postmark 25th Anniversary Dr. Who' in either blue or red. Once again, the covers could be obtained either in pristine form or signed by one of the Doctors. These may have been released after 1988.
OP: £5.95

SPI-003 Dalek Stamp
1999/06, Royal Mail, UK
As a part of the Millennium celebrations, the Royal Mail issued a set of four stamps every month during 1999. In June, the topic was 'Entertainers' and the Daleks were chosen to adorn the 44p stamp. An alternative design featuring Ena Sharples from Coronation Street was considered, however the Daleks won in the end. A postcard of the image on the stamp was also available for 25p.
OP: 44p

SPI-004a Dalek Stamp First Day Cover
1999/06, The Stamp Centre, UK
Officially licensed cover featuring the TARDIS in flight on the front and information about Doctor Who on the reverse. Signed by Tom Baker. Featured the set of 4 'Entertainers' stamps ('Mercury's Magic' – Freddie Mercury; World Cup; Dr Who; 'Chaplin's Genius' – Charlie Chaplin) and a special TARDIS postmark. 10 issued.
OP: £25   NM: £110

SPI-004b Dalek Stamp First Day Cover
1999/06, The Stamp Centre, UK
Officially licensed cover featuring the TARDIS in flight on the front and information about Doctor Who on the reverse. Signed by Tom Baker. Featured the Dalek stamp on the front, and a special TARDIS postmark. 3000 issued.
OP: £12   NM: £21 (signed by Tom Baker)
£25 (signed by Tom Baker and Frazer Hines)

SPI-001

SPI-002 (two versions)

SPI-003

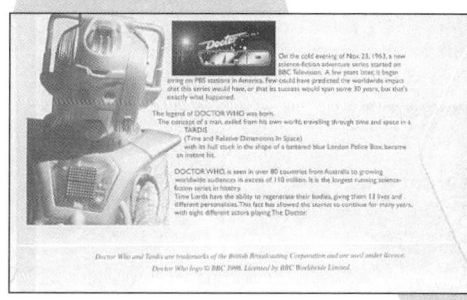

SPI-004b (front and back)

SPI-005

SPI-008

SPI-009 (one coaster)

SPI-011

SPI-014

SPI-015

SPI-005 Doctor Who at the Stamp Centre Cover
1999/06, The Stamp Centre, UK
A cover featuring a photograph of Tom Baker and the TARDIS outside The Stamp Centre shop in London's Strand. Commissioned by the *Doctor Who* Appreciation Society. 1000 issued. Featured the set of 4 'Entertainers' stamps ('Mercury's Magic' – Freddie Mercury; World Cup; Dr Who; 'Chaplin's Genius' – Charlie Chaplin) plus the special TARDIS postmark. Limited to 500 copies of the signed version.
OP: £17.50 (unsigned) £19.50 (signed by Tom Baker)
NM: £27.50 signed

SPI-006 Doctor Who and the Daleks – Dalek Stamp First Day Cover
1999/06, Cambridge Stamp Co., UK
Black and white photo from *Doctor Who* film. 100 issued.
REF: MC12 OP: £10 NM: £13.20

SPI-007 Doctor Who and the Daleks – Dalek Stamp First Day Cover
1999/06, Cambridge Stamp Co., UK
Colour film poster for *Doctor Who and the Daleks*. 100 issued.
OP: £10 NM: £20

SPI-008 Dalek Stamp Paperweight
1999/06, The Stamp Centre, UK
A clear glass paperweight with a Dalek stamp inside.
OP: £4.95 NM: £8

SPI-009 Dalek Stamp Coaster Set
1999, The Stamp Centre, UK
A set of six cork-backed heat resistant drinks coasters.
NM: £19

SPI-010 'Entertainer's Tale'
1999/06, Royal Mail, UK
A poster for the stamps released in the 'Entertainer's Tale' series. This poster features the Dalek stamp large and all four stamps in the series smaller below it.
OP: £9.95

SPI-011 'Stamps' from the 'Kingdom of Sedang'
1999/12/30, Bruce Grenville, AUS
Grenville creates and 'issues' stamps from the fictitious 'Kingdom of Sedang'. These are not genuine postal stamps and have no postal worth. They feature photographs from *Doctor Who*. The stamps are issued as mini-sheets of 10 stamps or as a first day cover with one stamp on it. $1 stamp features a Dalek; the $2 stamp features a Cyberman.
OP: Mint or 'cancelled' - $3; First Day Covers - $3.50

SPI-012 'Tom Baker' stamp cover
2000/05/22, The Stamp Centre, UK
A stamp cover featuring the Dalek stamp. The cover shows Baker and the TARDIS.
Variants:
Signed by Baker - £14.95
Signed by Baker and Louise Jameson - £19.95
REF: 4 OP: £12.50

SPI-013 'Sylvester McCoy' stamp cover
2000/05/22, The Stamp Centre, UK
A stamp cover featuring the Dalek stamp. The cover shows a photograph of the seventh Doctor plus photographs from some of his stories.
Variants:
Signed by McCoy - £17.50
Signed by McCoy and Sophie Aldred - £22.50
Signed by McCoy, Aldred, John Sessions and Stephen Fry - £39.50
REF: 5 OP: £12.50

SPI-014 'Battle of the Daleks' stamp cover
2000/05/22, The Stamp Centre, UK
A stamp cover featuring the Dalek stamp. The cover shows a montage of various Dalek images.
Variants:
Signed by Baker - £14.95
Signed by Baker and Elisabeth Sladen - £17.50
Signed by Nicholas Courtney - £12.50
Signed by Sladen - £12.50
Signed by Aldred - £12.50
Signed by Richard Franklin - £12.50
Signed by John Levene - £12.50
Signed by Frazer Hines - £12.50
Signed by Terry Molloy - £12.50
Signed by McCoy - £15.00
Signed by Jacqueline Pearce - £12.50
Signed by Louise Jameson - £12.50
Signed by Colin Baker - £15.00
Signed by Ken Dodd - £15.00
Signed by Maureen O'Brien - £15.00
REF: 6 OP: £12.50

SPI-015 'The Doctors United' stamp cover
2000/05/22, The Stamp Centre, UK
A stamp cover featuring the Dalek stamp. The cover shows photographs of the first seven Doctors, with facsimile signatures for the first three and genuine signatures for the latter four. Also features a commemorative postmark. Paul McGann is not featured. Limited to 1500 covers.
REF: 7 OP: £49.50 NM: £80

SPI-016 Tom Baker stamps
2000/05/22, The Stamp Centre, UK
Ten different designs available: a standard 1st class stamp with an adhesive image of Tom Baker attached. Produced exclusively by The Stamp Centre using technology on display at the 2000 Earl's Court Stamp Fair. The stamps were also available from The Stamp Centre as a set called 'smilers'.

SPI-017 'The Assistants United' stamp cover
2000/11/23, The Stamp Centre, UK
A stamp cover featuring the Dalek stamp. The cover shows a photograph of seven companions and is personally signed. Companions featured: Carole Ann Ford, Wendy Padbury, Caroline John, Elisabeth Sladen, Sarah Sutton, Nicola Bryant, Sophie Aldred. Limited to 500 covers.
REF: 8 OP: £49.50 NM: £65

SPI-018 'The Monster Montage' stamp cover
2000/11/23, The Stamp Centre, UK
A stamp cover featuring the Dalek stamp. The cover shows a collage of Chris Achilleos' *Doctor Who* artwork. Limited to 1500 covers.
Variants:
Signed by Achilleos and Tom Baker - £26.95
Signed by Baker, Anthony Ainley, Terry Molloy, Chris Achilleos - £39.95
REF: 9 OP: £12.50

SPI-019 Colin Baker stamp cover
2001/04/12, The Stamp Centre, UK
A stamp cover featuring the Dalek stamp. The cover shows a collage of Colin Baker images. Signed by Baker. Limited to 1500 covers. Designed by Ian Burgess.
REF: 10 OP: £12.50 NM: £16.50

SPI-020 'Unit Reunited' stamp cover
2001/04/12, The Stamp Centre, UK
A stamp cover featuring the Dalek stamp. The cover shows a collage of UNIT images. Signed by John Levene, Richard Franklin, Tom Baker and Nicholas Courtney. Limited to 1500 covers. Designed by Ian Burgess.
REF: 11 OP: £49.50

SPI-021 'Beauty and the Beast' stamp cover
2001/08/23, The Stamp Centre, UK
A stamp cover featuring the Dalek stamp. The cover shows a collage of images. Signed by Nicola Bryant. Limited to 1250 covers. Designed by Ian Burgess.
REF: 13 OP: £12.50 NM: £16.50

SPI-020

SPI-021

SPI-022

SPI-023

**SPI-022 'The Good, The Bad and the Ugly'
stamp cover**
2001/08/23, The Stamp Centre, UK
A stamp cover featuring the Dalek stamp. The cover
shows a collage of images. Signed by Tom Baker,
Anthony Ainley and Terry Molloy. Limited to 1000
covers. Designed by Ian Burgess.
REF: 15   OP: £37.50   NM: £45

SPI-023 'The Brigadier' stamp cover
2001/11/23, The Stamp Centre, UK
A stamp cover featuring the Dalek stamp. The cover
shows a collage of images from *The Green Death*.
Signed by Nicholas Courtney. Limited to 500 covers.
Designed by Ian Burgess.
REF: 14   OP: £12.50   NM: £16.50

SPI-024 'Ace Adventurer' stamp cover
2001/11/23, The Stamp Centre, UK
A stamp cover featuring the Dalek stamp and a collage
of images from *Ghost Light*. Signed by Sophie Aldred.
Limited to 500 covers. Designed by Ian Burgess.
REF: 16   OP: £12.50   NM: £16.50

SPI-025 'Louise Jameson' stamp cover
2002/05, The Stamp Centre, UK
A stamp cover featuring the Dalek stamp. The cover
shows a collage of images from *The Invisible Enemy*.
Signed by Louise Jameson. Limited to 1000 covers.
Designed by Ian Burgess.
REF: 17   OP: £12.50

SPI-026 'Sylvester McCoy' Stamp Cover
2002/05, The Stamp Centre, UK
A stamp cover featuring the Dalek stamp. The cover
shows a collage of images from *The Curse of Fenric*.
Signed by Sylvester McCoy. Limited to 1000 covers.
Designed by Ian Burgess.
REF: 18   OP: £12.50

SPI-027 'Talons of Weng-Chiang' Stamp Cover
2002/05, The Stamp Centre, UK
A stamp cover featuring the Dalek stamp. The cover
shows a collage of images from *The Talons of Weng-
Chiang*. Signed by Tom Baker and Louise Jameson.
Limited to 1000 covers. Designed by Ian Burgess.
REF: 19   OP: £12.50

SPI-028 'Matthew Waterhouse' Stamp Cover
2002/05, The Stamp Centre, UK
A stamp cover featuring the Dalek stamp. The cover
shows a collage of images from *The Keeper of Traken*.
Signed by Matthew Waterhouse. Limited to 1000 covers. Designed by Ian Burgess.
REF: 21   OP: £12.50

SPI-029 'Peter Davison' Stamp Cover
2002/05, The Stamp Centre, UK
A stamp cover featuring the Dalek stamp. The cover shows a collage of images from *The Caves of Androzani*. Signed by Peter Davison. Limited to 1500 covers. Designed by Ian Burgess.
REF: 22 OP: £12.50

SPI-030 'Jon Pertwee' Stamp Cover
2002/05/18, The Stamp Centre, UK
A stamp cover featuring the Dalek stamp. The cover shows a collage of images from *The Time Warrior*. Signed by Ingeborg Pertwee. Limited to 1000 covers. Designed by Ian Burgess. Commemorating the unveiling of a BBC plaque in honour of Pertwee.
REF: 20 OP: £12.50

SPI-031 'Katy Manning' Stamp Cover
2002/10/12, The Stamp Centre, UK
A stamp cover featuring the Dalek stamp. The cover shows a collage of images. Signed by Katy Manning. Limited to 1000 covers. Designed by Ian Burgess.
REF: 23 OP: £12.50

SPI-032 'Tom Baker' Stamp Cover
2002/10/12, The Stamp Centre, UK
A stamp cover featuring the Dalek stamp and a collage of images from *City of Death*. Signed by Tom Baker. Limited to 1000 covers. Designed by Ian Burgess.
REF: 24 OP: £12.50

SPI-024

SPI-025

SPI-026

SPI-027

SPI 028

SPI-029

SUNDRIES, POSTCARDS

POSTCARDS are among the earliest forms of *Doctor Who* merchandise to be released. Initially they were printed and issued free by the BBC as a form of publicity for their shows and stars, but they were stopped for *Doctor Who* when the market showed that postcards could be commercially sold. From that point, the production office would still send out signed photographs to fans, but these were the commercially available postcards rather than especially produced BBC ones. Other postcards have been produced by publishers and manufacturers for many purposes.

SPO-001 Publicity Cards
1963 – 79, BBC Television, UK
Free 'character' cards sent out by the BBC. Usually featured a black and white or colour photograph of the personality, with their name and space for a signature across the bottom. Proper 'postcards' rather than 'publicity cards' started to be issued for *Doctor Who* from around 1977, with postcards for Leela and the Doctor being among the first.
OP: free NM: £6.50 – £16.50 each

SPO-002 Daleks Postcard (14.8cm x 10.5cm)
1974, Larkfield Printing Co. Ltd, UK
Picture of two Daleks from a *Doctor Who* exhibition.
NM: £6.50

SPO-003 Tom Baker full length 'Happy Days' Postcard
1976, UK
This series of Tom Baker postcards was produced for the Longleat and Blackpool *Doctor Who* exhibitions.
NM: £6.50

SPO-004 Tom Baker full length 'Welcome to Blackpool' Postcard
1976, UK
NM: £6.50

SPO-005 Tom Baker full length 'Welcome to Longleat' Postcard
1976, UK
NM: £6.50

SPO-006 Tom Baker full length 'Wish "Who" Were Here' Postcard
1976, UK
NM: £6.50

SPO-007 Tom Baker head and shoulders Postcard
1976, UK
NM: £6.50

SPO-008 Leela (Louise Jameson) Postcard
1977, Larkfield Printing Co. Ltd, UK
The Larkfield Printing Co. were responsible for most of the *Doctor Who* promotional postcards produced for

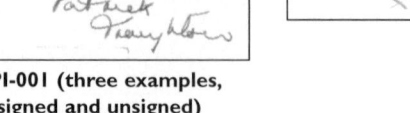

SPI-001 (three examples, signed and unsigned)

SPO-013

SPO-019

SPO-020

the BBC in the eighties but it is not known exactly how many they did. Prior to 1981 the cards were printed via a letterpress process on copper plates and thereafter the printers switched to a litho method. Cards were produced for all the various Doctors and companions featured in the series, and there were additional cards for *The Five Doctors*. Some characters had two different cards released: Tegan, Nyssa and Ace among them. NM: £6.50

SPO-009 K-9 Postcard (from *The Invisible Enemy*)
1978, Larkfield Printing Co. Ltd, UK
OP: 15p NM: £2.50

SPO-010 Tom Baker Postcard (pointing at lapel)
1978, Larkfield Printing Co. Ltd, UK
NM: £3.50

SPO-011 K-9 Postcard (from *The Horns of Nimon*)
1979, Larkfield Printing Co. Ltd, UK
OP: 15p NM: £1.50

SPO-012 Romana (Lalla Ward) Postcard (from *City of Death* – publicity)
1979, Larkfield Printing Co. Ltd, UK
NM: £4.50

SPO-013 Dr Who & the Daleks
1980 c., 'Editions cinema', France
Cut-out photograph of Tom Baker and Daleks (from *Genesis of the Daleks* press photograph) against a white background.
REF: EC 251

SPO-014 Adric Postcard (From *Full Circle*)
1980, Larkfield Printing Co. Ltd, UK
OP: 15p NM: £4.50

SPO-015 Daleks Postcard (From *Day of the Daleks*)
1980, Larkfield Printing Co. Ltd, UK
OP: 15p NM: £3.50

SPO-016 Fourth Doctor Postcard
1980, Larkfield Printing Co. Ltd, UK
There are two versions of this card; one features a pose with an obscured collar under the Doctor's scarf, while the other has both collars visible.
OP: 15p NM: £3.50

SPO-017 Nyssa Postcard (From *Logopolis*)
1980, Larkfield Printing Co. Ltd, UK
OP: 15p NM: £4.50

SPO-018 Tegan Postcard (From *Logopolis*)
1980, Larkfield Printing Co. Ltd, UK
OP: 15p NM: £4.50

SPO-019 The Master Postcard (From *Logopolis*)
1980, Larkfield Printing Co. Ltd, UK
OP: 15p NM: £4.50

SPO-020 Fifth Doctor Postcard (From *The Visitation*) (two diff)
1981, Larkfield Printing Co. Ltd, UK
OP: 15p NM: £3.50

SPO-021

SPO-021 Prime Computers Postcards
1981, Prime Computers, AUS
Postcards with a photo of the Doctor and Romana on from the Australian Prime Computers Advertisements. One features a close-up of both while the other depicts Romana seated at the computer with the Doctor entering the room.. The first ad, 'Dr. Who and the Aliens,' aired in New Zealand on Tuesday, 21 July 1981 at the ad break in 'Warriors' Gate' episode 2.
OP: free   NM: £3.50

SPO-022 Nyssa Postcard (Publicity shot – *Terminus* costume)
1982, Larkfield Printing Co. Ltd, UK
OP: 15p   NM: £1.50

SPO-023 The Master Postcard (Publicity shot)
1982, Larkfield Printing Co. Ltd, UK
OP: 15p   NM: £2.50

SPO-024 Turlough Postcard (From *Mawdryn Undead*)
1982, Larkfield Printing Co. Ltd, UK
OP: 15p   NM: £1.50

SPO-025 Sarah Jane Smith Postcard (From *The Five Doctors*)
1983, Acanthus Press Ltd, UK
Card withdrawn due to actress Elisabeth Sladen expressing dissatisfaction with the image.
OP: 15p   NM: £5.50

SPO-026 Susan Postcard (From *The Five Doctors*)
1983, Acanthus Press Ltd, UK
Card withdrawn due to actress Carole Ann Ford expressing dissatisfaction with the image.
OP: 15p   NM: £5.50

SPO-027 Tegan Postcard (From *Mawdryn Undead*)
1983, Larkfield Printing Co. Ltd, UK
OP: 15p   NM: £1

SPO-028 The Brigadier Postcard (From *Mawdryn Undead*)
1983, Larkfield Printing Co. Ltd, UK
OP: 15p   NM: £1.50

SPO-029 First Doctor Postcard (From *The Five Doctors*)
1984, Larkfield Printing Co. Ltd, UK
OP: 15p   NM: £1

SPO-022

SPO-024

SPO-027

SPO-028

SPO-030 Fourth Doctor Postcard (Publicity shot – Season 18 Costume, at least 2 diff)
1984, Larkfield Printing Co. Ltd, UK
One card features a portrait, the other a landscape photo.
OP: 15p   NM: £2.50

SPO-031 Peri Postcard (Publicity shot – *The Twin Dilemma* Costume)
1984, Larkfield Printing Co. Ltd, UK
OP: 15p   NM: £1.50

SPO-032 Sarah Jane Smith Postcard (From *K9 and Company*)
1984, Larkfield Printing Co. Ltd, UK
OP: 15p   NM: £2.50

SPO-033 Second Doctor Postcard (From *The Five Doctors*)
1984, Larkfield Printing Co. Ltd, UK
OP: 15p   NM: £3.50

SPO-034a Sixth Doctor Postcard (Publicity shot)
1984, Larkfield Printing Co. Ltd, UK
OP: 15p   NM: £2.50

SPO-034b Sixth Doctor Postcard (Publicity shot)
1984, JCS Printers Ltd , UK
Features a photo that is only slightly different from the Larkfield version above.
OP: 15p   NM: £2.50

SPO-035 Third Doctor Postcard (From *The Five Doctors*)
1984, Larkfield Printing Co. Ltd, UK
OP: 15p   NM: £3.50

SPO-036 Art Cards (9 different)
1985/09, Who Dares Publishing, UK
All art by Andrew Skilleter. Cybermen & Dark Tower; Davros and Daleks; Omega; K9; Sontarans; Cybermen; Sea Devil; Five Doctors; Sixth Doctor.
OP: 50p each, £3.50 set

SPO-037 Daleks Postcard (From *Resurrection of the Daleks*) Large Format
1985, Larkfield Printing Co. Ltd, UK
OP: 35p   NM: £3.50

SPO-038 TARDIS Console Postcard
1985, Larkfield Printing Co. Ltd, UK
OP: 15p   NM: £1

SPO-029   SPO-030

SPO-031

SPO-033   SPO-034a?

SPO-035

SPO-036 (full set)

SPO-040

SPO-039 Dalek Postcard
1986, BBC Enterprises, UK
Large format postcard.
OP: 65p

SPO-040 Dr What?
1986, Pictures Sales ltd, UK
Artwork by Rodney Matthews depicting a TARDIS-like ship and some aliens. This was part of the development work for one of the *Doctor Who* film treatments in the 80s. This also appeared in a calendar, but the details are unconfirmed at presstime.

SPO-041 Mel Postcard (from *The Trial of a Time Lord 9–12*)
1986, Larkfield Printing Co. Ltd, UK
OP: 15p NM: £3.50

SPO-042 Ace Postcard (from *Dragonfire*)
1987, JCS Printers Ltd, UK
OP: 15p NM: £3.50

SPO-043 Hologram Cards (7 diff)
1987, Light Fantastic, UK
Dalek; TARDIS; Cyberman; Sil; Sontaran; Sea Devil; Davros. Holographic images are of the Fine Art Castings models. The holograms were all images of Fine Art Castings' metal miniatures except the TARDIS which was artwork against a hologrammatic

SPO-042

  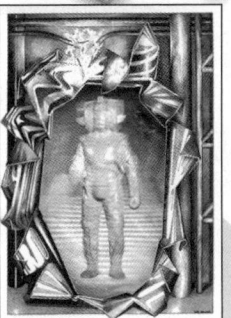 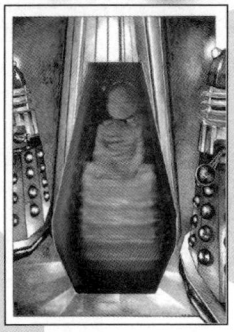

SPO-043

background. A promo of the Sea Devil card also exists with no border on the back and a differently angled picture of the Sea Devil.
OP: £1.95 unframed or £3.45 framed   NM: £2.50

SPO-044 Printpak
1987/03, Who Dares Publishing, UK
12 prints cut from the 1986 Calendar.
OP: £2.50

SPO-045 Seventh Doctor Postcard
1987, JCS Printers Ltd, UK
OP: 15p NM: £2.75

SPO-045

SPO-046 Ace Postcard (Publicity shot)
1988, JCS Printers Ltd, UK
OP: 15p NM: £2.75

SPO-047 Doctor Who Postcard Collection
1995/09/21, Boxtree, UK
Contains 21 photographic postcards. Introduction by Adrian Rigelsford.
REF: ISBN 0-7522-0731-8 OP: £5.99 NM: £5.50

SPO-046

SPO-047

SPO-048

SPO-050 (selected)

SPO-052

SPO-048 Doctor Who Movie postcards (10)
1996, Slowdazzle Worldwide /Forbidden Planet, UK
Only 2000 sets available.
OP: £4.99 set NM: £8

SPO-049 Doctor Who Movie postcards (10)
1996, Slowdazzle Worldwide /Radio Times, UK
Only 2000 sets available.
OP: £4.99 set NM: £8

SPO-050 Doctor Who postcards (32)
1996, Slowdazzle Worldwide , UK
Photographic postcards.
OP: 50p each NM: £1

SPO-051 *Radio Times Doctor Who* Covers Postcards
1996, Slow Dazzle Worldwide, UK
Set of 14 cards limited to 2000 sets. Could be bought separately at 50p each.
OP: 50p each

SPO-052 "Exterminate" Postcard
1997, R.P.M. Postcards, UK
© Rachel McCowat Taylor. Image of a Denys Fisher Dalek figure from the board game, *War of the Daleks* (see TYG-052).
REF: A06/01 NM: £1.50

SPO-053a Doctor Who Postcard book
1997/06/02, BBC Publishing, UK
Contains 16 photographic postcards from TVM.
REF: ISBN 0-563-40561-9 OP: £4.99

SPO-053b Doctor Who Postcards
1997/06, BBC Worldwide, UK
Set of cards promoting the launch of the BBC's new range of *Doctor Who* publications. Images as from the BBC's postcard book, but text on back differs. 16 cards in total. See also SPP-057.
OP: free

SPO-055 (two examples)

SPO-053a

SPO-054 TARDIS Art Postcards
1997, IB Productions, UK
12 images of a Police Box in various contrasting settings: Harvest Time, Outpost, Adrift, Encircled, Beached, Rockscape, Highland, Monoliths, Landfall, Ruins of Time, Open to Visitors, Snowscape. Also available as prints (see SPR-006).
OP: 70p each

SPO-055 Jon Pertwee Promotional Postcards
1998, UK TV, AUS
A series of postcards promoting the screening of Jon Pertwee stories on UK TV which commenced from 16 December 1998. One featured a picture of Jon being menaced by the Daleks under the heading of "Greetings from Skaro". On the back in a script font was "Food's great, weather's brill, shame the Daleks keep bothering me. Anyway see you soon on UKTV. The Doctor". Others featured a Sea Devil, a Sontaran and the male and female golden Axons.

SPO-056 Colin Howard Postcards (18)
1999, Slowdazzle Worldwide, UK
Set of postcards depicting Colin Howard's *Doctor Who* art from the books and videos: The TARDIS, *Logopolis, Mark of the Rani, Revelation of the Daleks, Frontier in Space, Inferno, Time Flight, Android Invasion, Time and the Rani, Planet of Evil, Monster of Peladon, The Sea Devils, Pyramids of Mars, The Five Doctors, Evil of the Daleks, The Three Doctors, The Tenth Planet, Doctor Who: The Movie*.
OP: £8.99 set. 50p each

SPO-057 Dalek Film Postcards
2002/10, Phoenix Publishing & Print Ltd, UK
Set of 9 postcards from the two Dalek films.
OP: £3.99

SPO-056 (Postcards 1-6)

SPO-056 (Postcards 7-18)

SPO-057 (seen in ad)

SUNDRIES, POSTERS & PRINTS

SPP-001 Poster (Third Doctor and IMC Robot Claw)
1972, Personality Posters, UK
This poster was withdrawn from sale after Jon Pertwee expressed concern that the image showed the Doctor looking afraid – giving the wrong impression to young viewers. It was replaced with an image from *The Sea Devils*. No 9 in set of 12.
OP: 50p   NM: £55

SPP-002 Poster (Third Doctor and Sea Devil)
1972, Personality Posters, UK
Image from *The Sea Devils* as on cover of the Piccolo *Making of Doctor Who* book (See also BFA-001a).
OP: 50p   NM: £35

SPP-003 Tom Baker Poster
1976, W. H. Allen & Co. Ltd, UK
Poster promoting the Target range of books.
OP: free   NM: £22

SPP-004 *The Amazing World of Doctor Who* Poster, Ty-Phoo
1976, Cadbury Ty-Phoo, UK
Poster onto which the 12 octagonal Ty-Phoo tea cards could be pasted. Poster artwork by Chris Achilleos. Only available mail order. See also STR-003 and BGE-007.
OP: 20p   NM: £22

SPP-005 Doctor Who and the Pescatons Poster
1976/07, UK
Given away to promote the record release.
OP: free

SPP-006 Poster (Fourth Doctor – artwork)
1977, for Crosse & Blackwell, UK
Poster given away at signings by Tom Baker to promote a special offer being run through the company's tinned goods.
OP: free   NM: £55

SPP-007 Doctor Who Posters (set of four)
1979, Denis Alan Print , UK
Four 18x24" photographic posters of Tom Baker. Two with K9 and one with a Dalek.
REF: DHP 101 – DHP 104
OP: 95p each £3.45 set   NM: £16.50

SPP-006

SPP-007

SPP-008

SPO-008 Keep Australia Beautiful Poster
1970s?, Keep Australia Beautiful, AUS
The 'Keep Australia Beautiful' organization did a campaign with Tom Baker as the Doctor which featured radio and newspaper advertisements. The newspaper advertisements had a picture of Tom Baker against a wall, which had the words 'Keep Australia Beautiful' scrawled on it. This also appeared as a pull-out poster in an issue of the TV magazine *TV Week*. For promotional purposes the organisation also produced a large poster version of the picture.

SPO-009 Fourth Doctor Posters (set of four)
1970s/1980?, Ian Nicoll, AUS
One poster was a Tom Baker head shot, two of them had Tom with K9 (one a full body shot and the other a close-up), and the final poster was of Tom reacting to a *Destiny of the Daleks* Dalek.

SPP-010 Prime Computers Poster
1981, Prime Computers, AUS
A close-up photo of the Doctor and Romana on from the Australian Prime Computers Advertisements.

SPP-011 Hospital Wall Chart
1981 – 1984, The Scottish Heath Authority, UK
Double sided poster featuring the Fifth Doctor and K9.
OP: free

SPP-012 'The World of Doctor Who' poster
1982, W H Allen, UK
Full colour poster advertising the range of Target novels.
OP: free

SPP-013

SPP-013 Tom Baker and K-9 Poster
1982, Madame Tussauds, UK
Poster to commemorate a *Doctor Who* waxwork exhibit. Poster featured the waxwork Baker and K9.
OP: £1.99   NM: £9

SPP-014 Black and white posters
1983 c., USA
11x17 Marvel comics Tom Baker, Five Doctors Cygnus Alpha
OP: $1.00 each

SPP-015 Docteur Qui - Tom Baker dans sans Tardis
1983 Spirit of Light Enterprises Ltd/Barbara Elder Corp, USA
Painted by someone who signs themselves 'SMcM', based on the Toulouse-Lautrec painting, 'Ambassadors'.

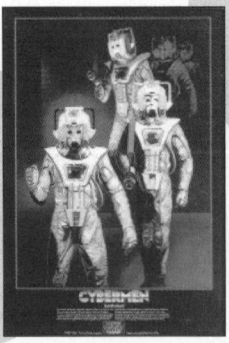

SPP-016

SPP-017

SPP-016 Profile Print – Cybermen
1983/04, Who Dares Publishing, UK
Text by Richard Landen. Painting by Andrew Skilleter.
Originally issued as a card-mounted print (with white
'Profile Print' logo). The laminated version was issued
in November 1983 with a coloured background to
the logo.
REF: PP1 OP: £1.25 (plain) £1.99 (laminated)
NM: £3/£5

SPP-017 Profile Print – Omega
1983/04, Who Dares Publishing, UK
Text by Richard Landen. Painting by Andrew Skilleter.
Originally issued as a card-mounted print (with white
'Profile Print' logo). The laminated version was issued
in November 1983 with a coloured background to
the logo.
REF: PP2 OP: £1.25 (plain) £1.99 (laminated)
NM: £3/£5

SPP-018 Portrait Poster – Patrick Troughton
1983/07, Robbaz Illustrations, UK
Black and white ink portrait
OP: 85p

SPP-019 K9 Print
1983/10, Who Dares Publishing, UK
Artwork by Andrew Skilleter/Russ French. Text by
Richard Landen. Also issued in a laminated version.
OP: £1.25 NM: £3

SPP-020 Portrait Poster – William Hartnell
1983/11, Robbaz Illustrations, UK
Black and white ink portrait
OP: 85p

SPP-021 Profile Print – The Sontarans
1983/11, Who Dares Publishing, UK
Text by Richard Landen. Painting by Andrew Skilleter.
REF: PP3
OP: £1.25 (plain) £1.95 (laminated) NM: £3/£5

SPP-022 Profile Print – The Master
1983/11, Who Dares Publishing, UK
Text by Richard Landen. Painting by Andrew Skilleter.
REF: PP4
OP: £1.25 (plain) £1.95 (laminated) NM: £3/£5

SPP-023 Gail Bennett B/W Art Prints
1984, Gail Bennett, USA
Master/Sarah/1 larry/Tegan/Brigadier/Third Dr/ 5 Drs
watching Space Shuttle/Fourth Dr/Sarah+Third
Dr+Fourth Dr
OP: £1.50 11x10 NM: £3.50

SPP-019

SPP-021   SPP-022

SPP-024 Gail Bennett colour prints
1984, Gail Bennett, USA
4x6 Hartnell, Troughton, Pertwee, T. Baker, Davison, C.
Baker, T. Baker with cat
OP: $1.00 each/£1.25 4x6; £5.25 8x10 NM: £3

SPP-025 Wanted posters
1984, USA
11x17 Jon Pertwee, Tom Baker, Peter Davison.
OP: $1.00 each

SPP-026 Art Posters (4 diff.)
1984, New Media, USA
OP: $3.00 each

SPP-027 Photographic Posters
1984, New Media, USA
8 diff.
OP: $3.00 each

SPP-028 Master Poster
1984, Spirit of Light Enterprises Ltd, USA
OP: $2.50

SPP-028

SPP-029 Posters
1984, Spirit of Light Enterprises Ltd, USA
'The Doctor Lives', 'Watch Out America … Who is here', Tom Baker (French), 5 Doctors
OP: $3.00 each

SPP-030 Posters
1984, Barbara Elder Corp., USA
At least seven released but full details not known:
GW5: Sixth Doctor and Peri by the TARDIS console;
GW7: Sixth Doctor in TARDIS.

SPP-031a TARDIS 21 poster
1984, Spirit of Light Enterprises Ltd, USA
TARDIS 21 was a USA convention to celebrate the 21st anniversary of *Doctor Who*.
OP: $1.50

SPP-031b TARDIS 21 poster with 17 signatures
1984, Spirit of Light Enterprises Ltd, USA
OP: $15.00

SPP-032 5 Doctors portrait set:
1984, Spirit of Light Enterprises Ltd, USA
11x14, full colour
OP: $5.00

SPP-029 (two styles shown)

SPP-030 (GW5 & GW7)

SPP-031a

SPP-032

SPP-033 K-9 Blueprints
1984, Star Tech, USA
2 sheets
OP: $1.00

SPP-034 Posters
1984, W. H. Allen & Co. PLC, UK
Five different 27" x 19" images. 'The World of Doctor Who' showing Davison kneeling in front of a Dalek with a background of *Doctor Who* book covers; a Dalek cut-away to show its insides; Photo of Pertwee struggling with Linx (*The Time Warrior*); Roy Knipe's 'Exploding Dalek' artwork from the cover of *Death to the Daleks*; Bill Donohoe's painting of two Cybermen from his cover for *The Cybermen*. The posters were offered for sale through the Target range of novelisations.
OP: £1.50 each

SPP-034 (set shown in advertisement)

SPP-035 Profile Print – Davros & the Daleks
1984/05, Who Dares Publishing, UK
Text by Richard Landen. Painting by Andrew Skilleter.
REF: PP5 OP: £1.95 (laminated only) NM: £4.50

SPP-036 Portrait Poster – Jon Pertwee
1984/08, Robbaz Illustrations, UK
Black and white ink portrait
OP: 85p

SPP-037 Profile Print – The Sea Devils
1984/11, Who Dares Publishing, UK
Text by Richard Landen. Painting by Andrew Skilleter.
REF: PP6 OP: £1.95 (laminated only) NM: £4.50

SPP-038 Sixth Doctor Print
1984/11, Who Dares Publishing, UK
Artwork by Andrew Skilleter.
OP: £1.95 (laminated only) NM: £2.75

SPP-039 The Five Doctors Print
1984/11, Who Dares Publishing, UK
Painting by Andrew Skilleter. Reproduction of his *Radio Times* cover for *The Five Doctors*.
OP: £1.95 NM: £5

SPP-040 FASA Role Playing Game Cover Art Poster
1985, FASA Corporation, USA
Promotional poster offered to stores to promote FASA game and products
OP: no price

SPP-041 Fourth Doctor Print
1986, Who Dares Publishing, UK
Painting by Andrew Skilleter.
OP: £1.50 (plain) £1.95 (laminated) NM: £3/£5

SPP-035

SPP-037

SPP-038

SPP-039

SPP-041

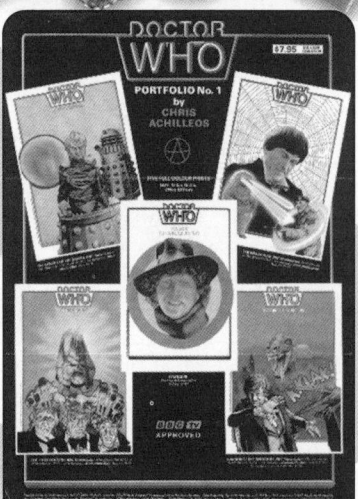

SPP-042 (set shown in advertisement)

SPP-047 (seen on the cover of DWM #140)

SPP-055

SPP-042 Art Portfolio No 1 by Chris Achilleos
1986/05, Titan Books Ltd, UK
Contains five A3-sized prints of Achilleos' *Doctor Who* art:
Genesis of the Daleks; *The Web of Fear*; *The Three Doctors*;
Invasion of the Dinosaurs; and *The Making of Doctor Who*.
REF: ISBN 0-907610-28-5 OP: £3.99 NM: £13.20

SPP-043 Sixth Doctor Poster
1986/12, John G. McElroy, UK
Photographic poster.
OP: £2.00

SPP-044 25th Anniversary Poster
1987, Lionheart, USA
OP: $8.00

SPP-045 USA Tour Posters
1987, Lionheart, USA
BBC *Doctor Who* USA Tour. Various photographic images.
OP: $3.00

SPP-046 *Planet of the Daleks* Poster
1988, MOMI, UK
Black and white photograph of the Doctor with a Dalek.
OP: £3.50

SPP-047 Doctor Who Poster
1988/08, Marvel Comics, UK
Painting by artist Lee Sullivan showed the Seventh
Doctor hanging onto the landing strut of a space-craft as
it flew over a volcanic landscape. Sylvester McCoy was
photographed hanging from some railings to get a realistic reference photograph for Sullivan to work from.
OP: £3.50

SPP-048 *Dr. Who and the Daleks* Film Poster
1989, MOMI, UK
A facsimile poster sold through MOMI.

SPP-049 *The Ultimate Adventure* Poster
1989/03, Mark Furness Ltd, UK
Released to tie in with the stage play. One poster
(March) featured Jon Pertwee while the other
(released in June) featured Colin Baker.
OP: £1.00 (s) £1.50 (l) NM: £4.50

SPP-050 Ghost Light Poster
1992/07, Dominitemporal Services Ltd, UK
A3 Print of Alistair Pearson's artwork for the Target
novelisation.
OP: £4.50

SPP-051 Ace Poster
1990/07, Mediaband, UK
An A2-sized photographic poster of Sophie Aldred as Ace.
OP: £2.99

SPP-052 Posters
1991, MOMI, UK
4 designs. These posters advertising the MOMI exhibition were intended for use on the London Underground, but when fans started taking the posters from the trains, MOMI decided to sell them in their shop as well.

SPP-053 Doctor Who Poster Book
1995/09/21, Boxtree, UK
Introduction by Adrian Rigelsford.
REF: ISBN 0-7522-0795-4 OP: £9.99 NM: £11

SPP-054 Key To Time Video Poster
1996, BBC Video, UK
A poster version of the artwork used on the spines for the Key to Time video releases. Art by Andrew Skilleter.

SPP-055 Doctor Who Poster
1996, Who Shop International, UK
Six Doctors and Monsters.
OP: £3.99 NM: £1.50

SPP-056 30th Anniversary Poster
1996, UK
30th anniversary logo in corner with all seven Doctors, Davros, Cyberman, TARDIS, white Dalek, and red movie Dalek.

SPP-057 Doctor Who posters
1996, Slowdazzle Worldwide/Eurodesign, UK
TARDIS from title sequence; The Master (Roberts); Tom Baker and Melkur; Daleks on Westminster bridge (photograph from the 30th anniversary documentary); McCoy and McGann (some signed by Paul McGann)
OP: £19.99 set
NM: Seventh/Eighth Dr: £5.50 (signed: £20); Master/Fourth Dr: £1.50; Daleks: £5.50; TARDIS: £2.50

SPP-058 *Doctor Who* Prints
1996, Eurodesign, UK
The Sea Devils, *The Seeds of Doom*, *The Curse of Fenric*, *Destiny of the Daleks*, *The Caves of Androzani*. 20x16" laminated poster prints featuring photographs and facts about each story.
REF: EUR001 – 5
OP: £6.95 each (all 5 for £30) NM: £2.75 each

SPP-059 *Doctor Who: The New Adventures: Happy Endings* Poster
1996, Virgin Publishing Ltd , UK
Painting by Paul Campbell. This is a large version of the cover image to the book. Poster offer within the book.
OP: £3.00 (+ £1 p&p) NM: £15

SPP-057 (two examples)

SPP-059

SPP-062

SPP-060 Poster (Third Doctor and Sea Devil)
1996, Slowdazzle Worldwide, UK
Same image as the 1972 Personality Posters.
OP: £5.99

SPP-061 Poster for TVM
1996, Radio Times, UK
Send-off offer in *Radio Times*.
OP: £4.99 NM: £9

SPP-062 Tom Baker on Bicycle Poster
1997/10/04, Forbidden Planet, UK
Photographic poster of Tom Baker on a bicycle with a
large horn device on the back. Given away by
Forbidden Planet in London to promote a signing by
Tom Baker of his autobiography.
OP: free

SPP-063 'Invisible' TARDIS Poster
2000, The Who Shop, UK
3foot by 2 foot poster of a polished steel Police Box
on display at the Whitechapel Art Gallery in London.
Due to the reflections, it appears to be almost invisible.
OP: £4.99

SPP-064 Posters
2001/05, Pyramid Designs, UK
Two designs: TARDIS in vortex and Daleks on
Westminster Bridge.
OP: £7.99 each

SPP-063

SPP-064 (both)

SUNDRIES, PRINTS LTD. ED.

THESE differ from posters in that they are usually of a higher quality, are limited and therefore cost more.

PORTFOLIO

SPR-001 Gary Stevenson Lithographs
1983, Big Thunder Publishing, UK
Set of 5 licensed heavy card stock prints: *The Doctor and K9, The Sontarans, The Zygons, The Pyramids of Mars, Davros and the Daleks*. Each measured 11" x 14".

SPR-002 Frank Bellamy Art Prints
1987/07, Who Dares Publishing, UK
Limited edition of 300. Came with a certificate signed by David Bellamy (Frank Bellamy's son). Set comprised full colour A2 reproductions of: the *Radio Times* cover art for *Day of the Daleks*; an internal *Radio Times* illustration for *Terror of the Zygons*; and a black and white illustration of *Jon Pertwee and the Daleks* originally used as part of *Radio Times'* *Doctor Who* competition promotion.
OP: £36.50

SPR-003 The Five Doctors
1983/11/23, DWAS, UK
Limited edition of 500. Signed and numbered colour print of artwork by Chris Achilleos used on the cover of a special DWAS magazine published in 1984, *The Making of The Five Doctors* edited by David J Howe.
OP: £4 NM: £55

SPR-004 The First Doctor
1989/01, Dominitemporal Services Ltd, UK
Limited edition of 500. Colour print of the First Doctor by artist Jeff Cummins.
OP: £8.00

SPR-005 Ian Scoones Prints
1994, Spacescapes, UK
Ian Scoones was a BBC visual effects designer who worked on several stories in the seventies. These prints are paintings based on his original design work for the show. Jagaroth Spaceship (*City of Death*); Prehistoric landscape (*City of Death*); Shuttle (*Invisible Enemy*); Citadel (*The Curse of Peladon*); Queen Spider (*Planet of the Spiders*). Limited edition of 2000 numbered and signed, A2 sized.
OP: £29.99 each or £119.96 for all five

SPR-001

SPR-006 (10 of 12 shown)

SPR-007

SPR-013 (seen in ad)

SPR-006 TARDIS Art Prints

1996, IB Productions, UK

12 images of a Police Box in various contrasting settings: Harvest Time, Outpost, Adrift, Encircled, Beached, Rockscape, Highland, Monoliths, Landfall, Ruins of Time, Open to Visitors, Snowscape. Also available as postcards. Released in two batches of six images each. See also SPO-054.

OP: £3.95 each

SPR-007 Tom Baker Limited Edition Costume Print

1999/10, Tree Root Productions Ltd, UK

A 38cm x 56cm reproduction of BBC costume designer June Hudson's 1980 costume design for the Doctor. Limited to 2500 prints. Each is individually numbered and signed by Hudson and Tom Baker. Came with a numbered certificate of authenticity.

OP: £39.99

SPR-008 Anneke Wills Art Prints

1999, Dapol, UK

Limited edition prints of artwork by Anneke Wills who played Polly in the TV series. Images available: A4 – Anneke Wills, Michael Craze, Sylvester McCoy. A3 – Jon Pertwee, Tom Baker, Colin Baker, Paul McGann.

OP: £25 each A4; £30 each A3

SPR-009 Invasion Dalek Print

2000/05, Simon Watson/The Toy Machine, UK

Limited edition print (of 100) showing the Daleks by the Houses of Parliament in London. Individually numbered and with a certificate of authenticity. Original oil painting by Simon Watson. A3 sized.

OP: £29.95

SPR-010 Duncan Gutteridge art prints

2000/10, Duncan Gutteridge, UK

Two images available: 4th Doctor and Davros; 3rd Doctor and the Master. Each print limited to 100 copies, hand signed and numbered by the artist.

OP: £15 A5; £25 A4

SPR-011 Chris Achilleos Art Print

2000/11, The Stamp Centre, UK

Limited edition of 50 copies, production proof art print of Chris Achilleos' Tom Baker/Target logo painting. A3 sized. This was a limited production run to test the market for future releases. Individually signed by Achilleos and Tom Baker. The final prints were never produced.

OP: £19.95

SPR-012 Duncan Gutteridge art prints

2001/04, Duncan Gutteridge, UK

Image of Sarah Jane Smith. Each print limited to 100 copies, hand signed and numbered by the artist.

OP: £15 A5; £25 A4

SPR-013 Julian Vince art prints

2001/08, Julian Vince, UK

Computer enhanced photographic art cards of Dalek models and scenes created by Julian Vince. Four cards produced intially: 1: Dalek Hovabout; 2: You Will Obey!; 3: Dalek Galaxy; 4: Ex-Ter-Min-Ate!. Also a special card: Dalek Patrol; issued to mail order customers.

OP: £10 set of 4

SPR-014 Art Prints

2001/08/23, The Stamp Centre, UK

Set of four 8x10" art prints: *Image of the Fendahl*; *Horror of Fang Rock*; *Pyramids of Mars* (all signed by Tom Baker); *Web of Fear* (signed by Nicholas Courtney). Designed by Ian Burgess. Limited numbered edition of 1000 copies of each print.

OP: £15 each

SPR-014 (*Image of the Fendahl* and *Pyramids of Mars* inset)

SPR-015

SPR-016

SPR-015 Tom Baker and the Daleks Art Print
2001/11/23, The Stamp Centre, UK
An 8x10" art print featuring Tom Baker and the
Daleks. Designed by Ian Burgess. Signed by Tom Baker.
Limited numbered edition of 1000 copies.
OP: £15

SPR-016 Sophie Aldred Art Print
2001/11/23, The Stamp Centre, UK
An 8x10 art print of Sophie Aldred (*Silver Nemesis*).
Signed by Aldred. Limited to 1000 copies. Designed by
Ian Burgess.
OP: £15

SPR-017

SPR-018

SPR-017 Carole Ann Ford Art Print
2001/11/23, The Stamp Centre, UK
An 8x10 art print of Carole Ann Ford. Signed by Ford.
Limited to 1000 copies. Designed by Ian Burgess.
OP: £15

SPR-018 Louise Jameson Art Print
2002/05, The Stamp Centre, UK
An 8x10 art print of Louise Jameson (*The Robots of
Death*). Signed by Jameson. Limited to 1000 copies.
Designed by Ian Burgess.
OP: £15

SPR-019

SPR-020

SPR-019 Sylvester McCoy Art Print
2002/05, The Stamp Centre, UK
An 8x10 art print of Sylvester McCoy (*The Greatest
Show in the Galaxy*). Signed by McCoy. Limited to 1000
copies. Designed by Ian Burgess.
OP: £15

SPR-020 Peter Davison Art Print
2002/05, The Stamp Centre, UK
An 8x10 art print of Sylvester McCoy (*The Greatest
Show in the Galaxy*). Signed by McCoy. Limited to 1000
copies. Designed by Ian Burgess.
OP: £15

SPR-021

SPR-022

SPR-021 Louise Jameson Art Print
2002/05, The Stamp Centre, UK
An 8x10 art print of Louise Jameson (*The Sun
Makers*). Signed by Jameson. Limited to 1000 copies.
Designed by Ian Burgess.
OP: £15

SPR-022 Talons of Weng-Chiang Art Print
2002/05, The Stamp Centre, UK
An 8x10 art print from *The Talons of Weng-Chiang*.
Signed by Baker and Jameson. Limited to 1000 copies.
Designed by Ian Burgess.
OP: £15

SPR-023 Matthew Waterhouse Art Print
2002/05, The Stamp Centre, UK
An 8x10 art print of Matthew Waterhouse (*Full Circle*). Signed by Waterhouse. Limited to 1000 copies.
Designed by Ian Burgess.
OP: £15

SPR-023

SPR-024 Richard Franklin Art Print
2002/05/15, The Stamp Centre, UK
An 8x10 art print of Richard Franklin (*The Web of Fear*). Signed by Franklin. Limited to 1000 copies.
Designed by Ian Burgess.
OP: £15

SPR-025 Robot Art Print
2002/05/15, The Stamp Centre, UK
An 8x10 art print from *Robot*. Signed by Baker and Courtney. Limited to 1000 copies. Designed by Ian Burgess.
OP: £15

SPR-026 Katy Manning Art Print
2002/10/12, The Stamp Centre, UK
An 8x10 art print of Katy Manning (*The Curse of Peladon*). Signed by Manning. Limited to 1000 copies.
Designed by Ian Burgess.
OP: £15

SPR-024

SPR-025

SPR-026

ADELPHI THEATRE

SRG-002

A Season of Doctor Who Television Material at the N.F.T.

SRG-004

SRG-005

SUNDRIES, PROGRAMMES

THEATRE and other presentation/production programmes can vary from a folded sheet of A4 paper to a more lavish colour booklet/magazine. We have listed here some of the more lavish examples.

SRG-001 *Curse of the Daleks, The*, stage play programme
1965/12, UK
A5 sized theatre programme.
NM: £90

SRG-002 *Doctor Who and the Daleks In Seven Keys to Doomsday* Programme
1974/12, UK
A5 sized theatre programme.
NM: £55

SRG-003 *Cinderella* Pantomime Programme
1982, Lovett Bickford Ltd, UK
Large-format A3 programme themed around *Doctor Who*. Pantomime was written and directed by John Nathan-Turner and starred Peter Davison and Anthony Ainley at the Assembly Hall Theatre, Royal Tunbridge Wells.
OP: 75p NM: £3.50

SRG-004 *Doctor Who – The Developing Art* programme
1983/10/29, British Film Institute, UK
Written by Jeremy Bentham. Illustrated by Phil Bevan. Cover by Stuart Glazebrook and Gordon Lengden. A4 programme to a weekend of screenings at the National Film Theatre in London October 29/30 1983.
REF: No ISBN NM: £11

SRG-005 The Doctor Who Celebration (programme)
1983/04, BBC Enterprises/The Warminster Press, UK
A4 programme for the 20th anniversary celebration at Longleat House.
OP: 50p NM: £16.50

SRG-006 Doctor Who USA Tour pamphlet
1987, Lionheart, USA
Given out at tour, shows a map of the exhibit and explanations of the characters, has a picture of Sixth Doctor, Peri, and Tegan.
OP: free

SRG-007a *The Ultimate Adventure* **souvenir brochure**
1989/03, Peter Griffiths Associates, UK
A4 programme. Version featuring a colour centre-spread with Jon Pertwee as the Doctor. Interior text by John Freeman. As well as the colour brochure, most theatres also issued their own programme for the play. These varied from single sheets of A4, to A5 magazines.
OP: £2.00 NM: £13.20

SRG-007b *The Ultimate Adventure* **souvenir brochure**
1989/06, Peter Griffiths Associates, UK
Version featuring a colour centre-spread with Colin Baker as the Doctor.
OP: £2.00 NM: £8

SRG-008 Bonham's Auction Catalogue
1991/05/11, Bonhams, UK
Quarto catalogue featuring many photographs from the series alongside a listing of what was being auctioned.
NM: £22

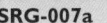

SRG-007a

SRG-008

SUNDRIES, STATIONERY ITEMS

STATIONERY items are among the hardest to try and categorise. This is mainly because they are very accessible and easy to produce, and so any company doing a promotion, or any exhibition, no matter how small, can, if they wish, produce a range of pens and other accessories to promote it. With *Doctor Who* the biggest outlet has been the BBC's permanent exhibitions at Longleat House and at Blackpool, but other exhibitions, like MOMI and Space Adventure, also produced their own items. We have tried to catalogue as many items as we can here, but as with Badges, there are almost certain to be some missing.

SSI-001 Dalek Pencil Sharpener
1965, Baileys Agencies , UK
A pencil sharpener in the shape of a Dalek.

SSI-002 Dalek Pencils
1965, Baileys Agencies, UK
NM: £27.50 each

SSI 003 Dalek Writing Pad, The
1965, Newton Mills Ltd, UK
Pad contained 30 ruled sheets. Two designs available.
OP: 1s

SSI-001

SSI-003

SSI-005

SSI-006

SSI-007

SSI-008

SSI-004 Dalek Pencil Craft Set
1966, Tower Press (London) Ltd, UK
A set of coloured pencils.
OP: 9s 11d

SSI-005 Doctor Who Space Mission Pad (Third Doctor)
1973, Naocraft Ltd, UK
This item was produced before it was realised that Pertwee was leaving. Withdrawn and replaced with a Fourth Doctor pad instead.
OP: 35p

SSI-006 Doctor Who Space Mission Pad (Fourth Doctor)
1974, John Morriss, UK
This was the first piece of merchandise to feature Tom Baker's Doctor, being produced several months in advance of his TV debut in *Robot*. The paper in the pads was specially treated so that a pen pressed on the top sheet would leave a copy on the lower one. The pad also included a code sheet, the idea being that the user could send coded messages to friends whilst retaining a copy. The pads were issued by John Morriss to support the Save the Children Fund. Only 5,000 units were produced.
OP: 35p

SSI-007 Doctor Who Data Printer
1978, Tangent Systems Ltd, UK
A standard 'Dymo' labeller with a *Doctor Who* logo on the letter dial, plus some strips of pre-cut black 'Dymo' tape and a BBC *Doctor Who* badge. The production run of these label makers was 40,000 units.
OP: 91p NM: £35

SSI-008 Doctor Who Poster Art Kit
1978/08, Thomas Salter Ltd, UK
This contained two 22 x 14" posters and five felt-tip pens (yellow, brown, red, green and blue) with which to colour them in. The posters consisted of simple line artwork of the Fourth Doctor and the Daleks.
OP: 99p NM: £55

SSI-009 Dr Who Pencil Sharpeners (set of four)
1979/04, H.C. Ford, UK
These featured the same *Doctor Who* mini-puzzles from 1974 set into the top of coloured plastic pencil sharpeners.
OP: 22p each NM: £3.50 each

SSI-010 Doctor Who Writing Set
1979 c., Ian Nicoll Enterprises Pty Ltd, AUS
10 envelopes, 20 letterheads. Colour artwork of

Fourth Doctor on envelopes and letterhead, with version of *Doctor Who* logo on back of envelopes. Came in a folder with Tom Baker's picture on the front. REF: DH 2200

SSI-011 Pencils
USA
10 colours.
OP: $8 per set

SSI-012 Eraser
BBC Enterprises, UK
On sale in the BBC exhibitions in the eighties.

SSI-013 K-9 Retractable Pens
BBC Enterprises, UK
Yellow, red and blue. On sale in the BBC exhibitions in the eighties.
OP: 60p each

SSI-009

SSI-014 Key Ring Pens
BBC Enterprises, UK
On sale in the BBC exhibitions in the eighties.
OP: 60p each

SSI-015 Pencils
BBC Enterprises, UK
Blue, white and yellow. .On sale in the BBC exhibitions in the eighties.
OP: 15p each

SSI-016 Retractable Pens
BBC Enterprises, UK
On sale in the BBC exhibitions in the eighties.
OP: 60p each

SSI-010 (full set)

SSI-010 (envelope front, back and letterhead samples shown with outside packaging)

SSI-020   SSI-021

SSI-022

SSI-027

SSI-031

SSI-037 (both versions)

SSI-017 Pen "This pen used to belong to the Doctor, now it belongs to one of his friends"
DWFCA, USA
OP: $2.50

SSI-018 Book Covers
USA
Two styles: 'Panoptikon Library Gallifrey' and 'Time Lords Academy'

SSI-019 'Doctor Who Rules the Universe' ruler
1982, BBC Enterprises, UK
On sale in the BBC exhibitions in the eighties.
OP: £1.25

SSI-020 TARDIS 3D Pencil Case
1982, Interwainer Handbag Co., UK
Dark blue with black windows and the front doors were on the same side as the zipper.
OP: £2.99   NM: £22

SSI-021 TARDIS 3D Pencil Case
1982, Hummingbird Productions Ltd, UK
A lighter blue, had white slashes on the windows and the doors were on the opposite side from the zipper.
OP: £1.75   NM: £22

SSI-022 Eraser
1983, A. B. & Son, UK
Blue and red.

SSI-023 Official TARDIS Technician pencil:
1984, USA
A rainbow finish, gold trim
OP: $1.25

SSI-024 Pen
1984, USA
Solid satin finish w/ gold trim, diamond logo, 'Property of Timelord Council'
OP: $1.50

SSI-025 Notepads
1984, Barbara Elder Corp., USA
2 colour, pastel, 5 1/2 x 8 1/2 pads of 100 sheets each. 4 different: diamond logo, TARDIS, Dalek, K-9. Art by Gail Bennett
OP: $2.00 each

SSI-026 Notepads
1984, Gail Bennett, USA
52 pages with five Doctors artwork
OP: £2.00 each

SSI-027 Dalek Pencil Case
1984, Interwainer Handbag Co., UK
OP: £3.30   NM: £16.50

SSI-028 TARDIS Flat Pencil Case
1984, Hummingbird Productions Ltd, UK
OP: £2.99

SSI-029 Ballpoint Pen in gold card box
1985, BBC Enterprises, UK
OP: £1.20

SSI-030 Ballpoint Pen in plastic box
1985, BBC Enterprises, UK
OP: 95p

SSI-031 Doctor Who Diary 1986
1985/09, International Scripts, UK
3" wide x 6" tall. Contains maps of the UK and
London, with listings of episodes and actors as well as
pages of dates to write appointments. Apparently
made for the US, as the dust jacket has an American
price. Dust cover features Andrew Skilleter's TARDIS
in webs artwork from the reprint book cover for
'Doctor Who and The Web of Fear'.
REF: ISBN 0-948234-00-8
OP: $6.95 (£2.95 import)   NM: £4

SSI-032 Pen: BBC *Doctor Who* USA Tour
1987, Lionheart, USA
OP: $2.00

SSI-033 Snap Pen
1987, BBC Enterprises, UK
Blue, white, yellow and red.
OP: £1.00

**SSI-034 'I've Journeyed through the World of
Doctor Who exhibition' Ruler**
1989, Space Adventure, UK
Space Adventure was a theme ride located in
London's Tooley Street next to the London Dungeon.
As well as the ride, they had a permanent exhibition
of *Doctor Who* props. Their shop therefore sold sever-
al *Doctor Who* related items.

SSI-035 Doctor Who Eraser
1989, Space Adventure, UK

SSI-036 Doctor Who Pencil
1989, Space Adventure, UK

SSI-037 Bookplates
1999, Bookmarks of Distinction, UK

SSI-042

Self adhesive full colour photographic bookplates. Two
designs: K9; The Three Doctors. Sold in sets of five.
OP: 99p each set

SSI-038 Hirschfeld Litho Note Cards
1990 c., USA
Offered on PBS pledge drives, note cards have reproduction of 'Seven Faces' litho. SEE COL-007.

SSI-039 MOMI Doctor Who Pencil
1991, MOMI, UK
OP: 40p

SSI-040 DSL Pens
1993, Dominitemporal Services Ltd, UK
Schaeffer 'no nonsense' pens with red, blue and black bar-
rels featuring 'Panopticon '93 Thirty Years of a Time Lord'
design on barrel and 'seal of Rassilon' logo on the cap.

SSI-041 TARDIS Pen
1994, Who Shop International, UK
TARDIS pen says 'Who at the Dock' in white.

SSI-042 Doctor Who 1996 Diary
1995, Mallon Publishing, AUS
A large format hardback week-to-view diary, printed in
full colour throughout. Exclusive to Angus and Robertson
Bookworld. The content of this diary was devised by
David J Howe, and written by Howe, along with Richard
Bignell and Graeme Wood. It featured fictional and factual
pieces for every week of the year, as well as several
'theme' photographic spreads. Designed by Pauline
McClenehan and edited by Anna Costello.
OP: $22.95 h/b   NM: £27.50

SSI-043

SSI-045

SSI-043 1997 Pocket Diary
1996, Dapol, UK
Maroon/Blue/Black
OP: £1

SSI-044 Notepad
1996, Dapol, UK
Purple notepad.

SSI-045 Address Books
1996, Dapol, UK
Diamond logo. Black/Red/White
REF: W035-001/2/3 OP: £2.50

SSI-046 Holographic Glitter pens
1996, Dapol, UK
Diamond logo. Gold/Purple/Silver/Red/Green/Blue.
REF: W032-001/2/3/4/5 OP: £1.75

SSI-047 Pencils
1996, Dapol, UK
Diamond logo and tip eraser.
Yellow/Gold/Blue/Green/Red
REF: W033-001/2/3/4/5 OP: 45p each

SSI-048 Wrapping paper
2000/11/23, The Stamp Centre, UK
A pack of six sheets of *Doctor Who* wrapping paper,
using the design from the 'Battle of the Daleks' stamp
cover.
OP: £5.95 pack

SSI-049 Rubber Stamp
2001/07, Prairie Rubber Stamps, Canada
Red rubber stamp of the TARDIS mounted on a
maple block with contoured edges.
OP: $2.50

SSI-050 Doctor Who Action Pens
2001/08/23, The Stamp Centre, UK
Three 'action' pens. When tilted, characters move
within a water/oil filled compartment. 4th Doctor and
TARDIS; Cybermen chase Ben and Polly; Dalek Attack.
OP: £7.50 set of three.

SSI-051 Sonic Screwdriver Pen
2002/05, The Stamp Centre, UK
A metal pen in the shape of the Doctor's Sonic
Screwdriver.

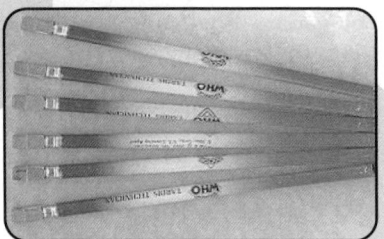

SSI-047

SSI-048

SSI-049

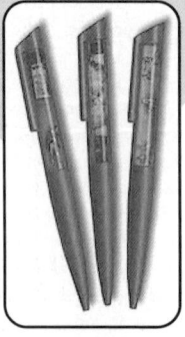

SSI-050

SSI-052 Doctor Who Action Pens
2002/12, The Stamp Centre, UK
Five 'action' pens. When tilted, characters move within a water/oil filled compartment. Davros; Daleks in Westminster; 4th Doctor and Skaroth; 5th Doctor; 3rd Doctor and Bessie.
OP: £1.50 each.

SSI-052 (close-up details)

SSI-051

SUNDRIES, STICKERS

SST-001 Doctor Who Exhibition Sticker
1976, BBC Enterprises, UK
OP: 25p

SST-002 Diamond Logo Sticker
1978, ABC, AUS
Free logo sticker advertised on Australian television after broadcasts of Doctor Who episodes. Demand was so great that a second print run of the stickers was quickly arranged.
OP: free

SST-003 Target Books Bumper Sticker
1980s, Target/WH Allen, UK
Black and neon green with a Dalek saying 'Exterminate Boredom!', the neon logo, and then a second Dalek saying 'Read Doctor Who Books'.

SST-004 Bumper Stickers
1983, Spirit of Light Enterprises Ltd, USA
'I Brake for Daleks', 'Travel With TARDIS', 'Who Is Here', 'I Love the Doctor', 'I Don't Brake for Daleks', 'This car protected by attack K-9 unit', 'Travel by TARDIS', 'Official Staff Car – Time Lord Council Authorised Use Only' (all have the diamond logo) silver foil.
OP: $2.00 each (£1.50 import)

SST-005 Day-Glo Stickers (Peter Davison, Cyberman)
1983/04, Image Screencraft, UK
OP: 75p each

SST-006 Bumper Sticker: Jelly Babies
1984, DWFCA, USA
Full colour reproduction of jelly baby box with 'Dr' to one side and 'Who' to the other.
OP: $2.00

SST-007 Doctor Who Exhibition Car Sticker
1984, BBC Enterprises, UK
OP: 25p

SST-004

SST-006

SST-007

SST-008 Bumper Sticker
DWFCA, USA
'I ♥♥ Doctor Who' (two hearts are used for love).
See also CBA-033.
OP: $1.00

SST-009 Stickers
USA
Different colours and came in small envelopes, with many of the same kind. diamond Logo, 'May you never lose the key to your Tardis', 'But I'm only 749 years old – life doesn't begin until…', 'Gallifrey Postal Service', 'Gallifrey Diplomatic Service', 'Caution – Tardis in Dematerialization Phase', 'Go Tardis – and Leave the Timing to Us!', 'The Key to Time is Mine!', 'Time Lords turn me on!', Doctor Who Logo (a strip of full colour stickers).

SST-0010a Save Doctor Who Stickers
1985/03, Sun Newspapers, UK
Given away by the Newspaper during a campaign to 'save Doctor Who' after the show's cancellation was announced in 1985. Sticker reads 'The Sun Says Save Doctor Who'. See also PRO-007.
OP: free NM: £3.50

SST-0010b Save Doctor Who Stickers
1985/03, Star Newspapers, UK
Given away by the Newspaper during a campaign to 'save Doctor Who' after the show's cancellation was announced in 1985. Sticker reads 'Save Doctor Who'. See also PRO-007.
OP: free NM: £3.50

SST-011 Bumper Stickers
1986, DWFCA, USA
'My TARDIS', 'Doctor Who', 'Save the Doctor'.
OP: $1.50 each

SST-012 McCoy Logo Bumper Sticker
1987, FasPrint?, UK
McCoy logo on white background. Available from Longleat.

SST-013 Bumper Stickers
1987, Lionheart, USA
'Doctor Who who's who', 'Who is aboard?', 'I ♥ the Doctor', 'Doctor Who w/logo'.
OP: $1.00 each

SST-014 Bumper Stickers
1988, Mere Dragons Inc., USA
'TARDIS EXPRESS – When it absolutely, positively, has to be there BEFORE you mailed it...' sticker has a

variation of the Federal Express logo; 'My Other Car is a TARDIS' is black ink on silver chrome vinyl; 'James Bond is realy a Time Lord' features a Bondian logo with the shadow of Tom Baker holding a sonic screwdriver and K9.
OP: $3.00

SST-015 Bumper Sticker
1992, Bally Midway, USA
'I NEVER Brake for Daleks' also came with two TARDIS stickers attached to the left side of the bumper sticker; given away at Visions '92.
OP: free promotional item

SST-016 'Triple M Rocks' Bumper Stickers
1990s, Triple M, AUS
As a promotional prize, radio network Triple M offered 200 bumper stickers with 'Triple M Rocks...' printed on. The winner would choose what town name would complete the phrase, but one winner chose 'Gallifrey.' The Doctor Who Fan Club of Australia subsequently contacted the network and had two more versions printed: 'Triple M Rocks the TARDIS' and 'Triple M Rocks the Daleks'.
OP: free promotional items

SST-017 Gallifreyan Institute Transfer
1990s?, USA?
Reverse clear transfer with gold ink. 'Parking Permit' in circle on the top, 'Gallifreyan Institute' on the bottom, and 'For Advance Temporal Studies' circling a TARDIS. Underneath there are three lines reading 'TARDIS: Class AA', 'Temporal Restrictions: None', and 'Spacial Restrictions: None'.

SST-018 Doctor Who Self Adhesive Transfers
1999/08, Dapol, UK
Set of twelve different self-adhesive transfer/stickers. Numbers 01 to 09 were released in August, and 10 to 12 in November.
Description: 01 – Gold 'Seal of Rassilon', 02 – Silver Cyberman, 03 – Red Dalek, 04 – Silver K9, 05 – Blue TARDIS, 06 – Grey Sontaran, 07 – Blue TVM logo, 08 – Red Question Mark, 09 – Silver Early Cyberman, 10 – Sea Devil, 11 – Zygon, 12 – Mandrel
REF: WS-01 – WS-12 OP: £2.99 each

SST-019 'I've experienced the Doctor Who Exhibition' car sticker
2000, Dapol, UK
Free with mail orders of the Early Dalek Gift Set. Also available on sale at the exhibition.

SSI-0010b

SST-016

SST-011 (one version)

SUNDRIES, STANDEES

STA-001 Police Box standee
2000/10, SlowDazzle Worldwide, UK
A small photographic card standee of the TARDIS.
Randomly included with the 2000 calendar.
OP: 99p

STA-002 Dalek standee
2000/10, SlowDazzle Worldwide, UK
A small photographic card standee of a Dalek.
Photograph provided by This Planet Earth, makers of
the full-size Dalek reproductions. Randomly included
with the 2000 calendar.
OP: 99p

STA-003 Jon Pertwee standee
2001, SlowDazzle Worldwide, UK
A small photographic card standee of Pertwee as the
Doctor, randomly included with the 2001 calendar.

STA-004 Tom Baker standee
2001, SlowDazzle Worldwide, UK
A small photographic card standee of Baker as the
Doctor, randomly included with the 2001 calendar.

STA-001

STA-002

STA-003

STA-004

STR-001a

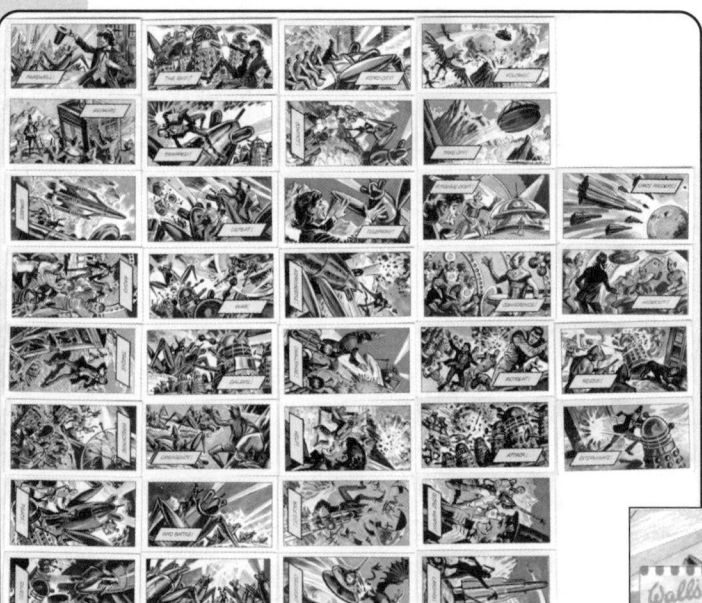

STR-002a

STR-002b

SUNDRIES, TRADING CARDS

STR-001a Dr Who and the Daleks Cards
1964, Cavenham Confectionery Ltd/Paramount Labs Ltd (Cadet), UK
Every box of ten sweet cigarettes (white candy sticks) contained a numbered picture card (art by Richard Jennings) from a set of fifty, telling the story of one of the First Doctor's many adventures with the Daleks (*TV Century 21* versions). Full colour front and black and white reverse. There was also an album into which the cards could be pasted, available for 1s plus five empty boxes. It is thought that the album was a generic one, not specifically produced for the Dalek promotion.
OP: 2d NM: £110 set, £2.50 singles

STR-001b Dr Who and the Daleks Cards
1983, Goodies, UK
In 1983 Goodies released some tubs of *Doctor Who* favourites bars as Christmas Candy. The tubs each included one of the 1965 Cadet Sweet Cigarette cards, re-printed by Goodies, but these were hastily withdrawn when the manufacturers realised that the Doctor was no longer played by William Hartnell. This set has 'Goodies' printed on the reverse, while the 1964 set has 'Cadet Sweets'. These re-issued cards are potentially far rarer as they were never really commercially released.
NM: £220 set, £4.50 singles.

STR-002a Dr Who's Space Adventure
1967, Sky Ray /T. Wall & Sons, UK
Cover and card artwork by Patrick Williams. There was also an album into which they could be pasted. Cards were as follows. Each card had a title on the reverse, and also a single word on the front. The front-word is shown in brackets where it differed from the title on the back:
Cards:
1 – Daleks on Zaos! (Exterminate!)
2 – Zaons to the Rescue! (Rescue!)
3 – Earth In Danger! (Hideout!)
4 – Emergency! Call Space Raiders (Space Raiders!)
5 – Landing on Zaos (Landing!)
6 – The Secret Weapon! (Secret Weapon!)
7 – Surprise Attack! (Attack!)
8 – Retreat!
9 – Conference
10 – The Hoverdrome (Strange Craft!)
11 – In Search of the Astrobeetles (Take Off!)
12 – A Perilous Journey (Volcano!)
13 – Collision!
14 – Bale Out!
15 – Rescue! (Help!)
16 – The Land of the Astrobeetles! (Challenge!)
17 – Dr. Who and the Astrobeetle! (Astrobeetle!)
18 – Mind Against Monster! (Telepathy!)
19 – Contact!
20 – Astro-City!
21 – Council of War (Allies!)
22 – Into Battle!
23 – Emergency!
24 – Daleks!
25 – The Daleks Weaken (War!)
26 – Defeat!
27 – Dr. Who in Danger (Trapped!)
28 – The End of Dr. Who? (The End?)
29 – Saved by the Astrobeetles (Saved!)
30 – Peace on Zaos (Peace!)
31 – Aftermath of War (Wreckage)
32 – TARDIS Wrecked (TARDIS)
33 – Radio for Help (Radio)
34 – Spares from Earth (Spares)
35 – Repairs to TARDIS (Repairs)
36 – Farewell!
OP: free NM: £90 set

STR-002b Dr Who's Space Adventure Book
1967, Sky Ray /T. Wall & Sons, UK
Cover by Patrick Williams. During the period of the promotion, every Sky Ray ice lolly contained a card from a series of 36. An album was available into which to paste the cards.
REF: No ISBN OP: free NM: £85

STR-003 The Amazing World of Doctor Who Cards
1976, Cadbury Ty-Phoo, UK
Octagonal ('space age shaped') cards given free in boxes of Ty-Phoo tea bags as a part of the *Amazing World of Doctor Who* promotion which ran from July through to September 1976. There was also a poster (onto which the cards could be pasted) – SPP-004 – and a hardbacked annual-type book – BGE-007. There was one card in a 36-pack, two in a 72-pack and four in a 144-pack.
Cards:
1 – Doctor Who (Tom Baker publicity shot)
2 – Sarah Jane Smith (from *Pyramids of Mars*)
3 – The TARDIS (from *The Seeds of Doom*)
4 – Alpha Centauri (from *The Monster of Peladon*)
5 – Davros (from *Genesis of the Daleks*)
6 – Sea Devils (from *The Sea Devils*)
7 – Daleks (from *Death to the Daleks*)
8 – Giant Robot (from *Robot*)
9 – Zygon (from *Terror of the Zygons*)
10 – Krynoid (from *The Seeds of Doom*)
11 – Ice Warrior (exhibition photo)
12 – Cyberman (from *Revenge of the Cybermen*)
OP: free NM: £35 set, £2.50 singles

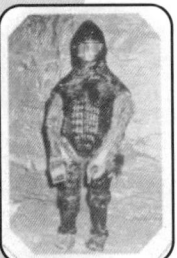
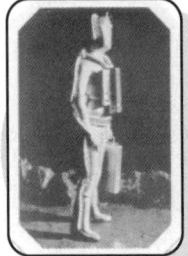

STR-003

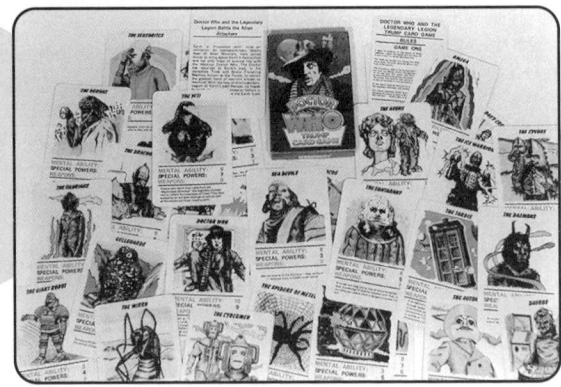

STR-004

STR-004   Doctor Who Trump Card Game

1978, Jotastar, UK

A boxed pack of cards. A set of Hero cards (Geronimo, Wyatt Earp, Davy Crockett, Robin Hood, Thor, Sherlock Holmes, Boadicea, Samson, King Arthur, Alexander the Great, Spartacus, Annie Oakley, Colonel James Bowie, Chaka/King of the Zulus, Shiao Chi/Samurai Warrior, Hercules, Doctor Who, The TARDIS, Lord Nelson, Parthian Warrior) against the Aliens (Cybermen, Ice Warriors, Yeti, Autons, Silurians, Sontarans, Sensorites, Mechanoids, Axons, Sea Devils, Dæmons, Omega, Draconians, Spiders of Metebelis, Gellguards, Giant Robot, Wirrn, Zygons, Davros, Ogrons). In the set the pictures for the Sea Devils and Ogrons are transposed.
OP: 70p   NM: £22

STR-005   Doctor Who Collectors' Cards

1993, CCC Ltd, UK

Set of 20 artwork cards. Seven 'special' cards were produced with a random card given away free on the front of Doctor Who Magazine #208. These special cards featured the Doctors' images but with a '30th Anniversary' flash at the top and 'Promotional Card' printed on the back.

Cards:

1 – The Daleks
2 – Davros
3 – The TARDIS
4 – Sea Devil
5 – Silurian
6 – Cyberman
7 – Yeti

STR-005

STR-005 (30th anniversary versions)

8 – Brigadier Lethbridge-Stewart
9 – K9
10 – The Master
11 – Ice Warrior
12 – 'Time Lord' (logo)
13 – Sontaran
14 – The First Doctor
15 – The Second Doctor
16 – The Third Doctor
17 – The Fourth Doctor
18 – The Fifth Doctor
19 – The Sixth Doctor
20 – The Seventh Doctor
OP: £50 set   NM: £5.50 set

STR-006 *Doctor Who* Playing Cards Set 1
1996/10/16, Jonder International Promotions, UK
Pack of playing cards with *Doctor Who* photographs on
them. Although further sets were promised, these
never appeared.
OP: £8.50 (inc. p&p)   NM: £9

STR-007 Doctor Who Trading Card album
1994, CMA, UK
Generic *Doctor Who* album. CMA are a UK based specialist trading card dealer and manufacturer.
OP: £14.00

STR-006 (box front and back)

STR-006 (assorted cards)

STR-008 Doctor Who Trading Card albums
1994, Cornerstone Communications, USA
Different albums produced for each set of cards.
OP: £14.00

STR-009 Doctor Who Trading Cards Series 1
1994/02, Cornerstone Communications, USA
110 base set. 7 Prism enhanced chase cards featuring
the 7 Doctors. Autograph cards of Anthony Ainley
(81), Sophie Aldred (84), Colin Baker (80), Peter
Davison (83), John Leeson (82), John Levene (82),
William Russell (57), John Levene (150 – gold signa-
ture cards only available in a special set).
See separate table for details of the cards available.
OP: £1.10 pack of 10
NM Set: £22
NM Gold Factory Set: £90
NM Singles: 20p each
NM Prism set: £40
NM Prism singles: £6.50 each
NM Autograph: £55 each
NM Uncut promo sheet: £50
NM Promo Cards: £1.75 each

STR-010 Doctor Who Trading Cards Series 2
1995/04, Cornerstone Communications, USA
110 base set. 6 Chromium enhanced chase cards (3
Dalek, 3 Cybermen). 9 Premiere UV coated cards.
Factory set includes a Davros Chromium card.
Autograph Cards: Sophie Aldred (113), Nicholas
Courtney (112), Jon Pertwee (112), John Levene (112).
See separate table for details of the cards available.
OP: £1.10 pack of 10
NM Set: £16.50
NM Factory Set: £22
NM Singles: 20p each
NM Foil set: £40
NM Foil singles: £6.50 each
NM Premiere Set: £8
NM Premiere singles: £1.50 each
NM Autograph: £55 each
NM Uncut promo sheet: £50
NM Promo Cards: £1.75 each

STR-011 Doctor Who Trading Cards Series 3
1996, Cornerstone Communications, USA
110 base set. 6 Premiere UV coated cards. 7 foil
enhanced chase cards featuring the 7 Doctors.
Factory set includes a 'the Master' foil card. Autograph
Cards: Michael Craze (90), Wendy Padbury (90),
Louise Jameson (90), Sophie Aldred (90), Sylvester
McCoy (90).
See separate table for details of the cards available.
OP: £1.10 pack of 10

NM Set: £16.50 each
NM Factory Set: £22
NM Singles: 20p each
NM Foil set: £45
NM Foil singles: £6.50 each
NM Premiere set: £8
NM Premiere singles: £1.75 each
NM Autograph: £55 each
NM Promo Cards: £1.75 each
NM Promo IT4: £11

STR-012 Doctor Who Trading Cards Series 4
1996, Cornerstone Communications, USA
90 base set. 7 foil enhanced chase cards featuring the 7
Doctors. Special Eighth Doctor foil signature card in
Factory Set. Special tribute cards of first three Doctors
and Pertwee with cases. Autograph Cards: Nicholas
Courtney (90), Caroline John (90), Nicola Bryant (90),
Elisabeth Sladen (90), Sylvester McCoy (90).
See separate table for details of the cards available.
OP: £1.10 pack of 10
NM Set: £16.50
NM Factory Set: £22
NM Singles: 20p each
NM Foil set: £35
NM Foil singles: £5.50 each
NM E1-E2 Foils: £11 each
NM Autograph: £70 each
NM Promo Cards: £2.50 each
NM Promo IT6: £3.50

**STR-013 Doctor Who: The Collectable Trading
Card Game**
1996, The Multimedia Group, UK
302 cards to collect in total. 1 card ('Exterminate') given
free in *Scrye* magazine #15 July 1996. Split between extra
rare (X-R), Rare (R), Uncommon (U) and Common (C).
All cards were 'black border limited edition'.
See separate table for details of the cards available.
OP: £7.50/$9.50 (starter deck of 60 cards),
£2.50/$2.95 (booster pack of 12 cards)
NM Common: 20p each
NM Uncommon: 25p each
NM Rare: 30p each
NM Extra Rare: £45 each
NM 'Exterminate': £45

STR-014 Trading Cards Series 1 Promo Set
2000/11, Strictly Ink, UK
PRI Set limited to 4000 editions. Came packaged in a
plastic case with gold limitation seal. Cards advertised
the release of the first series as December 2000. There
are cards in two states: one set on flimsy card (prepro-
duction samples) and one set on more sturdy card.

Card list:
SI-I – Promo card collage
PRI-I – The Cybermen Attack
PRI-2 – The 1st Doctor William Hartnell
PRI-3 – The 2nd Doctor Patrick Troughton
PRI-4 – The 3rd Doctor Jon Pertwee
PRI-5 – The 4th Doctor Tom Baker
PRI-6 – The 5th Doctor Peter Davison
PRI-7 – The 6th Doctor Colin Baker
PRI-8 – The 7th Doctor Sylvester McCoy
PRI-9 – The 8th Doctor Paul McGann (by TARDIS)
OP: £7.99 promo set

STR-015 Trading Cards Series 1

2001/05, Strictly Ink, UK
Originally announced for December 2000. 120 card
base set. 15 Autograph cards. 17 Radio Times Foil
Cards. 6 promo cards. 1 Autograph Redemption Card.
See separate table for details of the cards available.
OP: £15 set

STR-016 Binder

2001/07, Strictly Ink, UK
A padded binder in which to keep the Strictly Ink
cards. Binder comes with a special 'binder card': B-1:
'From One Doctor to Another'.
OP: £19.99

STR-017 Trading Cards Series 2 Promo set

2002, Strictly Ink, UK
PR Set limited to 999 editions. Came packaged with a
plastic band around the cards.
Card list:
PS2-1 – Jo's first steps into the TARDIS
PS2-2 – The Daleks prepare for Galactic War
PS2-3 – The Doctor On Trial
PS2-4 – Romana glimpses her destiny
PS2-5 – Leela
PS2-6 – The Men of UNIT
PS2-7 – Sontaran Invasion
PS2-8 – K9 and Companion
PS2-9 – Designed for Effect
PS2 10 – Promo card collage
OP: £7.99 set

STR-018 Trading Cards Series 2

2002/09, Strictly Ink, UK
120 card base set. 13 Autograph cards. 13 Comic
Strips Times Foil Cards. 5 Card 'DALEK' Subset. 9
promo cards. See separate table for details of the
cards available.
OP: £15 set

STR-013 (deck, display box and booster packs)

STR-015

STR-019 Binder

2002/06, Strictly Ink, UK
A second padded binder in which to keep the Strictly
Ink cards.
OP: £19.99

STR-020 Trading Cards Series 3 Promo set

2002/05, Strictly Ink, UK
Promo set of 10 cards. Numbered and limited to 999
sets. Came sealed in a plastic bag.
Card list:
PS3-1 – The Sixth Doctor
PS3-2 – The Doctor and Ace
PS3-3 – The fifth Doctor
PS3-4 – The Doctor and Tecker
PS3-5 – TARDIS
PS3-6 – four Doctors and a friend …
PS3-7 – The Rani
PS3-8 – John Friedlander Make-Up Effects
PS3-9 – The Doctor and Ace
PS3-10 – Tollmaster
OP: £9.99 set

STR-016 (binder with exclusive card)

STR-018

STR-019 (binder with exclusives)

STR-021

STR-021 Trading Cards Series 3
2002/07, Strictly Ink, UK
120 card base set. 21 Autograph cards. 9 Card
'Doctor Who' Subset. 14 card Merchandise Foil subset. 10 promo cards. See separate table for details of
the cards available.
OP: £15 set

STR-022 Trading Cards Series 4 Promo set
2002/11, Strictly Ink, UK
Promo set of 10 cards. Numbered and limited to 999
sets. Came packaged with a plastic band around the cards.
Card list:
PR1 – Friendly Yeti?
PR2 – Eighth Doctor & Grace
PR3 – Davros Make-Up
PR4 – DJ
PR5 – The Doctor & Jo
PR6 – Sea Devil
PR7 – Drawing Titles
PR8 – Leela ready to go …
PR9 – Radiophonics
PR10 – Promo card collage
OP: £9.99 set

STR-023 Trading Cards Dalek Films Promo set
2002/12, Strictly Ink, UK
Promo set of 10 cards. Numbered and limited to 999
sets.
Card list:
P1 – Dalek Minions
P2 – Dalek Spaceship
P3 – Exterminate!
P4 – Under Guard
P5 – Through the Wreckage
P6 – Captive
P7 – TARDIS
P8 – Attack
P9 – Nudge, Nudge … Wink, Wink
P10 – Promo card collage
Also available:
TP-3 – Inside the TARDIS (available from Tenth Planet
in the UK)
PTC-1 – Discovery (available from PC Trading Cards
in the UK)
SC-1 – Crash Landing (available from Steve Clark
Cards in the UK)
CI-6 – Deadly Enemy (available from Cards Inc in the UK)
AE-3 – (available from Cards Inc in the UK for £5 each)
RN-2 – (available from Cards Inc in the UK for £5 each)
DM-1 – No Escape (available from D&M cards)
OP: £9.99 set

CORNERSTONE TRADING CARDS

THE Cornerstone Trading Cards came in four series, with the cards from the first three series numbered consecutively, and covering every televised story, Doctor and companion, as well as exploring numerous tropes of the series.

The cards were all written by Karen Funk Blocher (with Tracy Ann Murray for Series One). Photographs came from the BBC's picture library as well as from private sources. Additional photographic assistance for Series One was from Jeremy Bentham. From Series Two onwards, David J Howe acted as consultant.

The autograph cards were all the same card, with AUTOGRAPH printed on the front and 'Congratulations! This is one of the very rare autographed cards!' on the back. These cards were very limited, with only around 100 of each signature card produced per series. There have been some fakes of these cards discovered, with unreadable signatures on.

The 'Inside Trader' cards were produced especially for members of Cornerstone's collectors club. Two *Doctor Who* IT cards were issued, the others being for different ranges of Cornerstone's cards. For Series 4, Inside Trader subscribers also received an unstamped version of the 5th Doctor foil signature card.

'Bonus Cards' could be found printed on the boxes the cards came in.

A 'Factory Set' is a special sealed and laminated set of the standard cards – minus any foil and premiere cards. These sets came with an additional card which was not available in the separate packs or sets of cards. There were also uncut sheets of the cards made available by Cornerstone.

Binders were made for all four series.

The following are the known quantities produced of the various card series.
- Around 37,000 sets of the Series 1 Promo cards were produced.
- Around 5,000 sets of the Series 2 Promo Cards were produced.
- Around 10,000 sets of the Series 3 Promo Cards were produced.
- 600 cases of Series 1 produced.
- 600 cases of Series 2 produced.
- 450 cases of Series 3 produced.
- 350 cases of Series 4 produced.

SERIES ONE

NO.	CARD TITLE
A1	Promo Card – Series One logo
A2	Promo Card – The Five Doctors
A3	Promo Card – Sarah and K9
Foil 1	William Hartnell
Foil 2	Patrick Troughton
Foil 3	Jon Pertwee
Foil 4	Tom Baker
Foil 5	Peter Davison
Foil 6	Colin Baker
Foil 7	Sylvester McCoy
Foil	'You Will Obey' – Glass Dalek (Only available with the Factory Set) Autograph Card: John Levene (150 – Gold ink, only available in a 'John Levene' set)

SI #1

CHECKLIST

SI #2

ADVENTURES

SI #5

ADVENTURES

SI #8

ADVENTURES

SI #10

ADVENTURES

SI #20

ADVENTURES

SI #33

ADVENTURES

SI #40

ADVENTURES

SI #44

NO.	CARD TITLE
	Autograph Card: William Russell (57)
	Autograph Card: John Levene (82)
	Autograph Card: John Leeson (82)
	Autograph Card: Peter Davison (83)
	Autograph Card: Colin Baker (80)
	Autograph Card: Sophie Aldred (84)
	Autograph Card: Anthony Ainley (81)
	Bonus Card: The Leisure Hive
	Bonus Card: 7th Doctor and Daleks
1	Checklist #1
2	Checklist #2
3	Checklist #3
4	Adventures: Marco Polo
5	Adventures: The Sensorites
6	Adventures: The Crusade
7	Adventures: The Celestial Toymaker
8	Adventures: The Tomb of the Cybermen
9	Adventures: The Abominable Snowmen
10	Adventures: The Silurians
11	Adventures: Colony in Space
12	Adventures: The Dæmons
13	Adventures: The Sea Devils
14	Adventures: The Three Doctors
15	Adventures: Frontier in Space
16	Adventures: The Time Warrior
17	Adventures: Death to the Daleks
18	Adventures: The Monster of Peladon
19	Adventures: Planet of the Spiders
20	Adventures: Robot
21	Adventures: The Ark in Space
22	Adventures: Terror of the Zygons
23	Adventures: Pyramids of Mars
24	Adventures: The Robots of Death
25	Adventures: The Talons of Weng Chiang
26	Adventures: The Image of the Fendahl
27	Adventures: The Invasion of Time
28	Adventures: The Ribos Operation
29	Adventures: The Pirate Planet
30	Adventures: The Stones of Blood
31	Adventures: The Androids of Tara
32	Adventures: Destiny of the Daleks
33	Adventures: Shada
34	Adventures: The Leisure Hive
35	Adventures: Meglos
36	Adventures: K9 and Company
37	Adventures: Castrovalva
38	Adventures: Four to Doomsday
39	Adventures: The Visitation
40	Adventures: The Five Doctors
41	Adventures: Warriors of the Deep
42	Adventures: The Awakening
43	Adventures: Frontios
44	Adventures: Planet of Fire

NO.	CARD TITLE
45	Adventures: The Twin Dilemma
46	Adventures: Attack of the Cybermen
47	Adventures: Timelash
48	Adventures: Revelation of the Daleks
49	Adventures: The Mysterious Planet
50	Adventures: Mindwarp
51	Adventures: The Ultimate Foe
52	Adventures: Dragonfire
53	Adventures: Remembrance of the Daleks
54	Adventures: The Happiness Patrol
55	Adventures: The Greatest Show in the Galaxy
56	Adventures: Battlefield
57	Adventures: The Curse of Fenric
58	Adventures: Survival
59	The Doctors: The First Doctor
60	The Doctors: Richard Hurndall as the First Doctor
61	The Doctors: The Second Doctor
62	The Doctors: His Future, His Past
63	The Doctors: Exiled to Earth!
64	The Doctors: 'Reverse the Polarity!'
65	The Doctors: His Future, Her Past
66	The Doctors: The Fourth Doctor
67	The Doctors: The Fourth Doctor
68	The Doctors: Lord President!
69	The Doctors: The Fifth Doctor
70	The Doctors: The Fifth Doctor
71	The Doctors: The Sixth Doctor
72	The Doctors: The Seventh Doctor
73	The Doctors: The Seventh Doctor
74	Companions: Ian Chesterton
75	Companions: Jamie McCrimmon
76	Companions: Victoria
77	Companions: Jo Grant
78	Companions: Sergeant Benton
79	Companions: K9
80	Companions: Leela
81	Companions: The Second Romana
82	Companions: Adric
83	Companions: Mel
84	Companions: Ace
85	The Villains: Employees of the Daleks
86	The Villains: Top Ten Ways to Kill a Dalek
87	The Villains: Enemies of the Daleks
88	The Villains: The Doctor and the Daleks
89	The Villains: Science of the Daleks
90	The Villains: The Toymaker
91	The Villains: Anatomy of a Cyberman
92	The Villains: Planets of the Cybermen
93	The Villains: Top 10 Ways to kill a Cyberman
94	The Villains: The Ice Warriors
95	The Villains: 'I Am The Master!'

SI #45

SI #50

SI #55

SI #65

SI #74

SI #77

SI #84

SI #93

S1 #94

S1 #99

S1 #109

S1 #110

S2 FOIL 2

S2 FOIL 4

S2 PREMIERE 2

S2 PREMIERE 6

NO.	CARD TITLE
96	The Villains: 'You Will Obey Me'
97	The Villains: Davros
98	The Villains: The Rani
99	The Villains: The Valeyard
100	The Legend: From Companion to Villain
101	The Legend: The Interplanetary Mining Corporation
102	The Legend: The Lost Episodes
103	The Legend: Bessie
104	The Legend: The 'Whomobile'
105	The Legend: Four out of Five Doctors
106	The Legend: Just Friends!
107	The Legend: Kamelion
108	The Legend: 'Shada' At Last!
109	The Legend: Sabalom Glitz
110	The Legend: The TARDIS

SERIES TWO

THE promotional cards for Series Two came with two different variant colour backs. 1200 uncut strips of the promo cards were distributed free to attendees of the Visions '94 convention.

NO.	CARD TITLE
B1	Promo Card – Series 2 Logo (Orange or Peach back)
B2	Promo Card – The Crusade (Purple or Light Green back)
B3	Promo Card – Dr, Leela & K9 (Yellow or Dark Green back)
B4	Promo Card – 7th Doctor (Blue or Pink back)
Foil 1	Operators of the Daleks
Foil 2	Designer of the Daleks
Foil 3	Creator of the Daleks
Foil 4	Scientist of the Cybermen
Foil 5	Lives and Times of the Cybermen
Foil 6	Cyberdad of the Cybermen
Foil 7	Davros Times Three (Only available in the Factory Set)
Premiere 1	2 out of 3 Doctors
Premiere 2	The 4th Doctor
Premiere 3	The 5th Doctor
Premiere 4	The 6th Doctor
Premiere 5	Time & the Rani
Premiere 6	The Master
Premiere 7	Ace
Premiere 8	Jo Grant
Premiere 9	A Sontaran
	Bonus Card: The Seven Doctors
	Bonus Card: Omega

NO.	CARD TITLE
	Autograph Card: Sophie Aldred (113 blue ink)
	Autograph Card: Nicholas Courtney (112 red ink)
	Autograph Card: Jon Pertwee (112 red ink)
	Autograph Card: John Levene (112 red ink)
111	Checklist #1
112	Checklist #2
113	Checklist #3
114	Adventures: 100,000 BC
115	Adventures: The Daleks
116	Adventures: The Aztecs
117	Adventures: Planet of Giants
118	Adventures: The Rescue
119	Adventures: The Romans
120	Adventures: The Space Museum
121	Adventures: The Chase
122	Adventures: The Time Meddler
123	Adventures: Galaxy 4
124	Adventures: The Massacre of St Bartholomew's Eve
125	Adventures: The Gunfighters
126	Adventures: The Tenth Planet
127	Adventures: The Highlanders
128	Adventures: The Moonbase
129	Adventures: The Evil of the Daleks
130	Adventures: The Ice Warriors
131	Adventures: The Web of Fear
132	Adventures: The Wheel in Space
133	Adventures: The Mind Robber
134	Adventures: The Krotons
135	Adventures: The Space Pirates
136	Adventures: Spearhead from Space
137	Adventures: The Ambassadors of Death
138	Adventures: The Mind of Evil
139	Adventures: Day of the Daleks
140	Adventures: The Curse of Peladon
141	Adventures: Carnival of Monsters
142	Adventures: The Green Death
143	Adventures: The Sontaran Experiment
144	Adventures: Revenge of the Cybermen
145	Adventures: The Seeds of Doom
146	Adventures: The Hand of Fear
147	Adventures: The Deadly Assassin
148	Adventures: The Face of Evil
149	Adventures: The Invisible Enemy
150	Adventures: The Sun Makers
151	Adventures: The Armageddon Factor
152	Adventures: The Horns of Nimon
153	Adventures: State of Decay
154	Adventures: The Keeper of Traken
155	Adventures: Kinda
156	Adventures: Earthshock
157	Adventures: Arc of Infinity

S2 BONUS CARD: THE 7 DOCTORS

S2 BONUS CARD: OMEGA

S2 #111

S2 #116

S2 #126

S2 #133

S2 #142

S2 #152

S2 #153

S2 #162

S2 #165

S2 #175

S2 #182

S2 #189

S2 #194

S2 #201

NO.	CARD TITLE
158	Adventures: Mawdryn Undead
159	Adventures: Enlightenment
160	Adventures: Resurrection of the Daleks
161	Adventures: Vengeance on Varos
162	Adventures: The Two Doctors
163	Adventures: Time and the Rani
164	Adventures: Paradise Towers
165	Adventures: Ghost Light
166	The Doctors: Doctor Who?
167	The Doctors: The Course of History
168	The Doctors: Doctor of What?
169	The Doctors: Agent of Gallifrey
170	The Doctors: The Man from UNIT
171	The Doctors: From Venus, with Love
172	The Doctors: The British Gallifreyan
173	The Doctors: The Wit and Wisdom of the Fourth Doctor
174	The Doctors: About that Scarf!
175	The Doctors: The Fifth Doctor and Cricket
176	The Doctors: On With the Motley
177	The Doctors: The Missing Episodes
178	The Doctors: Mixed Maxims
179	The Doctors: 'Who Are You?'
180	Companions: Susan Foreman
181	Companions: Vicki
182	Companions: Steven Taylor
183	Companions: Brigadier Alistair Gordon Lethbridge-Stewart
184	Companions: Zoe Herriot
185	Companions: Dr. Elizabeth (Liz) Shaw
186	Companions: Sarah Jane Smith
187	Companions: Nyssa
188	Companions: Vislor Turlough
189	Companions: Perpugillium (Peri) Brown
190	The Villains: Souvenirs of the Daleks
191	The Villains: Leaders of the Daleks
192	The Villains: Time Travel of the Daleks
193	The Villains: Abominations of the Daleks
194	The Villains: The Monk
195	The Villains: Planets of the Cybermen
196	The Villains: Cybermen and Cybermats
197	The Villains: The Master in Transition
198	The Villains: Omega
199	The Villains: The Sontarans
200	The Villains: Davros and the Thankless Child
201	The Villains: The Black Guardian
202	The Villains: Sil
203	The Legend: Another 'Unearthly Child'
204	The Legend: Another Time, Another World
205	The Legend: The Control Console
206	The Legend: The Vortex
207	The Legend: Regeneration
208	The Legend: 'Really, Doctor!'

NO.	CARD TITLE
209	The Legend: The Sonic Screwdriver
210	The Legend: History of the Transmat
211	The Legend: Doctors at Odds
212	The Legend: Politics of Gallifrey
213	The Legend: The Matrix
214	The Legend: Lord Borusa
215	The Legend: Relics of Gallifrey
216	The Legend: Commander Maxil
217	The Legend: Who is Ace?
218	The Legend: The Other Brigadier
219	The Legend: The Laws of Time
220	The Legend: ...And Relative Dimensions in Space

S2 #202   S2 #203

SERIES THREE

NO.	CARD TITLE
C1	Promo Card – Series 3 logo
C2	Promo Card – The Reign of Terror
C3	Promo Card – Bret Vyon
	Autograph Card – Michael Craze (90, red ink)
	Autograph Card – Wendy Padbury (90, red ink)
	Autograph Card – Sophie Aldred (90, red ink)
	Autograph Card – Louise Jameson (90, 10 red and 80 black ink)
	Autograph Card – Sylvester McCoy (90)
	Foil 1 – The First Doctor (Hurndall)
	Foil 2 – The Second Doctor
	Foil 3 – The Third Doctor
	Foil 4 – The Fourth Doctor
	Foil 5 – The Fifth Doctor
	Foil 6 – The Sixth Doctor
	Foil 7 – The Seventh Doctor
	Foil 8 – The Master (only available in the Factory set)
Premiere 10	The TARDIS
Premiere 11	Susan
Premiere 12	Romana
Premiere 13	Dalek Emperor
Premiere 14	Peri
Premiere 15	Romana Too
IT-4	Doctor on Wheels (Only available through Cornerstone's 'Inside Trader' club)
	Bonus Card: McCoy Logo
	Bonus Card: Kamelion
221	Checklist #1
222	Checklist #2
223	Checklist #3
224	Adventures: Inside the Spaceship
225	Adventures: The Keys of Marinus
226	Adventures: The Reign of Terror

S2 #218   S2 #220

S3 FOIL 6   S3 FOIL 7

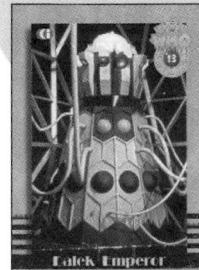

S3 PREMIERE 13   S3 PREMIERE 14

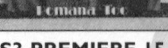

S3 PREMIERE 15

S3 #228

S3 #239

S3 #243

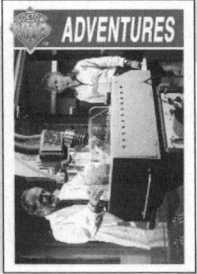

S3 #250

S3 #254

S3 #258

S3 #266

NO.	CARD TITLE
227	Adventures: The Dalek Invasion of Earth
228	Adventures: The Web Planet
229	Adventures: Dalek Cutaway
230	Adventures: The Myth Makers
231	Adventures: The Daleks' Master Plan
232	Adventures: The Ark
233	Adventures: The Savages
234	Adventures: The War Machines
235	Adventures: The Smugglers
236	Adventures: The Power of the Daleks
237	Adventures: The Underwater Menace
238	Adventures: The Macra Terror
239	Adventures: The Faceless Ones
240	Adventures: The Enemy of the World
241	Adventures: Fury From the Deep
242	Adventures: The Dominators
243	Adventures: The Invasion
244	Adventures: The Seeds of Death
245	Adventures: The War Games
246	Adventures: Inferno
247	Adventures: Terror of the Autons
248	Adventures: The Claws of Axos
249	Adventures: The Mutants
250	Adventures: The Time Monster
251	Adventures: Planet of the Daleks
252	Adventures: Invasion of the Dinosaurs
253	Adventures: Genesis of the Daleks
254	Adventures: Planet of Evil
255	Adventures: The Android Invasion
256	Adventures: The Brain of Morbius
257	Adventures: The Masque of Mandragora
258	Adventures: Horror of Fang Rock
259	Adventures: Underworld
260	Adventures: The Power of Kroll
261	Adventures: City of Death
262	Adventures: The Creature from the Pit
263	Adventures: The Nightmare of Eden
264	Adventures: Full Circle
265	Adventures: Warriors' Gate
266	Adventures: Logopolis
267	Adventures: Black Orchid
268	Adventures: Time-Flight
269	Adventures: Snakedance
270	Adventures: Terminus
271	Adventures: The King's Demons
272	Adventures: The Caves of Androzani
273	Adventures: The Mark of the Rani
274	Adventures: The Trial of a Time Lord 9-12
275	Adventures: Delta and the Bannermen
276	Adventures: Silver Nemesis
277	The Doctors: Grandfather!
278	The Doctors: Doctor 'Who'
279	The Doctors: The First Regeneration

NO.	CARD TITLE
280	The Doctors: Genius or Fool?
281	The Doctors: The Third Doctor
282	The Doctors: The Third Doctor and Authority
283	The Doctors: Quoth the Fourth Doctor…
284	The Doctors: Name Dropper!
285	The Doctors: CIA Agent
286	The Doctors: The Doctor and Money
287	The Doctors: The Fifth Doctor's Friends
288	The Doctors: Improved Performance
289	The Doctors: Quotations of the 6th Doctor
290	The Doctors: What we didn't see
291	The Doctors: The New Adventures
292	Companions: Barbara Wright
293	Companions: Katarina
294	Companions: Sara Kingdom
295	Companions: Dorothea ('Dodo') Chaplet
296	Companions: Polly Wright
297	Companions: Ben Jackson
298	Companions: Captain Mike Yates
299	Companions: Harry Sullivan
300	Companions: The First Romanadvoratrelundar
301	Companions: Tegan Jovanka
302	The Villains: The Dalek Invasions of Earth
303	The Villains: The Daleks Inside Out
304	The Villains: The Birth of the Daleks
305	The Villains: Metaphor of the Daleks
306	The Villains: Evolution of the Cybermen
307	The Villains: Invasions of the Cybermen
308	The Villains: Weapons of the Cybermen
309	The Villains: The Great Intelligence and the Yeti
310	The Villains: The Nestenes and the Autons
311	The Villains: Sea Devils and Silurians
312	The Villains: The Mind of Davros
313	The Villains: The Master Renewed
314	The Villains: The Mara
315	The Villains: Commander Gustave Lytton
316	The Legend: The Thals
317	The Legend: Bret Vyon
318	The Legend: The Mind of the Doctor
319	The Legend: Special Effects
320	The Legend: Actors and their Roles
321	The Legend: The Other TARDIS Control Room
322	The Legend: The Hitchhiker's Guide to the Doctor
323	The Legend: E-Space, N Space and CVEs
324	The Legend: The Cloister and its Bell
325	The Legend: The Watcher
326	The Legend: Rassilon
327	The Legend: The Continuity Game

S3 #267

S3 #274

S3 #280

S3 #284

S3 #287

S3 #292

S3 #300

S3 #312

S3 #313

S3 #316

S3 #317

S3 #321

S3 #328

S3 #330

S4 AUTOGRAPH CARD (front and back)

NO.	CARD TITLE
328	The Legend: Americans in Doctor Who
329	The Legend: Sorry – Our Mistake!
330	The Legend: Credits & Acknowledgements

SERIES FOUR

FOR this series, Cornerstone opted not to continue with the numbering from previous series and to re-vamp the look of the set. It was arranged in nine sub-sets of nine cards each, and the card backs were unrelated to the images on their fronts. The second two promotional cards have a different design of back to the first two. 3500 each were made of D1 and D2, while 15,000 of each were produced for D3 and D4. The 'tribute' cards, printed in France, are larger than the standard cards (10cm x 7.5cm as opposed to 9cm x 6.5cm). 250 of the double 'tribute' cards have been cut in half by dealers to give two cards. They were not supplied in this format. The foil cards carry a faximile signature from each of the actors to have played the Doctor.

NO.	CARD TITLE
D1	Promo Card – Series 4 logo
D2	Promo Card – The Two Doctors
D3	Promo Card – Behind the Scenes #1
D4	Promo Card – Behind the Scenes #2
IT-6	Keeping it in the Family (Only available through Cornerstone's 'Inside Trader' club)
	Autograph Card – Nicholas Courtney (90, blue ink)
	Autograph Card – Caroline John (90, blue ink)
	Autograph Card – Nicola Bryant (90, blue ink)
	Autograph Card – Elisabeth Sladen (90, blue ink)
Foil 1	The First Doctor
Foil 2	The Second Doctor
Foil 3	The Third Doctor
Foil 4	The Fourth Doctor
Foil 5	The Fifth Doctor
Foil 6	The Sixth Doctor
Foil 7	The Seventh Doctor
Foil 8	The Eighth Doctor (Only in Factory Set)
E1	Hartnell/Troughton/Pertwee tribute card (Only available within dealers cases as a double card with E2)
E2	Pertwee tribute card (Only available within dealers cases as a double card with E1)
	Bonus Card: 3rd Doctor and Friend
	Bonus Card: 3rd Doctor and Foe

THE FIRST DOCTOR

1 The Fallible Wizard
2 The Family Way
3 A Violent Child
4 Checklist
5 The Family Doctor
6 The Susan that wasn't, pt. 1
7 The Susan that wasn't, pt. 2
8 Ian and the Doctor
9 I was a teenage alien

THE SECOND DOCTOR

10 Memories of the Cybermen
11 Joining the Club
12 Victoria's Secret
13 Being Victoria
14 Into the Foam, pt. 1
15 Into the Foam, pt. 2
16 Behind the Sofa
17 The Yeti and the Dog
18 Missing the Episodes

THE THIRD DOCTOR

19 Stories vs Serials, pt. 1
20 Stories vs Serials, pt. 2
21 Presenting the Pertwees
22 Jon Pertwee the writer
23 The 'Stupid' idea, pt. 1
24 The 'Stupid' idea, pt. 2
25 The End of an Era
26 His Least Favourite Story
27 The UNIT Family

THE FOURTH DOCTOR

28 Tom Baker on K-9
29 Acting and Actors
30 The Autobiography, pt. 1
31 The Autobiography, pt. 2
32 The Autobiography, pt. 3
33 An Actor's Motivation
34 Fame and Failure
35 One, Two, Three Companions
36 The Doctor Who Archetype

THE FIFTH DOCTOR

37 Three Years and Out
38 Fashion Sense
39 Adric and the Children
40 Playing Cricket on Camera
41 Colleagues
42 Three's a Crowd
43 Still the Doctor
44 Tegan's Last Scene
45 A Matter of Perspective

S4 FOIL 1   S4 FOIL 2

S4 E1/E2

S4 #1

S4 #10

S4 #19

S4 #34

S4 #43

S4 #53

S4 #64

S4 #79

S4 #90

DOCTOR WHO: THE COLLECTIBLE CARD GAME

RARITY / TYPE / DESCRIPTION

XR	TIMELESS CREATURES (silver/white border)	Davros	£40
XR	TIMELESS CREATURES (silver/white border)	Doctor Who IV	£40
XR	RESOURCES (black border)	Doomsday Machine	£40
	FLASH (yellow border)	Exterminate!	
	Card given free with *Scrye* magazine. Not available in the packs.		£40
C	FLASH (yellow border)	Andromeda Sleepers	
C	PRESENT CREATURES (red border)	Autons	
C	PRESENT CREATURES (red border)	Bannermen	
C	FLASH (yellow border)	Barbed Wire	
C	RESOURCES (black border)	Bazooka	
C	PRESENT CREATURES (red border)	Bok	
C	FLASH (yellow border)	Brain Transformer	
C	PAST CREATURES (green border)	Brothers of Demnos, The	
C	RESOURCES (black border)	Chameleon Circuit	
C	FUTURE CREATURES (blue border)	Chumblies	
C	FLASH (yellow border)	Cloister Bell	
C	FLASH (yellow border)	Crusades	
C	FLASH (yellow border)	Cyber Bomb	
C	TIMELESS CREATURES (silver/white border)	Cybermat	
C	TIMELESS CREATURES (silver/white border)	Cybermen	
C	FLASH (yellow border)	Dalekenium Bomb	
C	TIMELESS CREATURES (silver/white border)	Daleks	
C	RESOURCES (black border)	Death Ray	
C	RESOURCES (black border)	DN6	
C	FUTURE CREATURES (blue border)	Draconian	
C	FUTURE CREATURES (blue border)	Drahvin	
C	FUTURE CREATURES (blue border)	Dulciens	
C	FLASH (yellow border)	Duranium Shield	
C	FLASH (yellow border)	Elixir of Life	
C	FUTURE CREATURES (blue border)	Exxilons	
C	FLASH (yellow border)	Eye of Orion, The	
C	PRESENT CREATURES (red border)	Fendahleen	
C	RESOURCES (black border)	Force Field	
C	FLASH (yellow border)	Fusion Booster	
C	PRESENT CREATURES (red border)	Giant Robot	
C	PAST CREATURES (green border)	Greek Hoplites	
C	FLASH (yellow border)	H.A.D.S.	
C	FLASH (yellow border)	Hal's Arrow	
C	FLASH (yellow border)	Happiness Patrol, The	
C	RESOURCES (black border)	Hydromel	
C	FUTURE CREATURES (blue border)	Ice Warrior	
C	FLASH (yellow border)	Keeper of Traken, The	
C	FUTURE CREATURES (blue border)	Krotons	
C	FUTURE CREATURES (blue border)	Menoptera	
C	FLASH (yellow border)	Metamorphic Symbiosis Regenerator	
C	FLASH (yellow border)	Mind Battle	
C	FLASH (yellow border)	Mind Drain	
C	PAST CREATURES (green border)	Mongol	

Card back

'Chameleon Circuit'

'Giant Robot'

'Mind Drain'

'Neanderthals'

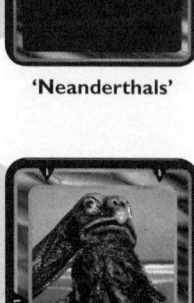

'Sea Devils'

'76 Totters Lane'

'Aztecs, The'

C	PAST CREATURES (green border)	Neanderthals
C	PRESENT CREATURES (red border)	Ogron
C	FLASH (yellow border)	P.C.M. Gas
C	FLASH (yellow border)	Particle Suppressor
C	PRESENT CREATURES (red border)	Policemen
C	FUTURE CREATURES (blue border)	Primitives
C	FLASH (yellow border)	Q Capsule
C	FLASH (yellow border)	Ransom Demand
C	FLASH (yellow border)	Raston Attack
C	RESOURCES (black border)	Records of Rasillon, The
C	PRESENT CREATURES (red border)	Robomen
C	FLASH (yellow border)	Robophobia
C	PAST CREATURES (green border)	Romans
C	PAST CREATURES (green border)	Rutans
C	FLASH (yellow border)	Sanctum
C	RESOURCES (black border)	Sea Base Four
C	PAST CREATURES (green border)	Sea Devils
C	FUTURE CREATURES (blue border)	Shrivenzales
C	RESOURCES (black border)	SIDRAT
C	PAST CREATURES (green border)	Silurians
C	FLASH (yellow border)	Space Special Security
C	RESOURCES (black border)	Space Station
C	FLASH (yellow border)	Star Base
C	RESOURCES (black border)	TARDIS
C	FLASH (yellow border)	Tartarus
C	PAST CREATURES (green border)	Terileptils
C	FLASH (yellow border)	Time Barrier
C	FLASH (yellow border)	Time Controller
C	FLASH (yellow border)	Time Eddy
C	FLASH (yellow border)	Time Stop
C	RESOURCES (black border)	Transduction Barrier
C	RESOURCES (black border)	Trionic Lock
C	RESOURCES (black border)	Underground Bunker
C	PRESENT CREATURES (red border)	UNIT Corporal
C	PRESENT CREATURES (red border)	UNIT Soldier
C	RESOURCES (black border)	Venom Gun
C	RESOURCES (black border)	V-Ship
C	RESOURCES (black border)	Web Gun
C	RESOURCES (black border)	X-Ray Laser Cannon
C	PRESENT CREATURES (red border)	Yeti
C	FUTURE CREATURES (blue border)	Zarbi
U	RESOURCES (black border)	76 Totters Lane
U	FUTURE CREATURES (blue border)	Adric
U	FUTURE CREATURES (blue border)	Aggedor
U	FLASH (yellow border)	Alliance, The
U	FUTURE CREATURES (blue border)	Alpha-Centauri
U	PRESENT CREATURES (red border)	Ambassadors, The
U	PAST CREATURES (green border)	Atlantean Fish People
U	EPISODES (purple border)	Aztecs, The
U	FLASH (yellow border)	Balarium Gas
U	PRESENT CREATURES (red border)	Barbara Wright
U	PRESENT CREATURES (red border)	Ben Jackson
U	FLASH (yellow border)	Bendalypse Gas
U	EPISODES (purple border)	Black Orchid, The

U	PAST CREATURES (green border)	Black Scorpion, The
U	FLASH (yellow border)	Blindfold
U	FLASH (yellow border)	C.I.A.
U	PAST CREATURES (green border)	Clanton Gang, The
U	FLASH (yellow border)	Cryogenics
U	RESOURCES (black border)	Demat Gun
U	PRESENT CREATURES (red border)	Dodo Chaplet
U	PAST CREATURES (green border)	Earp Clan, The
U	FLASH (yellow border)	Extortion
U	FLASH (yellow border)	Faster Than Light Propulsion
U	FLASH (yellow border)	Game of Rasillon, The
U	FLASH (yellow border)	Glitter Gun
U	FLASH (yellow border)	Great Fire of London
U	PRESENT CREATURES (red border)	Green Death
U	FLASH (yellow border)	Hexachromite Gas
U	FLASH (yellow border)	High Council Meeting
U	PAST CREATURES (green border)	Highlanders
U	PRESENT CREATURES (red border)	Ian Chesterton
U	PAST CREATURES (green border)	Irongron
U	PAST CREATURES (green border)	Jamie McCrimmon
U	PRESENT CREATURES (red border)	Jo Grant
U	RESOURCES (black border)	Kartz and Reimer Time Capsule
U	PRESENT CREATURES (red border)	Kastrians
U	RESOURCES (black border)	Kinda Jhana's Box, The
U	PAST CREATURES (green border)	Linx
U	PRESENT CREATURES (red border)	Liz Shaw
U	FLASH (yellow border)	Master's Presence, The
U	FUTURE CREATURES (blue border)	Mechanoids
U	FLASH (yellow border)	Meteorites
U	FUTURE CREATURES (blue border)	Monoids
U	PRESENT CREATURES (red border)	Morgaine
U	EPISODES (purple border)	Myth Makers, The
U	FLASH (yellow border)	Neurotrope X
U	FUTURE CREATURES (blue border)	Nimon
U	PRESENT CREATURES (red border)	Perpugilliam Brown
U	PRESENT CREATURES (red border)	Polly Lopez
U	PRESENT CREATURES (red border)	Prof. Clifford Jones
U	RESOURCES (black border)	Sacred Flame
U	PRESENT CREATURES (red border)	Sarah Jane Smith
U	FUTURE CREATURES (blue border)	Seers
U	RESOURCES (black border)	Siligtone Dome
U	PAST CREATURES (green border)	Skarasen
U	FLASH (yellow border)	Sonic Cone
U	FLASH (yellow border)	Sonic Toolkit
U	FUTURE CREATURES (blue border)	Sontarans
U	RESOURCES (black border)	Space Freighter
U	RESOURCES (black border)	Space Pod
U	RESOURCES (black border)	Spar 7.40
U	RESOURCES (black border)	Spectrox
U	FUTURE CREATURES (blue border)	Steven Taylor
U	PRESENT CREATURES (red border)	Susan
U	FLASH (yellow border)	T.C.E.
U	FUTURE CREATURES (blue border)	Tegan Jovanka
U	FLASH (yellow border)	Teleportation

'Black Orchid, The'

'Highlanders'

'Polly Lopez'

'Space Pod'

'U.N.I.T. Headquarters'

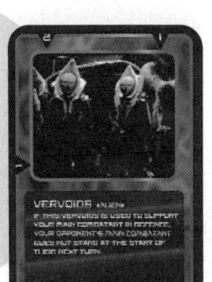

'Vervoids'

'Animus'

'Doctor Who V'

U	FLASH (yellow border)	Temporal Grace
U	TIMELESS CREATURES (silver/white border)	Tharils
U	FLASH (yellow border)	Thunderbolt Missile
U	FLASH (yellow border)	Time Acceleration Beam
U	FLASH (yellow border)	Time Loop
U	FLASH (yellow border)	Time Ram
U	FLASH (yellow border)	Time Scoop
U	FLASH (yellow border)	Time Travel
U	FLASH (yellow border)	Time Worn
U	RESOURCES (black border)	Tomb of Rasillon, The
U	RESOURCES (black border)	Total Survival Kit
U	RESOURCES (black border)	Trench
U	FLASH (yellow border)	Trisilicate
U	RESOURCES (black border)	U.N.I.T. Headquarters
U	FLASH (yellow border)	Venusian Aiki-Do
U	FUTURE CREATURES (blue border)	Vervoids
U	FUTURE CREATURES (blue border)	Vicki
U	PRESENT CREATURES (red border)	Victoria Waterfield
U	TIMELESS CREATURES (silver/white border)	White Dalek
U	TIMELESS CREATURES (silver/white border)	White Guardian
U	PRESENT CREATURES (red border)	Winifred Bambera
U	FUTURE CREATURES (blue border)	Woolfweeds
U	FUTURE CREATURES (blue border)	Zoe Heriot
U	PRESENT CREATURES (red border)	Zygons
R	PRESENT CREATURES (red border)	Ace
R	FLASH (yellow border)	Ancient Law of Gallifrey, The
R	FUTURE CREATURES (blue border)	Animus
R	EPISODES (purple border)	Ark In Space, The
R	TIMELESS CREATURES (silver/white border)	Black Dalek
R	TIMELESS CREATURES (silver/white border)	Black Guardian
R	FLASH (yellow border)	Blinovitch Limitation Effect
R	PRESENT CREATURES (red border)	Brigadier
R	EPISODES (purple border)	Castrovalva
R	EPISODES (purple border)	Claws of Axos, The
R	EPISODES (purple border)	Curse of Fenric, The
R	TIMELESS CREATURES (silver/white border)	CyberController
R	TIMELESS CREATURES (silver/white border)	CyberLeader
R	PAST CREATURES (green border)	Daemons
R	PRESENT CREATURES (red border)	Destroyer
R	TIMELESS CREATURES (silver/white border)	Doctor Who I
R	TIMELESS CREATURES (silver/white border)	Doctor Who II
R	TIMELESS CREATURES (silver/white border)	Doctor Who III
R	TIMELESS CREATURES (silver/white border)	Doctor Who V
R	TIMELESS CREATURES (silver/white border)	Doctor Who VI
R	TIMELESS CREATURES (silver/white border)	Doctor Who VII
R	FLASH (yellow border)	Double Time
R	EPISODES (purple border)	Earthshock
R	TIMELESS CREATURES (silver/white border)	Emperor Dalek
R	FUTURE CREATURES (blue border)	Emperor of Draconia
R	RESOURCES (black border)	Eye of Harmony
R	EPISODES (purple border)	Faceless Ones, The
R	FLASH (yellow border)	Fast Return Switch
R	RESOURCES (black border)	Fenric's Flask
R	FLASH (yellow border)	Flashback

R	EPISODES (purple border)	Genesis of the Daleks
R	FLASH (yellow border)	Genocide
R	EPISODES (purple border)	Ghostlight
R	TIMELESS CREATURES (silver/white border)	Gold Dalek
R	TIMELESS CREATURES (silver/white border)	Goth
R	PRESENT CREATURES (red border)	Great Intelligence, The
R	PRESENT CREATURES (red border)	Group Capt. Gilmore
R	PRESENT CREATURES (red border)	Gustave Lytton
R	FLASH (yellow border)	Harp of Rasillon, The
R	PRESENT CREATURES (red border)	Harry Sullivan
R	PAST CREATURES (green border)	Icthar
R	TIMELESS CREATURES (silver/white border)	K-9
R	PAST CREATURES (green border)	Kamelion
R	PAST CREATURES (green border)	Katarina
R	RESOURCES (black border)	Kontron Crystals
R	PAST CREATURES (green border)	Kronos
R	PAST CREATURES (green border)	Kublai Khan
R	RESOURCES (black border)	Lazar's Disease
R	PAST CREATURES (green border)	Leela
R	FLASH (yellow border)	Living Power Battery
R	FLASH (yellow border)	Malus, The
R	FUTURE CREATURES (blue border)	Marine Space Corps
R	EPISODES (purple border)	Massacre, The
R	TIMELESS CREATURES (silver/white border)	Master, The
R	RESOURCES (black border)	Master's Spaceship, The
R	TIMELESS CREATURES (silver/white border)	Meddling Monk, The
R	PRESENT CREATURES (red border)	Melanie Bush
R	EPISODES (purple border)	Mind of Evil, The
R	EPISODES (purple border)	Moonbase
R	FLASH (yellow border)	Movellan Logic
R	PRESENT CREATURES (red border)	Nestene
R	FUTURE CREATURES (blue border)	Nyssa
R	RESOURCES (black border)	Oracle, The
R	PAST CREATURES (green border)	Peking Homunculus
R	EPISODES (purple border)	Planet of Evil
R	FUTURE CREATURES (blue border)	Prapilus
R	FLASH (yellow border)	Random Laser Beam Emitter
R	TIMELESS CREATURES (silver/white border)	Rani, The
R	FUTURE CREATURES (blue border)	Raston Warrior Robot
R	EPISODES (purple border)	Revenge of the Cybermen, The
R	RESOURCES (black border)	Ring of Rasilon, The
R	EPISODES (purple border)	Robot
R	RESOURCES (black border)	Rod of Rasilon, The
R	TIMELESS CREATURES (silver/white border)	Romana
R	RESOURCES (black border)	Sash of Rasilon, The
R	PRESENT CREATURES (red border)	Sergeant Benton
R	EPISODES (purple border)	Silver Nemesis, The
R	TIMELESS CREATURES (silver/white border)	Sisterhood, The
R	RESOURCES (black border)	Sonic Screwdriver
R	EPISODES (purple border)	Space Pirates, The
R	RESOURCES (black border)	Tachyon Recreation Generator
R	FUTURE CREATURES (blue border)	Tetraps
R	FLASH (yellow border)	Time Corridor
R	RESOURCES (black border)	Time Dam

'Fenric's Flask'

'Harry Sullivan'

'Melanie Bush'

'Sisterhood, The'

'Vengeance on Varos'

R	EPISODES (purple border)	Time Warrior, The
R	FLASH (yellow border)	Time Winds
R	EPISODES (purple border)	Timelash
R	RESOURCES (black border)	T-MAT
R	RESOURCES (black border)	Tranquil Repose
R	EPISODES (purple border)	Vengeance on Varos
R	FLASH (yellow border)	Viral Destruction
R	FUTURE CREATURES (blue border)	Vislor Turlough
R	RESOURCES (black border)	Vorum Gas
R	FLASH (yellow border)	Warning
R	EPISODES (purple border)	Web of Fear, The
R	RESOURCES (black border)	Whomobile

'Vislor Turlough'

TIME Present VI

RARITY/TYPE		DESCRIPTION
C	TIME – Green	Past I (blue and white 'oil slick')
C	TIME – Green	Past II (triple spray from black hole)
U	TIME – Green	Past III (purple and black pos/neg 'ink blot')
U	TIME – Green	Past IV (purple spiral)
U	TIME – Green	Past V (rough figure '8')
U	TIME – Green	Past VI (mostly blue field with black mass in upper right)
C	TIME – Red	Present I (green spiral on orange)
C	TIME – Red	Present II (multi-coloured 'oil slick')
U	TIME – Red	Present III (purple/blue with white streamers)
U	TIME – Red	Present IV (green 'warp field')
U	TIME – Red	Present V (red spiral)
U	TIME – Red	Present VI (multi-coloured shapes)
C	TIME – Blue	Future I (small blue sphere circled by orange and purple)
C	TIME – Blue	Future II (multi-coloured bubble concentration)
U	TIME – Blue	Future III (green spiraling on purple). This card also available as a mis-print, with the letters 'TI' missing off 'TIME' on the card front.
U	TIME – Blue	Future IV (multi-coloured concentric circles)
U	TIME – Blue	Future V (green-orange-green horizontal bands)
U	TIME – Blue	Future VI (orange figure 8 at centre surrounded by red loops)
C	THE WATCHER – Green	Past I (globe with concentric circles)
U	THE WATCHER – Green	Past II (smudged green globe)
U	THE WATCHER – Green	Past III (brown and copper swirled globe on black and ochre expressionistic canvas)
C	THE WATCHER – Red	Present I (blue sphere with yellow spiral-star)
U	THE WATCHER – Red	Present II (blue and yellow swirled sphere)
U	THE WATCHER – Red	Present III (Green and white mottled globe)
C	THE WATCHER – Blue	Future I (red and green swirled sphere)
U	THE WATCHER – Blue	Future II (yellow sphere with blue swirl on upper left)
U	THE WATCHER – Blue	Future III (green-red sphere on sectioned ice-blue background)

THE WATCHER
Present III

STRICTLY INK TRADING CARDS

THE Strictly Ink Trading Cards came in three series to date, with the cards in each series numbered individually. The autograph cards were all individually printed for the subject, with a matt white band for the signature. The following are the known quantities produced of the various card series:

- Series 1 – 6000 boxes
- Series 2 – 4000 boxes
- Series 3 – 5000 boxes

SERIES ONE

IN addition to the standard sized cards, there is a 9-card 'boxtopper' set of double-sized cards. These are unnumbered, and the pictures are as follows:

Three Doctors
5th Doctor, Tegan and Turlough
Azal
Leela
The Brigadier
Morbius and Solon
Davros and the Daleks
The 6th Doctor being pulled into a barrel
Cyberman

Series One boxtopper (6th Doctor)

There are also two 'super large' cards (4 times the size of a standard card), available as 'case toppers':
7th Doctor and Ace
4th Doctor and Sarah

NO.	CARD TITLE
DI	Promo Card – Series 4 logo
B-1	From One Doctor to Another (free in Strictly Ink's first Collector's Binder) Autograph Redemption Card (never issued)
NS-1	The Doctor's Are Back (Card intended to be inserted in *Non-Sport Update* magazine Volume 12, Number 1, Feb/March 2001. This did not occur, however, and instead card CI-1 was included in the magazine instead)
CI-1	Exterminate
CI-2	The Doctors Are Back
DWM-1	The Daleks are Back (free with *DWM* 298)
DWM-2	The 8th Doctor Paul McGann (free with *DWM* 299)
SI-1	Collage
PR1-1	The Cybermen Attack

Series One case toppers

Series One DWM-1 (front and back)

Series One PRI-7   Series One A4

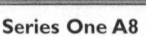

Series One A8   Series One A11

NO.	CARD TITLE
PR1-2	The 1st Doctor William Hartnell
PR1-3	The 2nd Doctor Patrick Troughton
PR1-4	The 3rd Doctor Jon Pertwee
PR1-5	The 4th Doctor Tom Baker
PR1-6	The 5th Doctor Peter Davison
PR1-7	The 6th Doctor Colin Baker
PR1-8	The 7th Doctor Sylvester McCoy
PR1-9	The 8th Doctor Paul McGann
A1	Tom Baker
A2	Peter Davison
A3	Colin Baker
A4	Sylvester McCoy
A5	Paul McGann
A6	Anneke Wills
A7	Deborah Watling
A8	Wendy Padbury
A9	John Levene
A10	Caroline John
A11	Katy Manning
A12	Elisabeth Sladen
A13	Sarah Sutton
A14	Nicola Bryant
A15	Sophie Aldred
R1	*Radio Times* February 22-28 1964
R2	*Radio Times* November 21-27 1964
R3	*Radio Times* February 13-19 1965
R4	*Radio Times* November 5-11 1966
R5	*Radio Times* September 2-8 1967
R6	*Radio Times* January 20-26 1968
R7	*Radio Times* January 3-9 1970
R8	*Radio Times* January 2-8 1971
R9	*Radio Times* January 1-7 1972
R10	*Radio Times* December 30 – January 5 1973
R11	*Radio Times* Special Autumn 1973
R12	*Radio Times* December 15-21 1973
R13	*Radio Times* Special Summer 1983
R14	*Radio Times* November 19-25 1983
R15	*Radio Times* November 20-26 1993
R16	*Radio Times* May 25-31 1996
R17	*Radio Times* November 13-19 1999
1	An Unearthly Child/100,000 BC
2	The Daleks
3	Inside the Spaceship
4	Marco Polo
5	The Keys of Marinus
6	The Aztecs
7	The Sensorites
8	The Reign of Terror
9	Planet of Giants
10	The Dalek Invasion of Earth
11	The Rescue
12	The Romans
13	The Web Planet
14	The Crusade

NO.	CARD TITLE
15	The Space Museum
16	The Chase
17	The Time Meddler
18	Galaxy 4
19	Mission to the Unknown
20	The Myth Makers
21	The Daleks' Master Plan
22	The Massacre of St Bartholemew's Eve
23	The Ark
24	The Celestial Toymaker
25	The Gunfighters
26	The Savages
27	The War Machines
28	The Smugglers
29	The Tenth Planet
30	The Power of the Daleks
31	The Highlanders
32	The Underwater Menace
33	The Moonbase
34	The Macra Terror
35	The Faceless Ones
36	The Evil of the Daleks
37	The Tomb of the Cybermen
38	The Abominable Snowmen
39	The Ice Warriors
40	The Enemy of the World
41	The Web of Fear
42	Fury the Deep
43	The Wheel In Space
44	The Dominators
45	The Mind Robber
46	The Invasion
47	The Krotons
48	The Seeds of Death
49	The Space Pirates
50	The War Games
51	The first Doctor
52	The second Doctor
53	The third Doctor #1
54	The third Doctor #2
55	The fourth Doctor #1
56	The fourth Doctor #2
57	The fourth Doctor #3
58	The fifth Doctor #1
59	The fifth Doctor #2
60	The sixth Doctor #1
61	The sixth Doctor #2
62	The seventh Doctor #1
63	The seventh Doctor #2
64	The eighth Doctor #1
65	The eighth Doctor #2
66	The eighth Doctor #3
67	The eighth Doctor #4

Series One A13

Series One R2

Series One R10

Series One R15

Series One 1

Series One 18

Series One 58

Series One 70

Series One 73

Series One 91

NO.	CARD TITLE
68	The eighth Doctor #5
69	The eighth Doctor #6
70	The eighth Doctor #7
71	Ben and Polly
72	Polly #1
73	Polly #2
74	Jamie #1
75	Jamie #2
76	Jamie #3
77	Victoria #1
78	Victoria #2
79	Victoria #3
80	Benton #1
81	Benton #2
82	Liz #1
83	Liz #2
84	Liz #3
85	Jo #1
86	Jo #2
87	Jo #3
88	Sarah Jane Smith #1
89	Sarah Jane Smith #2
90	Sarah Jane Smith #3
91	Sarah Jane Smith #4
92	Sarah Jane Smith #5
93	Nyssa #1
94	Nyssa #2
95	Peri #1
96	Peri #2
97	Peri #3
98	Peri #4
99	Peri #5
100	Ace #1
101	Ace #2
102	Ace #3
103	Ace #4
104	The Daleks #1
105	The Daleks #2
106	The Daleks #3
107	Davros #1
108	Davros #2
109	Cybermen #1
110	Cybermen #2
111	Cybermen #3
112	Cybermen #4
113	The Master #1
114	The Master #2
115	The Master #3
116	Time Lords #1
117	Time Lords #2
118	Time Lords #3
119	Checklist #1
120	Checklist #2

SERIES TWO

NO.	CARD TITLE
RN-1	It Takes Allsorts (available from Richard Nolan in Australia)
CI-3	Walkies …
CI-4	A Jaunt in Bessie
DWM-3	Doctor and the Monsters (not issued)
PH-1	Costume Test (available from Paul Hart Trading Cards in the UK)
AE-1	Behind the Mask (available from Alien Entertainment in the US)
WEB-1	The Doctor and Romana (available for customers who ordered the cards from Strictly Ink off the Web)
TP-1	Five Doctors (available from Tenth Planet in the UK)
NS-1	Jo Lends a Hand (available with *Non-Sport Update* magazine)
PS2-1	Jo's first steps into the TARDIS
PS2-2	The Daleks prepare for Galactic War
PS2-3	The Doctor On Trial
PS2-4	Romana glimpses her destiny
PS2-5	Leela
PS2-6	The Men of UNIT
PS2-7	Sontaran Invasion
PS2-8	K9 and Companion
PS2-9	Designed for Effect
PS2-10	Promo card collage
DALEK	5 card Dalek subset spelling the word 'DALEK' on the back
AU1	Lalla Ward
AU2	Tom Baker
AU3	Stuart Myers
AU4	Nicholas Courtney
AU5	Jackie Lane
AU6	Mary Tamm
AU7	Louise Jameson
AU8	Elisabeth Sladen
AU9	John Leeson
AU10	Mark Strickson
AU11	Ray Cusick
AU12	Ian Scoones
AU13	Anthony Ainley
F1	*TV Comic* Issues 674-683 'The Klepton Parasites'
F2	*TV Comic* Issues 784-787 'The Extortioner'
F3	*TV Comic* Issues 944-949 'The Arkwood Experiment'
F4	*Countdown* Issues 1-5 'Gemini Plan'
F5	*TV Action* Issue 104 'Who is the Stranger'
F6	*TV Comic* Issues 1204-1214 'Death Flower'

Series Two AU3

Series Two AU6

Series Two F2

Series Two F7

Series Two F8 (front)

Series Two F8 (back)

Series Two F11   Series Two F12

Series Two 15

Series Two 28

Series Two 40

NO.	CARD TITLE
F7	*Doctor Who Weekly* Issue 1-8 'The Iron Legion'
F8	*Doctor Who Monthly* Issue 61-67 'The Tides of Time'
F9	*Doctor Who Magazine* Issues 88-89 'The Shape Shifter'
F10	*Doctor Who Magazine* Issues 130-134 'A Cold Day in Hell'
F11	*Doctor Who Magazine* Issues 244-247 'Endgame'
F12	*TV Century 21* Issues 1-3 'Genesis of Evil'
F13	*Doctor Who and the Daleks* Issue 1 from Dell Comics
1	Spearhead from Space
2	Doctor Who and the Silurians
3	The Ambassadors of Death
4	Inferno
5	Terror of the Autons
6	The Mind of Evil
7	The Claws of Axos
8	Colony In Space
9	The Dæmons
10	Day of the Daleks
11	The Curse of Peladon
12	The Sea Devils
13	The Mutants
14	The Time Monster
15	The Three Doctors
16	Carnival of Monsters
17	Frontier In Space
18	Planet of the Daleks
19	The Green Death
20	The Time Warrior
21	Invasion of the Dinosaurs
22	Death to the Daleks
23	The Monster of Peladon
24	Planet of the Spiders
25	Robot
26	The Ark in Space
27	The Sontaran Experiment
28	Genesis of the Daleks
29	Revenge of the Cybermen
30	Terror of the Zygons
31	Planet of Evil
32	Pyramids of Mars
33	The Android Invasion
34	The Brain of Morbius
35	The Seeds of Doom
36	The Masque of Mandragora
37	The Hand of Fear
38	The Deadly Assassin
39	The Face of Evil
40	The Robots of Death

NO.	CARD TITLE
41	The Talons of Weng-Chiang
42	Horror of Fang Rock
43	The Invisible Enemy
44	Image of the Fendahl
45	The Sun Makers
46	Underworld
47	The Invasion of Time
48	The Ribos Operation
49	The Pirate Planet
50	The Stones of Blood
51	The Androids of Tara
52	The Power of Kroll
53	The Armageddon Factor
54	Destiny of the Daleks
55	City of Death
56	The Creature from the Pit
57	Nightmare of Eden
58	The Horns of Nimon
59	Shada
60	The Leisure Hive
61	Meglos
62	Full Circle
63	State of Decay
64	Warriors' Gate
65	The Keeper of Traken
66	Logopolis
67	Sontarans I
68	Sontarans II
69	Sontarans III
70	Sontarans IV
71	Silurians/Sea Devils I
72	Silurians/Sea Devils II
73	Silurians/Sea Devils III
74	Silurians/Sea Devils IV
75	Sil I
76	Sil II
77	Master I
78	Master II
79	Master III
80	Master IV
81	Master V
82	UNIT I
83	UNIT II
84	UNIT III
85	UNIT IV
86	UNIT V
87	UNIT VI
88	UNIT VII
89	UNIT VIII
90	UNIT IX
91	Companions Susan Foreman I
92	Companions Susan Foreman II
93	Companions Steven Taylor I

Series Two 59

Series Two 66

Series Two 77

Series Two 93

Series Two 99

Series Three AU1

Series Three AU7

Series Three AU12

NO.	CARD TITLE
94	Companions Steven Taylor II
95	Companions Zoe Herriot I
96	Companions Zoe Herriot II
97	Companions Leela I
98	Companions Leela II
99	Companions Turlough I
100	Companions Turlough II
101	Ray Cusick Set I
102	Ray Cusick Set II
103	Ray Cusick Set III
104	Ray Cusick Set IV
105	Ray Cusick Set V
106	Ray Cusick Set VI
107	Ray Cusick Set VII
108	Ray Cusick Set VIII
109	Ray Cusick Set IX
110	Ian Scoones Set I
111	Ian Scoones Set II
112	Ian Scoones Set III
113	Ian Scoones Set IV
114	Ian Scoones Set V
115	Ian Scoones Set VI
116	Ian Scoones Set VII
117	Ian Scoones Set VIII
118	Ian Scoones Set IX
119	Checklist I
120	Checklist II

SERIES THREE

NO.	CARD TITLE
CI-5	Hands Up
AE-2	Royal Connections (available from Alien Entertainment in the US)
TP-2	Disguise? (available from Tenth Planet in the UK)
RN-2	
PS3-1	The Sixth Doctor
PS3-2	The Doctor and Ace
PS3-3	The fifth Doctor
PS3-4	The Doctor and Tecker
PS3-5	TARDIS
PS3-6	four Doctors and a friend ...
PS3-7	The Rani
PS3-8	John Friedlander Make-Up Effects
PS3-9	The Doctor and Ace
PS3-10	Tollmaster

DOCTOR WHO	9 card subset spelling the words 'DOCTOR WHO' on the back
AU1	Colin Baker

NO.	CARD TITLE
AU2	Sylvester McCoy
AU3	Matthew Waterhouse
AU4	Richard Franklin
AU5	Jean Marsh
AU6	Peter Purves
AU7	William Russell
AU8	Paul Darrow
AU9	Mark Eden
AU10	Maureen O'Brien
AU11	Carole Ann Ford
AU12	Bonnie Langford
AU13	Lynda Bellingham
AU14	Ingrid Pitt
AU15	Kate O'Mara
AU16	Frazer Hines
AU17	Janet Fielding
AU18	Barry Newbery
AU19	John Friedlander
AU20	Peter Davison
AU21	Jacqueline Pearce
F1	1963: The Daleks
F2	1964: The Dalek Invasion of Earth
F3	1965: The Web Planet
F4	1966: The Celestial Toymaker
F5	1967: The Moonbase
F6	1968: The Web of Fear
F7	1969: The Krotons
F8	1970: Spearhead from Space
F9	1971: Colony in Space
F10	1972: Day of the Daleks
F11	1973: The Three Doctors
F12	1974: Invasion of the Dinosaurs
F13	1975: The Android Invasion
F14	1976: The Deadly Assassin
1	A Girl's Best Friend (K9 and Company)
2	Castrovalva
3	Four to Doomsday
4	Kinda
5	The Visitation
6	Black Orchid
7	Earthshock
8	Time-Flight
9	Arc of Infinity
10	Snakedance
11	Mawdryn Undead
12	Terminus
13	Enlightenment
14	The King's Demons
15	The Five Doctors
16	Warriors of the Deep
17	The Awakening
18	Frontios
19	Resurrection of the Daleks

Series Three AU17

Series Three F1

Series Three F5

Series Three F11

Series Three 6

Series Three 7

Series Three 37

Series Three 43

NO.	CARD TITLE
20	Planet of Fire
21	The Caves of Androzani
22	The Twin Dilemma
23	Attack of the Cybermen
24	Vengeance on Varos
25	The Mark of the Rani
26	The Two Doctors
27	Timelash
28	Revelation of the Daleks
29	The Mysterious Planet (The Trial of a Time Lord 1-4)
30	Mindwarp (The Trial of a Time Lord 5-8)
31	Terror of the Vervoids (The Trial of a Time Lord 9-12)
32	The Ultimate Foe (The Trial of a Time Lord 13-14)
33	Time and the Rani
34	Paradise Towers
35	Delta and the Bannermen
36	Dragonfire
37	Remembrance of the Daleks
38	The Happiness Patrol
39	Silver Nemesis
40	The Greatest Show in the Galaxy
41	Battlefield
42	Ghost Light
43	The Curse of Fenric
44	Survival
45	The Enemy Within (Doctor Who: the Movie)
46	Ian Chesterton I
47	Ian Chesterton II
48	Ian Chesterton III
49	Ian Chesterton IV
50	Vicki I
51	Vicki II
52	Vicki III
53	Sara Kingdom I
54	Sara Kingdom II
55	Ben Jackson I
56	Ben Jackson II
57	Harry Sullivan I
58	Harry Sullivan II
59	Harry Sullivan III
60	K9 I
61	K9 II
62	K9 III
63	K9 IV
64	Romana I I
65	Romana I II
66	Romana I III
67	Tegan I
68	Tegan II

NO.	CARD TITLE
69	Tegan III
70	The Master I
71	The Master II
72	The Master III
73	The TARDIS I
74	The TARDIS II
75	The TARDIS III
76	The TARDIS IV
77	The TARDIS V
78	The TARDIS VI
79	The Ice Warriors I
80	The Ice Warriors II
81	The Ice Warriors III
82	The Ice Warriors IV
83	The Autons I
84	The Autons II
85	The Autons III
86	The Yeti I
87	The Yeti II
88	The Yeti III
89	Omega I
90	Omega II
91	Set Design I
92	Set Design II
93	Set Design III
94	Set Design IV
95	Set Design V
96	Set Design VI
97	Set Design VII
98	Set Design VIII
99	Set Design IX
100	Special Make-Up I
101	Special Make-Up II
102	Special Make-Up III
103	Special Make-Up IV
104	Special Make-Up V
105	Special Make-Up VI
106	Special Make-Up VII
107	Special Make-Up VIII
108	Special Make-Up IX
109	Costume Design I
110	Costume Design II
111	Costume Design III
112	Costume Design IV
113	Costume Design V
114	Costume Design VI
115	Costume Design VII
116	Costume Design VIII
117	Costume Design IX
118	Checklist 1
119	Checklist 2
120	Header Card (John Nathan-Turner tribute)

Movie Preview Set P1-P10

MOVIE PREVIEW SET

NO.	CARD TITLE
TP-3	Inside the TARDIS (available from Tenth Planet in the UK)
PTC-1	Discovery (available from PC Trading Cards in the UK)
SC-1	Crash Landing (available from Steve Clark Cards in the UK)
CI-6	Deadly Enemy (available from Cards Inc in the UK)
DM-1	No Escape (available from D&M cards)
P1	Dalek Minions
P2	Dalek Spaceship
P3	Exterminate!
P4	Under Guard
P5	Through the Wreckage
P6	Captive
P7	TARDIS
P8	Attack
P9	Nudge, Nudge … Wink, Wink
P10	Promo card collage

SWA-002

TEL-001

SUNDRIES, WALLPAPER

SWA-001 Dalek Wallpaper
1965, The Wall Paper Manufacturers Ltd, UK
Showing numerous *TV Century 21*-style Daleks
whizzing about on their hoverbouts and firing their
guns. Made by The Wall Paper Manufacturers Ltd
(Lees Paper Staining Company Branch), a division of
Crown Wallpapers. First released in 1965, it was popular enough to remain in the catalogues until the end
of 1967, when it was discontinued.
NM: £110 roll

SWA-002 Wallpaper
1982/02, Colouroll, UK
One in the 'Play Mates' series of nursery pre-pasted
vinyls. A repeating image consisting of photograph of
Peter Davison, and artwork of three Daleks firing
their guns, the TARDIS and a Cyberman head against
a star-scape background.
REF: Pattern 150541 OP: £2.50 per roll NM: £46 roll

TELEPHONE CARDS

TEL-001 Doctor Who Phonecard Album
1995, Jonder International Promotions, UK
Album in which to keep the Jondar phone cards.
OP: £9.00

TEL-002 Doctor Who Phonecards
1994-1997 c., Jondar International Promotions, UK
A phonecard and an accompanying A5 information sheet
on a number of stories. Cards and sheets designed by
Steve Hampshire. Images were computer manipulated
photographs and screen shots. *100,000 BC, The Daleks,
The Aztecs, The Web Planet, The Dominators, The Invasion,
The Krotons, The War Games, The Silurians, Terror of the
Autons, The Curse of Peladon, The Planet of the Spiders, The
Ark in Space, Planet of Evil, Image of the Fendahl.*
OP: £7.50 each

**TEL-003 Doctor Who and the Daleks
Phonecards**
1998/07, P & J Promotions, UK
Set of four photographic phonecards, two from each of
the sixties Dalek films. Includes A5 plastic storage folders.
OP: £12.00 each

TEL-004 Doctor Who Phonecards
1999, USA
A series of $10 phonecards with images taken from
the Colin Howard video covers.

TEL-002 (phonecards)

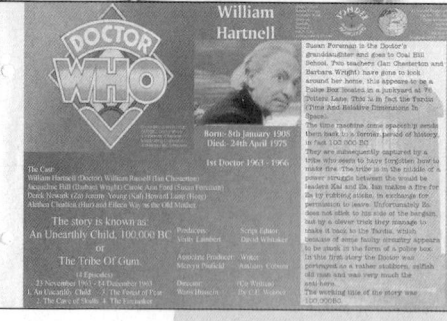

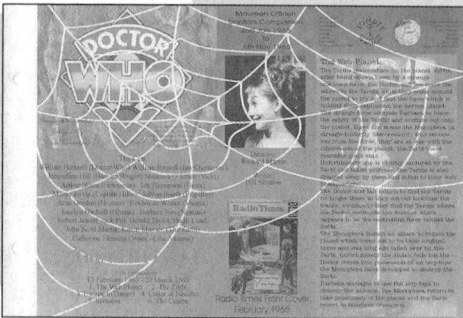

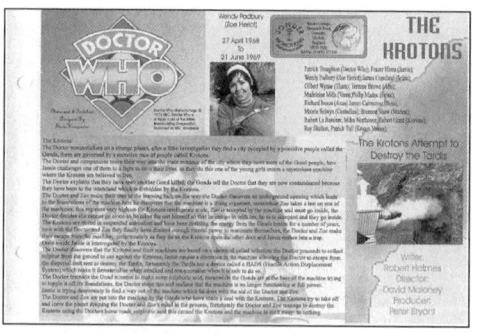

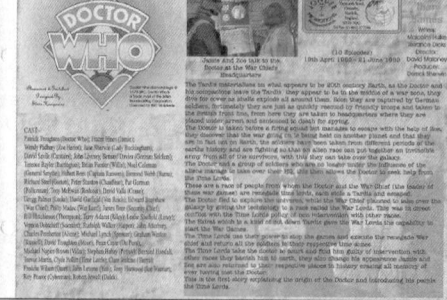

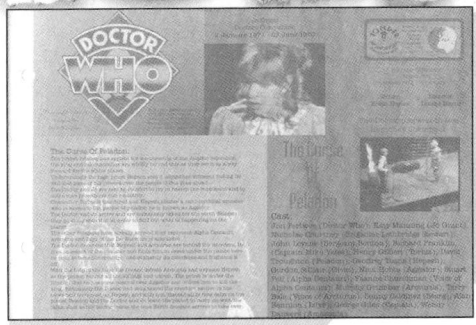

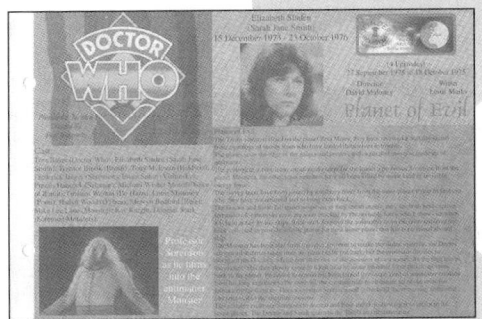

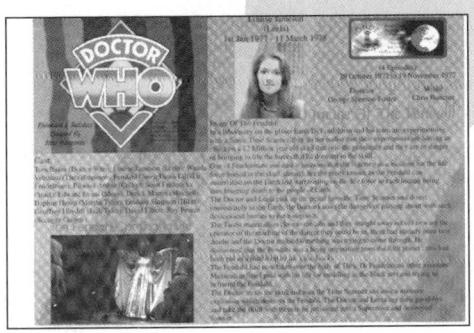

TEL-002 (information sheets)

TEL-003

TEL-004

TOYS, ACTION FIGURES

CONSIDERING the popularity of the action figure market, it is perhaps a bit surprising that there have been only a few of the larger format 'action man' type toys produced to tie-in with *Doctor Who*. The majority of the figures listed below have been produced by Dapol, and are smaller plastic figures with simple joints and basic attention to detail.

TYA-001a Cyberman
1977/09, Denys Fisher Toys, UK
The Denys Fisher range of toys were 'action man' sized (around 12"/24 cm tall) and came with clothes and accessories. Copyright dated 1976 but released in 1977. The Harbert versions are identical figures, but the boxes feature Italian text. Often referred to as the "Mego" figures in the US due to their similarity to other lines like Mego's *Six Million Dollar Man* toys, which were released under the Denys Fisher label in the UK.
OP: £2.50 NM: £250

TYA-001b Ciberniano
1979, Harbert, Italy
NM: £230

TYA-002a Dalek
1977/09, Denys Fisher Toys, UK
To this point, this was one of the most accurate representations of a Dalek in toy form.
OP: £2.50 NM: £275

TYA-002b Dalek
1979, Harbert, Italy
NM: £300

TYA-003a Doctor Who
1977/09, Denys Fisher Toys, UK
Came with hat, scarf and sonic screwdriver. This figure's apparent likeness to the character of 'Gambit' played by Gareth Hunt in *The New Avengers* is because the head *is* that from a Gambit doll. Before production started on the Tom Baker doll, the mould for the head was accidentally damaged and the Gambit head was used in its place.
OP: £2.95 NM: £125

TYA-003b Doctor Who
1979, Harbert, Italy
NM: £115

TYA-004a Giant Robot
1977/09, Denys Fisher Toys, UK
Figure held together with several elastic bands.
OP: £2.95 NM: £325

TYA-001a

TYA-002a

TYA-003a

TYA-004a

TYA-005a

TYA-004b Super Robot
1979, Harbert, Italy
NM: £350

TYA-005a Leela
1977/09, Denys Fisher Toys, UK
Came with knife.
OP: £2.95 NM: £225

TYA-005b Lella
1979, Harbert, Italy
NM: £240

TYA-006a TARDIS
1977/09, Denys Fisher Toys, UK
A large toy of the TARDIS scaled so that the Tom
Baker figure would fit inside it. By turning the 'light'
on the top of the toy, anything placed in the TARDIS
could be made to 'dematerialise'. Approx. 28.5 cm x
17.7 cm x 17.7 cm.
OP: £5.95 NM: £175

TYA-006b Cabina della Polizia
1979, Harbert, Italy
NM: £215

TYA-007 K-9 (friction-action)
1978, Denys Fisher Toys, UK
Scale model of K-9 with friction drive wheels.
OP: £2.99 NM: £175

TYA-006a

TYA-007

TYA-008 25th Anniversary Playset

1988/06, Dapol, UK

Dapol Model Railways Limited commenced trading in 1984 as a manufacturer of model railway products. In 1988 they approached the BBC and gained the license to make a range of *Doctor Who* toys. Over the years the range increased and as of writing the license is still held, with the range of Dapol *Doctor Who* products continually increasing. During 1998, the company diversified into allied *Doctor Who* products which included limited edition glassware and adhesive transfers within their range of BBC licensed products. In 1995, the company obtained a further licence to house and operate the *Doctor Who* exhibition. The exhibition is licensed until 2004 and attracts over 40,000 visitors every year. Visitors can also see the toys being made in the factory.

The playset was among the first items issued by Dapol. It featured a complete diorama of the insides of the TARDIS as well as some character figures. Contents: Seventh Doctor, Mel, TARDIS exterior, five-sided console and base, and a green-coloured K9 (now known to be available individually on a card as well as in this set). The five-sided console and base were also originally available to buy individually direct from the company by mail order. They did not come boxed apart from a thick cardboard tube around the central column to protect it in the post.

Dapol's license expired at the start of 2002.

OP: £39.95 NM: £65-£85

TYA-008

TYA-009a Seventh Doctor (Grey Coat)

1988/06, Dapol, UK

With umbrella.

REF: W001-1 OP: £2.99 NM: £7

TYA-009b Seventh Doctor (Brown Coat)

1988, Dapol, UK

With umbrella.

REF: W001-2 OP: £2.99 NM: £7

TYA-010a Melanie (pink jacket)

1988/06, Dapol, UK

REF: W002-1 OP: £2.99 NM: £6.50

TYA-010b Melanie (blue jacket)

1988/06, Dapol, UK

REF: W002-2 OP: £2.99 NM: £6.50

TYA-011 Tetrap

1988/06, Dapol, UK

REF: W003 OP: £2.99 NM: £7.50

TYA-012a K9 (Grey)

1988/06, Dapol, UK

REF: W004-1 OP: £3.25 NM: £7.50

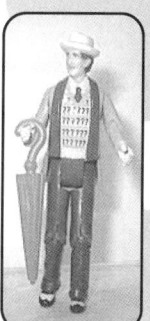

TYA-009a   TYA-009b   TYA-010a

TYA-011

**TYA-012a (top)
and TYA-012b (bottom)**

Details of TYA-012c & both versions of TYA-12d

TYA-013a

TYA-012b K9 (Green)
1988, Dapol, UK
REF: W004-1 OP: £3.25 NM: £7.50

TYA-012c K9 (20th Anniversary)
1996, Dapol, UK
Standard grey model with '20th anniversary' on side.
REF: W004-2 OP: £6.99 NM: £9

TYA-012d K9 (21st Anniversary)
1997, Dapol, UK
Standard grey model with '21st anniversary' on side.
Also offered at Longleat with '21st anniversary
Longleat' on the side.
REF: W004-3 OP: £6.99 NM: £9

TYA-012e Gold K9
2000/11, Dapol, UK
A gold variant of Dapol's standard K9 model produced
exclusively for the Trekker mail order firm in America.

TYA-013a TARDIS
1988/06, Dapol, UK
TARDIS features a flashing light. The base and interior
were only ever available as a part of the 20th anniversary gift set.
REF: W005 OP: £12.95 NM: £22

TYA-013b TARDIS
1998/11, Dapol, UK
Standard Dapol TARDIS with gold lettering and windows, '35th Anniversary' instead of 'Police Public Call
Box' and either 'Colin Baker', 'Sylvester McCoy' or 'Paul
McGann' printed on the door panel along with the
years they played the Doctor, to the right of the 'Pull to
Open' information panel. Some mis-prints available with
the Doctors' years mixed up with the names.
    This TARDIS model was also available in an edition
limited to 350, where purchasers could have their
own name printed on the TARDIS. These came with a
certificate of authenticity.
REF: W005 OP: £19.99

TYA-013c SoundFX TARDIS
2000/10, Dapol, UK
TARDIS model with 30 second sound effect of dema-
terialisation, in flight and materialisation. This is the
standard Dapol TARDIS model with a sound chip
linked to the flashing light circuit in the top section.
REF: W005SFX OP: £24.99

TYA-013d 'Tom Baker' TARDIS
2000/10, Dapol, UK
Signed and inscribed by Baker. Only 40 made.
REF: W005-XCLSV1 OP: £35.00

TYA-014 Master
1997, Dapol, UK
'Delgado' version.
REF: W006 OP: £3.99 NM: £6

TYA-015 Sea Devil
1998/07, Dapol, UK
Original version.
REF: W007 OP: £5.49 NM: £7

TYA-016a Dalek (white/gold)
1988/11, Dapol, UK
There are a plethora of Dapol Dalek variants with an
indeterminate number of colour combinations. Many
were repainted one-off specials for a particular event
(see some of the variants listed below), but some have
yet to be catalogued. Other colour combinations that
have been reported but not yet given their own listing
here include Brown/Gold; Green/Silver, Gold/Black,
Blue/Black with transparent dome (from gift sets); an
'American' Dalek in red, white and blue; and a
Christmas theme Dalek in green, red and gold. Further
information on these and other variations is welcome.
REF: W008-1 OP: £3.99 NM: £7

TYA-016b Dalek (black/gold)
1988/11, Dapol, UK
REF: W008-2 OP: £3.99 NM: £7

TYA-016c Dalek (black/silver)
1988/11, Dapol, UK
REF: W008-3 OP: £3.99 NM: £7

TYA-016d Dalek (grey/blue)
1989/10, Dapol, UK
REF: W008-4 OP: £3.99 NM: £7

TYA-016e Dalek (red/black)
1989, Dapol, UK
REF: W008-5 OP: £3.99 NM: £7

TYA-016f Dalek (red/silver)
1990, Dapol, UK
REF: W008 6 OP: £3.99 NM: £7

TYA-016g Dalek (red/gold)
1990, Dapol, UK
REF: W008-7 OP: £3.99 NM: £7

TYA-016h Dalek (grey/black)
1990/07, Dapol, UK
REF: W008-8 OP: £3.99 NM: £7

TYA-013c (note the sticker on
the box window)

TYA-014   TYA-015

TYA-016a   TYA-016c

TYA-016d   TYA-016f

TYA-016j (in video package)

TYA-016i

TYA-016k

TYA-016m

TYA-016n

TYA-016i Dalek (gold)
1992, Dapol, UK
Dalek with improved gun and eyepiece.
REF: W008-10 OP: £3.99 NM: £7

TYA-016j Dalek (blue)
1993, Dapol, UK
This Dalek was produced as a special commission from Boots the Chemist to make a Dalek in their corporate blue and silver colours. The 'Boots' Dalek was blue with silver spots and came in a blue box with a copy of the then current version of the *Five Doctors* video release. 80 of them were also released on the then standard 'rainbow' Dapol card.
OP: £3.99 NM: £22

TYA-016k Dalek (Grey/Gold)
1999/11, Dapol/BBC Manchester, UK
This Dalek was produced as a special commission from the BBC to help promote the *Doctor Who* Night on BBC2 on 13th November 1999. The Dalek came packaged with a special backing card which gave details of the schedule for the night. These Daleks were used as trade promotional items and also internally at the BBC.
NM: £33

TYA-016l Commemorative 'Tom Baker' Dalek
2000/10/28, Dapol, UK
Limited edition of 150 special backing cards produced to accompany a Dalek figure. Advertising states that the Dalek may vary in colour. Sample seen: Blue Dalek with gold spots, slats and eye.
REF: W005-XCLSV1 OP: £9.99

TYA-016m Dalek (Transmat)
2000/11, Dapol, UK
A clear plastic Dalek showing a green Dalek mutant inside. Another version exists with a yellow mutant.
REF: W008-11 OP: £5.99

TYA-016n Cancer Research Dalek
2000/12/01, Dapol, UK
A black dalek with pink head and arms and purple spots and slats – the Cancer Research Campaign colours. Came with a special backing card. Dapol donating £2.50 from each model produced to the charity.
OP: £5.99

TYA-017 Film Dalek (red)
1992, Dapol, UK
Dalek with claw arm, improved gun and eyepiece.
REF: W008-9 OP: £3.99 NM: £7

TYA-018a Cyberman
1989/08, Dapol, UK
REF: W009 OP: £2.99 NM: £6

TYA-018b Commemmorative 'Frazer Hines/Anneke Wills' Black Cyberman
2000/06, Dapol, UK
Limited edition of 1,000 special backing cards produced to accompany a black Cyberman figure with silver detail. Backing cards signed by Frazer Hines and Anneke Wills.
OP: £35

TYA-017   **TYA-018a**

TYA-019 Fourth Doctor
1991/01, Dapol, UK
This model was not issued with a scarf or hat.
REF: W010 OP: £2.99 NM: £6

TYA-020a Silurian
1998, Dapol, UK
REF: W011 OP: £5.49

TYA-020b Silver Silurian
1990s, Dapol, UK
Variant limited edition in silver with autographs; probably from Longleat.

TYA-021 Armoured Silurian
1998, Dapol, UK
REF: W012 OP: £5.49

TYA-019   **TYA-020a**

TYA-022 Ice Warrior
1990/04, Dapol, UK
With sonic gun. At least two shades of gun colour were produced, light green and dark green.
REF: W013 OP: £2.99

TYA-020b

TYA-021   **TYA-022**

TYA-023a   **TYA-023b**   **TYA-023d**

TYA-024   **TYA-025a**   **TYA-025b**

TYA-027

TYA-026

TYA-028

TYA-023a Gallifrey High Councillor (Brown Robe)
1998, Dapol, UK
REF: W014-1 OP: £5.49 NM: £8

TYA-023b Gallifrey High Councillor (Cream Robe)
1998, Dapol, UK
REF: W014-2 OP: £5.49 NM: £8

TYA-023c Gallifrey High Councillor (Burgundy Robe)
1998, Dapol, UK
REF: W014-3 OP: £5.49 NM: £8

TYA-023d Gallifrey High Councillor (Grey Robe)
1998, Dapol, UK
REF: W014-4 OP: £5.49 NM: £8

TYA-024 Ace
1990/06, Dapol, UK
With rucksack and baseball bat.
REF: W015 OP: £3.25 NM: £7

TYA-025a Davros (two armed)
1990/04, Dapol, UK
A two-handed version of Davros was initially issued in very small numbers (under 500) but this was hastily withdrawn when the mistake was realised and a one-armed figure released in its place. This figure is however still on sale in many outlets.
REF: W016 OP: £4.99 NM: £12-£24

TYA-025b Davros (one armed)
1990/05, Dapol, UK
A limited edition with gold trim instead of silver is also known to exist.
REF: W016 OP: £4.99 NM: £8

TYA-026 Third Doctor
1998/03, Dapol, UK
Limited to 5000.
REF: W019 OP: £5.49 NM: £7

TYA-027 Dalek Army Action Figure Play Set
1990/11, Dapol, UK
Seven Daleks (six standard, one 'special': blue with a black dome) and Davros.
REF: W021-1 OP: £32.50 NM: £45

TYA-028 Tom Baker Action Figure Play Set
1992, Dapol, UK
Fourth Doctor, Mel, Cyberman, TARDIS, Blue/Black Dalek, K9.
REF: W021-2 OP: £27.50 NM: £45

TYA-029 Action Figure Play Set 3
1992, Dapol, UK
Seventh Doctor, Ace, Cyberman, TARDIS, Green/Silver
Dalek, K9.
REF: W021-3 OP: £27.50 NM: £45

TYA-030 35th Anniversary Play Set
1998/11, Dapol, UK
Contains: Third Doctor, Time Lord, Master and 3 exclusive figures: TARDIS, Davros and K9. Only 350 produced.
REF: W022 OP: £44.99 NM: £55

TYA-031a Sontaran
1999/10, Dapol, UK
Comes with separate helmet. Black body with silver
collar, gloves and boots.
REF: W024 OP: £5.49

TYA-031b Sontaran Captain
1999/10, Dapol, UK
Comes with separate helmet. Silver body with black
collar, gloves and boots.
REF: W024-1 OP: £5.49

TYA-032 Melkur
1999/11, Dapol, UK
REF: W025 OP: £5.49

TYA-033 Early Daleks Gift Set
2000/08, Dapol, UK
Set of Daleks with backing scene. Four grey Daleks
with blue spots. One with Dalek mutant plunger, one
with standard plunger, one with seismic detector, one
with flame thrower.
REF: W030 OP: £26.99

TYA-034 "Self-Assembly" Dalek Kit/Make Your Own Dalek Kit
2000, Dapol, UK
Available at the Dapol shop in Llangollen. Consisted
of purple and pink parts from a 5" Dapol Dalek which
you could then assemble yourself. Exclusive to the
"Doctor Who Experience". Proceeds went to charity?
OP: £3.99

TYA-029

TYA-030

TYA-031a   TYA-031b   TYA-032

TYA-033

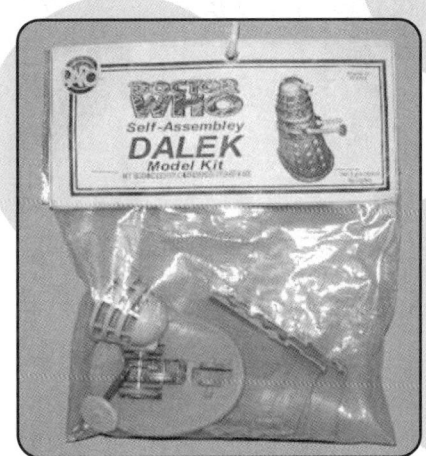
TYA-034

TYG-001

TOYS, BALLOONS

TYB-001 Dalek Balloon (large)
1965, Lewis Knight & Co. Ltd, UK
Exclusive to Woolworths stores.
OP: 6d NM: £110

TYB-002 Dalek Balloon (small)
1965, Sto-Rose Toys Ltd, UK
6 assorted colour balloons printed in two colours
with the design of a Dalek.
OP: 3d NM: £100

TYB-003 Doctor Who Balloons
1981, BBC Enterprises, UK

TYB-004 Doctor Who Foil Balloons
1985, Marlow Engineering Ltd, UK
NM: £3.50

TYB-005 Dalek Foil Balloons
1990s, Flex Metal, S.L. (International Balloons World), UK
Originally available at Longleat. Gold foil.
OP: £1.50

TYG-002a

TOYS, GENERAL

DOCTOR Who toys come in a great many forms. As
with all collectibles, where they originally came in
a box or bag, any damage to the packaging will
decrease the cost accordingly.

TYG-001 Dalek Dressing Up Costume
1964, Scorpion Automotives, UK
This is one of the rarest sixties items today, as in the
lead-up to Christmas 1964, the firm's Northampton
factory was apparently damaged by fire and the stocks
waiting to go to the shops, together with all the components to construct the suits, were destroyed.

  This costume had a plastic dome with side lights, a
realistic eyestalk, a neck section (through which the
occupant could see out) comprising two rings held in
place by vertical rods. The shoulder section was pat-
terned after the original Dalek design and the sucker
arm and gun stick fitted into sockets so that they could
be worked from inside. The outfit was finished off with
a PVC skirt, printed with the familiar pattern of studs.

  There were two versions of the costume produced.
The first was on wheels but this proved a safety hazard
and so the second was propelled by foot-power alone.
Another safety feature was that if the occupant should
trip and fall, the dome automatically came off, thus ensur-
ing that no one could get trapped inside.
OP: £8 15s 6d NM: £1350

TYG-002b

TYG-002a Cutta-mastic Doctor Who and the Daleks, The
1965, Bell Toys Ltd, UK
Box contains a heated wire tool, templates and several thin sheets of expanded polystyrene which could be cut into Dalek shapes and then painted.
OP: 29s 11d NM: £275

TYG-002b Cutta-mastic featuring Daleks, The
1966, Bell Toys Ltd, UK
Small boxed version of the Cutta-mastic toy.
NM: £300

TYG-003 Dalek
1965, Cherilea Toys Ltd, UK
These were approximately 3" tall models in three detachable sections – a base, a middle and a top – which came in several different colours. The appendages were also detachable and the top had two variations, slatted and solid. The idea was that children could swap the assorted body parts amongst themselves to create Daleks in a variety of different colour schemes. These toys were sold loose and initially came in three colours – black, light blue and silver – although more colours were added later.
OP: 1s NM: £55

TYG-003

TYG-004

TYG-004 Dalek
1965, Herts Plastic Moulders Ltd, UK
Sold exclusively through F. W. Woolworth stores, this silver/grey model stood about 7" tall and came in a plastic bag.
OP: 4s 11d NM: £235

TYG-005

TYG-005 Dalek (4.5" friction)
1965, Louis Marx & Co. Ltd , UK
Black or Silver. Boxed.
REF: 531 OP: 5s 11d NM: £220

TYG-006 Dalek (6.5" battery operated with robot action)
1965, Louis Marx & Co. Ltd, UK
Black or Silver. Boxed.
REF: 800 OP: 17s 11d NM: £250

TYG-006

TYG-007 Dalek (6.5" friction drive with siren and flashing lights)
1965, Louis Marx & Co. Ltd, UK
Black or Silver. Boxed.
REF: 540 OP: 12s 11d NM: £240

TYG-007

TYG-008

TYG-008 Dalek (bendy)
1965, Newfeld Ltd, UK
After meeting BBC representatives at a toy fair, American Charles Newfeld was sufficiently impressed with the Daleks and convinced of their market potential – the BBC was then trying to sell *Doctor Who* to America, and the film *Dr. Who and the Daleks* was already on release – that he became keen to add the creatures to his 'Bendy' toy empire. Consequently he produced a Bendy Dalek which came in one of three colours – black, grey or white.
OP: 10s 6d NM: £275

TYG-009 Dalek (mechanical)
1965, Cowan, de Groot Ltd, UK
Model moves along gradually turning itself through 360 degrees. At the same time the dome containing the eye, scans the horizon. Available in blue or black. Marketed as 'the mysterious clockwork Dalek'. Boxed.
REF: #1/7/22 OP: 15s 11d NM: £600

TYG-010 Dalek (scotchlite)
1965, Clifford Thomas Printing Co. Ltd, UK

TYG-011 Dalek (stand-up inflatable)
1965, Scorpion Universal Toys Ltd, UK
This was an inflatable punch-bag with a Dalek printed on it in blue, white and black.
OP: 21s NM: £165

TYG-009

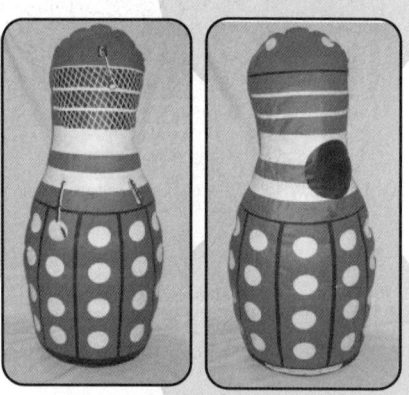

TYG-011

TYG-012

TYG-013

TYG-012 Dalek Construction Kit, The
1965, Louis Marx & Co. Ltd , UK
A seven piece boxed kit missing the drive mechanism
from the standard Marx toys.
REF: K110 OP: 6s 11d NM: £250

TYG-013 Dalek Eraza Board Set
1965, Bell Toys Ltd, UK
Box contains six double-sided cards of Dalek scenes
which can be coloured and then wiped-off.
OP: 8s 11d NM: £275

TYG-014 Dalek Glove Puppet
1965, The Chad Valley Company Ltd, UK
Moulded vinyl head and antennae with a fabric body glove.
OP: 8s 11d NM: £350

TYG-015 Dalek Kite
1965, Bowman Jenkins, UK
A plastic kite with wooden struts, plus a plastic tail.
Marketed as 'Dalek High Flying Space Kite'.
OP: 4s 6d NM: £165

TYG-016 Dalek Meteorite Storm
1965, Randall & Wood Ltd, UK
One of the 'Linda' range of TV character snowstorms
– a small scene inside a clear perspex dome filled
with water and tiny red particles which would swirl
like snow when it was shaken. The snowstorms are
believed to have come boxed, and several variants are
known to exist, with differing numbers of Daleks
making up the interior scene. The basic item consisted
of a landscape with a TARDIS in it, a fixed Dalek
beside the TARDIS and then two or three small
Daleks on hoverbouts which floated in the liquid.
OP: 2s 6d NM: £140

TYG-017 Dalek Money Box
1965, Cowan, de Groot Ltd, UK
Boxed Dalek with a slot in the top of the head, which
could also be removed to get at the saved money. This
toy was used as the basis for the illustrations of
Daleks on several products in the sixties, most
notably the Dalek crockery.
REF: #36/2 OP: 4s 11d NM: £180

TYG-018 Dalek Nursery Toy
1965, Selcol Products Ltd, UK
Blue plastic Dalek which could be filled with sand or
water to provide ballast. Arms and eye detachable.
Came in a plastic bag with header card.
REF: No 1052 OP: 5s 11d NM: £275

TYG-015

TYG-016

TYG-017

TYG-018

TYG-019

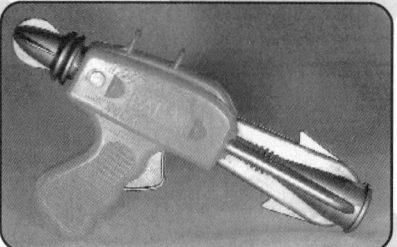

TYG-021

TYG-022

TYG-023

TYG-024

TYG-020

TYG-019 Dalek Oracle, The
1965, Bell Toys Ltd, UK
A variant of the popular 'Magic Robot' game. The playing board is divided into two adjacent circles, around one of which are dotted several questions. In playing the game, a small Dalek toy is placed in the centre of this first circle and turned to point to a given question. The Dalek is then moved to the second circle, surrounding which are the answers, and placed on a mirror at its centre. When released, it 'magically' spins to point to the correct answer. Operated by magnets, the boxed game contains several question-and-answer sheets.
OP: 9s 11d NM: £350

TYG-020 Dalek Playsuit
1965, Berwick Toy Co. Ltd, UK
Comprises a red PVC skirt printed with a white stud design, which fits over a silver, cardboard-slatted section topped with a plastic dome. Also provided are an eyestalk which can be fitted into a hole on the dome, and two 'arms' which can be held through suitably positioned holes in the skirt. Came packaged in a large cardboard box.
OP: 66s 6d NM: £375

TYG-021 Dalek Rocket Gun
1965, Lone Star Products, UK
In red and silver. Mounted on a card with two suction darts. A target is printed on the card. Pistol has a clip to hold the spare dart.
OP: 5s 11d

TYG-022 Dalek Shooting Game
1965, Louis Marx & Co. Ltd, UK
Box contains gun, corks, target board and four Dalek
targets.
REF: 680 OP: 16s 11d NM: £400

TYG-023 Dalek Skittles
1965, Randall & Wood Ltd, UK
NM: £70 each

TYG-024 Dalek Stencil Set
1965, Berwick Toy Co. Ltd, UK
Boxed set of Dalek scenes together with palette and
brush, two mixing bowls and five assorted paints.
OP: 4s 11d NM: £135

TYG-025 Dalek Transfers
1965, Tower Press/S. Guiterman & Co. Ltd, UK
40 transfers per sheet. 36 sheets to a single header
card. Pictures featured Daleks, Mechanoids, a Voord,
Menoptra, Zarbi, a Venom Gun, the TARDIS exterior
and the TARDIS console. Once cut from the sheet
and soaked in water, the images could be slid off their
paper backing and on to skin.
REF: No 1920 OP: 3d sheet

TYG-026 Dalek Wonder Slate
1965, Bell Toys Ltd, UK
A basic 'magic slate' consisting of a waxed tracing
paper placed on top of a dark shiny card. Drawing on
the slate with a blunt 'pen' causes the waxed paper to
adhere to the dark lower sheet, leaving dark lines and
marks which can be made to vanish by sliding a rule
down between the two sheets. The slate came either
on a backing card or in a box.
OP: 2s 11d NM: £220

TYG-027 Doctor Who and the Daleks
Bagatelle (large circular)
1965, Louis Marx & Co. Ltd, UK
9" high and 10" wide. Contains five coloured balls. Boxed.
REF: 1162 D OP: 7s 6d NM: £165

TYG-025

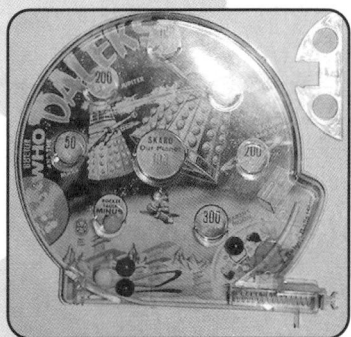

TYG-027 (in and out of box)

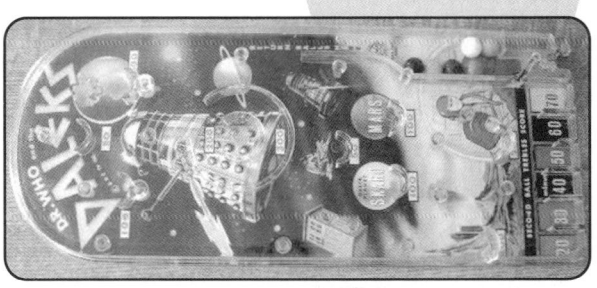

TYG-028 (shown sideways)

TYG-030

TYG-031

TYG-032

TYG-034

TYG-028 Doctor Who and the Daleks Bagatelle (oblong)
1965, Louis Marx & Co. Ltd , UK
A 15"-long arch-shaped game, available only from F. W. Woolworth. Contains five balls.
OP: 7s 11d NM: £155

TYG-029 Doctor Who and the Daleks Bagatelle (small circular)
1965, Louis Marx & Co. Ltd, UK
5" in diameter with three balls. Boxed.
NM: £140

TYG-030 Doctor Who Give-a-Show Projector
1965, The Chad Valley Company Ltd, UK
Battery-powered projector and 16 slide-strips in a box. The stories feature the Doctor, Ian and Barbara. The numbering reflects the total range of Chad Valley slides and these were the only *Doctor Who* related slides available. The slides which came with the projector had purple backgrounds to the text. Two slides (137 and 138) were available with red backgrounds to the writing in a Chad Valley Gift Set. The slides could also be bought separate from the set containing the projector in four sets of four.
Titles: 137: Dr Who in "Lilliput", 138: The Daleks Destroy the Zomites, 139: Dr Who on the Aqua Planet, 140: Dr Who in the Spiders Web, 141: Dr Who meets the Watermen, 142: The Defeat of the Daleks, 143: The Secrets of TARDIS, 144: The Daleks are Foiled, 145: Dr Who and the Nerve Machine (Daleks), 146: The Ice-Age Monster, 147: Rescued from the Daleks, 148: Escape from the Aquafien, 149: Where Diamonds are Worthless, 150: The Prehistoric Monster, 151: On the Planet Vortis (part 1 – story is a very basic version of *The Web Planet*), 152: The Zarbi are Destroyed (part 2)
REF: G344R OP: 29s 6d NM: £275

TYG-031 Doctor Who's 'Astro Ray' Dalek Gun
1965, Bell Toys Ltd, UK
This red and white plastic dart gun came with three suction darts and has a battery-powered ray beam. Boxed.
OP: 14s 11d NM: £440

TYG-032 Dr Who and the Dalek Rolykins
1965, Louis Marx & Co. Ltd, UK
Officially available in three colours – black, silver and red (released in 1966) – they stood about an inch tall and had detachable appendages. Their most distinctive feature was that they each contained a ball bearing in the base, which meant that they could glide down smooth inclines and be pushed along tabletops. Because of the modest price – only a shilling each – and the size of these toys,

TYG-035

seaside arcade machines were filled with them. The Rolykins were amongst the most popular of all Dalek items, with over a million units sold by October 1965. Examples also exist of Rolykins with a heavy domed base, allowing them to sway about in place, but no further information is available on this variant.
REF: 8350 OP: 1s NM: £55 each

TYG-033 Dr Who and the Daleks – The Great Escape Game
1965, Peter Pan Playthings Ltd, UK
A boxed ball-bearing maze game.
OP: 7s 11d NM: £275

TYG-034 Dr Who and the Daleks Top
1965, Selcol Products Ltd, UK
A children's spinning top which featured a TARDIS-shape in the centre, a rocky landscape image on the base of the encased spinning top and several 'flat' Daleks standing up from the base. Boxed.
OP: 19s 11d

TYG-035 Dr Who Dalek Painting by Numbers, The
1965, Peter Pan Playthings Ltd, UK
Box contains 6 scenes, a palette with 12 Reeves paints, a plastic water container and brush. Also a colour guide.
OP: 9s 11d NM: £220

TYG-036

TYG-036 Dr Who Money Box
1965, Raphael Lipkin Ltd, UK
Came in a yellow cardboard box featuring a black and
white photograph of William Hartnell as the Doctor.
The money box was TARDIS-shaped and was in blue
vinyl with yellow door and 'Police Box' banners.
OP: 4s 6d NM: £60

TYG-037 Dr Who's Anti-Dalek Fluid Neutraliser
1965, Lincoln International (London) Ltd, UK
A water-pistol gun.
OP: 3s 11d

TYG-038 Dr Who's Anti-Dalek Jet Immobiliser
1965, Lincoln International (London) Ltd, UK
A water-machine gun with rapid or single fire.
OP: 9s 11d

TYG-039 Dr Who's Anti-Dalek Neutron Exterminator
1965, Lincoln International (London) Ltd, UK
Bazooka gun. 3 foot long in metallic blue and silver.
Fires anti-Dalek missiles.
OP: 21s

TYG-040 Dr Who's Anti-Dalek Sonic Disintegrator
1965, Lincoln International (London) Ltd, UK
This plastic toy gun came in blue and white with a red
'firing' piece.
OP: 12s 11d

TYG-037

TYG-038

TYG-043

TYG-042

TYG-040

TYG-044

TYG-041 Dr. Who ... Dodge the Daleks Game
1965, Cowan, de Groot Ltd, UK
Box containing artwork cardboard board, counters, die
and throwing cup. The 'Dodge the Daleks' name originated in *The Dalek Annual* published by Souvenir Press.
REF: #1/8 OP: 6s 11d NM: £220

TYG-042 Mechanoid (large)
1965, Herts Plastic Moulders Ltd, UK
OP: 4s 11d NM: £375

TYG-045

TYG-043 Mechanoid (small)
1965, Cherilea Toys Ltd, UK
Came in three colours: Black, Light Blue, Silver.
OP: 1s NM: £85

TYG-044 Iron-on Transfer
1971, Dodo Iron-Ons, UK
A single transfer that could be applied to a T-shirt.
OP: 50p

TYG-045 Dalek (6.5", battery)
1974, Louis Marx & Co Ltd, UK
Came in two colours: Red or Yellow. Boxed.
REF: 800 NM: £155

TYG-046 Doctor Who Mini-Puzzles
1974, H.C. Ford, UK
A set of four small ball-bearing puzzles featuring artwork of the Doctor and some monsters.

TYG-047 Doctor Who Painting by Numbers
sets (six different)
1974, Airfix, UK
Each boxed set contained oil paint, two 190x250mm
pictures (plus painting guides) and a brush. Dalek
Invasion (75501-2); Dr. Who and his car (75502-5); Dr.
Who and the Snakebirds (75503-8); Dr. Who and the
Sea Monsters (75504-1); Dr. Who and the Robots
(75505-4); Dr. Who and the Octomen (75506-7).
NM: £85 each

TYG-047

TYG-048 Dalek (6.5", battery, talking)
1975, Palitoy Bradgate, UK
In two colours: red or silver. By pushing a button
located on the top of the dome, the Dalek could be
made to utter one of four pre-recorded messages: 'I
will obey'; 'Exterminate! Exterminate!'; Attack! Attack!
Attack!'; 'What are your orders?'. Boxed.
OP: £3.75 NM: £200

TYG-048 (both colors)

TYG-050

TYG-049a/b

TYG-051

TYG-052

TYG-049a Doctor Who
1975, Strawberry Fayre by Denys Fisher, UK
The box front bore a silhouette of the Doctor and the
TARDIS against a blue vortex, and inside were a board,
56 cards, four coloured 'Doctor' counters and a TARDIS
die shaker. The object of the game was to get around
the board, avoiding monsters along the way.
OP: £3.60 NM: £15

TYG-049b Doctor Who
1975, Strawberry Fayre by Denys Fisher, UK
Identical to TYG-049a except for the addition of a full
colour photographic sticker of Tom Baker to the box
front to make it more eye-catching.
OP: £3.60 NM: £15

**TYG-050 Doctor Who and the Daleks Transfer
(Dalek)**
1975, Imagine Transfers Ltd, UK
A single transfer that could be applied to a T-shirt.
OP: 50p

TYG-051 Doctor Who and the Daleks Yo-Yo
1975, Louis Marx & Co. Ltd, UK
Came on a backing card.
REF: Ref no 106 OP: 50p

TYG-052 War of the Daleks
1975, Strawberry Fayre by Denys Fisher, UK
Box contained eight plastic Daleks (four gold, four silver), a dynamic board and four player counters. The
object was to get to the centre of the board (Dalek

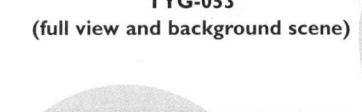

TYG-053
(full view and background scene)

Control) and destroy the Emperor Dalek, avoiding the patrolling plastic Daleks along the way. Later reissued with the new Denys Fisher logo replacing the Strawberry Fayre logo on both the box and rule book.
OP: £5.25 NM: £55

TYG-053 Doctor Who Dalek Invasion of Earth Transfers
1976, Letraset Action Transfers, UK
In 'Super Action Heroes' range. Featured a background and a single sheet of transfers featuring Daleks, spaceships, troops with guns, Sarah and the Doctor. Set came sealed in plastic.
OP: 55p NM: £27.50

TYG-054 Doctor Who Dressing Up Costume
1976, Berwicks Toys Ltd, UK
Consisted of a small plastic tunic, on which was printed a jacket and a scarf, and a plastic Tom Baker mask. It was discontinued in September 1977, at which point only 309 units had been sold.
NM: £110

TYG-054

TYG-055b

TYG-055a

TYG-055a Doctor Who Aim 'n' Shoot Bagatelle Game
1978, Jotastar, UK
Large version.
NM: £90

TYG-055b Doctor Who Aim 'n' Shoot Bagatelle Game
1978, Jotastar, UK
Small version.
OP: £1.49 NM: £70

TYG-056 Doctor Who Bagatelle
1978, Playtime, UK
OP: 75p

TYG-057 K-9 (battery, talking)
1978, Palitoy Bradgate, UK
Boxed K-9 model. By pushing the control panel on K9's back, the model could be made to speak one of eleven pre-recorded phrases: 'I am K9'; 'Affirmative Master'; 'Affirmative, understood'; 'Proceeding with caution'; 'Most satisfactory'; 'Weaponry set at stun level, firing now (gun sound effect)'; 'What are your instructions?'; 'Danger! Danger! Hostile life forms approaching'; 'Analysing atmosphere on planet surface, acceptable to humanoids'; 'Gravity reading normal'; and 'Mission accomplished'.
OP: £7.90 NM: £165

TYG-058 TARDIS Tuner
1978, Shortman Trading, UK
A radio with options to make various noises while lights would flash. Boxed.
OP: £19.95 NM: £110

TYG-059 Doctor Who 3-D Clay Picture
1979, Remus Playkits Ltd, UK
The idea of the boxed kit was to fill a plastic mould

TYG-057

TYG-058

TYG-059

TYG-060

with different coloured plasticine to create a '3-D' scene 'Dr Who Meets the Daleks' which could then be mounted against a coloured back-board to make a picture. This product did extremely well, with over 18,000 units sold.
REF: Prod No 1105 OP: £1.15 NM: £25

TYG-060 Doctor Who – The Game of Time and Space
1980, Games Workshop, UK
A 2-6 player boxed game. 'Each player, as a different incarnation of Doctor Who, must search the galaxy for the Key of Chronos. Daleks, Cyberman and other aliens protect the key; but with the help of his scientific know-how and assistants, each Doctor must fight the aliens, and maybe each other; in their struggle to save the galaxy.'
REF: 102102 OP: £6.75 NM: £27.50

TYG-061 Frisby
1980, Nightstar Corp., USA
White or yellow. A green one (pictured) with a notation on the disc, '10p.m. Mondays on Channel 10' may be from a different manufacturer.
OP: $4.00 each

TYG-062 TARDIS Tin – The Fourth Doctor
1980, Avon Tin, UK
The tins were available in two basic designs: the lid was hinged, or lifted straight off. These tins have, over the years, been sold as money boxes, tea-caddies, pencil boxes and storage tins. A metal tin with a printed exterior. Features the Fourth Doctor standing in the TARDIS doorway
OP: £1.65 NM: £35

TYG-061

TYG-062

TYG-063

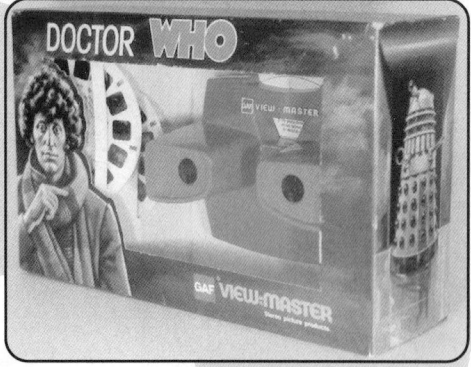

TYG-064 (front)

TYG-064 (back)

**TYG-065
(with box)**

**TYG-065
(window & console)**

TYG-063 Doctor Who Viewmaster: *Full Circle*
1981, GAF Corporation, UK
3 reels, 21 pictures. Viewmaster was a popular stereo-
scopic toy of the seventies and a great many picture
wheels were available on all manner of different subjects.
REF: BD 187-123 E OP: £1.95 NM: £25

TYG-064 Doctor Who Viewmaster Gift Set
1982, GAF Corporation, UK
A boxed set containing the Viewmaster viewer in a
box featuring pictures of the Daleks, a red coloured
TARDIS and the Fourth Doctor. as well as a set of the
Full Circle Doctor Who slides.
REF: Code No: 10 102 937 0 NM: £45

TYG-065 TARDIS Tent
1982, D. Dekker Ltd, UK
Boxed plastic vinyl tent and plastic tubular frame. Box
shows children dressed as the Fifth Doctor, Nyssa and
Tegan. Console printed on interior back panel. See-
through window in back panel. Top light is inflatable.
REF: T-WPH-1 OP: £15.99 NM: £95

TYG-066 TARDIS Tin – The Fifth Doctor
1982, Avon Tin, UK
A metal tin with a printed exterior. Features the Fifth
Doctor standing in the TARDIS doorway
OP: £1.75 NM: £27.50

TYG-067 Yo-Yo
1982, Nightstar Corp., USA
OP: $4.50

TYG-068 Doctor Who Viewmaster: *Castrovalva*
1983/04, View-Master International, UK
3 reels, 21 pictures. Dated 1982.
REF: BD 216-123 E TV & Movie NR.59
OP: £1.95 NM: £16.50

TYG-066

TYG-068

TYG-069

TYG-069 Cyberman mask
1983, Image Screencraft, UK
Flat cardboard mask with elastic to hold it to the head.
NM: £11

TYG-070 K-9 (Mark V) soft toy
1984, DWFCA, USA
OP: $60.00

TYG-071 K-9 (Mark VI) soft toy
1984, DWFCA, USA
OP: $45.00

TYG-072a Playmat
1984/08, S.P. Sport & Playbase Ltd, USA
39 x 29" rubber-backed one-piece playmat. Artwork
scene of the Fourth Dr and Leela by the TARDIS, surrounded by Daleks and Cybermen.
OP: $14.95 (£8.99 import) NM: £35

TYG-072a

TYG-072b Playmat
1985/05, S.P. Sport & Playbase Ltd, UK
Art and dimensions identical to TYG-072a except this
version features the Sixth Doctor and Peri.
REF: FSM5081/8 No 9 OP: £8.99 (I) NM: £27.50

TYG-072b

TYG-072c Playmat
1985/05, S.P. Sport & Playbase Ltd, UK
Two-piece playmat. Art identical to TYG-072b except
cropped and packaged in two separate pieces.

TYG-073 Binoculars
1987, Lionheart, USA
Plastic with Cyberman & Zygon, diamond and neon
logo. A design also exists with a Dalek & a Zygon.
OP: $6.00

TYG-072c

 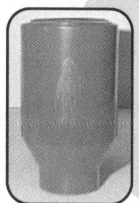

TYG-073 (front and side views)

TYG-075

TYG-074 Doctor Who YoYo
Vale Royal, UK
McCoy Logo and TARDIS.
NM: £2.75

TYG-075 Doctor Who Battle for the Universe
1989/06, The Games Team, UK
A boxed tactical strategy game. The product was apparently relaunched in 1990 at the lower price of £12.99.
OP: £14.99 NM: £16.50

TYG-076a Friction Drive Daleks – Black/Gold
1990, Dapol, UK
Based on the Louis Marx Dalek. Carded. As with other Dapol items, more colour combinations have been noted and are difficult to list in their entirety.
REF: W018-7 OP: £5.99 NM: £8

TYG-076b Friction Drive Daleks – Gold
1990, Dapol, UK
Based on the Louis Marx Dalek. Carded.
REF: W018-6 OP: £5.99 NM: £8

TYG-076c Friction Drive Daleks – Silver/Gold
1990, Dapol, UK
Based on the Louis Marx Dalek. Carded.
REF: W018-8 OP: £5.99 NM: £8

TYG-076f

TYG-076d Friction Drive Daleks – Black
1990/10, Dapol, UK
Based on the Louis Marx Dalek. Carded.
REF: W018-3 OP: £5.99 NM: £8

TYG-076e Friction Drive Daleks – Grey
1990/10, Dapol, UK
Based on the Louis Marx Dalek. Carded.
REF: W018-2 OP: £5.99 NM: £8

TYG-076f Friction Drive Daleks – Red
1990/10, Dapol, UK
Based on the Louis Marx Dalek. Carded.
REF: W018-1 OP: £5.99 NM: £8

TYG-076g Friction Drive Daleks – Silver
1990/10, Dapol, UK
Based on the Louis Marx Dalek. Carded.
REF: W018-4 OP: £5.99 NM: £8

TYG-076h Friction Drive Daleks – White
1990/10, Dapol, UK
Based on the Louis Marx Dalek. Carded.
REF: W018-5 OP: £5.99 NM: £8

TYG-077a Bump and Go Daleks – Black
1992/07, Dapol, UK
Based on the Louis Marx sixties Daleks.

TYG-077c

Numbered limited editions. 2500 (Black). Boxed.
REF: W020-3 OP: £19.99 NM: £27.50

TYG-077b Bump and Go Daleks – Silver
1992/07, Dapol, UK
Numbered limited editions 2501-5000 (Silver). Boxed.
REF: W020-1 OP: £19.99 NM: £27.50

TYG-077c Bump and Go Daleks – Red
1992/07, Dapol, UK
Numbered limited editions. 5001-7500 (Red). Boxed.
REF: W020-2 OP: £19.99 NM: £27.50

TYG-077d Bump and Go Daleks – Gold
1992/08, Dapol, UK
Numbered limited editions. 7501-10000 (Gold). Boxed.
REF: W020-4 OP: £19.99 NM: £27.50

TYG-078 Doctor Who YoYo
1992, Dapol, UK
Logo or TARDIS.
REF: W023 OP: £2.49 NM: £2.75

TYG-079 Doctor Who and the Daleks LCD game
1993, Systema, UK
Exclusive to Burton's Books but also available elsewhere
(Tesco's). A hand-held Liquid Crystal Display 'Frogger'-type
game. Came in a clear heat-sealed plastic shop display box.
REF: Model 8501 OP: £11.99

**TYG-080 Doctor Who In the Domain of the
Daleks**
1998/07, Bluebird Toys (UK) Ltd, UK
Part of the Bluebird Micro-Superstars Collection. This
playset was in the shape of a Dalek and, when opened
up, became the Daleks' headquarters complete with
Davros and TARDIS. There were separate figures of the
Fourth Doctor and a Dalek mounted on a ball-bearing
similar to the 1960s Rolykins. Came in a clear heat-
sealed plastic shop display box.
REF: Ref: 980511 OP: £7.99 NM: £15

TYG-078 (both versions)

TYG-079

TYG-080 (closed and open views)

TYG-080 (on card)

TYG-082

TYG-083a (four shown)

TYG-081   Doctor Who YoYo
1998, Dominitemporal Services Ltd, UK

TYG-082   Doctor Who: Invasion Earth
1999, Harlequin Miniatures, UK
A boxed tabletop conflict game devised and written
by Daniel Faulconbridge. Contains rulebook, set of 6
UNIT trooper metal miniatures, 4 Dalek metal miniatures, 6 full colour card buildings, counters, templates
and two dice. The initial release of the game was in a
thin card box.
REF: HMP0101   OP: £30

TYG-083a   Dr. Who and the Dalek Rolykins
2000/05, Product Enterprises Ltd, UK
Dalek Rolykin toys – a plastic Dalek model with a
ball-bearing mounted in the base allowing it to glide
over smooth surfaces. Packaged in a box with header
card attached. These are based on the design of the
original 1965 toys (see TYG-032).
Six released:
Imperial - Gold base/arm section;
White head/lower section; yellow arms and eye
Command - Grey base/arm section;
Black head/lower section; yellow arms and eye
Drone - White base/arm section;
Blue-grey head/lower section; black arms and eye
Supreme - Grey base; Black arm section;
Red head/lower section; yellow arms and eye
Battle - Black base; Blue-grey arm section;
Grey head/lower section; black arms and eye
Emperor - Red base/arm section;
Gold head/lower section; yellow arms and eye
OP: £3.99 each

TYG-083b   Dr. Who and the Dalek Rolykins
2000/08, Product Enterprises Ltd, UK
Four released. All with an additional sticker on the
header card saying 'Limited edition':
Gold Metal Chrome Plated – all gold except black base;
black arms and eye.
Silver Metal Chrome Plated – all silver; black arms and
eye.
Red Metal Chrome Plated – all red except black base;
black arms and eye
Crystal Clear Incubating Dalek with visible Dalek creature inside – clear plastic with yellow Dalek creature;
clear arms and eye. On this model, the head is loose
from the rest of the body. There were only 500 made
with the Dalek creature in yellow plastic. Thereafter the
creature was in green plastic. The green variant started
to be issued around November 2000.
OP: £3.99 each

TYG-083b

TYG-083c Dr. Who and the Movie Dalek Rolykins
2000/11, Product Enterprises Ltd, UK
Five released. Boxes redesigned to illustrate the
Movie Dalek, which has a large base and a choice of
sucker or claw arm.
Blue Head – silver body;
light blue head and base; black arms.
Silver Head – light blue body;
silver head; black base; red arms.
Gold – gold body and head; black base; black arms.
Red – red body and head; gold base; yellow arms.
Black – black body and head; gold base; light brown arms.
OP: £3.99 each

TYG-083c

TYG-083d Dr. Who and the Dalek Rolykins
2000/11, Product Enterprises Ltd, UK
Special colour Dalek produced for *The Day of the
Daleks* convention. Dull blue head and body; black
base; black arms.
OP: £3.99 each

**TYG-083e Dr. Who and the Dalek Rolykins –
Christmas Dalek**
2000/11, Product Enterprises Ltd, UK
Special metallic green Dalek produced for the Alien
Entertainment mail order store in America. Limited to
1000 numbered Daleks. This version does not have
the ball bearing, but has a small hook on the head and
a tie to affix it to a christmas tree.

TYG-083e

TYG-083f Dr. Who and the Special Weapons Gunner Dalek Rolykins
2001/04, Product Enterprises Ltd, UK
Gunner Dalek variant from *Remembrance of the Daleks*.
OP: £4.99 each

TYG-083g Dr. Who and the Dalek Rolykins
2001/06, Product Enterprises Ltd, UK
Steel Metal – light grey arms
Blue Metal – Yellow arms
Green Metal – Red arms
OP: £3.99 each

TYG-083f

TYG-083h Dr. Who and the Dalek Rolykins
2001/06, Product Enterprises Ltd, UK
Series of Special Edition toys:
Dalek Invasion of Earth Black Dalek with Sensor disk – Black arms
Dalek Invasion of Earth Silver Dalek with Sensor disk – Black arms
Dalek Masterplan Dalek with Pyro-Flame – Grey Dalek with black arms
The Chase Dalek with Electrode Unit – Grey Dalek with black arms
The Chase Dalek with Perceptor – Grey Dalek with Black arms
OP: £3.99 each

TYG-083i Dr. Who and the Movie Dalek Rolykins
2001/06, Product Enterprises Ltd, UK

TYG-083g

TYG-083h

TYG-084a

TYG-083i

Gold Metal – Black arms
Silver Metal – Black arms
OP: £3.99 each

TYG-084a Talking Daleks
2001/09, Product Enterprises Ltd, UK
Each Talking Dalek came tied into a display box. Around
17cm/7 inches tall. Three colours of Talking Dalek –
black, grey and red. Speaks when the oval between the
arms is pressed. Each says 5 phrases: 'Exterminate', 'You
Are An Enemy of the Daleks', 'Daleks Rule Supreme',
'Destroy the Doctor', 'Seek, Locate, Annihilate'.
OP: £25 each

TYG-084b

TYG-084b Talking Daleks
2001/11, Product Enterprises Ltd, UK
White/gold 'Imperial' design of Talking Dalek. Only
available via mail order from Product Enterprises and
from authorised partners. Limited edition of 3,000.
OP: £25 each

TYG-084c Talking Daleks
2002/10, Product Enterprises Ltd, UK
Grey and gold colours of the Talking Dalek. The pack-
aging was slightly redesigned, using the diamond
Doctor Who logo. Each says 4 phrases: 'Halt, Do Not
Move', 'You Will Obey', 'Locate and Destroy', 'Exterminate
the Doctor'. The fifth sound is an extermination blast.
OP: £19.99 each

TYG-084c

TYG-085 Dalek Rollamatic sets
2002/05, Product Enterprises Ltd, UK
Four blister packs, each containing three small Daleks around 6cm/2.5 inches high. They have a pull back and release mechanism in the wheels to make them roll along. Colour schemes: 2x grey/black, 1x black/silver; 2x blue/black, 1x gold/black; 3x white/gold; 3x silver/blue.
OP: £14.99 set

TYG-086 Talking Cyberman
2002/11, Product Enterprises Ltd, UK
Earthshock style talking Cyberman. Available as a Cyberwarrior' or 'Cyberleader' with black coloured handles on the side of the head. Each says 4 phrases: 'Destroy Earth', 'Excellent', 'Eradicate the Time Lord', 'Emotion is a Weakness'. Came packaged with a Cyber-gun, a Cybermat and two spare batteries.
OP: £14.99 each

TYG-087 Remote Control Dalek
2002/11, Product Enterprises Ltd, UK
Foot-high remote controlled Dalek in silver or black. Packaged in a display box with a remote control. Each colour Dalek was on a different frequency so they can be used together at the same time. Each says 4 phrases: 'Halt, Do Not Move', 'You Will Obey', 'Locate and Destroy', 'Exterminate the Doctor'. The fifth sound is an extermination blast.
OP: £69.99 each

TYG-086

TYG-085

TYG-087

VIDEO, BBC SPECIALS

VBS-001a *The Hartnell Years*
1991/06/03, BBC Enterprises Ltd, UK
Written and produced by John Nathan-Turner.
Photographic cover. 'U' certificate. Presented by
Sylvester McCoy. Contains a pilot version of *100,000
BC: An Unearthly Child*, *The Crusade: The Wheel of
Fortune* and *The Celestial Toyroom: The Final Test*. Re-
issued 1995/02/13 at £7.99.
REF: BBCV 4608 OP: £10.99 NM: £14.30

VBS-001b *The Hartnell Years*
1991, CBS/FOX, USA
REF: 3403 OP: $19.95

VBS-001c *The Hartnell Years*
1992/05/06, PolyGram, Aus
'G' rating. Deleted January 1996.
REF: BBC46802 OP: $29.95

VBS-001d *The Hartnell Years*
1992/06, PolyGram, NZ
'G' rating.
REF: BBC46802 OP: $29.95

VBS-002a *The Troughton Years*
1991/06/03, BBC Enterprises Ltd, UK
Written and produced by John Nathan-Turner.
Photographic cover. 'U' certificate. Presented by Jon
Pertwee. Contains episode 2 of *The Abominable
Snowmen* (edited by around 3 secs where the Doctor
first starts to examine the captured Yeti), episode 3 of
Enemy of the World and episode 2 of *The Space Pirates*.
Re-issued 1995/02/13 at £7.99.
REF: BBCV 4609 OP: £10.99 NM: £18.70

VBS-002b *The Troughton Years*
1991, CBS/FOX, USA
REF: 3402 OP: $19.95

VBS-002c *The Troughton Years*
1992/03/04, PolyGram, Aus
'G' rating. Deleted January 1996.
REF: BBC46092 OP: $29.95

VBS-002d *The Troughton Years*
1992/04, PolyGram, NZ
'G' rating.
REF: BBC46092 OP: $29.95

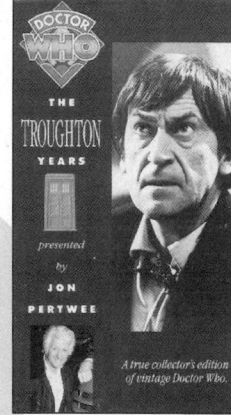

VBS-001b VBS-002b

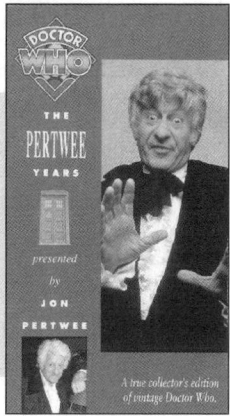

VBS-003b

VBS-003a *The Pertwee Years*
1992/03/02, BBC Enterprises Ltd, UK
Written and produced by John Nathan-Turner.
Photographic cover. 'PG' certificate. Presented by Jon
Pertwee. Contains episode 7 of *Inferno*, episode 6 of
Frontier in Space and episode 5 (in black and white) of
The Dæmons.
REF: BBCV 4756 OP: £10.99 NM: £18.70

VBS-003b *The Pertwee Years*
1992, CBS/FOX, USA
REF: 5732 OP: $19.95

VBS-003c *The Pertwee Years*
1992/10/20, PolyGram, Aus
'PG' rating. Deleted January 1996.
REF: BBC47562 OP: $29.95

VBS-004b

VBS-005b

VBS-006b

VBS-007d

VBS-008a

VBS-008c

VBS-003d *The Pertwee Years*
1992/11, PolyGram, NZ
'PG' rating.
REF: BBC47562 OP: $29.95

VBS-004a *Daleks – The Early Years*
1992/07/06, BBC Enterprises Ltd, UK
Written and produced by John Nathan-Turner.
Photographic cover. 'U' certificate. Introduced by
Peter Davison. Contains *The Daleks' Master Plan:
Counterplot*, *The Daleks' Master Plan: Escape Switch* and
episode 2 of *The Evil of the Daleks*. Re-issued
1994/02/14 at £7.99. Deleted 1996/05/09.
REF: BBCV 4810 OP: £12.99 NM: £35.20

VBS-004b *Daleks – The Early Years*
1993, CBS/FOX, USA
Does not note that it contains *The Evil of the Daleks*
episode 2.
REF: 4793 OP: $19.99

VBS-004c *Daleks – The Early Years*
1993/02/03, PolyGram, Aus
'PG' rating.
REF: BBC48102 OP: $29.95

VBS-004d *Daleks – The Early Years*
1993/03, PolyGram, NZ
'PG' rating.
REF: BBC48102 OP: $29.95

VBS-004e *Daleks – The Early Years*
1996/07/15, Roadshow Entertainment Ltd, Aus
'PG' rating.
REF: B00084 OP: $24.95

VBS-004f *Daleks – The Early Years*
1996/08, Roadshow Entertainment Ltd, NZ
'PG' rating. Deleted August 1999.
REF: Z00084 OP: $34.95

VBS-005a *Cybermen – The Early Years*
1992/07/06, BBC Enterprises Ltd, UK
Written and produced by John Nathan-Turner.
Photographic cover. 'U' certificate. Introduced by
Colin Baker. Contains episodes 2 and 4 of *The
Moonbase* and episodes 3 and 6 of *The Wheel in Space*.
Re-issued 1994/02/14 at £7.99.
REF: BBCV 4813 OP: £12.99 NM: £16.50

VBS-005b *Cybermen – The Early Years*
1993, CBS/FOX, USA
REF: 3494 OP: $19.99

VBS-005c *Cybermen – The Early Years*
1993/03/10, PolyGram, Aus
'PG' rating.
REF: BBC48132 OP: $29.95

VBS-005d *Cybermen – The Early Years*
1993/04, PolyGram, NZ
'PG' rating. Deleted January 1996.
REF: BBC48132 OP: $29.95

VBS-006a *The Tom Baker Years*
1992/09/07, BBC Enterprises Ltd, UK
Written and produced by John Nathan-Turner.
Photographic cover. 'PG' certificate. Presented by Tom
Baker who recalls his stories one by one and 'watch-
es' clips from them. Double tape. Contains clips but
no full episodes. Deleted 1996/05/09.
REF: BBCV 4839 OP: £19.99 NM: £55

VBS-006b *The Tom Baker Years*
1993, CBS/FOX, USA
REF: 3493 OP: $29.99

VBS-006c *The Tom Baker Years*
1993/03/10, PolyGram, Aus
'PG' rating. Released on one tape rather than two. The
two parts are very badly edited together on the tape,
though – the second one cuts in over the top of the
first just as it looks like the credits are about to roll.
REF: BBC48392 OP: $29.95

VBS-006d *The Tom Baker Years*
1993/05, PolyGram, NZ
'PG' rating. Released on one tape rather than two.
Deleted January 1996.
REF: BBC48392 OP: $29.95

VBS-006e *The Tom Baker Years*
1996/07/15, Roadshow Entertainment Ltd, Aus
'PG' rating. Released on one tape rather than two.
REF: B00085 OP: $24.95

VBS-006f *The Tom Baker Years*
1996/08, Roadshow Entertainment Ltd, NZ
'PG' rating. Released on one tape rather than two.
Deleted August 1999.
REF: Z00085 OP: $34.95

VBS-007a *The Colin Baker Years*
1994/03/07, BBC Enterprises Ltd, UK
Produced and directed by John Nathan-Turner.
Photographic cover. 'U' certificate. Presented by Colin
Baker who recalls his stories one by one and 'watch-
es' clips from them. No material is featured from

Attack of the Cybermen and *Revelation of the Daleks* as
writer Eric Saward witheld permission for clips to be
used. Contains clips but no full episodes. Made in
1992 but unreleased until 1994.
REF: BBCV 5324 OP: £12.99

VBS-007b *The Colin Baker Years*
1994/04/08, PolyGram, Aus
'G' rating.
REF: BBC53242 OP: $29.95

VBS-007c *The Colin Baker Years*
1994/05, PolyGram, NZ
'G' rating. Deleted January 1996.
REF: BBC53242 OP: $29.95

VBS-007d *The Colin Baker Years*
1994/08/23, CBS/FOX, USA
REF: 8144 OP: $19.99

VBS-008a *More than 30 Years in the TARDIS*
1994/11/07, BBC Enterprises Ltd, UK
Directed by Kevin Davies. Extended documentary of
the series made for the 30th anniversary in 1993.
Cover by Andrew Skilleter. 'U' certificate. The review
copies featured a Dalek Weetabix advert cut from the
final release.
REF: BBCV 5403 OP: £12.99

VBS-008b *More than 30 Years in the TARDIS*
1995/03/06, PolyGram, Aus
'PG' rating. Does not feature the foil print on the cover.
REF: BBC54032 OP: $29.95

VBS-008c *More than 30 Years in the TARDIS*
1995/09/20, CBS/FOX, USA
REF: 8293 OP: $19.99

VBS-008d *More than 30 Years in the TARDIS*
1996/03/11, Roadshow Entertainment Ltd, Aus
'PG' rating. Does not feature the foil print on the
cover.
REF: 17881 OP: $29.95

VBS-008e *More than 30 Years in the TARDIS*
1996/04, PolyGram, NZ
'PG' rating.
REF: BBC54032 OP: $29.95

VBS-008f *More than 30 Years in the TARDIS*
1996/04, Roadshow Entertainment Ltd, NZ
'PG' rating.
REF: Z17881 OP: $34.95

VBS-009a

VBS-009a *K9 and Company*
1995/08/07, BBC Worldwide Ltd, UK
Postcard. Cover by Andrew Skilleter. 'PG' certificate.
Diamond Logo. Release on video of the *Doctor Who*
spin off episode featuring K-9 and Sarah Jane Smith.
REF: BBCV 5635 OP: £9.99

VBS-009b *K9 and Company*
1995/11/08, PolyGram, Aus
'PG' rating.
REF: BBCV5635 OP: $24.95

VBS-009c *K9 and Company*
1996/04/15, Roadshow Entertainment Ltd, Aus
'PG' rating.
REF: 17892 OP: $24.95

VBS-009d *K9 and Company*
1996/05, Roadshow Entertainment Ltd, NZ
'PG' rating.
REF: Z17892 OP: $29.95

VBS-009e *K-9 & Company*
1998/11/03, CBS/FOX, USA
REF: 0131 OP: $19.99

VBT-001a   **VBT-001b**

VBT-001c

VIDEO, BBC TV RELEASES

BY the close of the seventies home video had become
more affordable than in the past and, although the price
of blank tapes was still very high in the UK (around £30
for a single 180 minute tape), many homes were equip-
ping themselves with video recorders.

The first *Doctor Who* TV story released by the
BBC was an edited version of season twelve's
Revenge of the Cybermen. The tape was released
towards the end of 1983, and the choice of story
had been made following a poll conducted at the
massive Longleat *Doctor Who* convention earlier that
year. Questionnaires had been distributed asking
which stories fans would most like to see, and the
Patrick Troughton story *The Tomb of the Cybermen*
had come out top. As this story did not at that time
exist in the BBC archives, the selectors theorised
that any Cyberman adventure would do as well.

The second release was a one-hour long edited version of *The Brain of Morbius* in 1984. *The Five Doctors* was
the next story to be issued on video, followed in 1985
by *Pyramids of Mars*, *The Seeds of Death* and *Day of the
Daleks* and in 1986 by *The Robots of Death*. All these

retailed at £24.95 and were available in both the VHS and Betamax formats. They were all edited in one way or another, with the opening and closing title sequences missing between episodes and seemingly random cuts made throughout the stories. The tapes were eventually re-released at the lower budget price, but the re-issued versions were identical in content to the original.

Perhaps due to the negative response from fan magazines to the editing of the stories, and perhaps due to the difficulty in obtaining clearance from all the cast members featured (for example *Pyramids of Mars* was held up allegedly because Bernard Archard's agents initially refused to accept the fee the BBC were offering), further additions to the range were brought out very infrequently up to the end of the eighties. In several cases commercial tapes were released overseas years before they were released in Britain (*Terror of the Zygons* and *Talons of Weng-Chiang* were released in Australia in 1987 while their UK release wasn't until 1988 and *The Deadly Assassin* was released in America in 1985 while the UK release did not occur until 1991).

In 1996, *The Hand of Fear* was released for two weeks only, as then all *Doctor Who* video releases were put on hold until the TV Movie aired. There was then a long gap before releases recommenced with *The Green Death*.

During 1993, several fans working within the VT and editing departments of the BBC started to offer their assistance on the BBC releases and this culminated in an extended edition of *The Five Doctors* in 1995, and the colourised versions of *Terror of the Autons*, *The Dæmons* and *Doctor Who and the Silurians*. Thereafter the group monitored and worked on the majority of the video releases, selecting the best tapes to use as masters, and cleaning up both picture and sound wherever possible. The best examples of their work can be found on the black and white releases which are significantly improved from any prior television transmission or video release.

At press-time, the last remaining stories to be released on video were appearing in the UK, ending one of the longest VHS runs in the market's history.

In the following listings, where no format is specified, then the tape was VHS only.

The New Zealand releases were in tandem with the Australian releases, however most of the video covers for New Zealand were altered to show a different catalogue number (starting Z).

VBT-001a *Revenge of the Cybermen*
1983/10/10, BBC Enterprises Ltd, UK
This first BBC video release was issued in an outsized box with the neon logo, a photo-montage cover by Sid Sutton which featured the Fourth Doctor, an *Earthshock*-style Cyberman head and shoulders and prismatic stars. It was then re-issued in 1983 in a standard VHS case with the diamond logo and a different photo-montage cover which featured a Cyberman from the story and Tom Baker's face from the title sequence. This second release cost £29.95. No certificate on packaging. Compilation version. Deleted 1984.
REF: BBCV 2003/BBCB2003
OP: £39.95 (VHS, Beta, V2000) NM: £16.50

VBT-001b *Revenge of the Cybermen*
1983, Pony Video, Japan
Japanese release of the story. In English with Japanese subtitles. Photo-montage cover. No certificate on packaging. The title translates as *Cyberman Counter-Attack* or *Counter-Attack of the Cyberman*. Video came with a brochure which contains details of the show, the characters and previous adventures – particularly *The Ark in Space*.
REF: V128F1331 OP: Y12,800

VBT-001c *Revenge of the Cybermen*
1984/05, BBC Enterprises Ltd, UK
A re-issue of the second 1983 tape. No certificate on packaging. Deleted 1986.
REF: BBCV 2003 OP: £24.95 NM: £16.50

VBT-001d *Revenge of the Cybermen*
1986/10/01, BBC Enterprises Ltd, UK
Re-issue as a budget video. Same cover image as previously. 'U' certificate. Deleted 1996/05/09.
REF: BBCV 4013 OP: £9.99

VBT-001e *Revenge of the Cybermen*
1987, Playhouse, USA
Playhouse was the children's video imprint of CBS/FOX and the first few US editions were released under that label.
REF: 3714 OP: $19.99

VBT-001f *Revenge of the Cybermen*
1987/01, Kerridge Odeon Amalgamated Video Services, NZ
'G' rating. Deleted January 1996.
REF: BBC20032 OP: $24.95

VBT-001g *Revenge of the Cybermen*
1987 c., PolyGram , Aus
'G' rating.
REF: BBC20032 OP: $29.95

VBT-001h *Revenge of the Cybermen*
1999/04/05, BBC Worldwide Ltd, UK
Unedited version. New photo-montage cover. 'U' certificate. TVM logo.
REF: BBCV 6773 OP: £11.99

VBT-001i *Revenge of the Cybermen*
1999/05, Roadshow Entertainment Ltd, NZ
'G' rating.
REF: Z00354 OP: $29.95

VBT-002a *The Brain of Morbius*
1984/07/23, BBC Enterprises Ltd, UK
Photographic cover. Diamond logo. No certificate on packaging. Compilation version. Edits story heavily edited into a one hour presentation. Deleted 1989.
REF: BBCV 2012/BBCB2012
OP: £19.95 (VHS, Beta) NM: £22

VBT-002b *The Brain of Morbius*
1987, Playhouse, USA
60 minute version.
REF: 3715 OP: $19.99

VBT-002c *The Brain of Morbius*
1987/11, Kerridge Odeon Amalgamated Video Services, NZ
'PG' rating. 60 minute compilation. Deleted 1990.
REF: BBC20122 OP: $24.95

VBT-002d *The Brain of Morbius*
1987 c., PolyGram, Aus
'PG' rating. 60 minute compilation.
REF: BBC20122 OP: $29.95

VBT-002e *The Brain of Morbius*
1990/07, BBC Enterprises Ltd, UK
Unedited Reissue. Edits: small section of soundtrack in Part One. Cover by Alistair Pearson. 'PG' certificate. Diamond logo. Re-issued 1994/02/14 at £7.99. Deleted 1996/01/02.
REF: BBCV 4388 OP: £9.99 NM: £33

VBT-002f *The Brain of Morbius*
1991, PolyGram, NZ
'PG' rating. Unedited version. Edits: small section of soundtrack in Part One. Deleted January 1996.
REF: BBC43882 OP: $29.95

VBT-002g *The Brain of Morbius*
1991 c., PolyGram, Aus
'PG' rating. Unedited version. Edits: small section of soundtrack in Part One.
REF: BBC43882 OP: $29.95

VBT-002h *The Brain of Morbius*
1997/02/11, CBS/FOX, USA

Unedited version. Edits: small section of soundtrack in Part One.
REF: 8456 OP: $19.99

VBT-003a *Pyramids of Mars*
1985/03, BBC Enterprises Ltd, UK
Photo-montage cover. Diamond logo. No certificate on packaging. Compilation version. Edits: approximately two minutes of cuts throughout story. Deleted 1987.
REF: BBCV 2014/BBCB2014
OP: £24.95 (VHS, Beta) NM: £16.50

VBT-003b *Pyramids of Mars*
1985/11/01, PolyGram, Aus
'G' rating.
REF: BBC20142 OP: $29.95

VBT-003c *Pyramids of Mars*
1985, Pony Video, Japan
Japanese release of the story. In English with Japanese subtitles. Photo-montage cover. No certificate on packaging. Title translates as *Pyramids Mars* or *Mars Pyramids*.
REF: V128F1440 OP: Y12,800

VBT-003d *Dr Who Marsin Pyramidit (Pyramids of Mars)*
1986?, Secam Video, Finland
Finnish release of the story. Subtitled.
REF: CVF 2017

VBT-003e *Pyramids of Mars*
1987, Playhouse, USA
Also re-issued in 1999 as a part of 'The Gateway Collection' priced at £14.95.
REF: 3713 OP: $14.95

VBT-003f *Pyramids of Mars*
1987/07, BBC Enterprises Ltd, UK
Re-issue. Deleted 1993.
REF: BBCV 5220 OP: £9.99 NM: £14.30

VBT-003g *Pyramids of Mars*
1987/12, Kerridge Odeon Amalgamated Video Services, NZ
'G' rating. Deleted January 1996.
REF: BBC20142 OP: $24.95

VBT-003h *Pyramids of Mars*
1994/02/14, BBC Enterprises Ltd, UK
Unedited version. Deleted 1994/09/30.
REF: BBCV 5220 OP: £7.99

VBT-004a *The Seeds of Death*
1985/07/17, BBC Enterprises Ltd, UK
Single tape. Photo-montage cover. Diamond logo. No certificate on packaging. Compilation version. Deleted 1987.

REF: BBCV 2019/BBCB2019
OP: £24.95 (VHS, Beta) NM: £27.50

VBT-004b *The Seeds of Death*
1987, Kerridge Odeon Amalgamated Video Services, NZ
'G' rating. Deleted January 1996.
REF: BBC20192 OP: $24.95

VBT-004c *The Seeds of Death*
1987/07, BBC Enterprises Ltd, UK
Re-issue. Deleted 1996/05/09.
REF: BBCV 4072 OP: £9.99 NM: £29.70

VBT-004d *The Seeds of Death*
1987 c., PolyGram , Aus
'G' rating. Re-issued on 1992/04/01 at the reduced
price of $29.95.
REF: BBC20192 OP: $39.95

VBT-004e *The Seeds of Death*
1989, Playhouse, USA
Other evidence suggests a catalogue number of 8294.
REF: 3716 OP: $19.99

VBT-005a *The Five Doctors*
1985/09/09, BBC Enterprises Ltd, UK
Cover by Andrew Skilleter (as used on the cover of *Radio
Times*). Neon logo. 'U' certificate. Edits: approximately 2
minutes of small cuts throught the story. Deleted 1988.
REF: BBCV 2020/BBCB2020
OP: £24.95 (VHS, Beta) NM: £16.50

VBT-005b *The Five Doctors*
1988/05/01, PolyGram, Aus
'PG' rating.
REF: BBC20202 OP: $29.95

VBT-001h

VBT-002a

VBT-002h

VBT-003c

VBT-003d

VBT-003e

VBT-004a

VBT-005a

VBT-006a

VBT-006b

VBT-007f

VBT-008d

VBT-009d

VBT-005c *The Five Doctors*
1988/08, Kerridge Odeon Amalgamated Video
Services, NZ
'PG' rating. Deleted January 1996.
REF: BBC20202 OP: $24.95

VBT-005d *The Five Doctors*
1989, Playhouse, USA
REF: 3717 OP: $19.99

VBT-005e *The Five Doctors*
1990/07/02, BBC Enterprises Ltd, UK
Reissue. Unedited version. Cover by Alistair Pearson.
Deleted 1995/08/14.
REF: BBCV 4387 OP: £9.99

VBT-006a *The Robots of Death*
1986/04/21, BBC Enterprises Ltd, UK
Photo-montage cover. 'U' certificate. Diamond logo.
Compilation version. Deleted December 1987.
REF: BBCV 2030/BBCB2030
OP: £24.95 (VHS, Beta) NM: £13.20

VBT-006b *Robots of Death*
1986, Pony Video, Japan
Japanese release of the story. In English with Japanese
subtitles. Photo-montage cover. No certificate on packaging. Title translates as *Robots Death* or *Death Robots*.
REF: V128F1485 OP: Y12,800

VBT-006c *The Robots of Death*
1987 c., Playhouse, USA
REF: 3726 OP: $19.99

VBT-006d *The Robots of Death*
1988/02/11, BBC Enterprises Ltd, UK
Re-issue. Deleted 1995/02/01.
REF: BBCV 4108 OP: £9.99 NM: £13.20

VBT-006e *The Robots of Death*
1988/03, Kerridge Odeon Amalgamated Video
Services, NZ
Deleted January 1996.
REF: BBC20302 OP: $24.95

VBT-006f *The Robots of Death*
1988 c., PolyGram, Aus
'G' rating.
REF: BBC20302 OP: $29.95

VBT-006g *The Robots of Death*
1995/02/13, BBC Enterprises Ltd, UK
Unedited release. Cover as before but with added
'unedited' logo.
REF: BBCV 5521 OP: £7.99 NM: £13.20

VBT-007a *The Day of the Daleks*
1986/07/21, BBC Enterprises Ltd, UK
Photo-montage cover. 'U' certificate. Diamond logo.
Compilation version. Deleted December 1987.
REF: BBCV 2036/BBCB2036
OP: £24.95 (VHS, Beta) NM: £20.90

VBT-007b *The Day of the Daleks*
1987/01/01, VPV, Aus
'G' rating.
REF: BBC20362 OP: $29.95

VBT-007c *The Day of the Daleks*
1987/07, Kerridge Odeon Amalgamated Video
Services, NZ
'G' rating. Deleted January 1996
REF: BBCV 4109 OP: $24.95

VBT-007d *The Day of the Daleks*
1987/10/01, PolyGram, Aus
'G' rating.
REF: BBC20362 OP: $29.95

VBT-007e *The Day of the Daleks*
1988/02/14, BBC Enterprises Ltd, UK
Re-issue. Cover as before but with added 'unedited'
logo. Deleted 1994/10/12.
REF: BBCV 5216 OP: £7.99 NM: £27.50

VBT-007f *Day of the Daleks*
1989, Playhouse, USA
REF: 5092 OP: $19.99

VBT-007g *The Day of the Daleks*
1994/02, BBC Enterprises Ltd, UK
Deleted 1996/05/09.
REF: BBCV 5219 OP: £9.99 NM: £24.20

VBT-007h *The Day of the Daleks*
1996/07/15, Roadshow Entertainment Ltd, Aus
'G' rating. Re-issue of the edited version.
REF: B00080 OP: $24.95

VBT-007i *The Day of the Daleks*
1996/08, Roadshow Entertainment Ltd, NZ
'G' rating. Re-issue of the edited version. Deleted
August 1999.
REF: Z00080 OP: $29.95

VBT-008a *Death to the Daleks*
1987/07/20, BBC Enterprises Ltd, UK
Photo-montage cover. 'U' certificate. Diamond logo.
Compilation version. Deleted 1994/10/26.
REF: BBCV 4073 OP: £9.99 NM: £14.30

VBT-008b *Death to the Daleks*
1987/12/01, PolyGram, Aus
'G' rating.
REF: BBC40732 OP: $29.95

VBT-008c *Death to the Daleks*
1989, Kerridge Odeon Amalgamated Video Services, NZ
'G' rating. Deleted January 1996
REF: BBC40732 OP: $24.95

VBT-008d *Death to the Daleks*
1991 c., Playhouse, USA
At this point, the US releases stopped closed captioning for a time.
REF: 5093 OP: $19.99

VBT-008e *Death to the Daleks*
1995/02/13, BBC Enterprises Ltd, UK
Cover as before but with added 'unedited' logo. There
are in fact two small edits in Episode 2 of material
present on the earlier compilation version.
REF: BBCV 5520 OP: £7.99 NM: £14.30

VBT-008f *Death to the Daleks*
1996/06/10, Roadshow Entertainment Ltd, Aus
'G' rating. Re-issue of the edited version.
REF: B00056 OP: $24.95

VBT-008g *Death to the Daleks*
1996/07, Roadshow Entertainment Ltd, NZ
'G' rating. Re-issue of the edited version. Deleted
August 1999.
REF: Z00056 OP: $29.95

VBT-009a *Spearhead from Space*
1988/02/11, BBC Enterprises Ltd, UK
Photo-montage cover. 'U' certificate. Diamond logo.
Compilation version. Edits: sound of Fleetwood Mac
song removed from factory scenes. Deleted 1994/10/26.
REF: BBCV 4107 OP: £9.99 NM: £13.20

VBT-009b *Spearhead from Space*
1990/04/01, PolyGram, Aus
'G' rating.
REF: BBC41072 OP: $29.95

VBT-009c *Spearhead from Space*
1990/05 c., Kerridge Odeon Amalgamated Video
Services, NZ
'G' rating. Deleted January 1996.
REF: BBC41072 OP: $24.95

VBT-009d *Spearhead From Space*
1991, Playhouse, USA
REF: 5421 OP: $19.99

VBT-009e *Spearhead from Space*
1995/02/13, BBC Enterprises Ltd, UK
Unedited release. Cover as before but with added 'unedited' logo.
REF: BBCV 5509   OP: £7.99   NM: £13.20

VBT-010a *Terror of the Zygons*
1987/04/01, PolyGram, Aus
'PG' rating. Released in Australia more than eighteen months prior to its UK release. The cover is a photograph of a Zygon.
REF: BBC20552   OP: $29.95

VBT-010b *Terror of the Zygons*
1988/09, PolyGram, NZ
'PG' rating. Deleted January 1996. All of the Kerridge Odeon releases became part of the PolyGram range when they took over distribution of the tapes in New Zealand in 1990.
REF: BBC20552   OP: $24.95

VBT-010c *Terror of the Zygons*
1988/11/04, BBC Enterprises Ltd, UK
Photo-montage/art cover. 'PG' certificate. Diamond logo. Compilation version. Re-issued 1994/02/14 at £7.99. Deleted 1994/11/02.
REF: BBCV 4186   OP: £9.99   NM: £16.50

VBT-010d *Terror of the Zygons*
1991, Playhouse, USA
REF: 5422   OP: $19.99

VBT-010e *Terror of the Zygons*
1999/06/07, BBC Worldwide Ltd, UK
Photo-montage cover by Black Sheep. 'PG' certificate. TVM logo. Unedited and episodic release. Includes footage of Tom Baker on *Disney Time* from 1975.
REF: BBCV6774   OP: £12.99

VBT-011a *The Talons of Weng-Chiang*
1987/04/01, PolyGram ,Aus
'G' rating. Released in Australia more than eighteen months prior to its UK release. The cover showed a photo of Mr Sin, Magnus Greel and the Dragon. Re-issued 1992/04/01 at the reduced price of $29.95. Deleted 1994/12/21.
REF: BBC20272   OP: $39.95

VBT-011b *The Talons of Weng-Chiang*
1988, Playhouse, USA
Also re-issued in 1999 as a part of 'The Gateway Collection' priced at £14.95.
REF: 5094   OP: $14.95

VBT-011c *The Talons of Weng-Chiang*
1988/07, PolyGram, NZ
'PG' rating. Deleted January 1996.
REF: BBC20272   OP: $24.95

VBT-011d *The Talons of Weng-Chiang*
1988/11/04, BBC Enterprises Ltd, UK
Photo-montage cover. 'PG' certificate. Diamond logo. Compilation version. Edits: cuts made to fight scenes in episode one. Deleted April 1996.
REF: BBCV 4187   OP: £9.99   NM: £33

VBT-012a *Ark in Space*
1989/01/01, PolyGram, Aus
Released in Australia several months prior to its UK release. The cover artwork is a photograph of a Wirrn. Also, the cover credits not only Tom Baker, but also Elisabeth Sladen and Ian Marter as stars, and also gives the title incorrectly as *Ark in Space*.
REF: BBCDW012   OP: $29.95

VBT-012b *The Ark in Space*
1989/06, PolyGram, NZ
'G' rating. Deleted January 1996.
REF: BBCDW012   OP: $24.95

VBT-012c *The Ark in Space*
1989/06/05, BBC Enterprises Ltd, UK
Photo-montage/art cover. 'U' certificate. Diamond logo. Compilation version. Deleted 1993.
REF: BBCV 4244   OP: £9.99   NM: £13.20

VBT-012d *The Ark in Space*
1991, Playhouse, USA
REF: 5420   OP: $19.99

VBT-012e *The Ark in Space*
1994/02/14, BBC Enterprises Ltd, UK
Unedited release. Photo-montage/art cover. 'U' certificate. Diamond logo. Deleted 1994/09/30.
REF: BBCV 5218   OP: £7.99   NM: £13.20

VBT-013a *The Daleks*
1989/06/05, BBC Enterprises Ltd, UK
Two tapes. Tape 1 (eps 1-4) subtitled: *The Dead Planet*. Photo-montage/art cover in black and white. Tape 2 (eps 5 – 7) subtitled: *The Escape*. Same image but sepia toned. Both tapes 'U' certificate. Diamond logo. Edits: final 'next episode' caption and closing moments of final scene removed. Also, a 'fade to black' in Episode 1 was shortened. Deleted 1995/08/14.
REF: BBCV 4242   OP: £19.99   NM: £57.50

VBT-013b *The Daleks*
1989/12/01, PolyGram, Aus
'G' rating. Released on two tapes, but housed in sepa-

rate cases.
REF: BBC42422 OP: $59.99

VBT-013c *The Daleks*
1990/01, PolyGram, NZ
'G' rating. Released on two tapes, but housed in separate cases. Deleted January 1996.
REF: BBC42422 OP: $59.90

VBT-013d *The Daleks*
1995/06/27, CBS/FOX, USA
REF: 8253 OP: $29.99

VBT-013e *The Daleks* [Remastered]
2001/02, BBC Worldwide Ltd, UK
Unedited. Photo montage cover. 'U' certificate. TVM logo.
REF: BBCV 6960 OP: £12.99

VBT-014a *The Time Warrior*
1989/03/01, PolyGram, Aus
'G' rating. Released in Australia several months prior
to its UK release. Cover features a photograph of
Lynx; also, the cover credits Elisabeth Sladen and
Nicholas Courtney as well as Jon Pertwee.
REF: BBCDW022 OP: $29.95

VBT-014b *The Time Warrior*
1989/04, PolyGram, NZ
'G' rating. Deleted January 1996.
REF: BBCDW022 OP: $24.95

VBT-014c *The Time Warrior*
1989/06/05, BBC Enterprises Ltd, UK
Photo montage/art cover. 'U' certificate. Diamond
logo. Compilation version. Re-issued 1994/02/14 at
£7.99. Deleted 1994/11/02.
REF: BBCV 4245 OP: £9.99 NM: £24.20

VBT-014d *The Time Warrior*
1991, Playhouse, USA
At this point, CBS/FOX shifted all the releases from the
Playhouse children's video imprint to the main label.
REF: 5423 OP: $19.99

VBT-015a *The War Games*
1990/02/05, BBC Enterprises Ltd, UK
Two tapes. Cover by Alistair Pearson. 'U' certificate.
Diamond logo. Deleted 1995/08/14. Edits: a "fade to
black" in Episode 7 is shortened by a second or two.
REF: BBCV 4310 OP: £19.99 NM: £60.50

VBT-015b *The War Games*
1990/06/01, PolyGram, Aus
'G' rating. Released on two tapes, but housed in separate cases.
REF: BBC43102 OP: $59.99

VBT-010d

VBT-010e

VBT-011b

VBT-012d

VBT-013d

VBT-013e

VBT-014d

VBT-015d

VBT-016d

VBT-016e

VBT-015c *The War Games*
1990/07, PolyGram, NZ
'G' rating. Deleted January 1996.
REF: BBC43102 OP: $59.90

VBT-015d *The War Games*
1991, CBS/FOX, USA
REF: 3400 OP: $29.99

VBT-016a *An Unearthly Child*
1990/02/05, BBC Enterprises Ltd, UK
Cover by Alistair Pearson. 'PG' certificate. Diamond
logo. Edits: final 'next episode' caption removed. Re-
issued 1994/02/14 at £7.99. Deleted 1994/12/02.
REF: BBCV 4311 OP: £9.99 NM: £27.50

VBT-016b *An Unearthly Child*
1990/07/01, PolyGram, Aus
'PG' rating.
REF: BBC43112 OP: $29.95

VBT-016c *An Unearthly Child*
1990/08, PolyGram, NZ
'PG' rating. Deleted 1996.
REF: BBC43112 OP: $24.95

VBT-016d *An Unearthly Child*
1991, CBS/FOX, USA
REF: 3401 OP: $19.99

VBT-016e *An Unearthly Child*
2001/08, BBC Worldwide Ltd, UK
Photo montage cover. 'U' certificate. TVM logo. Remastered
version. Final 'next episode' caption restored; a few frames
removed to 'tidy up' unclean edits on original print.
REF: BBCV 6959 OP: £12.99

VBT-017a *The Mind Robber*
1990/05/07, BBC Enterprises Ltd, UK
Cover by Alistair Pearson. 'U' certificate. Diamond
logo. Re-issued 1994/02/14 at £7.99. Edits: 'next
episode' caption at the end of Episode 5 has been
removed. Deleted 1996/01/02.
REF: BBCV 4352 OP: £9.99 NM: £27.50

VBT-017b *The Mind Robber*
1990/09/01, PolyGram, Aus
Deleted January 1996.
REF: BBC43522 OP: $29.95

VBT-017c *The Mind Robber*
1990/10, PolyGram, NZ
'G' rating.
REF: BBC43522 OP: $24.95

VBT-017d *The Mind Robber*
1994, CBS/FOX, USA
REF: 5945 OP: $19.99

VBT-018a *The Dalek Invasion of Earth*
1990/05/07, BBC Enterprises Ltd, UK
Two tapes. Cover by Alistair Pearson. 'PG' certificate.
Diamond logo. The end of the final scene of the last
episode, with the 'next episode' caption, has been
edited out. Deleted 1995/08/14.
REF: BBCV 4353 OP: £19.99 NM: £60.50

VBT-018b *The Dalek Invasion of Earth*
1990/11 c., PolyGram, Aus
'PG' rating. Released on two tapes in separate cases.
REF: BBC43532 OP: $59.99

VBT-018c *The Dalek Invasion of Earth*
1990/12, PolyGram, NZ
'PG' rating. Deleted January 1996.
REF: BBC43532 OP: $59.90

VBT-017d

VBT-018d *The Dalek Invasion of Earth*
1994, CBS/FOX, USA
REF: 5947 OP: $29.99

VBT-019a *The Web Planet*
1990/09/10, BBC Enterprises Ltd, UK
Two tapes. Cover by Alistair Pearson. 'U' certificate.
Diamond logo. Edits: final 'next episode' caption removed.
An entirely new end title sequence is subtituted for the
original on this closing episode. Deleted 1996/01/02.
REF: BBCV 4405 OP: £19.99 NM: £55

VBT-019b *The Web Planet*
1991/05/01, PolyGram, Aus
'G' rating. Released on one tape rather than two. Re-
issued on 1992/04/01 at the reduced price of $29.95.
REF: BBC44052 OP: $39.95

VBT-018d

VBT-019c *The Web Planet*
1991/06, PolyGram, NZ
'G' rating. Deleted January 1996.
REF: BBC44052 OP: $29.95

VBT-019d *The Web Planet*
1994/08/23, CBS/FOX, USA
Released on one tape rather than two.
REF: 8142 OP: $19.99

VBT-020a *The Dominators*
1990/09/10, BBC Enterprises Ltd, UK
Cover by Alistair Pearson. 'U' certificate. Diamond
logo. Edits: shots from three different death scenes
made by overseas censors to the print used to create
the video release. Re-issued 1994/02/14 at £7.99.
Deleted 1996/01/02.
REF: BBCV 4406 OP: £9.99 NM: £33

VBT-019d

VBT-020d

VBT-021d

VBT-020b *The Dominators*
1991/02/01, PolyGram, Aus
'G' rating.
REF: BBC44062   OP: $29.95

VBT-020c *The Dominators*
1991/03, PolyGram, NZ
'G' rating. Deleted January 1996.
REF: BBC44062   OP: $29.95

VBT-020d *The Dominators*
1994/08/23, CBS/FOX, USA
REF: 8141   OP: $19.99

VBT-021a *The Krotons*
1991/02/04, BBC Enterprises Ltd, UK
Cover by Alistair Pearson. 'U' certificate. Diamond logo.
Re-issued 1995/02/13 at £7.99. Deleted 1995/08/14.
REF: BBCV 4452   OP: £9.99   NM: £27.50

VBT-021b *The Krotons*
1991/07/01, PolyGram, Aus
'G' rating.
REF: BBC44522   OP: $29.95

VBT-021c *The Krotons*
1991/08, PolyGram, NZ
'G' rating. Deleted January 1996.
REF: BBC44522   OP: $29.95

VBT-021d *The Krotons*
1994/08/23, CBS/FOX, USA
REF: 8143   OP: $19.99

VBT-022d

VBT-023d

VBT-022a *The Curse of Fenric*
1991/02/04, BBC Enterprises Ltd, UK
Cover by Alistair Pearson. 'PG' certificate. Diamond
logo. Extended edition with around 7 minutes of
material added. Re-issued 1994/02/14 at £7.99.
REF: BBCV 4453   OP: £9.99   NM: £14.30

VBT-022b *The Curse of Fenric*
1991/07/01, PolyGram, Aus
'PG' rating.
REF: BBC44532   OP: $29.95

VBT-022c *The Curse of Fenric*
1991/08, PolyGram, NZ
'PG' rating. Deleted January 1996.
REF: BBC44532   OP: $29.95

VBT-024d

VBT-024g

VBT-022d *The Curse of Fenric*
1991, CBS/FOX, USA
REF: 3404   OP: $19.99

VBT-023a *Planet of the Spiders*
1991/04/02, BBC Enterprises Ltd, UK
Double tape. Cover by Andrew Skilleter. 'PG' certificate. Diamond logo. Deleted 1995/08/14.
REF: BBCV 4491 OP: £19.99 NM: £55

VBT-023b *Planet of the Spiders*
1991/09/01, PolyGram, Aus
'G' rating. Released on one tape rather than two. Reissued on 1992/04/01 at the reduced price of $29.95.
REF: BBC44912 OP: $39.95

VBT-023c *Planet of the Spiders*
1991/10, PolyGram, NZ
'G' rating. Deleted January 1996.
REF: BBC44912 OP: $29.95

VBT-023d *Planet of the Spiders*
1994, CBS/FOX, USA
REF: 8105 OP: $19.99

VBT-023e *Planet of the Spiders*
1996/06, Roadshow Entertainment Ltd, NZ
'G' rating.
REF: Z00055 OP: $39.95

VBT-023f *Planet of the Spiders*
1996/06/10, Roadshow Entertainment Ltd, Aus
'G' rating. Released on one tape rather than two.
REF: B00055 OP: $24.95

VBT-024a *City of Death*
1991/04/02, BBC Enterprises Ltd, UK
Cover by Andrew Skilleter. 'U' certificate. Diamond logo. Deleted 1995/08/14.
REF: BBCV 4492 OP: £10.99 NM: £38.50

VBT-024b *City of Death*
1991/09/01, PolyGram, Aus
'G' rating.
REF: BBC44922 OP: $29.95

VBT-024c *City of Death*
1991/10, PolyGram, NZ
'G' rating. Deleted January 1996.
REF: BBC44922 OP: $29.95

VBT-024d *City of Death*
1994, CBS/FOX, USA
Also re-issued in 1999 as a part of 'The Gateway Collection' priced at £14.95.
REF: 8102 OP: $14.95

VBT-024e *City of Death*
1996/07/15, Roadshow Entertainment Ltd, Aus
'G' rating.
REF: B00081 OP: $24.95

VBT-024f *City of Death*
1996/08, Roadshow Entertainment Ltd, NZ
'G' rating.
REF: Z00081 OP: $34.95

VBT-024g *City of Death*
2001/05, BBC Worldwide Ltd, UK
Photo montage cover. 'U' certificate. TVM logo.
REF: BBCV 7132 OP: £12.99

VBT-025a *The Masque of Mandragora*
1991/08/05, BBC Enterprises Ltd, UK
Cover by Alistair Pearson. 'U' certificate. Diamond logo. Deleted 1996/05/09.
REF: BBCV 4642 OP: £10.99 NM: £33

VBT-025b *The Masque of Mandragora*
1992/10/20, PolyGram, Aus
'G' rating.
REF: BBC46422 OP: $29.95

VBT-025c *The Masque of Mandragora*
1992/11, PolyGram, NZ
'G' rating. Deleted January 1996.
REF: BBC46422 OP: $29.95

VBT-025d *The Masque of Mandragora*
1994, CBS/FOX, USA
REF: 5948 OP: $19.99

VBT-026a *The Three Doctors*
1991/08/05, BBC Enterprises Ltd, UK
Cover by Alistair Pearson. 'U' certificate. Diamond logo. Deleted 1995/08/14.
REF: BBCV 4650 OP: £10.99 NM: £38.50

VBT-026b *The Three Doctors*
1992/09/01, PolyGram, Aus
'G' rating.
REF: BBC46502 OP: $29.95

VBT-026c *The Three Doctors*
1992/10, PolyGram, NZ
'G' rating. Deleted January 1996.
REF: BBC46502 OP: $29.95

VBT-026d *The Three Doctors*
1991, CBS/FOX, USA
REF: 3405 OP: $19.99

VBT-027a *The Sontaran Experiment/The Genesis of the Daleks*
1991/10/07, BBC Enterprises Ltd, UK
Double tape. Cover by Andrew Skilleter. 'PG' certificate. Diamond logo. Deleted 1998/08/21.
REF: BBCV 4643 OP: £19.99 NM: £49.50

VBT-027b *The Sontaran Experiment/The Genesis of the Daleks*
1992/07/03, PolyGram, Aus
'PG' rating. Released on two tapes in separate cases.
REF: BBC46432 OP: $59.95

VBT-027c *The Sontaran Experiment/The Genesis of the Daleks*
1992/08, PolyGram, NZ
'PG' rating. Deleted January 1996.
REF: BBC46432 OP: $59.90

VBT-027d *The Sontaran Experiment/Genesis of the Daleks*
1994, CBS/FOX, USA
REF: 5946 OP: $29.99

VBT-027e *The Sontaran Experiment/The Genesis of the Daleks*
1996/07/15, Roadshow Entertainment Ltd, Aus
'PG' rating. Released on two tapes in a single box.
REF: B00082 OP: $39.95

VBT-027f *The Sontaran Experiment/The Genesis of the Daleks*
1996/08, Roadshow Entertainment Ltd, NZ
'PG' rating.
REF: Z00082 OP: $49.95

VBT-028a *The Deadly Assassin*
1989, Playhouse, USA
Omits 'freeze frame' ending to Episode 3.
REF: 5419 OP: $19.99

VBT-028b *The Deadly Assassin*
1991/10/07, BBC Enterprises Ltd, UK
Cover by Andrew Skilleter. 'PG' certificate. Diamond logo. Re-issued 1995/02/13 at £7.99. 'Freeze frame' ending to Episode 3 partially restored. Deleted 1996/05/09.
REF: BBCV 4645 OP: £10.99 NM: £36.30

VBT-028c *The Deadly Assassin*
1992/03/04, PolyGram, Aus
'PG' rating.
REF: BBC46452 OP: $29.95

VBT-028d *The Deadly Assassin*
1992/04, PolyGram, NZ
'PG' rating. Deleted January 1996.
REF: BBC46452 OP: $29.95

VBT-029a *The Caves of Androzani*
1992/01/06, BBC Enterprises Ltd, UK
Cover by Andrew Skilleter. 'PG' certificate. Diamond logo. Re-issued 1995/02/13 at £7.99. Deleted 1996/05/09.
REF: BBCV 4713 OP: £10.99 NM: £36.30

VBT-029b *The Caves of Androzani*
1992/05/06, PolyGram, Aus
'PG' rating.
REF: BBC47132 OP: $29.95

VBT-029c *The Caves of Androzani*
1992/06, PolyGram, NZ
'PG' rating. Deleted January 1996.
REF: BBC47132 OP: $29.95

VBT-029d *The Caves of Androzani*
1992, CBS/FOX, USA
REF: 5733 OP: $19.99

VBT-030a *Robot*
1992/01/06, BBC Enterprises Ltd, UK
Cover by Alistair Pearson. 'U' certificate. Diamond logo. Deleted 1996/05/09.
REF: BBCV 4714 OP: £10.99 NM: £36.30

VBT-030b *Robot*
1992/07/03, PolyGram, Aus
'G' rating.
REF: BBC47142 OP: $29.95

VBT-030c *Robot*
1992/08, PolyGram, NZ
'G' rating. Deleted January 1996.
REF: BBC47142 OP: $29.95

VBT-030d *Robot*
1994, CBS/FOX, USA
REF: 8103 OP: $19.99

VBT-031a *Logopolis*
1992/03/02, BBC Enterprises Ltd, UK
Cover by Andrew Skilleter. 'U' certificate. Diamond logo. Deleted 1996/05/09.
REF: BBCV 4736 OP: £10.99 NM: £36.30

VBT-031b *Logopolis*
1992/09/01, PolyGram, Aus
'G' rating.
REF: BBC47362 OP: $29.95

VBT-031c *Logopolis*
1992/10, PolyGram, NZ
'G' rating. Deleted January 1996.
REF: BBC47362 OP: $29.95

VBT-031d *Logopolis*
1993, CBS/FOX, USA
REF: 4792 OP: $19.99

VBT-031e *Logopolis*
1996/07/15, Roadshow Entertainment Ltd, Aus
'G' rating.
REF: B00083 OP: $24.95

VBT-031f *Logopolis*
1996/08, Roadshow Entertainment Ltd, NZ
'G' rating. Deleted October 1999.
REF: Z00083 OP: $34.95

VBT-032a *Castrovalva*
1992/03/02, BBC Enterprises Ltd, UK
Cover by Andrew Skilleter. 'U' certificate. Diamond logo.
REF: BBCV 4737 OP: £10.99 NM: £19.80

VBT-032b *Castrovalva*
1992/09/01, PolyGram, Aus
'G' rating.
REF: BBC47372 OP: $29.95

VBT-032c *Castrovalva*
1992/10, PolyGram, NZ
'G' rating. Deleted January 1996.
REF: BBC47372 OP: $29.95

VBT-032d *Castrovalva*
1993, CBS/FOX, USA
REF: 4794 OP: $19.99

VBT-025d

VBT-026d

VBT-027d

VBT-028a

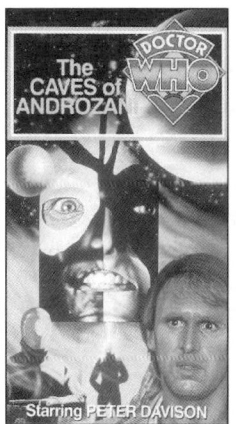

VBT-029d

VBT-030d

VBT-031d

VBT-032d

VBT-033d

VBT-034b

VBT-033a *The Claws of Axos*
1992/05/05, BBC Enterprises Ltd, UK
Cover by Andrew Skilleter. 'U' certificate. Diamond
logo. Re-issued 1994/02/14 at £7.99.
REF: BBCV 4742　OP: £11.99　NM: £16.50

VBT-033b *The Claws of Axos*
1992/10/20, PolyGram, Aus
'G' rating.
REF: BBC47422　OP: $29.95

VBT-033c *The Claws of Axos*
1992/11, PolyGram, NZ
'G' rating. Deleted January 1996.
REF: BBC47422　OP: $29.95

VBT-033d *The Claws of Axos*
1996/06/25, CBS/FOX, USA
REF: 8374　OP: $19.99

VBT-034a *The Twin Dilemma*
1992/05/05, BBC Enterprises Ltd, UK
Woolworths Only. Cover by Andrew Skilleter. 'U' certificate. Diamond logo. General BBC Release:
1993/02/08. Deleted 1996/05/09.
REF: BBCV 4783　OP: £10.99　NM: £27.50

VBT-034b *The Twin Dilemma*
1993, CBS/FOX, USA
Around this time, CBS/FOX accelerated the release
schedule and shipped *Who* videos in batches of 4-6
stories on a quarterly or semi-annual basis. By 1996,
they had caught up with the UK releases.
REF: 3491　OP: $19.99

VBT-035d

VBT-036d

VBT-034c *The Twin Dilemma*
1993/05/05, PolyGram, Aus
'G' rating.
REF: BBC47832　OP: $29.95

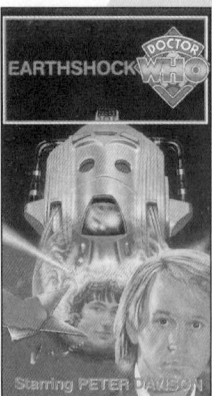

VBT-037b

VBT-038d

VBT-039d

VBT-034d *The Twin Dilemma*
1993/06, PolyGram, NZ
'G' rating. Deleted January 1996.
REF: BBC47832 OP: $29.95

VBT-035a *The Tomb of the Cybermen*
1992/05/05, BBC Enterprises Ltd, UK
Cover by Alistair Pearson. 'PG' certificate. Diamond logo.
Foil printing on cover. Includes a piece with the story's
director, Morris Barry, at the front. Deleted 1996/05/09.
REF: BBCV 4772 OP: £12.99 NM: £36.30

VBT-035b *The Tomb of the Cybermen*
1992/05/11, PolyGram, Aus
'G' rating, Cover does not feature foil printing.
REF: BBC47722 OP: $29.95

VBT-035c *The Tomb of the Cybermen*
1992/06, PolyGram, NZ
'G' rating. Deleted January 1996.
REF: BBC47722 OP: $29.95

VBT-035d *The Tomb of the Cyberman*
1992, CBS/FOX, USA
REF: 5731 OP: $19.99

VBT-036a *Shada*
1992/07/06, BBC Enterprises Ltd, UK
Video plus script book. Douglas Adams' royalties donated to Comic Relief. Photo-montage cover. 'U' certificate.
Diamond logo. Includes Tom Baker narrating the missing
parts of the story. Deleted 1996/05/09.
REF: BBCV 4814 OP: £19.99 NM: £58.50

VBT-036b *Shada*
1993/02/03, PolyGram, Aus
'G' rating. Video plus script book.
REF: BBC48142 OP: $39.95

VBT-036c *Shada*
1993/03, PolyGram, NZ
'G' rating. Video plus script book. Deleted January 1996.
REF: BBC48142 OP: $39.95

VBT-036d *Shada*
1992, CBS/FOX, USA
No script book included.
REF: 5730 OP: $19.99

VBT-037a *Earthshock*
1992/09/07, BBC Enterprises Ltd, UK
Cover by Andrew Skilleter. 'PG' certificate. Diamond
logo. Re-issued 1995/02/13 at £7.99.
REF: BBCV 4840 OP: £10.99 NM: £13.20

VBT-037b *Earthshock*
1993, CBS/FOX, USA
REF: 3492 OP: $19.99

VBT-037c *Earthshock*
1993/03/10, PolyGram, Aus
'PG' rating.
REF: BBC48402 OP: $29.95

VBT-037d *Earthshock*
1993/04, PolyGram, NZ
'PG' rating. Deleted January 1996.
REF: BBC48402 OP: $29.95

VBT-038a *The Aztecs*
1992/11/02, BBC Enterprises Ltd, UK
Cover by Andrew Skilleter. 'U' certificate. Diamond logo.
Edits: final 'next-episode' caption removed. Damage on the
print used for this release resulted in one line of dialogue
being cut short. Re-issued 1994/02/14 at £7.99.
REF: BBCV 4743 OP: £10.99

VBT-038b *The Aztecs*
1993/02/03, PolyGram, Aus
'G' rating.
REF: BBC47432 OP: $29.95

VBT-038c *The Aztecs*
1993/03, PolyGram, NZ
'G' rating. Deleted January 1996.
REF: BBC47432 OP: $29.95

VBT-038d *The Aztecs*
1994, CBS/FOX, USA
REF: 8100 OP: $19.99

VBT-039a *Mawdryn Undead*
1992/11/02, BBC Enterprises Ltd, UK
Cover by Andrew Skilleter. 'U' certificate. Diamond logo.
Re-issued 1994/02/14 at £7.99. Deleted 1995/08/21.
REF: BBCV 4874 OP: £10.99 NM: £33

VBT-039b *Mawdryn Undead*
1993/05/05, PolyGram, Aus
'G' rating.
REF: BBC48742 OP: $29.95

VBT-039c *Mawdryn Undead*
1993/06, PolyGram, NZ
'G' rating. Deleted January 1996.
REF: BBC48742 OP: $29.95

VBT-039d *Mawdryn Undead*
1994, CBS/FOX, USA
REF: 5949 OP: $19.99

VBT-040a *Terminus*
1993/01/04, BBC Enterprises Ltd, UK
Cover by Andrew Skilleter. 'PG' certificate. Diamond logo. Deleted 1996/05/09.
REF: BBCV 4890 OP: £10.99 NM: £36.30

VBT-040b *Terminus*
1993/06/04, PolyGram, Aus
'PG' rating.
REF: BBC48902 OP: $29.95

VBT-040c *Terminus*
1993/07, PolyGram, NZ
'PG' rating.
REF: BBC48902 OP: $29.95

VBT-040d *Terminus*
1994, CBS/FOX, USA
REF: 8101 OP: $19.99

VBT-040e *Terminus*
1996/07/15, Roadshow Entertainment Ltd, Aus
'PG' rating.
REF: B00089 OP: $24.95

VBT-040f *Terminus*
1996/08, Roadshow Entertainment Ltd, NZ
'PG' rating. Deleted August 1999.
REF: Z00089 OP: $34.95

VBT-041a *Enlightenment*
1993/02/08, BBC Enterprises Ltd, UK
Cover by Andrew Skilleter. 'PG' certificate. Diamond logo. Deleted 1996/05/09.
REF: BBCV 4891 OP: £10.99 NM: £33

VBT-041b *Enlightenment*
1993/05/05, PolyGram, Aus
'PG' rating.
REF: BBC48912 OP: $29.95

VBT-041c *Enlightenment*
1993/06, PolyGram, NZ
'PG' rating. Deleted January 1996
REF: BBC48912 OP: $29.95

VBT-041d *Enlightenment*
1994/08/23, CBS/FOX, USA
REF: 8145 OP: $19.99

VBT-042a *Image of the Fendahl*
1993/03/01, BBC Enterprises Ltd, UK
Cover by Andrew Skilleter. 'PG' certificate. Diamond logo. Deleted 1996/05/09.
REF: BBCV 4941 OP: £10.99 NM: £40.70

VBT-042b *Image of the Fendahl*
1993/07/07, PolyGram, Aus
'PG' rating.
REF: BBC49412 OP: $29.95

VBT-042c *Image of the Fendahl*
1993/08, PolyGram, NZ
'PG' rating. Deleted January 1996.
REF: BBC49412 OP: $29.95

VBT-042d *Image of the Fendahl*
1996/06/25, CBS/FOX, USA
REF: 8372 OP: $19.99

VBT-043a *The Dæmons*
1993/03/01, BBC Enterprises Ltd, UK
Colour reconstruction. Cover by Alistair Pearson. 'PG' certificate. Diamond logo. Re-issued 1995/02/13 at £7.99. Deleted 1996/05/09.
REF: BBCV 4950 OP: £10.99 NM: £46.20

VBT-043b *The Dæmons*
1993/07/07, PolyGram, Aus
'PG' rating.
REF: BBC49502 OP: $29.95

VBT-043c *The Dæmons*
1993/08, PolyGram, NZ
'PG' rating. Deleted January 1996.
REF: BBC49502 OP: $29.95

VBT-043d *The Dæmons*
1993, CBS/FOX, USA
REF: 4791 OP: $19.99

VBT-044a *Silver Nemesis*
1993/04/05, BBC Enterprises Ltd, UK
Extended edition with American produced documentary, 'The Making of *Silver Nemesis*' (hosted by Eric Luskin; see also VOT-002). Reflective photo-montage cover. 'PG' certificate. Diamond logo. Has had approximately 11 minutes of material added to it which was cut from the original BBC transmission due to time constraints. The American documentary has also been slightly edited to remove some clips from older stories for which clearance permission was refused.
REF: BBCV 4888 OP: £12.99 NM: £14.30

VBT-044b *Silver Nemesis*
1993/06/04, PolyGram, Aus
'G' rating. Cover does not feature the foil printing as on the UK release.
REF: BBC48882 OP: $29.95

VBT-044c *Silver Nemesis*
1993/07, PolyGram, NZ
'G' rating. Deleted January 1996.
REF: BBC48882 OP: $29.95

VBT-044d *Silver Nemesis*
1994/08/23, CBS/FOX, USA
REF: 8146 OP: $19.99

VBT-045a *Terror of the Autons*
1993/04/05, BBC Enterprises Ltd, UK
Colour reconstruction. Cover by Alistair Pearson. 'PG'
certificate. Diamond logo with '30th anniversary' flash.
Deleted 1996/05/09.
REF: BBCV 4957 OP: £10.99 NM: £41.80

VBT-045b *Terror of the Autons*
1993/06/04, PolyGram, Aus
'PG' rating.
REF: BBC49572 OP: $29.95

VBT-045c *Terror of the Autons*
1993/07, PolyGram, NZ
'PG' rating. Deleted January 1996.
REF: BBC49572 OP: $29.95

VBT-045d *Terror of the Autons*
1995/06/27, CBS/FOX, USA
REF: 8254 OP: $19.99

VBT-046a *Vengeance on Varos*
1993/05/04, BBC Enterprises Ltd, UK
Cover by Andrew Skilleter. 'PG' certificate. Diamond
logo with '30th anniversary' flash. Cover featured a
competition to win a trip to an American *Doctor Who*
convention. Also printed on *Keeper of Traken*? Re-
issued 1995/02/13 at £7.99.
REF: BBCV 4962 OP: £10.99 NM: £13.20

VBT-046b *Vengeance on Varos*
1993/08/04, PolyGram, Aus
'PG' rating.
REF: BBC49622 OP: $29.95

VBT-046c *Vengeance on Varos*
1993/09, PolyGram, NZ
'PG' rating. Deleted January 1996.
REF: BBC49622 OP: $29.95

VBT-046d *Vengeance on Varos*
1995/06/27, CBS/FOX, USA
REF: 8252 OP: $19.99

VBT-040d VBT-041d

VBT-042d

VBT-043d

VBT-044d VBT-045d

VBT-046d

VBT-047d

VBT-048d

VBT-049d

VBT-050d

VBT-051d

VBT-047a *The Keeper of Traken*
1993/06/07, BBC Enterprises Ltd, UK
Cover by Andrew Skilleter. 'PG' certificate. Diamond
logo with '30th anniversary' flash. Re-issued
1995/02/13 at £7.99.
REF: BBCV 4973   OP: £10.99   NM: £13.20

VBT-047b *The Keeper of Traken*
1993/09/03, PolyGram, Aus
'PG' rating.
REF: BBC49732   OP: $29.95

VBT-047c *The Keeper of Traken*
1993/10, PolyGram, NZ
'PG' rating. Deleted January 1996.
REF: BBC49732   OP: $29.95

VBT-047d *The Keeper of Traken*
1994, CBS/FOX, USA
REF: 5944   OP: $19.99

VBT-048a *The Invasion*
1993/06/07, BBC Enterprises Ltd, UK
Double tape. Cover by Andrew Skilleter. 'U' certificate.
Diamond logo with '30th anniversary' flash. Two missing
episodes linked by Nicholas Courtney's narration. There is
a small edit in the scene where Vaughan attacks Watkins
with the Cerebration Mentor. Deleted 1996/05/09.
REF: BBCV 4974   OP: £16.99   NM: £63.80

VBT-048b *The Invasion*
1993/10/13, PolyGram, Aus
'G' rating. Released on one tape rather than two. A
picture of Cybermen appears on the spine.
REF: BBC49742   OP: $29.95

VBT-052a

VBT-048c *The Invasion*
1993/11, PolyGram, NZ
'G' rating. Deleted January 1996.
REF: BBC49742 OP: $29.95

VBT-048d *The Invasion*
1995/06/27, CBS/FOX, USA
Released on one tape.
REF: 8251 OP: $19.99

VBT-048e *The Invasion*
1996/07/15, Roadshow Entertainment Ltd, Aus
'G' rating. Released on one tape rather than two.
REF: B00086 OP: $24.95

VBT-048f *The Invasion*
1996/08, Roadshow Entertainment Ltd, NZ
'G' rating.
REF: Z00086 OP: $34.95

VBT-049a *Doctor Who and the Silurians*
1993/07/05, BBC Enterprises Ltd, UK
Double tape. Colour reconstruction. Cover by
Andrew Skilleter. 'PG' certificate. Diamond logo with
'30th anniversary' flash. Deleted 1996/05/09.
REF: BBCV 4990 OP: £16.99 NM: £71.50

VBT-049b *Doctor Who and the Silurians*
1993/11/03, PolyGram, Aus
'PG' rating. Released on one tape rather than two. A
picture of Silurian appears on the spine.
REF: BBC49902 OP: $29.95

VBT-049c *Doctor Who and the Silurians*
1993/11, PolyGram, NZ
'PG' rating. Deleted January 1996.
REF: BBC49902 OP: $29.95

VBT-049d *Doctor Who and the Silurians*
1995/06/27, CBS/FOX, USA
REF: 8256 OP: $29.99

VBT-050a *The Curse of Peladon*
1993/08/02, BBC Enterprises Ltd, UK
Cover by Andrew Skilleter. 'PG' certificate. Diamond
logo with '30th anniversary' flash. Re-issued
1995/02/13 at £7.99.
REF: BBCV 4978 OP: £10.99 NM: £13.20

VBT-050b *The Curse of Peladon*
1993/11/03, PolyGram, Aus
'PG' rating.
REF: BBC49782 OP: $29.95

VBT-050c *The Curse of Peladon*
1993/11, PolyGram, NZ
'PG' rating. Deleted January 1996.
REF: BBC49782 OP: $29.95

VBT-050d *The Curse of Peladon*
1995/09/20, CBS/FOX, USA
REF: 8291 OP: $19.99

VBT-051a **Daleks boxed set**
1993/09/03, PolyGram, Aus
'PG' rating. The packaging appears to have been a
UK import. However the actual video tapes were
duplicated and manufactured in Australia. Price
reduced to $49.95 some time later, presumably to
clear.
REF: BBCV5005 OP: $79.95

VBT-051b **Daleks boxed set**
1993/09/06, BBC Enterprises Ltd, UK
Incorporating *The Chase* [5006] and *Remembrance of
the Daleks* [5007]. In a special 'Daleks' tin (4 variants:
photo on base from *The Dalek Invasion of Earth*, *Evil of
the Daleks*, *Genesis of the Daleks* or *Remembrance of
the Daleks*) plus booklet by Andrew Pixley. Cover artwork for *The Chase* by Andrew Skilleter. Cover artwork for *Remembrance of the Daleks* by Alistair
Pearson. Both tapes 'PG' certificate. Tapes in card
boxes. Deleted 1998/01/07.
REF: BBCV 5005 OP: £29.99 NM: £60

VBT-051c **Daleks boxed set**
1993/12, PolyGram, NZ
'PG' rating. Deleted January 1996.
REF: BBCV5005 OP: $85.95

VBT-051d **The Daleks Limited Edition Boxed Set**
1993, CBS/FOX, USA
No individual boxes for the two stories as above.
Simple card box with white cover and two tapes inside.
REF: 4795 OP: $39.95

VBT-052a *The Trial of a Time Lord*
1993/10/04, BBC Enterprises Ltd, UK
In a 'TARDIS' tin. 7 variants: photo on base of each of
the first seven Doctors. Cover artwork by Alistair
Pearson. 'PG' certificate. Diamond logo with '30th
anniversary' flash. Single card box contains three
videos. Tapes have the code number: BBCV5009.
Deleted 1998/01/07.
REF: BBCV 5008 OP: £34.99 NM: £66

VBT-052b *The Trial of a Time Lord*
1993/10/13, PolyGram, AUS
'PG' rating. The packaging appears to have been a UK import. However the actual video tapes were duplicated and manufactured in Australia. Price reduced to $49.95 some time later, presumably to clear.
REF: BBCV5008 OP: $99.95

VBT-052c *The Trial of a Time Lord*
1993/12, PolyGram, NZ
'PG' rating. Deleted January 1996.
REF: BBCV5008 OP: $99.95

VBT-052d *The Trial of a Time Lord*
1993, CBS/FOX, USA
This version was released in a card TARDIS cover, with no tin or picture box.
REF: 4790 OP: $49.99

VBT-053a *Resurrection of the Daleks*
1993/11/01, BBC Enterprises Ltd, UK
Cover by Colin Howard. 'PG' rating. Diamond logo with '30th anniversary' flash. This release features the four part version originally prepared for transmission rather than the two part version actually transmitted.
REF: BBCV 5143 OP: £10.99 NM: £13.20

VBT-053b *Resurrection of the Daleks*
1994/02/09, PolyGram, Aus
'PG' rating.
REF: BBC51432 OP: $29.95

VBT-053c *Resurrection of the Daleks*
1994/03, PolyGram, NZ
'PG' rating. Deleted January 1996.
REF: BBC51432 OP: $29.95

VBT-053d *Resurrection of the Daleks*
1994, CBS/FOX, USA
REF: 8104 OP: $19.99

VBT-053e *Resurrection of the Daleks*
1996/07/15, Roadshow Entertainment Ltd, Aus
'PG' rating. Apparently contains the edited four-part version broadcast by the ABC as opposed to the four-part version originally compiled by the BBC and included on the earlier release by PolyGram.
REF: B00088 OP: $24.95

VBT-053f *Resurrection of the Daleks*
1996/08, Roadshow Entertainment Ltd, NZ
'PG' rating. Deleted August 1999.
REF: Z00088 OP: $34.95

VBT-054a *The Two Doctors*
1993/11/01, BBC Enterprises Ltd, UK
Cover by Colin Howard. 'PG' certificate. Diamond logo with '30th anniversary' flash. Deleted 1996/05/09. Originally scheduled as a twin tape, this was released on a single tape.
REF: BBCV 5148 OP: £10.99 NM: £33

VBT-054b *The Two Doctors*
1994/02/09, PolyGram, Aus
'G' rating.
REF: BBC51482 OP: $29.95

VBT-054c *The Two Doctors*
1994/03, PolyGram, NZ
'G' rating. Deleted January 1996.
REF: BBC51482 OP: $29.95

VBT-054d *The Two Doctors*
1995/06/27, CBS/FOX, USA
REF: 8255 OP: $19.99

VBT-054e *The Two Doctors*
1996/07/15, Roadshow Entertainment Ltd, Aus
'G' rating. Contains the edited six-part version broadcast by the ABC.
REF: B00087 OP: $24.95

VBT-054f *The Two Doctors*
1996/08, Roadshow Entertainment Ltd, NZ
'G' rating. Deleted August 1999.
REF: Z00087 OP: $34.95

VBT-055a *Planet of Evil*
1993/12/29, BBC Enterprises Ltd, UK
Cover by Colin Howard. 'PG' certificate. Diamond logo.
REF: BBCV 5180 OP: £10.99

VBT-055b *Planet of Evil*
1994/03/09, PolyGram, Aus
'PG' rating.
REF: BBC51802 OP: $29.95

VBT-055c *Planet of Evil*
1994/04, PolyGram, NZ
'PG' rating. Deleted January 1996.
REF: BBC51802 OP: $29.95

VBT-055d *Planet of Evil*
1996/06/25, CBS/FOX, USA
REF: 8370 OP: $19.99

VBT-056a *Dragonfire*
1993/12/29, BBC Enterprises Ltd, UK
Cover by Bruno Elattori. 'PG' certificate. Diamond logo.
REF: BBCV 5181 OP: £10.99

VBT-056b *Dragonfire*
1994/03/09, PolyGram, Aus
'PG' rating.
REF: BBC51812 OP: $29.95

VBT-056c *Dragonfire*
1994/04, PolyGram, NZ
'PG' rating. Deleted January 1996.
REF: BBC51812 OP: $29.95

VBT-056d *Dragonfire*
1997/02/11, CBS/FOX, USA
REF: 8460 OP: $19.99

VBT-057a *Arc of Infinity*
1994/03/07, BBC Enterprises Ltd, UK
Cover by Pete Wallbank. 'PG' certificate. Diamond logo.
REF: BBCV 5199 OP: £10.99

VBT-057b *Arc of Infinity*
1994/04/08, PolyGram, Aus
'PG' rating.
REF: BBC51992 OP: $29.95

VBT-057c *Arc of Infinity*
1994/05, PolyGram, NZ
'PG' rating. Deleted January 1996.
REF: BBC51992 OP: $29.95

VBT-057d *Arc of Infinity*
1995/09/20, CBS/FOX, USA
REF: 8290 OP: $19.99

VBT-058a *Inferno*
1994/05/03, BBC Enterprises Ltd, UK
Double tape. Cover by Colin Howard. 'PG' certificate.
Diamond logo. Includes a short unbroadcast sequence
of the radio announcement voiced by Jon Pertwee.
REF: BBCV 5269 OP: £16.99

VBT-058b *Inferno*
1994/07/06, PolyGram, Aus
'PG' rating. Released on one tape rather than two.
REF: BBC52692 OP: $29.95

VBT-058c *Inferno*
1994/08, PolyGram, NZ
'G' rating. Deleted January 1996.
REF: BBC52692 OP: $29.95

VBT-058d *Inferno*
1995/09/20, CBS/FOX, USA
The box says the story is in B&W but it is in colour.
REF: 8292 OP: $29.99

VBT-053d

VBT-054d

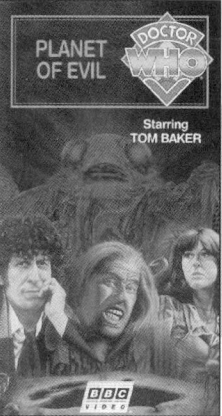

VBT-055d

VBT-056d

VBT-057d

VBT-058d

VBT-059d

VBT-060d

VBT-061d

VBT-062d

VBT-063d

VBT-064d

VBT-058e *Inferno*
1996/06/10, Roadshow Entertainment Ltd, Aus
'PG' rating. Released on one tape rather than two.
REF: B00052   OP: $24.95

VBT-058f *Inferno*
1996/07, Roadshow Entertainment Ltd, NZ
'PG' rating. Deleted August 1999.
REF: Z00052   OP: $39.95

VBT-059a *Ghost Light*
1994/05/03, BBC Enterprises ltd, UK
Cover by Colin Howard. 'PG' certificate. Diamond logo.
REF: BBCV 5344   OP: £11.99

VBT-059b *Ghost Light*
1994/07/06, PolyGram, Aus
'PG' rating.
REF: BBC53442   OP: $29.95

VBT-059c *Ghost Light*
1994/08, PolyGram, NZ
'PG' rating. Deleted January 1996.
REF: BBC53442   OP: $29.95

VBT-059d *Ghost Light*
1996/06/25, CBS/FOX, USA
REF: 8369   OP: $19.99

VBT-060a *The Visitation/Black Orchid*
1994/07/04, BBC Enterprises Ltd, UK
Double tape. Cover by Pete Wallbank. 'PG' certificate.
Diamond logo.
REF: BBCV 5349   OP: £16.99

VBT-060b *The Visitation/Black Orchid*
1994/08/08, PolyGram, Aus
'PG' rating. Released on one tape rather than two.
REF: BBC53492   OP: $29.95

VBT-060c *The Visitation/Black Orchid*
1994/09, PolyGram, NZ
'PG' rating. Deleted January 1996.
REF: BBC53492   OP: $29.95

VBT-060d *The Visitation/Black Orchid*
1996/06/25, CBS/FOX, USA
REF: 8373   OP: $29.99

VBT-061a *Destiny of the Daleks*
1994/07/04, BBC Enterprises Ltd, UK
Cover by Colin Howard. 'U' certificate. Diamond logo.
Deleted 1996/05/09.
REF: BBCV 5350   OP: £11.99   NM: £38.50

VBT-061b *Destiny of the Daleks*
1994/08/08, PolyGram, Aus
'G' rating.
REF: BBC53502 OP: $29.95

VBT-061c *Destiny of the Daleks*
1994/09, PolyGram, NZ
'G' rating. Deleted January 1996.
REF: BBC53502 OP: $29.95

VBT-061d *Destiny of the Daleks*
1997/05/06, CBS/FOX, USA
REF: 8493 OP: $19.99

VBT-062a *The Seeds of Doom*
1994/08/01, BBC Enterprises Ltd, UK
Double tape. Cover by Colin Howard. 'U' certificate.
Diamond logo.
REF: BBCV 5377 OP: £16.99

VBT-062b *The Seeds of Doom*
1994/10/04 , PolyGram, Aus
'G' rating. Released on one tape rather than two.
REF: BBC53772 OP: $29.95

VBT-062c *The Seeds of Doom*
1994/11, PolyGram, NZ
'G' rating. Deleted January 1996.
REF: BBC53772 OP: $29.95

VBT-062d *The Seeds of Doom*
1995/09/20, CBS/FOX, USA
Released on one tape.
REF: 8294 OP: $19.99

VBT-062e *The Seeds of Doom*
1996/06/10, Roadshow Entertainment Ltd, Aus
'G' rating. Released on one tape rather than two.
REF: B00054 OP: $24.95

VBT-062f *The Seeds of Doom*
1996/07, Roadshow Entertainment Ltd, NZ
'G' rating. Deleted August 1999.
REF: Z00054 OP: $39.95

VBT-063a *The Rescue/The Romans*
1994/09/05, BBC Enterprises Ltd, UK
Double tape. Cover by Andrew Skilleter. 'U' certificate. Diamond logo. Edits: *The Romans* is unedited, but
end scenes from *The Rescue* were removed. Deleted
1998/08/21.
REF: BBCV 5378 OP: £16.99

VBT-063b *The Rescue/The Romans*
1994/11/07, PolyGram, Aus
'G' rating. Released on one tape rather than two.
REF: BBC53782 OP: $29.95

VBT-063c *The Rescue/The Romans*
1994/11, PolyGram, NZ
'G' rating.
REF: BBC53782 OP: $29.95

VBT-063d *The Rescue/The Romans*
1996/03/26, CBS/FOX, USA
REF: 8338 OP: $29.99

VBT-063e *The Rescue/The Romans*
1996/06/10, Roadshow Entertainment Ltd, Aus
'G' rating. Released on one tape rather than two.
REF: B00053 OP: $24.95

VBT-063f *The Rescue/The Romans*
1996/07, Roadshow Entertainment Ltd, NZ
'G' rating. Deleted August 1999.
REF: Z00053 OP: $39.95

VBT-064a *Kinda*
1994/10/03, BBC Enterprises Ltd, UK
Cover by Colin Howard. 'U' certificate. Diamond logo.
REF: BBCV 5432 OP: £11.99

VBT-064b *Kinda*
1995/02/06, PolyGram, Aus
'G' rating.
REF: BBC54322 OP: $29.95

VBT-064c *Kinda*
1995/02, PolyGram, NZ
'G' rating.
REF: BBC54322 OP: $29.95

VBT-064d *Kinda*
1996/06/25, CBS/FOX, USA
REF: 8371 OP: $19.99

VBT 065a *Snakedance*
1994/12/28, BBC Enterprises Ltd, UK
Cover by Colin Howard. 'U' certificate. Diamond logo.
Deleted 1998/08/21.
REF: BBCV 5433 OP: £11.99 NM: £22

VBT-065b *Snakedance*
1995/02/06, PolyGram, Aus
'G' rating.
REF: BBC54332 OP: $29.95

VBT-065c *Snakedance*
1995/02, PolyGram, NZ
'G' rating. Deleted January 1996.
REF: BBC54332 OP: $29.95

VBT-065d *Snakedance*
1996/09/10, CBS/FOX, USA
REF: 8438 OP: $19.99

VBT-066a *The Android Invasion*
1995/03/06, BBC Enterprises Ltd, UK
Cover by Colin Howard. 'PG' certificate. Diamond logo.
REF: BBCV 5526 OP: £11.99

VBT-066b *The Android Invasion*
1995/03/06, PolyGram, Aus
'G' rating.
REF: BBC55262 OP: $29.95

VBT-066c *The Android Invasion*
1995/04, PolyGram, NZ
'G' rating. Deleted January 1996.
REF: BBC55262 OP: $29.95

VBT-066d *The Android Invasion*
1996/03/26, CBS/FOX, USA
REF: 8334 OP: $19.99

VBT-067a *Carnival of Monsters*
1995/03/05, BBC Worldwide Ltd, UK
3 collector's cards. Cover by Colin Howard. 'PG' certificate. Diamond logo. The back of the cover featured story information compiled by *Doctor Who Magazine*. Features an untransmitted version of episode two and episode four is cut at the end.
REF: BBCV 5556 OP: £11.99 NM: £16.50

VBT-067b *Carnival of Monsters*
1995/05/08, PolyGram, AUS
'G' rating. Evidence suggests this release was accompanied by a special card in remembrance of Jon Pertwee's death, but since Pertwee died a year after the release date listed above, this seems unlikely. Perhaps it was with another release or a later re-issue?
REF: BBC55562 OP: $29.95

VBT-067c *Carnival of Monsters*
1995/06, PolyGram, NZ
'G' rating. Deleted January 1996.
REF: BBC55562 OP: $29.95

VBT-067d *Carnival of Monsters*
1996/03/26, CBS/FOX, USA
REF: 8336 OP: $19.99

VBT-068a *The Ribos Operation*
1995/04/03, BBC Worldwide Ltd, UK
Cover by Colin Howard. 'U' certificate. Diamond logo. The back of the cover featured story information compiled by *Doctor Who Magazine*. The spine of these 'Key to Time' releases formed a picture by Andrew Skilleter. Deleted 1998/08/21.
REF: BBCV 5607 OP: £11.99 NM: £22

VBT-068b *The Ribos Operation*
1995/06/12, PolyGram, Aus
'G' rating.
REF: BBC56072 OP: $29.95

VBT-068c *The Ribos Operation*
1995/07, PolyGram, NZ
'G' rating. Deleted January 1996.
REF: BBC56072 OP: $29.95

VBT-068d *The Ribos Operation*
1996/09/10, CBS/FOX, USA
REF: 8435 OP: $19.99

VBT-069a *The Pirate Planet*
1995/04/03, BBC Worldwide Ltd, UK
Cover by Colin Howard. 'U' certificate. Diamond logo. The back of the cover featured story information compiled by *Doctor Who Magazine*. The spine of these 'Key to Time' releases formed a picture by Andrew Skilleter. Deleted 1996/02/21.
REF: BBCV 5608 OP: £11.99 NM: £22

VBT-069b *The Pirate Planet*
1995/06/12, PolyGram, Aus
'G' rating.
REF: BBC56082 OP: $29.95

VBT-069c *The Pirate Planet*
1995/07, PolyGram, NZ
'G' rating. Deleted January 1996.
REF: BBC56082 OP: $29.95

VBT-069d *The Pirate Planet*
1996/09/10, CBS/FOX, USA
REF: 8437 OP: $19.99

VBT-070a *The Stones of Blood*
1995/05/01, BBC Worldwide Ltd, UK
Cover by Colin Howard. 'PG' certificate. Diamond logo. The back of the cover featured story information compiled by *Doctor Who Magazine*. The spine of these 'Key to Time' releases formed a picture by Andrew Skilleter. Deleted 1998/08/21. Part two contains 38 seconds of untransmitted footage as De Vries and Martha run around the Hall screaming in terror.
REF: BBCV 5610 OP: £11.99 NM: £22

VBT-065d

VBT-066d

VBT-067d

VBT-070b *The Stones of Blood*
1995/07/10, PolyGram, Aus
'PG' rating.
REF: BBC56102 OP: $29.95

VBT-070c *The Stones of Blood*
1995/08, PolyGram, NZ
'PG' rating. Deleted January 1996.
REF: BBC56102 OP: $29.95

VBT-070d *The Stones of Blood*
1996/03/26, CBS/FOX, USA
Also re-issued in 1999 as a part of 'The Gateway
Collection' priced at £14.95.
REF: 8339 OP: $14.95

VBT-071a *The Androids of Tara*
1995/05/01, BBC Worldwide Ltd, UK
Cover by Colin Howard. 'PG' certificate. Diamond
logo. The back of the cover featured story information compiled by *Doctor Who Magazine*. The spine of
these 'Key to Time' releases formed a picture by
Andrew Skilleter. Deleted 1998/08/21.
REF: BBCV 5611 OP: £11.99 NM: £22

VBT-071b *The Androids of Tara*
1995/07/10, PolyGram, Aus
'G' rating.
REF: BBC56112 OP: $29.95

VBT-071c *The Androids of Tara*
1995/08, PolyGram, NZ
'G' rating. Deleted January 1996.
REF: BBC56112 OP: $29.95

VBT-071d *The Androids of Tara*
1996/03/26, CBS/FOX, USA
REF: 8335 OP: $19.99

VBT-068d

VBT-069d

VBT-070d

VBT-071d

VBT-072d

VBT-073d

VBT-076c

VBT-077d

VBT-072a *The Power of Kroll*
1995/06/05, BBC Worldwide Ltd, UK
Cover by Colin Howard. 'PG' certificate. Diamond
logo. The back of the cover featured story information compiled by *Doctor Who Magazine*. The spine of
these 'Key to Time' releases formed a picture by
Andrew Skilleter. Deleted 1998/08/21.
REF: BBCV 5612 OP: £11.99 NM: £22

VBT-072b *The Power of Kroll*
1995/08/28, PolyGram, Aus
'PG' rating.
REF: BBC56122 OP: $29.95

VBT-072c *The Power of Kroll*
1995/10, PolyGram, NZ
'PG' rating. Deleted January 1996.
REF: BBC56122 OP: $29.95

VBT-072d *The Power of Kroll*
1996/09/10, CBS/FOX, USA
REF: 8436 OP: $19.99

VBT-073a *The Armageddon Factor*
1995/06/05, BBC Worldwide Ltd, UK
Cover by Colin Howard. 'U' certificate. Diamond logo.
The back of the cover featured story information
compiled by *Doctor Who Magazine*. The spine of these
'Key to Time' releases formed a picture by Andrew
Skilleter. Deleted 1998/08/21.
REF: BBCV 5613 OP: £14.99 NM: £22

VBT-073b *The Armageddon Factor*
1995/08/28, PolyGram, Aus
'G' rating.
REF: BBC56132 OP: $29.95

VBT-073c *The Armageddon Factor*
1995/10, PolyGram, NZ
'G' rating. Deleted January 1996.
REF: BBC56132 OP: $29.95

VBT-073d *The Armageddon Factor*
1996/09/10, CBS/FOX, USA
REF: 8439 OP: $19.99

VBT-074a *The Mark of the Rani*
1995/07/03, BBC Worldwide Ltd, UK
Cover by Colin Howard. 'U' certificate. Diamond logo.
The back of the cover featured story information
compiled by *Doctor Who Magazine*.
REF: BBCV 5603 OP: £11.99

VBT-074b *The Mark of the Rani*
1995/10/04, PolyGram, Aus
'G' rating.
REF: BBC56032 OP: $29.95

VBT-074c *The Mark of the Rani*
1995/11, PolyGram, NZ
'G' rating. Deleted January 1996.
REF: BBC56032 OP: $29.95

VBT-074d *The Mark of the Rani*
1997/02/11, CBS/FOX, USA
REF: 8458 OP: $19.99

VBT-075a *Time and the Rani*
1995/07/03, BBC Worldwide Ltd, UK
Cover by Colin Howard. 'U' certificate. Diamond logo.
The back of the cover featured story information
compiled by *Doctor Who Magazine*. The titles for
episode 4 have been updated to the correct version:
on the BBC transmission, an earlier version was used
by mistake.
REF: BBCV 5617 OP: £11.99

VBT-075b *Time and the Rani*
1995/10/04, PolyGram, Aus
'PG' rating.
REF: BBC56172 OP: $29.95

VBT-075c *Time and the Rani*
1995/11, PolyGram, NZ
'PG' rating. Deleted January 1996.
REF: BBC56172 OP: $29.95

VBT-075d *Time and the Rani*
1995/09/20, CBS/FOX, USA
REF: 8295 OP: $19.99

VBT-076a *Frontier in Space*
1995/08/07, BBC Worldwide Ltd, UK
Double tape. Postcard. Cover by Colin Howard. 'U'
certificate. Diamond logo. The back of the cover fea-
tured story information compiled by *Doctor Who
Magazine*. Features an untransmitted version of
Episode 5.
REF: BBCV 5640 OP: £16.99

VBT-076b *Frontier in Space*
1995/11/08, PolyGram, Aus
'G' rating. Released on one tape rather than two.
REF: BBCV5640 OP: $29.95

VBT-076c *Frontier in Space*
1996/03/26, CBS/FOX, USA
REF: 8337 OP: $29.99

VBT-076d *Frontier in Space*
1996/04/15, Roadshow Entertainment Ltd, Aus
'G' rating. Released on one tape rather than two.
REF: B17941 OP: $29.95

VBT-076e *Frontier in Space*
1996/05, Roadshow Entertainment Ltd, NZ
'G' rating. Deleted August 1999.
REF: Z17941 OP: $39.95

VBT-077a *The Sea Devils*
1995/09/04, BBC Worldwide Ltd, UK
Double tape. Postcard. Cover by Colin Howard. 'PG'
certificate. Diamond logo. The back of the cover featured story information compiled by *Doctor Who
Magazine*.
REF: BBCV 5667 OP: £16.99

VBT-077b *The Sea Devils*
1996/07/15, Roadshow Entertainment Ltd, Aus
'PG' rating. Released on one tape rather than two.
REF: B00115 OP: $24.95

VBT-077c *The Sea Devils*
1996/08, Roadshow Entertainment Ltd, NZ
'PG' rating.
REF: Z00115 OP: $39.95

VBT-077d *The Sea Devils*
1997/05/06, CBS/FOX, USA
REF: 8495 OP: $29.99

VBT-078a *Warriors of the Deep*
1995/09/04, BBC Worldwide Ltd, UK
Postcard. Cover by Colin Howard. 'PG' certificate.
Diamond logo. The back of the cover featured story
information compiled by *Doctor Who Magazine*.
REF: BBCV 5668 OP: £11.99

VBT-078b *Warriors of the Deep*
1996/07/15, Roadshow Entertainment Ltd, Aus
'PG' rating.
REF: B00116 OP: $24.95

VBT-078c *Warriors of the Deep*
1996/08, Roadshow Entertainment Ltd, NZ
'PG' rating.
REF: Z00116 OP: $29.95

VBT-078d

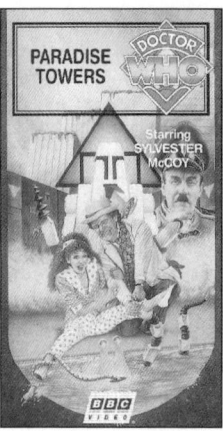

VBT-079d

VBT-080d

VBT-078d *Warriors of the Deep*
1997/05/06, CBS/FOX, USA
REF: 8497 OP: $19.99

VBT-079a *Paradise Towers*
1995/10/02, BBC Worldwide Ltd, UK
Postcard. Cover by Colin Howard. 'PG' certificate.
Diamond logo. The back of the cover featured story
information compiled by *Doctor Who Magazine*.
REF: BBCV 5686 OP: £11.99

VBT-079b *Paradise Towers*
1997/01/13, Roadshow Entertainment Ltd, Aus
'PG' rating. Cover incorrectly states that the rating is
for 'low level coarse language' when it is actually for
'low level violence'.
REF: B00049 OP: $24.95

VBT-079c *Paradise Towers*
1997/02, Roadshow Entertainment Ltd, NZ
'PG' rating.
REF: Z00049 OP: $29.95

VBT-079d *Paradise Towers*
1997/05/06, CBS/FOX, USA
REF: 8496 OP: $19.99

VBT-080a *Survival*
1995/10/02, BBC Worldwide Ltd, UK
Postcard. Cover by Colin Howard. 'PG' certificate.
Diamond logo. The back of the cover featured story
information compiled by *Doctor Who Magazine*.
REF: BBCV 5687 OP: £11.99

VBT-080b *Survival*
1996/11/11, Roadshow Entertainment Ltd, Aus
'PG' rating.
REF: B00050 OP: $24.95

VBT-080c *Survival*
1996/11, Roadshow Entertainment Ltd, NZ
'PG' rating.
REF: Z00050 OP: $29.95

VBT-080d *Survival*
1996/09/10, CBS/FOX, USA
REF: 8434 OP: $19.99

VBT-081a *The Five Doctors/The King's Demons*
1995/11/06, BBC Worldwide Ltd, UK
Extended/Special edition. Limited edition boxed set.
Includes collector's postcard album. Covers by Colin
Howard. 'U' certificate. Diamond logo. *The Five Doctors*
(BBCV5734) *The King's Demons* (BBCV5733). The back

of the covers featured story information compiled by *Doctor Who Magazine*. Individual tapes in plastic boxes. Some of the initial run of tapes had a fault on the Dolby Surround Sound. Deleted 1998/04/28.
REF: BBCV 5737 OP: £19.99 NM: £55

VBT-081b *The Five Doctors Collector's Edition/The King's Demons*
1997/02/11, CBS/FOX, USA
REF: 8455 OP: $29.99

VBT-081c *The Five Doctors/The King's Demons*
1997/07/14, Roadshow Entertainment Ltd, AUS
'PG' rating. Released on two tapes in a boxed set with a pack of *Doctor Who* playing cards. Individual catalogue numbers: *The King's Demons* – B00197, *The Five Doctors* – B00198.
REF: B00234 OP: $49.95

VBT-081b

VBT-081d *The King's Demons*
1997/08, Roadshow Entertainment Ltd, NZ
'PG' rating. This version has a statement on the cover alerting viewers to a fault on the tape 44 minutes into the story. This fault is not on the UK version. Released as an individual tape.
REF: Z00197 OP: $29.95

VBT-081e *The Five Doctors*
1997/08, Roadshow Entertainment Ltd, NZ
'PG' rating. Released as an individual tape.
REF: Z00198 OP: $39.95

VBT-082a *The Monster of Peladon*
1995/12/27, BBC Worldwide Ltd, UK
Double tape. Postcard. Cover by Colin Howard. 'U' certificate. Diamond logo. The back of the cover featured story information compiled by *Doctor Who Magazine*.
REF: BBCV 5781 OP: £16.99

VBT-081d

VBT-082b *The Monster of Peladon*
1997/05/06, CBS/FOX, USA
REF: 8494 OP: $29.99

VBT-082c *The Monster of Peladon*
1997/05/12, Roadshow Entertainment Ltd, Aus
'G' rating. Released on one tape rather than two.
REF: B00191 OP: $24.95

VBT-082d *The Monster of Peladon*
1997/06, Roadshow Entertainment Ltd, NZ
'G' rating.
REF: Z00191 OP: $39.95

VBT-082b

VBT-083a *The Hand of Fear*
1996/02/05, BBC Worldwide Ltd, UK
Postcard. Only available for two weeks due to the impending transmission of the Paul McGann TV Movie. Officially deleted 1998/08/21. Cover by Colin Howard. 'U' certificate. Diamond logo. The back of the cover featured story information compiled by *Doctor Who Magazine*.
REF: BBCV 5789 OP: £11.99 NM: £44

VBT-083b *The Hand of Fear*
1997/05/12, Roadshow Entertainment Ltd, Aus
'G' rating.
REF: B00182 OP: $24.95

VBT-083c *The Hand of Fear*
1997/06, Roadshow Entertainment Ltd, NZ
'G' rating.
REF: Z00182 OP: $39.95

VBT-083d *The Hand of Fear*
1997/02/11, CBS/FOX, USA
REF: 8459 OP: $19.99

VBT-084a *Doctor Who*
1996/05/22, BBC Worldwide Ltd, UK
UK transmission version of the Paul McGann TV Movie. Free postcards at W H Smiths. Glow in dark sleeve at Woolworths. Poster at other shops. Photographic cover. '12' certificate. Some sleeves exist with a '15' certificate on. TVM logo. Withdrawn 2001/05.
REF: BBCV 5882 OP: £14.99

VBT-084b *Doctor Who*
1996/11, Uni/CIC , AUS
'M15+' rating. The full and uncut version of the TVM. Box did not feature the foil-stamped logo, nor did it carry the BBC logo. Only the Universal logo appears.
REF: RFM1478 OP: $24.95

VBT-084c *Doctor Who*
1998/10, Uni/CIC , NZ
'M' rating. Effectively deleted soon after it became available in New Zealand as this was a one-off limited import from Australia.
REF: RFM1478 OP: $29.95

VBT-084d *Doctor Who*
1996 c., Kuraray, China
Similar to laserdisc and DVD versions, with Cantonese subtitles. Title translated as 'Murder in Space' or 'Death of Time'.
REF: RFM1478 OP: $24.95

VBT-085a *The Green Death*
1996/10/07, BBC Worldwide Ltd, UK
Double tape. Cover by Colin Howard. 'U' certificate.

TVM logo. Some of the covers for this release omitted the foil-stamped *Doctor Who* logo.
REF: BBCV 5816 OP: £16.99

VBT-085b *The Green Death*
1997/04/14, Roadshow Entertainment Ltd, Aus
'G' rating. Released on one tape. TVM logo.
REF: B00158 OP: $24.95

VBT-085c *The Green Death*
1997/04, Roadshow Entertainment Ltd, NZ
'G' rating.
REF: Z00158 OP: $39.95

VBT-085d *The Green Death*
1997/02/11, CBS/FOX, USA
REF: 8457 OP: $29.99

VBT-086a *The Leisure Hive*
1997/01/06, BBC Worldwide Ltd, UK
Cover by Colin Howard. 'PG' certificate. TVM logo.
REF: BBCV 5821 OP: £11.99

VBT-086b *The Leisure Hive*
1997/05/06, CBS/FOX, USA
REF: 4166 OP: $19.99

VBT-086c *The Leisure Hive*
1997/09/08, Roadshow Entertainment Ltd, Aus
'PG' rating. Diamond logo.
REF: B00213 OP: $24.95

VBT-086d *The Leisure Hive*
1997/10, Roadshow Entertainment Ltd, NZ
'PG' rating.
REF: Z00213 OP: $29.95

VBT-087a *The Awakening/Frontios*
1997/03/03, BBC Worldwide Ltd, UK
Double tape. Cover by Colin Howard. 'PG' certificate. TVM logo.
REF: BBCV 6120 OP: £16.99

VBT-087b *The Awakening/Frontios*
1998/03/09, Roadshow Entertainment Ltd, Aus
'PG' rating. Released on one tape rather than two.
REF: B00262 OP: $24.95

VBT-087c *The Awakening/Frontios*
1998/03/31, CBS/FOX, USA
Double tape set.
REF: 2777 OP: $29.99

VBT-087d *The Awakening/Frontios*
1998/04, Roadshow Entertainment Ltd, NZ
'PG' rating.
REF: Z00262 OP: $39.95

VBT-088a *The War Machines*
1997/06/02, BBC Worldwide Ltd, UK
Photo-montage cover. 'U' certificate. TVM logo. Article
on sleeve about the reconstruction work undertaken
on the story for the video release. Includes a BBC
globe, and a clip from the children's magazine programme *Blue Peter* featuring a War Machine in action. A
short out-take is included at the end of the tape of a
War Machine prop catching fire during filming. One
batch of tapes from this release had a fault on it.
REF: BBCV 6183 OP: £11.99

VBT-088b *The War Machines*
1998/01/05, Roadshow Entertainment Ltd, Aus
'G' rating. Diamond logo. Apparently, the original batch
of tapes were without the *Blue Peter* clip. Subsequent
batches had the mistake corrected.
REF: B00250 OP: $24.95

VBT-088c *The War Machines*
1998/02, Roadshow Entertainment Ltd, NZ
'G' rating.
REF: Z00250 OP: $39.95

VBT-088d *The War Machines*
1998/03/31, CBS/FOX, USA
REF: 2776 OP: $19.99

VBT-089a *The Happiness Patrol*
1997/08/04, BBC Worldwide Ltd, UK
Cover by Colin Howard (Kandy Man) and photo-
montage. 'PG' certificate. TVM logo.
REF: BBCV 5803 OP: £11.99

VBT-089b *The Happiness Patrol*
1998/03/31, CBS/FOX, USA
REF: 2778 OP: $19.99

VBT-083d

VBT-084a

VBT-085d

VBT-086b

VBT-087c

VBT-088d

VBT-089b

VBT-090b (three individual videos)

VBT-089c *The Happiness Patrol*
1998/05/11, Roadshow Entertainment Ltd, Aus
'PG' rating.
REF: B00266 OP: $24.95

VBT-089d *The Happiness Patrol*
1998/06, Roadshow Entertainment Ltd, NZ
'PG' rating.
REF: Z00266 OP: $29.95

VBT-090a The E-Space Trilogy
1997/11/03, BBC Worldwide Ltd, UK
Boxed set. Incorporates *Full Circle* [6230], 'U' certificate, *State of Decay* [6231] 'PG' certificate, and
Warriors' Gate [6232] 'PG' certificate. All photo-montage covers. Individual tapes in plastic cases.
REF: BBCV 6229 OP: £34.99

VBT-090b The E-Space Trilogy
1997, CBS/FOX, USA
REF: 7007/7008/7009 OP: $59.99

VBT-090c The E-Space Trilogy
1998/07/13, Roadshow Entertainment Ltd, Aus
'PG' rating. Released on three videos in a boxed set.
REF: B00293 OP: $69.95

VBT-090d The E-Space Trilogy
1998/08, Roadshow Entertainment Ltd, NZ
'PG' rating. Released on three videos in a boxed set.
Deleted 1999.
REF: Z00293 OP: $69.95

VBT-091a *Timelash*
1998/01/05, BBC Worldwide Ltd, UK
Photo-montage cover. 'U' certificate. TVM logo.
REF: BBCV 6329 OP: £11.99

VBT-091b *Timelash*
1998/03/31, CBS/FOX, USA
REF: 2781 OP: $19.99

VBT-091c *Timelash*
1998/09/14, Roadshow Entertainment Ltd, Aus
'PG' certificate. Apparently contains edited four-part
version broadcast by the ABC.
REF: B00280 OP: $24.95

VBT-091d *Timelash*
1998/09, Roadshow Entertainment Ltd, NZ
'PG' rating.
REF: Z00280 OP: $29.95

VBT-092a *Battlefield*
1998/03/02, BBC Worldwide Ltd, UK
Photo-montage cover. 'U' certificate. TVM logo.
Extended version with around 3 minutes of material
added.
REF: BBCV 6330 OP: £11.99

VBT-092b *Battlefield*
1998/03/31, CBS/FOX, USA
REF: 2775 OP: $19.99

VBT-092c *Battlefield*
1998/10/12, Roadshow Entertainment Ltd, Aus
'PG' rating.
REF: B00281 OP: $24.95

VBT-092d *Battlefield*
1998/10, Roadshow Entertainment Ltd, NZ
'PG' rating.
REF: Z00281 OP: $34.95

VBT-093a *The Mind of Evil*
1998/05/04, BBC Worldwide Ltd, UK
Double tape. Photo-montage cover. 'U' certificate.
TVM logo. Story in black and white. Existing colour
footage from episode 6 included.
REF: BBCV 6361 OP: £16.99

VBT-093b *The Mind of Evil*
1999/01/05, CBS/FOX, USA
REF: 0132 OP: $29.99

VBT-093c *The Mind of Evil*
1999/03/08 , Roadshow Entertainment Ltd, AUS
'PG' rating. Released on one tape rather than two.
REF: B00319 OP: $24.95

VBT-093d *The Mind of Evil*
1999/03, Roadshow Entertainment Ltd, NZ
'PG' rating.
REF: Z00319 OP: $39.95

VBT-094a *Horror of Fang Rock*
1998/07/06, BBC Worldwide Ltd, UK
Photo-montage cover. 'U' certificate. TVM logo.
REF: BBCV 6536 OP: £11.99

VBT-094b *Horror of Fang Rock*
1998/11/09, Roadshow Entertainment Ltd, Aus
'G' rating.
REF. B00311 OP: $24.95

VBT-091b

VBT-092b

VBT-093b

VBT-094d

VBT-095b

VBT-096d

VBT-094c *Horror of Fang Rock*
1998/11, Roadshow Entertainment Ltd, NZ
'G' rating.
REF: Z00311 OP: $29.95

VBT-094d *Horror of Fang Rock*
1999/03/02, CBS/FOX, USA
REF: 0129 OP: $19.99

VBT-095a *Planet of Fire*
1998/09/07, BBC Worldwide Ltd, UK
Photo-montage cover. 'PG' certificate. TVM logo.
REF: BBCV 6567 OP: £11.99

VBT-095b *Planet of Fire*
1998/11/03, CBS/FOX, USA
REF: 0133 OP: $19.99

VBT-095c *Planet of Fire*
1999/01/11, Roadshow Entertainment Ltd, Aus
'PG' rating.
REF: B00314 OP: $24.95

VBT-095d *Planet of Fire*
1999/01, Roadshow Entertainment Ltd, NZ
'PG' rating.
REF: Z00314 OP: $39.95

VBT-096a *The Ark*
1998/10/05, BBC Worldwide Ltd, UK
Photo-montage cover. 'PG' certificate. TVM logo.
REF: BBCV 6609 OP: £11.99

VBT-096b *The Ark*
1999/02/08, Roadshow Entertainment Ltd, AUS
'PG' rating.
REF: B00316 OP: $24.95

VBT-096c *The Ark*
1999/02, Roadshow Entertainment Ltd, NZ
'PG' rating.
REF: Z00316 OP: $39.95

VBT-096d *The Ark*
1999/03/02, CBS/FOX, USA
REF: 0157 OP: $19.99

VBT-097a The Ice Warriors Collection
1998/11/09, BBC Worldwide Ltd, UK
Special boxed set: 2 videos. Booklet by Paul Simpson.
Audio CD of the soundtrack to episodes 2 and 3.
Incorporates 6755 & 6766. Photo-montage covers to
card boxes. Includes a piece with Frazer Hines and
Deborah Watling at the start and a short section of

stills and narration by Frazer Hines to cover the missing episodes. Second video is *The Missing Years*, a documentary about 'missing' *Doctor Who* stories. Deleted 2000/02/25.
REF: BBCV 6387 OP: £24.99

VBT-097b *The Ice Warriors/The Missing Years*
1998/12/14, Roadshow Entertainment Ltd, AUS
'PG' rating. Released on one tape rather than two, and in a sturdy plastic case larger than those of normal releases, as it had to accommodate the tape, the CD and the book. These last two were apparently imported from BBC Worldwide for inclusion in the pack. Indeed, they feature the new logo rather than the diamond one as featured on the outer packaging. Also, only around 2000 units were sent. Cover incorrectly claims the PG rating is due to 'low level coarse language', but is actually due to 'low level violence', as is the usual case.
REF: B00312 OP: $39.95

VBT-097c *The Ice Warriors/The Missing Years*
1998/12, Roadshow Entertainment Ltd, NZ
'PG' rating. Deleted January 1999.
REF: Z00312 OP: $34.95

VBT-097d *The Ice Warriors*
1999/09/07, CBS/FOX, USA
Packaged in over-sized clamshell case with 'Collector's Edition' banner across top. Featured booklet and audio CD of episodes 2&3. Omits *The Missing Years* tape.
REF: 14722 OP: $34.99

VBT-098a *Nightmare of Eden*
1998/12/28, BBC Worldwide Ltd, UK
Photo-montage cover. 'PG' certificate. TVM logo.
REF: BBCV 6610 OP: £11.99

VBT-098b *Nightmare of Eden*
1999/03/08, Roadshow Entertainment Ltd, AUS
'PG' rating.
REF: B00322 OP: $24.95

VBT-098c *Nightmare of Eden*
1999/04, Roadshow Entertainment Ltd, NZ
'G' rating.
REF: Z00322 OP: $29.95

VBT-098d *Nightmare of Eden*
1999/05/04, CBS/FOX, USA
REF: 0195 OP: $19.99

VBT-097a (box set)

VBT-097a (individual videos)

VBT-098d

VBT-099c

VBT-100a

VBT-101a

VBT-102a

VBT-099a *The Keys of Marinus*
1999/03/01, BBC Worldwide Ltd, UK
Double Tape. Photo-montage cover. 'U' certificate.
TVM logo.
REF: BBCV 6671 OP: £16.99

VBT-099b *The Keys of Marinus*
1999/05, Roadshow Entertainment Ltd, NZ
'G' rating. Single tape.
REF: Z00324 OP: $39.95

VBT-099c *The Keys of Marinus*
1999/07/06, CBS/FOX, USA
REF: 14263 OP: $29.99

VBT-100a *The Face of Evil*
1999/05/03, BBC Worldwide Ltd, UK
Photo montage cover. 'PG' certificate. TVM logo.
Includes Louise Jameson (Leela) on *Swap Shop*, a BBC
Saturday morning children's programme.
REF: BBCV 6672 OP: £11.99

VBT-100b *The Face of Evil*
1999/06, Roadshow Entertainment Ltd, NZ
'PG' rating.
REF: Z00325 OP: $39.95

VBT-101a *The Crusade/The Space Museum*
1999/06/07, BBC Worldwide Ltd, UK
Special boxed set. Includes video of episodes 1 and 3 of
The Crusade and *The Space Museum*, 4 postcards and a
metal TARDIS key ring, plus a CD of the soundtrack of
episodes 2 and 4 of *The Crusade*. Photo montage cover.
'PG' certificate. TVM Logo. Video Number: BBCV 6888.
CD Number: BBC CRU CD. This release was prompted
by the discovery in late 1998 in New Zealand of the previously missing episode 1 of *The Crusade*. Includes linking
material by William Russell to cover the missing episodes.
REF: BBCV 6805 OP: £19.99

VBT-101b *The Crusade/The Space Museum*
1999/07, Roadshow Entertainment Ltd, NZ
'PG' rating. Deleted October 1999.
REF: Z00357 OP: $59.95

VBT-101c *The Crusade/The Space Museum*
1999, Roadshow Entertainment Ltd, AUS
In a flimsier cardboard box. No further information
available.

VBT-101d *The Crusade/The Space Museum*
2000, CBS/FOX, USA
Packaged in over-sized clamshell case.
OP: $34.99

VBT-102a *The Curse of Fatal Death*
1999/09/06, BBC Worldwide Ltd, UK
Photo montage cover. 'PG' certificate. TVM logo. Tape includes a behind the scenes documentary of the making of the *Children In Need* 1999 special, as well as three additional *Doctor Who* parodies from Lenny Henry, Victoria Wood and an untransmitted sketch by Dawn French and Jennifer Saunders.
REF: BBCV 6889 OP: £12.99

VBT-102b *The Curse of Fatal Death*
1999/10, Roadshow Entertainment Ltd, NZ
'G' rating.
REF: Z00362 OP: $29.95

VBT-103a Dalek Tin
1999/11/15, BBC Worldwide Ltd, UK
Metal tin featuring boxed tapes of *Revelation of the Daleks* (BBCV6927) and *Planet of the Daleks* (BBCV6828). The initial production run of tins was 20,000 units and these sold out almost immediately. A Jimi Hendrix song was removed from the *Revelation* soundtrack for this release. Episode 3 of *Planet* is in black and white.
REF: BBCV 6875 OP: £24.99 NM: £44

VBT-103b *Planet of the Daleks*
1999/12, Roadshow Entertainment Ltd, NZ
Story released individually.
REF: Z00382 OP: $39.95

VBT-103c *Planet of the Daleks*
1999, Roadshow Entertainment Ltd, AUS
Story released individually.

VBT-103d *Planet of the Daleks*
2001/09/11, Warner Home Video, US
Story released individually.
REF: E???? OP: $19.92

VBT-103e *Revelation of the Daleks*
1999/12, Roadshow Entertainment Ltd, NZ
Story released individually.
REF: Z00383 OP: $29.95

VBT-103f *Revelation of the Daleks*
1999/02/06, Roadshow Entertainment Ltd, AUS
Story released individually.
REF: E???? OP: $19.92

VBT-103g *Revelation of the Daleks*
2001/11/09, Warner Home Video, US
Story released individually.

VBT-104a *The Greatest Show in the Galaxy*
1999/09/02, CBS/FOX, USA
OP: $19.99

VBT-103a

VBT-103d

VBT-103g

VBT-104a

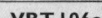
VBT-106a

VBT-105b

VBT-107a

VBT-106c

VBT-108a

VBT-104b *The Greatest Show in the Galaxy*
1999/09, Roadshow Entertainment Ltd, NZ
'PG' rating. UK release not until 2000/01/10.
REF: Z00346 OP: $29.95

VBT-104c *The Greatest Show in the Galaxy*
2000/01/03, BBC Worldwide Ltd, UK
Photo montage cover. 'PG' certificate. TVM logo.
REF: BBCV 6798 OP: £12.99

VBT-105a *The Invasion of Time*
2000/03/06, BBC Worldwide Ltd, UK
Photo montage cover. 'U' certificate. TVM logo.
REF: BBCV 6876 OP: £17.99

VBT-105b *The Invasion of Time*
2001/09/11, Warner Home Video, US
REF: E???? OP: $19.92

VBT-106a *The Edge of Destruction and Dr Who:
The Pilot Episode*
2000/05/01, BBC Worldwide Ltd, UK
Photo montage cover. 'PG' certificate. TVM logo.
Originally scheduled for release in March.
REF: BBCV 6877 OP: £12.99

VBT-106b *The Edge of Destruction and Dr Who:
The Pilot Episode*
2000/10, Warner Home Video, US
An early version of this tape, released in error. It contains non-restored and edited broadcast masters for
Inside the Spaceship and the final version of
100,000BC: An Unearthly Child rather than the pilot
version. There were two attempts to correct the
error before the correct version was released.
REF: E1497 OP: $19.92

VBT-106c *The Edge of Destruction and Dr Who:
The Pilot Episode*
2001/02, Warner Home Video, US
REF: E1578 OP: $19.92

VBT-107a *Time-Flight*
2000/07, BBC Worldwide Ltd, UK
Photo montage cover. 'U' certificate. TVM logo.
REF: BBCV 6878 OP: £12.99

VBT-108a Cyberman Boxed Set
2000/11, BBC Worldwide Ltd, UK
White tin box with an embossed photograph of a
Cyberman on it. Contains two videos: *Attack of the
Cybermen* (BBCV 7048) and *The Tenth Planet* (BBCV
6874). The latter is missing part 4, and so this has
been reconstructed on the video using photographs
from the story, plus a complete soundtrack. Videos
have photo montage covers. 'U' certificate. TVM logo.
REF: BBCV 7030 OP: £24.99

VBT-108b *Attack of the Cybermen*
2002/02/19, Warner Home Video, US
Story released individually.
REF: E1609 OP: $14.99

VBT-108c *The Tenth Planet*
2001/11/09, Warner Home Video, US
Story released individually.
REF: E??? OP: $14.99

VBT-109a *Delta and the Bannermen*
2001/03, BBC Worldwide Ltd, UK
Photo montage cover. 'PG' certificate. TVM logo.
REF: BBCV 7131 OP: £12.99

VBT-108b   VBT-108c

VBT-109b *Delta and the Bannermen*
2002/06/04, Warner Home Video, US
Photo montage cover. 'PG' certificate. TVM logo.
REF: E1649 OP: $14.99

VBT-110a *The Sun Makers*
2001/07/09, BBC Worldwide Ltd, UK
Photo montage cover. 'U' certificate. TVM logo.
REF: BBCV 7133 OP: £12.99

VBT-110b *The Sun Makers*
2001/09/11, BBC Worldwide Ltd, AUS/NZ
REF: BBCV 7133

VBT-110c *The Sun Makers*
2002/02/19, Warner Home Video, US
REF: E1607 OP: $14.99

VBT-111a *Four to Doomsday*
2001/09/03, BBC Worldwide Ltd, UK
Photo montage cover. 'U' certificate. TVM logo.
REF: BBCV 7134 OP: £12.99

VBT-109a   VBT-110a

VBT-111b *Four to Doomsday*
2002/06/04, Warner Home Video, US
Photo montage cover. 'U' certificate. TVM logo.
REF: E1648 OP: $14.99

VBT-112 Davros Boxed Set
2001/09/17, BBC Worldwide Ltd, UK
Card box containing re-issues of: *Genesis of the Daleks*
(BBCV 7251 – a remastered version different from the
original release); *Destiny of the Daleks* (BBCV 7252);
Resurrection of the Daleks (BBCV 7253); *Revelation of the
Daleks* (BBCV 7254); *Remembrance of the Daleks* (BBCV
7255). Videos have photo montage covers and the TVM
logo. All 'PG' rating except *Destiny of the Daleks* which is
'U'. Boxed set only available from W H Smith's stores in
the UK, and limited to 10,000 units.
REF: BBCV 7241 OP: £34.99

VBT-111a

VBT-112

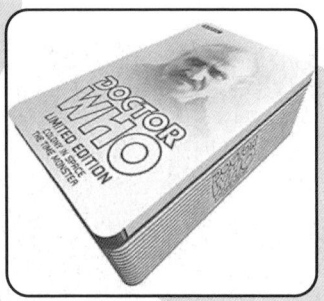

VBT-113

VBT-113 Master Boxed Set
2001/11/05, BBC Worldwide Ltd, UK
White tin box with an embossed logo and a photo-
graph of the Delgado Master. Contains two videos:
Colony In Space (BBCV 7176) and *The Time Monster*
(BBCV 7177). Videos have photo montage covers and
the TVM logo. 'PG' certificate.
REF: BBCV 7175 OP: £24.99

VBT-114a *Planet of Giants*
2002/01/07, BBC Worldwide Ltd, UK
Photo montage cover. 'U' certificate. TVM logo.
REF: BBCV 7263 OP: £12.99

VBT-115a *Underworld*
2002/03/04, BBC Worldwide Ltd, UK
Photo montage cover. 'PG' certificate. TVM logo.
REF: BBCV 7264 OP: £12.99

VBT-116a *The Ambassadors of Death*
2002/05/06, BBC Worldwide Ltd, UK
Photo montage cover. 'U' certificate. TVM logo.
Episodes 1 and 5 are in colour, while the other five
episodes are presented in a mixture of colour and
black and white. Also includes, in black and white, the
original trailer for the story.
REF: BBCV 7265 OP: £16.99

VBT-117a *The Creature from the Pit*
2002/07/15, BBC Worldwide Ltd, UK
Photo montage cover. 'PG' certificate. TVM logo.
REF: BBCV 7266 OP: £12.99

VBT-118a *The Invisible Enemy*
2002/09/02, BBC Worldwide Ltd, UK
Photo montage cover. 'U' certificate. TVM logo.
REF: BBCV 7267 OP: £12.99

VBT-114a

VBT-115a

VBT-116a

VBT-117a

VBT-118a

VBT-119

VBT-120

VBT-119 The Time Lord Collection
2002/10, BBC Worldwide Ltd, UK
Card boxed set exclusive to W H Smith stores in the
UK. Numbered and limited to 8000 sets. Contains *The
War Games* (BBCV 7363); *The Three Doctors* (BBCV
7364) and *The Deadly Assassin* (BBCV 7365). *The War
Games* was digitally remastered for this release. Videos
have photo montage covers and the TVM logo. All 'U'
rating except *The Deadly Assassin* which is 'PG'. The
'freeze frame' ending to Episode 3 of *The Deadly
Assassin* was fully restored for this release.
REF: BBCV 7346 OP: £27.99

VBT-120 The First Doctor Box Set
2002/11/04, BBC Worldwide Ltd, UK
Card boxed set. Contains *The Time Meddler* (BBCV 7275);
The Sensorites (BBCV 7276) and *The Gunfighters* (BBCV
7277). Videos have photo montage covers and the TVM
logo. All 'U' rating except *The Gunfighters* which is 'PG'.
REF: BBCV 7268 OP: £29.99

VDF-001

VDF-002a

VIDEO, DVD FILMS

VDF-001 *Doctor Who and the Daleks*
2001, Anchor Bay, USA
REF: DV11577 OP: $19.99

VDF-002a *Daleks Invasion Earth 2150 A.D.*
2001, Anchor Bay, USA
REF: DV11578 OP: $19.99

**VDF-002b *Les Daleks envahissent la Terre
(Daleks Invasion Earth 2150 A.D.)***
2001/11/14, Canal+ Video, France
OP: 20,99 Euros (some sources say 27,75)

VDF-002b

VDF-003a

VDF-003b

VDF-003c

VDI-001

VDI-002

VDF-003a *The Dr. Who Collection*
2001, Anchor Bay, USA
Card box including *Doctor Who and the Daleks, Daleks Invasion Earth 2150 A.D.* and *Dalekmania* DVDs cased in individual plastic DVD cases.
REF: DVI1958 OP: $40.00

VDF-003b *Doctor Who and the Daleks/Daleks Invasion Earth 2150 AD*
2001/05/09, Studio Canal, AUS
Photographic cover. 'PG' rating. Australia-only release on DVD of the two Dalek films. Also includes the *Dalekmania* documentary, photograph galleries from each of the films and the original theatrical trailers.
REF: 0782342 OP: $39.95

VDF-003c *The Daleks*
2002, Studio Canal, UK
Two DVD set containing *Dr. Who and the Daleks* and *Daleks Invasion Earth 2150 AD* and the *Dalekmania* documentary. *Dr Who and the Daleks* includes commentary by Jennie Linden and Roberta Tovey, theatrical trailer and DVD ROM feature: original theatrical Campaign Brochure. *Daleks Invasion Earth 2150AD* includes theatrical trailer and DVD ROM feature. The disk for the first film had a damaged audio track; initial replacement disks available from Warner (the distributors) were also faulty, but a second replacement disk was fine.
REF: ZI 38470 OP: £17.99

VIDEO, DVD INTERVIEWS

VDI-001 *The Doctors: 30 Years of Time Travel and Beyond*
2002, Waterfall Home Entertainment, UK
Straight re-issue?
REF: WHE 1066 OP: £8.99

VDI-002 *Big Finish Talks Back: Paul McGann – A conversation with the Eighth Doctor*
2002/09/07, Big Finish Productions, UK
DVD interview with Paul McGann and India Fisher recorded December 2001. DVD is region 0. Running time 90 minutes approx.
REF: BFPDVDTB02 ISBN 1-903654-91-2
OP: £15.99

VIDEO, DVD PROMOS

VDP-001 Promotional Disk
2001/10, BBC Worldwide Ltd, UK
Video-CD given free with issue 19 of *Starlog* magazine in the UK. Contains clips and features from the BBC's range of *Doctor Who* on DVD.
REF: BBFC VFC28749 OP: Free

VIDEO, DVD RELEASES

VDV-001a *The Five Doctors*
1999/11, BBC Worldwide, UK
DVD of the Special Edition release of *The Five Doctors*. Separate music track. No other extras. Regions 2 & 4.
REF: BBCDVD 1006 OP: £19.99

VDV-001b *The Five Doctors*
2001/09/11, Warner Home Video, USA
This DVD release differs from the UK release. It has an additional commentary track by Peter Davison and Terrance Dicks and 33 minutes of soundtrack music included. There are also 'Who's Who' biographies included.
REF: E1596 OP: $19.99

VDV-002a *Doctor Who The Motion Picture*
1996 c., Fox Video, Japan
Hong Kong DVD of the 1996 TV Movie. Cantonese soundtrack option.
NM: £220

VDV-002b *The Movie*
2001/08/13, BBC Worldwide Ltd, UK
Extras on the DVD: Commentary by Geoffrey Sax; Onscreen Production notes; photo gallery; music feature; behind the scenes footage; interview with Philip Segal. 12 certificate. Opening caption noting the movie is "based on" the original BBC series was removed from this release.
REF: BBCDVD 1043 OP: £19.99

VDV-003a *The Robots of Death*
2000/11/13, BBC Worldwide Ltd, UK
Extras on the DVD: Writer's commentary on the recording of the episode; 10 minutes of shots and footage of test runs on the models used in the story; image stills gallery; production notes; production team's floor plan.
REF: BBCDVD 1012 OP: £19.99

VDV-003b *The Robots of Death*
2001/09/11, Warner Home Video, USA
Extras as UK version. There is an additional feature on this edition, a 20 minute featurette of the intros and end of episode teasers narrated by Howard daSilva from the 1978 syndication of *Doctor Who* in America. There are also 'Who's Who' biographies included.
REF: E1120 OP: $24.95

VDV-001a   VDV-001b

VDV-002a

VDV-002b

VDV-003a   VDV-003b

VDV-004a   **VDV-004b**

VDV-005a   **VDV-005b**

VDV-006a   **VDV-006b**

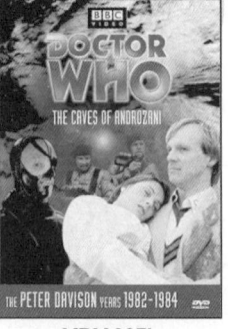

VDV-007a   **VDV-007b**

VDV-004a *Spearhead from Space*
2001/01, BBC Worldwide Ltd, UK
Extras on the DVD: Commentary by Nicholas Courtney
and Caroline John, UNIT recruitment film, Onscreen production notes, Trailers; photo gallery. A Fleetwood Mac
song was removed from the soundtrack for this release.
REF: BBCDVD 1033   OP: £19.99

VDV-004b *Spearhead from Space*
2001/09/11, Warner Home Video, USA
Extras on the DVD: Commentary by Nicholas
Courtney and Caroline John, UNIT recruitment film,
Onscreen production notes, Trailers; photo gallery.
REF: E1163   OP: $24.95

VDV-005a *Remembrance of the Daleks*
2001/02, BBC Worldwide Ltd, UK
Extras on the DVD: Deleted scenes and outtakes;
Multi-angle scenes; Music only option; BBC1 trailers;
Photo gallery; on screen production notes. A Beatles
song was removed from the soundtrack for this
release. Certain effects shots were inadvertently
included in incomplete form.
REF: BBCDVD 1040   OP: £19.99

VDV-005b *Remembrance of the Daleks*
2002/04, Warner Home Video, USA
Extras as UK version. This version restores the effects
shots missed from the UK release. There are also
'Who's Who' biographies included.
REF: E1608   OP: $24.95

VDV-006a *The Caves of Androzani*
2001/06, BBC Worldwide Ltd, UK
Extras on the DVD: Commentary by Peter Davison,
Nicola Bryant and Graeme Harper, 'Regeneration'
documentary, 'Making Sharaz Jek' documentary,
Photograph gallery, On-screen production notes,
story trailer and news features, music only feature.
REF: BBCDVD 1042   OP: £19.99

VDV-006b *The Caves of Androzani*
2002/04, Warner Home Video, USA
Extras as UK version. There are also 'Who's Who'
biographies included.
REF: E1183   OP: $24.95

VDV-007a *Vengeance on Varos*
2001/10/01, BBC Worldwide Ltd, UK
Extras on the DVD: Commentary by Colin Baker,
Nicola Bryant and Nabil Shaban; Onscreen Production
notes; photo gallery; music feature; behind the scenes
featurette. PG certificate.
REF: BBCDVD 1044   OP: £19.99

VDV-007b *Vengeance on Varos*
2002/???, Warner Home Video, USA
Extras as UK version. There are also 'Who's Who'
biographies included.
REF: E1718 OP: $24.95

VDV-008a *The Tomb of the Cybermen*
2002/01/14, BBC Worldwide Ltd, UK
Extras on the DVD: Commentary by Frazer Hines and
Deborah Watling; Introduction by Morris Barry; Behind
the scenes at BBC Visual Effects; 'Tombwatch'
Documentary; Unused title sequence tests and 8mm Cine
footage; Photo gallery and on-screen production notes.
REF: BBCDVD 1032 OP: £19.99

VDV-008a   VDV-008b

VDV-008b *The Tomb of the Cybermen*
2002/08/06, Warner Home Video, USA
Extras as UK version. There are also 'Who's Who'
biographies included.
REF: E1181 OP: $24.95

VDV-009a *The Ark In Space*
2002/04/08, BBC Worldwide Ltd, UK
Extras on DVD: Commentary by Tom Baker, Elisabeth
Sladen and Philip Hinchcliffe; CGI model footage of
the Ark; Ark schematic; Original BBC1 Trailer and
News report; Interview with Roger Murray Leach;
Unused effects footage; Photo gallery and on-screen
production notes.
REF: BBCDVD 1097 OP: £19.99

VDV-009a   VDV-009b

VDV-009b *The Ark in Space*
2002/08/06, Warner Home Video, USA
Extras as UK version. The 'easter eggs' are the same,
but hidden in different places on the disk. There is an
additional feature on this edition, a 15 minute featurette of the intros and end of episode teasers narrated by Howard daSilva from the 1978 syndication of
Doctor Who in America. There are also 'Who's Who'
biographies included.
REF: E1162 OP: $24.95

VDV-010a

VDV-010a *Carnival of Monsters*
2002/07/15, BBC Worldwide Ltd, UK
Extras on DVD: Commentary by Katy Manning and Barry
Letts; Extended and deleted scenes; Behind the scenes
footage; Model sequences; Using CSO documentary;
Alternative theme musis; Trailer for *The Five Faces of Doctor
Who*; Alternate episode 4 ending; Photo gallery and pro-
duction subtitles; TARDISCam sequence.
REF: BBCDVD 1098 OP: £19.99

VDV-011a *The Key to Time*
2002/10/01, Warner Home Video, USA
Card box containing DVDs for Season 16: *The Ribos
Operation* (E1336 Extras: Commentary by Tom Baker and

VDV-011a

VDV-011a (individual DVD cases)

Mary Tamm; onscreen production notes; Photo Gallery), *The Pirate Planet* (E1338 Extras: Commentary by Bruce Purchase and Pennant Roberts; raw location film footage; onscreen production notes; Photo gallery), *The Stones of Blood* (E1314 Extras: Commentary by Mary Tamm and Darrol Blake; onscreen production notes; photo gallery), *The Androids of Tara* (E1310 Extras: Commentary by Tom Baker, Mary Tamm and Michael Hayes; onscreen production notes; Photo Gallery), *The Power of Kroll* (E1337 Extras: Commentary by Tom Baker and John Leeson; onscreen production notes; Photo Gallery), *The Armageddon Factor* (E1340 Extras: Commentary by Mary Tamm, John Woodvine and Michael Hayes; onscreen production notes; Photo Gallery). The individual DVDs are also available separately at $24.95 each. There are also 'Who's Who' biographies included on each disk.
REF: E1692 OP: $124.95

VDV-012a *The Aztecs*
2002/10/23, BBC Worldwide Ltd, UK
Delayed from original release date of 7th October.
Extras on DVD: Commentary by Verity Lambert OBE, William Russell and Carole Ann Ford; Arabic soundtrack for episode 4; Interviews with John Ringham, Walter Randall and Ian Cullen; Interview with Designer Barry Newbery; The story of Cortez and Montezuma; Randomised introduction messages; Restoration featurette; TARDIS Cam; Photo Gallery and on-screen production notes.
REF: BBCDVD 1098 OP: £19.99

VDV-013a *Resurrection of the Daleks*
2002/11/18, BBC Worldwide Ltd, UK
DVD in a standard case but additionally packaged in a black plastic sleeve with the *Doctor Who* logo and TARDIS 'roundels' imprinted on. Presents a four-part version of the story rather than the two-part version originally transmitted.
REF: BBCDVD 1100 OP: £19.99

VDV-012a   VDV-013a   VFI-002b   VFI-002c

VIDEO, FILMS

THESE are video releases of the two *Doctor Who* cinema films. A large number of items were available to promote the Dalek films in the sixties. Among the items available to cinemas for the second film were linen banners which came in three sizes (10' x 3' [£3 3/ 6d]; 12'6" x 3' [£3 11/ 6d] and 15' x 3' [£3 17/ 6d]); Movie stills [8/ 6d for 8]; Quad posters (30" x 40" [3/ 6d each); Overprinted bags (30/- per 1000); paper serviettes (42/- per 1000); milk bottle collars (30/- per 1000); and photo blow-ups and star portrait posters. These items could be picked up from cinemas by enterprising fans but were not generally available to the public to buy.

VFI-002d

VFI-002g

VFI-001 *Daleks' Invasion Earth 2150 AD* **Super 8mm Home Movie**
1977, Walton Sound and Film Services, UK
REF: F741
OP: £133.04 (eight reels colour/sound) NM: £110

VFI-002a *Dr. Who and the Daleks*
1982, Thorn EMI, UK
Rating: 'U'. Deleted.
REF: TVC 90 0595 2 (VHS) TXC 90 0595 4 (Beta)
OP: £39.95 (Beta, VHS)

VFI-002b *Dr. Who and the Daleks*
1980s, Thorn EMI/HBO, USA
REF: TVB 3171 NM: $77

VFI-002c *Dr. Who and the Daleks*
No release date shown, King Video/Tohokushinsha Film Co., Japan
Title translates as *Invasion Earth War 2150*.
REF: K48V-15099 OP: Y14,800

VFI-002d *Dr. Who and the Daleks*
1988/06, Warner Home Video, UK
Deleted.
REF: PES 38024 OP: £9.99

VFI-002e *Dr. Who and the Daleks*
1989, Goodtimes Home Video, USA
REF: 9093 ISBN 1-55510-281-6 OP: $9.95

VFI-002f *Dr. Who and the Daleks*
1994, Lumiere/Republic, USA
REF: ISBN 0-7820-0291-9 0834 OP: $9.99

VFI-003

VFI-004c

VFI-002g *Dr. Who & the Daleks*
1996/02/26, Beyond Vision/Warner, UK
Widescreen Release.
REF: S038354 OP: £12.99

VFI-003 *Daleks' Invasion Earth 2150 AD* **Super 8mm Home Movie (Part 1)**
1977, Walton Sound and Film Services, UK
REF: A850
OP: £16.33 (one reel colour/sound) £5.49 (one reel b&w/silent) NM: £15-£25

VFI-004a *Daleks Invasion Earth 2150 A.D.*
1982, Thorn EMI, UK
Rating: 'U'. Deleted.
REF: TVC 90 0688 2 (VHS) TXC 90 0688 4 (Beta)
OP: £39.95 (Beta, VHS)

VFI-004b *Daleks Invasion Earth 2150 A.D.*
Thorn EMI/HBO, USA
OP: $69.95

VFI-004d   VFI-004f

VFI-006

VFI-009

VFI-004c *Daleks Invasion Earth 2150 A.D.*
No release date shown, King Video/Tohokushinsha
Film Co., Japan
Title translates as *Invasion Earth War 2150*.
REF: K48V-11559   OP: Y14,800

VFI-004d *Daleks Invasion Earth 2150 A.D.*
1988/06, Warner Home Video, UK
Deleted.
REF: PES 38025   OP: £9.99

VFI-004e *Dr. Who: Daleks Invasion Earth 2150 A.D.*
1994, Lumiere/Republic, USA
REF: ISBN 0-7820-0290-0 0833   OP: $9.99

VFI-004f *Daleks – Invasion Earth 2150 A.D.*
1996/05/13, Beyond Vision/Warner, UK
Widescreen Release. Free postcard at W. H. Smiths.
REF: S038353   OP: £12.99

VFI-005 *Daleks' Invasion Earth 2150 AD* **Super
8mm Home Movie (Part 2)**
1977, Walton Sound and Film Services, UK
REF: A851
OP: £16.33 (one reel colour/sound) £5.49 (one reel
b&w/silent)   NM: £15-£25

VFI-006 *Movie Double Feature: Dr. Who and the
Daleks; Daleks Invasion Earth 2150 A.D.*
1993, Warner Home Video, UK
Rating: 'U'.
REF: PES 38328   OP: £12.99

VFI-007 *Daleks' Invasion Earth 2150 AD* **Super
8mm Home Movie (widescreen)**
1977, Walton Sound and Film Services, UK
OP: £133.04 (eight reels colour/sound)   NM: £110

VFI-008 *Dr Who and the Daleks* **Super 8mm
Home Movie**
1977, Walton Sound and Film Services, UK
REF: F740
OP: £133.04 (eight reels colour/sound)   NM: £110

VFI-009 *Dr Who and the Daleks* **Super 8mm
Home Movie (Part 1)**
1977, Walton Sound and Film Services, UK
REF: A848
OP: £16.33 (one reel colour/sound) £5.49 (one reel
b&w/silent)   NM: £15-£25

VFI-010 *Dr Who and the Daleks* **Super 8mm
Home Movie (Part 2)**
1977, Walton Sound and Film Services, UK

REF: A849
OP: £16.33 (one reel colour/sound) £5.49 (one reel b&w/silent) NM: £15-£25

VFI-011 *Daleks Invasion Earth* **Super 8mm trailer**
UK
The film trailer.
NM: £15

VIDEO, INDEPENDENT DRAMAS

IN 1993, Bill Baggs, aided by money and resources from the BBC's own film club, made an independent video drama starring Colin Baker as 'The Stranger' and Nicola Bryant as 'Miss Brown'. The intention was that 'The Stranger' was the Doctor and 'Miss Brown' was Peri and the renaming of the characters was to avoid any BBC copyright issues. Despite this, the series of video dramas which followed actually had no connection whatsoever with *Doctor Who*, its characters or settings aside from the casting of actors known for their *Doctor Who* work.

These non-connected dramas were released as follows: *Summoned by Shadows* (1991), *More than a Messiah* (1992), *In Memory Alone* (1993), *The Airzone Solution* (1993), *The Terror Game* (1994), *Breach of the Peace* (1994), *Eye of the Beholder* (1995)

With *The Terror Game*, the true origins of 'The Stranger' start to be revealed and he is not the Doctor at all.

With the 'Stranger' concept being part-owned by the series co-funder, Metro Music International, BBV opted to diversify into other areas rather than continue with 'The Stranger' and so developed a second series, this time featuring the character of Liz Shaw from *Doctor Who*. The first of these true spin-offs was called *The Zero Imperative* (1994).

VID-001a *War Time*
1988/08/10, Reeltime Pictures, UK
The first ever independent *Doctor Who* drama video. Directed by Keith Barnfather. Written by Andrew Lane and Helen Stirling. Starring John Levene as Sergeant Benton and featuring Michael Wisher as his father.
REF: RTP0026 OP: £10.00

VID-001b *War Time*
1989, DHI Home Video, USA
Includes 'Panopticon VII' video.
OP: $19.95

VID-001c *War Time*
1997, Reeltime Pictures, UK
Sell-through edition. Includes 'making of' documentary.
REF: RTP0166 OP: £11.99

VID-002a *Downtime*
1995/09/02, Reeltime Pictures, UK
Written by Marc Platt. Directed by Christopher Barry. Features Nicholas Courtney (the Brigadier), Elisabeth Sladen (Sarah Jane Smith), Deborah Watling (Victoria Waterfield), and Jack Watling (Professor Waterfield). Also features John Leeson. A battle against the Great Intelligence and its robot Yeti. 1000 copies featured a signature sheet signed by the cast and crew. See also BVM-018.
REF: RTP0087 OP: £11.99

VID-002b *Downtime*
1996, S&J Productions, USA

VID-002c *Downtime*
1999, CBS Fox, USA

VID-001a

VID-001c

VID-002a

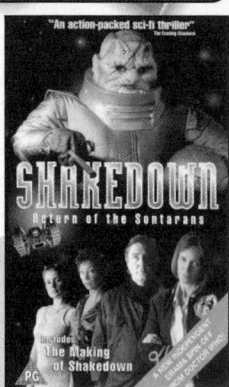

VID-003b   **VID-004b**

VID-005b   **VID-006**

VID-007   **VID-008a**

VID-003a   *The Zero Imperative*
1994, BBV, UK
Written by Mark Gatiss. Directed by Bill Baggs.
Features Caroline John (Liz Shaw), also Louise
Jameson, Jon Pertwee, Peter Davison, Colin Baker,
Sylvester McCoy and Sophie Aldred.
REF: BBV8 OP: £15.99 NM: £8.80

VID-003b   *P.R.O.B.E.: The Zero Imperative*
1994, S&J Video, USA
Another version with 'Special Limited Visions '94
Edition' on was also released.
REF: SJ006

VID-003c   *P.R.O.B.E.: The Zero Imperative*
1998/04/07, Reeltime Pictures, UK
REF: RTP0188 OP: £11.99

VID-004a   *Shakedown: Return of the Sontarans*
1994/11, Dreamwatch Media, UK
Written by Terrance Dicks. Directed by Kevin Davies.
Features the Sontarans and Rutans. A separate documentary 'making of' tape was also available at £11.99
in 1995. Also see BVN-045.
OP: £16.99

VID-004b   *Shakedown: Return of the Sontarans*
1996, Reeltime Pictures, UK
Includes 'making of' documentary.
REF: RTP0145 OP: £11.99

VID-005a   *The Devil of Winterbourne*
1995/08, BBV, UK
Two tapes. Written by Mark Gatiss. Directed by Bill
Baggs. Features Caroline John (Liz Shaw), also Louise
Jameson and Peter Davison.
REF: BBV11 OP: £15.99 each tape

VID-005b   *The Devil of Winterbourne*
1995, S&J Video, USA
Two tapes. Blank card boxes; final printed covers sup-
posedly offered by mail but never sent.
REF: SJ006 OP: $15

VID-005c   *P.R.O.B.E.: The Devil of Winterborne*
1996, Reeltime Pictures, UK
REF: RTP0146 OP: £11.99

VID-006   *P.R.O.B.E.: Unnatural Selection*
1996, Reeltime Pictures, UK
Written by Mark Gatiss. Directed by Bill Baggs. Features
Caroline John (Liz Shaw), also Louise Jameson. The second two PROBE tapes were not initially issued by BBV
and were co-funded by Reeltime Pictures.
REF: RTP0155 OP: £11.99

VID-007 *P.R.O.B.E.: Ghosts of Winterbourne*
1996, Reeltime Pictures, UK
Written by Mark Gatiss. Directed by Bill Baggs.
Features Caroline John (Liz Shaw), also Louise
Jameson and Peter Davison.
REF: RTP0157 OP: £11.99

VID-008a *Auton*
1997, BBV, UK
Written and directed by Nicholas Briggs.
REF: BBV16 OP: £15.00

VID-008b *Auton*
1998/03/02, Reeltime Pictures, UK
Includes 'making of' documentary.
REF: RTP0165 OP: £11.99

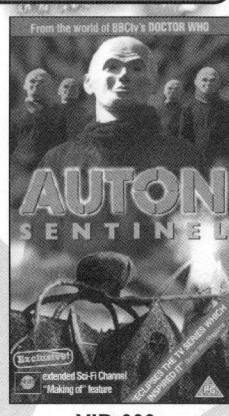

VID-008b

VID-009a

VID-009a *Auton 2: Sentinel*
1998, BBV, UK
Written and directed by Nicholas Briggs.
REF: BBV17 OP: £14.99

VID-009b *Auton: Sentinel*
1999, Reeltime Pictures, UK
Includes extended documentary.
REF: RTP0191 OP: £11.99

VID-010 *Mindgame*
1998/09/14, Reeltime Pictures, UK
Written by Terrance Dicks. Directed by Keith
Barnfather. Features a Draconian and a Sontaran.
Starring Sophie Aldred as an Ace-like human female. A
limited number featured a signature sheet signed by
the cast and crew.
REF: RTP0200 OP: £11.99

VID-009b

VID-010

VID-011 *Mindgame Trilogy*
1999, Reeltime Pictures, UK
Written by Terrance Dicks, Miles Richardson and
Roger Stevens. Directed by Keith Barnfather. Sequel
to *Mindgame*. Features a Draconian and a Sontaran.
Starring Sophie Aldred as an Ace-like human female. A
limited number featured a signature sheet signed by
the cast and crew.
REF: RTP0206 OP: £11.99

VID-012a *Auton 3*
1999/11, BBV, UK
Written by Arthur Wallace (Nicholas Briggs). Directed
by Bill Baggs. Third instalment in the Auton trilogy.
REF: BBV18 OP: £16.99

VID-012b *Auton: Awakening*
2000/04, Reeltime Pictures, UK
REF: RTP0224 OP: £11.99

VID-011

VID-012a

VLD-001   **VLD-002**

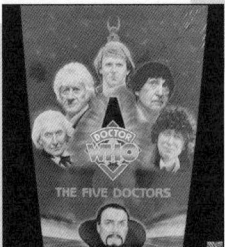

VLD-003b   **VLD-004b**

VLD-005   **VLD-006**

VLD-007

VIDEO, LASERDISCS

VLD-001 Revenge of the Cybermen
1983, BBC Video, UK
Photo collage cover by Sid Sutton.
REF: BBCL 2003 OP: £9.99 NM: £49.50

VLD-002 The Brain of Morbius
1984, BBC Video, UK
Photo cover.
REF: BBCL 2012 OP: £9.99 NM: £44

VLD-003a The Five Doctors
1991, UK
OP: £39.99 NM: £44

VLD-003b The Five Doctors
1991, CBS Fox Video, USA
89 minutes. Colour. Not rated. Cover features diamond logo and illustration taken from Andrew
Skilleter's *Radio Times* cover artwork. Back cover features diamond logo and four photos from the story.
REF: 3717-80 OP: £39.99 NM: £44

VLD-004a The Day of the Daleks
1992, CBS Fox Video, USA
Cover and content as on first BBC Video release.
OP: $34.98 NM: £66

VLD-004b Day of the Daleks
1997/04/14, Encore Entertainment, UK
Cover by Pete Wallbank. Delayed from 1997/02/19.
REF: EE1202 OP: £21.99 NM: £44

VLD-005 The Ark In Space
1996, Encore Entertainment, UK
Cover by Pete Wallbank.
REF: EE1158 OP: £23.99 NM: £44

VLD-006 Terror of the Zygons
1998/02/29, Encore Entertainment, UK
Cover by Pete Wallbank. A subsequent release of
Spearhead from Space was not done.
REF: EE1203 OP: £14.99 NM: £44

VLD-007 Doctor Who
1996 c., Kuraray, China
Photographic cover. Hong-Kong rental laserdisc of the
TV Movie. Features original soundtrack with Japanese
subtitles.
NM: £55

VIDEO, MYTHMAKERS

KEITH Barnfather had worked for the BBC and helped set up Channel 4 before leaving to start Reeltime Pictures, an independent video production company which specialised in corporate videos. As a sideline, and because Barnfather had been a fan of *Doctor Who* since the early days (he had organised the first ever *Doctor Who* convention in 1977), Reeltime also released a series of video interviews with people connected with the series. These were professionally produced and featured the companions, the Doctors, the production personnel, and even Marvel Comics.

The American releases were initially through Pleiades Corporation who released an initial eight tapes. These were then taken over by DHI Home Entertainment and more releases added. Some of the tapes had cases manufactured in the USA, while others used the UK video covers within white plastic video covers. More recently, distribution of some of the titles was undertaken by S&J Productions. The first ten tapes in the series were also available in the Betamax format. The initial batch of each tape was also available with a limited edition (usually 200 copies) signed and numbered label.

VMM-001a *Myth Makers 01: Michael Wisher*
1984, Reeltime Pictures, UK
Each of the *Myth Makers* videos features an actor or production person from *Doctor Who* being interviewed about their life and work for the show. The first two tapes were presented by Keith Harrison while actor Nicholas Briggs took over from the third tape onwards.
REF: RTP0001 OP: £8.95 NM: £14.30

VMM-001b *Myth Makers Vol 1: Janet Fielding/Michael Wisher*
1989, Pleiades Home Video, USA
Card box.
OP: $17.95

VMM-002a *Myth Makers 02: John Leeson*
1984, Reeltime Pictures, UK
REF: RTP0002 OP: £8.95

VMM-002b *Myth Makers Vol 2: Ian Marter/John Leeson*
1989, Pleiades Home Video, USA
Card box.
OP: $17.95

VMM-002c *Myth Makers 02: John Leeson*
1995, Reeltime Pictures, UK
Extended reissue.
REF: RTP0134 OP: £16.99 NM: £14.30

VMM-003a *Myth Makers 03: Nicholas Courtney*
1985, Reeltime Pictures, UK
REF: RTP0003 OP: £8.95

VMM-003b *Myth Makers Vol 3: Nicholas Courtney/John Levene*
1988, Pleiades Home Video, USA
OP: $17.95

VMM-003c *Myth Makers Presents The Men from UNIT Vol 3: Nicholas Courtney/John Levene*
1988, DHI Home Video, USA
Card box.
OP: $19.95

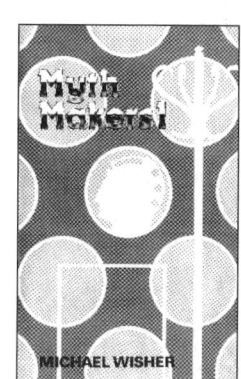

VMM-001a

VMM-001b

VMM-002a

VMM-003c

MEET THE STARS FROM THE BBC TV SERIES
DOCTOR WHO

MYTH MAKERS

Nicola Bryant/Michael Craze

VMM-008b

MEET THE STARS FROM THE BBCtv SERIES
DOCTOR WHO

SARAH SUTTON
NYSSA

VMM-009d

VMM-003d *Myth Makers 03: Nicholas Courtney*
1994, Reeltime Pictures, UK
Extended reissue.
REF: RTP0104 OP: £16.99 NM: £14.30

VMM-004a *Myth Makers 04: Carole Ann Ford*
1985, Reeltime Pictures, UK
REF: RTP0004 OP: £8.95

VMM-004b *Myth Makers Vol 5: Carole Ann Ford/Deborah Watling/Wendy Padbury*
1989, Pleiades Home Video, USA
OP: $17.95

VMM-004c *Women of the '60s: The Hartnell Era: Vol 17*
1992, DHI Home Video, USA
Contains Carole Ann Ford and Jackie Lane interviews.
OP: $19.95

VMM-004d *Myth Makers 04: Carole Ann Ford*
1996, Reeltime Pictures, UK
Extended reissue.
REF: RTP0143 OP: £16.99 NM: £14.30

VMM-005a *Myth Makers 05: Janet Fielding*
1985, Reeltime Pictures, UK
REF: RTP0005 OP: £8.95 NM: £14.30

VMM-005b *Myth Makers Vol 1: Janet Fielding/Michael Wisher*
1989, Pleiades Home Video, USA
Card box.
OP: $17.95

VMM-006a *Myth Makers 06: Nicola Bryant*
1985, Reeltime Pictures, UK
REF: RTP0006 OP: £9.99

VMM-006b *Myth Makers Vol 13: Nicola Bryant/Michael Craze*
1988, DHI Home Video, USA
OP: $19.95

VMM-006c *Myth Makers 06: Nicola Bryant*
1996, Reeltime Pictures, UK
Extended reissue.
REF: RTP0149 OP: £16.99 NM: £14.30

VMM-007a *Myth Makers 07: Wendy Padbury*
1986, Reeltime Pictures, UK
REF: RTP0007 OP: £9.99

VMM-007b *Myth Makers Vol 5: Carole Ann Ford/Deborah Watling/Wendy Padbury*
1989, Pleiades Home Video, USA
OP: $17.95

VMM-007c *Women of the '60s: The Troughton Era: Vol 5*
1989, DHI Home Video, USA
Contains Deborah Watling and Wendy Padbury interviews. 1987 date on box?
OP: $19.95

VMM-007d *Myth Makers 07: Wendy Padbury*
1994, Reeltime Pictures, UK
Extended reissue.
REF: RTP0112 OP: £16.99 NM: £14.30

VMM-008a *Myth Makers 08: Michael Craze*
1986, Reeltime Pictures, UK
REF: RTP0008 OP: £9.99

VMM-008b *Myth Makers Vol 13: Nicola Bryant/Michael Craze*
1988, DHI Home Video, USA
OP: $19.95

VMM-008c *Myth Makers 08: Michael Craze*
1996, Reeltime Pictures, UK
Extended reissue.
REF: RTP0150 OP: £16.99 NM: £14.30

VMM-009a *Myth Makers 09: Sarah Sutton*
1986, Reeltime Pictures, UK
REF: RTP0009 OP: £9.99

VMM-009b *Myth Makers Vol 6: Sarah Sutton/Peter Grimwade*
1988, Pleiades Home Video, USA
OP: $17.95

VMM-009c *Myth Makers Vol 6: Sarah Sutton/Peter Grimwade*
1988, DHI Home Video, USA
OP: $19.95

VMM-009d *Myth Makers 09: Sarah Sutton*
1994, Reeltime Pictures, UK
Extended reissue.
REF: RTP0114 OP: £16.99 NM: £14.30

VMM-010a *Myth Makers 10: Deborah Watling*
1986, Reeltime Pictures, UK
REF: RTP0015 OP: £9.99

VMM-010b *Myth Makers Vol 5: Carole Ann Ford/Deborah Watling/Wendy Padbury*
1989, Pleiades Home Video, USA
OP: $17.95

VMM-010c *Women of the '60s: The Troughton Era: Vol 5*
1989, DHI Home Video, USA
Contains Deborah Watling and Wendy Padbury interviews.
OP: $19.95

VMM-010d *Myth Makers 10: Deborah Watling*
1995, Reeltime Pictures, UK
Extended reissue.
REF: RTP0133 OP: £16.99 NM: £14.30

VMM-011a *Myth Makers 11: Victor Pemberton*
1990, Reeltime Pictures, UK
REF: RTP0018 OP: £16.99

VMM-011b *Myth Makers 11: Victor Pemberton*
1996, Reeltime Pictures, UK
Extended reissue.
REF: RTP0151 OP: £16.99 NM: £11.30

VMM-012a *Myth Makers 12: Ian Marter*
1987, Reeltime Pictures, UK
REF: RTP0019 OP: £9.99

VMM-012b *Myth Makers Vol 2: Ian Marter/John Leeson*
1989, Pleiades Home Video, USA
Card box.
OP: $17.95

VMM-012c *Myth Makers 12: Ian Marter*
1994, Reeltime Pictures, UK
Extended reissue.
REF: RTP0105 OP: £16.99 NM: £14.30

VMM-013a *Myth Makers 13: John Levene*
1987, Reeltime Pictures, UK
REF: RTP0021 OP: £9.99

VMM-013b *Myth Makers Vol 3: Nicholas Courtney/John Levene*
1988, Pleiades Home Video, USA
OP: $17.95

VMM-013c *Myth Makers Presents The Men from UNIT Vol 3: Nicholas Courtney/John Levene*
1988, DHI Home Video, USA
Card box.
OP: $19.95

VMM-013d *Myth Makers 13: John Levene*
1995, Reeltime Pictures, UK
Extended reissue.
REF: RTP0135 OP: £16.99 NM: £14.30

VMM-014a *Myth Makers 14: Peter Grimwade*
1987, Reeltime Pictures, UK
REF: RTP0027 OP: £9.99

VMM-014b *Myth Makers Vol 6: Sarah Sutton/Peter Grimwade*
1988, Pleiades Home Video, USA
OP: $17.95

VMM-014c *Myth Makers Vol 6: Sarah Sutton/Peter Grimwade*
1988, DHI Home Video, USA
OP: $19.95

VMM-014d *Myth Makers 14: Peter Grimwade*
1994, Reeltime Pictures, UK
Extended reissue.
REF: RTP0115 OP: £16.99 NM: £14.30

VMM-015a *Myth Makers 15: Jon Pertwee*
1989, Reeltime Pictures, UK
REF: RTP0030 OP: £15.00

VMM-015b *Myth Makers Vol 4: Jon Pertwee*
1988, DHI Home Video, USA
Photos by Jody Lynn Nye. Card box.
OP: $19.95

VMM-015c *Myth Makers 15: Jon Pertwee*
1996, Reeltime Pictures, UK
Extended reissue.
REF: RTP0160 OP: £16.99 NM: £14.30

VMM-016a *Myth Makers 16: Richard Franklin*
1989, Reeltime Pictures, UK
REF: RTP0031 OP: £10.00

VMM-016b *Myth Makers 16: Richard Franklin*
1996, Reeltime Pictures, UK
Extended reissue.
REF: RTP0152 OP: £16.99 NM: £14.30

VMM-017a *Myth Makers 17: Tom Baker*
1989, Reeltime Pictures, UK
REF: RTP0035 OP: £15.00 NM: £14.30

VMM-017b *Myth Makers Vol 8: Tom Baker*
1989, DHI Home Video, USA
OP: $19.95

VMM-017c *Myth Makers Vol 8: Tom Baker*
1989, Pleiades Home Entertainment, USA
Cover by Lucy A Synk.
OP: $19.95

VMM-018a *Myth Makers 18: Marvel Comics*
1989, Reeltime Pictures, UK
REF: RTP0036 OP: £10.00 NM: £14.30

VMM-018b *Myth Makers Vol 14: Marvel Comics*
1989, DHI Home Video, USA
OP: $19.95

VMM-019 *Myth Makers Vol 16: Sophie Aldred*
1991, DHI Home Video, USA
OP: $19.95

VMM-020a *Myth Makers 19: Colin Baker*
1990, Reeltime Pictures, UK
REF: RTP0038 OP: £16.99 NM: £14.30

VMM-020b *Myth Makers Vol 10: Colin Baker*
1990, DHI Home Video, USA
Copyright date on box is 1989. Probably not released until 1990.
OP: $19.95

VMM-021a *Myth Makers 20: David Banks*
1990, Reeltime Pictures, UK
REF: RTP0042 OP: £16.99 NM: £14.30

VMM-021b *Myth Makers Vol 11: David Banks*
1990, DHI Home Video, USA
OP: $19.95

VMM-022a *Myth Makers 21: Mary Tamm*
1990, Reeltime Pictures, UK
REF: RTP0050 OP: £16.99 NM: £14.30

VMM-022b *Myth Makers Vol 12: Mary Tamm*
1990, DHI Home Video, USA
OP: $19.95

VMM-023a *Myth Makers 22: John Nathan-Turner*
1990, Reeltime Pictures, UK
REF: RTP0055 OP: £16.99 NM: £14.30

VMM-023b *Myth Makers Vol 13: John Nathan-Turner*
1990, DHI Home Video, USA
Says 'Vol 22' on the tape.
OP: $19.95

VMM-024 *Myth Makers 23: Sophie Aldred*
1991, Reeltime Pictures, UK
REF: RTP0074 OP: £16.99 NM: £14.30

VMM-025a *Myth Makers 24: Jackie Lane*
1992, Reeltime Pictures, UK
REF: RTP0080 OP: £16.99 NM: £14.30

VMM-025b *Women of the '60s: The Hartnell Era: Vol 17*
1992, DHI Home Video, USA
Contains Carole Ann Ford and Jackie Lane interviews.
OP: $19.95

VMM-026 *Myth Makers 25: Barry Letts & Terrance Dicks*
1993, Reeltime Pictures, UK
REF: RTP0091 OP: £16.99 NM: £14.30

VMM-027 *Myth Makers 26: Anneke Wills*
1993, Reeltime Pictures, UK
REF: RTP0094 OP: £16.99 NM: £14.30

VMM-028a *Myth Makers 27: Louise Jameson*
1993, Reeltime Pictures , UK
REF: RTP0100 OP: £16.99 NM: £14.30

VMM-028b *Myth Makers 27: Louise Jameson*
1999, S&J Productions, USA

VMM-029a *Myth Makers 28: Sylvester McCoy*
1994, Reeltime Pictures, UK
REF: RTP0095 OP: £16.99 NM: £14.30

VMM-029b *Myth Makers 28: Sylvester McCoy*
1999, S&J Productions, USA

VMM-030 *Myth Makers 29: Barry Letts & Terrance Dicks Part 2*
1994, Reeltime Pictures, UK
REF: RTP0110 OP: £16.99 NM: £14.30

JON PERTWEE
THE THIRD DOCTOR

VMM-015c

MEET THE STARS FROM THE BBC TV SERIES
DOCTOR WHO

MYTH MAKERS

Tom Baker
Volume 2

VMM-017b

MEET THE STARS FROM THE BBC TV SERIES
DOCTOR WHO

MYTH MAKERS

Marvel Comics
Volume 14

VMM-018b

COLIN BAKER
THE SIXTH DOCTOR

VMM-020a

VMM-031a *Myth Makers 30: Caroline John*
1994, Reeltime Pictures, UK
REF: RTP0116   OP: £16.99   NM: £14.30

VMM-031b *Myth Makers 30: Caroline John*
1999, S&J Productions, USA

VMM-032 *Myth Makers 31: Frazer Hines*
1994, Reeltime Pictures, UK
REF: RTP0108   OP: £16.99   NM: £14.30

VMM-033 *Myth Makers 32: Peter Purves*
1995, Reeltime Pictures, UK
REF: RTP0130   OP: £16.99   NM: £14.30

VMM-034 *Myth Makers 33: William Russell*
1996, Reeltime Pictures, UK
REF: RTP0147   OP: £16.99   NM: £14.30

VMM-035 *Myth Makers 34: Verity Lambert*
1996, Reeltime Pictures, UK
REF: RTP0156   OP: £16.99   NM: £14.30

VMM-036 *Myth Makers 35: A tribute to
Jacqueline Hill*
1996, Reeltime Pictures, UK
REF: RTP0148   OP: £16.99   NM: £14.30

VMM-037 *Myth Makers 36: Mark Strickson*
1997, Reeltime Pictures, UK
REF: RTP0164   OP: £16.99   NM: £14.30

VMM-038 *Myth Makers 37: A tribute to Roger
Delgado*
1997, Reeltime Pictures, UK
REF: RTP0171   OP: £16.99   NM: £14.30

VMM-039 *Myth Makers 38: The Directors:
Christopher Barry & Paul Bernard*
1997/03, Reeltime Pictures, UK
REF: RTP0182   OP: £16.99   NM: £14.30

SOPHIE ALDRED
ACE

VMM-024

SYLVESTER McCOY
THE SEVENTH DOCTOR

VMM-029a

MEET THE STARS FROM THE BBC TV SERIES
DOCTOR WHO

CAROLINE JOHN
LIZ SHAW

VMM-031a

MEET THE STARS FROM THE BBC TV SERIES
DOCTOR WHO

THE DIRECTORS
CHRISTOPHER   PAUL
BARRY   BERNARD

VMM-039

VMM-041   **VMM-044**

VMM-051   **VOI-004a**

VOI-006 (all four)

VMM-040 *Myth Makers 39: Katy Manning*
1998/04/07, Reeltime Pictures, UK
REF: RTP0189   OP: £16.99   NM: £14.30

VMM-041 *Myth Makers 40: Shaun Sutton*
1998, Reeltime Pictures, UK
REF: RTP0194   OP: £16.99   NM: £14.30

VMM-042 *Myth Makers 41: Ray Cusick*
1998, Reeltime Pictures, UK
REF: RTP0197   OP: £16.99   NM: £14.30

VMM-043 *Myth Makers 42: Derrick Sherwin*
1998, Reeltime Pictures, UK
REF: RTP0201   OP: £16.99   NM: £14.30

VMM-044 *Myth Makers 43: William Hartnell*
1999, Reeltime Pictures, UK
REF: RTP0158   OP: £16.99   NM: £14.30

VMM-045 *Myth Makers 44: Donald Tosh*
1999/09, Reeltime Pictures, UK
REF: RTP0208   OP: £16.99   NM: £14.30

VMM-046 *Myth Makers 45: Jack Pitt*
1999/09, Reeltime Pictures, UK
REF: RTP0213   OP: £16.99   NM: £14.30

VMM-047 *Myth Makers 46: Barry Newbery*
1999/10, Reeltime Pictures, UK
REF: RTP0215   OP: £16.99   NM: £14.30

VMM-048 *Myth Makers 47: Doctor Who
Magazine 20th Birthday*
2000/01, Reeltime Pictures, UK
Recorded at *Doctor Who* Magazine's 20th anniversary
party in December 1999.
REF: RTP0218   OP: £16.99

VMM-049 *Myth Makers 48: Graeme Harper*
2000/05, Reeltime Pictures, UK
REF: RTP0228   OP: £12.99

VMM-050 *Myth Makers 49: Bob Baker & Dave
Martin*
2000/09, Reeltime Pictures, UK
REF: RTP0232   OP: £12.99

VMM-051 *Myth Makers 50: Elisabeth Sladen*
2000/12, Reeltime Pictures, UK
Specially extended edition for the 50th *Myth Makers*
release. Directed by Christopher Barry. Features a
'guest appearance' from Jeremy Bulloch. Limited edition with a signed inner sleeve.
REF: RTP0233   OP: £15.00

VMM-052 *Myth Makers 51: David Brierley*
2001/04, Reeltime Pictures, UK
Voice of K9.
REF: RTP0248 OP: £12.99

VMM-053 *Myth Makers 52: Yee Jee Tso*
2002/02, Reeltime Pictures, UK
Chang Lee in the TVM.
REF: RTP0259 OP: £12.99

VMM-054 *Myth Makers 53: A Tribute to Patrick Troughton*
2002/04, Reeltime Pictures, UK
REF: RTP0159 OP: £12.99

VMM-055 *Myth Makers 54: Tristram Cary*
2002/06, Reeltime Pictures, UK
Composer.
REF: RTP0270 OP: £12.99

VMM-056 *Myth Makers 55: Andrew Cartmel*
2002/09, Reeltime Pictures, UK
Script Editor.
OP: £12.99

VIDEO, OTHER INTERVIEWS

OTHER non-Reeltime Pictures *Myth Makers* series video interviews.

VOI-001 *An Interview with Tom Baker*
1984, Scorpio International Ltd, USA
23 min.
OP: (list: $74.95) $47.98

VOI-002a *Panopticon VII*
1986, Reeltime Pictures, UK
Video footage from the DWAS' annual convention.
REF: RTP0013 OP: £15.00

VOI-002b *The Panopticon Tapes 6*
1999, Reeltime Pictures, UK
Re-issued with new cover as the 6th tape in the series.
REF: RTP0013 OP: £16.99

VOI-003 *The Panopticon Tapes*
1991, Reeltime Pictures, UK
5 tapes. Selection of interviews from all the DWAS/DSL conventions. Re-issued in 1999 with new covers.
REF: RTP0056-001/005 OP: £16.99 each

VOI-004a *Myth Runner*
1987, Reeltime Pictures, UK

A selection of out-takes and especially recorded skits from the *Myth Makers* video series. Re-issued shortly after release with a new cover.
REF: RTP0016 OP: £15.00 NM: £14.30

VOI-004b *Myth Runner*
1987, Pleiades Home Entertainment, USA
OP: $17.95

VOI-004c *Myth Runner*
1987, DHI Home Video, USA
OP: $19.95

VOI-004d *Myth Makers Vol 7: Myth Runner*
1989, Pleiades Home Entertainment, USA
OP: $19.95

VOI-005 *Panopticon Highlights*
1992/09, DSL, UK
Very limited edition 30 minute tape of highlights from previous conventions. Only available at Panopticon 1992. DSLV002 was abandoned during production but was to have featured highlights from the 1992 'Tombwatch' event.
REF: DSLV001 OP: £5

VOI-006 *Panopticon Videos*
1994, DSL, UK
4 tapes: Highlights 1 and 2; Tom Baker live; Four Doctors live. Videos produced by DSL featuring material from their annual convention in 1993. Also available in NTSC format.
REF: DSLV003 (H1) DSLV004 (H2) DSLV005 (Baker) DSLV006 (4 Drs)
OP: £16.99 each tape

VOI-007a *A Sci-fi Audience with Tom Baker*
1997, JN-TV Productions, UK
Video release of Tom Baker's talk at MOMI on 15 February 1992.
OP: £10.99

VOI-007b *An Afternoon With Tom Baker*
1997/04, New Zealand Doctor Who Fan Club, NZ
Recorded on 25 January 1997 at St Andrew's Church Hall, Mission Bay, Auckland, New Zealand. A video record of Tom Baker's Q&A session held during the actor's visit to New Zealand to film the NZ Superannuation Services commercials (see PRO-010). The video also contains all the TV commercials, plus the full version of the TV1 interview with Baker conducted on the TARDIS set. First production run, 40 copies; second run, 35 copies.
REF: TSV Video 1 OP: NZ $16.00

VOI-008

VOT-002a

VOI-008 Where On Earth Is ... Katy Manning
1998/07/01, Reeltime Pictures, UK
Video diary of Katy Manning's trip to the UK in 1998.
A limited number featured a signed set of sleeve
notes. Directed by Keith Barnfather.
REF: RTP0195 OP: £16.99 NM: £14.30

VIDEO, OTHER VIDEOS

THIS section contains video tapes which are not
interviews, but nor are they dramas. Some of the
following contain interview material however.

VOT-001 Doctor Who in America
1983, Scorpio International Ltd, USA
57 minutes long. Hosted by Tom Carroll. Directed by
James B Brandt. A series of interviews with various
sociologists, intercut with clips from the show, plus
excerpts from an interview with Tom Baker, and
footage from a US convention.
OP: (list: $64.00) $45.00

VOT-002a The Home Whovian
1986, Lionheart, USA
The video itself says 'Copyright 1985,' but the box
says 1986. The New Jersey Network production, hosted by Eric Luskin (who also hosted 'The Making of
Silver Nemesis' special by NJN) is a 30 minute compilation of interviews with John Nathan-Turner, Jon
Pertwee, Tom Baker (in an edited convention appearance), Peter Davison and Colin Baker. On PBS stations, it aired as '*Doctor Who*: Who's Who.'
OP: $29.95 (also priced at $12.50)

VOT-002b

VOT-003c

VOT-002b The Home Whovian
2001/11, Reeltime Pictures, UK
First UK video release of a 1985 New Jersey
Network documentary about *Doctor Who*.
REF: RTP0258 OP: £12.99

VOT-003a Just Who on Earth is ... Tom Baker
1991, Reeltime Pictures, UK
Video documentary about Tom Baker directed by his
wife, Sue Jerrard.
REF: RTP0049 OP: £16.99

VOT-003b Just Who on Earth is ... Tom Baker
1991, DHI Home Video, USA
OP: $19.95

VOT-004a

VOT-005a

VOT-003c Doctor ... Who on Earth is Tom Baker
1996, Reeltime Pictures, UK
Re-issue.
REF: RTP0049 OP: £11.99

VOT-004a *Return to Devil's End*
1993/01, Reeltime Pictures, UK
Video documentary/interview tape about the making
of the Pertwee story *The Dæmons*. First 500 featured
a sleeve signed by the cast and crew. Directed by
Keith Barnfather.
REF: RTP0086 OP: £16.99

VOT-004b *Return to Devil's End*
1993, DHI Home Video, USA
OP: $19.95

VOT-004c *Doctor Who's Return to Devil's End*
1997/04, Reeltime Pictures, UK
Re-issue.
REF: RTP0170 OP: £12.99

VOT-005a *Dalekmania*
1995/07/24, Lumiere, UK
Tape celebrating the 1960s Dalek films. Rating: 'E'.
Directed by Kevin Davies. Deleted 1996/06/11.
REF: LUM2221 OP: £10.99

VOT-005b *Dalekmania Boxed Set*
1995/11/30, Lumiere, UK
Numbered limited edition. Box contains unboxed
Dalekmania video, two film posters, 'Dalekmania:
Doctor Who at the Cinema' booklet by Marcus
Hearn and 6 exclusive postcards. Deleted 1996/06/11.
REF: LUM2303 OP: £24.95 NM: £5.50

VOT-006a *The Doctors: 30 Years of Time Travel
and Beyond*
1995/09/25, Master Vision, UK
Documentary based on the Boxtree book of the same
name (see BFA-079). Special extended edition offered
through *Doctor Who Magazine* issue 230. This edition ran
for 80 minutes and included the full versions of some
8mm film footage of *Doctor Who* on the end of the tape.
Preview copies included footage of Tom Baker from
Panopticon 93 which was removed from the final version due to clearance problems. Directed by Bill Baggs.
REF: MV1004 OP: £12.99

VOT-006b *The Doctors: 30 Years of Time Travel
and Beyond*
1995, S&J Productions, USA
Released at Visions '95.

VOT-006c *The Stranger: Summoned by Shadows*
2000/06, Reeltime Pictures, UK
Re-issue. Includes Part one of *The Doctors*.
REF: RTP0209 OP: £12.99

VDF-005b

VOT-006a

VOT-006c

VOT-006d

VOT-007a

VOT-007b

VOT-008a

VOT-009

VOT-010

VOT-006d *The Stranger: More than a Messiah*
2000/06, Reeltime Pictures, UK
Re-issue. Includes Part two of *The Doctors*.
REF: RTP0210 OP: £12.99

VOT-007a *Bidding Adieu*
1996/04/27, BBV, UK
A video diary featuring Sylvester McCoy travelling to
Vancouver to take part in the 1996 *Doctor Who* TV
Movie. Produced by Bill Baggs.
REF: QL0008 OP: £11.99 NM: £8.80

VOT-007b *The Stranger: In Memory Alone*
2000/08, Reeltime Pictures, UK
Re-issue. Includes *Bidding Adieu*.
REF: RTP0211 OP: £12.99

VOT-008a *I Was A Doctor Who Monster*
1996/04/01, Reeltime Pictures, UK
Documentary presented by Sylvester McCoy celebrating *Doctor Who*'s monsters and the people who
played them. The first 1000 copies featured a sleeve
signed by a variety of the actors who appear in the
documentary. Directed by Keith Barnfather. Written
by Roger Stevens.
REF: RTP0109 OP: £10.99 NM: £20

VOT-008b *I Was A Doctor Who Monster*
1996, CBS Fox, USA

VOT-009 *Who is Tom Baker?*
1997/06, Visual, UK
Documentary about Tom Baker featuring interviews
with guests and fans at a *Doctor Who* convention, plus
an eighties home video interview with Tom.
REF: VSL-0129 OP: £12.99

VOT-010 *Doctor Who's Lust In Space*
1998/05/04, Reeltime Pictures, UK
Light-hearted documentary exploring the charge of
sexism against *Doctor Who*. Features Nicholas
Courtney, Mark Strickson, Katy Manning and Sophie
Aldred. Directed by Keith Barnfather. Written by
Roger Stevens.
REF: RTP0187 OP: £11.99

VOT-011a *The Few Doctors*
1998/12, DSL, UK
A comedy spoof in which all the Doctors (played by
fans) take part in a series of games at an old people's
home. Features appearances by John Nathan Turner
and Gary Downie.
REF: DSLV007 OP: £12.50

VOT-011b *The Few Doctors*
1998, USA
Released for Visions '98. Tape says 'NTSC ©1997'.

VOT-012 *Reverse the Polarity: A Day in the Life of Jon Pertwee*
2000/03, Archangel Media, UK
VHS. Video of Pertwee circa 1992. Contains extracts from the *Starwatch* promo.

VOT-013 *K9 Unleashed*
2000/11, Reeltime Pictures, UK
Documentary looking at the story of K9. Directed by Roger Stevens.
REF: RTP 0237 OP: £10.99

VOT-014 *An Englishman on Gallifrey*
2001/06, Reeltime Pictures, UK
Documentary about Mark Strickson's trip to the USA Gallifrey One Convention in 2001. Directed by Keith Barnfather.
REF: RTP 0241 OP: £12.99

VOT-015 *Longleat '83: The Greatest Show in the Galaxy*
2001/08, Reeltime Pictures, UK
Documentary about the Longleat 1983 *Doctor Who* Convention. Presented by John Leeson. Directed by Roger Stevens.
REF: RTP 0252 OP: £12.99

VOT-016 *Who's Who*
2001/09, Reeltime Pictures, UK
A 1985/6 New Jersey Network documentary about *Doctor Who*.
REF: RTP0257 OP: £12.99

VOT-017 *Then & Now*
2001/10, Reeltime Pictures, UK
A 1987 New Jersey Network documentary about *Doctor Who*.
REF: RTP0256 OP: £12.99

VOT-018 *ReUNITed*
2001/12, Reeltime Pictures, UK
Documentary made at the Chicago TARDIS convention 2001.
REF: RTP0253 OP: £12.99

VOT-019 *Doctor At Sea*
2002/01, Reeltime Pictures, UK
Documentary made at the *Doctor Who* sea cruise 2001.
REF: RTP0255 OP: £12.99

VOT-013

VOT-011a

VOT-014

VOT-015

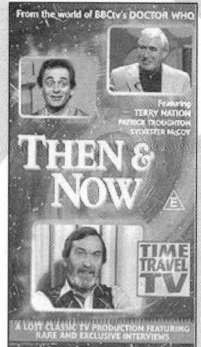

VOT-016

VOT-017

VOT-018   **VOT-019**

VOT-020 Katy Manning's World Down Under
2002/07, Reeltime Pictures, UK
Documentary of Manning in Australia.
REF: RTP0267 OP: £12.99

VOT-021 My Doctor Who Diary by Yee Jee Tso
2002/08, Reeltime Pictures, UK
Documentary of Tso in London.
OP: £12.99

VOT-022 The Megéve Experiment
2002/12, Reeltime Pictures, UK
Documentary of an event staged by Nextstage in
Megéve, France, to educate, instruct and entertain a
group of Doctor Who fans interested in acting and
directing. Featuring Sophie Aldred and Deborah
Watling, with Christopher Barry.
REF: RTP0271 OP: £12.99

VOT-020

VIDEO, STORAGE

VST-001 TARDIS Video Cabinet
1993/09, Harvard Associates, UK
A free- or wall-standing video case in the shape of the
TARDIS. Orders taken at the Panopticon '93 convention came with a commemorative plaque affixed to
the inside of one of the doors. The cabinet was also
available by direct mail order and advertised through
DWM. Holds up to 67 videos.
OP: £79.99 NM: £100

VOT-021   **VOT-022**   **VST-001**

APPENDIX A: COMIC STRIPS

THE following listing was originally based on information compiled by John Ainsworth for Marvel's *Classic Comics* series, and has been updated and revised with information from Finn Clark and Andrew Pixley, as well as by the authors of this book. It shows all the appearances of *Doctor Who* and *Doctor Who*-related comic strips in books and magazines. The titles listed are those shown on the strips themselves, however many early strips did not have titles. Titles marked + are based on those created by Jeremy Bentham for an article in issue 62 of *Doctor Who Magazine*. Titles marked * were given at the end of the preceding week's strip. Titles marked @ were given by the author on scripts. Where the artist or writer credit is absent, it means that the information is not currently known.

FIRST DOCTOR STRIPS

TITLE	ISSUES	ARTIST/INKER	WRITER
TV COMIC – published Mondays by TV Publications Ltd. (14/11/64 – 17/12/66)			
The Klepton Parasites+	674-683	Neville Main	
The Therovian Quest+	684-689	Neville Main	
The Hijackers of Thrax+	690-692	Neville Main	
On the Web Planet	693-698	Neville Main	
The Gyros Injustice+	699-704	Neville Main	
Challenge of the Piper+	705-709	Neville Main	
Moon Landing+	710-712	Neville Main	
Time in Reverse+	713-715	Neville Main	
Lizardworld+	716-719	Neville Main	
The Ordeals of Demeter	720-723	Bill Mevin	
Enter: The Go-Ray+	724-727	Bill Mevin	
Shark Bait+	728-731	Bill Mevin	
A Christmas Story+	732-735	Bill Mevin	
The Didus Expedition+	736-739	Bill Mevin	
Space Station Z-7+	740-743	Bill Mevin	
Plague of the Black Scorpi+	744-747	Bill Mevin	
The Trodos Tyranny+	748-752	John Canning	
The Secrets of Gemino+	753-757	John Canning	
On the Haunted Planet*	758-762	John Canning	
The Hunters of Zerox+	763-767	John Canning	
The Underwater Robot+	768-771	John Canning	
Return of the Trods+	772-775	John Canning	
The Galaxy Games+	776-779	John Canning	
The Experimenters+	780 783	John Canning	

TV COMIC HOLIDAY SPECIAL – published by TV Publications Ltd. (June 1965)
Prisoners of Gritog+   Neville Main

TV COMIC HOLIDAY SPECIAL – published by TV Publications Ltd. (June 1966)
Guests of King Neptune   John Canning
The Gaze of the Gorgon   John Canning

TITLE	ISSUES	ARTIST/INKER	WRITER

TV COMIC ANNUAL 1966 – published by TV Publications Ltd.

| Prisoner of the Kleptons+ | | Neville Main | |
| The Caterpillar Men+ | | Neville Main | |

TV COMIC ANNUAL 1967 – published by TV Publications Ltd.

| Deadly Vessel+ | | John Canning | |
| Kingdom of the Animals+ | | John Canning | |

DOCTOR WHO ANNUAL – published by World Distributors (Manchester) Ltd. (1966) **BAN-002**

| Mission for Duh | | Walter Howarth | |

DOCTOR WHO YEARBOOK 1994 – published by Marvel Comics Ltd. **BAN-028**

| A Religious Experience | | John Ridgway | Tim Quinn |

DOCTOR WHO MAGAZINE SUMMER SPECIAL: THE GENESIS OF DOCTOR WHO/ THE DESTINY OF DOCTOR WHO – published by Marvel Comics Ltd. (1994) **MAS-031**

| Are You Listening? | | Colin Andrew | Warwick Gray |

DOCTOR WHO MAGAZINE

| Food for Thought | 218-220 | Colin Andrew | Nick Briggs |
| Operation Proteus | 231-233 | Martin Geraghty | Gareth Roberts |

SECOND DOCTOR STRIPS

TITLE	ISSUES	ARTIST/INKER	WRITER

TV COMIC – published Mondays by TV Publications Ltd. to issue 850 and then by Polystyle Publications Ltd. (24/12/66 – 22/11/69)

The Extortioner+	784-787	John Canning	
(Strip title changes to *Doctor Who and the Daleks*)			
The Trodos Ambush+	788-791	John Canning	
The Doctor Strikes Back+	792-795	John Canning	
The Zombies*	796-798	John Canning	
Master of Spiders!*	799-802	John Canning	
The Exterminator+	803-806	John Canning	
The Monsters from the Past!*	807-811	John Canning	
(Strip title reverts to *Doctor Who* from issue 809)			
The TARDIS Worshippers!*	812-815	John Canning	
Space War III+	816-819	John Canning	
Egyptian Escapade!*	820-823	John Canning	
The Coming of the Cybermen+	824-827	John Canning	
The Faithful Rocket Pack!*	828-831	John Canning	
Flower Power!*	832-835	John Canning	
The Witches!*	837-841	John Canning	
Cyber-Mole+	842-845	John Canning	
The Sabre Toothed Gorillas!*	846-849	John Canning	
The Cyber Empire!*@	850-853	John Canning	Roger Noel Cook
The Dyrons!*@	854-858	John Canning	Roger Noel Cook

TITLE	ISSUES	ARTIST/INKER	WRITER
Dr. Who and the Space Pirates!*	859-863	John Canning	Roger Noel Cook (?)
Car of the Century!*@	864-867	John Canning	Roger Noel Cook
The Jokers!*@	868-871	John Canning	Roger Noel Cook
Invasion of the Quarks!*@	872-876	John Canning	Roger Noel Cook
The Killer Wasps+	877-880	John Canning	Roger Noel Cook (?)
Ice Cap Terror@	881-884	John Canning	Roger Noel Cook
Jungle of Doom!*	885-889	John Canning	Roger Noel Cook
Father Time@	890-893	John Canning	Roger Noel Cook
Martha The Mechanical Housemaid@	894-898	John Canning	Roger Noel Cook
The Duellists+	899-902	John Canning	Roger Noel Cook (?)
Eskimo Joe@	903-906	John Canning	Roger Noel Cook
Peril at 60 Fathoms@	907-910	John Canning	Roger Noel Cook
Operation Wurlitzer!*	911-915	John Canning	Roger Noel Cook
Action in Exile@	916-920	John Canning	Roger Noel Cook
The Mark of Terror!*	921-924	John Canning	Roger Noel Cook (?)
The Brotherhood!*	925-928	John Canning	Roger Noel Cook (?)
U.F.O.@	929-933	John Canning	Roger Noel Cook
The Night Walkers+	934-936	John Canning	Roger Noel Cook (?)

TV COMIC HOLIDAY SPECIAL – published by Polystyle Publications Ltd. (May 1967)

Barnabus+	Patrick Williams
Jungle Adventure+	Patrick Williams

TV COMIC HOLIDAY SPECIAL – published by Polystyle Publications Ltd. (June 1968)

Return of the Witches+	Patrick Williams
Masquerade+	Patrick Williams

TV COMIC HOLIDAY SPECIAL – published by Polystyle Publications Ltd. (June 1969)

The Champion+	Patrick Williams
The Entertainer+	Patrick Williams

TV COMIC ANNUAL 1968 – published by Polystyle Publications Ltd.

Attack of the Daleks+	Patrick Williams
Pursued by the Trods+	Patrick Williams

DOCTOR WHO ANNUAL – published by World Distributors (Manchester) Ltd. (1967) **BAN-003**

The Tests of Trefus	David Brian
World Without Night	David Brian

TV COMIC ANNUAL 1969 – published by Polystyle Publications Ltd.

The Time Museum+	John Canning
The Electrodes+	John Canning

DOCTOR WHO ANNUAL – published by World Distributors (Manchester) Ltd. (1968) **BAN-004**

Freedom by Fire	David Brian
Atoms Infinite	David Brian

TITLE	ISSUES	ARTIST/INKER	WRITER
TV COMIC ANNUAL 1970 – published by Polystyle Publications Ltd.			
Death Race+		John Canning	
Test Flight+		John Canning	
DOCTOR WHO ANNUAL – published by World Distributors (Manchester) Ltd. (1969) **BAN-005**			
The Vampire Plants		David Brian	
The Robot King		David Brian	

DOCTOR WHO MAGAZINE SUMMER SPECIAL: THE DEFINITIVE GUIDE TO THIRTY YEARS OF THE DALEKS – published by Marvel Comics Ltd. (1993) **MAS-028**

TITLE	ISSUES	ARTIST/INKER	WRITER
Bringer of Darkness		Martin Geraghty	Warwick Gray

DOCTOR WHO MAGAZINE

TITLE	ISSUES	ARTIST/INKER	WRITER
Land of the Blind	224-226	Lee Sullivan	Warwick Scott Gray

THIRD DOCTOR STRIPS

TITLE	ISSUES	ARTIST/INKER	WRITER
TV COMIC – published Mondays by Polystyle Publications Ltd. (17/01/70 – 06/02/71)			
The Arkwood Experiments+	944-949	John Canning	Roger Noel Cook (?)
The Multi-Mobile!*	950-954	John Canning	Roger Noel Cook
Insect+	955-959	John Canning	
The Metal Eaters+	960-964	John Canning	
The Fishermen of Carpantha+	965-969	John Canning	
Doctor Who and the Rocks from Mars@	970-976	John Canning	Alan Fennell
Doctor Who and the Robot@	977-984	John Canning	Alan Fennell
Trial of Fire+	985-991	John Canning	Alan Fennell
The Kingdom Builders+	992-999	John Canning.	Alan Fennell (?)

TITLE	ISSUES	ARTIST/INKER	WRITER
COUNTDOWN – published weekly by Polystyle Publications Ltd. (20/02/71 – 25/12/71)			
Gemini Plan	1-5	Harry Lindfield	Dennis Hooper
Timebenders	6-13	Harry Lindfield	Dennis Hooper
The Vogan Slaves	15-22	Harry Lindfield	Dennis Hooper
The Celluloid Midas	23-32	Harry Lindfield	Dennis Hooper
Backtime	33-39	Frank Langford	Dick O'Neill
The Eternal Present	40-45	Harry Lindfield(40,41), Gerry Haylock (42-45)	Dennis Hooper

TITLE	ISSUES	ARTIST/INKER	WRITER
COUNTDOWN FOR TV ACTION – published weekly by Polystyle Publications Ltd. (01/01/72 – 18/03/72)			
The Eternal Present (contd)	46	Gerry Haylock	Dennis Hooper
Sub Zero	47-54	Gerry Haylock	Dennis Hooper
The Planet of the Daleks	55-57	Gerry Haylock	Dennis Hooper

TITLE	ISSUES	ARTIST/INKER	WRITER

TV ACTION IN COUNTDOWN – published weekly by Polystyle Publications Ltd. (25/03/72)

The Planet of the Daleks (contd)	58	Gerry Haylock	Dennis Hooper

TV ACTION + COUNTDOWN – published weekly by Polystyle Publications Ltd. (01/04/72 – 13/01/73)

The Planet of the Daleks (contd)	59-62	Gerry Haylock	Dennis Hooper
A Stitch in Time	63-70	Gerry Haylock	Dennis Hooper
The Enemy from Nowhere	71-78	Gerry Haylock	Dennis Hooper
The Ugrakks	79-88	Gerry Haylock	Dennis Hooper
Steelfist	89-93	Gerry Haylock	Dennis Hooper
Zeron Invasion	94-100	Gerry Haylock	Dennis Hooper

TV ACTION – published weekly by Polystyle Publications Ltd. (20/01/73 – 18/08/73)

Deadly Choice	101-103	Gerry Haylock	Dennis Hooper
Who is the Stranger	104	Gerry Haylock	Dennis Hooper
The Glen of Sleeping	107-111	Gerry Haylock	Dick O'Neill
The Threat from Beneath	112	Gerry Haylock	Dick O'Neill
kcaB to the Sun	116-119	Gerry Haylock	Dennis Hooper
The Labyrinth	120	Gerry Haylock	Dick O'Neill
The Spoilers	123	Gerry Haylock	Dick O'Neill
The Vortex	125-129	Gerry Haylock	Dennis Hooper
The Unheard Voice	131	Gerry Haylock	

TV COMIC PLUS TV ACTION – published Mondays by Polystyle Publications Ltd. (01/09/73 – 22/12/73)

Children of the Evil Eye	1133-1138	Gerry Haylock	
Nova	1139-1147	Gerry Haylock	
The Amateur	1148-1149	Gerry Haylock	

TV COMIC – published Mondays by Polystyle Publications Ltd. (29/12/73 – 03/08/74)

The Amateur (contd.)	1150-1154	Gerry Haylock	
The Disintegrator	1155-1159	Gerry Haylock	
Is Anyone There?	1160-1169	Gerry Haylock	
Size Control	1170-1176	Gerry Haylock	
The Magician!	1177-1181	Gerry Haylock	

TV COMIC plus TOM AND JERRY WEEKLY – published Mondays by Polystyle Publications Ltd. (10/08/74 – 21/12/74)

The Magician! (contd.)	1182-1183	Gerry Haylock	
The Metal-Eaters!	1184-1190	Gerry Haylock	
Lords of the Ether!	1191-1198	Gerry Haylock	
The Wanderers	1199-1201	Gerry Haylock	

TV COMIC – published Mondays by Polystyle Publications Ltd. (28/12/74 – 04/01/75)

The Wanderers (contd.)	1202-1203	Gerry Haylock	

TITLE	ISSUES	ARTIST/INKER	WRITER

TV COMIC HOLIDAY SPECIAL – published by Polystyle Publications Ltd. (May 1970)

Assassin From Space+		Patrick Williams	Roger Noel Cook (?)
Undercover+		Patrick Williams	Roger Noel Cook (?)

DOCTOR WHO HOLIDAY SPECIAL – published by Polystyle Publications Ltd. (May 1973) **MAS-003**

Fogbound		Frank Langford	
Secret of the Tower		Alex Badia	

DOCTOR WHO HOLIDAY SPECIAL – published by Polystyle Publications Ltd. (May 1974) **MAS-004**

Doomcloud
Perils of Paris
Who's Who?

DOCTOR WHO MAGAZINE WINTER SPECIAL: UNIT EXPOSED – published by Marvel Comics Ltd. (1991) **MAS-026**

The Man in the Ion Mask		Brian Williamson	Dan Abnett

TV COMIC ANNUAL 1971 – published by Polystyle Publications Ltd.

Castaway+		John Canning	
Levitation+		John Canning	

COUNTDOWN ANNUAL 1972 – published by Polystyle Publications Ltd.

The Plant Master+		Jim Baikie	

COUNTDOWN ANNUAL 1973 – published by Polystyle Publications Ltd.

Ride to Nowhere		Frank Langford	

TV ACTION ANNUAL 1974 – published by Polystyle Publications Ltd.

The Hungry Planet		Jim Baikie	

DOCTOR WHO ANNUAL 1974 – published by World Distributors (Manchester) Ltd. **BAN-008**

The Time Thief		Steve Livesey	
Menace of the Molags		Steve Livesey	

TV COMIC ANNUAL 1975 – published by Polystyle Publications Ltd.

Petrified		Gerry Haylock	

DOCTOR WHO ANNUAL 1975 – published by World Distributors (Manchester) Ltd. **BAN-009**

Dead on Arrival		Edgar Hodges	
After the Revolution		Edgar Hodges	

DOCTOR WHO MAGAZINE

Change of Mind	221-223	Barrie Mitchell	Kate Orman
Target Practice	234	Adrian Salmon	Gareth Roberts

FOURTH DOCTOR STRIPS

TITLE	ISSUES	ARTIST/INKER	WRITER
TV COMIC – published Mondays by Polystyle Publications Ltd. (11/01/75 – 11/09/76)			
Death Flower!	1204-1214	Gerry Haylock	
Return of the Daleks!	1215-1222	Martin Asbury	
The Wreckers!	1223-1231	Martin Asbury	Dennis Hooper
The Emperor's Spy!	1232-1238	John Canning	
The Sinister Sea!	1239-1244	John Canning	
The Space Ghost!	1245-1250	John Canning	
The Dalek Revenge!	1251-1258	John Canning	
Virus+	1259-1265	John Canning	
Treasure Trail+	1266-1272	John Canning	
Hubert's Folly+	1273-1279	John Canning	
Counter-Rotation+	1280-1286	John Canning	
Mind Snatch	1287-1290	John Canning	
The Hoaxers+	1291	John Canning	
MIGHTY TV COMIC – published Fridays by Polystyle Publications Ltd. (18/09/76 – 12/11/77)			
The Mutant Strain+	1292-1297	John Canning	
Double Trouble+	1298-1304	John Canning	
Dredger@	1305-1311	John Canning	Geoff Cowan
The False Planet	1312-1317	John Canning	
The Fire Feeders	1318-1325	John Canning	
Kling Dynasty@	1326-1333	John Canning	
The Orb	1334-1340	John Canning	
The Mutants	1341-1347	John Canning	
The Devil's Mouth	1348-1352	John Canning	
TV COMIC – published Fridays by Polystyle Publications Ltd. (19/11/77 – 18/08/78)			
The Aqua-City	1353-1360	John Canning	Geoff Cowan
The Snow Devils	1361-1365	John Canning	
The Space Garden	1366-1370	John Canning	
The Eerie Manor	1371-1372	John Canning	
Guardian of the Tomb/The Living Mist!	1373-1379	John Canning	
The Image Makers	1380-1385	John Canning	
DOCTOR WHO WEEKLY – published Thursdays by Marvel Comics Ltd. (17/10/79 – 06/08/80)			
Doctor Who and the Iron Legion	1-8	Dave Gibbons	Pat Mills
City of the Damned	9-16	Dave Gibbons	John Wagner
Timeslip	17-18	Paul Neary	Dez Skinn
Doctor Who and the Star Beast	19-26	Dave Gibbons	Pat Mills
Doctor Who and the Dogs of Doom	27-34	Dave Gibbons	John Wagner
Doctor Who and the Time Witch	35-38	Dave Gibbons	Steve Moore
Dragon's Claw	39-43	Dave Gibbons	Steve Moore

TITLE	ISSUES	ARTIST/INKER	WRITER
DOCTOR WHO – published monthly by Marvel Comics Ltd. (09/80 – 01/82)			
Dragon's Claw (contd)	44-45	Dave Gibbons	Steve Moore
The Collector	46	Dave Gibbons	Steve Moore
Dreamers of Death	47-48	Dave Gibbons	Steve Moore
The Life Bringer	49-50	Dave Gibbons	Steve Moore
War of the Words	51	Dave Gibbons	Steve Moore
Spider-God	52	Dave Gibbons	Steve Moore
The Deal	53	Dave Gibbons	Steve Parkhouse
End of the Line	54-55	Dave Gibbons	Steve Parkhouse
Doctor Who and the Free-Fall Warriors	56-57	Dave Gibbons	Steve Parkhouse
Junk-Yard Demon	58-59	Mike McMahon/ Adolfo Buylla	Steve Parkhouse
The Neutron Knights	60	Dave Gibbons	Steve Parkhouse
DOCTOR WHO MAGAZINE			
Victims	212-214	Colin Andrew	Dan Abnett
Black Destiny	235-237	Martin Geraghty/ Bambos Georgiou (237 only)	Gary Russell
Doctor Who and the Fangs of Time	243	Sean Longcroft	

TV COMIC ANNUAL 1976 – published by Polystyle Publications Ltd.

Woden's Warriors		John M. Burns	

DOCTOR WHO ANNUAL 1976 – Published by World Distributors (Manchester) Ltd. **BAN-010**

The Psychic Jungle		Paul Crompton	
Neuronic Nightmare		Paul Crompton	

MIGHTY TV COMIC HOLIDAY SPECIAL – published by Polystyle Publications Ltd. (1977)

The Sky Warrior		John Canning	

TV COMIC ANNUAL 1977 – published by Polystyle Publications Ltd.

The Tansbury Experiment		John Canning	

DOCTOR WHO ANNUAL 1977 – published by World Distributors (Manchester) Ltd. **BAN-011**

The Body Snatcher		Paul Crompton	
Menace on Metalupiter		Paul Crompton	

MIGHTY TV COMIC ANNUAL 1978 – published by Polystyle Publications Ltd.

Jackals of Space!		John Canning	

DOCTOR WHO ANNUAL 1978 – published by World Distributors (Manchester) Ltd. **BAN-012**

The Rival Robots		Paul Crompton	
The Traitor		Paul Crompton	

TV COMIC ANNUAL 1979 – published by Polystyle Publications Ltd.

The Sea Devil		John Canning	

TITLE	ISSUES	ARTIST/INKER	WRITER
DOCTOR WHO ANNUAL 1979 – published by World Distributors (Manchester) Ltd. **BAN-013**			
The Power		Paul Crompton	
Emsone's Castle		Paul Crompton	
DOCTOR WHO ANNUAL 1980 – published by World Distributors (Manchester) Ltd. **BAN-014**			
Terror on Xaboi		Paul Crompton	
The Weapon		Paul Crompton	
DOCTOR WHO ANNUAL 1981 – published by World International Publishing Ltd. **BAN-015**			
Every Dog Has His Day		Mel Powell	
DOCTOR WHO ANNUAL 1982 – published by World International Publishing Ltd. **BAN-016**			
Plague World		Mel Powell	
DOCTOR WHO YEARBOOK 1994 – published by Marvel Comics UK Ltd. **BAN-028**			
Rest and Re-creation		Charlie Adlard	Warwick Gray
DOCTOR WHO SUMMER SPECIAL – published by Marvel Comics UK Ltd. (1995) **MAS-034**			
The Seventh Segment		Paul Peart	
DOCTOR WHO YEARBOOK 1995 – published by Marvel Comics UK Ltd. **BAN-029**			
The Naked Flame		Charlie Adlard	Warwick Gray
DOCTOR WHO YEARBOOK 1996 – published by Marvel Comics UK Ltd. **BAN-030**			
Star Beast II		Martin Geraghty	Gary Gillatt
Junk-Yard Demon II		Adrian Salmon	Alan Barnes

FIFTH DOCTOR STRIPS

TITLE	ISSUES	ARTIST/INKER	WRITER
DOCTOR WHO MONTHLY – published monthly by Marvel Comics Ltd. (02/82 – 01/84)			
The Tides of Time	61-67	Dave Gibbons	Steve Parkhouse
Stars Fell on Stockbridge	68-69	Dave Gibbons	Steve Parkhouse
The Stockbridge Horror	70-75	Steve Parkhouse (70-72),	Steve Parkhouse
		Mick Austin (73-75)/	
		Paul Neary (ex 72)	
Lunar Lagoon	76-77	Mick Austin	Steve Parkhouse
4-Dimensional Vistas	78-83	Mick Austin	Steve Parkhouse
The Moderator	84	Steve Dillon	Steve Parkhouse
THE OFFICIAL DOCTOR WHO MAGAZINE – published monthly by Marvel Comics Ltd.			
(02/84 – 04/84)			
The Moderator (contd)	86-87	Steve Dillon	Steve Parkhouse
DOCTOR WHO MAGAZINE			
The Lunar Strangers	215-217	Martin Geraghty	Gareth Roberts
The Curse Of the Scarab	228-230	Martin Geraghty	Alan Barnes

TITLE	ISSUES	ARTIST/INKER	WRITER

DOCTOR WHO ANNUAL 1983 – published by World International Publishing Ltd. **BAN-017**

On the Planet Isopterus		Glenn Rix	

DOCTOR WHO YEARBOOK 1995 – published by Marvel Comics UK Ltd. **BAN-029**

Blood Invocation		John Ridgway	Paul Cornell

SIXTH DOCTOR STRIPS

TITLE	ISSUES	ARTIST/INKER	WRITER

THE OFFICIAL DOCTOR WHO MAGAZINE – published monthly by Marvel Comics Ltd. (05/84 – 03/85)

The Shape Shifter	88-89	John Ridgway	Steve Parkhouse
Voyager	90-94	John Ridgway	Steve Parkhouse
Polly The Glot	95-97	John Ridgway	Steve Parkhouse
Once Upon A Time-Lord...	98	John Ridgway	Steve Parkhouse

THE DOCTOR WHO MAGAZINE – published monthly by Marvel Comics Ltd. (04/85 – 11/85)

Once Upon A Time-Lord... (contd)	99	John Ridgway	Steve Parkhouse
War-Game! Stockbridge	100-101	John Ridgway	Maxwell
Funhouse Stockbridge	102-103	John Ridgway	Maxwell
Kane's Story Stockbridge	104	John Ridgway	Maxwell
Abel's Story Stockbridge	105	John Ridgway	Maxwell
The Warrior's Story Stockbridge	106	John Ridgway	Maxwell

DOCTOR WHO MAGAZINE – published monthly by Marvel Comics Ltd. (12/85 – 10/87)

Frobisher's Story Stockbridge	107	John Ridgway	Maxwell

[Issues 104 to 107 formed a single story.]

Exodus	108	John Ridgway	Alan McKenzie
Revelation!	109	John Ridgway	Alan McKenzie
Genesis!	110	John Ridgway	Alan McKenzie

[Issues 108 to 110 formed a single story.]

Nature of the Beast!	111-113	John Ridgway	Simon Furman
Time Bomb	114-116	John Ridgway	Jamie Delano
Salad Daze	117	John Ridgway	Simon Ferman
Changes	118-119	John Ridgway	Grant Morrison
Profits of Doom!	120-122	John Ridgway	Mike Collins
The Gift	123-126	John Ridgway/ Tim Perkins (126)	Jamie Delano
The World Shapers	127-129	John Ridgway/Tim Perkins	Grant Morrison

TITLE	ISSUES	ARTIST/INKER	WRITER
DOCTOR WHO MAGAZINE			
Up Above The Gods	227	Lee Sullivan	Richard Alan

DOCTOR WHO – THE AGE OF CHAOS – published by Marvel Comics UK Ltd.
(October 1994) **BGR-008**

The Age of Chaos		John M.Burns,	
		Barrie Mitchell, Colin Baker	

SEVENTH DOCTOR STRIPS

TITLE	ISSUES	ARTIST/INKER	WRITER

DOCTOR WHO MAGAZINE – published monthly to issue 163 then every four Thursdays by Marvel Comics Ltd. to issue 236 and Panini UK Ltd. from issue 237 (11/87 – 08/96)

TITLE	ISSUES	ARTIST/INKER	WRITER
A Cold Day in Hell!	130-133	John Ridgway/Tim Perkins	Simon Ferman
Redemption!	134	Kev Hopgood/Tim Perkins	Simon Ferman
The Crossroads of Time	135	Geoff Senior	Simon Ferman
Claws of the Klathi!	136-138	Kev Hopgood/Dave Hine	Mike Collins
Culture Shock!	139	Bryan Hitch	Grant Morrison
Keepsake	140	John Higgins	Simon Ferman
Planet of the Dead	141-142	Lee Sullivan	John Freeman
Echoes of the Mogor!	143-144	John Ridgway	Dan Abnett
Time and Tide	145-146	Dougie Braithwaite, Dave Elliott	John Carnell
Follow that TARDIS!	147	Andy Lanning, John Higgins, Kev Hopgood, Dougie Braithwaite, Dave Elliot	John Carnell
Invaders from Gantac!	148-150	Martin Griffiths/Cam Smith	Alan Grant
Nemesis of the Daleks	152-155	Lee Sullivan	Richard Alan & Steve Alan
Stairway to Heaven	156	Gerry Dolan	Paul Cornell & John Freeman
Train-Flight	159-161	John Ridgway	Andrew Donkin & Graham Brand
Doctor Conkerer!	162	Mike Collins	Ian Rimmer
Fellow Travellers	164-166	Arthur Ranson	Andrew Cartmel
Darkness, Falling	167	Lee Sullivan/Mark Farmer	Dan Abnett
Distractions	168	Lee Sullivan/Mark Farmer	Dan Abnett
The Mark of Mandragora	169-172	Lee Sullivan/Mark Farmer	Dan Abnett
Party Animals	173	Mike Collins/Steve Pini	Gary Russell
The Chameleon Factor	174	Lee Sullivan/Mark Farmer	Paul Cornell
The Good Soldier	175-178	Mike Collins/Steve Pini	Andrew Cartmel
A Glitch in Time	179	Richard Whitaker	John Freeman
Evening's Empire (Part One)	180	Richard Piers Rayner	Andrew Cartmel
The Grief	185-187	Vincent Danks/ Adolfo Buylla (185), Robin Riggs (186-187)	Dan Abnett

TITLE	ISSUES	ARTIST/INKER	WRITER
Ravens	188-190	Brian Williamson/ Cam Smith (188), Steve Pini (189-190)	Andrew Cartmel
Memorial	191	John Ridgway	Warwick Gray
Cat Litter	192	John Ridgway	Marc Platt
Pureblood	193-196	Colin Andrew	Dan Abnett
Emperor of the Daleks	197-202	Lee Sullivan	Paul Cornell & John Freeman
Final Genesis	203-206	Colin Andrew	Warwick Gray
Time & Time Again	207	John Ridgway	Paul Cornell
Cuckoo	208-210	John Ridgway	Dan Abnett
Uninvited Guest	211	John Ridgway	Warwick Gray
Ground Zero	238-242	Martin Geraghty/ Bambos Georgiou	Scott Gray
The Last Word	304	Lee Sullivan	Gareth Roberts

THE INCREDIBLE HULK PRESENTS – published Saturdays by Marvel Comics Ltd. (07/10/89 – 01/01/90)

TITLE	ISSUES	ARTIST/INKER	WRITER
Once in a Lifetime	1	Geoff Senior	John Freeman
Hunger from the Ends of Time!	2-3	John Ridgway	Dan Abnett
War World!	4	Art Wetherell/ Dave Harwood	John Freeman
Technical Hitch	5	Art Wetherell/Cam Smith	Dan Abnett
A Switch in Time!	6	Geoff Senior	John Freeman
The Sentinel!	7	Andy Wildman	John Tomlinson
Who's That Girl!	8-9	John Marshall/ Steven Baskerville	Simon Ferman
The Enlightenment of Ly-Chee the Wise	10	Andy Wildman	Simon Jowett
Slimmer!	11	Geoff Senior/Mike Collins	Mike Collins & Tim Robins
Nineveh!	12	Cam Smith	John Tomlinson

DEATH'S HEAD – published by Marvel Comics Ltd. (1989)

TITLE	ISSUES	ARTIST/INKER	WRITER
Time Bomb!	8	Art Wetherell/ Steve Parkhouse	Steve Parkhouse

THE INCOMPLETE DEATH'S HEAD – published by Marvel Comics UK Ltd. (1993)

TITLE	ISSUES	ARTIST/INKER	WRITER
Connections	1	Simon Coleby	John Freeman & Dan Abnett
Mind Meet!	2-12	Simon Coleby/Sean Hardy, Niel Bushnell, Tim Perkins	Dan Abnett

DOCTOR WHO MAGAZINE SUMMER SPECIAL – published by Marvel Comics Ltd. (July 1991) **MAS-025**

TITLE	ISSUES	ARTIST/INKER	WRITER
Seaside Rendezvous		Gary Frank/ Steven Baskerville	Paul Cornell

TITLE	ISSUES	ARTIST/INKER	WRITER

DOCTOR WHO MAGAZINE WINTER SPECIAL: THE DEFINITIVE GUIDE TO THE TIME LORDS OF GALLIFREY – published by Marvel Comics UK Ltd. (1992) **MAS-028**

Flashback		John Ridgway	Warwick Gray

DOCTOR WHO CLASSIC COMICS: EVENING'S EMPIRE – published by Marvel Comics UK Ltd. (September 1993) **BGR-007**

Evening's Empire (including unpublished parts)		Richard Piers Rayner/ Vincent Danks	Andrew Cartmel

DOCTOR WHO MAGAZINE SUMMER SPECIAL: THE GENESIS OF DOCTOR WHO/ THE DESTINY OF DOCTOR WHO – published by Marvel Comics Ltd. (1994) **MAS-031**

Younger and Wiser		Colin Andrew	Warwick Gray

DOCTOR WHO WINTER SPECIAL – published by Marvel Comics UK Ltd. (1994) **MAS-033**

Plastic Millennium		Martin Geraghty	Gareth Roberts

DOCTOR WHO YEARBOOK 1992 – published by Marvel Comics UK Ltd. **BAN-026**

Under Pressure		Vincent Danks/Cam Smith	Dan Abnett

DOCTOR WHO YEARBOOK 1993 – published by Marvel Comics UK Ltd. **BAN-027**

Metamorphosis		Lee Sullivan	Paul Cornell

EIGHTH DOCTOR STRIPS

TITLE	ISSUES	ARTIST/INKER	WRITER

DOCTOR WHO MAGAZINE – published every four Thursdays by Panini UK Ltd. (09/96 –)

TITLE	ISSUES	ARTIST/INKER	WRITER
Endgame	244-247	Martin Geraghty/ Robin Smith, Robin Riggs	Alan Barnes
The Keep	248-249	Martin Geraghty	Alan Barnes
A Life of Matter and Death	250	Sean Longcroft, Martin Geraghty	Alan Barnes
Fire and Brimstone	251-255	Martin Geraghty/ Robin Smith	Alan Barnes
By Hook or by Crook	256	Adrian Salmon	Scott Gray
Tooth and Claw	257-260	Martin Geraghty/ Robin Smith	Alan Barnes
The Final Chapter	262-265	Martin Geraghty/ Robin Smith	Alan Barnes
Wormwood	266-271	Martin Geraghty/ Robin Smith	Scott Gray
Happy Deathday	272	Roger Langridge	Scott Gray
The Fallen	273-276	Martin Geraghty/ Robin Smith	Scott Gray
The Road to Hell	278-282	Martin Geraghty/ Robin Smith, Fareed Choudhury (282)	Scott Gray
TV Action!	283	Roger Langridge	Alan Barnes

TITLE	ISSUES	ARTIST/INKER	WRITER
The Company of Thieves	284-286	Adrian Salmon/ Fareed Choudhury	Scott Gray
The Glorious Dead	287-296	Martin Geraghty, Roger Langridge/ Robin Smith	Scott Gray
The Glorious Dead	287-296	Martin Geraghty, Roger Langridge/ Robin Smith	Scott Gray
The Autonomy Bug	297-299	Roger Langridge	Scott Gray
Ophidius	300-303	Martin Geraghty/ Robin Smith	Scott Gray
Beautiful Freak	304	Martin Geraghty/ Robin Smith	Scott Gray
The Way of All Flesh	306, 308-310	Martin Geraghty/ Robin Smith	Scott Gray
Children of the Revolution	312-317	Lee Sullivan/Adrian Salmon	Scott Gray
Me and my Shadow	318	John Ross/Roger Langridge	Scott Gray
Uroboros	319-322	John Ross/Adrian Salmon	Scott Gray
Oblivion	232-328	Martin Geraghty/ David A Roach/Adrian Salmon	Scott Gray

RADIO TIMES – published weekly by BBC Magazines (1-7 June 1986 – 22-28 March 1987)

Dreadnought	3775-3784	Lee Sullivan	Gary Russell
Descendence	3785-3794	Lee Sullivan	Gary Russell
Ascendence	3795-3804	Lee Sullivan	Gary Russell
Perceptions	3805-3814	Lee Sullivan	Gary Russell
Coda	3815-3816	Lee Sullivan	Gary Russell

CUSHING DOCTOR STRIPS

TITLE	ISSUES	ARTIST/INKER	WRITER

DR. WHO AND THE DALEKS – published by Dell Comics (1966) **MAS-001**

Dr. Who and the Daleks		Dick Giordano/Sal Trapani	Terry Nation

DOCTOR WHO MOVIE SPECIAL – published by Panini UK Ltd. (1996) **MAS-036**

Daleks versus the Martians		Lee Sullivan	Alan Barnes

BACK-UPS

Doctor Who strips have also appeared which do not feature the Doctor.

TV CENTURY 21 – published by City Magazines (23/01/65 – 13/01/67)
The Daleks comic strip ran for 104 issues and the stories were not titled. The titles listed here were developed by Jeremy Bentham and Jean-Marc Lofficer and are generally accepted. The stories were sporadically reprinted in both *TV Comic* and *Doctor Who Magazine*, and collected together in a Marvel special magazine (see MAS-032). It is believed that all were written by David Whitaker with occasional input by story editor Angus P Allen, although the Daleks' creator, Terry Nation, is credited.

TITLE	ISSUES	ARTIST/INKER	WRITER
The Daleks: Genesis of Evil	1-3	Richard Jennings	David Whitaker
The Daleks: Power Play	4-10	Richard Jennings	David Whitaker
The Daleks: Duel of the Daleks	11-17	Richard Jennings	David Whitaker
The Daleks: The Amaryll Challenge	18-24	Richard Jennings	David Whitaker
The Daleks: The PentaRay Factor	25-32	Richard Jennings	David Whitaker
The Daleks: Plague of Death	33-39	Richard Jennings	David Whitaker
The Daleks: The Menace of the Monstrons	40-46	Richard Jennings	David Whitaker
The Daleks: Eve of the War	47-51	Richard Jennings (47-49), Ron Turner (50-51)	David Whitaker
The Daleks: The Archives of Phryne	52-58	Eric Eden	David Whitaker
The Daleks: Rogue Planet	59-62	Ron Turner	David Whitaker
The Daleks: Impasse	63-69	Ron Turner	David Whitaker
The Daleks: The Terrorkon Harvest	70-75	Ron Turner	David Whitaker
The Daleks: Legacy of Yesteryear	76-85	Ron Turner	David Whitaker
The Daleks: Shadow of Humanity	86-89	Ron Turner	David Whitaker
The Daleks: The Emissaries of Jevo	90-95	Ron Turner	David Whitaker
The Daleks: The Road to Conflict	96-104	Ron Turner	David Whitaker

THE DALEK BOOK (1964) BGE-001

Invasion of the Daleks	R.Jennings, J.Woods, A.B.Cornwell
The Oil Well	R.Jennings, J.Woods, A.B.Cornwell
City of the Daleks	R.Jennings, J.Woods, A.B.Cornwell
The Humanoids	R.Jennings, J.Woods, A.B.Cornwell
Monsters of Gurnian	R.Jennings, J.Woods, A.B.Cornwell
Battle for the Moon	R.Jennings, J.Woods, A.B.Cornwell

THE DALEK WORLD (1965) BGE-003

The Mechanical Planet	Jennings, Woods, Cornwell, Wiggins
Treasure of the Daleks	Jennings, Woods, Cornwell, Wiggins
The Invisible Invaders	Jennings, Woods, Cornwell, Wiggins
The Orbitus	Jennings, Woods, Cornwell, Wiggins
The World That Waits	Jennings, Woods, Cornwell, Wiggins
Masters of the World	Jennings, Woods, Cornwell, Wiggins

THE DALEK OUTER SPACE BOOK (1966) BGE-005

The Dalek Trap
Sara Kingdom, Space Security Agent
The Super Sub
Secret of the Emperor
The Sea Monsters
The Unwilling Traveller
Chris Welkin Planeteer
The Brain Tappers

TITLE	ISSUES	ARTIST/INKER	WRITER
DALEK ANNUAL 1976 – published by World Distributors (Manchester) Ltd. **BAN-022**			
Planet of Serpents		Edgar Hodges	
Flood!!!		Edgar Hodges	
DALEK ANNUAL 1979 – published by World Distributors (Manchester) Ltd. **BAN-029**			
The Human Bombs		Walter Howarth	
Island of Terror		Walter Howarth	

DOCTOR WHO WEEKLY

As well as the main strip, *Doctor Who Magazine* occasionally featured a back-up *Doctor Who* strip.

TITLE	ISSUES	ARTIST/INKER	WRITER
The Return of the Daleks	1-4	Paul Neary/ David Lloyd (1-3), David Lloyd (4)	Steve Moore
Throwback: The Soul of a Cyberman	5-7	Paul Neary(5), Steve Dillon(6-7)	Steve Moore
The Final Quest	8	Paul Neary	Steve Moore
The Stolen TARDIS	9-11	Steve Dillon	Steve Moore
K9's Finest Hour	12	Paul Neary	Steve Moore
Warlord of the Ogrons	13-14	Steve Dillon	Steve Moore
Deathworld	15-16	David Lloyd	Steve Moore
Abslom Daak ... Dalek Killer	17-20	Steve Dillon	Steve Moore
Twilight of the Silurians	21-22	David Lloyd	Steve Moore
Ship of Fools	23-24	Steve Dillon	Steve Moore
The Outsider	25-26	David Lloyd	Steve Moore
Star Tigers (episodes 1-4)	27-30	Steve Dillon(27-29), David Lloyd(30)	Steve Moore
Yonder ... the Yeti	31-34	David Lloyd	Steve Moore
Black Legacy	35-38	David Lloyd	Alan Moore
Business as Usual	40-43	David Lloyd	Alan Moore

DOCTOR WHO

TITLE	ISSUES	ARTIST/INKER	WRITER
Star Tigers (episodes 5-7)	44-46	David Lloyd	Steve Moore
Star Death	47	John Stokes	Alan Moore
The Touchdown on Deneb 7	48	David Lloyd	Paul Neary
Voyage to the Edge of the Universe	49	David Lloyd	Paul Neary
Crisis on Kaldor	50	John Stokes	Steve Moore
4-D War	51	David Lloyd	Alan Moore
The Greatest Gamble	56	Mike McMahon	John Peel
Black Sun Rising	57	David Lloyd	Alan Moore
Skywatch-7 (episode one)	58	Mick Austin	Maxwell
Stockbridge			
The Gods Walk Among Us	59	David Lloyd	John Peel

DOCTOR WHO MONTHLY

TITLE	ISSUES	ARTIST/INKER	WRITER
Devil of the Deep	61	John Stokes	John Peel
The Fires Down Below	64	John Stokes	John Peel

TITLE	ISSUES	ARTIST/INKER	WRITER
DOCTOR WHO MAGAZINE			
Conflict of Interests	183	Richard Whitaker/ Cam Smith	Dan Abnett
The Cybermen: The Dead Heart	215-220	Adrian Salmon	Alan Barnes
The Cybermen: The Flesh Unbound	221-223	Adrian Salmon	Alan Barnes
The Cybermen: The Black Sky	224-226	Adrian Salmon	Alan Barnes
The Cybermen: The Hungry Sea	227-229	Adrian Salmon	Alan Barnes
The Cybermen: The Dark Flame	230-233	Adrian Salmon	Alan Barnes
The Cybermen: The Future Perfect	234	Adrian Salmon	Alan Barnes
The Cybermen: The Ugly Underneath	235-238	Adrian Salmon	Alan Barnes
The Daleks: Return of the Elders	249-254	Ron Turner	John Lawrence
Unnatural Born Killers	277	Adrian Salmon	Adrian Salmon
Character Assassin	311	Adrian Salmon	Scott Gray

DOCTOR WHO – A MARVEL WINTER SPECIAL – published by Marvel Comics UK Ltd. (1981) **MAS-009**

Skywatch-7 (episode two) Stockbridge		Mick Austin	Maxwell
Minatorius Stockbridge		John Stokes	Maxwell

DOCTOR WHO SUMMER SPECIAL – published by Marvel Comics UK Ltd. (1982) **MAS-010**

A Ship Called Sudden Death		Dave Gibbons	Steve Parkhouse

[Has no direct *Doctor Who* content but features the Freefall Warriors from issues 56-57 of *Doctor Who Magazine*.]

The Fabulous Idiot		Steve Parkhouse, Geoff Senior	Steve Parkhouse

[Has no direct *Doctor Who* content but features Dr. Ivan Asimoff from issues 56-57 of *Doctor Who Magazine*.]

DOCTOR WHO MAGAZINE HOLIDAY SPECIAL: WHO IS SARAH-JANE SMITH – published by Marvel Comics Ltd. (August 1992) **MAS-027**

City of Devils		Vincent Danks	Gary Russell

FUNNIES

This is not a complete list of spoofs, but it includes the most famous spoof of all: Steve Parkhouse's first *Doctor Who* comics work, in *Mad Magazine*.

TITLE	ISSUES	ARTIST/INKER	WRITER
MAD MAGAZINE – published by General Book Distributors Ltd. (September 1975)			
Doctor Ooh	161	Steve Parkhouse	Geoff Rowley
(Note: This was in the UK edition only)			

DOCTOR WHO MONTHLY			
Doctor Who?	64-84	Dicky Howett	Tim Quinn

THE OFFICIAL DOCTOR WHO MAGAZINE			
Doctor Who?	85-98	Dicky Howett	Tim Quinn

TITLE	ISSUES	ARTIST/INKER	WRITER
THE DOCTOR WHO MAGAZINE			
Doctor Who?	99-106	Dicky Howett	Tim Quinn
What if Doctor Who was produced by…?	103	Dicky Howett	Tim Quinn
Enlightenment	105	Dicky Howett	Tim Quinn
DOCTOR WHO MAGAZINE			
Doctor Who?	107-225	Dicky Howett	Tim Quinn
The Doctor Who History Tour	108, 110, 113, 115, 117, 119, 122, 129, 135	Dicky Howett	Tim Quinn
The Comic Assassins: Ghost Light	157	Kev F & Stanton	
The Comic Assassins: The Five Doctors	163	Kev F & Stanton	
The Comic Assassins: The Curse of Fenric	167	Kev F & Stanton	
Doctor Who? The Year Ahead	169	Dicky Howett	Tim Quinn
The Comic Assassins: The Dominators	173	Kev F & Stanton	
The Comic Assassins: Doctor Who's Grating Adventures	175	Kev F & Stanton	
The Comic Assassins: The Deadly Assassin	179	Kev F & Stanton	
The Comic Assassins: The Two Nits From UNIT	181	Kev F & Stanton	
Doctor Who? 92 The Year Ahead	182	Dicky Howett	Tim Quinn
The Comic Assassins: Number Eight	192	Kev F & Stanton	

DOCTOR WHO SUMMER SPECIAL – published by Marvel Comics UK Ltd. (1982) **MAS-010**

So You Think You'd Make A Good Companion		Dicky Howett	Tim Quinn

DOCTOR WHO – A SUMMER SPECIAL – published by Marvel Comics UK Ltd. (1983) **MAS-012**

The Next Twenty Years		Dicky Howett	Tim Quinn

DOCTOR WHO WINTER SPECIAL – published by Marvel Comics UK Ltd. (93/94)

An Unearthly Child The Unscreened Edition		Dicky Howett	Tim Quinn

DOCTOR WHO 25th ANNIVERSARY SPECIAL – published by Marvel Comics UK Ltd. (1988) **MAS-022**

Doctor Who? The Auditions for the seven Doctors		Dicky Howett	Tim Quinn

THE DOCTOR WHO FUN BOOK (1987) **BHU-001**

Doctor Who?		Dicky Howett	Tim Quinn

DOCTOR WHO: IT'S BIGGER ON THE INSIDE! (1988) **BHU-002**

Doctor Who?		Dicky Howett	Tim Quinn

FRAGMENTS

From time to time, incomplete fragments of *Doctor Who* comic strip stories have appeared. These are some of them, and include advertisements for other products which feature a comic strip.

TITLE	ISSUES	ARTIST/INKER	WRITER
RADIO TIMES (10 – 16 April 1971)			
Colony in Space	2474	Frank Bellamy	
DOCTOR WHO WEEKLY			
Doctor Who and the Turgids			
(for the TARDIS Tuner)	Issue 2+		
Advert for the *Genesis of the Daleks* LP	Issue 8+		
DOCTOR WHO MAGAZINE			
Masque of Mandragora	161	Colin Howard	
Terror of the Autons	164	Colin Howard	
Terror from the Deep	167-168	Gerry Dolan	John Freeman
Deceptions	272	Lee Sullivan	Gary Russell
The Daleks: Deadline to Doomsday	276	Ron Turner	John Lawrence

A series of previews for Big Finish's *Doctor Who* audio CDs appearing in DWM also featured a fragment comic strip drawn by Lee Sullivan to illustrate the piece.

THE COMIC RELIEF COMIC – published by Fleetway Publications (March 1991)
A single story written and drawn by numerous writers and artists.

The Comic Relief Comic		John Ridgway	

DOCTOR WHO – CYBERMEN (1988) **BFA-021**

Cyberhistory		Andrew Skilleter	David Banks

REPRINTS

Doctor Who comic strips have often been reprinted. Sometimes they were partly re-drawn for the reprint; for example, some Troughton and Pertwee stories had Tom Baker's face redrawn on them by John Canning. These appeared in *TV Comic*, the *Mighty Midget Doctor Who Comic* and the 1977 *Doctor Who Winter Special*.

TITLE	ISSUES	ARTIST/INKER	WRITER
TV COMIC – published Fridays by Polystyle Publications Ltd. (08/07/78 – 18/08/78)			
The Duellists+	1386-1389	John Canning	
The Amateur	1390-1392	Gerry Haylock	
TV COMIC with **TARGET** – published Fridays by Polystyle Publications Ltd. (25/08/78 – 13/10/78)			
The Amateur (contd.)	1393-1396	Gerry Haylock	
The Magician! [untitled]	1397-1400	Gerry Haylock	

TITLE	ISSUES	ARTIST/INKER	WRITER
TV COMIC – published Fridays by Polystyle Publications Ltd. (08/07/78 – 18/08/78)			
The Magician! [untitled] (contd.)	1401-1403	Gerry Haylock	
The Wanderers	1404-1408	Gerry Haylock	
The Metal Eaters!	1409-1415	Gerry Haylock	
Moon Exploration			
(Lords of the Ether!)	1416-1423	Gerry Haylock	
Size Control	1424-1430	Gerry Haylock	

DOCTOR WHO HOLIDAY SPECIAL (1974) **MAS-004**

The Daleks: Power Play		Richard Jennings	David Whitaker
[Black and white, re-laid out and re-lettered]			

THE AMAZING WORLD OF DOCTOR WHO (1976) **BGE-007**

The Psychic Jungle	Paul Crompton	
Neuronic Nightmare	Paul Crompton	
The Daleks in a Fresh Start (Eve of the War)	Richard Jennings, Ron Turner	

MIGHTY MIDGET – DOCTOR WHO COMIC (1977) **MAS-005**

Doomcloud		
[Third Doctor re-drawn as the Fourth]		
The Daleks: Power Play	Richard Jennings	David Whitaker
[Black and white, re-laid out and re-lettered]		

DOCTOR WHO WINTER SPECIAL (1977) **MAS-006**

The Labyrinth	Gerry Haylock	Dennis Hooper
Invasion (The Threat from Beneath)	Gerry Haylock	Dick O'Neill
The Spoilers	Gerry Haylock	Dick O'Neill
Who is the Stranger	Gerry Haylock	Dennis Hooper

DALEK ANNUAL (1977) **BAN-022**

The first two stories were reproduced in colour, but 'The Quest' was in black and white.

The Daleks: The Envoys of Evil (The PentaRay Factor)	Richard Jennings	David Whitaker
The Daleks: The Menace of the Monstrons	Richard Jennings	David Whitaker
The Daleks: The Quest (The Archives of Phryne)	Eric Eden	David Whitaker

TV COMIC HOLIDAY SPECIAL (1978)

Story overdrawn by John Canning with the fourth Doctor's likeness.

The Unheard Voice	Gerry Haylock	

DALEK ANNUAL (1978) **BAN-023**

The Daleks: [The] Rogue Planet	Ron Turner	David Whitaker

DOCTOR WHO – ADVENTURES IN TIME AND SPACE (1981) **BGE-015**

Mission for Duh	Walter Howarth	
The Vampire Plants	David Brian	
Dead on Arrival	Edgar Hodges	
Menace on Metalupiter	Paul Crompton	

TITLE	ISSUES	ARTIST/INKER	WRITER
The Traitor		Paul Crompton	
The Power		Paul Crompton	
Emsone's Castle		Paul Crompton	

DOCTOR WHO WEEKLY
All reproduced in black and white.

The Daleks: Genesis of Evil	33	Richard Jennings	David Whitaker
The Daleks: Power Play	33-34	Richard Jennings	David Whitaker
The Daleks: Duel of the Daleks	35-36	Richard Jennings	David Whitaker
The Daleks: The Amaryll Challenge	36-37	Richard Jennings	David Whitaker
The Daleks: The PentaRay Factor	37-39	Richard Jennings	David Whitaker
The Daleks: Plague of Death	39-40	Richard Jennings	David Whitaker
The Daleks: The Menace of the Monstrons	40-42	Richard Jennings	David Whitaker

DOCTOR WHO
'Eve of the War' and 'The Archives of Phryne' were reproduced in black and white.

The Daleks: Eve of the War	53-54	Richard Jennings, Ron Turner	David Whitaker
The Daleks: The Archives of Phryne	54-55	Eric Eden	David Whitaker
The Daleks: Rogue Planet	56, 58-60	Ron Turner	David Whitaker

DOCTOR WHO MONTHLY

The Daleks: Impasse	61-66, 68	Ron Turner	David Whitaker
A Ship Called Sudden Death	84	Dave Gibbons	Steve Parkhouse

THE OFFICIAL DOCTOR WHO MAGAZINE

Skywatch 7	85	Mick Austin	Maxwell
Stockbridge			

DOCTOR WHO MAGAZINE
'Business as Usual' was redrawn to be presented by Sylvester McCoy instead of Tom Baker.

Hunger from the Ends of Time	157-158	John Ridgway	Dan Abnett
The Daleks: Genesis of Evil	180-182	Richard Jennings	David Whitaker
The Fires Down Below	181	John Stokes	John Peel
Spider God	182	Dave Gibbons	Steve Moore
The Daleks: Power Play	183-188	Richard Jennings	David Whitaker
Business as Usual	184	David Lloyd	Steve Moore
The Daleks: Duel of the Daleks	189-193	Richard Jennings	David Whitaker
Flower Power!	307	John Canning	
The Witches	308-312	John Canning	

DOCTOR WHO SUMMER SPECIAL – published by Marvel Comics UK Ltd. (1980) MAS-007

Doctor Who and the Iron Legion		Dave Gibbons	Pat Mills
K9's Finest Hour		Paul Neary	Steve Moore

TITLE	ISSUES	ARTIST/INKER	WRITER

MARVEL PREMIERE – published bi-monthly by Marvel Comics Group [US] (12/80 – 06/81) **MAG-007**
All stories coloured.

Doctor Who and the Iron Legion	57-58	Dave Gibbons	Pat Mills
K9's Finest Hour	58	Paul Neary	Steve Moore
City of the Cursed			
(City of the Damned)	59-60	Dave Gibbons	John Wagner

STAR-LORD THE SPECIAL EDITION – published by Marvel Comics Ltd. [US] (February 1982)
This story was coloured.

Spider-God	1	Dave Gibbons	Steve Moore

THE VERY BEST OF DOCTOR WHO (MARVEL SUMMER SPECIAL) – published by Marvel
Comics UK Ltd. (1981) **MAS-008**

Timeslip		Paul Neary	Dez Skinn
Business as Usual		David Lloyd	Steve Moore

DOCTOR WHO – A SUMMER SPECIAL – published by Marvel Comics UK Ltd. (1983) **MAS-012**

Junk-Yard Demon		Mike McMahon/	Steve Parkhouse
		Adolfo Buylla	
Abslom Daak – Dalek Killer		Steve Dillon	Steve Moore

DOCTOR WHO COLLECTED COMICS – published by Marvel Comics UK Ltd. (1986) **BGR-002**
Painted colour for this edition by Gina Hart.

The Shape Shifter		John Ridgway	Steve Parkhouse
Polly The Glot		John Ridgway	Steve Parkhouse

DOCTOR WHO – published monthly by Marvel Comics Group (10/84 – 8/86) **MAG-008**
This was a US format comic book, reprinting coloured versions of the *Doctor Who Magazine* strips.

Doctor Who and the Star Beast	1-2	Dave Gibbons	Pat Mills
The Return of the Daleks	1	David Lloyd, Paul Neary	Steve Moore
Throwback: The Soul of a Cyberman	2-3	Paul Neary, Steve Dillon	Steve Moore
Doctor Who and the Dogs of Doom	3-4	Dave Gibbons	John Wagner
The Final Quest	3	Paul Neary	Steve Moore
The Stolen TARDIS	4	Steve Dillon	Steve Moore
Doctor Who and the Time Witch	5	Dave Gibbons	Steve Moore
Warlord of the Ogrons	5	Steve Dillon	Steve Moore
Dragon's Claw	6-7	Dave Gibbons	Steve Moore
Abslom Daak – Dalek Killer	6-8	Steve Dillon	Steve Moore
The Collector	8	Dave Gibbons	Steve Moore
Dreamers of Death	8	Dave Gibbons	Steve Moore
The Life Bringer	9	Dave Gibbons	Steve Moore
Star Tigers	9-12	Steve Dillon, David Lloyd	Steve Moore
War of the Words	10	Dave Gibbons	Steve Moore
Spider-God	10	Dave Gibbons	Steve Moore
The Deal	11	Dave Gibbons	Steve Parkhouse
End of the Line	11-12	Dave Gibbons	Steve Parkhouse

TITLE	ISSUES	ARTIST/INKER	WRITER
Doctor Who and the Free-Fall Warriors	12	Dave Gibbons	Steve Parkhouse
Junk-Yard Demon	13	Mike McMahon/	Steve Parkhouse
		Adolfo Buylla	
Yonder The Yeti	13	David Lloyd	Steve Moore
The Neutron Knights	14	Dave Gibbons	Steve Parkhouse
A Ship Called Sudden Death	14	Dave Gibbons	Steve Parkhouse
The Fabulous Idiot	14	Steve Parkhouse,	Steve Parkhouse
		Geoff Senior	
Black Legacy	14	David Lloyd	Steve Moore
The Tides of Time	15-18	Dave Gibbons	Steve Parkhouse
Business as Usual	15	David Lloyd	Steve Moore
Ship of Fools	16	Steve Dillon	Steve Moore
Devil of the Deep	17	John Stokes	John Peel
Crisis on Kaldor	17	John Stokes	Steve Moore
Timeslip	18	Paul Neary	Dez Skinn
Twilight of the Silurians	18	David Lloyd	Steve Moore
Stars Fell on Stockbridge	19	Dave Gibbons	Steve Parkhouse
The Touchdown on Deneb 7	19	David Lloyd	Paul Neary
The Outsider	19-20	David Lloyd	Steve Moore
The Stockbridge Horror	20-22	Steve Parkhouse,	Steve Parkhouse
		Mick Austin/Paul Neary	
The Greatest Gamble	20	Mike McMahon	John Peel
Skywatch-7	21-22	Mick Austin	Maxwell
Stockbridge			
The Gods Walk Among Us	21	David Lloyd	John Peel
The Fires Down Below	22	John Stokes	John Peel
Lunar Lagoon	23	Mick Austin	Steve Parkhouse
Voyage to the Edge of the Universe	23	David Lloyd	Paul Neary
An Unearthly Child :			
The Unscreened Edition	23	Dicky Howett	Tim Quinn

DOCTOR WHO SPECIAL (JOURNEY THROUGH TIME) (1985) **BGE-018**

Mission for Duh	Walter Howarth
Dead on Arrival	Edgar Hodges
The Power	Paul Crompton
Emsone's Castle	Paul Crompton
On the Planet Isopterus	Glenn Rix

DOCTOR WHO – 1985 SUMMER SPECIAL CLASSIC – published by Marvel Comics Ltd.
(June 1985) **BGR-001**
Painted colour for this edition.

Doctor Who and the Iron Legion		Dave Gibbons	Pat Mills
K9's Finest Hour		Paul Neary	Steve Moore

TITLE	ISSUES	ARTIST/INKER	WRITER

VOYAGER – published by Marvel Comics UK Ltd. (1985) **BGR-003**
Painted colour for this edition by Gina Hart.

TITLE	ISSUES	ARTIST/INKER	WRITER
The Shape Shifter		John Ridgway	Steve Parkhouse
Voyager		John Ridgway	Steve Parkhouse
Polly The Glot		John Ridgway	Steve Parkhouse
Once Upon A Time-Lord…		John Ridgway	Steve Parkhouse

CAPTAIN BRITAIN – published by Marvel Comics UK Ltd. (01/85 – 11/85)

Abslom Daak – Dalek Killer	1-11	Steve Dillon	Steve Moore

DOCTOR WHO MARVEL ADVENTURE COMICS (November 1986) **MAG-010**
Coloured versions of strips from *Doctor Who Magazine*, although they have also been redrawn and re-laid out, and Peri has been removed from all the frames.

Revelation (contains 'Revelation' and 'Genesis')	1	John Ridgway	Alan McKenzie
Fun House Stockbridge	2	John Ridgway	Maxwell
War Game Stockbridge	3	John Ridgway	Maxwell
Once Upon A Time Lord	4	John Ridgway	Steve Parkhouse
The Shape Shifter	5	John Ridgway	Steve Parkhouse
Voyager Dreams of Eternity (Parts 4 & 5 of the 'Voyager' story)	6	John Ridgway	Steve Parkhouse

THE INCOMPLETE DEATH'S HEAD – published by Marvel Comics UK Ltd. (01/1993 – 12/1993)
All stories coloured.

The Crossroads of Time	1	Geoff Senior	Simon Ferman
Keepsake	4-5	John Higgins	Simon Ferman
Time Bomb!	9	John Ridgway	Jamie Delano
Party Animals	12	Mike Collins/Steve Pini	Gary Russell

THE MARVEL BUMPER COMIC – published fortnightly by Marvel Comics UK Ltd. (02/10/88 – 21/01/89)
Not certain if the magazine lasted past issue number 9.

Claws of the Klathi!	1-6	Kev Hopgood/Dave Hine	Mike Collins
Keepsake	7-8	John Higgins	Simon Ferman
Culture Shock!	9	Bryan Hitch	Grant Morrison
Salad Daze (Part 1)	11	John Ridgway	Simon Ferman

DOCTOR WHO – CYBERMEN (1988) **BFA-021**
Reproduced in black and white only.

Test Flight+		John Canning	

THE MARVEL BUMPER COMIC HOLIDAY SPECIAL – published by Marvel Comics UK Ltd. (Summer 1988)

The Crossroads of Time		Geoff Senior	Simon Ferman

TITLE	ISSUES	ARTIST/INKER	WRITER

ABSLOM DAAK – DALEK KILLER – published by Marvel Comics UK Ltd. (1990) **BGR-004**

These stories were redrawn to be presented by Sylvester McCoy instead of Tom Baker and also to draw Daleks over the Kill-Mechs of 'Star Tigers' (part six).

TITLE	ISSUES	ARTIST/INKER	WRITER
Abslom Daak – Dalek Killer		Steve Dillon	Steve Moore
Star Tigers		Steve Dillon, David Lloyd	Steve Moore
Nemesis of the Daleks		Lee Sullivan	Richard Alan & Steve Alan

DOCTOR WHO CLASSIC COMICS – published every four Thursdays by Marvel Comics UK Ltd. (09/12/92 – 07/12/94) **MAG-009**

This was a full colour magazine, with black and white stories being computer-coloured.

TITLE	ISSUES	ARTIST/INKER	WRITER
Gemini Plan	1	Harry Lindfield	Dennis Hooper
Timebenders	1	Harry Lindfield	Dennis Hooper
The Vogan Slaves	1-2	Harry Lindfield	Dennis Hooper
The Daleks: The Amaryll Challenge	1-2	Richard Jennings	David Whitaker
The Klepton Parasites+	2	Neville Main.	
The Daleks: The PentaRay Factor	2-3	Richard Jennings	David Whitaker
The Extortioner+	3	John Canning	
The Celluloid Midas	3	Harry Lindfield	Dennis Hooper
Backtime	3-4	Frank Langford	Dick O'Neill
The Daleks: Plague of Death	3-4	Richard Jennings	David Whitaker
The Arkwood Experiments+ (?)	4	John Canning	Roger Noel Cook
The Eternal Present	4-5	Harry Lindfield, Gerry Haylock	Dennis Hooper
The Daleks: The Menace of the Monstrons	4-5	Richard Jennings	David Whitaker
*Sub Zero	5	Gerry Haylock	Dennis Hooper
Death Flower!	5-6	Gerry Haylock	
The Planet of the Daleks	6	Gerry Haylock	Dennis Hooper
The Daleks: Eve of the War	6	Richard Jennings (47-49), Ron Turner (50-51)	David Whitaker
The Daleks: The Archives of Phryne	6	Eric Eden	David Whitaker
A Stitch in Time	7	Gerry Haylock	Dennis Hooper
The Ordeals of Demeter	7	Bill Mevin	
Enter: The Go-Ray+	7	Bill Mevin	
The Daleks: Rogue Planet	8	Ron Turner	David Whitaker
The Trodos Tyranny+	8	John Canning	
Return of the Trods!	8	John Canning	
The Trodos Ambush+	8	John Canning	
Dr. Who and the Daleks	9	Dick Giordano, Sal Trapani	
The Neutron Knights	9	Dave Gibbons	Steve Parkhouse
The Tides of Time	10-11	Dave Gibbons	Steve Parkhouse
Shark Bait+	10	Bill Mevin	
The Doctor Strikes Back+	11	John Canning	
The Therovian Quest+	12	Neville Main	
The Enemy from Nowhere	12	Gerry Haylock	Dennis Hooper

TITLE	ISSUES	ARTIST/INKER	WRITER
The Daleks: Impasse	12	Ron Turner	David Whitaker
The Hijackers of Thrax+	13	Neville Main	
On the Web Planet	13	Neville Main	
The Ugrakks	13-14	Gerry Haylock	Dennis Hooper
Woden's Warriors	14	John M. Burns	
Planet of the Dead	14	Lee Sullivan	John Freeman
The Daleks: The Terrorkon Harvest	14	Ron Turner	David Whitaker
Steelfist	15	Gerry Haylock	Dennis Hooper
A Christmas Story+	15	Bill Mevin	
Zeron Invasion	15-16	Gerry Haylock	Dennis Hooper
The Daleks: Legacy of Yesteryear	15-16	Ron Turner	David Whitaker
Exodus	16	John Ridgway	Alan McKenzie
Revelation!	16	John Ridgway	Alan McKenzie
Genesis!	16	John Ridgway	Alan McKenzie
The Gyros Injustice+	17	Neville Main	
The Zombies*	17	John Canning	
Return of the Daleks!	17	Martin Asbury	
The Daleks: Shadow of Humanity	17	Ron Turner	David Whitaker
The Daleks: The Emissaries of Jevo	18	Ron Turner	David Whitaker
Master of Spiders!*	18	John Canning	
Deadly Choice	18	Gerry Haylock	Dennis Hooper
Stars Fell on Stockbridge	18	Dave Gibbons	Steve Parkhouse
The Daleks: The Road to Conflict	19	Ron Turner	David Whitaker
The Wreckers!	19	Martin Asbury	Dennis Hooper
Who is the Stranger	19	Gerry Haylock	Dennis Hooper
Kane's Story Stockbridge	19	John Ridgway	Maxwell
Abel's Story Stockbridge	20	John Ridgway	Maxwell
The Glen of Sleeping	20	Gerry Haylock	Dick O'Neill
The Exterminator+	20	John Canning	
Challenge of the Piper+	20	Neville Main	
The Stockbridge Horror	21-23	Steve Parkhouse, Mick Austin/Paul Neary	Steve Parkhouse
The Warrior's Story Stockbridge	21	John Ridgway	Maxwell
Once in a Lifetime	21	Geoff Senior	John Freeman
Frobisher's Story Stockbridge	22	John Ridgway	Maxwell
Moon Landing+	22	Neville Main	
Time in Reverse+	22	Neville Main	
The Monsters from the Past!*	22	John Canning	
Lizardworld+	23	Neville Main	
The Threat from Beneath	23	Gerry Haylock	Dick O'Neill
The Didus Expedition+	24	Bill Mevin	
The TARDIS Worshippers!*	24	John Canning	
kcaB to the Sun	24	Gerry Haylock	Dennis Hooper

TITLE	ISSUES	ARTIST/INKER	WRITER
War World!	24	Art Wetherell,Dave Harwood	John Freeman
Technical Hitch	24	Art Wetherell, Cam Smith	Dan Abnett
A Switch in Time	25	Geoff Senior	John Freeman
The Labyrinth	25	Gerry Haylock	Dick O'Neill
Space War III+	25	John Canning	
Doctor Who and the Star Beast	25-26	Dave Gibbons	Pat Mills
Egyptian Escapade!*	26	John Canning	
The Coming of the Cybermen+	26	John Canning	
The Spoilers	27	Gerry Haylock	Dick O'Neill
The Vortex	27	Gerry Haylock	Dennis Hooper
The Unheard Voice	27	Gerry Haylock	
Timeslip	27	Paul Neary	Dez Skinn

THE MARK OF MANDRAGORA (1993) BGR-006

All stories coloured for this graphic novel, with 'Fellow Travellers' also being relettered with extra dialogue.

Train-Flight	John Ridgway	Andrew Donkin & Graham Brand
Doctor Conkerer!	Mike Collins	Ian Rimmer
Fellow Travellers	Arthur Ranson	Andrew Cartmel
Darkness, Falling	Lee Sullivan/Mark Farmer	Dan Abnett
Distractions	Lee Sullivan/Mark Farmer	Dan Abnett
The Mark of Mandragora	Lee Sullivan/Mark Farmer	Dan Abnett

THE DALEK CHRONICLES – published by Marvel Comics UK Ltd. (August 1994) MAS-032

The Daleks: Genesis of Evil	Richard Jennings	David Whitaker
The Daleks: Power Play	Richard Jennings	David Whitaker
The Daleks: Duel of the Daleks	Richard Jennings	David Whitaker
The Daleks: The Amaryll Challenge	Richard Jennings	David Whitaker
The Daleks: The PentaRay Factor	Richard Jennings	David Whitaker
The Daleks: Plague of Death	Richard Jennings	David Whitaker
The Daleks: The Menace of the Monstrons	Richard Jennings	David Whitaker
The Daleks: Eve of the War	Richard Jennings, Ron Turner	David Whitaker
The Daleks: The Archives of Phryne	Eric Eden	David Whitaker
The Daleks: Rogue Planet	Ron Turner	David Whitaker
The Daleks: Impasse	Ron Turner	David Whitaker
The Daleks: The Terrorkon Harvest	Ron Turner	David Whitaker
The Daleks: Legacy of Yesteryear	Ron Turner	David Whitaker
The Daleks: Shadow of Humanity	Ron Turner	David Whitaker
The Daleks: The Emissaries of Jevo	Ron Turner	David Whitaker
The Daleks: The Road to Conflict	Ron Turner	David Whitaker

APPENDIX B: UNRELEASED ITEMS

EVERY so often an item of merchandise is announced or advertised which, for various reasons, is then never released. This listing attempts to detail the majority of these and is intended to act more as a guide as to what not to look for.

UNRELEASED/CANCELLED ITEMS

TITLE	YEAR	NOTES
Doctor Who Discovers Inventors, Doctor Who Discovers Miners, Doctor Who Discovers Pirates (assumed title)	1978	Three books in Target's *Doctor Who Discovers* series that were not produced due to poor sales. Cover proof and internal sheets exist for the *Inventors* book, and just cover artwork for the *Miners* and *Pirates* books.
Leatherbound edition of *The Doctor Who File*	1986	ISBN 0-491-03993-X. Leatherbound edition announced but not produced.
The Sontarans FASA Role-Playing Supplement	1986	The FASA 1986 Spring catalog and the orange FASA product order form sheet with prices effective until July 1986 included a listing for a *Doctor Who Role-Playing Game* supplement on the Sontarans. The supplement was apparently never printed, but it was advertised along with the Cybermen supplement, which was released. ISBNs can be batch issued for upcoming products, so it appears this supplement was planned so far as to be assigned an ISBN number. REF: ISBN 0-931787-74-2 #9104 OP: $11
Doctor Who Classics: Seeds of Death/The Krotons	1989	Cover proof produced but range cancelled.
Ameron US Hardback novels	1980s	Although two hardback novels were issued by Ameron (*The Giant Robot* and *Day of the Daleks*) several others were planned but not released: *Revenge of the Cybermen*, *The Android Invasion*, and *Genesis of the Daleks*.
Black Light II - The Remixes (Dominic Glynn)	1990	An LP/CD of Dominic Glynn's music was never released. Mentioned on the free flexidisk on *Doctor Who Magazine* #167.
Doctor Who and the Sea Devils	1992	1992 re-issue by Virgin. Cover proof exists of the John Geary Artwork against a pink background. Intended as a tie-in to the BBC repeat of the story but never published.

The Davison Years/The McCoy Years	1992/3	The last two volumes in the *Years* tapes series, planned by video specials producer John Nathan-Turner but never made or released.
Delgado, Cyberman, Hartnell model kits	1993	Amarang/Comet Miniatures suggested doing these kits after the success of the Tom Baker and Troughton kits.
Doctor Who **Character Tankards/K-9 Teapot**	1994	The Lustleigh Pottery/Aidee International Ltd planned further tankards and a K-9 teapot after their range of seven Doctors tankards completed. Characters proposed included The Rani, The Master, Rassilon, Omega and Borusa.
Paperback edition of *The Key to Time*	1995	Intended to be released by Virgin along with paperbacks of *A Celebration* and *The Time Traveller's Guide*. These were released, but *The Key to Time* was not.
Memories and Magic **(David J Howe)**	1995	Book proposed and cover proofed by Salamander Press. To have been written by David J Howe. Cancelled due to change in editorial staff at the publishers and a subsequent loss of American distributor.
The Making of The Dark Dimension **(Adrian Rigelsford)**	1995/09	Book proposed and cover proofed by Boxtree. To have been written by Adrian Rigelsford, but cancelled. REF: ISBN 0-7522-0964-7 OP: £14.99
'Light and Sound' Badges	1995	Alpha Marketing had two 'light and sound' badges scheduled for release but evidently the sound chips proved too expensive and the badges were not produced before the licence expired. The two designs were a TARDIS with roof light and dematerialisation sound, and a Dalek with a spoken 'Exterminate!' and light-up dome lights.
Resurrection of the Daleks & Revelation of the Daleks	1996	Eric Saward was originally commissioned by Virgin, then Paul Leonard (*Resurrection*) & Gareth Roberts (*Revelation*) were working on the novelisations for scheduled publication in October & November 1996. Saward refused permission for these versions, and the Missing Adventures *Speed of Flight* and *The Potters* by the same authors were commissioned in their place.

Doctor Who **Movie Cake**	1996	Licensed by Elizabeth the Baker's. Advertised but not produced due to a fire at the factory.
Classic Who: The 500 Year Diary - The Essential Behind-the-Scenes Guide to the Longest Running SF Series Ever (Marcus Hearn)	1996/06/24	A book proposed and cover-proofed by Boxtree. The book was cancelled allegedly due to a dispute over crediting between Hearn, the publishers and Adrian Rigelsford who was acting as consultant to Boxtree's range of *Doctor Who* titles. REF: ISBN 0-7522-0193-X OP: £9.99
Dr Who - The Scripts: The Abominable Snowmen	1996	Was to have been the ninth book in the Titan script book series. Cover artwork was produced and still exists. An ISBN number for this release is also known to exist.
Dr Who - The Scripts: The Pirate Planet **(Douglas Adams)**	1996/06/30	Was planned as a later release in the Titan script book series. Adams had apparently planned to rewrite the *Pirate Planet* scripts to present a version he was happy with. The release was planned for whenever an agreement could be reached with Adams, which never came to pass. REF: ISBN 1-85286-518-0 OP: £4.99
Doctor Who **Collectors Cards**	1998	Proposed series of mail order collectible cards by Orbis. Test advertised in selected UK regions but never produced due to lack of interest.
Spearhead from Space **Laser Disk**	1998	Encore Entertainment planned this release.
War Machine from *The War Machines*	1998/08	Harlequin Miniatures. Originally a part of Release 10. This was not actually issued as the mould broke during manufacturing. Scheduled for 2000.
The Beginning	1999/11	Video box set of the first three stories and the pilot episode restored and remastered. The stories were subsequently released individually.
Dapol Whomobile	199?	A prototype was produced. It was pictured in a Dapol catalogue and noted in *Doctor Who Magazine* before it was pulled from the schedule.
Unofficial Doctor Who Internet Guide	2000	United States item. Offered at $10, but delayed from its original scheduled publication in March 2000.
Classic Who: The Barry Letts Years **(Adrian Rigelsford)**	?	To have been published by Boxtree.

Logopolis/Castrovalva **CD**   ?   Planned by Silva Screen but not released.
Product Enterprise Toys   2001?   A variety of additions to Product
                                                            Enterprise's toy line were planned,
                                                            prototyped and announced but never
                                                            released, including a Mechanoid and
                                                            Dalek hoverbout scaled to match the
                                                            Dalek Rolykins, and a re-creation of the
                                                            classic '60s Dalek Swapit toys.

Unreleased Product Enterprise toys: Mechanoid (top left), Dalek hoverbout (top right),
and Dalek Swapits (bottom).

APPENDIX C: WORKING TITLES

SOME books were announced under working titles which differed from those they eventually
appeared as. Some of these are listed here. This is not intended to be a list of all working titles, as
the vast majority of books are announced under their final title.

WORKING TITLES

WORKING TITLE	RELEASED TITLE
Doctor Who and the Sea-Monsters	*Doctor Who and the Sea Devils*
Doctor Who and the Yeti	*Doctor Who and the Abominable Snowmen*
The Will of Zandarr	*The English Way of Death*
The Genesis of Terror	*The Scales of Injustice*
Stripper	*Demontage*
Chains of Commands	*Business Unusual*

ABOUT THE AUTHORS

DAVID J HOWE

DAVID has been involved with *Doctor Who* research and writing for over twenty years. He has been consultant to a large number of publishers and manufacturers for their *Doctor Who* lines, and is author or co-author of eighteen factual titles associated with the show. He also has one of the largest collections of *Doctor Who* merchandise in the world.

David is contributing editor to *Starburst* magazine and has edited the book reviews column for that magazine since 1984. He is also reviews editor for *Shivers* magazine. In addition he has written articles, interviews and reviews for a wide number of publications including *Fear*, *Dreamwatch*, *Stage and Television Today*, *The Dark Side*, *Doctor Who Magazine*, *The Guardian*, *Film Review*, *SFX* and *Sci-Fi Entertainment*.

He is on the committee of the British Fantasy Society and has edited their bi-monthly newsletter as well as editing and publishing several books for them, including the British and World Fantasy Award shortlisted *Manitou Man*, a limited edition hardback and paperback collection of short fiction by horror author Graham Masterton.

He wrote the book *Reflections: The Fantasy Art of Stephen Bradbury* for Dragon's World Publishers and has contributed short fiction to *Peeping Tom*, *Dark Asylum*, *Decalog* and *Perfect Timing* and factual articles to *James Herbert: By Horror Haunted* (Hodder & Stoughton, ed. Stephen Jones).

ARNOLD T BLUMBERG

ARNOLD has been a *Doctor Who* fan since 1986, and his collection pales in comparison to David's. When he's not hunting for that elusive Troughton annual, he serves as Editor of Gemstone Publishing, where he edits and oversees production of *The Overstreet Comic Book Price Guide* and *Hake's Price Guide to Character Toys*. He has also co-authored *The Overstreet Comic Book Grading Guide,* and co-designed and assembled almost all of the Gemstone guides.

Arnold also serves as Senior Editor for *Cinescape Magazine* (www.cinescape.com), where he provides all of the comic book industry coverage and also writes extensively about science fiction, horror, and fantasy entertainment. He has also written articles for *Overstreet's FAN*, *Comic Book Marketplace*, *Collector's Showcase*, *Dreamwatch,* and other on-line and academic venues.

He authored the on-line guide to sci-fi collecting available in the "Sci-Fi-O-Rama" section of the eBay auction site (www.ebay.com), and has contributed short fiction to the *Doctor Who* charity anthologies, *Missing Pieces*, *The Cat Who Walked Through Time*, *Walking in Eternity,* and the forthcoming *The Cat Who Walked Through Time II*, for which he also read another contributor's tail (heh heh) for inclusion on a bonus audio CD.

He teaches courses in comic book and time travel literature at the University of Maryland Baltimore County. He is currently pursuing a doctoral degree in Communications Design at the University of Baltimore, and yes, that means friends and family will soon be required to call him "Doctor." You can find out the latest on all his projects at www.atbpublishing.com.

www.galaxy4.co.uk

Official Doctor Who Merchandise Suppliers

GALAXY FOUR 493 Glossop Road Sheffield S10 2QE
0114 2684976 0845 166 2019 drwho@galaxy4.co.uk

Official Doctor Who Merchandise Suppliers

Time is NOT the enemy.
LACK OF INFORMATION IS...

Some people will tell you that once a particular generation leaves us, the collectibles they were interested in become worthless (or at least worth less).

Is that what happened with Monet? Renoir? Beethoven?

Is that what happened with Washington, Jefferson and Lincoln?

Is that what happened with Howdy Doody, Elvis or Marilyn Monroe?

How about the Lone Ranger, Tom Mix or Buck Rogers?

Collectibles are alive and well. The only enemy is ignorance.

Get your free weekly inoculation against lack of information – delivered painlessly straight to your e-mail box – from Scoop! Each week Scoop brings you news, auction results, interviews and insights into collecting. And did we mention it's free?

Visit http://scoop.diamondgalleries.com/signup/ to get your free subscription!

Cult TV Guides from Telos

BEYOND THE GATE
The Unofficial and
Unauthorised Guide to
Stargate SG-1
BY KEITH TOPPING

A DAY IN THE LIFE
The Unofficial and
Unauthorised Guide to
24
BY KEITH TOPPING

LIBERATION:
The Unofficial and
Unauthorised Guide to
Blake's 7
BY ALAN STEVENS
& FIONA MOORE

Beyond the Gate is an indispensable unofficial and unauthorised guide to the *Stargate* universe. Author Keith Topping breaks down each of the series' 100-plus episodes, analysing the elements and recurring themes that make it so popular.
288pp. A5 paperback original   £9.99 UK

A Day in the Life chronicles the critically acclaimed first season of the innovative TV thriller, *24*. Author Keith Topping offers his distinctive breakdown of each episode, with behind-the-scenes details and examples of when the show's logic went off course.
192pp. A5 paperback original   £9.99 UK

The publication of *Liberation: The Unofficial and Unauthorised Guide to Blake's 7* coincides with the 25th anniversary of *Blake's 7*. The book offers analyses of every episode, examination of key episodes from their genesis to the final version, and excerpts from original scripts and interviews with people involved in the production.
250pp. (approx.) A5 paperback original   £9.99 UK
Signed and numbered limited ed. hardback   £30 UK

Available from **Telos Orders, Beech House, Chapel Lane, Moulton, Cheshire, CW9 8PQ, England**. Please add the following p&p to the prices above: Single title ordered: UK: £2.50; Europe: £4.00; USA/Canada: £7.50; Rest of World: £8.50. Two or more titles ordered: UK: £4.00; Europe: £5.00; USA/Canada: £10.00; Rest of World: £11.00. Please make cheques (in pounds sterling only) payable to **Telos Publishing Ltd**. All Telos titles can also be ordered online by credit card. Visit **www.telos.co.uk** for more information.

Coming in 2004 From Telos Publishing

HOWE'S TRANSCENDENTAL TOYBOX UPDATE 2003

BE THE MASTERS OF THE DOCTOR WHO
COLLECTIBLES UNIVERSE WITH THE FIRST
REGULAR UPDATE TO THE TOYBOX,
CATALOGUING ALL THE WHO MERCHANDISE
RELEASED IN 2003,
THE 40TH ANNIVERSARY YEAR!

ALSO FEATURING NEW PHOTOS AND A FEW SURPRISES!

Visit www.telos.co.uk or www.tardis.tv
for ordering information

TELOS
.CO.UK